The World As I Found It

The World As I Found It

BRUCE DUFFY

TICKNOR & FIELDS
New York 1987

For information about permission to reproduce selections from
this book, write to Permissions, Ticknor & Fields,
52 Vanderbilt Avenue, New York, New York 10017.

Library of Congress Cataloging-in-Publication Data
Duffy, Bruce.
The world as I found it.
I. Wittgenstein, Ludwig, 1889–1951 — Fiction.
I. Title.
PS3554.U31917W6   1987   813'.54   87-6443
ISBN 0-89919-456-7
ISBN 0-89919-808-2 (pbk.)

Printed in the United States of America

P 12 11 10 9 8 7 6 5 4 3

The author gratefully acknowledges the editors and publishers
of the following magazines, in which chapters of this novel have
appeared: *Formations, Conjunctions,* and *The Antioch Review.*

Thirteen lines on page 359 from *The Duino Elegies* by Rainer
Maria Rilke, translated by Stephen Garmey and Jay Wilson.
Translation copyright © 1972 by Stephen Garmey and Jay Wilson.
Reprinted by permission of Harper & Row, Publishers, Inc.

Epigraphs on pages 17 and 257 from *Herakleitos and Diogenes* by
Heraclitus of Ephesius and Diogenes, the Cynic, translated from
the Greek by Guy Davenport. Copyright © 1976 by Guy
Davenport. Reprinted by permission of Grey Fox Press.

For Marianne

If I wrote a book called *The World As I Found It,*
I should have to include a report on my body, and
should have to say which parts were subordinate
to my will, and which were not, etc., this being a
method of isolating the subject, or rather of showing
that in an important sense there is no subject; for it
alone could *not* be mentioned in that book. —

— Ludwig Wittgenstein,
Tractatus Logico-Philosophicus

Preface

This is a work of fiction: it is not history, philosophy or biography, though it may seem at times to trespass on those domains. Although the book follows the basic outlines of Ludwig Wittgenstein's life and character, it makes no attempt at a faithful or congruent portrayal, even if such were possible — or desirable for the aims of fiction.

Fiction cannot, by definition, be completely factual or historically accurate. "True fiction" is a contradiction in terms. But there is one very practical reason why fiction that makes use of real life and history cannot usefully serve the prevailing standards of biography or history. This is fiction's inherent need for narrative compression. Fiction that shrinks from changing fact, that dilutes itself in an expository effort to faithfully duplicate factual circumstance and chronology in all its detail, cannot help but lose narrative force and acuity, if not its very claim as fiction. So my aim is not to usurp the rightful place of history or biography, or to somehow mimic the work of the historian or biographer. Fiction must do its work differently, making up its own rules and moving the fence line where necessary to suit its own special purposes.

For example, I have Wittgenstein meeting Bertrand Russell one year later than he did, I give Wittgenstein two sisters rather than three, and I have G. E. Moore marrying three years earlier than he actually did. Fiction also allows the author to fill in holes and even largely make up the personalities of certain obscure real-life figures, and this I have done as well. Nevertheless, the book does basically follow the trajectory of Wittgenstein's life and work — and that of Moore's and Russell's — in pretty much the sequence of events and basically within the broader frame of history.

As I have come to realize, one has to be fairly well versed in the facts before one can effectively change them. To freely write about historical figures one also must be willing to borrow. Those familiar with Wittgenstein's work will readily recognize my debts and misunderstandings, not to mention my periodic use of his words and ideas. The same will be true for my debts to the thinking of Russell, Moore and others who appear in the book, or who influenced me in the writing of it.

The hole, too, is part of the doughnut, and so I would hope the witting and unwitting holes in this account will infuse it with a necessary fictional space. We are all composite lives and minds living in a composite world so fraught with times, claims and voices that it seems we are forever in the process of forgetting. But forgetting is also the work of memory. Truly we forget in order to remember, and in memorializing this unruly world, I have scrupulously forgotten and mixed up the facts so this book will not be mistaken for anything but what it is — fiction.

Prologue

I once said, perhaps rightly: The earlier culture will become a heap of rubble and finally a heap of ashes, but spirit will hover over the ashes.

— Ludwig Wittgenstein, *Culture and Value*

Duck-Wabbit

THE PHILOSOPHER loved the flicks, periodically needing to empty himself in that laving river of light in which he could openly gape and forget.

Following one of his three-hour lectures, exhausted by his own ceaseless inquiries, he would hook one of his young men by the arm and ask with a faintly pleading look:

Care to see a flick?

The Tivoli was just down the street from Trinity College, Cambridge, rarely crowded. Wanting to avoid chance meetings in the queue, the philosopher would let the film start before he went stalking down the darkened aisle, audibly saying in British English with a German accent:

For this you must get *up close* — fourth aisle at least.

They were watching *Top Hat*. Craning back, spellbound as Fred twirled Ginger "Cheek to Cheek" under a temple of sound stage moonlight, the philosopher turned to his companion and said delightedly: *Wonderful*, how the light empties over you. Like a *shower bath*.

The young Englishman, precise in inflection, his top button buttoned, carefully smiled in the affirmative as his mentor continued:

Now, no one can dance like this Astaire fellow. Only Americans can do this sort of thing — the English are entirely too stiff and self-conscious. Astaire always gets the girl and of course it's utterly *without pretense*. Oh, it makes no sense whatsoever. Like the antics of that American mouse and his animal acquaintances —

The young man perked up. Mickey Mouse, you mean?

Yes, that one. Entirely creditable and charming. Also the duck. I very much like the duck. A *wise guy*, as the Americans would say.

Donald Duck, you say?

No, no — A quick up-down look, amazed that a young man could be so removed as not to know this. Not Donald — *Daffy*.

But then the philosopher wondered if the young man was instead making a veiled philosophical point about the indeed curious fact that these two excitable ducks spoke with sputtering lisps. *Ah*, thought the philosopher. His companion was pointing out that the two ducks were of ambiguous, even synonymous, identity, like the curious duck-rabbit he had shown in his lectures, a drawing that could be seen as either a duck or a rabbit before it dawned on the viewer that it was both or neither, or just one continuous line.

Oh, brother! lisped the philosopher, this to immediately fix in mind the duck in question. But don't you think it curious, he probed, pressing this obscure young man to make his point. I mean that neither of these ducks can speak *without spitting*. Assuming we could even *understand* a duck who could speak. But *spitting* —

The young man, accustomed to the philosopher's unorthodox mind, ogled around.

That is rather odd, isn't it.

On the screen, meanwhile, it was pure stage business — the usual boy-girl stuff before the next dance number. Dispense with the duck. Broadly hinting now, the philosopher said:

And the rabbit. I *like* that rabbit. Or *cwazy wa-bbit*, as they say.

Bugs? asked the young man carefully.

It was quite hopeless. He didn't get it. Ginger, meanwhile, was in another snit. Fred, crestfallen, was pacing in his dressing room, hands stuffed in his tuxedo pockets. Glancing around distractedly, the philosopher said:

Bugs the rabbit, yes.

The young man was squinting, looking troubled. Under the lapping light, the philosopher hardly heard him at first when he asked:

But *as art*, Dr. Wittgenstein?

Art? Suddenly, the magisterial Dr. Wittgenstein looked profoundly uncomfortable. Whatever do you mean?

These films. Do you consider them art?

Fred, by then, was chasing Ginger across a moonlit bridge. Bathed in that powdery light, Wittgenstein screwed up his nose as if he'd whiffed Limburger:

To speak of these flicks as *art*? This I would view with the highest suspicion.

At this time, in the later forties, Ludwig Wittgenstein, not unlike the duck-rabbit, was himself an object of ambiguity and suspicion in many philosophical circles.

It came as no surprise to Wittgenstein that his ideas were misunderstood and misrepresented. In his shunning contempt for philosophy and philosophers, he almost consciously encouraged this reaction. Publishing his late work could have done much to boost his reputation and erase his mystery-man image, but despite his periodic waverings and the pleadings of his friends, Wittgenstein could not bring himself to bring out his new work — not in his lifetime. Instead, his ideas were repeated by word of mouth or passed around as transcripts of the shorthand notes that his students doggedly took down during his lectures.

Lectures! Séances was more like it. Wittgenstein held these classes twice a week in his two small, bare rooms in Trinity's Whewell's Court. The door would be open, and his students would enter as into a chapel this room furnished solely with an army cot, a shelf of books and manuscripts and the folding card table on which he wrote. Seated near the window, deep in a funk of thought, Wittgenstein would be facing partly away, like a figure posing for a life study. They would not have dreamed of greeting him, much less of bothering him with questions or small talk. He wanted no tourists or gapers, and none dared come late. Perched on the folding gunmetal chairs on which he expected them to remain for two or three hours *without squeaking,* they were not to talk, smoke, raise their hands or, in short, do anything that might distract him. The session would "begin" promptly at four, but another ten or fifteen minutes might pass before, without warning, he erupted into words. Grimacing, grasping the metal seat of his own chair, cast in the forcing house of their expectant gaze, he might talk brilliantly for the entire session, without a single note. These were the good days. But there were also the slow, halting or bad sessions, when he would sit there mentally whipping himself for his torpidity, snorting, Come — *on!* Oh, this is *intolerable.* As you can see, I'm perfectly stupid today . . .

People would watch him and wonder. Was he happy? Sad? A troubled man beneath? But what could the outer world know of the inner? Morning and evening, when the light was most intense, the most transitional, they would see him barging through the Cambridge Backs, a wild expanse of cattails and lilystems, impossibly green, through which the River Cam glides under ductile willows. Even then, late in his life, Wittgenstein looked a good ten years younger than fifty-eight. He was a trim man of average height, with a sharp nose, flat, literal lips, and curly brown hair graying at the temples. His eyes were dark and piercing, and he often carried a bamboo cane, not as a crutch, but as a foil and pointer. About him there was a vaguely martial air, a certain cleanness and sobriety, like that of a priest on an off Sunday. His dress was functional, meticulous and, above all, *consistent*: an old tweed coat or a worn leather jacket, a shirt open at the collar. The dark flannel trousers were worn but carefully pressed, and the cracked leather of his old oxfords was buffed to the burnished hue of an old pipe bowl.

Often one of his young friends would accompany him on these walks. These were, as a rule, self-effacing, innocent young men from middle- or lower-middle-class families, the type who took the early school prizes and were duly brought under the wing of some lonely master who made it his cause to get the lad into Oxford or Cambridge. But besides being innocent and brainy, Wittgenstein's young men were slender and good-looking. More beguiling still, for Wittgenstein, they were often as not quite unaware of their looks and indeed of sex in general. Oblivious to the pull of mirrors, they were themselves mirrors — deep, drowsing pools of innocence in which Wittgenstein could lose himself while feeling, in certain fundamental respects, more innocent himself.

He craved their companionship. Like a possessive mother, he fussed over them and read their fate like tea leaves: to marry late, if ever, and be forever tied to him. A few years before, in fact, Wittgenstein had even taken one of these young men with him to Russia — for Wittgenstein the spiritual land of Tolstoy and Dostoyevsky — with the idea of their emigrating there to study medicine in preparation for a life spent treating the poor. They went quietly, secretively, but of course stories got out that Wittgenstein was a Red or a Marxist, while others snottily said that the former aeronautical engineer had taken his young shadow to Russia so they might get their wings — their angel's wings.

But Russia was not what Wittgenstein wanted. Whatever its merits, philosophy wasn't what he wanted either, not when life offered so many other useful pursuits. Certainly he did not advise his students to become philosophers; that was the last thing he would have suggested. No, he warned them to avoid at all cost the trap of academic life — at least if they planned to do any honest or original thinking of their own.

On the surface, this might have seemed hypocritical, coming as it did from a man with a tolerably comfortable chair at a great university. But

Wittgenstein was not advocating a path he had not himself followed, for he had done many things in life besides philosophy. After the First World War, where he fought with the Austrian army on the Russian front, Wittgenstein had even abandoned philosophy for ten years, dispensing with a sizable fortune he had inherited and going off to live a life of servitude and penury as a rural schoolmaster in a poor Austrian village. Hard as he tried, though, he was not cut out for life among stunted village folk, and he left a few years later. He then worked for a time as a gardener in a monastery and even considered taking vows until the abbot wisely talked him out of it. With that, he returned to his native Vienna, where he put his early engineering background to use designing and building for his wealthy older sister a splendid modernist home of angled steel and stone, whose chaste, rigorous lines suggested the ascending logic of a tone poem. In the Vienna telephone directory at this time, during the late twenties, he even listed himself as *Ludwig Wittgenstein: Architekt*.

But architecture couldn't hold him either. Philosophy, he was forced to realize, was his supreme gift, yet when he returned to philosophy in 1929, his mind never entirely settled there. Still, much as he hated Cambridge, he instinctively knew that college life, and the relative freedom it afforded him, was more conducive to his work than a life spent on the Russian steppes, tending an endless line of human misery. But because he couldn't settle on anything, the young men around him couldn't really settle, either. And so this, too, was his legacy: to leave them and, later, philosophy deluged with his huge, half-conscious will, which, like a sweeping flame, sucked up all the oxygen.

This influence wasn't an entirely conscious thing on Wittgenstein's part. On the contrary; because it was so deeply rooted in his character — because it was not overtly selfish or deliberately manipulative — the bond he created was all the more powerful. And strong as this bond was in life, it was that much stronger after his death, when in the collective memory of those who knew him he would become a sort of splatched and angled concatenation of images, wishes, evasions, running feuds, regrets. For some who knew him, his name would evoke pains such as old men feel — sharp, bunionlike pangs that would shoot out at the mention of *Witt-gen-stein*, that fractious weather system of remembering and forgetting which finally consumes the life of the thing remembered.

For years, Wittgenstein had been engaged in a struggle with language, examining — and indeed exhaustively auditing — language in its variety to discern its endless games and guises. He was discouraged to hear of

Einstein's continued effort to bring the forces of gravitation and electro-magnetism under a single law. How, he wondered, could so great a mind succumb to the will-o'-the-wisp of mere *unity*? The world, he was now convinced, defied reduction or summary, despite his own attempts in that direction as a young man. Philosophy needed no more dinosaurs, no more grand systems. His own intentions were as humble as the words "table," "lamp," "door."

As he saw it, the rightful course of philosophy was not the pursuit of elegance or the distillation of intoxicating mathematical essences. Our natural craving for generality, for the handy rule of thumb, was precisely the problem. Our crude rules were only hammers, when we also needed chisels and screwdrivers — when we needed a whole toolbox, as well as an encyclopedia and a taxonomy of the things we say, and what we *think* we mean by them. A language, he said, is nothing more than a collection, and to understand it, we must plow over the whole ground of language, examining it in all its particular crotchets and uses. For the philosopher, he felt, the problem was much like that of seeing the rabbit within the duck — that is, seeing with the freshness of *second sight,* holding in mind the image of what one first saw while yet bringing to it the force of what one saw later, since one was always seeing more in the picture. Still, in an age addicted to scientific leaps, he knew the ambiguous, ongoing, nec-essarily fragmentary nature of the search was not exactly a cheering pros-pect. Like many a stealthy thinker who presents something difficult and vaguely uncongenial, he was often at some pains to make himself clear, at times even dropping broad hints. Once, for instance, he told a friend that where the usual thinker wants to show unexpected resemblances, his task was rather to show many discrete *differences* among the various families of language, families that each have their own resemblances and eccentricities, their rules and disguises. Their duck-rabbits, so to speak.

In contrast to his early hostility to Freudian thinking, Wittgenstein now spoke of himself as a disciple of Freud but warned that Freud had to be read extremely critically. Since when, asked a young man to whom he had given this advice, had he ever read *anything* uncritically? Witt-genstein laughed. But here was another hint, and he was pleased when someone later remarked that the seemingly unordered remarks that com-posed his *Philosophical Investigations* and other late works had the cu-mulative effect of a kind of linguistic psychoanalysis designed to help the analysand overcome the muddles that cloud understanding. Suspicious of the dubious virtues of order and equally suspicious of how order could lead to error and intellectual complacency, Wittgenstein found this a fair analogy. Still, it was a somewhat guilty explanation: despite his misgivings, he and others had expended much labor in a fruitless effort to organize his ideas. But the river would not be diverted: he could not change the course of his mind. Like analysis, and indeed like thinking itself, the method was not linear but circular, obsessively returning to the same general concerns: concepts of meaning and understanding, states of consciousness, logic, the nature of propositions and philosophy and, above all, the "games" through which language is acquired and transmitted. A question would appear, disappear, then resurface again a few pages later in altered form, clouded as thought, tricky as talk. Yet he still felt that the indeterminacy of his method was oddly appropriate to the very ambiguity and indeterminacy of the subject, his point being to present thought as a *process*, rather than a canned result to be read and forgotten. And finally for him, these investigations went even beyond the more parochial concerns of philosophy. After all, he asked, what was the use of studying philosophy if it did not improve your thinking about important questions of everyday life? The investigation is eternally open, longer than life, as endless. Thinking is begetting. We do not practice philosophy, or think, in order to forget.

Wittgenstein often spoke of the "bewitchments" of language, but he was far less mindful of the bewitchments of his own personality.

Surely, nothing could have been more disagreeable to him than the mounting spectacle of his own influence, engulfing other minds. The last thing he wanted was to found another school or movement, yet he could plainly see it coming and, wittingly and unwittingly, he fostered it. He hated to see his students unconsciously mimic his gestures and parrot his expressions, and he was even more distressed to see his unpublished ideas pirated and distorted. Indeed, at times, he feared he would leave nothing but a collection of mannerisms: the Do-This-in-Remembrance-of-Me School.

Inevitably, he had his rivals and detractors, chief among them his former teacher and mentor, Bertrand Russell. It pained Wittgenstein to think that he and Russell should be doomed to bear this antagonism through the rest of their days. Still, it could have ended only this way. Their natures were too disparate. Besides, their reputations had both grown too large, and there was now much else at stake — fundamental values and beliefs, not to mention the added goad of vanity.

Difficult to say how this emnity had come about. Attribute it to time, time and the misunderstandings of time, ingrown. Russell had long felt that Wittgenstein disapproved of his life, of his couplings and anti-Christian beliefs, of his politics and popular writings, his easy socializing and celebrity. Russell was not entirely wrong in his suspicions. Wittgenstein did disapprove, but not as sternly as Russell thought. On Wittgenstein's end it was the same. In the twenties, when he was off in that Austrian backwater teaching school, Wittgenstein fancied that Russell felt him to be more misguided and confused than in fact he did. Besides, Russell had a family by then. He had more on his mind than Wittgenstein.

Time was the breach, then. Friendship, it seemed, wasn't long or durable enough for time. Slowly, almost inevitably, they lost sight of one another. And they changed — they changed more than they knew, accepting all too readily those ways in which they felt they had changed for the better and spurning what they had lost or discarded as the price of becoming something else. It was a very human amnesia, this spewing of the past while hungrily swallowing the future. Like colliding waves, they broke and fell away.

But to think: Russell had once called the twenty-three-year-old Wittgenstein his philosophical heir, the most brilliant man he had ever met. Now Russell called him tragic, a brilliant failure. Russell said many cutting things, especially as Wittgenstein's influence in certain circles began to eclipse his own. This was what was beginning to happen by 1946. Russell's philosophical work was then undergoing one of those periodic declines of reputation. Indeed, his reputation was suffering the aftershocks of his own hegemony and grandeur as a thinker. He was too gargantuan; his successors had to throw him off, had to debunk and devalue him so their own work could proceed, unintimidated. But beyond that, Russell was a victim of his own fame and success, qualities that to those who were unknown or, worse, only marginally successful meant he must now be a smug old fraud who was happily coasting — and cashing in — on his name. Russell simply did too many things well, wore too many hats — educator, journalist, sexual revolutionary, libertarian, gadfly, pundit, peace advocate and moral leader. And these were by no means all his hats. To his now venerable head, others would have sooner fastened goat's horns and plastered his forehead with scarlet letters proclaiming "Atheist," "Philanderer," "Pervert," "Public Pest."

This was the same Russell who corresponded with Einstein, Gandhi and Niels Bohr, who hectored and advised kings, premiers and presidents and who had long shown an intransigent willingness — if not an appetite — to be jailed if necessary in the cause of peace and the free exchange of civil beliefs. Russell didn't just have detractors, he had sworn enemies.

The press loved and hated him, but early on Russell had been shrewd enough to see that, in the long run, the periodic black eyes they gave him made no difference and sometimes even worked in his favor. All that really mattered, he realized, was that he be provocative and quotable. *He was the story;* the papers were only the mouthpiece, and he plied them like a master ventriloquist so that no matter how they distorted or vilified him, they spoke with one voice, blabbing the universal praise of publicity.

Russell was a master of the bon mot and the slogan, of the seemingly good-natured slight, fraught with élan and bonhomie, which fizzed up like a fatal heartburn in the person slighted. In Wittgenstein's case, the old fox knew better than to show himself as a bitter old man nursing a grudge against a now famous associate. His tone was not angry. Rather, it implied a wistful *what if* as he shook his hoary head with the thought of all Wittgenstein might have been. Ah, it was a tragic loss. Yes, he opined, it must have been the First War — why, it would have been enough to unhinge anyone, let alone so finely tuned a mind. And then there was the long absence from philosophy, the deliberate isolation from his colleagues. Sad, very sad.

Yet without fail there came the *but,* and then the blow. Tragic, Wittgenstein's influence. Incalculable, the damage he had done. Russell — and now most emphatically *Lord* Russell — was now penning his memoirs. Yes, Lord Gadabout Russell was talking more freely than ever. I'm an old goat but I don't butt or bite, he would playfully tell students and reporters. *Ask,* I say! That's all. You have only to ask.

Aristocratic and elegant, wearing a rumpled chalk-striped suit, Russell was persuasive and charming, even seductive. A mist of dry white hair swept back over his oblong skull. The face was long and drawn, and the nobbed upper-class chin, though receding, was still hard, rearing back like a ball-peen hammer when he laughed. Then there was the pipe with its gurgling and popping. Thumbing the pipe, then knocking it against the wide heel of his palm. Locking it back between his discolored molars where it seemed a slot had formed. Grinning. Just grinning.

His voice was Whig-BBC, a little shrill when excited. Yes, he said, Wittgenstein had brought chaos, beguiling many naive young men, not to mention many older philosophers who ought to have known better. Worse, added Russell, betraying a little testiness, there were Wittgenstein's beliefs. Take his disingenuous, Tolstoyan fantasy that philosophy can be conducted solely with *ordinary* language. Russell threw up his arms. As if an ordinary person would bother to read — let alone comprehend — a word Wittgenstein has written! Yet Wittgenstein acts as if employing a more precise, technical vocabulary is a sin against democracy!

Russell sighed. For the life of me, I can't fathom his concerns. Really now, who cares what silly people mean when they say silly things? If I were to say, I see the table, Wittgenstein would ask, But in what sense of the word "see"? Oh, I can just see him, biting the word like a piece of bad money. Well, life is simply too short for that sort of nonsense, don't you agree?

Realizing he was getting nigh into a rant, Russell reined himself in. Look at me, he said, dropping his shoulders with a smile. Here I am going on about Wittgenstein and the poor fellow hasn't published a word in twenty years — why, twenty-five years at least. But of course, conceded Russell, grinning out the side of his mouth, a humble man like Wittgenstein can hardly be concerned with mere publishing. *Jesus* never published, after all . . .

People were only too happy to carry and embellish Russell's words — or invent them. One way or another, though, the words always returned to Wittgenstein, harsher and more stinging. Wittgenstein wasn't one for mudslinging, but he made an exception in Russell's case. In response to Russell's barb likening him to Jesus, Wittgenstein retorted that Russell, like the old Tolstoy, had fallen victim to his own insane celebrity. Celebrity had driven him to the point that he could hear only his own voice. Why, said Wittgenstein, you could hardly turn on a radio broadcast without hearing Lord-Help-Us Russell spouting nonsense on the revolting BBC *Brain Trust* program. What a life! Publicly whining about the atom bomb while popping around the world collecting fat lecture fees, having his picture taken and eating lavish suppers! Well, if nothing else, said Wittgenstein, I, unlike Russell, am a *practicing* philosopher. No wonder Russell finds philosophy so easy now. The man has done no real philosophical thinking in thirty years.

In a bruised way, Russell and Wittgenstein relished these snipings, which, paradoxically, made their former closeness all the more apparent. The last time they saw each other, as it turned out, was at a meeting of the Cambridge Moral Science Club in 1946, five years before Wittgenstein's death and four years before Russell's Nobel.

It was appropriate that G. E. Moore should have been presiding over the meeting. For years, Moore had acted as a sort of buffer between Wittgenstein and Russell.

Wittgenstein had assumed Moore's chair at Cambridge when Moore had retired, and the two were still on quite friendly terms. Wittgenstein found the judicious Moore a good sounding board for his ideas, and he met with the old don every Tuesday to discuss philosophy, music, literature or anything else that struck their interest. The two men also met once a month at the Moral Science Club, where Wittgenstein would appear like a guilty conscience to brain a visiting Reputation or silence some mouthy young twit.

Moore ran a civil meeting, thoughtfully introducing speakers and rapping his gavel whenever a discussion got out of hand. A boyish, courtly, paunchy man of seventy-three, with fine white hair and rosy little chaps for cheeks, Moore was the most unvain of men, especially great men. In this respect alone, he could not have been more unlike the contentious Russell. Since their undergraduate days at Cambridge they had known each other, and for almost as long they had been rivals. Typically, this rivalry was more Russell's doing than Moore's, but it was largely quiescent now, not from any change of heart or, Lord knows, from the supposed softening of age, but as a purely practical matter. After all, the two men almost never saw each other. They moved in completely different orbits, and though they did not want to admit it, they both knew their best work was behind them. As elder statesmen secure in their reputations — indeed, as men whose names were even commonly linked because of their early alliance in demolishing the idealism of Bradley, the reigning *ism* when they were both coming up at Cambridge in the late 1890s — they knew there was nothing to be gained from squabbling. To Russell, Moore did not present the threat he had forty years before, when the young author of *Principia Ethica* stood as the moral guide and example to a generation of young England's finest young minds, including Maynard Keynes, Lytton Strachey and Leonard Woolf. And faster than either of them cared to imagine, they were becoming history now — captive spirits.

Between them, then, was the tacit understanding that each would speak appreciatively, if briefly, about the other should his name come up. An innocent anecdote or thoughtful parenthesis, a thoughtful smile — that would do it. Moore admirably disguised his dismay when he learned that Russell would be attending that night's meeting. The speaker, a visiting professor from the University of Chicago, might as well have stayed home. It was Wittgenstein and Russell they came to see, and the normal audience of two or three dozen swelled to a standing-room crowd of more than a hundred.

Russell was the first to arrive, accompanied by a little throng of students and several dons. Russell observed the etiquette: straightaway, he went up to Moore and warmly shook his hand. The master courtier asked about Dorothy, Moore's wife. He asked about Moore's two sons, just demobilized, then turned, in passing, to ask of Moore's health and work. Well . . . said Moore, reaching for a comparable question (wondering, that is, which wife or mistress Russell was on). Tell me, resumed the politic Moore, altogether sidestepping the sensitive question of woman. How are *your* children?

Very well — oh, very well indeed . . .

And so they stood, making bland small talk, waiting for Wittgenstein while answering the usual nervous questions from people who nosed up like frightened fry, searching for some pretext to shake Russell's hand — longing to feel the heat of his genius while inwardly marveling or carping at the least things he said, as if genius must always be radiantly manifest, like the emanations from some true magnetic north.

The voltage jumped when Wittgenstein arrived with his contingent. He walked right up to Russell, the way parting before him. The two men observed the same etiquette, shaking hands and whispering inaudible pleasantries, all too aware of the eyes upon them. It was too civil for words — too civil to last, Moore saw. He quickly called the meeting to order.

The speaker was a large, balding, petulant man. His paper, entitled "The Articulation of Moral Rules," was a thicket of grammar and conjecture grown over assorted categorical holes in which rabbits consorted with porcupines to produce polecats. The speaker knew Wittgenstein's reputation as a spoiler, and when Wittgenstein raised his hand immediately afterward, the man was gunning for him.

Looking up thoughtfully, Wittgenstein said, These categories you have for moral values. It's all so tidy, everything in its place, as in an apothecary's shop. Leaving aside this questionable business about articulation, I am quite confused by these categories.

Well, retorted the speaker, anxious to land the first punch. I understand you're confused by a great many things, Dr. Wittgenstein. In fact, from what I understand, you've done an admirable job yourself in the confusion department.

The gloves were off. Staring holes through him, Wittgenstein said, It's your work we're discussing tonight, not mine. And I would say you've built your edifice by exercising what I would call *air rights*. First, you must lay a foundation — something *on the ground*.

Wittgenstein did not react to the guffaw he got at *air rights*. The crowd was roused. Russell, meanwhile, was chafing to wade in and single out

Wittgenstein, but the discussion between Wittgenstein and the speaker grew so heated he couldn't get a word in.

Russell was almost panting. He kept opening his mouth, snatching gulps of air, waiting for his chance to seize Wittgenstein by the ears. Moore was raising his gavel. The speaker was on the mat; he knew he was about to get trounced and he was stalling. Sweat gleamed on his forehead. Red in the face, he leaned down ponderously, his wattling cheeks shaking as he uttered, All I've heard from you are charges, generalities! Again, Dr. Wittgenstein. Ask me something *specific*.

I'd be happy to, said Wittgenstein. He was getting ready to make a point — one several steps down the line — and in so doing, he had absent-mindedly picked up a poker from the hearth beside him. Wittgenstein did not brandish or even point the poker at the speaker. He just held it abstractly and said, Good. We'll have no more confusion. Here is a direct and highly *specific* question. Just give me *one* example of an unassailable moral rule.

One? roared the speaker, grasping the sides of the podium menacingly. Just *one*, you ask? Yes, *Herr Doktor*, I'll be happy to! *Never threaten speakers with pokers!*

The audience gasped. Moore's gavel banged down. Wittgenstein was completely shocked to see every eye upon him as if he had indeed thrust the poker in the man's face. His eyes blazed at the speaker — later, some said they thought he would hurl the iron at him. *Clang!* People jumped as the iron rang on the hearth. Jaw set with fury, Wittgenstein lunged for the door, his legs moving like whips.

Wittgenstein! called Moore, standing up. Moore called him a second time, and not unsympathetically, seeing that Wittgenstein had meant nothing by the poker. But Russell drowned him out as he jumped up, shouting, *Wittgenstein!* Come-back-at-once!

Lord Russell! remonstrated Moore, rapping the gavel.

Russell couldn't hear him. Never had they seen the unrufflable Russell in such a state. Why, they thought the old boy would charge out and drag Wittgenstein back, so furious was he at being cheated of the last word. But of Russell's sudden, extravagant anger, what they most remembered was how he shook his fist at Wittgenstein's departing back, bellowing:

Run away, then! But it's *you,* Wittgenstein! *Yooooou* are the source of confusion!

BOOK I

The Foreworld

All men are equally mystified by unaccountable evidence, even Homer, wisest of the Greeks. He was mystified by children catching lice. He heard them say, What we have found and caught we throw away; what we have not found and caught we still have.

— Heraclitus

Strong Wind

WITTGENSTEIN'S association with Russell began, not with philosophy or logic, but as an outgrowth of his study of aeronautics in England, at the University of Manchester. It was the summer of 1912, another season of international air shows, crackups and aviation records. Wittgenstein was twenty-three. André Gobe had flown a breathtaking 459 miles, Jules Védrines, attaining 90 m.p.h., had broken the record Nieuport had set seven months before and Roland Garros, piloting a Blériot, had set a world altitude record of 12,960 feet. Wittgenstein had been working on propeller designs — a basically mathematical task — and experimenting with various wing surfaces, which had led him into work with kites.

But Wittgenstein was also thinking that summer of branching off into the study of philosophy, specifically, the philosophy of logic. This was not as sudden and unaccountable a change as it seemed to his father, Karl Wittgenstein, who by then had concluded that Ludwig would remain a dilettante just like his other sons, the gifted pianist Paul and the woeful Kurt, who was interested in little more in life than French cooking, stamps and opera.

But though Karl Wittgenstein might ridicule, hector or ignore — though he might wax "philosophical," painting himself as a sorry Job cursed with boils for boys — whatever else, he was not about to repeat the fatal mistake of cutting one of them off. Karl Wittgenstein groaned when his son announced his intention of leaving aeronautical engineering — a course he had hardly greeted with enthusiasm — for the study of logic and philosophy. Wittgenstein knew his father was about to give him the treatment. His father opened his mouth, then stopped himself. He lowered his head and thought for a moment. He was quite, *quite* calm now. Very well, he said, blinking at a notion so clearly imbecilic. But please tell me: if I should be asked, what title shall I give your new profession? *Aviator-philosopher?*

Karl Wittgenstein was a wealthy steel magnate, a peer of the Krupps and a good friend of his American counterpart and fellow philanthropist Andrew Carnegie. During Austria's economic expansion in the 1880s and 1890s, Karl Wittgenstein almost single-handedly modernized the empire's decrepit, ill-organized steel industry, earning himself the sobriquet "The Rationalizer of Industry." But Karl Wittgenstein was equally prominent in Vienna as a patron of the arts. As a result of his daughter Mining's early association with the painter Gustav Klimt, Karl Wittgenstein, in the late 1890s, had largely underwritten the cost of building Vienna's Secession Hall, where the bold new artists, breaking with the bankrupt classical historicism of the salons, proclaimed their objective of showing modern man his own face. Karl Wittgenstein was even better known as a patron and impresario of music. Brahms and Mahler, Josef Labor and Bruno Walter, the young Pablo Casals — these and other artists were featured in Karl Wittgenstein's soirees at the Palais Wittgenstein, where as many as three hundred of Vienna's wealthy and prominent would be in attendance.

In that ancient, hierarchical city, names and titles for even the lowliest were an obsession. Families schemed and groveled for two and three generations to get the noble *von* affixed to their names, yet Karl Wittgenstein did the unthinkable when he declined the emperor's offer to ennoble the Wittgenstein family in recognition of his contributions to the empire. It was not modesty that led Karl Wittgenstein to do this; quite the contrary, he believed the title to be superfluous to his noble nature, which he felt was manifest in the very grandeur of his achievements.

Karl Wittgenstein's human grandeur and vaunted standards were no less evident in his home, where his seven children and thirty-odd servants lived in fear of his periodic eruptions. Typically, these rages occurred as a result of some peccadillo or misunderstanding, the culprit summarily tried and hanged with no last words or stay of execution. Besides being a stickler for deportment, Karl Wittgenstein was fond of drilling his children in Latin, Greek, geometry, history or musical theory at the dinner table — this while three servants stood by, ready to leap lest a soup drop soil his cravat or his scrupulous cuff scrape a butter pat embossed with the regal W. Like gifts from the East, each successive course would be brought to him first for tasting. Hot from the spirit lamp, steaming in their silver chafing dishes and quickly swaddled in crisp linen by a white-gloved butler — Behold, sir, a *Vorspeise* of crayfish in dill — followed, in season, by roast boar or perhaps a golden carp fattened in the cook's tub for a week before being steamed and smothered, Czech style, in a pungent black sauce. Course after course it came, poached squab and veal tongues, hot puddings and brook trout *au bleu*, all expiring as if with a squeal into the master's trembling nostrils. The father never tired of this presentation ritual. The liveried butler would produce a gleaming spoon, and all would breathlessly watch as Karl Wittgenstein brought it to his bearded lips, his eyes gliding up quizzically while his sensitive palate discerned whether he would praise or dress down the head cook or perhaps write a patronizing two-page disquisition to the *Mehlspeiseköchin*, the dessert cook, on the proper presentation of a soufflé or the secret to glazing a *Sachertorte*.

The father seemed massive at the head of the table, which was covered with an embroidered damask cloth and bathed under the light of three fiery candelabras. Wittgenstein remembered the room as being dizzyingly overwarm, the rich food heavy with flour-thickened gravies and sauces, with sour cream and *Schlagobers* that raised his temperature under his thick woolen suit until his itchy starched shirt was soaked through. His head, by the fifth course, would sometimes feel almost insupportable. And then his feet would be going to sleep in the tightly laced high boots that his manservant had blacked and set out with his clothes, which were laid across the bed like an inflatable replica of himself that he was expected to stuff with food and knowledge, growing, like his father, to impossible size.

His mother, Poldy, was an intelligent, loving woman and an accomplished organist, but for the life of him Wittgenstein could not remember her ever saying a word at that table except in those extreme instances when she felt compelled to defend one of the children from their father's wrath. Through interminable courses they were admonished not to eat too slowly or too fast. Moreover, *des Vaters* food was to be eaten properly, almost sacramentally, without frivolous talking, slumping or giggling. At the same time, they were expected to adopt a "philosophical" — meaning, serious-minded — attitude as they discussed Karl Wittgenstein's latest hortatory economic essay in *Das Neue Wiener Tageblatt* or sat through his brilliant, though stultifying, monologues on Goethe, Brahms, the industrial dynamism of America (where he had lived several years as a young man) or the chronic need to reassess the crippling effect of the government's tax and tariff policies.

Even the vaultlike Palais Wittgenstein seemed an extension of Karl

Wittgenstein. Three stories tall and imperial in its pretensions, it was a glacier of Baroque stone and stucco that seemed to have slid over mountains, palaces and assorted shrines before skidding down Vienna's tree-lined boulevards to the fashionable Allegasse, where it finally came to rest, by then encrusted with every kind of pillar, gargoyle and relief that human imagination had ever concocted after a dyspeptic night. Ugly or not, the house did have wonderful acoustics. It rang with music. Karl Wittgenstein played the cello, and his wife played the piano, of which the house had four, along with a pipe organ and a harpsichord. All of the Wittgenstein children were musical, and often as a Sunday divertissement Karl Wittgenstein would lead his versatile family ensemble through Haydn trios or Schubert quartets, sometimes managing to get through an entire composition without indulging in a thirty-minute diatribe on tempo or proper *feeling* that would leave them all red in the face or near tears.

No one in the family could have found these lectures more odious than Wittgenstein's two oldest brothers, Hans and Rudolf. Both were musical prodigies, and both, despite Karl Wittgenstein's astounding ability to ignore the fact, were homosexual. Looking back on it, Wittgenstein felt his older brothers were perhaps too musical, too feverishly overbred and severe for this life. For them it proved impossible to live under the interdict of this father, who loomed before them like the Last Judgment. The oldest, Hans, committed suicide by syringe in Cuba in 1902, when Wittgenstein was thirteen. By all appearances, Karl Wittgenstein managed to almost completely expunge this tragedy from his consciousness. Hans's life was his own, he said, willfully forgetting that Hans had been deeply depressed after his father banished him for his defiant insistence on a career in music and not in that bold consortium of coal, iron ore, steel plants and capital known as the Wittgenstein Gruppe. The Rationalizer of Industry was somewhat less successful in his rationalizations two years later when Rudolf took his own life under similar circumstances. Wittgenstein's sister Gretl once said she felt like a lump of coal, living under such a mountain of a father. The mountain produced some diamonds, she said, but they were brittle diamonds and some had shattered, or very nearly shattered. Wittgenstein very nearly shattered several times. Music and philanthropy weren't the only traditions in the Wittgenstein family.

Hitler was born in Austria in the same year Wittgenstein was, 1889. Catholic Vienna was a cosmopolitan but anti-Semitic city, and around this time anti-Semitism was becoming an increasing force in its politics and consciousness. One of the most successful politicians of the period was the Christian Social party's Karl Lueger, who served as mayor from 1897 to 1910. "Handsome Karl," who wanted Jews barred from all participation in public life, was more anti-Semitic in his rhetoric than in practice, but he was still successful in bringing anti-Semitism once more to the forefront of public discourse. The other force in the city was the paunchy, mutton-chopped old Hapsburg emperor, Franz Josef, who on his birthday would don full military regalia of scarlet and plumes and ride through the city in an open carriage while the women waved their lace hankies and the men gravely doffed their top hats and bowlers. The emperor, while mildly anti-Semitic in outlook, was careful to keep silent on the subject. But the ambitious and opportunistic Lueger troubled himself with neither scruples nor coherence, whipping up a misty confection of democracy, social reform, anti-Semitism, Catholicism, concern for the little man and sheer personality. The emperor loathed Lueger so much that he refused to ratify his election as mayor in 1895. Sigmund Freud, no supporter of the monarchy, smoked a cigar in celebration of the emperor's courageous decision. It was only a temporary reprieve. Two years later, the emperor caved in to the popular tide for *den schönen Karl,* beautiful Karl with the waltzing walk and golden side whiskers. Thereafter, Franz Josef did little to oppose Lueger or the brand of demagoguery he found so barbaric and irrational. Still, Lueger's politics could hardly be less bankrupt than the woolgathering of the old order, a monarchial bureaucracy whose values were by then as dull and ceremonial as the sabers the nobles gravely dragged across sundry palace rugs, ballrooms and reviewing stands. Distasteful as it was, Lueger's splattering, red-faced oratory *was* effective — indeed, the mayor was one of Hitler's earliest influences.

Lueger's ascendancy also roughly coincided with the trial of Captain Alfred Dreyfus, the Jewish French army officer accused of treason. But of course Dreyfus was only a pawn, a proxy: it was not Dreyfus but Europe's Jews who were on trial, and though Dreyfus was eventually acquitted, Europe's Jews were not.

Covering the Dreyfus trial in Paris for the *Neue Freie Presse,* the young journalist Theodor Herzl became convinced that assimilation would never work and, upon his return to Vienna, revived the old dream of creating a Jewish state in Palestine. Many prominent Gentiles agreed with Herzl's estimation of the Jewish question. Why, they were even so generous as to provide him with money and introductions to courts and politicians, regarding the extraordinary young revolutionary as a kind of Pied Piper sent to rid Europe of her Jews.

Karl Wittgenstein wanted no part of these mass delusions or of Herzl's messianism. He accepted the fact that there would be periodic flare-ups of anti-Semitism, yet on the whole he preferred to continue along the assimilationist course, having accepted the Devil's proposition that people are, on the whole, more reasonable than they are unreasonable. Vienna, after all, was a city of converts who had put off the old clothes, the old language and ways, to, if not exactly embrace, then at least go through the motions of Christianity. Karl Wittgenstein had been baptized a Protestant at an early age, while his wife was a baptized Catholic. Poldy insisted the children should be baptized Catholic, and since this was the most practical religion from a purely social standpoint, Karl Wittgenstein ceded to her wishes.

So it was that Wittgenstein and his brothers and sisters were raised to receive communion under the instruction of Monsignor Molke, who frequently served mass at the Palais Wittgenstein for the family and servants. Still, there were reminders of the family's Jewish past in the guise of their bearded paternal grandfather, Hermann Wittgenstein, and several decrepit aunts and uncles who clung to the old ways, whispering in Yiddish and reading their obscure Hebraic newspapers. This was charming, if distant, like the Menorah, the fringed prayer shawl and the ancient leather-covered prayer book that could be found in the library, locked in a chest of unvarnished oak carved with apocalyptic creatures. Still more haunting to the boy were the cracked daguerreotypes in their frames, wobbly photographs the color of muddy water, showing the dark, wild-looking *shtetl* ancestors dressed in black gabardine and gazing out fearfully at the camera. Looking at them, the boy would feel that through some black keyhole of time they were staring out *at him* — wondering at this child with the slick brown hair and modern white shirt, sitting with his books on the tassled sofa in the tall, wainscotted library.

His Jewish roots were hardly a constant concern, and yet as a boy it had sometimes troubled Wittgenstein to realize that his family had not always been the same people, as if one time or faith had been true and the other a lie. They were a becoming people, the Wittgensteins. Later in life, he would recall this queer sense of a family remembering forward, with the past a kind of becoming that might be skillfully retouched, unraveled and re-remembered with the fiery Yule tree, the greens that wreathed the door and, outside, the eerie little manger with its garishly painted wise men — not joyful tidings, it seemed, but talismans to ward off danger and hasten the tide of becoming.

Unfortunately, in Vienna it took several generations at least before one was considered completely assimilated, so far as one was ever assimilated. For some, this purgatorial process took longer than for others, and for some like Wittgenstein, the effects were delayed for years as the Christian scraped bones with the vestigial Jew within. But there was another, somewhat parallel legacy for Wittgenstein to overcome, one that began when his brother Hans took his life in Cuba. Hans was guilty of the elementary sin: the sin of despair. Banished, scuttled with sin, lost even from God, Hans had not just poisoned himself or his hated father; in that act of revenge, he had poisoned a whole family and even the future. Life was the fold into which Hans could not assimilate, but then Hans was hardly the only one in that fomenting city to fail at this task. Like caged canaries sunk in a mine shaft, other raw and excitable souls were beginning to smell the fumes of that futurity.

Odd how the impossible negation of death — the sudden absence of life where once there was promise — can stimulate an early philosophical bent. In Wittgenstein's case, it was a growing sense of precariousness — indeed, a profound suspicion — of what until then had seemed life's givens. From earliest childhood, Wittgenstein had been haunted and frightened by the morbid Hans, but then one day in 1902 the boy was suddenly told that his old tormentor and nemesis, that aesthete's aesthete, was dead. Yet how did he know this for certain? There was no body. His brother returned from Cuba as a funeral urn, a ghastly hunk of crusted Spanish silver that would have turned Hans's sensitive stomach.

The boy had no doubt that the obsessive Hans had composed a death that would yield the utmost in pain and ambiguity. When they finally interred his ashes in the family crypt, even their friend Monsignor Molke, by then archbishop of Vienna, could not officially bury the suicide. All the priest could offer was a few mumbled *ave*s and a faint pass of the hand. Wittgenstein stood huddled in a clump with his ruined siblings and their inconsolable mother, who was shrouded beneath a tent of black veils. As a family they were broken, but the boy could see that his father was by no means broken: Karl Wittgenstein's face was a pink wall of wanton health. Was the father not relieved, in a way, to be rid of this miserable invert, this Judas goat who had defied him? Had the boy not heard his father say with a sigh to an uncle that it was probably all for the best?

That day in 1902, the boy stood watching his father with something like loathing that burned his stomach. If his father could not feel sorrow, thought the boy, he might at least feel shame. But Karl Wittgenstein betrayed no shame for the simple reason that he felt, or said he felt, no guilt or responsibility for Hans. The truth was, Karl Wittgenstein betrayed no discernible emotion then or any day after save a kind of vague, chaste disgust — an almost aesthetic reaction, as if his son had committed a breach against good taste. And all the while the boy kept wondering if the ashes were really Hans's, or if the Cubans had merely shoveled dirt into that ugly urn which seemed so impossibly small to contain his brother.

By the time Wittgenstein decided to leave aeronautics for philosophy ten years later, his relationship with his father was even more tense and tangled. During that period, Karl Wittgenstein had changed as a father, loosening the reins while growing ever more cautious and shrewd. Now an indefatigable man of sixty-five, he had no need of edicts or ultimatums. Diplomacy has other, more subtle means, and so it continued, with the father and son conducting their affairs like two rival heads of state, albeit a big state over a little one.

What had never changed in those ten years were his father's expectations, which were heavier for being unspoken. Contrary to Karl Wittgenstein's accusations, his son had not failed to consider his father's feelings in his latest decision, nor was this course as illogical and precipitous as the old man wanted to believe. Wittgenstein had already given three years of study to Bertrand Russell's *Principles of Mathematics*. More recently, he had been poring over the first volume of the book's successor, *Principia Mathematica*, a mountainous three-volume work on the logical foundations of mathematics that Russell and Alfred North Whitehead were completing after nearly a decade of labor. Besides studying Russell, Wittgenstein had been reading Russell's most immediate predecessor, the virtual inventor of modern symbolic logic, Gottlob Frege. Earlier that summer, in fact, Wittgenstein had traveled to Jena, a medieval university town in central Germany where Frege was a professor, to consult the old logician about his future.

Before their meeting, Wittgenstein sent Frege a courtly letter praising his work and declaring his interest in logic. Frege, in turn, sent Wittgenstein a brief reply, thanking him for his letter and saying that he would be pleased to meet him if he cared to come to Jena. Literalist that he was, Wittgenstein took Herr Professor Frege at his word: a month or so later, Frege's housekeeper answered the door only to find a young man dressed in a dark and expensively tailored suit and carrying under his arm a box of cigars. The housekeeper looked askance when he asked for the professor and curtly presented his card: he looked young for a card, especially for so expensive a card, slender and embossed and edged with gold.

As someone who had been raised with servants, the young man knew how to handle the housekeeper; it was clear from his subdued and correct manner that he was not to be trifled with. At the same time, the housekeeper had her station. She did not keep house for just anybody, she kept the house for a famous university professor who received many important visitors, and she was apt to take her sweet time, or even to tell the person to call later if she didn't like his manner or looks. But few visitors were so refined, or so finely dressed, as this young man. And fewer still came with their own cards, much less bearing expensive cigars. She fetched Herr Professor Frege.

Coming around the staircase several minutes later, still putting on his rumpled little suit jacket with his stubby hands, Frege was a trifle dismayed to see the owner of the card standing so darkly and fiercely correct, with his springy hair standing on end like a waxwing's crest. Frege knew at a glance what the housekeeper knew: the young man sprang from wealth and social position.

As for Wittgenstein, he could hardly hide his dismay when he realized the author of the great *Begriffsschrift* was this pudgy, elfin old man with a grizzled beard and white hair. At least, thought Wittgenstein, Frege might have kept his suit coat brushed and his cravat in better repair. In this respect Wittgenstein was still his father's son, still the *haute* Viennese. Such things still mattered to him then.

Wittgenstein made a slight bow and presented Frege with the cigars. These were princely cigars, choice Havanas wrapped in tissue paper and rollers of shaved cedar. Frege was delighted, though he protested that such a lavish gift was entirely unnecessary — and yet the warm tropical fumes as he opened the well-fitted humidor on its brass hinges. Glorious! he groaned, sticking his blunt nose into the box. If Frege did not expect cigars, neither did Wittgenstein expect the great logician to luxuriantly sniff the length of one as if it were a rind of ripe cheese.

Sensing the young man's hauteur — and nervousness — Frege then took him down a peg, saying, Well, you're certainly *punctual*, Herr Wittgenstein — though I can't say by whose clock. But, please, sir, come into my study.

The interview began stiffly, but Wittgenstein soon showed the logician his mettle. Within minutes, Wittgenstein was pacing the floor, declaiming.

Unwrapping one of the Havanas, Frege licked it with a practiced twirl, then set it to match, saying with a smile, You didn't say I was going to have to work for this nosegay, Herr Wittgenstein.

The young man's ideas were half-baked, and Frege duly gave him a theoretical bruising. But what Wittgenstein said wasn't so important; it was how he fought Frege's mind, how he fought for the primacy of his own understanding — *this* was what seized Frege's attention. Manners fell by the wayside; there wasn't time. The young Viennese was stubborn and argumentative. Worse, he had a bad habit of interrupting. *No!* protested Wittgenstein, and then he stopped himself. It cannot be ... I just — *I don't know!* he snapped, and then he turned away, the blood blurting up into his face, blinded by the shame of *not seeing*, at once forty steps ahead and forty behind. But even more, Frege saw how the young man would not let go, saw his tremendous, irascible impatience to get at it — at what he could not quite see but vividly intuited.

The pungent cigar was faintly narcotic. Sitting slumped in his heavy, overstuffed chair, the cigar raised like an exclamation point, Frege inwardly flagged then. Now a man over sixty, he felt a vague melancholy sifting over him, saddened, in the face of this rampant youth, to realize his own diminished energies. He simply didn't have the strength, not for this one. This one, he saw, needed a younger man to take him in tow. Frege puffed out his cheeks with smoke, then exhaled, saying in a low, rasping voice, *Rus-sell.*

Wittgenstein looked up quizzically. Watery eyed with the smoke, Frege said, Work with Russell at Cambridge. He's the one doing the new work now. Write to him. You may use my name.

Frege roused himself from the chair and cleared his throat. Wittgenstein was still staring when the old logician looked back in good-natured dismay and said, On second thought, I will send Russell a note myself. Not to recommend you, you understand, but to warn him. That's all. Just a friendly note of warning.

Wittgenstein took Frege's advice: he wrote to Russell. Russell replied favorably, and by early September Wittgenstein was officially enrolled at Cambridge. Karl Wittgenstein, meanwhile, was fulminating over his son's latest letter formally notifying him of his intentions. Wittgenstein was in England finishing up his aeronautical work when he received his father's reply — a warning shot across the bow:

5. September 1912

My Son,
    Your latest letter, like our last interview, was unsatisfactory. As usual, there was your own natural — I want to say *willful* — difficulty and reticence and my own inclination to want to seize a certain pass and plow through various recurrent objections, which, as I see it, are just that — stubborn objections.

To philosophy you bring a certain irritating skepticism and the uncanny ability to make others feel self-conscious. But can these truly be called *gifts?*

You would say, "I cannot have my gifts guaranteed *in advance.*" Quite true. No man could do anything if he first had to vouch for his priority. God, I told the Royal Guild, grants no charters; one takes that out for oneself. But to fish one requires at least a stout boat; it is not enough to express mere inclination to fish or eat fish. If this were the case, every young man of quality in Vienna who did not have to shift for a living would be an artist; the rest would be rich idlers. The world has already too many artists with their kits and claims, their astounding pretensions. I do not mistake the rightful place of philosophy. Philosophy *is* an art but has an even more tenuous claim to truth than does Art itself, which at least claims to be nothing more than it is. No philosophical system has ever proven anything. All a philosophy shows are the presumptions and proclivities of the philosopher, who simply cuts the coat to fit the cloth. Do not speak to me of Absolute Truth. At best the effect is only beautiful or evanescently satisfying in the way of myth. Goethe is more believable and a thousand times more honorable than any philosopher. Forget your beloved Schopenhauer, that latter-day Ecclesiastes. Schopenhauer can open his wrists and call it literature because he did not have to toil for a living or offer the world anything but vain groanings. We need men who bring STEAM to the world; we need, if anything, another Goethe, and you — need I say it? — are no Goethe.

Would it surprise you if I said I, too, had wanted at one time to be a philosopher? True to say, in my published writings I have touched, shall we say, on a *civil* philosophy of an obdurate variety that puts steel in the foundation and ensures a certain code of civil workmanship, with the finest of materials and work that goes according to some foreseeable SCHEDULE. But I realized much earlier than you — now, I might add, in your twenty-third year — that it was not in my veins to be a philosopher, not at least as Kant is a philosopher, or Goethe a poet-philosopher. What of your case? You are abundantly *talented.* But to think of you as a philosopher . . . I am skeptical because I know what thinking went into the formation of your character. You did not just fall into the world; it was with long and exacting deliberation that I planned the education of you and your siblings, and why, indeed, I concluded that my children could be educated only under my roof with hand-picked tutors.

It DISTRESSES me, dear son, to see you, a man of enviable intellect and talent, flounder in this way. I wish I could be more sanguine in this, yet you see, I did not found a family not to know that family, and if I should raise an eyebrow at your latest fancy, please understand that it is in the interests of a resolute *efficiency.* I, too, have traveled this path, and I do not believe the way of the Wittgensteins goes there.

I trust you will give my words some CONSIDERATION.

Your concerned Father

This little *pensée*, as his father was wont to call these thunderbolts, fell on Wittgenstein's chest with the weight of ten atmospheres. With anybody else, Wittgenstein's rebuttal would have been quick and sure, but this was not to be thrown off so quickly. He suffered three days and five drafts before he replied.

13.9.12.

Dear Father,

First, you vastly exaggerate my love of Schopenhauer and degrade my love of Goethe. You make other erroneous assumptions. Halley's Comet appeared two years ago. It is probable that it will return in 74 years, but it is not a matter of *logic* to assume so; it is only an expression of statistical belief.

I make this point in reference to your comments on Goethe. Do not wait for him, nor Schiller nor Beethoven. If Goethe were to return with the comet, we would not recognize him because we expect him in the guise of the last coming. In fact, as with all artists or thinkers, he comes — *if* he comes at all — as a wolf in wolf's clothing, obstinate and himself, different than expected, *wrong*. Please do not put words in my mouth. I do not look, as you suggest, for Absolute Truth. No truth is absolute, not even a star in the sky like our Goethe.

I see I already regret this letter. Please, can we avoid turning this into one of those feuds one finds waged across editorial pages? If I must, *if only for now*, follow this path, you might at least humor me so the journey might be easier. Do you believe one's life is entirely a matter of conscious choice? Is the mule merely stubborn? — or does he instead find his hooves stuck in the mud of unyielding necessity?

Your respectful son

After this letter, Wittgenstein returned to his kites, but the sick feeling persisted and with it a certain floating anxiety. And so he buried himself in his work, looking *out* into the phenomenological world to keep the worsening weather of his boiling inner world contrite and contained.

These were big, aerodynamically curved kites he was flying, wide wings in need of galloping winds. For such winds, the University of Manchester had established the Upper Atmosphere Kite-Flying Station near Absdell, a cottage standing on a point where the headlands shear off into the Irish Sea.

For two days Wittgenstein had been there. For two days this feeling had been building. The kite, a ten-foot-tall red dihedral of laminated spruce and doped silk, had taken him four weeks to build, and in the twenty-knot wind it took right up, the stretched silk rattling like a jib sheet as it tore line from a winch wound with four thousand feet of 150-pound piano wire.

The sky was wreathed with cirrus. The wind was blowing out to sea. Behind him the brass cups of an anemometer whirled. He had a barometer and stopwatch, inclinometer and notebook, science and its methods — all forgotten now as he watched the kite sweep away.

Air desires. Water encircles and engulfs. The scourging waves recurred and pulled, seamlessly merging like stairs, without human meaning, without ever ending. As he looked down from that bluff, the waves seemed as meaningless and futile as the generations, no sooner surging than they were wiped clean of what they had just brought, falling back into an oceanic blackness, with a slow explosion of all that had passed before. Ocean or air — it was either the engulfment of will or the steady pull of desire that destroyed him. As a boy, and even now, he had suffered periodic bouts of agoraphobia, a fear not of height but of space. This fear came in different guises. At times he felt he would actually dissolve, perishing like an open flask of ether into the world's greater volume. Then at other times he saw it was not space he feared but the queasy feeling of *not knowing what he would do,* imagining that, like an unstable substance, he would somehow explode if ever fully exposed to the concupiscent air.

In the rising wind, spears of sharp sea grass were whirring like scissors. Clouds covered the sea and waves battered the rocks, spurting up in steamy plumes as the last birds beat back to shore. Across the sky, like a cornea filling with blood, came a fearful darkening. The piano wire was humming, and ever so faintly he was trembling, thinking what a thing it was to dread one's own self — to see the self as enemy or other, not as companion, guide, sanctuary.

Why is the will so powerless to stop the thing that life has set in motion? he wondered. Did he suppose that if he were to find value, some gloss of value might rub off on him? In all the sea there is a single pearl. In all the world there is a single, mirroring form that binds and reflects all other things. Desire was his crime, he saw. His father was right: surely, it was vain and sinful to want this thing. Surely, for this presumption punishment awaited. The ocean need not be deep for one to drown, nor need the grapes be high to be just past reach and hence all the sweeter. The dream is incomparably stronger than the dreamer.

His stomach sank with the barometer. Sore from thinking, sore from wanting — to him it seemed that even sex was easier. In his head a hum, a rhythm was hovering. On his lips, a question was forming . . .

Where in the world is value to be found?

It was the question of his life. Using logic as his calculus, he thought he would work progressively *out* from what could be said intelligibly until he reached the limits of what could *not* be said. And once having drawn this arc or limit, he would be able to better behold the logical form, or structure, of the world, isolating it in much the way a sculptor chisels down a block of alabaster, seeking to reveal the form glowing within.

A vain presumption, he thought. He was no better than Archimedes boasting that he could lift the earth if only he had a lever long enough and a planet to serve as a fulcrum. But these self-reproaches did not make the dream desist, they only made it all the more powerful. He could see himself in his vision, which had dimension and depth like a body of water. His vision was so strong that he felt he could stand right out of it. Ascending a ladder of propositions, he would plant his shoes on the last possible rung. And looking down, he would peer, as if through sheer form, into another world darkly mirrored under the aspect of eternity.

Yet how was this undertaking to be practically achieved? Was it to be had in the human heart for desiring — in the will for willing? He saw all too well that will has no power over the world, or its own reckless willing. The dissembling will only blames the hand, which blames the mind, which in turn blames the loins — dumb but no less turgid. And so the thirsting will turns on itself, curtailing itself from the misery of willing by deputizing the hand with its magnetic attraction to poison and sharp objects, to push and precipice and philandering air . . .

He closed his eyes, wishing his expanding will to be smaller, milder, more reasonable. But the will was not compliant; it would not be ordered about like some cringing subordinate. SAY, ventured the riddling will or mind. SAY, said the soul, which is as various and contrary as it is many. SAY this kite is your will, with this much line and this much scope under the general sky. And just as in an aeroplane there is thrust and drag, so the thrust of will must be factored over fear, chiefly the fear of rampant willing, that hell-bent runaway. And then, as Wittgenstein realized this, he pictured in his mind the following equation:

$$\frac{W}{F} = S$$

With: *W* being Will
        F being Fear
        S being Scope

It was the same old story. Here and no farther, God commanded the waves. Stand without and come no closer, said He to the barrier clouds, those lifebreakers that separate the earth from what lies beyond.

Wittgenstein could smell the squall, could taste it on his tongue, bitter as blood and rusted iron. Higher and higher rose the silver waves, heaving down and exploding up the beach as the clouds bumped with a fulminating green light. Facing the sky, Wittgenstein thought of the myth he had made up as a boy to explain his life. It was the story of how souls connect with bodies to become people. Before birth, the newly washed soul, then a snowy, sexless nothing, waits for a body. The soul has but one chance. If the soul moves one way, it becomes a male, if another, a female. But if the soul moves wrong or clumsily, the person takes on the impulses of both, so that he is never free or far from torment.

He then remembered how, as a boy, he had watched girls jumping rope, two twirling and a third swinging her arms, waiting to start jumping. Rhythmically, the rope slapped the pavement, walloping through the air. That rope would have sliced him in two, but for the girl it was easy. She was free. She watched the rope, not the intimidating sky. Effortlessly, she jumped in and out, chanting and stamping, turning four-square to the world that spun so tunelessly. And each time he saw how, as she jumped in, she closed her eyes, not in dread but joyously, seamlessly merging with the fatal ebb and slippage of life; chanting:

> My bird, it has a red, red ring,
> It sings the end of everything.

Straining and humming, the heavy wire curved up into the covering storm. Clouds concealed the kite. Pain congealed in his heart. He saw he'd never vault that chasm. The kite was all out, and the will was at its ecliptic — it would not be denied or cranked down. Rain splashed through his skull. His clothes filled with wind. The cable was stretching, and he could feel his clenched teeth grinding and sparking. Flashing through the lightning glints, the world shone before him like a lucid lake. For one wondrous moment, he could actually *see* it — could actually feel the lightning coils pooling in the hot blackness. In the hollows and vacuums, surges of value were collecting to infuse the loss, the pooling pain. In those holes, eternal value was welling, then exploding into thunderclaps of life. He was less already than the air — his pleasure when the cable snapped was almost obscene. Rain lashed his face, and drumming in his ears he heard that child's chiding chant:

> My bird, it has a red, red ring,
> It sings the end of everything.

The Distance from Thee to You

THAT SAME SUMMER, on a beach on the south coast of England, Bertrand Russell was witnessing a very different conflagration. Splashing down the shingle, a pack of pranksters were carrying on their shoulders Queen Mab, "Her Modesty" having no sooner been coronated with a seaweed wig and tin-can crown than the young ninnies plunged her, heartlessly, into the cold ocean.

Stop! Dropping her jeroboam scepter, Mab spat and sputtered, pulling slimy green strings of weed from her face. You're all w-orrrr-ible!

Chief among Mab's happy train were some healthy lads clad in woolen black one-pieces. Supple and young, infused with champagne, they stumbled along, their polished limbs glowing like amber in the gritty August sunshine. With these were other friends, prudent dears who by day never went unclad, yet who were so caught up in the merriment that they had dropped their Chinese parasols and soaked their creamy flannels in the waves. Down the beach, meanwhile, several prying neighbors, already wise to Mab and her weekend mob, could be seen peering, hands shading their eyes. Anxious not to further damage her reputation, Mab — Bertrand Russell's new love, Lady Ottoline Morrell — cried, Enough! Put me down!

Mab had relished this play at first, but now she had reverted to the imperious voice of *m'lady,* wife of an MP and mother. Lytton! she cried to the instigator, Lytton Strachey. Do you hear me? Then, in despair, she called out, *Bertie!*

But Bertie just stood there, the lump. Such a dry bob, that Bert, so aghast and emphatically *un*drunk in his white shirt, braces and trousers. Sad, was he, with his big, droopy brown mustache? Sad and feeling — what?

Old? Jealous? A little left out in love's drains, was it, captive to Ottoline's artistic friends? Seeing her on their shoulders, he was reminded of an ungainly nesting bird perched over this clutch that she, mother hen, had laid, as it were. And all men! And all of them young — younger than he, a lovesick forty. And suddenly he felt angry, not at his adored Ottoline, but at her husband, Philip — angry that Philip should be such a blasted fool to permit his wife the dangerous impropriety of a weekend virtually alone with him and six other men, at least if one didn't count her cousin Adelaide and some older woman who apparently wrote novels. But come to think of it, thought Russell, Philip wasn't such a fool after all. As Ottoline obviously knew, there was safety in numbers. Russell had scarcely had a moment alone with her, nor did he dare among such gossips.

By then the lads had had their fun. Setting her down, they fell in a clump on the sand, panting and laughing. Ottoline took her chance to get away. In a long and dripping French bathing gown with puffed sleeves and wadded cotton flowers, she walked emphatically toward Russell. Giggling and swallowing his hiccups, acting the part of Caliban, that professional guest and sporadic author Lytton Strachey called back, Oh, O. Don't be in a wax now.

Then honking like gulls came the others: Now O . . . Ottolinoscoska! *Dearest, darling O.*

Don't O me, she said, whirling around. It went too far. Then turning to Russell, she said with a sniff, Much help you were.

Me? he retorted. The others were near so he kept his voice low, saying, Obviously, you loved it.

How dare you, she hissed. I did not love it. She began walking down the sand.

No? he asked, picking up beside her. If you do not love it, then why are they here, the lot of them? We were supposed to be alone — foreign as you seem to find the concept.

How was I to know they'd come?

Of course. A prisoner to your guests. As usual.

She glared at him. *Spontaneous!* Do you even understand that principle? *Spont-aneity?*

He could feel her crumple then. Instinctively, she was retreating before he could trap her with some piddling point, using his mind first as a scalpel, then as a bludgeon, mocking and cold. Ottoline feared his mind — he was painfully aware of that — and here, as ever, he felt he had to retreat to show her the delicate clay feet of his love. This love was a new experience for him. Almost all his most logical important ideas had come unbidden, in moments of sudden insight. But these moments were then followed by months and even years of labor to find *reasons* for these truths, which he hoped would stand like the stars. His love, by contrast, was beyond revoking or reason, and he now had no way of knowing whether it was advancing or receding, whether it would stay, or what, at this rate, would ever become of it.

Ottoline, meanwhile, was looking out to sea, where the dull, gray waves were stippled with light, like the barnacled humps of whales. Russell looked, too, but then instinctively his eyes dipped, deft and hungry as mosquitoes, to the cleft where the clinging wet silk made a fold over Ottoline's noble buttocks.

Oh, drop it, she resumed. She turned and looked at him weakly. They'll be gone tomorrow, most of them.

Glumly, he added, Yes, and then I'll be gone myself. He looked at her miserably, then said, I've half a mind to leave tomorrow. This is doing neither of us any good.

Her piled hair, an earthy dark red, as variegated as wool, was coming unbound. Long face, dark eyes, full lips. Lank supple shanks of legs and slender feet with long, bony toes. As he often did, he was studying her in wonderment, unable to decide whether she was impossibly beautiful or possibly somewhat ugly. She saw him looking, anatomizing her, and again she told herself that she wouldn't be bullied or manipulated by him. In a flash of irritation, she said coldly, Then why don't you? *Go*, if it's so unpleasant. Really —

Russell's face creased with pain. Knowing he had pushed her too far, he wasted no time backpedaling:

I'm not going, and you don't want me to go. I just find it unendurable at times — to love you this much and be surrounded always by people. I am *so* sick of it, he said, and then stopped himself, feeling his eyes starting to fill.

Seeing he was coming undone, she said quickly, I know — just a while longer. We'll have our day together tomorrow.

And even then, like figures in a comical film, jerking and gesticulating, they felt themselves having to speed up their emotional exposition because the others were lurching toward them, mock penitents now, their legs spavined with drink as they said, Now there, Mabby. Don't be an old crabby . . . Is there more wine at the house? . . . Will supper be served soon?

No, their little holiday had not turned out at all as he had planned. They were to have been alone — alone meaning with two maids, the cook, the chauffeur and one or two odd guests thrown in to make it all tidy.

In the six months that Russell and Ottoline had been lovers, there had been various trysts, all of them hasty and increasingly furtive — nothing like this long weekend was to have been. This time she would not have to run back to her husband, Philip, or her daughter, six-year-old Julian. Here there would not be the endless luncheons, dinners, teas, at-homes, parties and charity bazaars that made it almost impossible for her to meet him. For weeks, Russell had been waiting for this, pining for her like a schoolboy waiting for the holidays. After ten unhappy years, married to a woman whom he now could hardly suffer, Russell felt like a man freed from prison. Hang discretion. Die, Wife. Die, old life. Stand and deliver, Philip Morrell, your wife and child, and repair to your constituency to fade away in genteel obscurity.

So raged Russell's enraptured ego, that great claymore which longed to chop the legs from under his wife, Alys, Philip and anyone else who dared stop him. Still, it wasn't just his wife whom Russell found blocking his path. There was his own former self, that drudge poisoned by musty chastity like an Inquisition priest; that heart so shrunken that he sometimes felt his head had swelled like a globe in compensation, revealing supreme forces of concentration — and avoidance — that expanded his already considerable mental powers tenfold. Who was that man who had produced the mammoth *Principia Mathematica*? Who was that dispassionately analytical man who, while riding his bicycle one day ten years before, had come to the almost arithmetical conclusion that he no longer loved his wife?

Russell had not been thinking of Alys when this had happened. Pedaling along, he was thinking of a seemingly unrelated logical problem when he looked up, as if he had suddenly seen the time, and realized that his marriage would never again be the same.

Alys immediately sensed something was wrong when he returned. They had always prided themselves on their honesty, and the next day, dizzily, he told her the truth, not that there was another woman, for there was none, but that he had somehow fallen out of love with her. He thought Alys would at least be thankful for his honesty, but she was impaled. All that night she wailed and wept. She was an American Quaker, five years his senior, and after that she prayed that his heart would change. Several times, unable to stand the tension — that feeling of airlessness and entrapment with no relief — he broke down, telling her and himself that his heart *might* change. But once his senses cleared, he told her, and continued to tell her, that there was absolutely no hope, that his feelings would never change. *Thee cannot predict the future!* she would shriek, slamming the door and choking back sobs that sounded as if she were punching herself in the stomach.

Finally, it made no difference what he said. In spite of his hatred and nullity, in spite of all reason, she passionately believed his love would rise from the dead if only she were patient and forgiving. Poor woman. Poor, deluded woman, he would write in his diary, filling page after page with unctuous tones and fairy tale nobility, the scribblings of a man in shock.

But increasingly she wore on him, as he did on her, until he began to loathe her for her insane patience and submissiveness, suspicious that even her innocence was malign. And gradually over those next years, as if to fulfill his fallen estimation of her, she lost what luster she had, until in his eyes she was nothing at all. By then he found it impossible to imagine that he had ever found her beguiling, this the first woman ever to have paid attention to him when he met her as a prig of seventeen. Even harder to imagine was that he had so dutifully saved himself for her — saved himself even during a year in Paris, passing purblind the frizetted whores and the Moulin Rouge before marrying her as a prig of twenty-two.

Alys was — or once had been — a courageous and freethinking public woman, a champion of women's suffrage, social reform and workers' groups. Early on, she had been a tremendous influence on him, helping him research his first book, *German Social Democracy*. Nor was she without strength of character. Daughter of an evangelist, she would take a podium with the indomitable moral fearlessness of a saint mounting a gibbet to say a few defiant words, and never allowing herself to sink into despair. How he had once loved the charm of her sectarian *thee*s and *thous* — it was as if they had their own language, ancient and intimate. Now, though, he associated them with hysterical outbursts — pleas that made him feel like Henry VIII with Anne Boleyn clutching his knees, begging for her life.

Still, he had been practical in those first years of their alienation. Divorce was not an acceptable expedient; it would have been social and professional suicide. Besides, Alys wouldn't have granted him a divorce. Instead, he buried himself in his work, and over the next years they found a *modus vivendi*. Alys managed his household and saw after his every need, setting food before his closed door as for a spirit. To Russell, she was like a piece of furniture, a heavy oak bureau he was careful not to collide with. It occurred to him, and not unpleasurably, that she must have wondered if she still had a face or hips or if, in his mind, she even existed. But for all his mental powers he could not make her vanish. Like the chambers of a heart, their two small bedrooms were separated by a wall through which he could hear her, shuffling, coughing, bumping, a clumsy woman deep in want, craving love and a child — forgiveness.

Affection he might shirk, but sex he could not avoid. Sex was his conjugal duty, and as an aristocrat, he strongly believed in duty. Alys knew this, and periodically, with what seemed a subconscious desire to torture him, she would beg him to come "lie" with her. He could not stave her off forever. Feeling himself a life shirker and a bedroom criminal, he would flog them both by lumbering over her, mashing his face into the pillow so as not to see her. She was a heavy woman, with white, doughy skin, freely perspiring. His slack penis was bent like a thumb, and unwilling. Not a word passed between them. For him, there was only nullity as he rocked and hated and punished her, thinking of mathematical entities, flaccid abstractions, empty sets. And failing, mightily failing. Hearing her gently ask, with the faint catch of a sob, *Thee cannot?* and wanting then to strike her. Jumping up, he would walk quietly into his room and note in his diary, as if he were making an entry in a ledger, that he had made his "sacrifice" and thus had earned his reward: three months absolved from suffering her touch.

Then came Ottoline. Russell had first met her the year before while campaigning for Philip Morrell, a liberal candidate who was trying to win a seat in Burnley. Philip won the election, and sometime later, when Russell was attending a dinner at their home in Bedford Square, in the heart of Bloomsbury, Philip was suddenly called away. There were several other guests, but when they left, Russell, without quite knowing why, remained, sitting by the fire with Ottoline. He did not plan or anticipate what happened. They were quietly talking when out of nowhere he said cryptically, There is always a tragedy in someone's life if one knows where to look for it. He remembered Ottoline looking at him, not knowing what to say. He was surprised himself and suddenly found himself telling her of the misery of his marriage and the vile emptiness of his life.

They slept together soon enough, but for him not often enough. He was in rut — completely mad for new life, mad to jettison Alys and wrest Ottoline from Philip. He was living apart from Alys then, having taken rooms in Cambridge, where he had been given a lectureship at Trinity. But Alys refused to give up. On the contrary, she was so desperate that friends feared she would kill herself or ruin them all in court if she caught whiff of the affair.

Hang her. He didn't care. All instincts of self-preservation were gone. In those first flushed months, he was completely reckless. Ottoline was nothing like Alys; he didn't know what she was. Russell could see at a glance that she was not a true intellectual, did not think logically or sequentially, and indeed was not, even for an upper-class woman, especially well educated. Yet she was everything he was not: sensual, when he was still unawakened; attracted to beauty, which he thirsted for but feared; and drawn to art, which, in its seeming irrationality and subjectivity, he still did not entirely understand. It seemed he told her everything at once, wanting to conquer not only her body but even her mind and memory. He overwhelmed her. She felt he was far too brilliant for her to be of any conceivable interest to him except sexually. Yet in another way, it seemed they had always known each other. She knew all about his illustrious family, especially his formidable grandfather, Lord John Russell, a prime minister under Victoria. He would say, Of course, my grandfather. And she, nodding, would say, Of course, the story evoking the bare outlines of a tale she already knew, like a nursery rhyme. Of course, the Russells. Of course, the Balfours and Lansdownes. The world, within certain realms, was small, and she had been taught to be more at ease where she could say of course and to be wary where she could not.

Yet even so she was wary. Ottoline liked fire in a man, but she didn't want the fire to get out of control. At bottom, she knew that she was not about to risk her husband and daughter, not to mention her freedom and reputation, for a man who wasn't sure he could even get a divorce and who would be penniless if he did. And what was the need when she could eat her cake and have it, too? If Ottoline was more conscious than he was of society's rules, this was because as a woman she had more to lose. Besides, if the rules were at times a farce and a bother, they were there for her protection. They were something to play against, offering a favorable backdrop for her high coloratura life. Ottoline knew she was skating on thin ice, yet if she was something of a maverick, she was nonetheless a cunning and practiced skater who knew just how much the ice would decently bear. Russell had been planning to give her a lesson in logic, but she, in turn, was teaching him social skating on the scrim, with some hard lessons yet to come that weekend down in Studland.

Analyzing Certain Signs

IN FACT, Ottoline was on the thinnest of ice, having said good-bye only hours before Russell arrived to that most special of her young friends, the painter Henry Lamb.

Several times Ottoline had offhandedly mentioned Lamb's name to Russell, but she did so more from caution than candor, figuring that by treating Lamb casually, Russell would be less suspicious if ever his name popped up. And actually she told Russell the same story about Lamb that she told both Philip and Lamb about Russell — that he was a wounded bird in need of tending.

Highly principled and methodical, if somewhat bland, Philip was not dense or blind, just very tolerant. Much as Ottoline craved the company of blazing men, Philip knew as well as she did that she did not want a blazing man for a husband. He also recognized that these so-called wounded birds were the price of keeping Ottoline.

In its restrained way, it was very tender and intimate, the unspoken way she and Philip both knew this, though it was a different, mostly unconscious kind of knowing. For Philip it was not a matter of what he knew but of what he emphatically did not *want* to know in the way of wounded birds or other fictions. As for Ottoline, she knew, in a way, that he knew, yet she was never quite sure, which was chafing, sometimes anguishing; she did not on any account want to hurt him. Feeling the high gratitude of guilt, a sensation not unlike biting one's tongue, Ottoline frequently told herself how very fortunate she was in having someone as loving and considerate as Philip to come back to. Distraught — yet for all that faintly titillated — she would say to Russell, I *know* he knows now. Then, the next week unsure again, she would say as if it had just struck her, You know, I'm not sure he *does* know. And then the next time he saw her she would say in confoundment, What does he think? He *must* know. How could he possibly *not* know?

Around and around she would go, grinding these worry beads, grinding them not only for the thrill and the guilt but to prove to herself that she was a woman of established, even notorious, desirability, even as she fretted that in two or three years more she would be a little less desirable, and then less desirable after that.

Philip, for his part, went along, never quite sure that his wife was doing anything more than her easy, not-entirely-plausible stories suggested. Besides, if these adventures were only flirtations, he did not want to wound her vanity by showing them to be only innocent nothings. And it was agreeable to know, wasn't it, that others found one's wife desirable?

In any event, it was out of the question that Philip Morrell would ever make a scene: cuckolds and asses make scenes, not gentlemen. It was treacherous and difficult for him, this foggy art of not knowing, but with his very considerable powers of self-control and subordination to prin-

ciple, Philip was able to carry it off with panache — so much so that
Ottoline sometimes wondered if he wasn't almost grateful for the intimacy she conferred on him with her white lies. Russell wasn't the only
one versed in neat distinctions. If she lied, Ottoline reasoned, this was
because she cared enough not to inflict pain. Her fibs, then, were not
really lies, but rather obverse truths — truths that in her mind gradually
assumed a certain moral plausibility, like the whitest of kindnesses.

Before coming to Studland, it had never crossed Russell's mind that he
faced any rival but Philip. Why, he would have found the idea physically
and emotionally inconceivable. It was all Ottoline could do to handle
him. Like a drunk, he blithely assumed that she, too, was drunk. Passionately he believed they were *destined,* not realizing that he was suffering from the powerful illusion that his love was reciprocated in kind and
intensity.

No, until that weekend, Russell had never thought twice about Henry
Lamb. But then against his will certain realizations were progressively
forced on him. The first inkling came just after he arrived, when Ottoline
brought him down to his quarters in the old caretaker's cottage, now a
guest house.

Russell was in a bad mood then, and not without cause, considering
that he had just discovered that two of their three days would be filled
with interlopers, and some obnoxious ones at that. Arriving in the station
fly, he saw her guests bivouacked on slat chairs below the big stone and
stucco house, in that trellised garden whose concentric flowerbeds rolled
in marcel waves toward the sea. God, the gall of them! They were asking
about *him,* turning up their hat brims to get a better look as they impertinently pressed Ottoline: O? Now, O, who is *this?*

Approaching with a *mea culpa* smile, Ottoline was a sylph in lavender
and red silk, with her long red hair bound in a scarf like a Gypsy. And
then he was trapped, forced to play the smiling guest, getting names
straight and shaking hands until they escaped, ostensibly for a tour of
the house. Upstairs, as he was getting into a rant, she suddenly pulled
him into the library, kissing him wildly and telling him how she wanted
him — wanted him two days hence, once the others had left. Then came
the recriminations, and then the sex bartering — the pound of flesh, as
she called it.

Finally, she took him down to the guest cottage, which she said he
would have all to himself. She implied she was doing him a great honor,
putting him here, away from the others. This, he thought, was only his

due, yet in spite of himself he was flattered and vaguely mollified. But then this too was dashed when, stepping under the low lintel, he smelled the odor of a gamy man, then saw painted on the wall across the little cottage room an image that he took at first for the Blessed Virgin. It took him a moment to place who it was in that blue cloak, with those placid, whorish eyes and lewd red lips.

Good God, he said, turning around. It's *you!* Who painted this?

That? asked Ottoline offhandedly, as if he had noticed some knick-knack in the corner. Henry painted that.

Henry?

The painter Henry Lamb. You've heard me speak of him.

Like a curtain, her silk skirt swept across the floor as she moved around the room, opening windows. She felt his eyes on her back but pretended not to notice as she chirpily continued. Henry wintered here last year. He needed a place to work and we needed someone to watch over the place, so —

And Philip, asked Russell suddenly. Philip saw this?

Ottoline looked at him curiously. He saw it, yes. Didn't get it. The joke, she added, as if to compliment Russell for the fact that he had.

But Russell did not get it, or want to. Making a mouth, he said, It seems a work of anger if you ask me. It mocks you. You don't find it mocking?

Mocking? asked Ottoline, raising her eyes. No, I find it rather amusing.

Do you? He eyed her with a look of incomprehension. As if to taunt him, Ottoline continued moving around, straightening.

Bowing his fingers by his sides, he was snappish. Quit — Will you kindly quit that and look at me?

Yes? she asked — a forbearing yes.

Stuffing his rage back like a jack-in-the-box, he resumed: It's mocking and cruel — like a slap. Like some vicious caricature in *Figaro*. There's certainly nothing to be *gotten* in it — don't be deluded on that account. Even the draftsmanship is slapdash and cynical.

Oh, stop, she replied, attempting a smile. I find it very . . . *Lambian*. Very much the naughty boy and punster. It's not a finished, considered work. Henry was bored, that's all. He probably couldn't stand the bare wall.

Russell was so patronizing. She could see his contempt; it was smeared all over his face. He wanted her to see it, too. He wanted to break her of her obstinance and stupidity. His rival, he saw, was not just Lamb, or

Lamb's stench, but this ugly, defacing portrait. In a flash of anger, he said, Well, I think it ought to be painted over! Blotted out! And why not? Do you think that because an *artist* did it it's somehow sacred? I needn't be a critic to see it's muck. It has not the mark of the *Lamb,* it has the smell of the *goat!*

Oh! she shot back. How witty!

His eyes got squinty. I'm not trying to be *witty,* I'm trying to make you *see!* I'll tell you what it says. It *says* — he hesitated — it says, *There, you bitch!*

Ottoline jumped as if a gun had gone off. *Oh!* Don't you dare use that horrid word around me!

Don't blame the word, blame the work. It's the work that profanes you. I won't have you mocked! I'll paint it out!

You won't paint anything! Moving toward him then, she was like a wave, with that propulsive power, flushed and smelling of the sun. Before her he was amazed and aroused as she beat him back, saying, You'll not come here, to *my* home, and dictate terms to me. There's a spare room up at the house if this isn't satisfactory. There's also an inn nearby and a train tomorrow if that isn't to your liking . . .

Don't be angry just because I won't have you mocked, he said sullenly.

I'll be the judge of what mocks me. Ottoline shook her head. You don't know how patronizing you are, do you? For you, it's a given that I'm a blind idiot, accepting anything.

That's not true. He felt his jaw trembling. It's just you're too close to it.

Not knowing what else to do, he opened his bag and started unpacking. It was the wrong thing to do. To her, the sight of his folded clothes was like a glimpse of stained bedding.

I should leave, she said suddenly.

He smiled a coaxing smile. Don't be silly. Look at you. You'll allow this on the wall, yet you want to flee in dread of possibly seeing my undergarments.

I have guests.

They'll get along. Then, compulsively, knowing her answer even as he opened his mouth, he thought to ask — But no, he told himself, leave it be. The look on his face was that of a small animal furiously digging. Pausing then, telling himself not to be a fool, he had the sensation of raising a hammer while knowing full well that he would squash his thumb. And yet in spite of himself he raised that hammer, feeling a bit squeamish but faintly exhilarated as he brought it squarely down, sug-

gesting, You know, we *could* . . . Just once — briskly. We might both be
better for it.

Her head rocked back. Folding her hands over her lips, she said with
delighted sarcasm, You're priceless! You won't have me mocked, but then
you're ready to have do in broad daylight with some of the worst tongues
in England about. You ought to take up *painting.*

Yes, mock me!

Not mocking. Just pointing out your own contradictions — since you
so love to point out mine. Now, she said chidingly, put your things away
and come up to the house. She stopped at the doorway. You will be coming, won't you?

He was bent with deep care over the suitcase. Without looking up, he
replied, In a few minutes.

Good, she said, pleased to have won this round. Good.

Ottoline's need to nurse wounded birds was not the only thing about her
that Russell and others failed to fully understand. Equally misunderstood
was Ottoline's need to surround herself with lions, literary and otherwise.

Already some were calling her a huntress. Russell was not yet famous,
but in Ottoline's lair were famous and accomplished men such as Henry
James, the art critic Roger Fry and the painter Augustus John — magnets
who helped attract younger talents such as Lytton Strachey and Henry
Lamb. Along with these came many a Sunday painter and poetaster —
the inevitable dross that any search produces — and these Ottoline, no
sentimentalist in such things, usually cut from her list after a visit or two.

In any case, Ottoline's vocation as a patron was not as sudden or opportunistic as it seemed to others. Beneath these pursuits there was a
charitable impulse that had been a distinct part of her character since
girlhood.

Her father, a general, had died suddenly when Ottoline was six, forcing the family to live for a year under drastically reduced circumstances.
But after this period of relative privation, the family's fortunes suddenly
reversed when her father's cousin, the fifth duke of Portland, died, his
estates and title passing to Ottoline's twenty-one-year-old half brother,
Arthur.

Ottoline never forgot Arthur's orgy with that sudden money. Still in a
lather from another frenzied day of buying and fittings, Arthur took her
into Cremer's toy shop in London and *ordered* her to buy anything —
anything and as much as she wanted. A spooky, skinny, religious girl, she

knew even then that this was not a gesture of generosity. Instead of feeling grateful or excited, she felt panicky and oddly destitute, paralyzed to think of all the poor waifs she would see without even shoes or a penny pie. Arthur had a temper, and he was immediately incensed that the girl did not want to take part in this potlatch of his new wealth. Do you see nothing? he asked in disbelief, as if she were a traitor to her class. Look here! Dolls and doll houses . . . stuffed horses and small carriages. Arthur turned with disgust to their mother. What is *wrong* with her? Will she have *nothing*?

She was no happier when her mother, just made a peeress by Arthur's importuning of Disraeli, took her to live on her stepson's vast estate in the Midlands. Welbeck Abbey was a tribute to the mania of her uncle, the duke, who was known throughout the region as the "Burrower" or "Hedgehog." Beneath the stone piers and projections of the misshapen stone manor house were the catacombs and warrens that had taken two hundred navvies twenty years of excavation and blasting to complete. Through a tunnel that coiled like a bowel, there was a cavernous underground ballroom whose rotting pink walls resembled the lining of an enormous stomach, this followed by a charming grotto chapel where the water dripped darkly, it was said, like Christ's blood.

The morbidly religious girl didn't have to imagine what hell was like, living over ground bored through like a foul cheese. For Arthur, though, the duke's rat runs were a distinct social asset. Once Prince Edward and his court toured Arthur's hellhole, Welbeck was on the map of fashion, with London's chief nabobs and sycophants flocking to tour its dungeons and attend Arthur's underground masques, where he would appear as Mephistopheles in black tights, pointy slippers and a cocked hat with one greasy black feather. Ottoline hid in her room and prayed, wishing she were Florence Nightingale and reading *The Imitation of Christ*. She hated Arthur's life. Hated the endless, stupid guests. Hated the bloated, daylong eating and constant dressing. Hated the men trooping out to blast Arthur's now imported partridges, and hated the ladies chattering and eating crystallized violets before joining their ladies' maids to dress for yet another stultifying dinner.

Ottoline could no more pick a sweetmeat from Arthur's gaping table than she could pick a paltry doll. Shy, gawky, hypersensitive about her as yet unfocused appearance, she grew steadily more pious, with a mother confessor and a thirst to help the poor, who on Arthur's lands were as plentiful as once the native partridges had been.

Arthur found her a frump and a nuisance and wished she would marry.

Instead of enjoying herself and finding herself a good match, Arthur said, all she did was waste her time praying, distributing food parcels and teaching footmen how to read. Unable to stand her chronic gloominess, Arthur finally packed her off to Italy with two chaperones. With its warmth, light and beauty, Italy marked the slow demise of her old life. Italy also marked her first affair. Ottoline became so bold that her chaperones, fearing for their reputations, fled, saying that they would pray for her.

She married in 1902, at the age of twenty-nine, and she changed as people do, in certain ways fundamentally, in other ways not at all. In her there was still much of Florence Nightingale. Art was her Crimea, and she was still the libidinal nurse, ministering to these penniless young scribblers and painters who manned the barricades against boors like Arthur.

Art was her creed, and people were her palette. In her mind, then, Ottoline was not a camp follower but, say, an artist of life. Skillfully arranging these colors and textures, the dull with the vibrant and the rough with the smooth, she hoped to create a salon that would rival that of Madame de Staël or George Sand. But still there were the critics, not the least of them being those whose careers she had most advanced, calling *her* an opportunist and adventuress. It made her furious! Was this mere self-promotion? she would ask herself. After all, who but a fool would be so generous toward artists who, as a class, were almost invariably ungrateful, self-centered and two-faced? Why, this was saint's work she was doing. But where, for God's sake, were the saints?

Russell complied with Ottoline's wishes. After putting away his clothes, he walked, grumbling, up to the house, where he heard the strum of a guitar and saw the party still gathered in the garden. I'm not prepared for this, he thought. With that, he slipped into the empty house to compose himself with a browse among the books he'd seen downstairs.

Furnished in a mode of calculated deshabille, the house was pure Ottoline, very inviting and eccentric. There was a wing where Ottoline and the family slept, and there was a paneled guest's gallery lined with bookshelves and furnished with a tumble of doggy-smelling chairs with arms rubbed smooth and cushions molded, like distinctive hats, by a succession of rumps. Meandering about this room, Russell wasn't looking for anything particular when he stopped before a wall hung with a sort of rogue's gallery of drawings and caricatures done by Studland's artists and habitués. Russell wasn't consciously looking for Lamb's work; somehow, Lamb's etched pencil portrait found him. He immediately recognized the style as Lamb's, and he knew from the subject's smug look that it was a self-portrait. Russell's stare was like a knife driven into the wall. And then he jumped — Lytton Strachey was standing right behind him. Spooky Lytton, so fond of looming. His large nostrils flared with the scent of prey as in a deep, strangely inflected voice he intoned:

Heavenly Henry . . . God hate him for being so gorgeous.

Lytton smiled. As usual, he was standing just a little too close, peering into Russell's face through circlets of horn rim that were much too small for his tall Chinese lantern of a head. Russell could hear the air whistling through his nose, could see his equine jaw working. Such a gaping, thoroughly homely man with this cadaverous skin and livid, patchy red beard. And now Russell felt Lytton stuff words in his mouth as he said with a sigh, God gives some the looks and some the brains, eh, Bertie?

Deflected Russell, And to some, like ourselves, he gives both.

Lytton snorted. He wasn't fooled by this dodge. Pointing to a drawing on the wall opposite, he said, There's the one Henry did of Ottoline.

Russell was noncommittal as he idled over. Umm . . .

Russell had known Lytton Strachey for over ten years, yet for all the young man's frivolousness in certain company, Russell never mistook for a moment his intellect, wit or social cunning. At thirty-two, Strachey was eight years younger than Russell, but they knew each other fairly well, both belonging to the Cambridge Conversazione Society, better known as the Apostles. Having numbered among their members the likes of Tennyson, Whitehead and Moore, the Apostles had, since 1820, secretly elected to their brotherhood Cambridge's most brilliant undergraduates. The brothers had no hesitation whatsoever in electing Lytton, nor in electing his good friends Leonard Woolf and Maynard Keynes. For a time, Russell hoped Strachey might become a protégé, but the appearance of Moore's *Principia Ethica* in 1903 burst that bubble. In a single stroke, most of the younger brethren went over to Moore, taking up his ethics just as resoundingly, it seemed to Russell, as they ignored his logic, which sought to assault the same mountain from the other side.

As a result, Russell was inclined to feel chafed around Strachey, not only because of Strachey's allegiance to Moore but because of his now egregious homosexuality, which he and other Apostles of similar leanings, having taken Moore's Platonic aesthetics at the expense of his morals, had redubbed the "Higher Sodomy." Left alone, with none to ignore or impress, Strachey could have given Russell hours of remarkable conversation, but amid the excitement and distraction of these young men it was hopeless: Strachey was like a stallion set loose among the mares.

Russell could feel Lytton probing as he studied Lamb's pencil sketch. Skillfully executed, with brassy, etchinglike strokes, this one was not mocking or cynical. This time Ottoline was transfigured, with a nimbus of dark hair setting off the prowlike chin and large, sensuous lips. Beyond flattering, thought Russell, wondering if it didn't suggest more than the usual involvement of a painter with his subject.

Carefully setting the hook, Lytton remarked, Excellent draftsmanship, don't you agree? God, he was a scandal at dinner last night. Oh, what a romp we had.

Who's that? asked Russell, affecting not to have heard.

Why, Henry, chirped Lytton.

The faint constriction of Russell's face told the fisher what he had been fishing for. With that, winsome Lytton drifted out through the french doors, saying moonily, Ahh, Lamb, Lamb. Who made thee?

Lytton didn't have to complete the line; Russell's mind did the rest, only his emending brain changed Blake's refrain from "God bless thee" to "God damn thee, Henry Lamb."

Ottoline was stunned when Russell found her just after this and said to her accusingly, Lamb stayed down at my cottage, didn't he? He was just here, wasn't he?

Ottoline's eyes widened, as if to ask what the problem was. Yes, of course he did. I told you. He stayed there all last winter.

Right. But you neglected to say he was just here last night. In the place you reserve for your *special* guests —

Ottoline eyed him with pity. I think you're reading much more into it than is there. If I neglected to tell you, that's because Lamb *isn't* so important next to you. With a wronged look, she added, I've never taken you for the jealous type. You've certainly no reason to be.

Russell was asking for reassurance, and by now she knew exactly what to say. Russell was like a child, as grateful and relieved as Philip was when she told him the same tales.

Russell felt much better then. And for that next hour until they sat down to dinner, he was fine, fine. But as they were taking their places at the table, he found his seating card, not two or three, but *five* places down from Ottoline's, the more to emphasize that he was no one in particular — and this while that Cheshire, Lytton, sat to her right, opposite her cousin Adelaide.

Ottoline, disguising her trail, flashed him a sympathetic glance, but it did no good. She was not there for him, not now. Ottoline was her hard public self tonight, having strapped on not a dress but a mailed suit of social armor. This dinner was not mere play, it was her occupation, dead in earnest. Holding court at the head of the table, flushed and slightly sunburned, Ottoline was a dark, flashing sapphire, wearing a long blue velvet dress with a dove-colored panel and a mantilla of black lace. The cooks and serving maids had been deployed and given their instructions, and when she rang her diminutive brass bell, out with its accompanying sherry came the first course, *consommé froid à l'Indienne*. For her centerpiece that artist of life had arranged around her a bunch of young flowers, including Philip Ritchie, Jules Coolcomb, the young painter Duncan Grant and Lytton's latest, the crapulous first son of the earl of Farnsworth, who plucked his eyebrows and insisted on being called Eddie.

Down the table, meanwhile, trying to strike a youthful air, Russell was defiantly dressed in a new and, as it seemed under candlelight, glowing pink shirt. Despite his anxieties, he was trying to be gay, but in this ill-chosen shirt, with his neck funneled up in a high celluloid collar, he felt like a target in a penny-a-pitch stall. Lytton was the first to have a throw, saying, Well, aren't we looking *colorful* tonight.

Eddie, drinking since noon, went into titters, crumbs of bread sticking to his lips.

Trying not to smile, but delighted in spite of herself, Ottoline said, I think it's very becoming, Lytton. If you can wear a cape, Bertie can certainly wear a pink shirt if he likes.

Eminently fair, said Lytton, raising his glass as Eddie, smirking, whispered something behind his artfully drawn napkin. A *nice* choice.

Well, on that account, replied Russell icily, I thank you.

On any other night, Russell would easily have fended this off, but instead he fought back with brute intellect. Current expenditures for dreadnoughts in relation to German naval expansion? Home rule for Ireland? The failure of Robert Scott's polar expedition? Was there anything under the sun he did not know or did not have an opinion on? He was brilliant, but it was the brilliance of anger — the light he gave off was too hot and white for people who had drunk several glasses of wine. They didn't want a tutorial; they wanted to be merry. Besides, Russell was a hopeless latecomer to Ottoline's life. Oh, said the looks, such a crashing bore he was! Tiresome how he missed the private jokes and references. Irritating how he had to be filled in on names and nicknames and old stories, when the party was straining to hear the latest morsels from London. Russell was jealous not just of Lamb but of Ottoline's past. In his urge to consume her, to internalize her as his creation, he chafed at the idea that she had a whole life prior to him. Anxiously, he remarked — he thought terribly aptly — I feel as if I'm in the midst of a Russian novel where everyone has three names! But this was greeted with looks of genteel incomprehension and the conversation turned elsewhere.

For the life of him, he couldn't get his footing with these people. Where his own jokes ignominiously misfired, theirs were thought wildly amusing. No sooner would he sink his teeth into a topic than Ottoline would say, But Bertie, we're talking about suffragism now.

Soon, he was grabbing at straws. When Lytton — someone — mentioned Nietzsche, that then fashionable subject, he jumped on it, launching off on a discussion of "Homer's Contest":

Even early on, we hear Nietzsche talking about the generative, life-giving properties of conflict. Envy, for the Greek, is a virtue — it spurs him on to greatness. But Socrates, you see, is just too much for the Athenians. Because he towers above the rest — because he *ends* the contest — they scotch him, feed him the hemlock. Oh, yes, Nietzsche does raise an interesting point. But what I detest is how he revels in the contest, especially at this rather advanced stage of history. And it's anything *but* generative or life giving — it merely feeds this hateful Darwinism of contending peoples and nations, militarism and all the rest. If you ask me, it's exceedingly savage and destructive.

As is life, chided Lytton. Nietzsche's raising laurels, not distributing alms to the ordinary. Besides, he's really speaking of individuals, not nations.

Oh, yes, added Eddie, looking up sloppily from his port. The Superman and so forth.

True, said Russell, directing his comment solely to Lytton, since it was only Lytton he was contesting. This may be true of Nietzsche's *intentions,* but what of the results? People do not read so discriminatingly. The egotist will find his truth, and the militarist his. The result in both cases is predictably brutal. Not only do the strong subjugate the weak, but the strong grapple with the strong to the general destruction of all. And of course for Nietzsche the weak don't count anyway. For him, millions of ordinary lives are not worth one Napoleon — or, I presume, one Nietzsche. Hateful, megalomaniacal thinking. It only justifies the idea that the great feed upon the ordinary, that history, like an infernal factory, is designed to produce certain great *products* — Christ, Beethoven's Ninth, the aeroplane.

Sensing the general restlessness, Lytton spoke for the table as he remarked with a dry smile, Speaking of *great products,* we may have to banish you, old man, if you persist in being much more brilliant tonight.

Oh, hardly! scoffed Russell. And then he laughed, *hoof hoof.* But he was gored. Sitting at the head of the table like Helen herself, even Ottoline, the prize of this contest, was staring him down as he gulped from his goblet, wanting to die.

It was downhill after that. He remembered them playing charades, starting with Lytton, who did a rakish Leda and the Swan. Gloriously beating the air with his wings, Lytton had them thinking he was not Zeus buggering Leda but Christ impaled on the cross. Eddie was shrieking with laughter. Russell could not bear it. Pleading sleep, he left, but not before seeing Ottoline as Marie Antoinette. Here was a cozy image to take to bed — this one rivaled Lamb's fresco of Whore Mary. Ottoline gesturing. Eating yards of cake, then merrily cradling her severed head as they called out:

Mary Queen of Scots!
The Headless Horseman!
Cronus eats his young! Or was it Rhea?

Eats his young? gasped Eddie, catching his chest. Eats his —
And with that, Eddie cut loose with another shriek.

Russell's Paradox

BUT WHY would you concern yourself for three years with a paradox about a Cretan who said all Cretans were liars?

Oh, more than three years, said Russell, delighted with Ottoline's incomprehension. Five years I spent — God, more, once I started wrestling with such nonsense as the round square and the present king of France. The problem with these last two, the king and the square, is how denoting phrases like these can describe, with seeming verisimilitude, nonexistent squares and monarchs. To the layman, it sounds silly, wasting one's time on puzzles like this, but you see such absurdities are the experiments of the logician. A theory can't hold if it works only part of the time or works only in certain isolated cases. The absurdity, the exception, no matter how trivial, belies the crack in the theory that sends the good ship *Ars Logica* to the bottom . . .

It was a warm, overcast day, and they were sitting on the sand, talking as the waves coughed and sloughed to their feet. Things between them were better now that the two last guests, Lytton and Eddie, were gone. That morning, Russell had left on the same train with them, traveling as Eddie's guest in his first-class compartment. Ottoline's house staff were on the same train, third class. Russell didn't travel far. When they reached Winchester he got off, saying he was stopping there to visit an aunt. It was an indifferent story — Lytton certainly didn't swallow it — but Russell didn't care. It was enough for decorum's sake.

Before noon he was back at Studland, and now, except for Ottoline's personal maid, Brindy, they were alone. Better yet, they were feeling that sense of repose that comes after having made love — once urgently in his cottage, and then again outside, this time against a tree, his trousers round his ankles as he struggled to roll a condom over his plumb bob before she changed her mind or thought she heard someone coming. Russell was still picking bark from his palm.

They both agreed it was better, infinitely better. With less than a day left, they were now working hard at putting a gloss on the weekend, both eager to forget the tension and remember instead this *one perfect day.* Sitting there, Ottoline felt she saw with fresh eyes this brilliant, difficult man whom, for all her doubts, she still loved. With marked detachment, and some pleasure, she had watched him suffer at dinner the night before, but now, having purged herself of resentment, she was nursing him so he could withstand those barren weeks without her in his Cambridge bachelor rooms. Yet even here, her impulse was not entirely selfless: as she well knew, the happier he was when they parted, the less demanding he would be when she turned her attentions once more to Lamb.

As for Russell, he was determined to be cheerful and optimistic. He would not dwell on his imminent departure, nor on thoughts of Lamb or other petty jealousies. He very much wanted to be diverted, and he was flattered when Ottoline asked for her first lesson in logic so she might better understand his mind and work. Even if it was a bit of a sop to assuage his bruised ego, she was genuinely curious. He, on the other hand, was anxious to improve her mind, and he wasn't starting from nothing. Some years back in Edinburgh, much to her brother Arthur's annoyance, Ottoline had spent a year in college, where she had taken a general course in logic. Unfortunately, Ottoline had done badly in the course, further diminishing her already precarious sense of her abstract mental abilities. But here Russell was quick to put her at ease, promising to be simple and clear and to start at the beginning. So saying, he began by telling her that the logic she had studied was of the old, Aristotelian kind, no doubt employing syllogisms of the sort called Barbara:

> All men are mortal.
> Russell is a man.
> Therefore Russell is mortal.

Russell was saying: This kind of reasoning dominated Western logic for two thousand years, and in some quarters, especially church quarters and the schools, it still dominates logic and severely hampers it. Aristotle employed many other types of syllogism besides Barbara, and if all logic were syllogistic, this would be splendid. But real progress came only with the modern recognition of asyllogistic processes, which of course confound syllogistic reasoning. Leibnitz made some progress, but even he had too much respect for Aristotle to break his hold. So the real modern period of logic dates from the publication of Boole's *Laws of Thought* in 1854. But Peano and Frege, working independently, were the ones who made the biggest contribution to modern logic.

And not yourself? asked Ottoline cattily.

Well, he said with an embarrassed smile, I'm getting to my place in things. But to return to Peano and Frege: one great contribution they made was to show that propositions that traditional logic thought to be of the same form were in fact quite different. Take the propositions "Socrates is mortal" and "All men are mortal." Aristotelian logic would say they are of the same form. But consider: "Socrates is mortal" has Socrates — a single man — for its subject, whereas "All men are mortal" takes as its subject a universal class consisting of all men. The persistent failure to grasp fundamental logical distinctions like these made for all manner of bad metaphysics and generally bad philosophy. Modern logic has finally uncovered many of these problems, and one way it achieved this was through the development of logical notation.

So saying, Russell took a stick and drew on the wave-smoothed sand:

> ∽ stands for *not*
> ∨ stands for *or*
> • stands for *and*
> ∴ stands for *therefore*

Hence, he said, you might write in signs:

$$(p \lor q) \cdot \sim p \therefore q$$

Meaning: either *p* or *q*; and not *p*; therefore *q*.

Ottoline rolled her eyes. And for you this is as simple as one, two, three.

One gets used to it, he demurred. I can't use it to order supper.

Mmmm . . . Or to mind your p's and q's.

In any event, he resumed, silently drawing other signs in the sand, as you can see, there are other symbols and more complex propositions. The advantage here is that the signs are more easily taken in at a single sweep. Avoiding the connotations of words, they isolate the sheer logic — the bones — of a statement, showing something that is at once simple and highly abstract.

I see, I see, said Ottoline, rubbing her arms. It *is* getting abstract, isn't it.

No, not so abstract, soothed Russell. Just listen, please . . . Now, where was I? Right! Frege and Peano came to logic through mathematics. I also came to logic through mathematics, but with a more philosophical bent. You see, mathematics is most philosophical in its beginnings, when we ask such general questions as how we can deduce one thing from another, or what logic even is.

Anyway, I had long wanted to systematically reduce mathematics to logic. Even as a boy I can remember asking my brother why a mathematical axiom was so, only to hear him reply, Because it is so. In college, I found this lack of a foundation in mathematics even more bothersome. Hegel's *Greater Logic* I thought was muddled nonsense. I found Kant's contention that mathematics and logic are independent of experience equally unsatisfactory. Why was I to believe that arithmetic consists of empirical generalizations that somehow work? I couldn't tolerate it. What I wanted to establish was a way of deducing mathematics that was rigorous, defensible and scientific. At the Paris conference in 1900, Peano and his students very much impressed me — their discussions were so extraordinarily precise! Well, part of the reason was the logical notation that Peano used. So taking Peano's notation, I invented my own, more extensive notation for logical relations. It was like a microscope. Suddenly, I was able to see to the root of questions that hitherto had eluded me. Russell sighed. What I didn't know then was that Frege had already covered much of the same ground.

Oh, how awful! said Ottoline.

Well, said Russell, betraying a slight smirk of satisfaction. As things turned out, it was rather worse for Frege. You see, in 1901 Cantor made a proof that there was no greatest cardinal number —

Cardinal number?

Don't concern yourself with that. All you need to know is that while working with Cantor's proof, I discovered a contradiction having to do with classes. This posed no small problem — in my mathematics, I had defined number in terms of class, with classes of classes, and classes of classes of classes, and so forth. So it wasn't a silly little logician's conundrum at all. It was really quite fundamental. And the question was, if we had a class — say, the class of odd numbers — could that class be a member of itself?

Wait, protested Ottoline dizzily. Please, you mustn't run on like this. You must go more slowly.

No, no — Already he was gesturing. Really, it's not that hard to see. It goes back to our Cretan — the one who called all Cretans liars. Consider: if what the Cretan says is true, then he's a liar and his statement is false. If what he says is a lie, on the other hand, then he's telling the truth while at the same time lying. The same principle applies to the contradiction I found in Frege's mathematics.

Ottoline sat there, closing her eyes. I feel so stupid, so miserably stupid.

Don't, he said, smoothing her arm. Consider it another way. You can say a man is part of the class of men. But the *class* of men is not itself a *man*.

She blinked. Right . . .

So: the class of men is not itself a man. Thus, it's a class that does not belong to itself, just as the Cretan is a liar telling the truth, or vice versa. It was this problem with classes that undermined Frege's mathematics. Well, I was reading Frege's *Foundations of Arithmetic* when I realized this. So I sent Frege a letter telling him how much I admired his work, and what a great influence it had had on me and so forth —

Here Ottoline made a sudden leap. And you told him his classes were all wrong?

Russell looked at her with surprise. Well, not so bluntly. But yes, I told him about the paradox, certainly.

But how vile of you! Ottoline jumped up and stared at him. First you praise the poor man, then you tell him his work is all wrong?

Not *all* wrong. But very much eroded by this paradox — at least with regard to this theory of classes.

Ottoline continued staring at him. But didn't you feel dreadful, ruining his work like that?

Russell was at something of a loss. Well, I wouldn't say *ruin*. But, yes, I suppose I felt sorry, somewhat. Not that Frege blamed me, you understand. Oh, he was most gracious about it — more than gracious. There was something very noble in his reaction. He sent me a letter that went on for several paragraphs with mundane business about offprints and such — and then, almost by the bye, he said my discovery left him beyond words — left him quite thunderstruck, in fact. Yes, said Russell, looking up musingly. Those were almost his exact words. He said he felt thunderstruck because my discovery had undermined the basis on which he had hoped to build his mathematics — especially as his next volume was just ready for publication.

Ottoline dropped her arms in stupefaction. And you *knew* that?

No! No, I didn't know that — But as I say, Frege was extraordinarily dignified about it. There was something superhuman about it, really. He reacted almost with pleasure, intellectual pleasure at my discovery.

Oh, please! Ottoline winced. It couldn't have been that pleasurable!

Nervously fingering his mustache, Russell asked, Well, what would you have had me do? Not to have told him would be unthinkable. Was Copernicus to hide his contention that the earth revolved around the sun out of respect for Ptolemy?

Well, he didn't write Ptolemy in the guise of a friendly letter and say, Oh, by the way, old boy, everything you think is wrong! And wait! Before you even say a word, I'm aware they weren't contemporaries.

Standing there with his hands hanging limp and a pleading look, Russell said, Please, understand this. If I overlooked something in my work, I certainly wouldn't wish to persist in my delusions. I would very much want to be told about it.

You would? she asked skeptically.

Oh, absolutely. Not that I'd enjoy it, of course.

Not enjoy it? But you just said Frege reacted with pleasure.

Frege, I said — not me.

But it must have given you great pleasure, didn't it? Getting the old general to surrender his sword to you like that?

Why, no! That wasn't the spirit at all. With a look of pain, he asked, Why are you suddenly attacking me like this — and here on my last day! I thought we were talking about logic.

We were — are. It's just that you say the most extraordinary things sometimes. I mean, for you to say that Frege would not have been devastated. Or that you, a young man hardly launched in his career, would not have been gratified to upset his applecart. Why can't you admit it?

Admit what? he asked, hedging. I've always thought I would want to behave as Frege did when it happens to me. And someday, no doubt, it will happen. I know that. It's the natural order of things. I owe a great debt to Frege.

So you do, said Ottoline with a faint edge of smile. But then Frege owes you a great debt, too.

They walked on after that, a little bruised and gloomy. Climbing the hill, they could see the sea rippling in the distance like a flying rug. The sea was only water, and the sky was less than the sea. Russell felt cut adrift. It was all he could do to believe in their love or compatibility, let alone be sanguine about the future. Ottoline didn't share his fears. If Ottoline was not worried about the future, that was because she wasn't thinking of it, or at least not with him.

I'm ready to eat, she said, and so, on a lofting hill above the sea, they spread their blanket, then opened their basket filled with cold poached chicken, wine and other good things. Uncorking the bottle, Russell told himself not to be so dour. He told himself that he and Ottoline were, in the main, *happy*, and that with time they would be even happier, rising higher and higher in their happiness, like a tire being pumped with air. Kissing him, Ottoline said they would quarrel no more, and they clinked their glasses. But then as they were eating, she said he must finish his story about the round square and the present king of France.

Do you really want to go into this? he asked, a little wearily.

Ummm, she said, wiping her lips. If it's not too terribly complicated.

No, it's not too complicated. Really, the problem with the round square and the present king of France is rather apparent. As I said, the problem here is of denoting statements that have a sense but no reference: you can't point to the present king of France in the way you can the king. The problem, then, is how a nonexistent thing or person can be the subject of a true or at least grammatically orthodox proposition. And you see, this curiosity can easily lead to metaphysical misadventures. Thus we had Meinong arguing that because we can say "the round square does not exist," there must be such an object as the round square, but that it must be a nonexistent object, dwelling, one must suppose, in that Platonic realm where nonexistent kings confer with round squares.

Russell took a bite and finished chewing. But first let me complete my earlier discussion. For the paradox suggested by the Cretan, I developed my theory of types. What this did was to break such statements down into smaller classes that, in effect, avoided this paradox of a class that wasn't a member of itself. This way I was able to avoid the trap of having to pronounce a statement like the Cretan's to be either true or false. Instead, I could say that the statement was not true or false but *meaningless*. Ah, you smile! Well, this may sound arbitrary, just a logician's trick, but I think it is a truly great advance in sheer common sense. At least it doesn't leave logic at the same impasse.

Umm, minced Ottoline, as if to say that for her these weren't problems at all.

But Russell ignored this. Magisterially holding his half-eaten drumstick, he pushed on:

Now, as to the round square and the present king of France, these gave rise to my theory of descriptions. In a way, the theory of descriptions is analogous to the theory of types, in that it recasts a problem into terms in which it can more readily be understood. Essentially, the theory of descriptions is a method of descriptive translation: it casts the troublesome phrase into a form that doesn't contain the original confusions. Hence, I can translate "The present king of France is married" into "*Exactly one thing reigns over France and nothing that reigns over France is not married.*" This says what the first statement does. True, it requires more words, but it does so without the more or less direct suggestion of some entity presently sitting on a nonexistent throne. It also shows that we cannot assume that each separate word or phrase has significance on its own account.

But wait, said Ottoline, laying down her fork. I don't see what you changed with the second statement. You merely said only one person presently reigns over France. Isn't that tantamount to saying he's the present king?

It's a subtle distinction. But it's a distinction just the same. I'm not saying "the king" in the confident way I say "George the Fifth, by the grace of God!" It also helps me better see what I am saying. I can see the grammar of it while making these other confusions more or less disappear.

But here again, for some reason, he felt himself inwardly sag. Closing his eyes then, he asked, Might we continue this lesson some other time? We're both a bit tired now. At least I am.

Of course, darling, she said solicitously. Putting her hand on his, she said with a look of alarm, Was I horrid talking about Frege? I was horrid, wasn't I?

No. He put his hand on her knee. Really, you weren't. If we'd been alone these past two days, I'm sure it wouldn't have happened. I'm convinced of that, aren't you?

I don't know . . . She canted her head from side to side, thinking. We might have quarreled a little. About sex, most likely.

Do you really think so? he asked, brightening a bit. About sex?

She saw he was looking at her strangely, and before he could even ask she said with mock vehemence, Don't you dare think of it! Twice is quite enough for one day.

He grinned. Did you like it back there, against the tree?

Ummm. Most novel . . .

He was still smiling at her funny.

And the answer is still no!

Why, my darling, he demurred, with a foolish grin. I wasn't even asking.

He was feeling so much better as they walked home. He didn't know why, in the midst of such good feelings, he should have thought of his wife.

But then Russell realized it was the present king of France that had reminded him of Alys. This was the problem he had been grappling with that day ten years before while out riding his bicycle.

The king of France is bald . . . The king of France is married . . .

Riding along that afternoon, the young logician was fully as unreal and abstract an entity as the nonexistent monarch. But then in the midst of this otherwise logical process, his mind substituted for the king the equally troublesome phrase: *The husband who loves his wife pedals up Chertnam Road.*

And then as he puffed along under the greening trees, he heard, like an echo, his voice call back in translation:

Exactly one thing is on that bicycle on Chertnam Road, and on that bicycle there is no one *and* no thing *that loves his wife.*

Grasping the handlebars, with his pipe clenched in his teeth and legs revolving so uselessly, the logician felt upside-down. He was fairly suspended in air as he sailed over the rise, then dipped down that ditchy lane into the coming kingdom. Indeed, the Cycling Husband then saw that he was not one man but two: the one who had loved, and the one for whom the word "love" now had a sense but no apparent reference — a fraud and a fiction like the hollow king.

Walking along with Ottoline now, Russell was thinking hard about that earlier, humbug self who had fallen from grace that day in 1902.

Like cows returning from pasture, he and Ottoline were being driven home from that Eden of their one day together. They were holding hands, yet they were somehow separate, just as he himself was cut in two, one foot in this new land, the other in that place where Alienated Affections consort with Nonexistent Kings. These two Russells, then, were walking abreast of their mistress, who was herself a being of opposite minds, like a child with an ice cream in each hand. And so, all of them were walking home that summer day, not long before the Messrs. Russell were to meet that other illogical assemblage, the Messrs. Ludwig Wittgenstein.

Letters

LIKE A GUILTY CONSCIENCE, Karl Wittgenstein's letter was waiting in Cambridge when Wittgenstein arrived there in late September for the start of Michaelmas term. His work had not even begun, thought Wittgenstein, yet here it was — the next shot and probably the deadliest now that his father was taking deliberate aim.

23. September 1912

My son,
    Your last letter offers little but artful evasions. Let me offer you, if I may, something more in the way of *provender*.
    Families are not static things, and when you have lived as long as I have, you will note in them a certain progression, especially in those of Hebrew lineage. In the latter case, they begin, as we ourselves did, as peddlers and artisans; they accumulate money, which is like a stream of water that eventually grooves its own bed to the noble sea, wherein power resides; and there, in that sea, they acquire influence and visibility until, at length, the children do not have to work and indeed have to do precious little of anything. Freed of the burden of securing the requisite material comforts, the spoiled heirs feel the mercantile is no longer good enough; they think it grubby and pedestrian, and they crave the life of art (or philosophy, which amounts to the same thing). Again, I say, in the Jew, there is the dual tendency to understand and even crave art *in more or less direct proportion to his own inability to express himself as an artist.* Mahler is a good practitioner, with sometimes wonderful effects, but he has not, it seems to me, the depths of Christian artists. I would not presume to tell you why this is, but all the same — *it is.* It is quite empirically true, as you will readily see by simply asking yourself

how many of our greatest artists have been Jews. Few. Precious few. And fewer still philosophers.

But I have veered off the track. As I say, for these heirs, they suffer from a kind of spiritual hemophilia, increasingly seduced by art and other fancies, which, I again emphasize, *did not bring their people to that succès d'estime.* And then begins the downward motion, just as one sees in certain degraded countries, such as France and Italy. The farmer divides his fields among his sons, whilst the merchant or industrialist divides his holdings, until the family's power declines and comes to nothing, whereupon the cycle begins again, as do those other cycles of weal, woe and war that the stockbroker senses in the way a farmer does fluctuations in the weather. Evolution thus begets dilettantes — cows who give no milk, beget neither true art nor commerce but only vanity books, vain thrashings, debauchings and worse.

Now, it is quite true that we Wittgensteins are not what we once were, nor will we be, in fifty years' time, what we are now. My enemies have accused me of trying to found a house of Rothschild — apparently in reaction to certain admittedly shrewd speculations I have made. This, as surely you know, is absurd. What concerns me is OBLIGATION. No doubt you think your work is an obligation, if one patently self-proclaimed. But if you truly had such a vocation, I am convinced, *the world already would have found you.* This has not been the case, as is evinced by your own telling lack of conviction; or perhaps by a fear that, beneath it all, you may only be *ordinary.* (You are not, and will never be, *ordinary.*)

Please understand that I am trying not to be harsh. But, I beg you, please ask yourself what you will do to advance the dreadnought of culture? She needs steam, not pretty streamers and whirligigs. For all its manifold guises and disguises, progress is quite fearfully simple: it goes FORWARD, just as I ask you, as my son, to go FORWARD.

Let me leave you with a little story of my own patrimony that I do not believe I have ever shared with you. My father once asked, "Do you like me? I mean, on a purely human basis, as one man to another?" This was a difficult pass. Certainly, I did not want to hurt my poor father; yet I saw I must be truthful. A minute passed before I offered tentatively, "I respect you." Father drew up his lips and said, "I thought you would say that. But that is quite all right. As a man, I don't like you, either."

Please don't suppose I am "fishing" if I mention this trifle. I would not presume to put to you this hard question, because I know, and have always known, the answer. Moreover, I am convinced that it is like this with all sons and fathers. All the same, you ought to listen to me. I was once a latecomer like you, but I now know more of the story.

Father

The effect was that of pigeons bursting from a booming belfry. When Wittgenstein finished the letter, his ears were hot and his chest was constricted; he could not catch a good breath. It seemed so unjust! So unbelievable! They had been all through this before he left home. Little had been said directly — in that house, little was ever said directly. It was like an Oriental language, all intonations and silences.

As a man of transcendent technical understanding, Karl Wittgenstein was profoundly resourceful in this regard. He knew that, as with a hydraulic pump, only a little force need be applied to a subject mind: overburdened with the past, the mind would vastly magnify the original force, until it succumbed with the merest tap, a word, a look, a letter.

Yet *was* this actually what happened? As an engineer, Wittgenstein was forever trying to devise a kind of dynamic model for this relationship, something that might account for how it could be so compressed and reserved, then so shrill with all the bitterness and chaos of a long-interred silence. For years, Wittgenstein had wondered to what extent his father's behavior was intentional and to what extent it was just a blind aspect of his character, as unaccountable as a force of nature. By his fourth reading of the letter, in fact, Wittgenstein could hear, with a little straining of his captive mind, his father trying to *restrain* and even *temper* his language. With two more readings, Wittgenstein could even feel his poor father's palpable distress as he wrote out the word "FORWARD" in wobbly capitals in his otherwise heartlessly regular hand.

And, really, how could he blame his father for being himself? Wittgenstein did not want to prolong the agony, did not want to wound his father or further poison his last years on earth. Nor could he on any account bear the thought of seeing his proud father, such a shaker of a man, humbled. Yet what did his father want? To install him in his offices? To groom him so that he could eventually assume his place in the world? Surely, his father must have known they couldn't have worked a single day together. The idea was ludicrous.

So how were they to end it? Short of agreeing with everything his father said, Wittgenstein had no good response to this letter — certainly none that his father would have accepted. Not to acquiesce was to defy; and to acquiesce would be gnawing — killing.

His turmoil was all the worse for his being a stranger in Cambridge, where it seemed all were in a state of glad intoxication in those first days before term started. But there was another reason why Cambridge — any school — was strange to him. Wittgenstein had not been educated at the *Gymnasium,* nor at any other normal school where boys clack along well-greased rails, passing regular milestones toward careers and eventual manhood. No, like his siblings, Wittgenstein had been educated at home, cultivated like a hothouse plant with no classmates but his brothers and sisters, who by then were mostly grown anyway.

Karl Wittgenstein's reasons for doing this were not at all easy to discern. Education at home was, by then, an antiquated, somewhat antisocial idea, especially in the liberal tide that was sweeping Vienna at the turn of the century. But it was not politics that drove Karl Wittgenstein to keep his children at home. He had nothing against this state-run bureaucracy that stamped *Gymnasium* boys into budding bureaucrats who would fit like blocks into that byzantine edifice of patronage. On the contrary, Karl Wittgenstein highly approved of the *Gymnasium* system, where boys were, above all, thoroughly drilled in Latin and Greek classics and grammar in the belief that this would instill in them logical thought patterns, noble values and mental discipline. Built upon the useful principle of fear of one's superiors and a corresponding drive to strike fear into one's subordinates and social inferiors, the system was like life itself. All Karl Wittgenstein's subordinates were *Gymnasium* products, shrewd but thoroughly tractable men trained from boyhood to endure hours of stupefying memorization — finely honed, zealously detailed men who feared and revered the Direktor and passed his thinking down like the Eucharist.

No, Karl Wittgenstein educated his sons at home so he could be sure, as he did with his steel, exactly what materials and pedagogical processes had been used to mold the character and intellect. What he wanted was absolute, cartellike control of the quality, durability and ultimate destination of the product. That he kept his children at home also had to do with romantic but largely misunderstood and ill-executed ideas that he had gleaned from *Emile*. It was the idea of one teacher for one boy. Also that line from Rousseau he was so fond of quoting, that a father owes to his species men, to society sociable men and to the state *citizens*. There was, moreover, the classical ideal of the peripatetic school, wherein genius might achieve a strolling, Grecian repose, viewing the world as through the cool sanctum of a temple. Yes, Karl Wittgenstein's school would build true Greeks and Renaissance men, men born to rule and dispose of wealth in the furtherance of a city that would be, in the truest sense, *their* city, a tableau vivant of the mind.

Such plans were not to be left to chance, certainly not to a state-run system still infested with priests. Unfortunately, Karl Wittgenstein made one fatal miscalculation. Virtually all the tutors he employed were gifted *Gymnasium* products. Yet, clearly, had they been less whimsical and eccentric, they would have been *teaching* at the *Gymnasium*. It was odd that Karl Wittgenstein, a man much renowned for his foresight, did not anticipate this fairly obvious drawback to his plan. Tutored by gifted, independent-minded men, his sons were anything but the *Gymnasium* products that Karl Wittgenstein wanted in his heart of hearts. As Karl Wittgenstein put it, the genius of his sons was like water, running everywhere, and in all the wrong directions.

But the isolation of this education at home had another effect on Wittgenstein: having never been a boy among boys, he was ill prepared for life among young men, especially among young Englishmen. Wittgenstein had had a difficult time adjusting at Manchester, but here at Cambridge, where the traditions were at once more exaggerated and more obscure, his extremity was even more pronounced. Here he was thrust in among a race of public school boys who had been hazing, fagging, footballing and palling with each other since early boyhood at Harrow, Eton and assorted other forcing houses of the middle and upper classes. Among them, Wittgenstein's strange charisma counted for little, and his values counted for even less, stamping him as nothing but *queer*. He had none of that jaunty grace or pluck they loved, none of that shallow tone that marked their heroes. No power on earth could have made him English, or rather not foreign — why, even by Austrian standards, he was foreign.

Consciously, Wittgenstein had no interest in crashing their world, but all the same he suffered from it. The young Englishmen who lived on his hall were gay, athletic, clannish, smug — everything he was not. Among them, he felt old beyond his years; to him it seemed that Austrian years counted twice for English years. To them, on the other hand, this scowling Teuton (a German was German, after all) was an *odd duck*. More than odd — he was a damned recluse. They hardly saw him.

Through his window, Wittgenstein could hear the glad cries and nicknames, the happy horsing and talking. Looking out, he could see his fellow students in bunches trotting off to breakfast, and then off again to spend a few hours engaged in the sweaty, bullying athletics that he found as incomprehensible as he did fearful. At night, he could see them going off in evening attire to attend the dinners and functions given by the various clubs. And later, once the pubs had closed, he would hear them lumbering back in raucous knots, caroling down the lane.

He envied them, to be so charged and glowing, so increased by the same abrasive air that seemed to wear him down to nothing. Outside his room, he could feel them eyeing him, tentatively returning his own awkward nod. And then as he went down the stairs, he could imagine them smirking — bursting into laughter because he was so alien and forbidding, and not just on account of his accent.

In his state of mind, even the veilish, drizzly fall beauty of Cambridge failed him. Standing on King's Bridge — that pale stretch of stone that bows across the River Cam — looking at the punts gliding along under the willows, he felt it was a sin for such beauty to be lost on him and he on it. Why was he even here in England? His father was right. It was like aeronautics, another whim that would come to grief or nothing. For an hour, he would continue on this tack, and then he would turn about, telling himself that he must stay, if only for his own survival. And all the while he would be reproaching himself for not introducing himself to Bertrand Russell, who surely thought him intolerably rude for not making the requisite visit that advisers expected of new students. Yet how could he face Russell in his present state of mind? In those days before classes started, he avoided Russell like a contagious person.

At last then, after brooding over his father's letter for two days, Wittgenstein replied with a postcard. He wrote not to strike back, of course, but simply to give a good account of himself — by striking back:

2.10.12.

Dear Father,

The closing story of your last letter — the one about you and Grandfather — puts me in a bind. It is not a matter of liking someone, it is more a matter of understanding another's mind. I wish I could put this better. No doubt you will see this as a lack of technical facility on my part. Nothing new here. Learned or well-reasoned arguments do not work with fathers.

As for the rest, the less said, I think, the better. As you say, I will do what I want. But again I would remind you that this isn't necessarily a matter of CHOICE. (Emphasis yours.)

Your Son

As he expected, his father wasted no time responding, this time with a postcard, mimicking his son's favorite medium.

11. October 1912

My Son,

Very well, a card. (YOUR emphasis.) I will be succinct to the point of being EXTINCT. (Again, YOUR emphasis.) Your card, like the rest, is long on evasions but short on *reason*. My father, to repeat, once asked me a difficult question, but times change. I see I must ask my son NO QUESTIONS.

Faithfully yours in brevity,
Father

P.S. *Will* you be coming home for the holidays?

This time, Wittgenstein took his time responding. Three weeks later he replied, but he did so by letter.

12.11.12.

Dear Father,
   Your last letter leaves me even less to say. Words are not limitless. They do run out at a certain point, and then the less said the better — so I see it, anyhow. I do not expect it will always be this way between us, but at present this is how I find it. I DO recognize this is not easy for you.
   As for the holidays, I think for this year it would be better if I remained in England, to weather through some things. It is for the best, and I am NOT angry or sulking. Without undue advertising, my work goes well, and I am reasonably happy. I have struck up a kind of friendship — or at least understanding — with my teacher Bertrand Russell. I don't think he knows what to make of me either, but he is trying. He is young, barely forty, but he will, I believe, one day be considered of a rank with Kant — or Locke, if you like. My English is slowly improving.
   A longer letter, after all.

                                                    Your respectful Son

   The next round surprised him. Instead of responding himself, his father managed to draw Wittgenstein's sister Gretl into the fray. Gretl had long been the family mediator, simply by virtue of her being the only one left in the family willing to defy their father. But as Karl Wittgenstein also knew, Gretl was the one who could best penetrate the stubbornness of his youngest son.
   Eleven years older than Wittgenstein, Gretl was for him something of a mother figure, doting, brilliant, gay, at times even a bit silly. Long had she told him to do as she did with her father — ignore him. Oh, don't be so serious! she would say in her throaty voice, mugging into Wittgenstein's eyes until he would have to laugh and turn away. At home, she took him out to the cafés, where it seemed that everybody — all the painters, writers and musicians — knew her. She was so madcap and brilliant, such a plump little whirlwind in her couture clothes of bronze-like fabrics designed by her friend Klimt for the house of Flöge. A formidable woman, some said admiringly. Entirely too bold, said others, including her own father. In the papers, Gretl had been the subject of more than one high-flown feuilleton and the butt of several more satires. It didn't daunt her, nor did it especially daunt her husband, Rolf, a wealthy industrialist and financier. Frau Margarete Stonborough cut a wide swath, quite unmistakable in pearl and diamond chokers, sharp-

toed French shoes, and hats with sprays of alert feathers that trembled with her laughing and talking, her broad gestures. Yet for all her barreling strength and heartiness, Gretl had her troubles. She, too, was her father's child, and so she was Freud's patient, seeing the doctor four mornings each week. But still, she was so very Viennese in her ability to kid her little brother out of his moods, to wink at those unpleasantries that from earliest youth they had both seen staring them in the face.

Ordinarily, Wittgenstein thrived on her letters, but this time, sensing he had shaken down a hornet's nest, he could feel his stomach gurgling as he opened the embossed vellum envelope and read:

My Dear Hardheaded Brother,

Father is FURIOUS. Even Mother is angry — strike that, *upset* by your stubbornness about the holidays. Might you realize that people other than Father wish to see you? Sooner or later you will, and must, come home, and then it will only be worse. You have not made a serious point. All you have succeeded in doing is making Father still more suspicious and angry — and, I might add, have done so at the expense of the rest of us. And before you jump to conclusions, I am *not* suggesting that you simply give in to him. I DO, however, urge you to adopt a more intelligent approach. As your apologist, I do wish you would do a little better by me. I really think you are being — forgive me — SILLY. How are we to take you? You hardly seem to know how to take yourself.

I remember on the telephone — how you would always have to be the first to hang up, presumably before the other person hung up on you. I told Dr. Freud this, and he said, "Clearly, your brother has a fear of being spurned."

I told him another story as well. Do you remember when you were eight — that snowy day when that man with the bloody nose accused you of having struck him in the face with an icy snowball? Father was outraged when the man dragged you home. I remember my shock at how strenuously he defended you against the man's accusations. He said you were not at all the type to do such a thing. I suppose the man, some tradesman, thought he would get some money, and I have no idea how Father got rid of him, finally. But afterward, Ludi, I found you in a rage, thrashing your pillow. You said you had not done it, had been wrongly accused. But then, a few days later, you said you had done it, and then you broke down again — apparently because you were not sure then whether in fact you *had* done it. Everyone knew you had done nothing; yet for weeks, you would not speak to anyone — even Father was uncharacteristically understanding, saying that it was just one of those unpleasant things in life that one must forget.

It seems extraordinary to me. I think you never did forget it and have ever since been trying to blame yourself for something you did not do, looking, I wonder, for things you may not even want in response to an unsolicited question that fate (an irate man) put into your head. I think, beneath, you are either very sad or angry. I know for years I was both. I am still angry now, but certainly I am less angry; at least I do not suffer the same headaches and fears. That is something, don't you agree?

All goes reasonably well here. At the Secession, I am on the select committee to judge this year's younger artists; I also am getting to know Kokoschka, who is a delight and a terror — fascinating. You really should, at least, write Mother.

Please, more than two words. You mustn't hang up on us.

Affectionately,
Gretl

He could not reply to her with the same heat. But he could not give in to her either — or to her irksome recollections.

My Dear Sister,

Your memory is extraordinary — or at least eleven years longer than mine. The problem is, I don't believe in the *UNconscious* any more than I do in such chimeras as water-ice or iron-wood. I believe in mental states — conscious states, some happy, some sad. I am sad sometimes, and I *know* I am sad. That is the end of it. But *UNconscious*? Your Freud is speaking absurdities, Schopenhauer's Will notwithstanding.

I am sorry but I will not be home at Christmas. Believe me, this will be better for us all, and you really should not worry. Why, on second thought, don't you come to England? It would be wonderful to see you here. I would take you to see all the sights worth seeing, including Mr. Russell.

Your Hardheaded Brother

Wittgenstein may have written to his sister, but his father, for then at least, had the last word, sending him a Christmas card that was purposely saccharine and frilly. Inside, beneath the powdered glass snowflakes and sugarplums, was a lump of coal.

23. November 1912

My Son,

Wishing you FAR IN ADVANCE a joyous year in all your pointedly cerebral enterprises.

Good will to men.

Father

Cambridge

LATER, Wittgenstein would say that what could be said about logic must be capable of being said *all at once*. And later, much later, it would seem to Russell that he had seen Wittgenstein's genius all at once, as if Wittgenstein were the visitation of some forgotten, vanquished or extinct version of himself. Who recognizes an heir all at once? Who doesn't deny or quarrel with the likeness or say that the heir comes *too soon*? It took Russell longer than all at once to see who his new student was, yet within a matter of months he would cease to think of him as a student and would regard him as something the likes of which he had never seen.

Russell had received Frege's letter recommending Wittgenstein. Not long after, he received Wittgenstein's own courtly letter in clumsy English saying that he greatly admired his *Principia* and wanted to follow in his footsteps, clarifying logical points Russell had raised in his great work. *Clarifying what?* wondered Russell aloud. Not that he thought his book was the last word on the subject, but what cheek! For a mere *student* to fancy improving ten years of intensive thinking — much less the thinking of two men!

On second thought, though, it occurred to Russell that the gaffe was perhaps unintentional — the fumbling of a man with an imperfect command of English. In a more positive vein, Russell was intrigued to hear that Frege's candidate was an engineer. Thanks to Poincaré and Einstein, among others, science had been steadily gaining hegemony over mathematics and philosophy, disciplines whose results were less quantifiable and certainly less tangible than aeroplanes, light bulbs and miracle serums. As a philosopher who wanted to make logic and mathematics achieve the rigor and method of a science, and who moreover hoped to make philosophy a sort of *governess* over the methods and suppositions of the sciences themselves, Russell had long wished that he and his pupils were better grounded in mechanics and other more empirically based subjects. He now felt this especially keenly, working in the shadow of Cambridge's Cavendish Laboratory, which was directed by the great J. J. Thomson, discoverer of the electron and Nobel laureate in 1906. Cavendish had also given rise to the New Zealander Ernest Rutherford, another recent laureate, who in collaboration with Thomson had done pioneering work with x-rays to explore the nature of the atomic nucleus. Working at Cavendish now was Charles Wilson, nicknamed "Cloud" Wilson, who had developed a cloud chamber for observing ions. There was William Lawrence Bragg, a young man who was doing an x-ray study of the structure of crystals. And now, with a young Dane named Niels Bohr, Rutherford was attempting to plot out the structure of the atom. Russell had good reason to feel physics breathing down his neck.

Leaps in progress were much like cyclones, it seemed to Russell. He hoped a kind of cyclone might just be touching down at Cambridge, perhaps with him at its center. Russell, the scientist manqué, even dreamed of becoming another Aristotle, founder of a school that would produce a new breed of thinker: the scientist-philosopher.

For these reasons, Russell was especially intrigued with Wittgenstein. But Frege further incited Russell's curiosity — and his sense of competition — when he wrote that this Wittgenstein was fearless and unrelenting in discussion, that he had in him not only the bulldog but originality.

On the strength of this, Russell recommended admission — he even smoothed the admissions process by agreeing, sight unseen, to be the student's adviser. It was hardly incumbent on Russell to do this. By virtue of mere gratitude and civility — or, failing that, by virtue of sheer grubbing, apple-polishing practicality — a student would have repaid his benefactor with a courtly visit. At least the student would have sent his master an appreciative note.

But Russell received nothing. In matters of manners and Cambridge punctilio, Russell was less hidebound than most, but still he was disappointed, especially when he found that his German (he had forgotten that Wittgenstein was Austrian) had taken charge of his rooms.

"Still no sign of my German," he wrote Ottoline in one of his daily letters. "Frege said he was guilty of impetuosity, but he said nothing about his being ill-mannered. Well, we shall see . . ."

Like Wittgenstein, Russell was intensely aware of the excitement around Cambridge with the start of the new year. He found these annual rites pleasant, even nostalgic, but in his uncertainty about Ottoline his feelings had a way of turning on him unexpectedly, with memories of his own youth at Cambridge — memories mixed with the irony of *not knowing* in a place where he had been elevated precisely in the expectation that he did indeed *know* something, that he was not still struggling, confused and burdened by doubt.

How very odd it was at times for Russell to find himself a victualer of knowledge in a place where formerly he had been a consumer. Trinity had not changed so much in twenty years. True, the students were more worldly and less innocent — certainly, they were less religiously inclined and guilt plagued than they had been in his day. But the place itself never changed, not outwardly. With its mix of styles, Trinity College, like the rest of Cambridge, was a piece of architectural legislation cobbled over centuries by various kings, queens, bishops, architects and ages. In one direction, there were spires and Renaissance balustrades, in another, castle keeps notched with archer's roosts. Inside the walled battlements of Great Court, which enclosed a three-hundred-foot green, there was Neville's fountain, the very center of Trinity. Built in 1602 in a High Renaissance style, it was a pedestaled cupola of carved stone that, at a distance, looked like ivory, almost translucent in the deepening afternoon light. But Great Court was most beautiful at sunset, when the red stone walls, having soaked up the day's sun, suddenly released their color, filling the air with the warm, glowing effulgence of old claret.

At times now, walking along the same paths, almost against his will, Russell would remember Alys as a fresh thing, would remember that time when it seemed he could see the whole of life as an unsegmented green distance. Heraclitus was wrong, he thought. All was not in flux; nothing ever changed. Looking down, he could see his feet, the same feet clad in virtually the same shoes, below what seemed the same flapping trousers that he had worn at age twenty. And not only did his feet look no different but they seemed to fall into the same pools of shadow, as if at each stage of life there were stirrups in which one mechanically inserted each successive step. All one's life mounting the same predestined path, the same rungs, inhaling the same smells and the same scenes, which hung like smoke, then dispelled in the broader gaze. And always the way the red stone glowed at dusk, and how, when one looked up, the moon appeared like a coin seen through very deep water, and then the way the light nested on the same feathery layers of creepers that bearded the library and underhung the archways, beneath which had passed Bacon, Newton, Thackeray and a host of others who surely had trod these same paths, staring at their feet while mulling these same doubts, hopes and griefs.

Russell sometimes found it a bit oppressive to be among these confident young believers — to see them all so excited and flushed, so full of themselves, strutting about in their new wools, silk neckties and tweeds. What a thing it was to watch them, newly enfranchised into adult life and duly empowered in their allowances, with money for the washerwoman and tobacconist and for the sundry purveyors of spirits, not to mention the tailor, bookseller and grocer. For some there would even be money for manservants and motorcars, private dinners in their rooms and larks to London to consort with expensive whores — in short, to begin laying in the store of memories and regrets that would dog them, too, when they were forty and passing down some too-redolent path. Walking through Great Court, Russell could feel the whole year unfolding. Here were the freshmen being ragged and run around. Here were the big sportsmen in their flannels and magnificent sweaters. At night, around banging pianos, there would be voices raised in song. In Hall, on audit night, they would merrily taste the new ale, as well as Trinity's own pale sherry and the Bucellus of Magdalene. Dressed in caps and gowns with Geneva bands under their chins, the proctors would stroll the streets along with their top-hatted proctor's men, or "Bulldogs," searching for miscreants who might be out carousing late, riding bicycles without lamps or flinging lumps of sugar at the borough constabulary. A few of the more idle, obstreperous or drunken would be sent home to rusticate, but for the others, the gay progress would swell into the next term and the next. And such a grand time it was. All the clubs would now be starting up, the choristers, dramatists, and *littérateurs,* the scullers and Trinity's own Foot Beagles, all groping for evanescent trophies and laurels, all putting out their innocent hopes like flags. Such youthful enthusiasm! Come join us. Do be like us. All the world is a stage. All life is the hearty fellowship of rowing, footballing, cricketeering, debating, singing, scribbling, chess playing and carousing. No, thought Russell, doggedly sniffing for the trail he had lost. All life is, is getting started. Just getting started.

Still, there was tradition to fall back on.

As a rule, Russell frowned on tradition, but at Trinity it was a different story. In class, students and dons alike wore the mortarboard and long black scholar's robes, though only the dons wore the red ribbons that distinguished and exalted them. And Russell did find a certain grandeur to it, strutting along like one newly coronated in his flapping black gown. So, too, was it reassuring to be addressed in the diffident voice of the Cambridge student, the voice of men who, even when they were absolutely positive of something, would say with collegial, English tentativeness, *It would seem . . .* or *One might reasonably wonder if . . .*

As someone accustomed to such consideration, Russell was surprised when, entering class on the first day, he saw a young man with a tuft of brown hair lift his gown and reach into a suit jacket of decidedly German tailoring. Avoiding Russell's gaze, the young man dropped his gown and, with a baleful look, conspicuously sat down in the last row. And still not a word? thought Russell. What cheek! Russell felt it like a taunt, amazed that the German would even have the gall to show himself.

Russell took a good, long look at the young man as he walked presidingly to the front and began his course on philosophy and the foundations of logic. The German looked younger than he had expected. And, to his discomfort, he was staring. He had a copybook open, but never once did he pick up his pen — this as the other students, with typical first-day zeal, raced to take down Russell's every word.

On the first day, it was important for the don to captivate — in short, to *stun*. Here Russell was in his element. Talking quickly and zestfully, tearing at the subject in gleeful hunks, throwing out seemingly insurmountable questions only to swat them down like flies, Russell did indeed stun, at least to judge by their wide-eyed looks as they filed out afterward.

All except his German, that is. The German was still sitting. With his head craned up to the ceiling, he seemed oblivious to the fact that class had ended. What was his problem? Russell wondered. The language? At several points during the lecture, Russell had seen him squinting up at the ceiling, mouthing his words suspiciously, like some foreign food. At yet another point, the German had squeezed his eyes shut, wincing painfully, as if he had heard a screech beyond human frequency. But now Russell decided to put him out of mind. Let the rude German come to me if he has difficulties, he thought. He left.

The windy green of Great Court was filled with what looked like a flock of fluttering blackbirds as students and dons winged by in their black gowns. Striding along, Russell heard a guttural voice:

Sir . . . Sir . . .

Turning, he saw it was the German. The young man did not excuse himself but straightaway said, I am Wittgenstein. From the class. And I must say, sir, I think you are wrong, quite. This cannot be so. To my satisfaction you have not proved that we can know *anything* of the world. Not with such certainty. *Spoken* proposition, yes. This much I will admit. This much I can accept. But the rest you say with such a confident — no, I cannot . . .

To openly confront a don on one's first day like this — it was so astounding that Russell had to smile. Almost baiting him, Russell replied, Oh, do you?

The young man shrugged. The German was staring right through him, not angry or afraid. Clearly, he was not even aware of his abrasiveness as he nodded and said, Yes, I am sure. Quite sure.

Oh, I see, said Russell. Cocksure.

Gogksure? Squinting. The German didn't know this word.

Russell was staring him down now, trying to beat him back. But the German wouldn't budge. Wanting once and for all to bring matters under control, Russell was brusque: Well, I suppose I should be happy we've at last had a chance to speak. I rather had thought you would visit me. The German was still looking right through him, so Russell added punitively, In my rooms. It's customary to come over. I am your adviser, you know.

Good! A hint of embarrassment and chagrin. The German nodded hopefully. Yes, I am pleased and honored, sir. Of course, of course. His facial expression altered again. But about my assertion. Your answer does not satisfy me, no.

Oh, does it not now? asked Russell, taking a step back. Well, we can take that up later, I think. I'm very sorry, but I must be off now.

Russell turned to resume walking, but the young man followed him, saying, If it is all right, sir, I will walk, thank you. Now, I will say . . . And again he launched into an explanation of his contention that nothing was knowable but spoken propositions.

Breaking in, Russell said, Why are we even talking, Mr. Wittgenstein? After all, if you *know* only what *you* know or say — why speak at all?

Your *thoughts* I can consider.

Oh! huffed Russell. Well, that's most kind of you. But it does hurt my feelings that you won't admit *I* exist.

Russell was mistaken if he thought this would throw off the German. When he sped up, the German sped up, too. Looking around, Russell saw the German's head bent like a whirling grindstone, throwing up a shower of sparks as he bore along, arguing and waving his arms.

Later that night, once freed from the German's grip, Russell wrote in a letter to Ottoline:

Today I met my German. Frege was right about his bullheadedness. He accosted me after class & argued with me until I reached my rooms — and this with an uncomprehending force and belligerence that I have never seen. I must write to Frege. The German's English is poor & his manners are even poorer.

Several days later he wrote:

My German threatens to be an affliction. He came back again after my lecture & argued with me until dinnertime — obstinate & perverse, but I think not stupid.

Then:

My German ex-engineer is a fool! He ought to go back to flying kites. He was very argumentative & tiresome today. Also, I think, distraught about something. It is as if there were a lid over him, which, when opened, releases the forces of hell! The other undergraduates clearly think him odd, as indeed he is. I think they fear him — nor do I blame them, the way he wrestles the discussion in class. I really must speak to him; this disruption cannot continue.

Then two weeks later:

My lecture went off all right, but then my German ex-engineer, as usual, came back and maintained his thesis that there is nothing in the world except stated propositions. I told him, rather dryly, that it is too large a theme for his paper. He replied, "Too large for whom?"

Several weeks later, though, there was a slight change in tone:

Again today, my German was riding his hobbyhorse that nothing empirical is knowable — a contention that traditionally appeals to the angry young. It was very curious. It is one thing to argue such a thing philosophically, but I wondered if he didn't somehow *believe* it. I told him he made me feel as if we were two empty blocks of air, conversing. My German smiled a bitter smile, then sd. that I was a block of light & himself a block of darkness, & sd. this, mind you, in a way that made me recoil in recognition, reminding me exactly of my own morbid moments. I remember him smiling faintly & nodding, as if to say, "I know you, Russell, I know you better than you think." I don't know, my darling, my German may be right — if one is un-happy, then perhaps one *is* better off invisible.

By the following week, there was a distinct change:

I think I was wrong about my German, who, as he told me pointedly yesterday, is not German but Austrian. We are really on much better terms. At his invitation, I went with him as his guest last night to hear a chamber recital of Mendelssohn music given by the Cambridge University Musical Society. His attention to music is extraordinary. He sat there staring up with the unfocused fixity of a blind man — I rather got the impression that he was sight-reading the score in his head. It seems it is not only my lectures he finds fault with, for after the piece was ended, he sd., "Please wait a moment. I must speak to these men." Forthwith he went up to the musicians, very much on his high horse as usual, & began with great deliberation to criticize their playing! Poor devils, he was the same with them as he is with me. The leader was at first quite vexed, & then seemed to grasp his point, especially when Wittgenstein whistled a few bars in absolutely perfect pitch & then proceeded to dissect the movement. By the time he finished, they were listening to him. They apparently accepted his authority on the subject & suggested — quite sincerely, I think — that he attend their practice sessions, an offer he readily accepted.

Now that we are more comfortable together and can talk about matters other than logic, I see he is really very literary, very musical & pleasant mannered (being Austrian), & I think *really* intelligent. I rather hope I will see more of him.

This warming trend continued. At the end of November, Russell wrote:

Another concert with Wittgenstein. Having dutifully attended practice sessions, he liked this concert much better. Finally ventured to ask of his family. Apparently, they also are very musical, & also very wealthy & prominent, as Frege himself implied, & as is evident by Wittgenstein's own extreme cultivation (at least once one gets to know him). He sd. two of his brothers were musical geniuses. "Were?" I ventured. Pokerfaced, he sd. yes, they were dead, but clearly he did not want to elaborate, & I did not ask, noticing his discomfort. The same was true when I enquired about his father. Wittgenstein sd., in a rather unwarranted argumentative tone, "My father is a very great man. In Vienna he is very well known." I sd., "I imagine he is happy you are at Cambridge." At this he shrugged & sd. that, on the contrary, his father was very displeased & thinks logic an utter waste of time. I wish I had left it. Wittgenstein became quiet & lumpish after that. It rather spoilt the evening.

Big Woman

THE VACATIONS were drawing near, but Russell was not much looking forward to them. It would be his first Christmas with Ottoline — or rather, *without* Ottoline, who was as usual squirming with an overbooked calendar, including the requisite charity functions and Christmas parties, not to mention time for Julian and Philip. Her extreme kindness to Russell — the kindness of one who has nothing else to give — only deepened his gloom about his relative importance in her life. In the end, Russell had just one afternoon with her that holiday, and this was spent in the Nabob, a run-down hotel in Maida Vale, where, if they were sure not to be recognized, they were equally sure to be depressed.

Still, Russell tried to put the best face on it. For days he racked his mind about what to get her for Christmas, worrying about what she could wear as a sign of his love without inviting questions. He had no instincts for these things. Finally, frantically, barely an hour before they were to meet, a jeweler talked him into a brooch of sapphires set in gold filigree. Russell wasn't sure — it seemed a bit unlike her — and later, in their tatty, half-bob room, his doubts were confirmed. Oh, it's lovely! she bubbled, but there was a catch in her voice as she held it up to her breast. Much too crusted and clumsy. Here, he said, giving her a hopeful kiss as he fastened the pin. But you don't like it, do you? I can easily bring it back —

But of course I like it! she protested, giving him a peck. It's lovely, lovely. And I shall think of you when I wear it. But still he could see it was wrong, tugging like a burr at her bodice. Worse, it was more than he could afford, what with Alys demanding money for the doctor and repairs to the house.

Ottoline sensed his mood but was determined not to succumb to it. *Now,* she said in a spritely voice as she stubbed out her cigarette. Now you must open your gift!

With that, she watched with anticipation as he tore off the wrapping and opened a felt-covered box containing — what? A gold-nibbed pen? She could think of nothing better than *this*?

Why, a pen! he said weakly. Obligingly, he held it in his writing hand.

It's engraved, too, she prompted, turning the pen over in his hand. See there, on the barrel? And he looked, hoping to see their initials coyly entwined, but found only his own scripted name.

He didn't know what struck him then. Seeing these gifts, he started inwardly to pine, thinking of their poor human hopes, pinned to such trivial things. And he was desperately trying to be gay — he had to be gay, he thought, if he didn't want to drive her off. But looking at these offerings, then considering as well their two bodies, the meager bottle of wine and the two filmy glasses the old porter had brought up — seeing all this, he turned away, surprised and ashamed as tears sprang to his eyes.

I did-not-want-this, he gulped, pinching the bridge of his nose. I did *not* —

Huffing, out of breath, he was staring out the window as she came from behind and gave him a squeeze, doing her best to console him. But she had a dinner engagement with Philip and their time was running out. I hate leaving you like this, she said, coaxing him toward the bed. Please, darling.

But all he heard was, *Look! Here it is — here's what you want.* So ready to offer herself up, he thought cynically. A little Christmas charity between the sheets. No, he thought resolutely, he had principles, he was much too heartbroken for sex. Instead, he told her he wanted only to lie together, to talk and hold each other. He genuinely believed this, but once she had calmed him his penis gorged like a tulip bulb and, lo, he wanted sex, too.

But I *can't* now! she pleaded, her voice turning scratchy. I *wanted* to — you saw that I did — but now we haven't the time. Honestly! I cannot . . .

He had his way finally, but he hurt her. She was not ready, and he was too jabbing and eager. And then she fell apart, too, softly crying as she bent beside the rusty sink, slapping water up into herself. And not just washing herself, he felt, but washing *him out.* And failing again. Mightily failing.

He endeavored to apologize. Straining, he tried to suggest how it might be better next time — as if there would be a next time, he thought, as he looked out the window onto the steep, icy street where even the draft horses were struggling in their harnesses, even the horses.

Having little to look forward to, Russell was hoping to derive some vicarious pleasure from Wittgenstein's holiday plans when he asked several nights later, So . . . I expect you'll be going home for Christmas?

Evidently, Wittgenstein did not relish the question. I will be here, he said, with the same reticence and rigidity he had shown when Russell had asked about his family.

Pretending not to notice the look that darkened Wittgenstein's eyes, Russell persisted. Any plans in particular?

I may travel to Scotland. I have not thought about it.

Ah. Russell brightened. Then I take it you will be here part of the time? In that case, we might see each other.

Yes. Wittgenstein nodded as if this had just occurred to him. This would be good. He nodded again.

Probing once more, Russell asked casually, You just decided this? To remain here for the holidays?

No. Wittgenstein held back as before. I have for some time decided.

Oh. Raising his eyes, Russell broadly affected to be content with this answer, but there was mutual discomfort, the conversation slowly sinking like a punctured tire, bringing them to what, by now, was a familiar impasse. Their relationship had reached the point where they could be neither formal nor entirely familiar, where it was not clear if their association was that of student and don, budding colleagues, friends or accomplices. As the don, Russell was uneasy as to the nature of his role and obligations; or rather, he was queasy about the more basic question of who was on top. But obscuring this was the increasingly confusing matter of who was who. Wittgenstein was such an impenetrable thicket of character that Russell couldn't put him in any apparent context. Even Wittgenstein's most ordinary gestures — the way he slapped his forehead, his figures of speech, recurring images he used — struck Russell in a weird and distant way as an uncanny translation of himself: a translation of a translation. Wittgenstein's English further confused matters. At times, when Wittgenstein was struggling to make a point, Russell would insist, *Speak German.* Yet hearing this other voice, so elegant and clear, Russell would stop cold, as if he had glimpsed his own sunstruck image in a shop window: one's appalling *otherwise.*

But the problem was not just Wittgenstein. Wittgenstein was merely the catalyst for something else Russell felt stirring within him. Other selves — discarded ideas — were rising to the surface, showing their silvery undersides like startled leaves in a warm wind mouthing rain. But there was also the fear of seeing unearthed what one had so assiduously smothered, the inchoate confusion of the new in its unprecedented raiment. And so, while watching Wittgenstein perform some ordinary act, Russell would find himself thinking, *Who* are *you?*

If only Russell could have struck some balance, a truce of some kind. He didn't want to pry, but now he felt no more comfortable inquiring than he did keeping silent. And wittingly or unwittingly, Wittgenstein was tantalizing him. For the last month, Wittgenstein had been steadily enticing him with a trail of crumbs. His two older brothers, for instance. Wittgenstein was briskly, oppressively matter-of-fact when he mentioned them, saying that they were dead but offering no other details. Russell wouldn't stoop to pick it up, not then. Yet he resented Wittgenstein's silence, which nagged at him for days until in an anxious moment he said, If I might inquire, Wittgenstein, what happened to your two brothers?

Eyeing him, Wittgenstein replied disdainfully, They had their lives taken.

Took their lives, you mean?

Russell didn't mean to correct his English. But then as he saw Wittgenstein's black look of affirmation, Russell found himself emotionally back-pedaling. I'm very sorry . . .

No need to be *sorry*, retorted Wittgenstein, correcting in turn Russell's emotional grammar. They have not died yesterday.

This stung but Russell took it, not saying another word. And absurd as this apology was, it was no less absurd than Wittgenstein's need to imply that his was a great and otherwise normal family. Not, Wittgenstein seemed to hastily add, that their greatness had in any way rubbed off on him, the most unworthy of their subjects. Nor, Lord knows, was this to imply any criticism of his august father. At the mere mention of his father's name, Wittgenstein's voice would drop to the muted tones of a courtier anxious that his sire appear in the best possible light — meaning, so far as Russell could see, in no light whatsoever.

There was something else that nagged Russell: the nature of Wittgenstein's character.

Specifically, he was mystified by this insular, fugitive quality in Wittgenstein. Russell could see it wasn't mere reserve, nor the manner of a young man who invests himself with a false air of tragedy. Without being able to explain how or why, Russell sensed that Wittgenstein's beliefs and character were all of a piece. After all, for Wittgenstein to refuse to admit the existence of anything except spoken propositions — this, as Russell saw it, went beyond the stubbornness of the usual self-styled solipsist or nihilist. Another young man might have said this to be bizarre or fanciful, to butt horns with authority. But in Wittgenstein it seemed part of a deeper rupture. Wittgenstein didn't just argue, he argued for his life.

But why all this thrashing to arrive at new ideas? Russell wondered. It was a question Russell might as easily have asked himself. In logic, there is the law of identity, by which whatever is, is. There is the law of contradiction, by which nothing can both be and not be. And there is the law of excluded middle, by which everything must either be or not be. Besides these laws, there is also Ockham's razor — more a practical aesthetic than a law — by which logical entities are not to be multiplied more than necessary. But for the thinker, Russell saw, there is what might be called Willy-Nilly's law, by which the act of seeking or desiring, like a kind of propulsion, is accompanied by a simultaneous avoidance or dread. Seeking, Russell knew, was never simply seeking in itself; it was not only that one blessed thing in the distance but also the momentum behind it, adding exponentially to the eventual impact.

Whatever else, Russell sensed danger, and yet he found it oddly thrilling. But here Russell forgot the corollary of Willy-Nilly's law, namely, that this condition was far more thrilling for him, the observer, than it was for Wittgenstein, for whom this necessity was something else, something else entirely.

There was another capacity in Russell, however, that was antithetical to Wittgenstein's character — namely, his sublime ability to ignore certain unpleasant areas of his life.

This was not a mere difference in temperament; it was also a function of their difference in age. Unlike Wittgenstein, Russell had attained that age at which men are adept at psychically treading water, treading for days and sometimes weeks on end. Emotionally, he might be lost in the middle of the North Atlantic, but it *wasn't so bad*. Cozily bobbing along as a wave hits . . . *pfffftttt* — gasping. Then another wave. And another.

At times it was hardly a dog paddle, barely keeping his head above water. And lately, Russell was so busy swimming along that he hardly noticed this new current that was slowly sweeping him out to sea. Besides, it was this fear, this heroic struggling in the foam of experience — this was the fatal discharge whereof life is created. *This* was what he lived for. And, blast it, the point was, he *was swimming*. Yes, in a pinch all Noah's critters swim, but none tread water better than shipwrecked, middle-aged men.

Wittgenstein was a different story. He was a ghost who would appear at Russell's door late at night, unable to sleep.

For two and three hours at a stretch, sometimes, the ghost would talk and pace. During these vigils, Wittgenstein could be brilliant, both in what he said and in that passion and excitement that Frege had first noticed. Just as often, though, he would be slack and boring — depleted. But never did he drift contentedly. He was too young not to fight the current.

Russell would be struggling not to nod off, his eyes watering as Wittgenstein endlessly paced the floor, locked on some idea or other. Russell had never seen the like of him. He himself had worked *with* logic, but until Wittgenstein he had never had the sense of someone locked *inside* logic, struggling to escape like Houdini shackled inside a trunk. For Wittgenstein, logic was not merely a problem, it was the *problem of his life*. Sometimes Russell would try to prod him out of it, saying in a kindly voice, I'm not sure what you expect, Wittgenstein.

But of course I expect everything.

And again, Wittgenstein would raise his eyes, flashing that bitter little smile, so fatal and dark. Wittgenstein was daring him, Russell thought, and again he would feel that thrill, and *pffffttt* — another wave. Carrying him out farther still.

But then Russell was approaching the task from another angle, one of British liberal parlor empiricism mixed with an Enlightenment sense that most things in life could eventually be explained or justified by virtue of reason. The skepticism was there, of course, but it was a comparatively sober skepticism leavened with a quipping practicality that blew away so much moon dust while accepting the not unreasonable premise that, at any given time, fully nine-tenths of the world's business was pointless lunacy in the cause of general employment. For this world view, Russell could thank the Russell legacy and in particular his paternal grandmother, who on the flyleaf of the Bible she had given him as a boy had written the injunction, *Thou shalt not follow a multitude to do evil.*

In Russell's character, there was also the agnostic, freethinking tradition of his parents, especially that of his father, Lord Amberley, who knowingly scotched his political career by supporting birth control. Russell was very much a man in his father's mold, and had he not been orphaned, he certainly would have grown into a much different man. But first his mother and sister died of diphtheria, and then a year and a half later, his quietly inconsolable father, prematurely aged and depressed, followed them into the ground.

Russell was three then, not yet old enough to fully understand but old enough to remember in the way that sorrow remembers. His father left Russell and his older brother, Frank, in the care of a tutor who shared his unconventional views, but their grandmother's solicitor soon put an end to that. Instead, Lady Russell took the boys to Pembroke Lodge, a grace and favor house outside London that the queen had granted to their grandfather, Lord John.

Twice prime minister under Victoria, Bertie's grandfather had counseled Napoleon at Elba and shot grouse with Bismarck. The old earl was also the same slippery politician whom Henry Adams remembered as such a liar and intriguer, soothing the American legation in London while conspiring with Gladstone to aid the Confederate cause. But those days were far behind Lord John. Lost in the forests of bewildering, compounding age, the old man paid scant notice to the boy, who best remembered him either immersed in his old parliamentary papers or dozing as a footman perambulated him down the garden path in his rickety bath chair.

The force in the family was Lady Russell, a hardtack puritan who eschewed ease and derided joy for its vanity and transitory nature, advocating cold baths, plain food and service to men who, like the beasts, needed to be governed. God for her was impersonal, but for a Russell the British government was anything but impersonal. It was through his grandmother that Russell learned to think of England as *his* England and to speak of the government in the royal *We.*

For some reason, Lady Russell felt it critical to the boy's moral development that she disguise her love, and she was very, very good at it. He was too clever by a deuce, she said, and she kept him in line with dry ridicule, that sovereign sport of adults. What is mind? she would ask with a prim and joyless smile when he first evinced an interest in philosophy. What is mind? — *sniff* — no matter. What is matter? — *sniff* — never mind.

Life, she seemed to say, had been duly debated and decided by elders who knew far better than he, a callow boy, what bore serious examination. For Lady Russell, even words were an extravagance to be parceled out parsimoniously, as if each day one was granted a hundred, of which ten were worth anything. The boy felt like a snuffed candle in her house. Brought out in tumbrels like the condemned, ideas rumbled down that long dinner table to the old woman's docket, there to be duly affirmed or denied, then forever banished with a little catch phrase, a hollow nugget meant, so far as the boy could see, to spare the trouble of further thinking. Yes, Lady Russell once said distastefully, Darwin was indubitably *correct,* punctuating this pronouncement with her off-with-his-head sniff; subject closed.

Being of the opinion that public schools were morally corrupting, Lady Russell kept the young boy home under the instruction of governesses and tutors — mediocrities whose main qualifications were solemn adherence, or at least lip service, to Her Ladyship's religious views. The tutors were quite unnecessary. Her Ladyship's joyless prig of a grandson soon required no supervision, and with an inward sneer he learned nothing from them. Lord Russell's vast library was the boy's school, and this too took its toll. Cold, clever, solitary, the budding polymath kept a diary and even developed a sort of mathematical code to hide his teeming inner life from his grandmother's prying eyes. In this code, the boy recorded his first impure thoughts, analyzing his emotions in much the way that Galvani used electrodes to stimulate the legs of dissected frogs. In code, he plumbed the laws of dynamics and the ontological argument; in code he despaired and fell from faith; and in code he began to seriously contemplate suicide, deciding, after due deliberation, that he most preferred the idea of throwing himself under a train. Her Ladyship's visitors did find the boy a bit unreal, but they approved of his tireless industry as he sat at his grandfather's big bureau, working away at his trifling boy's doings. Dour, diligent Bertie — one more product of a sentimental education at home.

Still, Russell was learning not to always take Wittgenstein's pronouncements at face value — that is, he was learning to listen not merely for what Wittgenstein said but for what he implied.

For instance, at one time or another, Russell had seen most of his philosophy students flirt with the idea of solipsism as an extreme metaphysical possibility. He had done so himself. But it was not until he met Wittgenstein that he had heard anyone argue it as a deeply felt predicament.

Several nights when Wittgenstein was in a bad way — raw and restless, distracted — Russell saw it: nothingness made palpable. Russell had long felt that there was something fearful and disfiguring in solipsism, a willful blinding, like Oedipus dashing out his eyes. And it pained him to see Wittgenstein clawing to get a foothold on something, a crevasse of life or logic — himself. At night in his rooms sometimes, Russell could see Wittgenstein's eyes welling up with the doubt and drift of that murky ocean. They told one story, and they also suggested the other, unspoken part of the story: the part about death, the ultimate solipsism.

What the solipsist *says* — that the world is *his* world — this seemed to Russell disagreeable and somewhat boring; above all, it was *lonely*. But still it contained more than a grain of truth about the nature of our lives, of how we view life from the inside, peering out through crabstalk eyes. Wittgenstein talked and talked about this, but that he spoke at all, Russell thought, gave the lie to his contentions. If he spoke at all, it seemed to Russell, then he must believe there are ears to listen. For Russell it was an article of faith: despite what the solipsist says, people's hopes and sensations *must* somehow be connected, however haphazardly, like beads on the slenderest of threads.

Listening to Wittgenstein, Russell was reminded of the old dictum that says to trust the tale and not the teller. Wittgenstein was the proverbial Cretan calling himself a liar in the service of a truth about the unknowable inwardness of our lives — that and the fundamental obscurity of lives not our own. The Cretan warned of how the soul may crimp under the life that cannot break its own shell. And equally the Cretan showed how the life that does burst free may eventually be smothered by its own dark fullness, to the point that it speaks and sees darkly, singing like a mockingbird to populate the night.

In this vein, Wittgenstein began talking one night about the Grimms' fable of Rumpelstiltskin.

So distasteful, chided Russell. Clearly a folktale about the usurious Jew extracting his pound of flesh.

But Wittgenstein did not respond to this. Instead, he said, But such a great truth it shows! Do you remember the story?

Vaguely.

Remember it? To the king the grinder boasts —

You mean the *miller* boasts —

Miller, yes! To the king the miller boasts that his daughter can spin to gold the straw. So the king locks her in a room full with straw and tells her to spin it into gold. If not, she will be killed. Wittgenstein's eyes grew wide. She despairs! She cannot spin gold! Then the little dwarf Rumpelstiltskin comes and says he will spin to gold the straw in return for her first-born child. There is nothing she can do. She agrees and, ziff! — Wittgenstein snapped his fingers — the room is filled with new gold.

And then she marries the king, prompted Russell, recalling the outlines of the tale.

And she has a son, resumed Wittgenstein. And then the little man, he returns one day to take the child. Now! Here we get at the meat of the tale. The queen begs and cries. Very well, says Rumpelstiltskin. You can keep the boy if my name you can tell me. *Grimelthorpe? Grimelwald? Osward?* Name after name she tries. She sends men across the land to find new names. The little man, so happy he is . . . *No name works!*

Looking up impishly, Wittgenstein recited, *Ach, wie gut, dass niemand weiss, dass ich Rumpelstilzchen heiss* — Oh, how good it is, that nobody knows that *I* am called Rumpelstiltskin. And as Wittgenstein said this, Russell felt that the truth was that he, Wittgenstein, was the confounding Rumpelstiltskin! *He* was the riddle, withholding the magic name. And, like the dwarf, Wittgenstein saw, quite in spite of his more shrinking impulses, that he did indeed have Russell in his thrall as he said, Profound Truth! Just like her, we are, Russell. Just like her we work to break this spell upon us! The logic of our language, this is our confounding Rumpelstiltskin — this is what keeps us in its spell. And only the right — the perfect answers will free us.

But there you go! cried Russell, leaning forward in his chair. For you the answer must be *perfect* — why? Can there be no middle or temporary ground while we whittle away at the problem?

But no! cried Wittgenstein. This is the point, there must be *the* key. You do not *half* unlock the lock — the door opens either or it does not. And then, Russell, said Wittgenstein with a grin, then you must hope we have not spent our life struggling to open the wrong door!

———————

Of course, Russell had other things on his mind besides Wittgenstein: holiday worries, money worries and now even deadline worries connected with writing, for money, his first fast and popular book, *The Problems of Philosophy*.

Aware of his continuing difficulties, the Whiteheads insisted that he have Christmas dinner at their house, and Russell readily agreed, accepting with more relief than pride would have permitted him in better times. But then having gotten himself a berth for the holiday, Russell thought guiltily of Wittgenstein, who no doubt would be spending the day alone. Might he angle an invitation for him also? Considering the complaining he had done to Whitehead about Wittgenstein earlier in the term, Russell thought this might be a ticklish undertaking, but he was confident he could manage it. Once he thought about it, though, what really surprised Russell was that he would even be asking Wittgenstein to Christmas dinner.

In fact, the unconventional quality of the relationship — and the speed at which it was changing — rather shocked Russell now that he really thought about it. Russell was a popular don, and he prided himself on being on good terms with his students. His better students flocked to the Tuesday morning "squash-ups," when he was available in his rooms to discuss anything with anyone who cared to come. Yet for all the seeming openness of this concept, these sessions were resoundingly closed by virtue of the gulf between what Russell knew and what they knew. But the real difference was not so much *what* they knew or didn't know but rather *how* they knew it. Indeed, Russell saw that it was not intellect or even imagination they lacked, but that clawing, irrational desire to know. This Russell could not teach, and not through any effort in the world could they acquire it. And not from mere lack of ability, but for a simpler, chicken-crossing-the-road kind of reason: unlike Wittgenstein, they had no real need to make the crossing.

And really, thought Russell, what could he hope to teach Wittgenstein in a classroom, especially when the Austrian had arrived having closely read him, and Frege as well? In class, Wittgenstein had now come full circle. In contrast to his temperamental outbursts in the beginning of term, railing about point after point he could not accept, he now said hardly a word. Not out of arrogance or petulance, he assured Russell, but because it was unfair for the two of them to carry on a dialogue that the other students could only half follow.

This partly explained why Wittgenstein dropped by Russell's rooms at all hours, sometimes as late as midnight. This at least was how Russell explained it to Parkham, the old don next door, when he commented on it. But how was he to explain Wittgenstein's Germanic sense of exclusivity, his tendency to expect, and exact, radically different terms than his other students? In anybody else, Russell would have found such expectations outrageous, but in Wittgenstein they somehow seemed commensurate with his character. Arrogance fit him. To Russell, even Wittgenstein's unreasonableness seemed relatively reasonable, as if he were subject to forces under which life's normal standards did not apply.

Still, Russell could see this was begging the issue. Obviously it was through his own witting or unwitting complicity that they had reached this point. Russell, after all, was the don. He could define the relationship — or could he? Because faster than Russell knew, Wittgenstein was reaching that point of being his equal, or even exceeding him in pursuit of what seemed a single unbounded dream. Russell knew this would only grow more difficult as Wittgenstein's powers came more sharply into focus — or rather, thought Russell fatalistically, as his own powers further diminished. Strangely, though, Russell found himself not caring so much. It was a gentle, natural process, not unlike falling asleep. True, he had a vague sensation of failing, but it wasn't so much a ruined kind of failing. Rather, it was a sense of ripening and unfolding, like a stream of light dissolving into the brighter stream of day.

At times, Russell thought he ought to resist this impulse in himself, but then he would wonder why, since it was inevitable. With feelings of envy mixed with apprehension and gratitude, he would look at Wittgenstein and think, He is like me, only more so. He is like me, but, unlike me, he has no practicality, no ability or willingness to compromise to the terms of life.

Still, there was more affinity here than perhaps Russell was willing to admit. Why, only a week before, after that unhappy afternoon in the hotel with Ottoline, Russell had seen his other woman. She came on him in Liverpool Street Station, on his way back to Cambridge. Russell felt the platform shake, then saw the blinding metallic glare, the Cyclops stare of the light at the head of the throbbing engine. A bell was slowly clanging. Flogging the air, spewing steam and blasting gritty black smoke, she was closing on him like an ecstasy. Russell shut his eyes and let her murderous darkness cover him. Like a giantess exploding with rage and hate, she sucked and enveloped him, crushing his frail bones under her tons of boiling, pummeling destruction. Inching closer to the platform, eyes clenched shut, Russell could feel that tidal pull, an urge terrific in its sweep to do the dark thing. But something stopped him. *Still too weak,* she chided. *Such a puling, pitiful weakling.* And then as the train stopped, with a long, sickening screech, he opened his eyes and found himself still standing so correct in his black Homburg and umbrella — standing there when, but for a few feet, he would not have been boarding his train but spraddled under her, hugging her oily black darkness like the thighs of a big woman.

Gastronomicus Philosophicus

BUT JUST as Wittgenstein was becoming the embodiment of Russell's dreams, others were getting wind of him. It started with Moore, who at supper in Hall near the end of term said:

Well, I understand your German is showing promise.

It was a perfectly innocent remark, and Moore, who as yet had not met Wittgenstein or even thought of making his acquaintance, meant nothing at all by it. Finding the chair beside Russell unoccupied, Moore was simply making a bit of conversation as he settled down to eat. Moore wasn't the first to ask Russell about Wittgenstein, who was already earning a reputation as a spoiler. Having heard Russell's earlier complaints about the German, Moore was merely expressing mild surprise that Russell's estimation of Wittgenstein should have changed so quickly.

In his present state of mind, however, Russell did not take Moore's remark so innocently. Quite the contrary. Russell was immediately suspicious, thinking that Moore was prospecting, looking to bring Wittgenstein over to his side. Concealing his unease with joviality, Russell said, Well, he has improved. We are getting along much better. But he's anything but easy. He's very volatile sometimes.

Russell quickly speared a bite of boiled turnip, chewed, swallowed. There was something staccato in his talk just then, as if with each phrase he were listening for an echo in Moore. Russell took a few more hasty bites, then continued. My word, he gave me a fit at first. A thoroughgoing skeptic. Extremely hardheaded. But he's really very bright, I think, and serious. Pleasant, too, once you get to know him. And incidentally, he's Austrian, not German. Trying to strike that balance between saying too much and saying too little, Russell added, I must say I was surprised to find he's quite cultivated — quite literary. Here Russell stopped himself from saying that Wittgenstein was musical, a fact that would have piqued the curiosity of the musical Moore, who loved nothing more than to sing lieder for friends in a stalwart tenor.

Flanked by portraits of Byron and Newton and seated before a High Gothic wall of ornately carved oak, they were eating at High Table, that long table that sat on a dais overlooking the echoing Hall, where the undergraduates supped beneath their noble eyes. Even before the meal began, the air would be steamy close with the enfolding smells of meats boiled to string and long-suffering vegetables whose culinary misfortunes were disguised in a menu of faultlessly spelled French. All gownsmen would rise as the dons, in procession, entered the beamed Hall. Like a college of cardinals in their black gowns, each clutching his cap under his right arm, they would assemble behind the long, polished table, then stand in prayer as the proctor, Sir Ambrose Preece, nicknamed Demosthenes, mumbled his way through Latin grace. *Pāx* came the last word, followed by a crash as two hundred gownsmen sat down. Then commenced a louder din of knives and forks and hurling voices as platoons of waiters and kitchen trouts in greasy caps and aprons came slogging out with trays laden with hot serving dishes and pitchers slopping with water, milk and ale.

Moore had arrived late for this ritual in a rumpled, lint-specked gown and a mortarboard missing a tassel. Russell was already halfway through his supper, while Moore, famished as usual, was just settling down to his meal, his kneading stomach gurgling like bagpipes. Moore was not much for conversation while eating, though afterward, when he could smoke his pipe over a full belly, he was happy to talk at length with most anyone. Russell knew Moore's quirks but kept talking, partly to find out why Moore had mentioned Wittgenstein, and partly, in a half-conscious way, to devil him by keeping him from his supper.

But Moore had aplomb. *He* was not deterred. Draping a napkin over his paunch and asking those to his right and left to begin, please, the passing, Moore got down to the serious business of eating. For Moore, there could be nothing passive or fainthearted about such eating. It was not enough to tease off the lids of the serving dishes. Moore had to really get his nose down, so that the steam could envelop his face and start the digestive juices pumping. And it was a good meal today. Today and every day the food was good. *Whomp*, one glop of potatoes. *Whomp*, *whomp*, two more. And this while inclining his ear to Russell as if to say, Carry on, while he piled his plate with a bounty of boiled beef and onions, cauliflower still stewing in its own slime-gray juices and an equally indistinct compost of boiled turnips and carrots, topped off with a slab of bread impastoed with butter. Then, trying to quiet Russell with this Wittgenstein business, Moore said, Well, that's *good*. It's gratifying when, after all, they turn out. Changing the subject, he added, And I trust you're well this raw day?

A bit overworked with papers.

Ummm, said Moore with an eloquent shrug as the first heaping forkful found his mouth.

Compared to Moore, Russell was a gastronomical abstinent, hasty and largely indifferent to the mystical properties of food. Oh, Russell could be enticed by an especially good or elegant meal, especially if the fare was French or Italian, but he had not that love of quotidian, bland or even marginal food that is the mark of the truly stouthearted eater. Moore had, first off, serious *form*: the elbows squarely planted on the table, the gut pressed against the board, the plates well organized for maximum displacement of *food mass*. But Moore was no mere glutton; he was a gastronomical poet. There was a distinct tenderness in the way he would slide his knife under a cutlet or a slab of fish on a platter, gently lifting it with a wriggle so it came away intact, with full breading or skin. Moreover, Moore displayed impressive utensil technique, swiping the tines of his fork with his knife, *whisk-whisk*, like a chef sharpening a knife. There was the way he embedded peas in potatoes, not to mention the dexterity with which he herded together a burst egg yolk or an unruly pool of gravy, sopping up the leavings with a heel of bread, then sucking his fingers in that final *frisson* of finishing.

Moore was part of a long and lofty tradition there at High Table, that oak trencher dark with the grease and drippings of forebears who for some three hundred years had chopped and slopped, sawed and spooned, or sat in solitary mastication while plumbing the meaning of Milton's inversions or the upper strata of Aquinas's *Summa contra Gentiles*. Several of the sundry schools of eating were in evidence there that night. Sitting on Moore's right, for instance, was his fellow Apostle and former teacher, the philosopher and idealist John McTaggart. McTaggart, as a boy, had rebelled against God, denying his authority while yet fearing his space, which squashed him like a bug viewed through the wrong end of the ontological telescope. Because he was agoraphobic, McTaggart had spent his life stooping and as a result was bent and twisted, with a crab-like walk that caused him to rub and rebound along walls, leaving his gowns and suit jackets scuffed and shiny and daubed with chalk.

Using the dialectic of Hegel, the rebellious anthropocentric McTaggart had sought to prove that there was a heaven of Platonic souls so bound by love that God was *superfluous* — nothing more for the frail metaphysician to uphold, nevermore to be stooped like Atlas, struggling to support a hellish pack of air. But God had not broken the back of McTaggart's dialectic; Moore and Russell had. Having learned his dialectical method, Moore, aided by Russell, had unhorsed poor McTaggart more than a decade ago, relegating his method and his idealism to a nook in the whatnot of philosophical curios. But McTaggart bore no grudge, and he ate like a true dialectician. Taking a portion, he would halve it, then halve it again, eating the quarter of the first part, then a quarter of the second, which he then halved again before moving on to another portion, halving and halving to the point that he never finished anything.

Among other eaters in evidence, there was also the old historian McDougal, a leveling reductionist long due for pasture, who mixed the all with the all — carrots, meat and cauliflower — making of it an unholy mush of meaning. Then, far down from him, there was Cecil Goodhart, stoic, classicist and xenophobe, for whom all had to be separate, like air, earth and fire, with each food group, and even its juices, free of the contagion of the other.

Besides these men, there were of course more orthodox palates. And among these, too, were a few inspired eaters, men with stomachs like bosoms, who didn't dabble or *despair* of life — men who kept eating when others had choked or fagged out, saying with a baleful glance, Does anyone wish anything more? And looking as if they'd stab the hand of anybody who did.

But Moore, Moore went these eaters one better. It was not enough to merely empty dishes. Moore must have *Moore*, went the joke, Russell's line. Having polished off two plates, Moore would snag a trout or waiter or would go back himself into the steamy, dark recesses of the kitchen, past the scullions toiling over the stacked havoc of the meal. Moore had good rapport with the head cook, to whom he would always pay his considered compliments. Smoking over the bubbling pots, as filthy and sweaty as he was savvy, the swarthy, ale-quaffing cook was pleased to have good Mr. Moore, the Reverend, as he called him, appreciatively lift the lids of the simmering pots and generally preview the next meal. Happily, Moore would examine the cuts in their bloody brown paper and smell the melon bungs in season. Brushing away the shaved ice, he would prod the stacked cod, reeking and slimy, checking for the color of the scales and the clearness of the eyes. Moore knew the correct saffron hue of a good fresh pullet, and he likewise loved to appraise the leanness and savoriness of the bacons, bringing his nose down so close that he could see the little black stubs of unshaved bristle visible under the brownish skin. As a treat, the cook would sometimes take out his big black knife and cut Moore a cheese end, a choice, smelly rind tough as a toenail paring, which Moore would stuff in his pocket with a look of pure gratitude. With stacked plate, Moore would emerge from the hot kitchen as from a cathedral, knowing, as do the wise, that sweet as the present meal is, there is none sweeter than the next.

Despite his prodigious appetite, though, Moore was not really fat — or not except for his kangaroo's stomach, which bowed out under a mis-buttoned vest lashed together with a heavy gold watch chain. Moore's suit was always loose and rumpled, and his dark blue tie — one of the maybe three he owned — was greasy at the knot and bunched about his curling, fraying collar. At thirty-nine, he was an odd mix of a man, with a slack, middle-aged body and a boyish face, which still carried with it surprising sweetness and innocence. His cheeks were ruddy, and his smooth, cowlicky brown hair curled down like a comma over a high, strong forehead, which seemed not to have formed a single line of worry.

He was extraordinarily unselfconscious, with none of that haughty reserve and guardedness that envelops many a man as he gets older. Around Russell, though, Moore had learned from hard experience to be cautious. So as he finished his dinner that night, Moore was frankly wondering why Russell, normally off like a shot once he had finished, was lingering over his second cup of tea. Moore was not wrong to wonder. Sure enough, Russell turned to him and asked the question that had been nagging him for the past thirty minutes.

By the way, Moore, who told you about Wittgenstein?

Moore wiped the grease from his lips. Lytton did. Several days ago I guess it was.

No need for Russell to wonder where Lytton Strachey had heard it. Already, Russell was composing the wounded letter he would dash off to Ottoline.

As for Moore, he sensed Russell's irritation and resolved to face it squarely, asking, Is something the matter?

Giving Moore an up-down look, Russell said with a trace of irony, No, merely curious.

Oh. Moore nodded as if this were sufficient, but of course it wasn't. And so they sat there, both inwardly glowering. No, it didn't take much these days, not with these two.

Two Hills

MOORE AND RUSSELL frequently found themselves at this point, not openly warring but just vaguely dissatisfied, each sensing in the other some hard-to-define intransigence.

Both would have shrunk from calling it a rivalry. The last thing either of them would have wanted was for anyone to feel that between them was envy or jealousy, not only because these were unseemly emotions but because it would have been tantamount to admitting that there was *reason* for jealousy.

But of course it was not so simple. If asked, neither Moore nor Russell would have hesitated to say — and say truthfully — that the other was the greatest single influence on his work. Nor could either lose sight of the fact that they were very much tied to each other professionally. Besides reading, commenting on and supporting each other's work, they exchanged ideas and watched each other's flanks, each standing ready, when the need arose, to defend the other with a well-placed letter or review, or perhaps a few politic words in the right ear.

It was a convenient if unspoken pact, and Moore, for his part, would have been most content to leave it be had Russell not always been jockeying for position. A modest man, Moore could not understand Russell's need to vie with him. Moore had never understood Russell's contentiousness, but he especially didn't understand it now. Here while his fame was on the wane, if not long past, Russell's fame, at least within philosophical and scientific circles, was steadily growing. After all, his own *Principia Ethica* was now nine years old; Russell's *Principia Mathematica* was the new work now. Besides, Moore would have been the first to point out that of the two books (and ignoring their obvious differences in subject matter) Russell's was indisputably the more ambitious and important.

True, with those of Keynes and Strachey's generation, Moore's influence remained, but his ideas were hardly in vogue. Yet Moore did not especially seem to regret the fact. This in itself irked Russell: to Russell, Moore's seeming lack of concern with fame and plaudits had always seemed unreal, if not faintly disingenuous. But perhaps what really rankled Russell was that Moore had been famous first, and famous young, when barely thirty. Harder still for Russell to take was Moore's guise of never seeming to notice that, in a single sweep in 1903, the young men had flocked to the moralist, seeking his counsel perhaps for the very reason that he did not hunger for fame or disciples in the famished way that Russell did.

What Russell also had trouble swallowing at the time was the irony of being the one who had first encouraged Moore to study philosophy. Russell had been among the first to recognize and promote Moore's special gifts, and it was a great service he had done, too, since Moore would have been the last to suppose he had a special talent for anything, least of all philosophy. Moore had always been a slow starter, yet in a queer way his pokiness — his tendency to maunder and stare at ideas that others had glibly accepted and sped by — was a fundamental part of his genius for philosophy, which he took up only after his usual period of doubt and deliberation. Having come to Cambridge to read classics, Moore continued for some time in that vein, expecting nothing more than to one day join that bedraggled corps of rumpled, pipe-smoking bachelors who teach at the public schools — monastic men who spent August on the moors and perhaps a solitary Christmas in Switzerland, while despairing of ever having money enough to marry.

No, in his first years at Cambridge, Moore didn't have the foggiest idea who he was. Besides being a cox for a rowing team, he knew he liked to read, and he liked to talk with the other fellows and sing in the Trinity choir. Tobacco he had discovered. Also the pleasures of alcohol, with which one might get talkative and silly, spending a rousing evening round the piano with the fellows, singing *Ta-ra-ra BOOM-de-ay* and the raffish street tune *Wot Cher*. Later, as a coda to this rambunctiousness, Moore would do several solos for the lads, holding them all transfixed with each bugling note of *Foggy, Foggy Dew* and *Missy Mine*, singing so achingly about these misty lasses that one never would have guessed he didn't have the faintest idea about women — not a clue. Not that Moore disliked girls; he just didn't *know* any. For him women didn't even seem to exist. But even more unbelievable to the other lads was the fact that Moore didn't seem to suffer the slightest urge or pang.

Russell did not fail to respond to Moore's unearthly innocence during their early undergraduate days together. After all, as a man engaged to an older woman, Russell could not help but feel somewhat superior in experience to this brilliant but naive boy two years his junior in academic standing. Russell knew there was something otherworldly and strangely beautiful about Moore's innocence; he really did feel that Moore was the blood incarnation of some Platonic type. Still, it seemed to Russell that if his protégé was ever to progress as a thinker, this Eden musn't persist. Besides, it irked Russell to behold a soul so pure and unpurloined by bodily urges. For a man of ordinary drives like Russell, it was a sour provocation, like an unspoiled hill of snow before a boy's new boots.

Russell's opportunity came one summer when he and Moore, virgins both, were on a walking tour of the Lake District. There they were, two hardy but both untried pilgrims, carrying their Wordsworth and talking the wafting truths of idealism as they walked over fields as glistening green as lily pads in the sun. Walking, Moore would talk and talk, his flushed young face rising like a balloon toward the evolving light. But it wore on Russell that one could be so free and untroubled, and finally one night at an inn, Russell saw a mirthful pair of eyes peering over a mug of porter and knew he'd found the man who could bring an abrupt end to Moore's innocence. He was an older man of about forty-five, a former classicist, with bulgy eyes and a long, soft, raveling beard that he fingered like a waist. An underwriter for Lloyd's, the man had traveled widely in India and the Far East. With a game grin, he said he had had some interesting experiences there. For the first two hours, Moore found him a charming companion, surprised and a little bewildered by the way the man laughed, throwing his head back so that his voice boomed off the ceiling. A born raconteur, the man loved the trick and taste of words, reveling in their spill and off-rhymes, their lingering odor. Waving his French cigarettes, drawing the words from his rather coarse lips, he twatted them forth like outrageously large bubbles, gaily laughing as they blew high into the air, then settled with unseemly little pops on the noses of his mesmerized listeners. He also liked his wine and, to Russell at least, it was clear he had an ogle eye for the ladies, what with the way he fingered his beard and wound his almost prehensile mustache whenever a full bum bustled by. Content to talk about Homer and Ovid, Moore had no idea about the man, who had already co-opted Russell with sly little winks, implying that the two of them, as much wiser sorts, could draw out the youngster.

Later, in Moore's room, the innocent hardly noticed as the talk slowly began to change, turning to the bisexual Catullus, then to Petronius's *Satyricon* and Apuleius's *Golden Ass*, classics that Moore, flushing, said he had never read. Oh, but you should, said the man, giving him an insinuating pat on his knee. And with that, he launched off on an ode about the surpassing beauty and feline cleanliness of the Oriental woman. Moore did not quite get the point, or not consciously. With evident feeling, he began talking about the corporeal lines of *horses*.

But sir, laughed the roué, so that his wooden chair gave a sharp crack. You must mean the *mares*! With that, he returned, allusively, to the most beautiful of all God's burthened beasts, the ingenious ladies of the Orient. But hardly had he warmed to his theme than Russell surprised Moore even more by volunteering how long and hard he had looked on the ladies of Paris, particularly the trollops, who were so incredibly bold, mooning up out of the night of his venereal fears, saying, *Tu viens?* . . . *Viens avec moi?* . . .

Moore was frozen in his seat; at first he didn't quite seem to know what was happening. Emboldened by Russell, the roué gave Moore a goose on the knee as he hissed:

But the whores of Paris must be paid more, you know, if you've a taste for *novelty*. I'm speaking here of their — and he looked at Moore the Latinist — their *cloacal* opening. *Sewer?* asked Moore, just to be sure he had heard the man correctly. *Sewer!* roared the man, throwing back his head in disbelief at one so live and green. Growing more animated, he leaned forward, almost lisping in his urgency as a little piece of dry white spittle jumped from lip to lip. You know, lad, the sweetest meat is the netherest. Oh, it's cat clean when you slide it in, so slick and sweet . . .

Moore's cheeks were inflamed. He could not move as the roué, with his big face, bent closer, in a voice crackling like a freshly wrapped candy. Well you know, laddie, how in Hong Kong the girls take it? Well, as you pump and pump away, they busy themselves shoving a knotted string up your arse, then, when you're ready to blow? *RRRrrrippp* — The antic roué tore his hand away. Why, they give it a Jack the Ripper! *God!*

Moore looked as if he'd been stabbed. He gaped at the man, then at Russell, a film forming in his eyes. Russell remembered it struck him as funny, seeing his friend so pigstuck. Russell and the roué did not have long to smile. Jumping up, Moore bellowed:

You're both depraved! Get *out*! Both of you!

What do you mean, boy? demanded the man, angrily. Sit down.

I'll not sit down! *Out*, do you hear me! shouted Moore, hauling him up by the sleeve. You're not a man, you're a filthy beast! You don't deserve to live, to breed such rottenness! Nor you, Russell! Both of you! *Out!*

Russell thought Moore was going to strike the man or start throwing things, he was so enraged. With oaths, the man left, but to Russell's disbelief, Moore would not hear him out then, nor even the next morning, when Moore announced that he was continuing on alone.

Why are you being this way? protested Russell. I've never in my life done or even dreamed such things as he described. I was only using him to draw you out as a lesson. You're much too naive.

Moore smacked his fists together. What right have you to presume what *I* need? Malice and depravity! Ignorance! That's all I saw last night. And it's a side of you I loathe, Russell, thinking yourself so superior! What has *filth* to teach? A sloppy raw egg! That's your morality. Man of the world! A *boy* was all I saw, a puling milkfed boy hiding behind a false sheen of rationality. I'm off. I'm off, and not another word from you!

In time, they managed more or less to put this behind them, but it was never the same — never as free or resilient, never with the same innocent trust. Actually, they came fairly early to a grim understanding, of sorts. One day before a group of their friends, Russell succeeded in demonstrating their moral objectivity — and in testing Moore's already mythic honesty — when he pointedly asked:

Moore, do you like me?

Anyone else would have felt sorely put on the spot by this challenge. Moore felt no such awkwardness, however, and he treated it like any other question. Moore answered neither quickly nor painfully, but he did answer succinctly and with his usual candor when he replied:

No.

In a twisted way, Russell was pleased with his answer, which confirmed his anxieties and certainly proved his premise about Moore's sometimes eerie honesty. The others present were highly uncomfortable, but Russell and Moore both took perverse pride in their ability to continue the discussion in seeming amicability. Still, this was a question that only unformed boys could have put to each other, before they were grown men with well-entrenched vanities and reputations to protect. This would be another injury, especially for Moore, who suffered to dispense honesty at another's whim. Yes, this, too, would go down in his debit book on Russell.

For his part, Russell had been able to see Moore with much greater clarity in those early years, in the 1890s, before contention and pride clouded his vision. Russell could readily see that Moore, with his clear, boyish freshness of face, was far handsomer than he. And despite his conflicting feelings, Russell promoted Moore. Championed by Russell and duly approved by McTaggart, Moore was easily elected to the Apostles. And then on the night of his initiation, when it was customary for the newcomer to give a speech, Moore stunned them not merely with his brilliance but with his uncanny ability to project the power and beauty of his character.

They had been talking about the Cambridge life, whether the skepticism and cynicism they learned there wouldn't later render them unfit for the normal round of offices and courtrooms, newspapers and government posts. Moore had done no preparation. It all just poured out of him as he took the stage, saying excitedly, On the contrary, gentlemen! Skepticism is what renders us most fit for life! Skepticism ought to be our religion! A permanent condition!

They had all had some wine, and they thought at first he was drunk, to be so excited. No one, not even Moore, knew what came over him that night. He hadn't felt this way since, as a boy of eleven, he had joined the Children's Special Service Mission, the evangelical crusade then sweeping England. In those days, nothing could have been more beautiful to the boy than saving a soul. Even at Brighton for a seaside holiday — while other boys in boaters and sailor suits went for donkey rides or ate ices — there he would be, dressed in his hot, ill-fitting black suit and lugging his heavy black Bible. In his zeal to save souls, he was unstoppable, gladly suffering the pulled ties and bloody noses. Let them jeer him as a hake and a bum sucker, they could not break him. So mighty was the boy preacher's passion that he even succeeded in converting older, cynical boys, reducing some to tears when he confronted them, demanding like God's own Highwayman that they renounce sloth and tobacco and forthwith surrender their lives to Christ.

That patently religious faith was now gone, but as he stood before the Apostles that night, the young agnostic could still feel that preacher's power. In his exultation, Moore looked as if he would catch the air in his arms. It wasn't a speech so much as a series of titanic outbursts.

Yes! avowed Moore. Skepticism was the soul of truth — why, it was the most beautiful quality in the world! Truth could not be *told* simply. Truth could not exist in the mind unless it was examined personally and hard won — unless every statement was defended against its antithesis, like a gladiatorial contest! And not just every statement, he declared, but *every single man* — here Moore's eyes got big — *every man must defend himself against HIMSELF!* He must defend himself against his own proclivity for dishonesty! And if he does *not*, he swore with a gasp, if he does *not* defend himself against humbug, then he ought to be laughed at! Just, said Moore, taking another lunging breath, just as you are laughing at *me*! And as, indeed, I am laughing at myself! Oh, I know it, he laughed, wagging a knowing finger. I *know* I am a silly. *I am an unholy ass! I* know this, but *you,* my fellow asses, this you must also know of yourselves!

They were all laughing, not at him but rather at the truth of this, swept up in all the Dionysian joy and exultation of truth that Moore seemed to embody like a young god. It wasn't even so much what he was saying as the life and joy they felt swelling within him, fit to explode. Moore was laughing uncontrollably. He was so full and boiling with life that life was snapping off him. Like electricity, it was ripping across the room, this divine discharge.

Moore was so infused with laughter, in fact, that they feared he would suffer an apoplectic fit. First his eyes got big. Then, like a cuckoo, his tongue shot out. And then he suddenly covered his mouth and, in his fullness, turned and pressed his blazing forehead against the cool marble of the mantelpiece behind him.

It was a beautiful, unpremeditated gesture, a gesture of submission and respect, like a priest kissing the altar stone — a gesture beautiful even for the fact that Moore's fanny was in the air as he bent down, panting for breath. The laughter abruptly stopped and anxious looks flew round the room. Was he all right? McTaggart, shuffling along the wall, was starting to go to Moore when the novice abruptly turned, smiling with such ripe, rubicund fullness that it was clear to all in the room that there was nothing more to say; and then, without another word, he shyly sat down.

That night Russell wrote Alys, saying that if Moore did not die or go mad he would be a great genius — perhaps the greatest genius the world had ever known. Not only did Russell believe this, but he believed it without reservation, never thinking what it implied about himself, much less where he might be ranked relative to Moore one day. They were still that young. Two unblemished hills, and not yet a thought about which was the higher.

The Suitor

BUT IF IT SEEMED to Russell and others that Moore's genius emanated from an innocence that provided him a moral fulcrum from which to ply his analytical brilliance; if indeed Moore's innocence was what was best and most original in him, it did not always seem so to Moore himself, who feared he might after all be only a silly. He put no garnishings on it. He was not, as Lytton avowed, a divine silly — no latter-day Socrates — but just your ordinary, naive, vacillating ninny. And not just a ninny, either. As things looked now, he was a plain fool who was about to embarrass himself by proposing to a young woman nearly twenty years his junior.

Leaving Hall from dinner that night, Moore was still smarting over Russell's maneuverings and general overbearingness. Moore wasn't bothered about Wittgenstein; it was Russell's whole manner — his overweening confidence — that needled him. Worse, Russell's attitude only showed Moore his own native wooliness, his endless shilly-shallying. And in a way, Moore envied Russell. *Russell* wasn't burdened with this useless Hamletizing. *He* never shrank from going after what he wanted, nor from using whatever casuistry was necessary to justify his actions. But even this, Moore saw, was just another evasion. For him it was not, after all, a matter of *justifying* his actions but of for once going after what he wanted, namely, Miss Dorothy Ely.

The problem was, Moore wasn't entirely sure, or couldn't entirely justify to himself, that he *knew* what he wanted. It was abominably complicated. As he had shown in his *Principia*, it was not a matter of shalts and shalt nots. There were no logical *proofs* by which one could arrive at the Good. A moral law, Moore had found, had the guise not of a law but of a *prediction* of what will generally produce the greatest *sum* of good. That was all. Moore admitted that it was at first a little dispiriting to realize that ethics was really a matter of brokering, in a given instance, something better than worse, and likely rather worse than good. Not, it's true, that one did not always keep the Good shining over one's shoulder like the sun. But still, thought Moore, dogging his way home now from High Table — why did it fall on *him* to be the broker in this case? Why was it that the *man* was saddled with all the moral burden of proposing? Think of the ramifications! Did he, George Moore, wish to take Miss Dorothy Ely freely and simply and lovingly, or was he merely trying to satisfy himself that some woman would have him? That is, did he want Dorothy *as a love*, purely and simply, or did he rather want her as an *end*, a *product* of his affections made flesh, so to speak, by virtue of some flimsy *word*? And besides, wasn't he merely indulging a vanity, seeking to satisfy some agreeable image or ideal of himself as a husband ensconced in a domicile with wife, children, chattels? *Children!*

Down the lane now, under the yellow streetlamps, men far younger than Moore — vigorous young men Miss Ely's age — were walking along briskly in the cold air. Moore looked at them striding hungrily into their own steaming breath, eating and inhaling life like fire, not forever analyzing it like a gas. Yet straightaway Moore reverted to the philosopher, asking himself again what it properly *meant*, to love? In his *Principia*, he had written of the Ideal as consisting of certain timeless mental states in which one contemplated truth, beauty, good works, love: sister states of the all-encompassing Good. But man and woman love — this he had skirted almost entirely, and no wonder. What had he known then, in 1903, of love, much less of loving a real flesh and blood woman? Why, even now I hardly know a thing! he thought, inwardly giving himself another good kick. You were describing Platonic doves and halos, you oaf, not people of flesh! Why, even that poor thwarted monk Abelard knew more — vastly more! At least Abelard *knew* he loved!

All the way back to his rooms Moore kicked himself. And once there he dawdled. Looking at himself in the mirror, he thought his suit looked rumpled and shabby, old. He had a good dark suit for special occasions, but this was so predictable — Miss Ely would see him coming a mile off, all ready with her rejection. Christ, where was Smyth, his gyp? Gone for the night and his shoes unshined, and no clean white shirt, either. And even after Moore wiped his shoes with a rag, and wet and combed his hair — even after he reluctantly put on his best suit and brushed his teeth, he still felt a fool, and at that a rather dastardly one for wanting to palm himself off on a former student foolish enough to have trusted him.

Moore had met Miss Ely the year before, when she took his course in moral logic. Miss Ely did well in the course — better than many of his men in fact — but he did not remember thinking much about her until several months later, when he saw her coming out of a seamstress shop on Bridge Street. She looked different outside the classroom, in the daylight. Had she cut her hair? They stopped and spoke, but of course it was the rather dismally formal don-to-undergraduate sort of chat. Moore felt himself straining to seem natural, to appear aboveboard and donlike, rather than a hungry man sniffing. Nevertheless, he noticed her handsome self-sufficiency and her dark straight hair, which she tied up around her close and slender ears with a thin strand of black ribbon. Miss Ely had large, dark eyes, deeply set, and Moore was amazed, from the relative vantage of age, how youthfully clear her features were, as if she were part of the foreground while he was modestly receding. He remembered thinking that she had the most lovely hairless white hands, plump at the palm and slender at the fingers, with fine white slivers of nails. She struck him, correctly as it turned out, as a father's girl, independent and quiet, shy. Why hadn't he asked her out then? He had a sense of her routine. Awkward, stalking, stammering a hasty greeting as he flew by her, Moore kicked himself for the next two weeks for his shyness. Finally, though, after two days of internal arguments and counterarguments, he almost pushed himself in her path, suggesting, sucking his tongue, that they *might* go walking — *if* she didn't mind, of course. Oh! Any day, really, would be fine . . .

Tomorrow? she asked.

Well, he thought afterward, she must be at least *somewhat* interested to suggest the next day, out for a walk in the Backs. But then Moore's mind sued for the counterargument, that she was just curious or simply felt sorry for him, an aging bachelor down on his luck.

He was terribly nervous that day as they crossed King's Bridge, pausing to gaze at the dark hummocks the arches cast over the river, beneath their own shining reflections. It was a fine June afternoon, not long after a shower, and the willows, pale and flossy with rainlight, were stretched down, dripping faint circles into the tea-dark water. Miss Ely tended to be quiet when she was nervous, but Moore, he was a talker. Couldn't shut up. He sounded as if this were a refresher course in philosophy rather than your basic courting business. And when Moore found out that she was but twenty, his mouth popped open.

Oh! Moore stuffed his guilty hands in his pockets. I didn't know.

Didn't know what? asked Miss Ely.

That you were so young. Moore was in the soup then. Quickly backtracking, he hedged. Or rather, not because you are so young — I do not want to say that — but rather, well, because —

But here he stopped again, not wanting to scotch his chances by suggesting he was too old for her. And despite her years, Miss Ely in this instance was far more knowing and worldly than he. Frankly, she said, I am surprised you would even concern yourself with age, Mr. Moore. If, as you suggest in your *Principia*, affection is basically a mental state, then what does it matter the relative ages of the two minds concerned?

Oh! Well, that is *true*, said Moore, stuffing his hands more deeply in his pockets.

But still he lollygagged. He took her home that day, and almost accidentally mumbled something about their doing it again — em, going for a walk or something. Fortunately for them both, Miss Ely recognized his extremity and suggested — rather boldly, it seemed to him — that they go to the fair the next week.

But their second outing was even harder for him. Walking with her through the reeking straw, looking at the prize cattle and horses, Moore wondered what he ought to do. He liked her awfully much, but he was such a duffer. Why, he couldn't even win a penny dish, while she won three. They ate ices, and then they came to a black tent painted with yellow zodiacal signs, where Miss Ely had her palm read. She was smiling when she emerged. What did she say? he asked, suddenly anxious, as if these divinations might concern him. Just never you mind, she said, rather saucily. It wouldn't come true if I told you, now would it, Mr. Moore?

He didn't know why that chastened him. He was in the most awful muddle. And didn't she have the most comely buttocks, switching under her long skirt as he caught up to her after losing his hat. Should he kiss her? Would that be too forward — or was it not forward enough? God, he didn't know. He didn't know what the older set did, let alone this younger set. The impossible truth was, he'd never kissed a girl before — not in earnest, anyhow.

Bubbles in his stomach. The moment of truth at her door. Grasped her hand was all, only her hand! You *ass*! Stupid, silly ass! Storming down the lane, kicking himself.

Moore next saw Miss Ely a week after the fair, this time for a picnic on the Cam. This was the day of truth, he told himself, and he manfully took charge of the situation, babbling on about his days as a cox as he scooped muddy rainwater from the bottom of the punt.

There now, he coached as he helped her in. Step to the center. Easy now . . .

Miss Ely was as competent as he in handling a boat, but she was wise enough to let him play cox that day. And he caught the most awful guilty eyeful when she boarded — a flash of black stocking and petticoat as she was scissoring her sturdy legs around, getting herself situated. Miss Ely must have been rather nervous herself, because as he pushed off, he noticed little spots of sweat, like raindrops, bleeding through the back of her white blouse. Having manfully rolled up his sleeves, he was poling from the back, his straw skimmer cocked like a cymbal, and curls of his still golden hair darkly dripping sweat over his brow. I feel like a gondolier, he said, and for effect began faintly singing *Ave Maria*. Such a beautiful voice, Miss Ely said. You'll have to sing for me sometime. I play the piano.

He felt so happy then, so hopeful. Like a lily, the sun lay on the water, and as Miss Ely peered down into the greeny-brown depths, he saw the reflections dancing on her throat, then on her face as she turned, shading her eyes, and smiled at him. And a nice swell of bosom, too — umm, rather fuller than he thought, actually. Why did he think even then that he loved her? He hardly knew her. And what was he to do now? First he was out of songs. Then out of jokes, desperately looking for a place to put in and do it finally — kiss her. Yes, and then what? *And what if she refused?*

Stowing the pole, he sat and began paddling, his heart pounding as he ominously thought, *At this next willow . . .*

With one good swirling stroke, he aimed the punt for the branches. He felt the leaves brush his face as he stealthily removed his skimmer. In the air, globes of midges fluttered. In the water, he saw water striders swarming. It's like a tent! she cried, and then she was all sun dappled, the light falling like tiddlywinks through her hair as, crouching, he lumbered forward, ostensibly to secure the rocking boat. *Go on*, prodded some animus within him, and he felt an electric shock as she turned toward him, eyeing him so openly. What was she *doing*, he wondered, to stare at him so frankly and innocently? *Go on*, urged the voice, and he rested his sweaty palm atop hers on the gunwale, then squeezed it. She did not draw away, and the boat rocked then as he kissed her — awkwardly at first, then more passionately, until at last he was on his knees to get better purchase, squeezing her tighter with each sally. Then she was all over with light, and afterward, as he sat back on the rocking seat, he saw he had wet the knees of his trousers. Look at me, he said, leaning forward for a second helping, then another, until she said, Mr. Moore, I think we ought to go ashore now. I'm afraid you'll capsize us.

It was only later in their courtship that Miss Ely told Moore that she had taken Russell's course concurrently with his. Moore tried to seem pleased that she would avail herself to the ideas of a respected colleague, but Miss Ely saw through him. And she rather liked his jealousy, saying, I know it was awful of me. First I would ask Mr. Russell a question in his class and record his answer, and then I would ask you the same question and write your answer beside it.

What? asked Moore, his face like a teakettle. You did *what?*

I meant no harm by it, said Miss Ely, turning a shade provocative. Mr. Russell's answers were more succinct. But I felt yours were more thorough and — I don't know — more true.

Well! he blustered. Certainly I wasn't asking you to *judge.*

But Mr. Moore, she soothed. I didn't know you then. And you came off exceedingly well in the comparison.

But I wasn't *asking* to be compared! he thundered. Comparisons advance nothing. Russell and I understand and respect one another. That's what's important.

Never in his life had Moore been so jealous — until Miss Ely, there had been no reason. Yet here he was, as in a shilling romance, with fantasies of Russell trying to steal Miss Ely away and him, the Wronged Suitor, shouting, *Scoundrel! Have you concealed from the lady in question the fact that you are married!*

Moore even harbored fears that Russell might steal Miss Ely away just to spite him. In his anxiety, Moore turned fatalistic. If he was going to lose her to Russell, he thought, it might as well happen sooner rather than later. With this weighing on him, he even pointedly told Russell about Miss Ely. But far from being jealous, Russell, just then feeling the first flush of love for Ottoline, seemed delighted for him.

It did no good. Still Moore suffered. Even near forty, the author of *Principia Ethica* couldn't bypass that feeling of first love. Guarded, self-absorbed and easily embarrassed, Moore was as sensitive as a youth, and as moony.

All that summer Moore saw her. Eight months he'd now spent with her, walking and reading and singing lieder to her, sweat pouring down his face as she accompanied him on the piano. Moore supposed she liked him all right, yet he found it almost impossible to imagine that she would ever have him as a husband. This was not entirely Moore's fault, however. Dorothy said she never expected to marry — she never wanted to depend on anybody. Still, she knew, as Moore did, that her education would soon be completed, at which point she planned to get a job. She said she liked the idea of earning her own living.

Moore didn't know what to believe. Still less did Moore know what he wanted, let alone how to ask for her hand. For three months he had been thinking of asking, but still he slunk along, asking himself if he really loved her, and if he was good enough for her — more delaying tactics. Two months before, all set to ask, he had stalled. A week before, desperate, he had set out once more for her boarding house — stalled again. Yet now, at probably the worst time and at virtually the last possible minute, Moore had gone farther than he ever thought possible. Not only was he standing on the stoop of her boarding house, he was actually knocking on the door. Had he not been so terrified, he would have known from the landlady's smile that she knew his purpose. Upstairs packing, Dorothy scoffed when Mrs. Boylan ran in saying that Mr. Moore had come to propose.

He's merely come to say good-bye, said Dorothy nervously. I told him I don't want to marry.

In ordinary circumstances, Moore might have spent two hours coming to the point. But when Dorothy entered the parlor, he stood, then went white, saying, I've come late, I know. But — I want you to marry me. Drawing himself up, he said, I've examined my feelings — I've examined them, I *think*, from every possible angle, and I can *assure* you of — that I do love you . . .

She looked frightened, suddenly standing there so naked. Before he could say another word, he felt her go quite automatic, as she said miserably, But I told you . . . I want to make my own way. Then, in response to his stricken look, she interjected, Not because I don't care for you. I *do* care for you, it's just —

He sat down abruptly. The chair was so low, and his knees so high — he looked like a boy. Nervously scrubbing his hands, he said loudly, Well, what are you saying?

Well, nothing about *you*, Mr. Moore.

He didn't know why her use of "Mr." suddenly annoyed him then. Please, he said sharply. Don't you think we could at least dispense with this Mister and Miss business, seeing how I've asked you to be my wife?

We might, I suppose . . . She bit her lip. Only I don't like the name George.

Gaping at her, he said, But that *is* my Christian name, you know.

I realize that, she said, looking around the corner to make sure they were entirely alone. But I don't like it. I never fancied I'd know a George.

Harrumphed Moore with rising irritation, George or no, I *have* asked you to marry me! And my name *is* George.

Please do lower your voice, she said with a panicky look. I just don't fancy George. You don't even *look* like a George.

Well, he labored, call me *G.E.*, then. Call me *Moore*, I don't care —
The question is, *Will you have me or not?*

Her eyes went blank; it was as if she had dropped something on the
floor — his name, her career — anything to avoid the real issue as she
protested, I just didn't expect this. Especially when I was leaving. I suppose I thought I would always be off by myself. Making my own way,
you know.

I've been at it twenty years longer than you, said Moore glumly. I don't
advise it. And why won't you have me? I mean, do you love me? There's
a start.

She nodded.

Well? he boomed.

Will you *kindly* lower your voice. Yes, she hissed. Yes, I love you, and
then her eyes bit together and she squeaked out that difficult *darling.*

Well, he said, that's a damned sight better than George!

Bill, she resumed distractedly. She had hit on it. We could call you
Bill —

Bill?

Right. What about Bill? I rather like Bill.

He looked at her. Then you'll have me?

Yes — And she sort of hiccupped, her voice breathy now that it was
dawning on her. Yes, of course I'll have you.

Well, then it's Bill, he said, thinking that it was so absurdly appropriate, a new name for his new life in the way Saul became Paul, and
George, Bill.

Vacations

IN THE FACE of his father's silence, punctuated by squibs from Gretl,
Wittgenstein was rather pleased with the resolve, obstinance, spite or
whatever it was making him stick by his decision to remain in England
over the vacations. But in the first week of December, just when he
thought his break was a fait accompli, he received an appeal from an
unexpected and influential quarter: his mother.

As if to underscore her own distress over the matter, Frau Wittgenstein
so far had not mentioned his intentions in her letters. But then at the end
of a typically newsy letter, she put her foot down, saying:

... I have tried to leave you alone, but I am sorry, I am losing my patience with you and your father. Why is it that you cannot come home this month? I told your father that I want peace in my family, and furthermore secured his promise that he will say nothing to you while you are here about your as yet unresolved course of a career. Now, please, will you come home for the Yuletide?

His mother, who typically abstained from feuds such as this one over his choice of career, had an almost diplomatic gift for couching displeasure in a few subdued words. But because she so seldom raised her voice or offered her opinion, her rare pronouncements carried considerable weight. Describing his career as "unresolved" was an instance of her knack for strategic understatement, and it was more wounding than she probably realized or intended. Wittgenstein's attachment to her was filial and deep, but it was anything but simple, one practical problem being that he rarely could think of much to say to her. It was not from any apparent malice that he had so little to say, it was just her helplessness, the way she existed in that house like the Virgin Mary, loving, sentient, suffering, even interceding when necessary, but mainly looking down ever more helplessly from her pedestal while fate took its course.

In one sense, Wittgenstein grimly understood the impotence of his mother's position, yet in another, deeper sense, her silence and ineffectuality angered him more than perhaps he realized. He knew how pliable she was, just as he knew his father's knack for eliciting her entreaties when his own efforts failed. But because his mother spoke softly and suffered, Wittgenstein could almost never refuse this woman who had never quite recovered from her sons' deaths, this silent figure sitting at the far end of the dinner table, encased in that sticky, stealthy cocoon that grief had slowly secreted over her.

And in a way, Wittgenstein was relieved to be done with it, this stab at independence. Why had he even tried? he wondered. It was bound to fail. Not wanting his mother to suffer another day, he sent her a telegram, saying that he would be home after all.

In her joy and relief, his mother sent him a telegram in return. But then, in her excitement, Frau Wittgenstein unwittingly put another noose around his neck, writing in her next letter:

... Now, do not be stern with me. Do you remember Berthe Ketteler? I had her and her daughter, Hilde, over the other day. We had a little *Jause*. I don't suppose you've seen Hilde in ten or fifteen years. She is a year younger than you and is going to the university. She has turned into quite a lovely young lady, very pretty and quite, quite smart, exceptionally literary and musical — all the things you like. Gretl saw her and was quite favorably impressed. I would like you to at least meet her. Think about it, do. But please, a word before next week — please, or I shall be most embarrassed, as I told Frau Ketteler I would ask you, and I should not want to disappoint Hilde, who saw your recent photograph and seemed quite intrigued with you. (She also adores Schopenhauer.)

He replied:

Dear Mother,
   Isn't it enough that I agreed to come home? If you MUST, I will meet Hilde, but please do not expect anything to come of it. Despite your apparent feeling that my career is "unresolved," I will be in England for some time, studying philosophy with Herr Russell; as such, it would not do to form an "attachment." And please, no more talk of Schopenhauer. If you want to know those who are the sun to me, then speak of Herr Russell or Frege (the logician with whom I had an interview in Jena last summer). These are great men, but real, human men with genuine clay feet. Just the other day, when Russell and I were arguing a point, he said I was an obstinate ass and had the pride of Lucifer! We were reconciled by nightfall, but this is what I mean by real, human men. The best influences are those who can rail back at you. My work goes well, and I look forward, after all, to seeing you and Father and the rest of the family.

With deep affection,
Ludwig

Despite the disguising sunniness at the end, he reviled himself for this nonsense about not wanting to form an attachment. Still, perhaps his mother's meddling was a blessing. Now at least he had something besides his father to dread. Now there was also Fräulein Ketteler.

One night around this time, Russell was more than taken aback when McTaggart turned to him at supper and said, Well, what about Moore, eh?
   Waiting for the other shoe to drop, Russell rested his fork, then asked, What about him?
   McTaggart's dark brows beetled above a supercilious smile. Why, about him getting married of course.
   Moore? Russell canted his head, incredulous. I hadn't heard. But Russell made a quick recovery. Peering prankishly down the long, warped

table to where Moore was supping, he said, Well, haven't you been cunning. That's right — *you*, Mr. Moore! Beaming as Moore looked around, bland as a cropping beef, Russell said, McTaggart says you're to be married!

With a look of embarrassment, Moore swallowed and said, I was going to tell you. I couldn't think of how to go about announcing it — without making too much of a *thing* about it, I mean.

Well, this is wonderful! exclaimed Russell. And then, looking up and down the Olympian table to better broadcast his happiness, he said it again as Moore began to squirm.

Moore got the full treatment then. Rising from his chair, Russell squeezed along the carved wall, past the other banqueters, and heartily shook his hand, saying, Absolutely delighted for you, Moore, really I am. You'll make a marvelous husband. I mean that, he said, clenching Moore's hand again to make it sure. And do, please, give Miss Ely my best wishes. A long and happy life together. Most happy.

Moore's hand was uncharacteristically limp. Russell could see he was touched; for a moment they both were. And soon Moore was a bubbling brook, saying, It's been so, I don't know, *overwhelming*. Cheeks flushed, Moore reached a big breath, still clearly dazed by his good fortune as he continued, Just asked her the other night. Horribly nervous — really didn't know if I'd be able to go through with it. Awfully glad I did, though. Don't know what I'd have done if I hadn't. Well, I might have lost her! Oh, yes. She was *leaving*, you know . . .

And as Russell stood there listening to Moore talk happily about his vacation plans, so full with parents and family — as he listened to Moore carry on, hunched like a kangaroo over his blousing belly, Russell felt correspondingly smaller, to behold one still so unspoiled by griefs and disappointments, and hence so open to love. Russell watched Moore with that twisting bafflement which only the dispossessed unhappy can see in the face of happiness, wondering how Monday could possibly have been so good when Tuesday is so bleak. Moore had no notion then of how Russell admired and envied him; in his happiness Moore had no sense of himself whatsoever. Exposed at the cuffs, Moore's plump, white wrists were turned up like an offering amid the dinner clutter. Russell, meanwhile, felt himself wavering like a tree, lost at that point where words and good wishes peter out.

Well, said Russell, capping off this rampant well-wishing. Do give her my very best. And I want to hear more of it. And if you need help of any kind —

Oh! Thank you.

Moore's chair groaned as he stood up, hastily wiping his hands on his napkin. For both of them now, it was quite unexpected, this sudden surfeit of warmth and glad tidings. But it was more than a surge of Yuletide bonhomie, and they both hung there, each wanting to say something further, when Moore, realizing that they had spoken only of him, said suddenly, And you, Bertie? You'll be here for the holidays?

Oh, in and out, you know. Relatives and visits . . .

Good, said Moore, a little unsure. Good, and he pumped his hand again, wanting, after all, to be glad in return, this being the least a happy man can do.

It would have been too easy for Russell to say that he was glad for Moore and have that be the end of it. After all, Russell didn't want to deny Moore a long-awaited draft from the trough of domestic happiness. But inevitably for Russell there came the sourness of envy, the frustration that Moore's courtship should seemingly end so easily while his dragged on and on, with no good end in sight.

Russell hated feeling like this; it seemed so mean-spirited and Scrooge-like. Still, he was happy that Wittgenstein would be there with him over the holiday. Russell had even succeeded in getting him invited to Whitehead's for Christmas dinner, and Wittgenstein had gratefully accepted, saying he would get them some good wine and something else to show a little Viennese *Gastfreundlichkeit*. Russell thought he might suggest the idea of their going together to Scotland. But then four nights before the end of term, Wittgenstein knocked on Russell's door around nine, a little earlier than usual. Russell could see he was agitated, and Wittgenstein came straight to the point:

I will be going home to Vienna, Mr. Russell. I am very sorry, but that is decided. He looked up. I will send to the Whiteheads the wine I was to bring. I will send them also a note for being so kind, to invite me. Thursday morning I leave.

But why? asked Russell. Then, realizing this was the wrong tack, he reversed himself, saying, Excuse me. That is certainly none of my concern.

It is for only my mother I am going, said Wittgenstein irritably. It is really very annoying.

His English was fuzzy now, like a bird molting new feathers. First an "awkwardism," or "Teutonism," as Russell joked, then a phrase in fine syntax, with faint British inflections.

Fishing, Russell said, Well, I'm sure you'll make her happy.

It was completely selfish for me to remain here! said Wittgenstein suddenly. Intolerably selfish — Wittgenstein was now pacing, whirling back and forth.

Well, said Russell, perhaps too soothingly. I would not call you *selfish*. That is only something you have imagined about yourself.

Glaring, Wittgenstein retorted, Then you do not know me! *At all!* I *am* selfish. And not only selfish! In fact, I am filled with the pettiest, vilest thoughts! *All the time!* Don't look at me like that — it is true! It is better that I go home. If I cannot do for myself any good, I can at least do for someone else some good.

Russell had no desire to argue with him, but Wittgenstein wouldn't be ignored. In a sudden leap of logic, Wittgenstein demanded, Now, tell me once and for all. Have I *any* talent as a philosopher?

Russell didn't know what he was saying. Fending him off, he replied, Why do you ask?

Because, groaned Wittgenstein. If I do not have any *real* talent — then I will become an aeronaut.

Aeronaut? Russell felt the blood draining from his head. But then, with a guilty thrill, Russell took a stab, asking, Why? Because an aeroplane would afford you a better chance to kill yourself?

It was a taunt, but Wittgenstein just stared him down with a long and unsentimental look — chilling, as he quietly replied, If I were *whole* or *healthy*, Russell, I would not even *be* a philosopher. Nor you.

Russell did not deny it. And in the oddest way, he felt they had just exchanged the deepest intimacy, each looking at the other, thinking, *So you, too, are this way.*

But with that, there was awkwardness again. Wittgenstein was still waiting for a reply to his question, and Russell, reverting back to his English need to tidy after an upset, was brisk and businesslike as he resumed. Well, in answer to your question, yes, I *do* think you have genuine philosophical talent. But *how much* talent — this, unfortunately, I cannot tell as yet. But if you will write a paper on any logical or philosophical subject that you choose — Russell took a deep breath — I will answer your question as truthfully as I can. But, cautioned Russell, wondering if he dared scatter the crockery again, you will not have your answer in time to see your father.

For two months Russell had been probing this nerve, and now he had found it. Scalded, Wittgenstein shot back, It is not for *him* I ask! Wittgenstein's hands grappled together. Then came that morbid wrist wrenching. And sure enough, Wittgenstein reversed course, saying, Still, it *is* correct for my father to *wonder* — to wish his son to be of some *use* to the world. This much is clear, Mr. Russell: we are not put here to have a good time.

But at the risk of sounding pedantic, labored Russell. If philosophy has no value to your father — well, what does your talent matter? You cannot win.

I told you! railed Wittgenstein. *He* is not the point!

But here was one argument that Wittgenstein could not challenge or refute; to rebut this, he had only silence, angry silence. And it was so odd for Russell to see before him then not the invincible zealot of his dreams but just a bitter, confused young man. Yes, Russell had to remember, he was still a young man, after all. Just a young man.

Soon after this, Wittgenstein left, but outside his door the next morning, Russell found two meticulously wrapped packages containing a tin of expensive tobacco and a quarto edition of Schiller. Attached to it was a note that expressed what Wittgenstein could not have said in Russell's presence:

Dear Mr. Russell,

Please accept this — a better good-bye, and my fond wishes for the holiday and the New Year. Last night, as usual, I was abrupt and willful — my usual stupidity. *Despite* what you think, it will be good for me at home, and I DO look forward to seeing my family. You must not judge them. No one, as I think, knows a man like his family. This is both good and bad but it is true.

I thank you for your many kindnesses this term, and I will await your *objective* judgment when I return.

Yours ever,
Ludwig Wittgenstein

Bitter Herbs

THE FIRST SIGN was at the symphony.

For Wittgenstein, the symphony was a supreme pleasure, and under normal circumstances this program at the Musikverein featuring a Mozart piano concerto followed by Schubert's monumental Ninth would have propelled him into that state of almost mathematical attention with which he followed music. Yet sitting high above the hall in their family's third-tier box with his sisters Gretl and Mining and his brothers Paul and Kurt — peering down obliquely, he felt he had to pit his feet against the face of the box, had to push back as if to displace space or this dizzying sensation he had of yawning *down*, but ever so slightly, into that volcano blazing with light and music.

Once trained as an engineer, one could never shed that sense of the world as a mechanistic system, a conceptual mesh built out of a given system of axioms that somehow must account for all that pervades the physical sphere, that concatenation of flux, heat, pressure, stress and limits — those snowblind limits that somehow buttress and support piers, pillars and arches, not to mention opera boxes precariously projecting from walls already bearing a vast domed roof and, over that, heavens groaning with the last days of a future mounting like an avalanche. But to try to *see* beneath the incredibly fine mesh of these physical concordats; and truly, to feel this enveloping one's chest, with the heart swelling like an organ fugue, elliptically and ineluctably, into the all-pervading *form* of the world; and to attempt to see all of this *tonight, all at once* and *all of one piece,* as if the world had been built in a single day, and not seven, out of one numinous strand of purest crystal — this was a soul-breaking task. In the tilting salient of the spotlights, Wittgenstein could see dust rising, whole clouds billowing up, cleaved by the crossed lights into conic sections. Terrific layers of heat caused the dust to rise. Looking up, he wondered what tons of air were displaced by the horns alone, not to mention the thermal layer rising from three thousand bodies, stuffed with rich dinners and wine, and all of them vibrating with a sonic, emotive barrage that made him feel as if he were clinging to the stretched outer skin of a dirigible inflated with insupportable expectations, a burgeoning that was rising, in rapid gasps, to the rupture of crescendo . . .

His foot was tapping and his bladder, the other pressure, was slowly filling with the three cups of strong Turkish coffee he had drunk in the Lindser Café, where his brothers and sisters had taken him so he might *relax,* of all things. At supper, his father's careful questions about England, so pattering and pleasant, so emphatically *neutral,* had had all the hallmarks of a prosecutor's putting a witness at ease before the real questioning began. And of course, his father saw in him what they all saw: the tensed shoulders, the constriction of the neck, the unnatural deliberation before each answer. For his sisters and brothers — for his mother sitting pokerfaced at the end of the table — there was no telling what

Karl Wittgenstein was leading up to with this lengthy, conversational *proof*. Wittgenstein could not suppress the feeling that his father would suddenly shoot out at him like a jack-in-the-box, shouting, AH-HA! then exposing the cause of his dysfunction.

Of course, it would have been all too easy to say his father was being spiteful or malicious. Plainly, it was the family's own rising concern that was prompting this investigation, insofar as the father knew what he was doing or the worsening effect these questions had on his son. As a student of comparative industry, Karl Wittgenstein had traveled widely in England, especially in Staffordshire and other industrial areas, where he had toured steel plants, looking for improved processes and equipment. He liked English theater, especially Shaw, and knew the British Museum by heart. His English was flawless — far better than his son's. And he probably had a better grasp of the English people, whom, as with people everywhere he traveled, he felt quite free to stop — perfect strangers — and question at length as if they were workers in his own factories. People answered him, too. Yes, Wittgenstein found it most troubling how his father commanded such immediate docility in the human herd.

There was, in short, little Wittgenstein could have told his father about England. But still the old man continued with these circling questions as he worked away at an enormous welcoming meal that featured *Jungschweinsbraten,* a young roast pork loin covered to its crackling with a thick cream sauce, and that culminated some five courses later with a snowy meringue *Spanische Windtorte* — four pounds of sugared egg whites that he couldn't look at when it appeared, vaguely polar, through the lapping candlelight.

And the food at Trinity? asked Karl Wittgenstein conspicuously, noting his son's lack of appetite.

It is food, replied Wittgenstein, who, perhaps in reaction to his father, had always shown a certain indifference to food, an indifference not unlike his coolness about meeting Berthe Ketteler's daughter the following afternoon.

Wittgenstein continued. I eat simply. Vegetables, mainly. Meat disagrees with my digestion.

A misstep, this; his mother carefully daubed her lips with her napkin, leaving it to his father to ask, There is something wrong with your digestion?

Wittgenstein waited three beats, then replied, Not if I eat as I should.

And the food *here*? asked his father pointedly. It is too rich for your digestion?

A pleasant change, replied the son agreeably, though he felt his smile curdle.

Resumed his father helpfully, A change before you go back to your bland fare, you mean — so you will know the difference. Barbishly, his father then quipped for the benefit of the table, Ever the philosopher — our latter-day Epictetus. Then, seeing his son's withholding look, Karl Wittgenstein asked, You have not read the Stoics?

Wittgenstein froze, as if it were natural to expect that, as a student of philosophy, he must be conversant with every facet of the subject. Gathering his forces, Wittgenstein replied, I understand the basic outlines of the Stoic creed. That is enough.

His father stared at him. They don't teach the Stoics at Cambridge? he asked, as if to say, *The English are so debased?*

They teach the Stoics, replied the son patiently. *If* one is reading philosophy in the Tripos or studying the classics. But that is not what I'm about.

Oh? asked his father, saying only oh, but by that meaning, *Pray, then, tell us what you* are *about?*

Boldly, Wittgenstein brushed this aside, pointedly asking, You were asking about food at college?

Yes! his father chimed. Rising up on his elbows, Karl Wittgenstein seemed pleased that his feckless son was finally showing some backbone. And perhaps this, Wittgenstein reflected, was his reason behind this inquisition — not necessarily because it was a good reason, but because it was necessary for Wittgenstein to believe that his father actually *had* a reason.

But then, having asked his son how he liked English food, Karl Wittgenstein answered his own question. Well! he said. For myself, I really do think English food is amply deserving of its reputation for dreadfulness. At least in the main. The wealthy, of course, do not really eat English food. They still lick the boots of the French — French cuisine is the rage. Even their menus are in French, though they do persist, especially at breakfast, in serving grilled lamb kidneys, herrings and other solidly English offal.

Out to charm his family now with observations far more picturesque and amusing than any his son could have made, Karl Wittgenstein added with a look of astonishment: But do you know what? The English do not know how to bake! Oh, there you would find nothing like this magnificent *Spanische Windtorte,* and certainly none executed so beautifully (eyeing his youngest son, who had hardly touched his). It's quite true, he said, looking around the table with raised brow. Their baked goods have none of our subtlety, none whatsoever! Like lead. Rather like Jewish baked goods, I'd say.

Karl Wittgenstein drew his hand over his beard as if he would yank it down, smiling as his children set their jaws against him. Such a dinnertime provocateur! With the table his stage, Karl Wittgenstein then launched into a penetrating, high-spirited discussion of national traits as revealed in the art of baking and desserts: the hardtack English, so stoical and unimaginative, with their runny trifle and puritanical plum puddings caked with hard sauce; the larcenous French, all hot air and flummery, as shown by their own pale imitations of Viennese pastry; and the unregenerate Italians, so oily and *lazy*, with those doughy pastries, swimming like sodden meatballs in fruity sugar water.

But, said Karl Wittgenstein, raising one finger. Compare to this, if you will, our own *Torten*, so lively, layered and varied in texture; and yet, he added contrapuntally, yet so reliably and indeed densely honest! Consider the sheer compositional variety of, say, the *Indianer Torte, Josephinentorte, Pralinentorte*, the *Neapolitaner* and *Breslauer*. A veritable library of baking, one might say. Why, it is a culture even conscious of its history, what with the *Nelsontorte* and *Austerlitztorte*. And of course, Karl Wittgenstein suggested with a wave of the hand, he could go on. And on. Yes, even that raconteuse Gretl had a hard time competing with her father at his own table.

Later, at the café before the symphony, though, Gretl was typically scathing about her father's suppertime antics.

And that nonsense about the Stoics! Go on, she urged Wittgenstein, look by his bed. I'm sure he's reading the Stoics — Kant and Hegel, too, and everything else he'll want to throw at you while you're home.

Paul was sitting opposite Gretl, beside Mining. As for Kurt, he was sitting at the end of the table with his legs crossed, pulling at his little waxed mustache while reading — much to Gretl's annoyance — one of the café's spindled newspapers.

Must you read that now? Gretl asked suddenly.

Crumpling the paper together, Kurt said with a devilish smile, But I'm listening! Of course I'm always listening to you. That's what we're all here for, aren't we?

Said Gretl oversweetly, We might listen to you, too, Kurt, if you put down that mask of a newspaper.

Well, said Kurt glibly, laying down the paper and moving his seat toward the table. Here I am.

Still, he offered nothing, and Gretl, seeing no other takers, resumed these digs at their father. But instead of boosting Wittgenstein's spirits, her barbs only made him more uneasy. Nor was he the only one. Covering her mouth politely, Mining was laughing in spite of herself at her renegade sister. For Mining, who was devoted to both Karl Wittgenstein and Gretl, it was a strained and dangerous laughter. As her father's favorite, Mining had always found herself caught in the middle. Between Gretl and Wittgenstein. Between Gretl and Paul. Between her father and everybody else.

Of all Karl Wittgenstein's children, Mining was the most balanced and mild, with the least desire to hurt him. But Mining paid for her father's love. At thirty-nine, she was, and would forever be, unmarried, a fact obvious to all but Mining, who had never extinguished dreams of marriage and children, clutching them ever more doggedly the more unattainable they became. This rankled Karl Wittgenstein, who as usual had it both ways, reproaching her for not marrying even as his daughter subconsciously held back from attachments, knowing how devastated he would be to lose her.

A heavy, maternal woman, Mining had a habit in conversation of shyly dropping her head inconsolably, like a cow deprived of her calf. Wearing a round, drab dress and perforated old lady's shoes, she made Gretl seem all the more vibrant and secular. But for all their differences, the sisters were inseparable, Gretl depending on Mining's calm good sense and Mining sustaining herself on the life of her flamboyant younger sister, who it seemed could have everything in life that she couldn't, including a husband and a son of three on whom Auntie Mining doted.

Gretl was getting carried away with her claim that their father carefully researched his dinnertime disquisitions. And as she had always done, Mining patiently pulled her back, saying, *Gretl . . . Gretl,* now you're exaggerating. You know you are.

But this only egged Gretl on. What do you mean? she retorted. At night before dinner when we were small, I used to see him in the library. We were all so stupid. He'd pick out a volume of the encyclopedia! One night it was *arthropods,* the next *Borneo,* then *dodo birds. We* were the dodos!

Stop, said Mining, smirking in spite of herself.

It's *true,* said Gretl, whose voice squeaked when she got really excited. Gretl loved raising the dust around her, clapping her hands together, her eyes teary with laughter. In her excitement then, Gretl was like a sputtering balloon. She carried on, saying, I'm sure I could show you the book he read tonight before supper. You know his tricks, Mining. I showed you once — I know I did!

Gretl, said Mining doubtfully. Gretl, this is pure fancy.

Wittgenstein's brother Paul did not take Gretl's remarks so playfully. Priggishly correct, he said flatly, Oh, nonsense. Why must you delude yourself with this?

Paul's angry because he never caught on to him, mocked Gretl. Mugging for the others, she quipped, Poor Paul, he thought Papa was an authority on arthropods, too.

Replied Paul with disgust, Yes, and on artful dissembling.

This did not deter Gretl. Turning to Wittgenstein beside her, she said, Listen to me. Go into the library before dinner tomorrow. Tonight I'm sure it was desserts or baking. They could feel the gears turning as Gretl looked round the table, then exclaimed, Honestly! Don't we have a book on desserts or something? Why, I think we do!

Challenged Paul, Please, show me this book. I very much want to see this book.

But Gretl wasn't about to be pinned down. As usual, she had just spied somebody she knew, desserts forgotten as she said, Please, will you all excuse me a moment? I know we have to leave, but I must say a word to this person. I'll get my coat. I won't be a minute . . .

A word, muttered Paul. Thanks to Gretl, we can all be late.

Oh, *shush,* said Mining, laying her hand on top of his. Shall we go, then?

It had been Gretl's idea to get the siblings together that evening, and as they left the café she was remembering why such gatherings never worked.

As a group, there had probably never been much symmetry among them, but now what moorings they had once had as a family had torn loose. For the Wittgenstein children, this was partly a function of age and changing interests, but there was more to it than that. Gretl had a genius for human and family politics — this as opposed to the scrapping of purely political politics. Being a profoundly social creature, the perspicacious Gretl was able to see people in configuration and arrangement like hues of color that had definite orders and values, with harmonious blends and also some unexpected combinations. Gretl loved nothing better than to make bold and unexpected pairings of people, and she was not afraid to experiment. But with her family, Gretl found her social gifts sorely thwarted: so little worked. She, Mining and Ludwig got on well; Mining and Paul also got along, as did Paul and Ludwig. Between herself and Paul there was friction, but less if Mining was there as a buffer. As for Kurt, he got along with everyone and no one. The man was a shell. He wasn't really there.

Gretl wasn't the only one who felt this frustration. They all knew something was wrong, and because the deaths of their brothers loomed largest in their memories, they tended to feel that this must be the main problem. The answer must be simple — simple as a child's answer. And so they would find themselves wondering what life would be like had their brothers lived, as if the dead could somehow complete or recompense the living for having died.

But suppose their two dead brothers *had* miraculously returned. Suppose the crippled body of the Family Wittgenstein regenerated these two missing limbs. Yet this was impossible! Such a miracle would have struck the Wittgenstein children as *wrong*, and not merely because the dead do not return to life. Above all, they would have found it grossly unfair, after all those years away, that their brothers should get off scot-free, leaving them to bear on five backs what was meant for seven.

If logic was the text, grief was the subtext of this equation that Wittgenstein was now beginning to unearth. More than life separates the dead from the living, and more than logic separates this world from the next: with logic there is illogic, too. As a philosopher, Wittgenstein was just coming to the realization that logic cannot make anything *more* logical: a thing is either logical or it is not; there is no in between. Likewise, he had concluded that all sentences are well formed and intelligible, insofar as we have *given* them sense. But what sense was he to make of his own grief, so ill formed and seemingly unintelligible, with neither words nor limits, nor any reason but that it is grief and never entirely goes away.

These are the bitterest herbs, that we should so resent the malingering dead. In its first grips, grief makes itself a felt thing, but then, like an ice face, it shears off, sliding beneath the waves, as fathomless and deep as an iceberg. Wittgenstein's drive to survey the limits and interior of logic, then, was not unlike this deeper need to survey the buried mass of his own grief, that hazy curtain dividing sense from non-sense. And entangled with this grief was guilt. Once having consigned the dead to the ground, the living do not wish the dead to return, not really. They feel that the dead are strangers to life, and especially to the present. Still wearing their old suits and gowns, and burdened with their outdated notions and former bad habits, the dead are like discharged servants: they have found another situation.

This was the most unspoken truth around that table. Not only were the dead brothers not needed, they were not even wanted. For them to have returned would only have botched and complicated matters. Yet, in their minds, Wittgenstein and his siblings would periodically revert to these magical half-conscious wishes that said *if only if* and *had not* and if one could only make right these things that *ought* but *aren't* and *can't* and *never will be.*

Wittgenstein would not soon, or perhaps ever, disentangle the grammar of these illogical propositions. In some his father was the subject, in some the predicate, but in none was his father a logical, complete or entirely human entity. Further, Wittgenstein's grief was complicated by the fact that while the dead brothers had been troubled, scarred and indeed wretched creatures, they had never been even remotely likable. If Wittgenstein as a boy had merely disliked Rudi, he had thoroughly despised Hans, who was forever tormenting him with his cruel, belittling remarks.

Still, a brother is a brother. As much as Wittgenstein's anger at his brothers weighed on him, their youth made them heavier still, the young suicide being, next to a parent, the heaviest of all the dead, and far and away the most illogical.

Wittgenstein's two living brothers were another matter.

Contrary to what their father had said at the table earlier that evening, it was Wittgenstein's brother Paul, a year older than he, who was the real stoic in the family. Nothing could have driven Paul to suicide. For Paul, life itself was a wedge against his father; there was no need to scatter mere words against him, as Gretl did. Paul had no tolerance for what he saw as Gretl's wasteful and frivolous troublemaking. A consummate rationalist, Paul, like Wittgenstein himself, was especially contemptuous of Gretl's lay psychologizing now that she was on Freud's couch. Invoking the satirist Karl Kraus, who regularly excoriated Freud and his followers in his weekly paper *Die Fackel,* Paul said the science of the "soul doctor" was the disease of emancipated Jews. Inside the ghetto, Kraus said, there was the business mentality; outside it, there was the soul doctor, just another manifestation of the Jewish business spirit, robbing men of their souls. As a Jew who believed he had expunged from his character all objectionable Jewish traits, Kraus regularly exhorted his fellow Jews to be less Jewish. All educated Vienna, including Kraus's many enemies and detractors, read him religiously. Once an avid reader of *Die Fackel,* Gretl had now come to hate the satirist's astounding denials. Paul and Wittgenstein loved him, though. They reveled in Kraus's self-appointed mission to cleanse the Augean stables of the German language; and they took special delight in his vow to kick the "Austrian corpse," which Kraus swore still had life in it, in spite of all signs to the contrary.

It was not Freud but Kraus who was the disease, Gretl told Paul. Kraus's much-vaunted word play did not impress her. She said he reminded her of a child who had opened his diaper and begun playing in it. Oh! crowed Paul. How analytical! The soul doctor could not put it better himself! And so Paul would persist in his Krausian misanthropy and sloganeering, needling her till inevitably things took an ugly turn, as they did one day when Gretl told her brother that he was bound in an invisible corset. You ought to let it out, she snipped. It might help your piano playing.

Gretl immediately apologized for this remark, but characteristically Paul withdrew in icy contempt. No one in the family was colder or more tightly reined in; even Karl Wittgenstein was unnerved by his son's seeming air of invulnerability. Yet how else could Paul, having assumed that death warrant of a musical career, have withstood his father? After years of exercise, Paul's spiny, almost double-jointed fingers had grown almost reptilian in length. Tense as a bow, grimacing, he even enunciated with his fingers, flexing them with a slow and awful cracking, as if his whole rachitic psyche were on the rack. In this respect, Gretl was quite correct about his playing. While technically superb, it was too cold and tense, lacking that surrender necessary to overcome the corset of mere technique.

Kurt, six years older than Wittgenstein, was another story. Woeful Kurt. Even his father was willing to concede that somewhere Kurt had been lost, or dropped on his head. By any standards Kurt was well above average intelligence, but by Wittgenstein standards he was deficient, and Karl Wittgenstein made no effort to conceal the fact. Not that this fazed Kurt. To him, it seemed his father's standards were meaningless, and yet this patent denial had also taken its toll: with no apparent will to combat his father, Kurt's personality had gone from a liquid to a gaseous state. He was perfectly pleasant and intelligent, but he was a counterfeit. Karl Wittgenstein even had a gesture for him: a vague pass of his hand, as if he could merely waft his fingers through Kurt's ghostly head.

The irony was that Kurt had never defied his father. Having entered the business, he was following his father's wishes to the letter. But because Kurt had no real brains or backbone, Karl Wittgenstein found him only another disappointment. With the help of a ghost manager, Kurt ran one of Karl Wittgenstein's lesser steel factories on the eastern outskirts of the city. Once a month or so, usually on a Sunday, Kurt would spend the day at home, burying himself in the paper or affably moping. Otherwise he lived alone and collected stamps — at least, his father said, when he was not collecting dust.

Like compass points, the three brothers faced in different directions, while all veering away from that force field emanating from the head of the table. The two other brothers were installed above in a now bygone constellation called *The Empty Chairs,* two staring holes where once stars had flickered.

All this and more was weighing on Wittgenstein as he sat there pitted against the face of his box, the symphony imploding below him with Schubert's Ninth. And then he could wait no longer. He had to relieve himself.

He dreaded this in public, especially the pressure of doing so during intermission — having to *produce,* with a line of uncomfortable men butting up behind him. Turning to Gretl, he whispered, My leg is cramping. I must get up now. I will see you by the stairs at intermission.

He knew, and she knew, why he was leaving. Wittgenstein saw his sister's disappointment, that he should still be suffering this anxiety, but then in his urgency he was gone, walking stiff-legged down the gilt and marble foyer, hoping to find the lavatory empty now as the orchestra was storming to crescendo.

And he was in luck! The lavatory was deserted, and he whisked in, clasping the stall shut as he spread his black tails and dropped his trousers. But just as he was settling himself on the seat, the lavatory door opened, and he heard someone lock the next stall. Trying to relax, he closed his eyes and thought of *water* — clear, free, running water, as his knotted bladder unclenched, draining into the ringing porcelain. But when he opened his eyes, Wittgenstein suffered a shock: beneath the marble divider, he saw in the next stall not trousers but a skirt and high-heeled shoes.

His first thought was, The poor woman, she took the wrong door. But then he heard the lavatory door open again, this time with women's voices! But how was this possible? He yanked up his trousers and crouched atop the seat with his knees hiked to his chin, certain he would be exposed, arrested!

And no escape! Outside now he heard applause, then the hubbub of the intermission crowds, a sound like rushing surf down the foyer. Quick! What to do? Hide as if the stall were out of order? Run?

He did not run. Flushing the toilet to cover his escape, he walked out like a gentleman, ramrod straight, eyes half closed. Up went a gasp, a cry! A fox was in the hen house! Amidst those clotted pink walls, he had a fleeting sensation of angry geese, of threatening white crinoline wings warding him off. He flinched as a woman looming under a gigantic nebula of hat veered toward him with a sound of either excited clucking or choking. Huddled in the corner, another woman covered her face.

Shrieks and cries as he burst out the door and pushed through the clotted bodies, slipping down the stairs, past the attendant, then out the doors and down the darkened street, where, against all principle, he started running, his forked tails flying as he tore like a thief through the dirty December snow.

On the Origins of Charity

ONCE SAFELY down the street, he felt soiled. Deranged. Not daring to return for fear of being recognized, he took a cab to the palais, where he telephoned the concert hall to ask that his family be told that he had been taken ill and was now resting at home.

Hardly had he hung up than his mother appeared, having been alerted by her excitable maid, who had been told by the night butler — in spite of Wittgenstein's explicit orders not to disturb his parents — that her red-faced son was so terribly ill and in such a state that he had come home in a cab, *gnädige Frau, without even a coat and hat!*

What-*is*-the-matter? demanded his frantic mother, indignant to find him sitting up in his condition.

Please, he said. I'm really all right. I became ill.

Ill? she sputtered, as if to say he surely must be gravely ill to appear at this hour hatless and coatless and plainly absent of his senses. Where is Gretl? she asked, looking around.

Dabbing his eyes, he said very softly, I called the hall. She's there still.

Frau Wittgenstein was incredulous. *You left and did not tell them?*

And he, laboring now, I told you . . . I felt too ill.

Ill! she cried. What is this, *ill*! *How* are you ill?

But here he was stuck: in all the ruckus, he had had no time to concoct an alibi, and so he found himself in the double bind of having to find an illness serious enough to justify his sudden departure yet not so grave that he would be plagued for days with questions and solicitude. At the same time, he dared not make things any fishier by hesitating, so he said, I vomited. But in that flash of his mother's eyes, he saw his error.

I knew it! she cried, knitting her frayed fingers together. With over-work and this needless stoicism of yours, you have given yourself a nervous ulcer.

It's not *stoicism*, he said irritably. Those are Father's words. A stomach is not a creed, it's only a stomach.

Don't be clever, his mother reprimanded. You never had such a stomach in my house. Did you see blood in your sputum?

Blood?

His father's voice. Rushing in still slick from his evening bath and swaddled in his smoking jacket, Karl Wittgenstein was leading a brigade consisting of the guilty maid and the butler, who was carrying a chest filled with enough bandages and medicinals to have supplied a polar expedition.

What blood? demanded his father.

No blood. Peeved at him for barging in and taking over as usual, Frau Wittgenstein was unusually snappish. I asked if he vomited blood.

He vomited *blood?*

And he said no, insisted Frau Wittgenstein. *No.*

Well, the father demanded, shaking his arms. Then what *did* he vomit?

My *dinner,* groaned the son.

Oh. The father nodded. Our *dinner,* was it?

It hardly helped matters when, in the midst of this now heated medical inquest, Gretl arrived, throwing off her fur in alarm as Wittgenstein stared her down, directing her with his emphatic eyes not to make this any more of a scene.

Fifteen minutes later, it was all he could do to convince his father not to summon the family physician out of bed, and this only after promising he would see him in the morning for a complete physical examination. Still, for Karl Wittgenstein to persuade his son to see the doctor after the fact was hardly as gratifying or demonstrative as taking action *now,* even if it only meant picking up the telephone. Karl Wittgenstein found few acceptable opportunities to show fatherly solicitude. These moments were rare as eclipses, yet despite their bungling, awkward quality, the feeling in them ran deep, so deep that Karl Wittgenstein finally burst from the room, wounded that his ungrateful son should deny him even this. Wittgenstein called after him appreciatively, while for his mother, who seemed sure he was hemorrhaging, he contrived to swallow some buttermilk. Then, with a worried, suspicious look, Frau Wittgenstein also left, off to quell her wounded husband.

Once they were alone, Gretl managed to pry the truth from him. But almost as soon as he began, she broke in, saying, Please, don't be offended at this. But so you won't accuse me later of pretending to know after the fact what happened, let me tell you what I think it was.

Fine, he said bitterly, sure she would never guess. Tell me.

All right, she said, taking a breath. You somehow found yourself in the women's lavatory. Seeing him go white, Gretl hastily added, Lest you worry, nobody recognized you, and no one told me this. But I heard about a man in the ladies' room and — I don't know — I had a feeling.

But why a hunch about *me*? Why *me*? He was grasping the armrests, his head swaying back and forth. Do you even know what you're saying?

Ludi, she said, laying her hand on his arm. I'm certainly not suggesting you make a habit of it. But I *knew* — I just did. Knew even from how you looked when you got up — so chased, and nothing I could do. Why else do you think I kept Mining and Paul from going to the management to find you? I was afraid they might make the connection.

Oh, God, he moaned. You *told them*?

I had no *choice*. Otherwise they would have made inquiries. They're upstairs now. They agreed it would be best if we spoke alone.

A long, anguished wince. He *was* sick now, pale and trembling sick, his voice stumbling, saying, It was a mistake . . . a horrible accident. You *do* know it was an accident, don't you?

Well, of course.

But Gretl agreed a little too easily, with that telltale squeak in her throaty voice. He could hear the gears churning now. Protesting in advance, he said, I'm telling you that it was an accident. Oh, I know, you'll say it was a dark wish — an unconscious wish to return to the womb or something.

Well, she said carefully, there are accidents and accidents.

I *told* you, I was distracted! I merely reached for the wrong door.

Distracted? Her voice turned accusatory. Is that the word? Distracted to walk through a completely different door, a door on the opposite side of the hall, no less? And to walk not only through the wrong door but through a pink powder room filled with feminine settees and mirrors? *Distracted?*

Is it necessary, he broke in breathlessly, is it necessary to make me feel any worse than I do already?

I'm sorry, she squeaked. I am. But tomorrow, I think we ought to talk about it — I do.

But you forget, he said bitterly. Tomorrow I'm to meet Fräulein Ketteler.

Gretl's eyes flew up. That's right! I'd forgotten about her.

Oh, I see! he said sarcastically. Now I understand, Herr Doktor. Those were *her* shoes I saw in the stall beside mine.

Shoes? sleuthed Gretl. Whose shoes?

This was too much. He jumped up. Oh, yes! You really must go work for the shoe doctor.

Soul doctor, you mean.

Oh! He winced. Soul — sole! *Good!* This is getting *good,* isn't it! And he started to laugh, a long, ripping, seasick laugh that boiled up out of him, until she cried, *Stop it!* And he did stop. He stopped with a hiccupping bump. But he still was not rid of it, that expectoration. It was not his stomach that was sick, it was his soul, his soul.

Gretl more or less managed to work a truce before he went off to bed. Feeling as if his pockets had been turned out, he moved like a sleepwalker across the glassy parquet. And then as he was gliding down the darkened hallway, he saw a crease of light beneath the door of the library, where his father was no doubt sulking, having again found himself too late with his useless medicine.

As he hesitated there, blurry and trembling as a flame, it occurred to him that he might undo the lock, might unfreeze the past and go to his father. Physically, it was possible. But to knock on that door with the vain expectation of explaining, apologizing or offering solace — this was impossible, and not just impossible but downright shameful: to do this, he felt, would be to expose some part of his father or himself as he had been tonight exposed, hobbled in that coven, with his trousers wrapped around his ankles.

And later, lying in bed, stifled under blankets and his own burden of darkness, Wittgenstein saw something else he had overlooked downstairs, namely, his father's love. It was a love so turgid and disfigured as to be almost unintelligible, but still it was there, struggling like a spring shoot to dislodge a winter of snow. And what of that chest of medicinals? he thought. This seemed a relatively new development. Was it crude insurance so his father would be ready this time to snatch his flesh from the flames? But this, too, was smothering, and again Wittgenstein wondered why he should feel pricked and besmirched by the blackthorn of his father's thwarted love. And then he remembered how as a child he had gone through a period in which he feared toe-snatching elves and giants, nights when he would cry out, *Wasser, Wasser, bitte.* His kindly old Iglauer wet nurse, who slept in the next room, would dutifully bring him his water cup, soothing him as he gulped it down. But one night, when it came to his father's attention, Karl Wittgenstein told the nurse that *he* would bring the boy his water. One glass his father gave him, one glass with a scolding that he was not to cry out again, so big a boy as he. His father must have waited outside the door, because when the boy cried out again, he appeared in the darkness with another glass, beading and sparkling in the liquid darkness. Wittgenstein could distinctly remember his father's gleaming white collar points as he came forward with that glass of liquid succor, saying, You want *water*? Here is your *water*! and throwing it cold in his face.

It taught him. The child learned. Never again did he call out in the night, and so it was now, when the man would neither ask for forgiveness nor offer it.

Crystal Logic

THE NEXT MORNING was more of the same. Asleep around four, up at eight. Down at nine to the invalid's breakfast, bland and milky. Saying, *Ja,* to the concerned mother, wringing her napkin, Much, much better. Then propping himself up for his father, who it seemed could levitate with his expectant eyes. Eating the good, good food, and happily, to show his newfound wellness. Talking the bland, bland news to appear happy and voracious, so they could see he was committed to a definite course in life and, yes, ready, too, to meet Fräulein Ketteler — and all the while wondering why they did not foist her on his brother Paul, that feather-bedder sitting at the end of the table, distinct and erect of posture, with his single boiled egg.

Then it was off to the doctor, rousted out this Saturday to inspect the sickly scion. Directed to the waiting automobile, where the chauffeur, puffing steam and stamping his freshly polished boots, grasped the silver handle, then carefully tamped shut the black door. Joy to the world. Piles of old snow and the fog snared in the bare branches as they motored round the drive, past the manger, with the empty crib still waiting for the ceramic Christ child from Florence with the queer moorish skin and chipped nose. Then past the two brass angels standing on the gateposts, and down the Allegasse, where over imposing walls could be seen other vaultlike homes with wreaths on their doors. But on this street there were also a few like the Feines and Schupps who did not go along, who did not mark their doors for the wraiths of Yule and so were thought by their neighbors to be closed and somber, somehow vaguely *forbidding*.

A few blocks later, the rubber tires were thumping on the cobbles of the Ringstrasse, that great gyre in the heart of the city that had been built over what formerly had been its fortifications. Begun with the emperor's proclamation in 1857, the Ringstrasse was now, some fifty years later, lined with heavyset buildings bedecked in the polyphonous, often cacaphonous strains of historicism, Greek and Roman, then a *Götterdämmerung* of neo-Gothic and Baroque — heavy, heavy brick and stone already soaking up the coal soot and pigeon streaks of days. In that city, all was embellishment. Having razed one fortress, they had erected another. These walls and steeples were really the ramparts of Germanic, cosmopolitan *Kultur* struggling to remain ascendant over a racial cauldron brimming with Czechs, Ruthenes, Slovaks, Slovenes, Poles, Serbs, Croats, Romanians, Italians, Hungarians and Diaspora Jews. Beauty upon beauty, delirium upon delirium, the stones rose up in a lapidary confection, with piers giving way to columns, columns rising to spandrels and spandrels vaulting to imposts and roofs of beaten copper where stood the three Fates, winged cherubs and basilisks spewing rainwater.

Beautiful, improbable city, where the electric trams perambulated around an architectural circus wreathed with trees and iron-cupolaed kiosks splattered with bills clarioning every conceivable offer and entertainment. Sitting in the rear of the car, Wittgenstein saw but blankly the incomprehensible weave of this coat of far too many colors. But still, life happened along, switching like the tail of that indolent dray horse clopping just ahead, carelessly dropping his burden. And didn't Wittgenstein want to ooze down the seat as they passed the Musikverein from which he had fled the night before. Then on past columned Parliament, whose roof was piled like a necropolis with deities and winged chariots. In the fountain, amid stone waves and leaping dolphins, various sages tried with oars as useless as lollipops to steer a course through that brimming Styx. And standing powerfully over them all, holding forth a bronze-headed spear, was Athena, protectress of the polis and — to Wittgenstein's still smoldering eyes — the sworn avenger of ladies' toilets.

Five minutes later, he was mounting the stairs to Dr. Friedhof's office. He hated doctors, and it was an excruciatingly long visit, which did not fail to make him feel any less criminal. After the usual ahhhing, thumping and groin poking, Dr. Friedhof inserted his stubby hand in a greased glove and thoughtfully plumbed the patient's rectum before sending him off, suspiciously sound, with a homily about overwork and a prescription for paragoric.

Once out, Wittgenstein was hardly anxious to rush back home for more. Discharging the driver, he started walking. Two blocks later, with a sense of rising impatience, he jumped a tram, which slowly whirred around the Ring, past the Stadtpark, over the Danube Canal, and then up to the Praterstern, where, above the holiday crowds, he could see the park's giant Ferris wheel, a familiar sight that now conjured a gurgling deep in his bowels that Dr. Friedhof had dislodged but not seen.

So he was walking, but now it was a different walk, a feral, hungry, faintly feline walk. Down he passed through the dirty, slushy snow, down the wide cobbled avenue of the Praterstern, past the untold people, open mouthed as groupers. Ahead was the great iron Ferris wheel. Moaning like a loom, it gravely rose up, astonishingly swift, the glassed-in cars swinging out, the people pointing and waving in that one whooping instant at the apogee — then sinking down so swiftly that, as he watched, he had the glutted sensation of having swallowed himself.

He continued on. Cinders crackling underfoot. Dried, the sap of the summer. Brittle, the winter twigs. The Sacher restaurant was still open inside, but closed and withered was its vinous trellis garden. This was another place he found forbidden, but in a different way. Here in midsummer, he would see wealthy officers and ladies drinking and eating the rich, dark *Sachertorte* under shady thatch arbors filled with the strains of lugubrious violins, a sound that to him suggested the odor of melons left too long in the sun. One look and he would turn away, repulsed, expelled.

On he walked through the snow, through the vestiges of the old season. The sour-smelling outdoor *Bierstuben* were closed, as was the Wurstel Prater, the children's amusement park, where tarps cloaked the merry-go-round, the Velocipede and the Ghost Train. Then on past the closed Panopticum, its canvas façade painted with ghastly pictures of the wax figures inside. If only he could have fastened on something, some diversion. But there was nothing now. The roving clowns and witches, jugglers and Gypsies, the puppet shows — all were gone. No sharp smells of burned almonds or stringy Turkish taffy. No cracks from the shooting gallery or whoops from the games of strength or skill. Like smoke he hung in the air, ready to be moved by the slightest breeze, when he heard the clop of hooves. Wearing greatcoats and black-billed shako hats, two young officers, bloods both, trotted by on horseback. Wittgenstein watched as they passed two pretty lower-class girls, seamstresses or shop-girls, most likely — good for an adventure. Then came the treatment. Reining their mounts so they clopped a sideways prance and champed at their snaffles as the bloods tipped their hats, hoping to snag an eye.

As at the Sacher Garden, Wittgenstein felt that he was peering into another world — an impossibility. And walking on then, he saw his life as an imprisoning *form*. From that gray, organizing sky, his life was fall-ing like a stray snow crystal, a piercing sliver of the same crystal logic. But why was he *this*? he wondered. Why caught in this structure, tied with these invisible sutures? Unlike him, these folk could go home and be themselves; they could live an easy, seemly, unmeditated life in accor-dance with rules that more or less held, and held always. They did not see these hungry spirits treading the broken snow, panting with smoking breath. No, it was not *you*, Wurstel Prater, nor you, Ferris wheel. It was not you, Herr Vendor, selling bags of stale crumbs to feed the wintering geese on the chill pond, nor, heaven knows, was it you, innocent children, out today for a walk with your nanny —

No, it was you, scowling Herr Kollege, saber scarred and swaggering with your vituperative cane, away for a few hours from your brothers in the dueling fraternity. It was you, Game of Strength — you, the burly sausage maker or bricklayer. And it was you, too, away for an hour from your wife and family, away from the privation and anxiety of Christmas. Yes, and if you weren't so slight — if you were darker, rougher, more menacing — it well might be you, young man, swatting your leg, mysti-cally nodding about something that could be had, and had fast, among these shrouding firs . . .

No, Wittgenstein didn't have to venture as far as the firs that day. The point was to go just far enough to singe himself without tasting, to smudge his nose against the window of that world. That was the day's objective, and having satisfied it, Wittgenstein turned back dizzily, leav-ing them as he found them, padding back and forth like caged lions in the pocked snow.

Menorah

BACK AT THE PALAIS WITTGENSTEIN, meanwhile, the final preparations for Christmas and Fräulein Ketteler were under way. Sitting in a
ring, happily gabbing, the ladies of the house staff were weaving paper
festoons, while in the main reception room a group of footmen armed
with crooked sticks and stepladders under the supervision of the chief
butler, Herr Stolz, were hauling up the tree, a twenty-foot fir that this
season would be fitted for the first time with a fearfully expensive set of
electric lights.

Elfin shoes clopped like woodblocks across the freshly buffed parquet.
Slow down! blustered Karl Wittgenstein as, through a black forest of
bulbous chair legs, his three-year-old grandson, Stefan, mouth smeared
with cake batter, ran up and gave his arriving uncle a sloppy kiss. Wittgenstein returned the kiss, then saw his father eyeing him, alerting him
that he was late.

You had business after the doctor? asked his father as the child struggled in his arms.

I went for a walk, said Wittgenstein, winding the boy up over his
shoulder.

I see, said his father, plainly making an effort to be evenhanded this
festive day. At six? he asked suddenly. Is that when the Kettelers are to
arrive? Karl Wittgenstein knew perfectly well when they would be over;
this question was solely for his son's benefit, to reassert his paternal control. But then, for the benefit of Stefan's father, Rolf Stonborough, now
emerging from the drawing room, Karl Wittgenstein added officiously:
And, please, don't let the boy run. He's much too overheated and excitable today.

Quite true, chimed Rolf with a deft smile. And Stefan's not the only
one.

Karl Wittgenstein was not pleased with this playful dig, but he took it.
And it had its desired effect, for he then lumbered off, passing his own
imposing equestrian portrait as he went to meddle elsewhere.

The capable Rolf! A well-respected financier, Gretl's husband was a
cheerful, modest, highly cultivated man of forty-two, with full brown

hair and deepset blue eyes. Genial and amusing but more reserved than Gretl, Rolf was for her the perfect foil. He adored his wife's titanic energy — her flights — yet he always stood ready, when the need arose, to pull her gently back to earth. A clubman active in city affairs, Rolf was on occasion an amusing feuilletonist; and like Karl Wittgenstein, he wrote periodic essays on political and economic questions — matters on which the two men seldom agreed. Rolf was also something of a *Wandervogel* — he loved to walk the mountains and sometimes, much to Gretl's dismay, shot stag in Hungary, where he and his family had extensive business interests, chiefly in coal, which of course coincided with Karl Wittgenstein's own interests, though not always happily.

Charming, self-contained Rolf, a man immune to Karl Wittgenstein in ways that seemed miraculous to his mum son. Many times Wittgenstein had thought that Rolf was exactly the sort of son his father would have wanted. Yet even so, the old bull could not easily cede his territory to this affable intruder. And so there was always the prodding and probing, the old man implying that while what Rolf said was perfectly true and even rather shrewd — at least so far as it went — it was still a little, well ... *off the mark*. Not through any intrinsic fault of his, Karl Wittgenstein would affably suggest. After all, Rolf could hardly be held accountable for the fact that he still lacked seasoning and some requisite — but, for him, probably unobtainable — information. Still less could Rolf compensate for lacking that comprehensive and indeed synoptic view that came with more years than he, unfortunately, would ever have, because of course Karl Wittgenstein would always have more years and, moreover, would carry to his grave the wisdom that worked in the days when the world truly worked as it should — that is, before irresponsible bunglers like Rolf got their hooks into things.

Karl Wittgenstein's sons might brook this treatment, but Rolf would not. For all his good-natured forbearance, he would press back when Karl Wittgenstein pressed too hard, questioning Rolf's business judgment or suggesting that he might exert more control over his excitable wife and their equally excitable son. Oh, Rolf would groan fatuously, if only I had consulted you! Again and again, I ask myself — I ask my staff — now what, *what* would Karl Wittgenstein do?

Wittgenstein found this shocking. But even more stunning was how, after jabbing back, Rolf would go on eating, not wounded or angry and not harboring any apparent resentment against his father-in-law. And Karl Wittgenstein took it! True, he would be hot under the collar, but never was there the kind of fiery eruption that his son expected. Even with this probably inevitable tussling, Wittgenstein could see that the two men clearly did like and admire each other. Like the horsemen he'd just seen in the Prater, they were men of another world who operated and communicated according to rules, assumptions and manners that clearly he did not, and never would, entirely understand. Hard as this was for Wittgenstein to accept, he still could see it, just as he could grudgingly see that Rolf was the perfect rudder for his sister, a woman who would have overwhelmed a lesser man. In this last respect, Karl Wittgenstein wasn't the only rival Rolf faced. Rolf's biggest rival in the family was Wittgenstein himself. There was no way for Wittgenstein to rationally approach the matter; there was nothing rational about it at all. He was completely allergic to Rolf. Couldn't stand him.

Everyone in the family was aware of this, especially Rolf. Still, knowing where these feelings sprang from, Rolf didn't really hold it against his young rival. But for Gretl this emnity toward her husband brought no end of awkwardness, unhappiness and frustration. Wittgenstein felt bad about this, and in his way he did try to get along with Rolf, especially now that Stefan was approaching an age where he could intuit adult feelings. But it was no good. Even now, standing there, Wittgenstein could feel his palms perspiring as Rolf approached.

Ludwig, said Rolf easily, extending his hand.

Frohe Weihnachten, replied Wittgenstein, trying to show some seasonal friendliness. But this concealed nothing, Wittgenstein thought with chagrin; Rolf could sense his true feelings through his clammy, perspiring palm. Then they were talking, talking easily and inconsequentially, it seemed. Yet Wittgenstein had to stop himself, realizing that he was faintly rising up and down on his toes, as if to measure himself against his brother-in-law, who was actually shorter than he. The manly Rolf did not bounce or squirm. Rolf did not suffer. Rolf, he felt, had perfect emotional aplomb. *He* would never prowl the Prater or wind up in the ladies' toilet.

Fortunately for Wittgenstein, this conversation was cut short when Gretl entered the room, followed by her father, who was saying, Fine. If you like it so much, then display it in your home.

It is displayed in my home, she said, holding up a Menorah. Why can't we have one here?

Putting Rolf on the spot, Karl Wittgenstein then turned to him and said, You're her husband. Please, tell me. Am I being unreasonable?

Oh, I don't know, offered Rolf diplomatically. It is your home.

Gretl shot him a dirty look, then turned to her father and continued, I can't see the harm in it. We used to light it as children.

Cor-rect, Karl Wittgenstein injected. When you were children, it is true we lit a Menorah on several occasions when your grandfather and aunt were here. It was for them — for believers — that we did this. But now there are no believers.

What do you mean? asked Gretl. There's a half believer in me. Wittgenstein saw her turn to him for support, but he looked away, irked that she should press the matter when their father was in his usual state over the holiday preparations.

All right, Gretl conceded. There are no relatives here. But that's more a circumstance than a reason. I'm sorry, I suppose I'm still trying to discern your reason.

Oh, *of course,* Karl Wittgenstein sniffed. Always you want reasons. Very well. It's *unnecessary.* There's your reason.

Oh, please — Gretl's face tightened with frustration. That's an evasion, not a reason.

Karl Wittgenstein stood there, plainly wondering whether to pursue this. Finally he said, Gretl, if you wish to join the Allianz or the B'nai B'rith and help Galician refugees, this is your right. If you wish to convert, this is your right also. But that has no place here, not in this house. That affair is over. This is a Christian house, and this is Christmas, not Chanukah.

But why not a Menorah? she asked, and Wittgenstein flashed her a look for pressing it.

Why? he returned, indicating by his bearing that he'd heard quite enough. Why? Because it's — *inconsistent.* Karl Wittgenstein nodded, so pleased with this answer that he even repeated it, saying, That's my point. It's inconsistent.

Leaning out over her toes as if she had just found herself at the edge of a precipice, Gretl said, Oh. Just, Oh, and then, to everyone's surprise, she left without another word and put the Menorah away.

The Blocker

THEN IT WAS TIME to dress for Fräulein Ketteler, time to stand as his father's champion since all others had fled the field. This was barrier enough, but as Wittgenstein mounted the scrolling, red-carpeted stairs, he encountered one more obstacle.

Wittgenstein could remember how Hans, some nine years his elder, used to block his way on the stairs when he was a child of four or five. Oh, excuse me, Hans would say, stepping in his way. Oh, excuse me again, as he stepped the other way. Excuse me and excuse me, until his little brother would burst into tears, flailing and screaming. This was all the Blocker wanted: with the first cry he would be gone, leaving Wittgenstein, the Blocked, wailing on the vertiginous red stairs.

Eventually, of course, the Blocker was caught and punished, but he just found other ways to block, sometimes enlisting his younger brother Rudi as an accomplice. Wittgenstein would be lying in his bed when he would see the door, hooked by an unseen wire, slowly but inexorably slam shut. *Stop! Stop!* Jumping up, he would hurl himself against the door, frantically pushing and beating as if all the air were slowly being extinguished. *Bitte, Hans,* he would sob. *Please, let me out . . .*

Nothing. Not a sound as he pressed his ear against the cold wood, nothing but the jammed door and the ceiling crowding down. He knew, if he had any sense, he would wait out the Blocker. But this was impossible — never could he hope to outwait the Blocker. Almost immediately, his bladder would be ignominiously bleating and then he would panic, fearing that it wasn't the Blocker but a ghost, or that the house was on fire! *Hans!* Beating and begging until fear turned to rage. Heaving himself against the door until it finally burst open, and he pitched headlong over the chair Hans had propped against it.

But what Wittgenstein most remembered was how Hans would "steal" his nose, tearing it off, then displaying it, a beet-red thumb pinched between his middle and index finger. *See the nosy? See?* Even at age three, the boy half knew it was a thumb and not his nose, but still he begged and grabbed for it, finding it intolerable that with mere words his brother could steal a piece of him.

This was much the same feeling Wittgenstein would have at seven or eight, when for long spells Hans would so thoroughly ignore the boy that he would begin to wonder at his own existence, as if Hans had snuffed his soul. But the Blocker himself was blocked. Looking back on it, Wittgenstein imagined that even Hans must have felt sickened at his compulsion to steal innocence from a child. Hans would be caught periodically, but this, too, seemed part of the game. Wittgenstein could still see his brother, smiling like a malign saint as his father whipped him with his stinging braces, smiling in the sweet knowledge that he had inflicted more pain than he received, as if experience were an exchange bank in which one might somehow profit on the margin. It got very confused. Sometimes the boy would strike back at the Blocker, but the Blocker always struck harder and more deeply. At first, retribution was swift, but then the Blocker learned he could torment his brother even more by withholding punishment. *Somewhere . . . sometime,* the Blocker would threaten, his Adam's apple bouncing with that gargling, girly voice, the manhood that was being withheld from him. Sometime, I'll get you for this, *Liebchen,* and I won't even tell you what I'll do . . .

Unable to bear the suspense, the boy would break down, begging for forgiveness or punishment, begging to be given back his purloined nose or soul, which assumed an even more radical form once religion took root. In his catechism, the boy had heard Monsignor Molke describe sin as a nail driven into the soft wood of the soul. Confession could remove the nail but not the mark of the nail. The only thing that could do this was purgatory, which the boy imagined as a simmering pot in which soiled souls were placed to cleanse these suppurating wounds that kept them from heaven. The boy knew his soul was filled with gaping holes, but these were nothing compared with the Blocker's soul. The Blocker's soul, the boy told himself, was black with nails — a hairy black corset of nails. Wittgenstein wasn't entirely sure where, or at what age, he formed this image of Hans in a corset, but there was more to it than this. As he dressed for Fräulein Ketteler, Wittgenstein recalled how, at age eight, he and Paul, along with several other girls and boys from the neighborhood, were given waltzing lessons by an Italian dancing master named Herr Passarelli. Yet here, too, the Blocker called the tune. Finding his younger brother dressing upstairs, the Blocker would pull him close, saying in an overheated voice, I am the dancing master and you must dance with *me!* Oh, my dear, he would say, swaying as he pushed him, pinioned, around the floor. Oh, but don't you love to dance . . . And you love to waltz with . . . that's right — with a jerk — that's right, you love to waltz with *boys,* is it? With wee *little* boys? Oh, no, no! It is with big, *big* boys you love to waltz!

Wittgenstein could still feel that dog clutching, dancing so close sometimes that he imagined he could feel the nails of Hans's soul scraping his face. Downstairs later, his mother would play for them on her piano, sometimes even singing in a wavering contralto. *Und hier, und hier,* would come Herr Passarelli's monotonous voice as the boy fumbled along, holding the sweaty hand and sweatier back of some equally nervous girl. And even then he would see the Blocker loitering by the french doors, slyly nodding, as if to say, *I* know with whom you wish to dance, *Liebchen,* oh, yes, I know . . .

•

The Blocker was still with him that night as he stood with his parents at the threshold of the great room before the glowing tree and the rustling fire. More palpably there was also the person of his father, slick as a whiskered seal in his white tie and tails. Showing his son how these things were done, Karl Wittgenstein was insufferably charming, especially to Fräulein Ketteler, a comely redhead with a long, dramatic throat and hazel eyes. Wittgenstein could feel her excited expectancy, slightly tremulous as he made his little bow and wanly took her hand. And later, by the fire while his father carried on like a one-man band, he saw her snitch looks at him, the promised, as he inwardly asked her, *What's wrong with you? . . . Don't you know what I am? . . . Don't you know yet?*

Supper was interminable. Yet here again Fräulein Ketteler, sitting opposite him, seemed to be drawn to him almost in direct proportion to his own aloofness as he answered, with mounting irritation, her parents' excruciatingly correct questions. And why was he studying logic? And why, of all places, in England?

Why were they even asking these questions? he wondered. If Fräulein Ketteler herself didn't see, didn't *they?* And after England? asked Herr Ketteler, making Wittgenstein feel like a piece of meat that was not only to be consumed but was expected to attest to its own wholesomeness. But it was Karl Wittgenstein who acted as his son's advocate, wisely saying to Herr Ketteler, Well, we *change* in youth, don't we? The strong suggestion being that this philosophy nonsense would soon run its course. Why, to hear him, his son was still a chrysalis with foggy eyes; with several years and a good woman, he would come around. He had the blood. The brains, too. Yes, with time, Karl Wittgenstein suggested, he would become a stout man of affairs, just like his father.

Well, as I say, added Karl Wittgenstein, it never pays to fish behind another man's nets.

It was not clear from the context what his father meant, nor did Herr Ketteler seem to know himself. But this did not prevent these two successful older men from exchanging as a countersign that hearty, knowing smile which is its own benediction, as Herr Ketteler chimed in, So true! And so do we learn not to fire one arrow vainly after another.

Here, here. Tut, tut. And so again the two fathers, wine warmed, enjoyed another pregnant moment while the stewing suitor flushed crimson over his own, specially bland soup.

And then came the part Wittgenstein dreaded most, when he and Fräulein Ketteler — "the young folk" — were nervously ushered like stud and mare into the library, there ostensibly to talk their young talk while the old people waited, wondering if their blood would take. Wittgenstein might as well have blundered once more into the powder room for all the competence he felt here, sitting with his knees clasped together, mired in his own impossibility. And again, imagining himself as a kind of fact betrayed by its own self-evidence, he thought, *Doesn't she see?* Yet to judge by Fräulein Ketteler's talk about opera and museums, *Die Fackel* and the latest novels — broad hints about shared interests and things they might do together — clearly Fräulein Ketteler did not *see* at all. But if not, he thought, wasn't it possible that he might see her? Surely, life could evolve. It wasn't just Fräulein Ketteler or respectability he craved, it was being propelled into new life — being freed of the imprisoning form of the old. And a push, a mere push was all he needed. After all, he told himself, there was no need to plunge straight to the bottom; like cold water, intimacy with a woman could be entered slowly. She would be patient. Over a few years, he might get on, might even marry and father children — might, in short, be a credit and not an encumbrance to his family, perpetuating their name. Fräulein Ketteler was not a life prowling the Prater meadows; Fräulein Ketteler was a chance. But here again, these fantasies were broken by an image of a slender figure standing by the french doors. It was the Blocker, and he was nodding, smiling in the knowledge that by taking his own life he had stolen forever another life, which he still dangled before his little brother like his own nose.

The Golem

CHRISTMAS PASSED. Fräulein Ketteler passed. Further notes from his father passed, but this feeling of failure, this seeming interdict on his life, did not pass. And then, not long before Wittgenstein returned to England, Gretl took him out again, this time to a play.

It was Gretl's idea, and he was immediately suspicious when she told him the play was to be a surprise. Still, Wittgenstein went along, until Gretl's driver, who had been heading northeast around the Ring, crossed the Danube Canal into the heart of the Leopoldstadt. This was Vienna's main Jewish district, once the old ghetto, and it was near no theaters that Wittgenstein knew of. Still, Gretl managed to quiet him until they reached the Hotel Stefanie, a worn-out place on the Taborstrasse with a dark façade of glazed block and narrow, smeary windows hung with tessellated curtains.

What is this? he asked, looking at the crude billboard with its clotted Hebrew lettering. Along the sidewalk, people were gathered under the dangling light globes that lined the hotel's façade like an old string of beads, some dully aglow, some missing.

This is my surprise, said Gretl. It's the Jüdisches-Theater Variété — Yiddish theater. Tonight they're hosting a production of *The Golem of Prague*.

Wittgenstein felt betrayed: he thought Gretl was deliberately trying to trap him. Tell me, he demanded. Why did you bring me here?

Why do you think? she retorted. Already, her voice was getting squeaky. I thought you might *enjoy* it. Then accusingly, Are you going to spoil the evening?

It's already spoiled. Shaking his head. A jargon play.

Gretl made a face. Don't use that word. And you can follow the Yiddish, you can. She laid her hand on his arm. Ludi, would I bring you here just to antagonize you?

He softened at this sisterly appeal. And he was tired, so tired. He did not want to fight with Gretl, but neither did he want to go in and be enveloped with these people who conjured images of fever, overcooked cabbage and quibbling. Here with their wives in their lumpy furs were more assimilated Jews, solid burghers in their Homburgs and cravats. And here, too, were the *shtetl* Jews, bearded peddlers and traders fresh from Galicia, Bukovina and Moravia, in their black felt hats and long frock coats. The men stood in a huddle, talking animatedly while their round wives, wrapped in shawls and bunchy coats, stood off at a respectful distance. Now all these people were casting glances at the long black car with its gleaming grille and bulbous tires. Already he could feel them staring at him, fingering their mossy beards. Looking away, he said:

Gretl . . . Gretl, honestly I'm not —

Oh, stop it! Do you ever listen to yourself? Ever since you've been home you've been like this.

His eyes were swimming, he was so furious. Why do you think I wanted to stay in England? Did it ever occur to you — to any of you — that I might have known what was best? I was fine in England.

Stop! You were not fine in England. You were not fine last summer.

What do you know? You just can't imagine I'd be fine for long away from them. *Or* you.

Or me — You know, she said, shaking her finger at him, you know, I resent being implicated in your absurd, imaginary scourges. All of us against you! All of us guilty! What were you looking for when you went into the ladies' toilet? Oh, I realize it's not abstract and complicated enough for your mind. Of course it's easier to think about logic than about your life — it's certainly much safer, don't you think, *ummm*? You know, she said scathingly, in his own inimitable and wrongheaded way, I think Father's basically right about you.

Oh, I know! he said, taking an involuntary hop in his seat. And of course it's so easy, now that you've sold your soul to the doctors. Yes, do lure little brother to a jargon play so he can wallow in *your* fears and *your* preoccupations. *Ummmmm?* This is your misery, your Menorah — not mine. He turned away. Go light your own candles.

Fine! In her fury, Gretl's eyes fluttered as she seized the speaking tube and told the driver to take them around the block.

Not a word as the car crept through the ghetto quarters, past the darkened shops with their rolled awnings and signs in jagged Hebrew. Gretl was content to leave, but then, spitefully, he was insisting that he wanted to go. No! Gretl said. Absolutely not. But still he persisted, so cocksure that it became a kind of mutual dare, one following the other into this haunted house to prove there was no such thing as ghosts.

But the ghosts were real. Even as they entered, he could feel the place envelop him like a vapor with a smell of heavy, overcooked food, privation and dust. The lady taking tickets, old and wigged, with big bosoms, conspicuously switched from Yiddish to German, putting the interlopers on notice that they had been spotted. Eyeing the overblown placard for the play, showing a giant Jew with maniacal eyes throttling some stricken Gentile, he again wondered, Why did they huddle so, these people? And all the while he kept hearing this coarse, splattery jargon, so animated, with that catarrh as though a fishbone were stuck in the throat. There was a man selling hot tea from a samovar and another vending sticky cakes and ices. And the eating — everybody eating, gnawing apples and chewing sweet crackling dumplings from greasy sheets of brown paper. And that marshy barn-warmth of people huddling. It was too close for him.

Can't we sit down? he asked suddenly.

If you wish. Gretl faced him. You're all right?

This was his chance, but as they entered the little theater, his pride prevented him from admitting that he felt ill. Doubling as a hall for weddings, brisses and bar mitzvahs, it was a dusty little place that had the feeling and smell of a gutted pumpkin, what with the peeling paint and tattered wall coverings. On the stage, behind an open halfhearted curtain, was a crudely painted backdrop of a ghetto scene — listing huts and stoops, a fence.

Gretl, incorrigible guide, was saying: The play is based on the legend — you've heard it, the legend of the golem of Prague? It has a factual basis. In Prague in the 1700s, the Jews were being blood-libeled by Christians. It happened quite routinely. A Christian might swear a Jew had stolen his child to use the blood to make matzos. There would be a pogrom or the Jew might be burned at the stake —

Yes, yes, he said suddenly. You needn't rehearse this for me.

Fine! Gretl swung around.

Sorry for his rudeness, he said, I didn't mean to be short with you. Striving for a more conciliatory tone, he said, The golem — it's a kind of beast or something, isn't it?

But Gretl wouldn't answer, and he sat there, feeling impossible even to himself while trying to graciously decline some sort of seed cake that an agreeable but insistent old man was pushing at him. Then, in the din of the outer hall, a man could be heard shouting — the play was about to start. The crowd flooded through the doors. People were squeezing in around them, when Wittgenstein suddenly realized he was much too close to the coal stove, which a man had just stoked, giving the grate a good rattle as he spat and clamped it shut. The room was packed. Wittgenstein didn't think he'd be able to stand this heat pulsing along his back as the lights dimmed and the play began. Lumbering across the stage, bent low, a black-bearded butcher with a bloody smock was hauling over his back the papier-mâché carcass of a slaughtered pig. Already Wittgenstein was hating it, feeling a hot constriction. Beast! cried someone in the front row. The audience hissed. Muttering his foul plans, the villainous butcher stole into the graveyard, where he stuffed the body of a Christian child into the pig's carcass, then left it where one of his henchmen would claim to find it — the bloody work of the Jew.

The play was bad, but the schtick acting was even worse, as false and buffoonish as the actors' puttied noses, horsehair beards and gestures heavenward at the least provocation. No art here. This was no play, and this was not the famed Vilna Troupe. These actors were only people cut from the herd to act out the fears of the herd huddled here to be told of their humiliations, disasters and small triumphs between disasters. Listing and crooked, billowing with every draft, even the slapdash huts of that ghetto backdrop took on an unintended nightmarishness to Wittgenstein, in whose mind the play paradoxically carried more weight than even the playwright knew, let alone these actors. Unable to take refuge behind critical judgments, Wittgenstein now found himself naked before the legend, the heat licking up his back as Rabbi Loew, known as the *Maharal,* dreamed of creating a golem who would destroy the butcher, the sorcerer-priest Thaddeus and all the enemies of Israel.

Resisting the onslaught of this stealthy dream, Wittgenstein closed then opened his eyes, felt his hands tingle and the blood slowly drain from his head while the rabbi and his cohorts met in the darkness to create their golem. Sweeping a pile of dust into the form of a man, they walked seven times around the mound, circling from left to right while reciting cabalistic incantations. When the spotlight went out, a woman in the audience let out an involuntary cry; then in the audience there was a nervous buzzing and rattling of paper as onstage, under a growing stain of light, the dust pile began to move.

Behold! howled the *Maharal. Behold!* trumpeted Isaac ben Shimshon ha-Cohen, clutching his breast the better to upstage the *Maharal,* as meanwhile Cohen's disciple, Jacob ben Chayyim ha-Levi, tripped on his flowing robes. Rearing back in stupefied grease-paint amazement, they looked up, their fingers like gnarled branches, as he drunkenly arose on woodblocks, a gaping giant seven feet tall.

Yosele Golem, the people called him. Mindless mute idiot. Being without soul. A heavy lump with a fringe of dark hair, the young man who played the golem had no talent, but then the part called for a lifeless nothing. Wittgenstein was overwhelmed. It was not what the actor brought or didn't bring to the role; it was Wittgenstein's own emptiness that brought the golem to life. The proscenium disappeared: down came the screen that shields the viewer from the engulfment of seeing. This was not a matter of disbelief willingly suspended. Wittgenstein was now so inexorably drawn to the golem's pain that there was nothing to hold him back, his mind guttering like a candle as the play lumbered along.

Yosele Golem, he knew nothing, did nothing but what he was told, clopping along so trustingly on clubbed feet. When the *Rebbitzen,* the *Maharal's* wife, told the golem to carry water, he carried it, bucket after bucket, until she opened the door and was blown back with a whoosh of imaginary water. *Oy!* Up went the hands, more schtick. Even for Gretl this was too much. Feeling the heat herself, she nudged him, whispering that she was ready to leave. But he waved her off. Why? she asked. He was staying only to spite her, as the golem predictably caught the butcher red-handed, then exposed the wicked priest Thaddeus.

Ludi, she whispered, giving him a nudge. Can't we go, *please?*

But he still didn't hear, knowing no more than the golem did why he carried these empty buckets. What happened then? Why did Wittgenstein feel this paralysis when onstage the *Maharal* said that the golem, having avenged Israel, must return like Adam to the dust. And why was the golem so compliant, showing an almost stupefied relief when the rabbi bade him lie down so they could unweave his frail life. Dumb and trusting, the golem just lay there, staring up almost sweetly as they circled him, this time walking in the opposite direction while covering him with crumbling pages torn from old prayer books.

Gretl's first thought was that Wittgenstein was mocking the ending when he lapsed back in his seat with his arms sprawling. Everything stopped then. Looking around helplessly as some men laid him, pale and sweating, across three chairs, Gretl realized that the whole play had stopped. Even the golem was watching, sitting up in his nest of paper, when Wittgenstein himself finally sat up, saying in a groggy, underwater voice, I'm fine . . . Thank you, I'm fine . . . Please, let me up . . .

For five minutes he was captive to their solicitousness. For five hard minutes he *was* the play, Yosele Golem. Later, Wittgenstein remembered a bald and bespectacled doctor peering in his eyes as some woman brought up a cup of warmish water and a cookie for his blood sugar. Staring into that bower of faces, his ears tipped red with piquant mortification, Wittgenstein felt like a figure in a manger. Out of the sky he had fallen in with these queer folk and their play. Happy applause when it was announced the young man was all right. Under dimming lights, the play then resumed. And then once more the crumbling paper came flaking down, mounting and drifting like old dust, slowly covering the golem's somnolent face as one dream seamlessly merged with the other.

Bipolarity

A FEW WEEKS LATER, Russell excitedly wrote Ottoline:

Today Wittgenstein brought me that paper he was to write so I could decide whether he is to be a philosopher or an aeronaut. I am pleased to report that, after reading his paper, I strenuously advised him to pursue the former course. The paper was short — 2 pp. only — & as usual, he merely stated his conclusions — fairly picked from the air — shown with some equations. His main idea, in essence, is that propositions have a true & a false pole. By this he means — I *think* — that to truly understand a proposition, we must know what it means to be true & false. Thus propositions contain, in advance, both senses of truth & falsity. He says this means that logic is devoid of subject matter — a sort of empty hole that can accommodate events & nonevents alike. In connexion with this point, Wittgenstein then drew two boxes as follows:

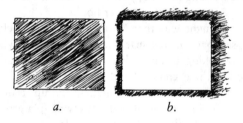

a.   b.

a. here wd. correspond with a *negative* fact, a solid body with no room within it for a body or possibility; & *b.* with a *positive* fact, one that has room for a body or possibility.

Understand that the ideas are germinal & still a bit jumbled. Nor are either of us entirely clear on all the ramifications of the foregoing. Nevertheless, this is, I think, a truly original & important contribution that may give us another look into the hole of logical form. One thing we see is that a proposition is not a name for a fact. The reason for this is that there are *two* propositions corresponding to each fact. Suppose it is a fact that Socrates is dead. You have two propositions: "Socrates is dead" & "Socrates is not dead." And with those two propositions corresponding to the same fact, there is one fact in the world wch. makes one true & one false. That is not accidental, & it shows how this two-pole relation of a proposition to a fact is a totally different one from the one-to-one relation of a name to the thing named.

To the layman, these ideas may seem evident, even trivial, but like many an important discovery we forget that somebody had to think of it. He is a lightning rod — it gives me chills to hear him & I feel what it is to be young again & vital. "Two poles!" he shouted. "Every proposition has two poles!" I thought for a moment he wd. smash the furniture, he was so excited.

He was so pent up — I gather he had an awful holiday since he virtually refused to discuss it. I thought of sharing with him some of my *own* new ideas, but then I held back, knowing the ferocity with which he treats germinal ideas — except of course his own. He told me then that he has further ideas — so much is coming free in him. I suppose I should have held my tongue, but I sd. that while intuition is the seed of many great ideas, he ought not simply state what he thinks is true but also give the proper arguments. But he sd. arguments wd. only spoil its beauty; he wd. feel he was dirtying a flower with muddy hands, especially one still only days old. Wittgenstein does so appeal to me — the artist in intellect is so very rare. I told him I hadn't the heart to say anything against that, & that he had better acquire a slave to state his arguments. But he was in no mood then to be lectured, even if it was well intentioned. Joking, I sd., "You don't suppose I will write out your arguments for you, do you?" He sd., "How could you? Then they wd. be your ideas. Which is to say they would be your problems." I sd., feeling rather hurt, "Do we not share the same problems?" He looked so pained, so concerned for me, then sd. rather mysteriously, "I certainly hope for your sake we do not."

It made me melancholy for some reason, this wish that we might shoulder the same burden. Could I reconstruct Wittgenstein's vision from a fragment in the way a paleontologist might produce a whole mammal from a knucklebone? I suppose it's my fear that he shall not last, & that I shall have to do something of the sort. I do fear for him.

But still, my love, there are limits to induction & I am happy I have you, if only reconstructed from a scented letter. But this is, as you say, a Sir Philip Sidneyism — a mild reproach to one's fair mistress. Still, I need more than a lock to rape or handkerchief to hold. So when, prithee, shall it sithee? Saturdee? . . .

Russell had the results — the knucklebone — but, as Wittgenstein said, Russell did not have the history that gave rise to the life, of which bipolarity was just a fragment. Perhaps this was why Wittgenstein was so evasive when Russell asked how he had come upon his idea. Acting as if it was quite beside the point, Wittgenstein said, I was walking in the Prater. I wasn't *looking* for the idea, if that is what you ask.

Perhaps Russell should have asked not how or where but why and at what cost Wittgenstein's idea had come to him. No answer, Wittgenstein would come to realize, is a virgin birth; every answer comes as a response to a discrete set of problems. An answer, like a life, is a prism. Seen one way it seems sound, a complete solution. Seen from another vantage point, however, it is only a further bewitchment, one step forward and one step back.

Still, Wittgenstein had told the bare truth. The concept of bipolarity had come to him while he was walking in the Prater. This was several days after *The Golem of Prague,* and Wittgenstein was still haunted by that image of the empty golem hauling the *Rebbitzen's* heavy buckets. Pain was in the buckets. The buckets were as brimming full as Wittgenstein was empty. In one hand was a bucket full for the living; in the other hand was an empty bucket for the looming dead who block the path of the living. And then the door opened, and out burst bountiful white water, the grass inundated. To have a thought is one thing, but it is another to say what that thought means or portends. Full or empty, both buckets were as full with meaning as he, the hauler of buckets, was then hollow enough — receptive enough — to divine their meaning.

It had been dusk when he returned to the Prater, that hour when respectable people are bundled up and heading home. In the early winter darkness, the Ferris wheel, that whirling constellation of lights, pitched down for its last ride, and then the white lights blinked out. The sun was almost spent. Looking up, he saw a weak red light that just tinged the treetops, and above that, a dry winter sky sliding beneath a hazy half circle of moon. Ahead, across the meadows, he could dimly see the distant peaks of the easternmost Alps, as his mind, like a dog sled, pulled him along, still thinking, he solemnly told itself, about logical form and the mystery of negation. He remembered thinking that the problem was really one of a profound simplicity, a thing so simple that it seemed almost insurmountable. And then in that unaccountable way in which things dawned on him, appearing as if planned in queer relief, he looked down and noticed how the snow outlined an empty footprint. White space had formed around a black space where once a foot had stood. The logical space might admit the foot; or it might negate it by saying, The foot must not stand in this spot. And then, feeling as if he had touched cold iron, it struck him: the sublime oddity of being able to say, *This is* not *how things are, and yet we can say* how *things are* not.

The space of logic was large, offering both unlimited space and possibility — or no possibility. It was the Blocker again, holding the purloined nose just close enough to elicit belief yet not close enough to dispel doubt. And then, with a shiver, Wittgenstein saw the trees had also lost their light as the wind reared up and the boughs cast down their bony branches. *Tack tack tack* came the wind across the crystallized pond, and he pulled his head down into his coat. No evading it. His eyes now settled on a spot where he saw not empty footprints but a pair of formless boots filled with stout legs. Here was a possibility, one before which he saw no possibility. And as with that empty footprint, Wittgenstein then saw a logical space that he would fill, crouched before this stranger who now approached like Mammon, giving no name as he unburdened himself in the roaring darkness.

Walking home later, not so much sorry as empty, Wittgenstein wondered if a man might build around his life a machine by which he might become decent. The full bucket, this was easy to fathom; but to realize that in emptiness also there was pain — this he did not expect. Nor was it much recompense when his germinal idea came to him, and he saw, like a piece of logic, what it is to be both true and false, as well as empty.

Furniture

WITH WITTGENSTEIN'S DISCOVERY, then, Russell ceased to think of him as a student. From this time on, he treated him as a full equal, if not sometimes more than an equal. Yet with this acceptance other tensions emerged as the two put their heads to the same questions.

They were tremendously idealistic. As they both saw it, ego and pride had no place in a great collaboration. To differing degrees, they both recognized the dangers but felt that with humility there was certainly room enough in the wide world (and one full of such tremendous technical problems) for two to fit into the same trousers — at least so long as they could agree on the cut.

Fortunately, Russell was an experienced collaborator. And collaboration was so very modern: it was the method of science, that collegial relay race of progress. After all, for a single mind to try to unite all the spheres of philosophy or put forth one unassailable view that the world is like *this* — that was the legacy of the *old* philosophy, of the system builders in whose fantastic contraptions logical error cavorted with religious belief, superstition and blind prejudice. In a sense, Russell was like the proverbial general fighting the last battle and the last enemy: even now, years later, he was still beating back those now vanquished idealists like McTaggart, who held that the external, physical world was but a figment of the mind. Surely, Russell felt, it was most pleasant to sit in the parlor with our teacups perched on our knees while imagining the world as a phantasmagorical dance animated by the brain. Perhaps, as Dostoyevsky opined, men do crave miracle, mystery and authority, but if Ars Philosophia was ever to stroll with Dame Science into the sunlight of this new century, Russell felt that philosophers would finally have to pledge themselves to sobriety — to renounce their mundane personal desires for power, salvation and the *presto* of metaphysic. Still, Russell found it hard to take his logical-empirical philosophical science cold. Increasingly now, the scientist had to taste, nay, to squeeze the bosomy grapes of mystery.

Having endured years of abstinence plying abstract mathematics, Russell found it hard to curb this sudden desire to seize the pulpit and speak baldly from the heart. Wittgenstein was still young. He remained fresh and uncompromising in his fervor, not yet realizing that, at its ecliptic, the mind must bend like the rainbow, stretching always back to earth. And really, it was a difference of style: whereas Russell was the Enlightenment man who felt that everything could be rationally discussed and attained through diligent effort, Wittgenstein, that most impatient of men, was the desert mystic subsisting on bread, rainwater and silence. Professing to expect nothing, preaching only patience and submission, Wittgenstein was like a child peeping through a blindfold, hoping against hope to be granted his guilty metaphysical wishes.

If anything, Russell was incomparably more modest and earthbound in his expectations. Wittgenstein's power, by comparison, was the priest's power, a distillation of abstinence and self-denial. Better, thought Wittgenstein, to fast — to anticipate that meal — than to wolf it down and still be hungry. Better a fresh promise than a bitter afterward, cursing the barren tree.

As Wittgenstein saw it, Russell had broken fast over the holidays, first completing *The Problems of Philosophy,* a popular book on the subject that he had begun that summer, then writing an article entitled "The Essence of Religion." Russell gave Wittgenstein *The Problems of Philosophy* almost as soon as it came back from the typist. And, predictably enough, Wittgenstein disliked it, feeling it was impossible to provide a popular treatment that wasn't more misleading than illuminating. But above all, Wittgenstein hated the book's final chapter, "The Value of Philosophy."

How can you *say* that philosophy has a *value?* he asked. This you can *say* no more than a proposition can *say* it is correct. It is not for the proposition to say; it is for the proposition to be judged. With philosophy it is the same. Either a person sees its value or he does not. Philosophy does not need *you* to say it has a value. You only muck it up.

Wittgenstein was even more shocked by "The Essence of Religion." The moment Russell put the manuscript in Wittgenstein's hands, he knew he had made a mistake. Three hours later, Russell heard an urgent knock. In burst Wittgenstein, the typescript flapping in his hand.

I'm sorry, he said, taking a deep breath. I'm very, very sorry . . .

You don't like it, said Russell, trying to soften the blow.

Like it? Wittgenstein threw down his arms. *I detest it!*

There was silence then, that trapped, hopeless look as Wittgenstein brought up more words:

It's completely glib — superficial. Your terms — they're wholly inexact. What do you mean, *freedom from the finite self*? What self is this you speak of? Here we work to build a world *based* on something — and then you write *this*! I am very sorry, but, please, you must not print this. Even if they want to publish it, you must not . . .

As Wittgenstein was making his ultimatum, Russell could hear this same criticism well up from some buried annex within him. In a gush of ego and arbitrariness, Russell felt he should at least defend himself against this onslaught. And yet it was queerly agreeable, like his fantasies of being crushed beneath a train. Later, in his nightly letter to Ottoline, Russell wrote:

I must stop, I must. Much as I hate to admit it, Wittgenstein is right about the paper, & I have already written the journal, requesting that it be withdrawn. I had planned to expand it into a book, but I see this is quite impossible; & damn it, he *is* right — I am sure it is for the best. I understand your concern, my love — I know at times he can be destructive, but he does not intend it. In his way, he is really very gentle, & he was so hurt to think badly of me, that I could write such a thing.

As for your other fears, I agree that I am influenced by him, but not, I think, overly. Harsh as it may be, truth is never harmful. If Wittgenstein is right, then he is right, & that is the end of it. I can hardly complain if he is right, can I?

So Russell abandoned the book. And with that he began to cede even more to Wittgenstein. To Wittgenstein he would bequeath the purely logical end of their work. Let Wittgenstein undertake those questions which require youth and freshness of approach — that is, the purely philosophical pursuit of what propositions are and what forms they take, as well as the related problem of developing a system of logical notation by which one logical form could never be mistaken for another.

But Russell had another reason for giving ground. He was restless. More and more now, Russell wanted to rove in places where the field was still open, where the sod was not broken by his own repeated attempts. With this in mind, Russell was now interested in taking logic into the realm of matter and epistemology, searching for a more scientific understanding of the great question of whether humans can really *know* anything, and, if so, what?

Not long after the publication of *The Principles of Mathematics* in

1903, Russell had retreated from his belief that every phrase in a sentence achieves its meaning by denoting something that in some way exists. The problem, again, was the one raised by denoting phrases like *the present king of France,* which give rise to those never-never zones where fictions run pell-mell with absurdities.

Russell's theory of descriptions was a method of logical code breaking: it broke down a troublesome expression like *the present king of France* into sensible substatements; or at least made its patent nonsense more apparent. More recently, Russell had tried to take matters a step further — and to a rather different vantage point — by developing a model of the act of judging. As with the theory of descriptions, Russell was partly concerned with problems of nonsense: specifically, how one can judge what is not the case. Unlike the theory of descriptions, however, the theory of judgment was not fully elaborated but rather a still rough sketch of the directions such a theory might take. Yet now, with Wittgenstein freeing him to pursue other things, Russell wanted to rework his judgment theory, the idea being to create a model that could embrace not only the logical relation of, say, $A = B,$ or even the comparatively uncomplicated acquaintance of an ego with an object. Instead, Russell wanted a theory that could encompass the additional, and still more complex, mental act of *judging* that relation. In this way, Russell hoped to connect the judging mind with logic and the external world, thereby wedding the abstract concept of, say, "greenness" with the physical particulars of real grass — fragrant, new-mown grass redolent of grass and greenness, the whole whiffed through the sensorium of eye, nose and mind. Indeed, this quest had even assumed a certain parallel with Russell's conflict with Ottoline. Russell did not want a rarefied idealist's world that would remain locked like a virgin in the tower of the mind; he wanted Rapunzel to let down her hair, revealing a world that might be climbed, ravished, eaten.

But again Russell was practical. He knew these questions would only be solved progressively, with a theory and then an improved theory, and so on.

Wittgenstein had no such practicality. He put no stock in the notion that he was part of that trumped-up tinker's guild known as a *profession.* He found repugnant the notion that he was to work in fraternal amity and cooperation with learned colleagues who purportedly shared the same general aspirations, and who, with time, would help him perfect his ideas, and even extend them.

Never!

For Wittgenstein the work had to be delivered whole and complete! A virgin birth, no more, no less.

He was such a bloody perfectionist — so utterly lacking in that blithe English sense of getting on with it that Russell had in abundance. Refusing to accept compromise of any kind, lashing himself, Wittgenstein was driving himself to the verge of illness with his infernal bucket bearing. It irked Russell that Wittgenstein should persist in this stubborn fast. On the other hand, it sorely irked Wittgenstein to see Russell publish what was less than perfect and indeed often flawed. But in Wittgenstein's reaction there was also more than a hint of jealousy. The truth was, it pained him to see how effortlessly Russell slipped through the world.

Despite appearances, though, Russell was slipping by with mounting difficulty. One big problem was his craving for Wittgenstein's imprimatur, as when he asked Wittgenstein to read the proofs for the third volume of his *Principia Mathematica*. Russell all too readily accepted Wittgenstein's judgment that the book was riddled with errors. If anything, Wittgenstein was more distraught about it than Russell, sick to always be the bearer of bad news. Russell tried to put the best face on it, but for Wittgenstein this only made things worse — he hated Russell's need to put a pleasant face on everything. Surely, Russell said, Wittgenstein could help him put the proofs to right. Yes, Wittgenstein agreed, he *could*. But Wittgenstein also strongly implied that this offended his sense of personal responsibility, his belief that the author alone must deliver the work, and deliver it whole, *without blemish*.

Wittgenstein could be insufferably arrogant about this. So self-righteous as he remonstrated, I can't help you avoid difficulty — or effort.

Having braved the *Principia*, Russell wasn't about to suffer this. He shot back, Tell me this when *you* produce a work. And by *work* I mean something more than two pages!

At this, Wittgenstein burst from his rooms. Russell, fearing the worst, caught him and apologized. Please — it's really not your fault. Nor mine. It's just nerves, don't you see — nothing but nerves.

It's not alone that! Arms akimbo, squeezing himself, Wittgenstein looked as if he were in a straitjacket. Don't you see? The difference is fundamental. *Fundamental!*

I'm *tired*, sighed Russell. Can't you see I'm tired? I've read these proofs again and again. My head *swims* when I see them.

Russell managed to calm him down, and for days afterward they tread on cat feet, blistering at the need for this scaly, false politeness. Adversaries had to be easier than this. And hardest of all they had to be not just colleagues but friends, loving and civil. To regain their equilibrium, they would involve themselves in neutral activities. But even when Wittgenstein suggested a seemingly innocent outing, such as helping him select bedroom furniture, these conflicts emerged in another guise.

Wittgenstein was hardly one to flaunt his wealth, but where furniture or aesthetics was concerned, Russell saw that money was no object. Rather, the problem was finding pieces that satisfied Wittgenstein's severe criteria of harmonious balance, purity of line and absence of ornament, not to mention his equally impossible standards of workmanship. They went to one shop, then another. One chest of drawers had legs too long, another had ugly pulls. Another he found sheathed in almost seamless veneer — a scandal, he said, to have one thing masquerade as another.

Good God, groaned Russell. How organic must a form be? Do you expect oaks to grow in the shapes of chairs and bureaus?

See here, said Russell with a conspiratorial eye to the salesman, an older, balding man of uncommon patience. Russell gestured at a dresser, a magnificent piece. Constructed of red cherry, well lacquered, it was a veritable Stradivarius, with slender, tapering legs and drawers that slid silently on hard rubber castors. But immediately Wittgenstein found a flaw. Attached to the back of the dresser was a piece carved in an elegant fan design. This time, however, the salesman was ready:

But see here, sir. It's a quite functional design, ter keep yer things from falling down behind the wall.

Utterly unnecessary, scolded Wittgenstein, moving away. I can pick a penny from the floor.

Well, look here, said the salesman. If you do not like the piece, you can simply remove it like so. Three small screws is all. No one will know, sir.

Please — Wittgenstein was already walking away. I'm sorry. I will not have it.

But sir, pressed the salesman. Three little screws and you'll have what you want. I'll even knock off a quid for the piece you don't want.

Hear him, pleaded Russell.

Wittgenstein looked at Russell in amazement. Do you suppose you can just — *pull* it off? Forever it is fixed. Good day, good day. And off he went, dismissing them both.

Now listen, said Russell, following him out the belled door. All morning we've looked and you've found nothing. Nor will you —

Then I will have nothing. I will go to London.

Go to London! Russell stopped in the narrow lane. *Three screws.*

Three too many! Wittgenstein resumed walking. God does not grant us limitless chances.

What on earth do you mean, *God*? Standing in the King's Parade with outstretched arms, Russell said, You said you don't even *believe* in God! But when it's expedient, then you drag God into it.

God is *there*, said Wittgenstein, pointing up at the sky. *Here*, he said, snapping his fingers at the ground. *Here* is no God. Still we have God's expectations. And God *expects* perfection — the *first* time.

Well, I wish you well!

It is not *good wishes* — *nor* God.

Good! Russell fumed, striking off. Then let *God* make your furniture!

Wittgenstein could be harsh and imperious, but this took its toll on him. Back in Russell's rooms, once they had hastily reconciled, Russell told Wittgenstein, apropos of this furniture, that he must not wait for perfection before publishing. Russell expected a fight, but instead Wittgenstein turned away for shame, his voice wheezing as he blurted, I know. I *know* I will have nothing! But the problems we face, they are *not* nothing — even if I am nothing.

Russell stood there frozen. Wittgenstein was swaying like a tree. And then Wittgenstein whirled around, his voice pleading.

You must not on any account abandon me! Even if I do come to nothing. As I must! You must not!

But of course not, Russell insisted. Never . . .

Not knowing what to do, Russell did what he had never done: he placed his hand on Wittgenstein's arm and gave him a paternal pat. It was fearful to see Wittgenstein's mood swerve from imperious certainty to abject fear and helplessness. But what most struck Russell was this fleeting sense he had of tenderly consoling Ottoline or some woman. But even more unsettling was Russell's sense that, at bottom, he was only consoling *himself*. It was himself Russell saw before him, the incarnation of his own suspended judgment.

Other Orbits

OTTOLINE, meanwhile, was growing increasingly concerned for both Russell and Wittgenstein. Not incidentally, she was also thinking of herself: these storms that rocked Russell spilled over on her, too.

Not that Ottoline found such pressures entirely unwelcome. Despite her incessant complaints about her social responsibilities, she obviously relished the task of balancing so many geniuses, near-geniuses and neurotics. Julian at least had a governess. For these others, Ottoline often felt that she was the governess.

Considering her schedule, Ottoline was amazed that she managed to give Russell the time she did. Why, just to answer his letters took two and three hours a day, and this wasn't even counting what he expected her to read. At the moment, Ottoline felt like a music hall juggler, the kind who sets plates spinning on bamboo rods, then dashes madly back and forth trying to keep them all from crashing down. Chief and worst lately, there was Lamb, triumphantly working for two days, then grandly pouting for a week in preparation for a show in May, where he knew he would be denied the public outcry his genius so richly deserved. So here would be Mummy O, dropping by his studio (the same she had found and furnished for him) with little gifts and sops of hasty sex when Lambykins was feeling needy. He was a pill. Oh, O, I'm so this, he'd purr on the telephone. Oh, O, I can't . . . Oh, O, I need . . . And there she'd be, sending her own maid on odd days with brooms and cooked food from her kitchen. Or dispatching friends to his studio that they might cheer him on, marveling at his desultory, half-finished canvases, each a Sistine Chapel, to hear him.

There were in Ottoline's gallery a half dozen other young men, all in various unfinished, promising, declining or disheveled states. These were more casual, Platonic friendships, but inevitably these ill-defined attachments also harbored vague sexual tensions that required from Ottoline an endless round of letters, pick-me-ups, strategic remembrances and not a few small deceptions.

And last, there was Lytton — a special category. Despite his own incessant demands, Lytton was a great confidant; and best of all, he came without the usual snares and unease resulting from S-E-X. In the process of beginning *Eminent Victorians* now, Lytton was in need of pleasant, painterly places. And Ottoline's London residence, Bedford Hall — this, Lytton said, was his Watteau and Gainsborough! Bedford Hall ranked high on Lytton's list as he made his robin rounds, staying here a week and there a month until his welcome wore thin, or he got bored.

Aside from Lytton's brilliance and charm as a guest, gossip was his stock in trade, and, like a pack rat, he always carried off a whiff of scandal for every thorned nosegay he left. Ottoline had learned her lesson, burned once already when her innocent remarks about Wittgenstein got back to Russell, via Moore. Bertie scandalized! Bertie betrayed! Ottoline did think Bertie's indignant letter was a bit much. What was the harm if Moore knew about Wittgenstein? she wrote back. It was a matter of confidence, he replied: his comments were not for public consumption. And besides, he said, Wittgenstein was better off in a smaller circle. *Smaller* circle? replied Ottoline sarcastically. You're only a circle of *two*!

Flimsy as Russell's reasons were, Ottoline had still been embarrassed. But now, it was late January and Lytton was over. And the weather was so interminably dreary, like old porridge, mucking cold and gray. And, *per favore*, they were both trying to be gay that afternoon, she and Lytton, the better to banish these winter weeds! *Sì*, they were being Italian today, which suddenly made everything seem sunny, so warm and carefree. They could get so silly together — such fun a man and woman could have when sex was not lurking. After a morning spritzer of brandy with soda, Lytton, whose moods were like layers of water, warm over cold, declared he would have made a fetching woman. To prove his point, he wriggled into his hostess's high heels, rolled his trousers past the knee, then pranced before the wall-length mirror.

I am naughty Francesca. *Whoopsidaisini!* he cried, almost toppling over. I have most wicked legs, no?

Oh, *sì*, enthused m'lady, who had sprawled back on the bed, shrieking. *Molto hairy.*

Such fun they had, trading secrets and mimicking everyone. After they had pilloried half of London, Ottoline told her hushed guest that she had something else to tell him — *if* he could keep his cursed mouth shut. Lyttonni — for that was his *nom de biche* today — Lyttonni was, but of course, the very soul of discretion. Crossing himself, he said he was a veritable priest in Her Ladyship's confessional.

Oh, assolutamente! From me, Bella, not one *solo mio*!

I'm *seriosa*! warned Ottoline. You get me in trouble again, and I'll never tell you another secretini, *capire*?

Oh, *sincero, signora*! said Lyttonni with caressing hands. *Sincero.*

He wore her down with his entreaties. And of course she wanted and intended to tell him — and why not? It was not really gossip, not in the sense of being malicious. And she had Lyttonni's word. So, she unburdened herself. It was this Wittgenstein, she said. He was so tragic and tormented. A suicidal genius. And poor Bertini, she moaned. Wittgenstein was driving him to distraction with his criticisms and insistent demands as they strove to solve questions that, to hear her tell it, sounded almost Newtonian in their implications.

Lyttonni was so understanding, so full of pungent ideas. And so it was decided: for Bertie's own good, this Wittgenstein really must be given other outlets. Air was needed. He must broaden his horizons. Lyttonni, for one, wanted to meet him — *very*. So, no doubt, would Keynes. But in the meantime, Lyttonni had an idea that was, on second thought, *splendido!* Ottoline would tell Bertie that Wittgenstein ought to meet Moore and perhaps even take his course. Moore, reasoned Lytton, would be the perfect counterbalance to Russell, and all concerned would benefit — Russell, Wittgenstein and the *signora*.

It was a brilliant stroke. And such a load off her mind. But Lyttonni, he was a wee curious? This Wittgenstein, he asked with a wry wink, he is handsome? . . . Does he . . . I mean, *signora, is* he . . . ?

Stop! chided O, the tease. I don't know.

Bella! pleaded Lyttonni.

I don't *know,* she insisted. Stop —

Oh, Ottoanaschini, *soccorra me!*

Looking away, she waggled her fingers like a marionetteer. *Comme ci, comme ça.*

Trulyoso?

I don't know! I mean, Bertie won't quite say. And not a word! You never heard a *word* from me! *Not one!*

Oh! Lyttonni brushed his lips. Of this there need be no mention. Of this there was no question.

Much as it galled him at bottom, Russell did see the sense of Ottoline's suggestion that he introduce Wittgenstein to Moore. Broader exposure probably would be good for Wittgenstein now. Certainly, Russell did not want to feel selfish, nor to invite charges of being exclusive with a strong prospect. And it was safe now, he thought; the bond between them was too strong for Moore to threaten it. Besides, he doubted that Moore had much to offer Wittgenstein, Moore being more at his depth in metaphysics, ethics and psychology. Moreover, Russell was fairly sure — gleefully so — that Moore's elaborate, sometimes plodding style of lecturing would quickly frustrate Wittgenstein.

Still, in almost inverse proportion to his confidence here, Russell felt a superstitious urge to test Wittgenstein's loyalty. Russell was sporting about it, though. Talking to Wittgenstein about Moore, Russell gave his colleague every chance, making a good many left-handed compliments and pointing out how Moore's tortoise tactics had fooled many a quicker adversary, including himself. Russell even gave Wittgenstein a copy of

Principia Ethica, saying what a stir the book had caused ten years before. And when, two days later, Wittgenstein returned the book, saying that it gave him headaches — saying that Moore, in his circuitous, Latinate style, said over and over in pages what could have been said in a single paragraph — why, poor, shocked Russell was warmed to the heart.

As for Moore's class, Russell told Wittgenstein not to expect to be immediately stunned, and lo, Wittgenstein was not stunned. Still, he withheld judgment, remembering Russell's promise that Moore, like a magician, would soon whip away the black cloth, revealing Truth in all its pearly effulgence.

But, for God's sake, *when?* By the third class Wittgenstein was still waiting as Moore held forth with the sweat streaming down his brow. Why was Moore so infernally cautious? Wittgenstein wondered. Why, when Moore had considered every conceivable facet of a question, why did he immediately return to it the next class, unable to proceed until he had banished every possible confusion? Wittgenstein remembered Russell telling him that Moore's effect was cumulative, but this was more on the order of geological ages!

That was essentially what Moore did in those opening periods: he catalogued the world, leading the entities two by two into that ark in which he sought to memorialize all we know, think we know, and don't or can't possibly know.

If only Wittgenstein had watched Moore tunneling his way through a plate heaped with food — then he might have understood how Moore's mind grazed through this bounty that is the world. Moore had his philosophical gospel. It was the Gospel of Common Sense, of cutting the *nonsense* and plunging forthwith into the baptismal font of what we know, and know truly, despite all protests to the contrary.

To begin with, testified Moore, it seems clear that there are in the universe an enormous number of material objects of one kind or another. We know, for instance, that besides our own bodies, the bodies of millions of other men inhabit the earth. We know also that there are billions of animals and plants. There are an even greater number of inanimate objects — mountains and all the stones upon them, grains of sand, different kinds of minerals and soil, and all the drops of water in the swelling rivers and the sea. We recognize that there are also a multitude of objects manufactured by men, and we now accept the idea that the sun and moon, and those bright grains that are the visible stars, are themselves great masses of matter, most of them many times larger than our earth. And besides these material objects, Moore continued, we know that there are other phenomena. We know, for instance, that men possess minds, and that in this world, we encounter not just our own minds but *other* minds — minds not our own and often indeed almost nothing like our own . . .

It was such a long catalogue Moore enumerated; it was such an ungodly, prognathous mess of experience he was heaping up. Still, it was just and necessary, said Moore, that we cautiously examine these things. Through civil looking and thinking, he seemed to suggest, we could heft and smell these mental melons and cabbages — we truly could behold their phenomenological essences and so perhaps discern our own. But just as difficult and important as making judgments, he added, is the art of *withholding* judgment — of not precipitously surrendering to the ego's gluttonous caviling to be *right,* so it could eat and spew more. For surely it was folly to plow through the world simply to be through it.

In his ruminating rootedness, Moore had a positive genius for withholding judgment, for that relentless, often exasperating analysis necessary to prepare these victuals for proper beholding. Still, in his own good time Moore could make his point, could even startle with his point. Like Russell, Moore was still fighting those old skirmishes against the Hegelian idealists, those rebels against the Gospel of Common Sense. And so, harrumphed Moore, isn't it curious that skeptics routinely believe what is most fabulous and discount what is most obvious and indeed under their very noses? And let us also ask ourselves how it is possible that *material* philosophers have held that *material* objects do not exist. For, after all, argued Moore, if this view is true, then it follows that no philosopher has ever held it, since philosophers are themselves material objects —

Sir —

Up went the hand. Looking up, Moore acknowledged the arrogant-looking chap in the fifth row, the one with his mortarboard cocked like a wedge and a bit askew. Moore knew all too well who it was, having waited over a week for the inevitable objection.

Sir, said Wittgenstein, with yet a glimmer of admiration. Your point is certainly *interesting.* But tell me, please, what *material* difference it makes? Whether I am material or immaterial — why should this affect the truth of what I say? If something is true, then it is true. We do not judge its truth by asking by what *medium* does it come to us. Do I say I will not consider your argument because you use *spoken* words only? I might say I believe only in the written word.

Moore did not bridle or evade. On the contrary, he was quite struck by this objection and said straightaway, Your point is well taken. Moore's eyes went up into his head, then he continued. I had not considered that objection, but it is certainly a serious objection and perhaps reduces my statement from an argument that holds water to a more or less interesting point that only sprinkles a little water. Having said that, I hope you will at least concede that it is somewhat *odd* that we would entertain on material pages the thoughts of men who denied the material existence of, well, *pages.*

Yes, Wittgenstein conceded. I suppose it is odd. But —

There was laughter then as, from the back of the hall, someone said, Professor Moore? Did I just hear a voice? Did someone in this room just put a question to you?

He did, agreed Moore with a smile. Do you not see my interrogator?

I heard only a voice, a voice was all, said the student amid the general titter. I — I confess I do not see him.

Nor do I see you! muttered Wittgenstein, whirling around on the clown. I *see* nothing worth *hearing.*

Zounds! exclaimed the clown. It's that ghostly *voice* again.

Facing back around, Wittgenstein could still see an afterimage of his tormentor, rubicund and handsome, with a supercilious smirk. But even more infuriating to Wittgenstein was the red-haired runt sitting beside the clown, delightedly snorting into his clenched hand.

Very well, harrumphed Moore. Let us continue now.

And with that, Moore resumed his catalogue, but for the rest of the period Wittgenstein sat there, burning, burning . . .

Pinsent

IF RUSSELL had figured on Wittgenstein's meeting Moore, and perhaps even Strachey and Keynes, he hadn't counted on other rivals. But then one unseasonably warm day in late February, Wittgenstein was energetically walking along the Backs when he saw the red-haired runt from Moore's class — the one who'd laughed at that clown who professed not to see him.

The clown was not the first to have taken on Wittgenstein's mounting notoriety, but he was the only undergraduate to have effectively silenced him. Even now, before class, the clown would fumble blindly past Wittgenstein's chair, his mouth gaping in mock terror as he intoned in mongrel echoes of Shakespeare, Is this a *doubter* I see before me, head turned toward my face? Is this indeed my seat? Am I — *I*? Oh, fie, fie, Fleance!

Wittgenstein made a few desultory comebacks, but none that met with any success: the clown was much too clever to stray from his own comic ground. And the red-haired runt — Red Hair, Wittgenstein called him — took such delight in Wittgenstein's frustration; he seemed to have it in for him. Several times Red Hair had rushed to Moore's defense, displaying more terrier courage than savvy as he countered Wittgenstein's arguments. For someone so young, Red Hair had not argued badly. Grudgingly, Wittgenstein could see there was brilliance in him. Worse, Moore seemed to have taken Red Hair under his wing. Several times, Wittgenstein had seen them walking across the Common, impetuous Red Hair holding forth while Moore shambled along, sucking his pipe.

Wittgenstein had considered asking Moore just who this Red Hair was, but he held back, not wanting to admit having noticed him. Wittgenstein felt the same reluctance today. Red Hair was standing below him on the grassy banks of the Cam near King's College. Red Hair was staring at the upper branches of a tree, looking — at what? A bird? A bird. A brown, sharp-beaked bird with a spotted white breast.

Why even approach on such a flimsy pretext? Wittgenstein asked himself. He so dreaded the spring, that feeling of the world straining once more to break forth, wheezing under the boggish damps and drizzle like an air-starved hurdy-gurdy. On his chest, Wittgenstein felt that weight like a croup, a weight such as trees must feel, struggling to evince new leaves. He was in a bad way. Another quarrel with Russell. More "nerves" and misunderstanding, the two of them like a pair of crossed eyes, with neither focus nor perspective.

Why this need to talk to this stranger? Why even try when Red Hair seemed so callow and obnoxious? Drawing closer, Wittgenstein saw from the state of his clothes that Red Hair was rather poor. His dull brown shoes were cracked with old polish, and his short, square trousers bore the sheen of too many pressings. But what Wittgenstein most noticed was the bunchy blue blazer that Red Hair was wearing. It was a boys' school blazer: Wittgenstein could still see the outlines of a school crest on the breast pocket. Think of his shame, thought Wittgenstein, to have to wear this boys' school relic among his well-heeled peers. With his ruddy, chubby cheeks, all Red Hair needed to complete the picture was a striped cap and Eton collar.

Red Hair started as Wittgenstein approached. His very vulnerability emboldened Wittgenstein, who said in an unconsciously martial tone, The bird — Tell me, please, what kind is this?

Pinsent, came Red Hair with a queer, twitchy look.

A *pinsent*? asked Wittgenstein quizzically. This is what you call this bird?

Beg your pardon? replied Red Hair, scowling. And then, cocking his head, he made a sudden turn so that Wittgenstein flinched involuntarily, thinking, for a moment, that Red Hair meant to strike him. In a huff now, Red Hair demanded, What! *What d'ye say?*

In the pressure of the moment, this colloquialism delivered in such a furious rush rattled Wittgenstein, who nervously parroted, What? *What?*

Spreading his fingers impatiently, Red Hair emphatically enunciated, I *asked*, What is it you *said*?

And I *asked you* what is this bird, and you said it was a *pinsent*? Correct?

I'm Pinsent, said the boy, rolling his eyes. That's a *mistle thrush.* Just in early for the spring, you know. A *harbinger.*

But — Wittgenstein was twisted up again — a thrush, it is a harbinger?

No, a *thrrr-ush* is a *thrrr-ush.* Rolling the R's, the intonation harsh and British. Red Hair continued, A *harbinger* is one thing that signals the approach of another. The *thrrrush* that presages the approach of spring.

Stung, Wittgenstein said almost sorrowfully, It is for me a new word. Wittgenstein closed his eyes as if he were fixing these words like photographic exposures into his memory. But when he opened them, he saw the boy still eyeing him, owlish, guarded. And then Wittgenstein had that awkward feeling of embarrassed silence, of privacy having been breached. He would have fled then had not Pinsent asked peevishly, Do you really *believe* the things you say in Moore's class?

Wittgenstein found the question so incredible that he leaned forward, his eyes widening. Believe them? Whatever do you mean?

I dunno . . . You seem so . . . *ar*bitrary. Arbitrary for the sake of being arbitrary.

Do I? retorted Wittgenstein, glaring. Well, *you* seem to me rude, to laugh at me. And no understanding. So very rude. You and your friend — that fool.

He's not my friend. Red Hair gave a sassy squint. And he's no fool, either.

He is so amusing, do you think? What does he offer, is it? Rudeness. Rubbish and stupidity only. Jokes are not arguments.

Pinsent smiled foolishly. No, but they're funny.

Are they? Well, you will have to tell me, please, your own ideas. They are, I am sure, very original, to make such jokes.

As is your bullying. Red Hair held his ground. You do excel at that.

Normally, Wittgenstein would have broken away in disgust, but he wasn't about to let himself be beaten, not by this one. And despite Red Hair's defiance, Wittgenstein sensed he was winning. The boy was not so confident. Wittgenstein could see the wavering eyes, the hesitancy — the boy could be cracked, and Wittgenstein dearly wanted to crack him. They were on his ground now; Wittgenstein would teach this youngster a lesson. And it worked, his glacial stare. Pinsent did waver. Only a momentary failure of nerve, but exploitable.

Somewhat chastised, Pinsent offered, We *laugh* because you're so awfully serious — so cocksure of yourself. Especially compared to Moore. It's not just Moore's arguments, you know. It's Moore's *spirit* you don't understand.

I understand Moore. Nodding huffily. As much as necessary.

There you go! Pinsent turned his scattery red hair against the wind. What an egregiously arrogant thing to say!

With what scowling relish did Pinsent chew and spit out the word "egregiously." Regretting this show of ill temper, Wittgenstein was more conciliatory as he asked, You are a friend of Moore's?

Pinsent eyed him uneasily. I suppose I am.

Then I am sorry. Wittgenstein reverted to formality. I was wrong to speak this way.

Oh, *please* — you needn't be polite.

It is not to be *polite* merely. Wittgenstein's jaw tightened. I *do* respect Moore. Not that I agree with him much.

No, offered Pinsent after a moment. You do not.

They were stuck then, each unsure how to continue but neither stepping away, until Wittgenstein finally ventured, A first-year man, you are?

Second, said Pinsent, looking a little hurt. Then with a glance he added, I was put forward a form. In school, I mean.

Oh. Wittgenstein nodded, then asked suddenly, Will you walk on?

We can, replied Pinsent, dubious. He looked rather surprised.

Wittgenstein had started walking slowly, when Pinsent looked up, clouds reflected in his thickish glasses as he asked, Might you walk to this side of me? To my *right*, I mean. I don't hear well in my left ear. In fact, I can hardly hear in it at all. That's why I mistook your original question — about the bird.

Oh — Startled, Wittgenstein turned like someone leading an unsteady foal as Pinsent, with a peculiar clopping gait, picked up behind him, pricking up his one good ear.

The Wall

WITHIN A WEEK, they were almost inseparable.

Between classes or going to supper, they could be seen together, Wittgenstein walking in clipped strides, speaking and gesticulating, and Pinsent racing after him with that clumsy clop step, his head turned as from a blow as he raised his stubby arm in objection.

"'His Master's Voice,'" Russell wrote Ottoline, describing the two. "Wittgenstein's new friend reminds me of the white dog pictured on the Victrolas in the way he inclines his head to the stream of words issuing from Wittgenstein. I haven't the faintest who the lad is & haven't asked. Suppose I must wait until I'm introduced."

Felt a bit left out, Russell did. Nor did Wittgenstein help matters with his awkward secrecy. Russell tried to be understanding about it, telling Ottoline and himself that it was only healthy for a young man to have friends his own age. But still it nagged him, as did Moore's own growing interest in Wittgenstein.

I can well understand your high opinion of him, Moore told Russell one night at supper. At my lectures, Wittgenstein always looks puzzled. Nobody else looks so puzzled as he does. In my third class he lodged a very serious objection, and then two more the next. Then in his laconic way Moore added, It's evident he's much cleverer than I.

I wouldn't say that, protested Russell. It struck Moore as distinctly odd, Russell's scandalized air: Russell acted as if Moore had said this of *him*.

Oh, no. Moore waved him off. It is true. Wittgenstein is cleverer. More profound as well, I expect. I don't mind about it.

Moore didn't mean to elicit protests to the contrary; he was merely stating a fact. Russell didn't take it as such. To him, Moore was only flaunting his legendary lack of vanity. And couldn't Moore bill and coo now, thought Russell, with his wedding but a month away. Oh, Russell got the point, all right. Moore was saying, *Unlike you, Russell, I have another life now. Unlike you, I am not saddled with ambition. Unlike you, I can marry and have children.*

These little incidents, the chaff of days, piled up, and Russell continued to brood. One day, for instance, Moore remarked on his surprise that Wittgenstein was musical.

I had no idea, said Moore. Wittgenstein, I think, was rather surprised to learn that I sing. We talked a good while about that, and I said I would have to get my music sometime. I thought Miss Ely — *Dorothy,* I mean — em, perhaps she might play for us. Moore smiled. Wittgenstein said he can whistle anything — even piano and violin parts. Have you ever heard him whistle?

Whistle? The vestigial scold and prig appeared from behind the arras, saying with evident disdain, No, never.

Russell thought he sounded impeccably neutral, if with a slight edge, but to Moore, who was now hearing things himself, the translation was, *We've better things to do than whistle.* Again, Moore sensed in Russell that unmistakable air of ownership. Always that need to remind him that Wittgenstein was *his* student, *his* future. As if Moore had designs on him! As far as Moore was concerned, Russell could have Wittgenstein! Disturbing as this possessive air was, Moore was just as alarmed by Russell's seeming blindness to Wittgenstein's darker currents. But Moore's chief concern now was Wittgenstein's mounting influence on Pinsent.

Russell bridled when Moore raised his fears one wet day as they passed on the Common. Like dust, the blowing mist clung to their black gowns. Stooped under the black eave of his umbrella, his hair dripping, Moore resembled a bust of Cicero. It was hardly a place to talk, but Moore asked Russell rather suddenly if he didn't think Wittgenstein was — well, unhappy. Moore was exceedingly cautious in how he couched it, but Russell still took it personally. For Russell, there was no distance now. Moore was implying that Russell was acting selfishly and irresponsibly, saddling Wittgenstein with his own frustrations and disappointments. The problem, Russell heard Moore saying, was not Wittgenstein but *him.*

Please, emphasized Moore, who could see this was going over badly. Don't take this wrongly. But do you think Wittgenstein is entirely stable?

Oh, no. He's quite *mad!*

Hoping to combat absurdity with absurdity, Russell then said testily, Come, now. Do you think it's all that grim? Hovering there with a queasy look, Moore wasn't at all attuned to Russell's lacerating attempt at satire. Well, of course I'm *joking!* Russell added with a flaring grin. What I mean is, you must know Wittgenstein on *his* terms. As opposed to *my* terms. *Or* your own.

Knowing he had overreacted, Russell ventured another laugh, to show his easy unconcern. But the patronizing tone that capped off this laugh only antagonized Moore, who waded in, saying, Well, all the same, *I've* wondered. Also, a student of mine, David Pinsent, mentioned some things.

What things?

Again, Moore felt that irritating proprietal tone. With a look of discomfort, he hedged. I misspoke just now — I was told in confidence. Nothing awful, you understand, but still matters of concern.

This student, asked Russell, inclining his head under his umbrella, he's red haired? A short fellow?

That's him. You've met?

No, but I've seen them together. Your student, is he?

No, he's not *my* student, said Moore, giving a dig in return. I'm his adviser. Pinsent's also reading philosophy. He took a first in mathematics in his Little Go last year — quite gifted. Moore's eyes moved up and down. I rather thought you knew him.

Well, I don't —

Well, said Moore, drawing up his shoulders. This can be kept between us, I think. My concern is that Pinsent is young — three or four years younger than Wittgenstein. Wittgenstein's already made a sufficiently strong impression on him, if you know what I mean. I'd hate to see Pinsent — shall we say, knocked off course. That's *roughly* my concern —

Feeling that he had made his point, Moore abruptly stopped. Unfortunately, he had said too much and not enough. All he'd done was raise Russell's hackles.

No, Russell wasn't giving in to this meddling. With all the focused attention of a boy pulling the wings off a fly, Russell slowly nodded, watching a bead of rain inch down Moore's brow before he gave a frosty *Good afternoon.*

It did not sit well at all with Russell that Pinsent was one of Moore's lads — one of his "fleas," as he called them. And this still left begging the fact that Russell was seeing Wittgenstein less at a time when Russell increasingly needed him, and not just professionally.

Russell tried to put it all in proportion. The problem was not them, he thought, it was the nature of the work, advancing one moment, collapsing the next. The work had the nature of a wall — he and Wittgenstein both spoke of it so, saying after a good night's work, There's another piece of the wall we've pulled down.

Russell had long held this image of a wall sundering him from the truth, an intolerable wall that he must pull down. Characteristically, he imagined that he and Wittgenstein must share the same wall, but this was wishful thinking: their walls were not the same, nor could they be. Moreover, their respective walls were always changing in form, shifting in the way of a dream. The problem was plural, one of evolving dimensions: the wall was not one but many, or perhaps many walls that made up one Great Wall. Before a wall one was too close to say.

At least Russell felt he had allies and forebears. Unlike Wittgenstein, he saw himself as part of a tradition, one of a line of thinkers who had stared at various walls, wondering what remained to be done — or more likely demolished.

By persistence or brute force a wall might be assaulted, but it would not be breached by imagining it was not really so high or formidable. Still, even Wittgenstein would wonder at times if a given wall even existed — that is, if a problem was truly a *philosophical* problem, and not instead one of the wards of psychology or science. Russell, by contrast, was more wily. Philosophy, he would say with a wink, was traditionally a case of weighing theft — the theft of assumptions and givens — over honest toil. Wittgenstein despised this attitude. He said the problems must be squarely confronted, not sent a Trojan horse. And here Wittgenstein would see himself as both the betrayed and the betrayer, knowing, as Russell did not, that their walls were really quite different. Shameful arrogance, but true, Wittgenstein would think. Russell did not have his ear to this wall, and if he did, he could not hear it surging with the outer sea.

For Wittgenstein the biggest obstacle was a more all-pervasive problem. For lack of a better term, he thought of it as the riddle of life — his life, life in general, it was pretty much the same. The problem, in any case, was not just one of finding an answer but of first posing the correct question, or questions. And part of the problem, he saw, was the very logic of language, that Great Mirror, which could describe the world but not itself, blinded by its own reflected radiance. One root problem, it seemed, was the mystery of logical form. In even the most basic tautology this form was present. The self-evidence of tautology was of course trivial. But the *principle* of tautology — the logical ability to say that *this* is *this* — was a fundamental logical truth that no one could deny. Cat is mightily cat. George is England's king. Either it is raining or it is not raining.

Clearly, Wittgenstein told Russell, one could hardly disagree that it is either raining or not raining. This was intelligible but it was empty: it said nothing about the weather. But here Russell interjected that a Hegelian idealist might say it was neither raining nor not raining, but rather only *drizzling* — they so love a synthesis. Wittgenstein laughed — Russell was always breaking the tension with jokes — but then he was still lost in that drizzly parenthesis. Stumped.

Like a mountain pushed up from the sea, a wall will sometimes rise out of a life, rising to see the world arrayed below like paradise. But ultimately the wall prevails, while the life becomes at best a kind of residue — the mortar squeezed out between the wall's blocks, or the lowly grass at its foot. Bang the wall. Talk to the wall. A wall remains. A *wall* that is a *wall* that is a *wall* . . .

Sleep

BENEATH A WALL is the life, and the life, unlike the wall, must sleep.

Russell hated putting Wittgenstein out late at night, but there was no point continuing. The wall wasn't giving. Even Wittgenstein's own mind had put him out. The life must sleep.

The suicide is sly, he is so secretive he hardly knows himself what the plotting mind has set in store. So many ways to make a hole in the dark, so many ways to slip out of the world. Dread of the razor. Dread of the length of rope or the tower. Lowering guilty eyes while passing the chemist's shop, where a quietus could be had for a half bob and a fib.

They were both so coy about this, Wittgenstein and Russell. To himself each would wonder if the other shared the same shameful dream. One night, seeing Wittgenstein's gloomy look, Russell asked, Are you thinking about logic or your sins? And he felt a thrill when Wittgenstein replied without a hint of irony, Both.

Nowadays Russell fell easily to sleep, the sand running swiftly out his ears; he slept more soundly than he had in years. Still, it was galling for Russell to feel that another must come and undo what he had done — to feel that in some fundamental way he had been reduced. Worse, Russell often could not quite see what Wittgenstein was getting at in his statements about logic, much less how they might agree on a point yet derive from it wholly different conclusions. But what most disturbed Russell was how Wittgenstein's ideas would seem like ideas he himself had once had, dream ideas long discarded or forgotten but now brilliantly recast. It seemed unfair. With the imperviousness of something shattered, Wittgenstein spilled himself only to find himself replenished, brimming over with new thoughts.

But this was another instance of Willy-Nilly's law: Wittgenstein didn't at all see himself in such heroic terms. Breathless, sleepless, he would dream of death, of long-fingered Clotho stripping the life from him, a milty, guilty cloud billowing in the teeming dark. It was a fatal pill upon his lips, this life and its word. Explain, illogician, why loss and past is *form*, and *forever fixed*. Explain, please, why loss, which after all is about nothing, is still somehow *something*. And once you have explained this, then explain why — though we gulp experience whole and molt it as quickly, handling our past like slippery snakeskin — explain, if you can, why nothing is forgotten or forgiven, or why a wave scarcely recedes before there comes its repetition.

Dreams, like walls, do attain different sizes. Dreams do exceed our capacity to contain them. As so as a boy, and even now, Wittgenstein had imagined an acid so corrosive and pure that no vessel could contain it. Error was the sin. Suicide was the result and cause, and life was the first error, an infinite regress. He couldn't stop it. Clear through his ulcerous heart the acid ate, burning through the bedding and dripping blackly on the rug, burning down through the floor and ages of coal, burning clear down to hell where devils dance, then falling through space and never cooling, and never ridding itself of the cutting virulence of truth, black heart, falling and falling and never stopping . . .

Logic is not forgiving.

Faith

THERE WAS a more benign variation of this dream. Lying in bed, Wittgenstein would think of how Jesus, standing like an apparition on the stormy sea, bade Peter to step from the boat and walk to him across the unquiet water. Wittgenstein would imagine himself stepping out on the waves, finding them first solid as planks, then mushy cold like a wet snow in which he sank to his knees, then, abruptly, to his Adam's apple. But unlike Peter, he never cried out. His arms flew up, and he was sucked beneath the waves, blind as a stone and never caring, sinking and sinking and never sleeping because he had no faith, no faith.

The Making of a Scholar

BUT WHILE RUSSELL FRETTED, then put a nice face on things — declaring it all nerves, evanescent melancholia, unhappiness — in the meantime, David Pinsent, not unlike the Victrola fido, was pricking up his good ear and keeping a careful diary in a precise, piercing hand:

14.III.13

W. asks me today, & rather suddenly, about my past & family. Awfully nosy of him, I think; but I answer, & of course it is rather easy in the main, as there is only Mother. Don't think much about it — tell him she's rather dotty, frankly. Wittgenstein screws up his face; doesn't know this English word. I say, "She's, how should I say, crazy. Eccentric, if you like." W. thoroughly displeased at this. Very sudden: "This is not for you to say — a son." "Why?" I ask. "She's my mother, not yours. You've never laid eyes on her." W. scolds. "This does not matter; it does not in the least!" "As you wish. But I'd venture to say you didn't have to be a parent to your mother." W: "What! Whatever do you mean?" I say, "I mean I was never left to be a child; I was always raising my mother."

W. is abrupt, hushed; clearly, this comes at tremendous cost. "I am sorry," he says. "I did not know. *Still* —"

W. silent then. So I tell him about myself. One would naturally assume W. would tell me about his family, but when I ask, he says, "I cannot burden you with that." "Why should it burden me?" I ask. W: "It is burden enough." I'm angry then: "Well, you know, I wouldn't even ask if you hadn't asked me first — I mean, we've hardly met. Still, fair's fair, don't you think?"

W. weighs this — *irritatingly* long pause — then says: "Very well, I should not have asked about your family. All the same, I will not burden you."

Outrageous! Ought I to have pressed it? I was uneasy, rather. Suddenly he must go. I watch him hurtling off, his head cast down, as if he's counting the pavement stones; & all the while I feel in him this tremendous *compression*. I see I do not understand my new friend at all.

While playing his own cards close to his chest, Wittgenstein meanwhile was learning a good deal about his new friend. Besides seeing anew Pinsent's contrariness, Wittgenstein confirmed his initial impression that the young man was poor and a public school boy. Once the ice was broken, Pinsent told Wittgenstein all about life before Cambridge — how he'd bounced from school to school, preceded by a well-deserved reputation for taking school prizes, and making trouble.

I never did get on, said Pinsent with a shrug. Because I was so silent, the masters always thought me sneaky and arrogant. Coming in as a scholarship boy did me no good, either. The clever boy was always taken for a swot — anything intellectual was so much rubbish to the other fellows. All that mattered was athletics and *tone* and trousers of the right cut.

To the average public school master, brilliance in a boy was one thing, but brilliance mixed with originality was most troubling, definitely to be discouraged. More disturbing still to the school constabulary was this stubborn impudence, for which the lad was given many a vigorous birching, as when he refused to attend vespers. Like hangings, these floggings were public humiliations, with the school captain and other senior boys present to attest that the headmaster did not break the law by raising the freshly cut switch over his head.

Pitched over, forced to grasp his own trembling ankles, the boy was hardly the first miscreant to fear he might foul his breeches during a twenty-count. Ah, yes, Pinsent said, it gave one perspective to view the world upside-down. Peering between his outstretched legs, he did not miss the rapt, sometimes aroused grimaces of his mates as the master paused at sixteen to dab his fleshy forehead.

In every school there were dozens of written and unwritten shibboleths governing dress and deportment: the proper vocabulary to use, where and precisely how one was to walk in the hall and how one was to defer to prefects and the various "bloods," those school heroes and Adonises who were adored by boys and masters alike. In this two-tiered jail system of master and boy justice, at least the masters were bound by civil code. The boy justice was worse, far worse, and soon Wittgenstein saw why, beneath it all, his bantam friend was so tough and unyielding.

Pinsent was funny and bitter describing these experiences, of which he was perversely proud, like one who has survived a war. He could tell about Cramburne, a school heavy on Latin, where he was caught writing satires and was compelled to conjugate in the pluperfect subjunctive while Mr. Caedmon spiritedly flogged him. Or about a master there who supervised rugger and combed his curly side whiskers like laurels over his temples. *Lupus Dementia*, the boys called him for the way he would foam at the mouth at football matches, shouting, *Piger stulte! Dele plumbum, Higgins! Jugula! Jugula!* rallying his toughs like Caesar to his cohorts, as in the mud they battled the pugnacious Gauls of Chigwell, Brighton and Leatherhead.

Once Pinsent got over his initial reluctance to speak of his life, he could laugh himself sick over these stories, telling them half to see Wittgenstein's horrified expression. Less funny was the part about how Pinsent had been born with a twin a month premature; and how his brother Alfred died of the croup at three, while he himself nearly died of the fever that took his hearing in one ear. With Alfred's death, his mother, always flighty and depressed, went to pieces. This was her first stint in the "loony bin," as Pinsent called it. His father, who sold machine tools and traveled, wasn't much for caring for children, and anyway, Pinsent said, he wasn't much around. The boy was sickly pale and a picky eater. So while his mother was wheeled about in a bath chair, heavily sedated, he was left in the care of an old nurse who craw fed him like a goose, screamed in his deaf ear for being ill attentive and bound his left hand when he favored it, calling it "the devil's hand."

Still a lefty, Pinsent said, gamely holding up his hand.

Things didn't get much better. When his mother returned from the sanitarium, she found the boy partially deaf and stuttering, though somehow along the way he had taught himself to read and do long sums in his head. Sent to a day school that next autumn, the boy was teased for his speech, which worsened, and also for his peculiar way of running. This proved another affliction: as a very young child, imitating a rider on a horse, Pinsent had learned to run by rhythmically patting himself on the rump, *ti-tump, ti-tump*, a habit for which he was called "Bumbeater," "Switch," and "Nickers."

Still, the school was not bad. Things really might have been all right had not his father died of a brain hemorrhage a few years later. This loss paralyzed his mother, who suffered her third, and worst, breakdown. So, after dumping her in the asylum, the relatives collected some money and finally packed the little rotter off to Bondock, a third-rate public school rabid on football.

It was my uncle's idea, said Pinsent. Guess he thought Bondock would toughen the little sissy up. Teach him to run proper, you know.

And your mother? Wittgenstein asked. For you, she could do nothing?

Her? Pinsent jerked his thumb. She couldn't even dress herself.

The boy had always hated athletics. Worse, he arrived in the middle of term, a hopeless time for the newcomer, when all alliances have been forged and an inviolable pecking order established. Pinsent clutched his stomach even as he described it: the sickening smell of the greasy food, and for pudding always that boarding school standby, the cursed *Spotted Dick*. Worse were the dripping, gutterlike stalls of the lavatory, where pecker holes had been gouged by countless pent-up penknives.

Pinsent best remembered the first day, when, dressed in his enormous blue blazer emblazoned with Bondock's golden crest, he was introduced to the schemers, dolts and bullies who were to be his new mates. They showed him good cheer, all right. No sooner did the master leave than a sneering inquisition began. Trapped under a circle of faces, the boy was asked a riddle that he naturally muffed — his first offense.

Oh-oh, said the smirking faces as a plate was passed forward. Hungry, was he? *Ooops!* Chucky pudding dribbled down his front. Then came a helpful hand, smearing it the length of his blazer.

Filthy scob! shrieked a towering senior boy with cracked teeth, the leader. Soiling the school colors! You'll be firked for this!

So saying, he jacked the boy's tie past his throat, watching his bulging eyes glaze over before he cut it off — a Bondock tradition that ended with whistling jeers, fists on the back and the unanimous decision that he should fag for four and pass along all desserts and home parcels or else be beaten senseless.

The boy couldn't run or talk properly, knew nothing of fisticuffs; but they wouldn't beat him, he promised himself that. Brought down to the playing field in his new cleats and jersey later that afternoon, he could see the lads waiting for him, furiously rubbing dirt and spit into their palms. He remembered standing there, feeling incredibly stupid and inert as a ball struck him hard in the ribs, a glancing blow that spun him sideways. The boy clutched his ribs but did not cry. Regaining his balance, he stood for a moment, watching the grinning, sniggering boys. And then at that moment, at age eleven, he made a decision that would dictate his entire life. He lay down in the cold mud and stared at the sky.

'Ey, scob! they screamed at the boy who would not play. Ge' up before yer get a foot in the face. 'Ey, scobber!

It was amazing. For a moment, they didn't know what to do. There was name calling and threats, then a kick in the back that finally flushed tears. Still he didn't move. They stood him up, but when they took their hands away he fell in a heap. They threw him in the mud, dragged him by the hair; and then, with retching coughs of disgust, the spitting started, warm gobbers drooling down his face and muddy glasses. The boy felt the worst was behind him by then. Beyond terror, he realized that he had wet himself and wondered if his aunt had packed extra drawers. Also, there was God — he still believed in God — and as the jeering circle closed, he started to pray, thinking that soon it would all be over.

Had not the coach seen the pack closing and heard their blood chant, the Bondockers might have done the lad serious harm. But all this stopped with a groan like bagpipes as the football master punched his blood-red upside-down head through that bower of teeth and taunts.

Up! he barked. Up right now!

To the recumbent boy it seemed most strange that this enraged and powerful man did not simply haul him up by the arm. But no: the coach believed in rules; he wanted the boy to rise by his own volition. In a curious way the boy wanted to comply, but in him there was a stronger side, which clamped its jaws on his mind like a bulldog on a windpipe, choking off this impulse to survive at sufferance of another's will. *They'll not make me.* That was more or less what he remembered hearing, this accompanied by a distinct sensation of choking, as if by smothering himself he might destroy them as well.

And they were losing. As the football master began his second ten-count, the boy triumphantly saw it was not he but *they* who were powerless. It was an eleven-year-old's revelation. *They did not know what to do.*

That afternoon, after being hauled by his muddy hair before the headmaster; after being ordered, then compelled, to grasp his ankles while the sap-laden whip softened his will; after being told that no boy had ever, *ever* done what he had, which was comparable to a king's soldier deserting the field under fire; and after being assured by the headmaster that he would not disgrace his family or Bondock, and that he would, make no mistake about it, *play* — after all this, the boy was shut in the headmaster's library for his own safety, with a vow that early the next morning he would have one last chance to redeem his sullied honor.

This threat the headmaster did carry out. The next morning, after further warnings and before what seemed the entire school, the boy lay down again. This time there was not a sound, just the keening November wind and the feeling that he was present at his own funeral. Of that day, Pinsent especially remembered the silent, shamed expressions of the boys and how the headmaster then turned to the football master and muttered, This will not do.

The boy got his way. Two days later, he was packed back to his uncle, who sent him to another school, where he didn't fare much better. And so came the pattern: the obstinate nose-thumbing at authority, and later the contempt even for God, finding himself in and out of the soup the way his mother was the loony bin. They were poor. Worse, they were beholden to relatives, to the church and the various charities. Since the boy had no pater and no reverence, it was his job to be brilliant. Thus he learned mathematics, taking prizes and scholarships in that and classics, and always making a point of being more brilliant than he was difficult. This pattern lasted until age fourteen, when he landed at Glengalerry, the first school loose enough to suit him and wise enough to basically leave him go his own way.

Wittgenstein lacked such wisdom. Overtly or covertly, Pinsent felt the same doughty need to fight Wittgenstein. For the boy who would not play, the circumstances had changed, but not the fundamental conditions of his life. For Pinsent, the question was how long he could hold his breath — suspend his life — while remaining submerged beneath another's will.

Jottings

No, Pinsent was no pushover. He fought Wittgenstein, but even here he felt himself fall short. Still, as Pinsent noted, he wasn't the only one:

. . . In discussion with Moore & Wittgenstein today — more skeptic talk. We are in M.'s office, & M.'s mouth keeps popping open, so shocked that W. will not admit to knowing for certain that any but himself or his sensations exist. M. as delighted as he is pained by W.'s pigheadedness. From time to time I jump in, &, alas, usually more in M.'s favour than W.'s. Most of all, I am trying not to laugh — for all its seriousness, there is a distinct air of ridiculousness about it. W., meantime, is putting M. through his paces, rejecting one by one M.'s arguments in favor of common sense.

M. sees he's getting nowhere, so he ably turns the question to a *reductio ad absurdum,* saying, "Very well, Wittgenstein, will you at least admit there is not a rhinoceros in this room?" Wittgenstein emphatically shakes his head no. *"In this small room?"* asks Moore, scratching his head. "Indeed, a rhinoceros in here? Ought we not run?" In an effort to further shame him, M.

stands, peeks under the desk, peers in the corner. M. looks everywhere for this beast but where it is — glowering in W.'s seat.

Between Pinsent and Wittgenstein, more personal conflicts were also beginning to emerge, and Pinsent kept a steady record of these, too.

20.III.13

Ask W. if he is walking out w/ anyone. He smiles at my cheek & says, "No, are *you*?" I say with some shame, "No . . . not at present." "At *present*?" he asks, & I think he has caught me in a logical/linguistic absurdity (the effect of feeling one's fly is undone). But actually, this is a lie; I never had a girl. Why can I not say this? "Well, no, I do not have one — yet. But I suppose I shall . . . sometime."

W. still smiling. "And what will you do then, David?" And again, I find myself looking at him, wondering what he *means* — alarmed. Not knowing what better to say, I interject, "You do not like women?"

W. stops smiling; the cat now finds himself the mouse & is furious, sputtering, as he says, "You ask astonishingly impudent & asinine questions! I thought you were just young — naive. But I see you really are an ass! Just an ass!" "Yes," I retort, "and you are extraordinarily cruel!" "After all," he says, "still a boy!" & storms off, his head down.

Ashamed because I see I fear him. Is it possible that Russell tolerates this behaviour? Better away from him, I think, then wonder if it is not him but *me*. Never had much luck with friendship. Too much the lone duck.

20.III.13 (midnight)

W. comes to apologize. Feel angry. Don't want to see him, but I let him in, he looks so desolate. Straightaway, he says, "I was shameful. Shameful. But now perhaps you *see* me, how it is I am . . .

He crumbles off (his English gets poorer, esp. in pronunciation, when he is upset). At length he's tongue-tied, stuttering, "I have no tolerance. Smaller — less understanding I have . . ."

Think he is trying to get rid of me nicely. Then think he's only trying to beg sympathy, then am just angry & afraid. Why must I fight him? Why do I get close to tears when I am furious?

God, but he talks & talks. And he is persuasive — fearfully. Then we are reconciled & I am afraid again, thinking it will only happen again; as it must happen — his mind in a perpetual state of war. All the while I keep feeling this need to fight him. Fighting & the exhaustion of fighting, wch. am no good at for always seeing both sides, as w/ Mother. Ever since a boy, I have been this way. Always using myself against myself, like that Oriental jujitsu by wch. a man defeats his opponent by turning the opponent's own force against him.

Then W. says, "I will tell you now of my family." Before he even speaks, I
see I do not *want* to know. I see why he kept silent about his family — terrible
business about his brothers . . . He is so factual. Surgical. No details how he
felt, wch. makes it that much worse. So gloomy and Germanic, I think. An
Englishman would offer no more but wd. be more blithe & resigned to it.

Finally, I ask him why his father put his brothers out, but W. bridles at
this. "That's quite irrelevant. It happened. That is all that can be sd.!" "Yes,"
I say, "but it might not have happened had your father given them a chance."
W. retorts: "My father is a perfectionist — as I am." And I think, *God help
you both.*

28.III.13

Today we are walking & I say, "Why don't we sit down?"

We are on a hill — wide & green, with a red church steeple in the distance
over the early green of the trees & the smell of things germinating. I can
smell the grass in the sun, an empty-headed gazing. Not W. Not for a single
moment can he stop thinking. Apparently, he and Russell have had another
row & he looks ill. Seeing him looking at me, I shrink; & then he looks even
worse. With his knees drawn up to his chest, he looks as if he's floating on a
chunk of ice — adrift. "Are you ill?" I ask. He shakes his head & says with
some effort, "Might we move back a bit?" Seeing my quizzical look, he adds,
"The space sometimes, it makes me dizzy." "Space?" I ask. "*Open* space."

We draw back then, but still W. remains frozen. Sitting there, he keeps
trying to make himself smaller, focusing himself under the sun's beams like
a specimen beneath a microscope.

3.IV.13

We go out punting on the river, wch. is high with spring, & we see a man
with his friend. The man is fishing & he either has the biggest fish in the
world (wch. he doesn't) or he is caught on the bottom. Seeing our curiosity,
the fisher & his friend wave us away. "We've hooked a huge one — huge!
Please! You must give us berth, else we'll lose him!"

Others on shore and in boats are looking at the comical pair — the Simple
Simon hooked on the bottom & the ass leaning over the water w/ his little
net, patiently waiting to boat this mammoth. For half an hour, the two asses
fight this fish, when the line breaks! From the shore come condolences, clapping, jeers. "Too bad!" "Bad luck, mate!" They stand up then, the two simpletons. So proud they are, the worthy fight over, holding out their empty
hands. Even W. is laughing.

Watching the pair row home, Wittgenstein looks at me & says, "Friendship is like that. There is no sense to it, no practicality whatsoever. Imagine — that two fools could teach me more about friendship than any book."

W. he looks at me then, smiling, & I see his point in relation to our own budding friendship. But then I see that likely he'll be the one fishing & I the poor fool holding the net.

7.IV.13

Money. Another disagreement about it.

W. has money — his family has a huge pot of it, apparently, whilst I have little or none & no prospects. Ought to be grateful for his generosity, yet it galls me, that he always pays. Forever bringing me little gifts. In spite of myself, I like this — yet it makes me feel helpless, little Davie, that he always pays & I cannot. Whether W. knows it or not, this money is just one more thing that he can control. I have always hated money & people's hidden strings in giving it — Uncle Howard & that lot. That rotten beholdenness, to see Mother have to suck up to them & account for every rotten farthing.

W. is uncomfortable & guilty w/ his money, as though it were a third party between us about whom I am apparently not to remark. I feel him scrutinize the state of my clothes, wch. must shame him, he is so careful in his dress — tie & suit, shoes always faultlessly shined. Every time we pass a clothier, I feel he would drag me inside. Worse, I wish in a way he would & feel like a sponger. Cursed money.

At supper, without thinking, W. says, "My manservant, Klaus, he used to say —" Then, flushing, he stops himself, saying, "Forgive me. This is stupidity — boasting." I say, "That is your life. You cannot help being wealthy." But this comes off badly. He will say nothing more about it & then the cheque comes. Feeling my palms sweat. A guilty gulp as he pays.

12.IV.13

Walking with W. See an exceedingly beautiful woman & remark on her, feeling as always that mixture of awkwardness & impossibility & shyness. W. does look at her, but as someone might assess a statue — very abstract, none of that longing. I want to say, "But do you not suffer from such a woman!" But he does not, I see. He suffers from other things, & once more I feel that sense of inadequacy, because I suffer & he does not. In a way, I would to be independent like him & not suffer. Yet he suffers. Plainly he suffers, but not from female beauty. In him there is an indescribable longing, but not, I think, for sex. In music I can see his sensual side, though that is not the word. Certainly he is infinitely more spiritual than I am, though that is not the word, either . . .

15.IV.13

W. in a funk again. His expression says do not ask, yet plainly he wishes me to ask. I ask if it is R., but he shakes his head. It is a letter from his father, he says. *This* much he wants me to know; anything more he will not discuss.

Yet he says I really must meet his father, saying this as if he would introduce me to the Kaiser. God help me if I speak ill of his father; then I have profaned. Or Russell — a god, to hear W. talk.

Outside again, W. hugs the periphery of the trees. Walking at a crawl. Daren't sit. Daren't stop. The sky looms.

17.IV.13

This is odd. W. & I at a recital of the Cambridge Chamber Society. W. is standing before the loo, looking puzzled. Turns to me and asks — though the legend GENTLEMEN on the door is quite plain — "This *is* the one for men, is it not?"

25.IV.13

W. & I at the cinema — an American cowboy film, *Bronco Billy and the Cowpunchers*. It's Bronco Billy with his trick horse, Teepee. A typical cowboy film — farcical fisticuffs & grimacing villains clutching their chests as they fall back, shot.

I'm bored, but for W. this American cowboy muck is utterly simple & beautiful, beyond the ken of mere art. It is, he says, "ethically instructive." With longing, he says: "Imagine if one were always good. If one were good virtually by definition. Would it not be wonderful — to be so good that one had no choice? To be so good that nothing evil or unfortunate could ever befall you?" "But that would be terribly boring!" I insist. "One perpetual Sunday." "*You!*" he says forbiddingly. "This you would not understand. You are naturally good." "I'm not so good," I say. "Less good than you are guilty."

W. shocked that I would see this. He looks at me almost approvingly. For once, it seems, I am right. But for now, in the cinema, W. is free & good & not guilty, & I watch him yawn back, astounded, as the posse gallops over our heads.

Inquiries

BUT PINSENT didn't have Wittgenstein to himself for long. Soon others besides Russell were after Wittgenstein, starting with Lytton Strachey.

28.IV.13

W. to tea today with Lytton Strachey & Maynard Keynes. W. very offhand, as if this were nothing. I met Keynes and Strachey December last, in M.'s office. Both were so formidable. In their eagerness to talk to M., they quite passed over me. Couldn't very well blame them. M. pushed several questions my way, but I was blocked — they were so dashing & sure. Also, Strachey made me nervous, he leaned so close; also his laugh — extravagant, forced, a bit overbearing. Keynes dark & glowering & aloof — arrogant, I hear, & justly so if this be true. M. says he's fully as clever as Russell. (Naturally, M. would eliminate himself from the running.)

Later, W. returns from this tea. Says they wish him to come to a meeting of the Apostles, where he is to talk on a subject of his choosing, wch. he cannot disclose. Frankly, I'm surprised W. would go, tho' he treats this as nothing — a courtesy, nothing more. He deludes himself: it is hardly a courtesy to accept an invitation to meet with the brilliants of Cambridge's mysterious & elect club. But here I see I am jealous, & then am ashamed to be jealous. Still, I am not so shamed as Wittgenstein is of his own ambition. This W. conceals even from himself, like his wealth. Nonetheless, he is wealthy. And ambitious.

When Wittgenstein told Russell about this invitation two days later, he took this same offhand attitude. But like Pinsent, Russell saw through it. It rankled Russell to hear of it two days after the fact, but what bothered him even more was that the Apostles had not consulted him before extending the invitation. After all, thought Russell, what did Strachey and Keynes — or Moore, for that matter — know about Wittgenstein? They saw only the energy and potential; they knew nothing about his volatile nature. Then there was Russell's more general discomfort with the Society, which had become less a culture of Moore and more one of Strachey, who had brought the homoerotic wing of the Society out of its early period of latency into the more aggressive politics of the Higher Sodomy. This, for Strachey, was the intellectual sublimity and indeed supremacy of male love — of Patroclus with his arm around the immortal Achilles — and of the glory of the ancient Greek theater, where men, in a dream of androgyny, rendered womankind superfluous, playing the parts of both men and women. This, then, had hastened Russell's departure. As for Moore, who for years had thought sodomy had died with the ancients, he cast something of a half-blind eye on this. But then of course when *the Divine* Moore was present among the randys, there weren't the droll looks and pats, the brittle jokes and esoterica about tight bums and buggery.

Even as Wittgenstein sat there with his legs twisted around, Russell could feel his tension building. Wittgenstein was asking him, in effect, if it was all right to join the Society — if it was not vain and foolish.

Russell was brusque. Well, go, he said. Go, by all means. At least see if you like it.

Wittgenstein's eyes wandered, then he asked suddenly, You were a member, were you not?

Russell shrugged. Oh, some years ago. It's been four or five years since I turned in my wings — angels, we're called, the older fellows who have taken degrees and gone on. Strachey and Keynes are angels — *fallen* angels, he added with a snort, wondering if Wittgenstein would catch his drift, or if indeed this might be Wittgenstein's drift. Probing, Russell added vaguely, Moore's still active, I believe.

Yes. Wittgenstein looked up suddenly. Moore named me.

Oh? Russell turned to light his pipe, the match flaring as he poked it into the bowl.

Wittgenstein saw Russell's sly look but misread it, wondering if Russell was really the one behind it. Then *you* recommended me to Moore? Wittgenstein asked pointedly.

Indeed, no. Russell grimaced with the pipe fixed between his teeth. *I* had nothing to do with it. Strachey's the one who runs the show now. Moore's a mere figurehead. They said nothing to me.

But now Wittgenstein got a different feeling, a hint of censure that bled into a hue he was at peril to discriminate. Rising again, Wittgenstein asked edgily, Well, what do you think? Ought I to join? *If* I am asked, I mean?

Well — Russell began to speak, then checked himself, saying with dubious conviction, Go.

Wittgenstein turned, circled, turned, sat. His indecision dance.

I mean that, repeated Russell. Go —

But why? Do you care?

Care? Why, of course not. Again, a moment's hesitation, then a cloud of smoke as Russell added, On the other hand, I don't want anyone to think I told you *not* to go.

But why would anyone think that? Wittgenstein looked as if he were sitting on a cake of ice. Why ever would you advise me against it?

Cautiously offhand, Russell said, Because I'm no longer active. I don't know. They're a suspicious lot in ways.

Suspicious?

In the way of a coterie, suspicious. Nothing very unusual in a group, the cliquishness and little intrigues.

And Moore?

What about Moore?

He takes part in this?

Dear me, I don't know. A dry smile. Moore is Moore.

But then Wittgenstein felt a different edge to this, causing him to ask, Then you've quarreled, you two?

No, we haven't quarreled. An indignant look. Another cloud of smoke. Go — You'll see soon enough what you like.

See what?

Go!

Wittgenstein wasn't the only one who felt Russell's spurs. By the heavy swing doors, on his way to Hall for breakfast the next morning, Russell finally caught up with Moore. Russell strode straight up to him.

I understand Wittgenstein has been invited to the next Apostles meeting.

Moore eyed him up and down. That's correct.

You initiated it?

Come to quarrel with me this morning, have you?

Not to quarrel, to inquire.

Well, your manner is fast making me angry.

I'd like to know why I wasn't informed.

You're no longer active. Why was I obliged to inform you?

As a courtesy if nothing else. I'm a member in good standing.

Former member. And a former member who, I fear, is a bit off course this morning.

Am I? asked Russell, leaning closer so this wouldn't be heard. I venture you'd feel the same if it were Pinsent.

Pinsent goes his own way, said Moore measuredly. Thanks to Wittgenstein, he's gone it quite completely, actually.

Russell stood there nodding. And this is my fault, is it? That your game, is it? To use the Apostles to pry Wittgenstein away from Pinsent?

This was so absurd that Moore hardly knew how to respond. Craning forward, he said, I believe that will be quite enough this morning, thank you.

Yes, by all means. Russell dropped his shoulders. By all means.

That was all. Separately, they strode down the corridor into Hall, where the hazy sun was streaming through the stained glass, warming the ancient oak of the trenchers, where breakfast was already under way. And there, at opposite ends of High Table, not a pistol shot away, the two dons chopped and swallowed in silence, their stomachs gurgling with early morning acid.

•

Getting nowhere with Moore, Russell then did the next worse thing: like Paul Revere, he went to Strachey and Keynes to warn them of the *danger* of electing Wittgenstein.

Normally, Russell was effective in the counselor's role, but this time he was in a sorry state. Lytton, always able to see the worst, thought Russell was in a shambles — old as Methuselah, with his haggard grimace and hair singed white. Such a crashing bore Bertie was, with his dire predictions. Why, the old boy was practically panting as he ran on with mounting frustration.

You simply don't *know* Wittgenstein as I do. I'm convinced he'll find the Society an utter waste of time. And really, he added impoliticly, you both must admit the Society is not what it once was.

I wouldn't say that, interjected Keynes, who for five minutes had listened in silence to this diatribe. Keynes felt the edge of this just as keenly as Strachey did, and he was not one to be toyed with. Keynes's tapping foot was like the switching tail of a cogitating cat as he continued. To every angel I'm sure the next generation seems debased — less this or that. But I can assure you the Brethren are quite impressive. Especially this latest crop.

Very well, then, said Russell, straining to be conciliatory. I stand corrected. But I still tell you — Wittgenstein may go along for a meeting or two, but then he will leave. Of that I'm certain.

And what if he *does*? asked Lytton impatiently. If you don't mind my asking, Bertie, of what consequence is it to you?

Me? Why, it's nothing to *me*. Russell felt himself inwardly wince at this transparent denial. It's Wittgenstein I'm concerned about. There's quite enough turmoil in him.

Keynes's foot set once more to tapping, and Strachey, taking his cue, asked still more pointedly, Just turmoil in Wittgenstein, is it?

Russell was moved to anger, but looking into Strachey's raw, bearded face he thought better of it, seeing to his humiliation that he was defenseless. He had no good answer; even for himself, he had no good answer, let alone one that these two partisans would have accepted. Retreating toward the door, Russell could only repeat his warnings.

As a statistician, Keynes had a first-rate logical mind — frequently he and Russell conferred on matters of mutual interest. Hanging by the door then, Russell was hoping that Keynes, with his courtier's demeanor, might come to his rescue — might artfully change the subject, perhaps even invite him to tea. Instead, the unstintingly correct Keynes ushered him out with that mild solicitousness reserved for dotards and cripples, saying, Well, good day, old man, good day . . .

And as the door swung closed, Russell had a distinct sense of social slippage, feeling — quite correctly, it turned out — that he would soon be the butt of half of Cambridge, with Ottoline pulling the strings like Pallas Athene.

But Russell didn't stop there. Starved for information, he boldly went up to Pinsent one day and introduced himself. Pinsent wrote:

4.V.13
At last I meet Russell. Russell, rather, meets me — waylays me. "You're D.P., aren't you? — Wittgenstein's friend?"
Feel cool to him. R. says how much he has wanted to meet me. W. has told him so much. "Has he?" I ask. "Oh, indeed," R. assures me. I look at him, wondering what W. has said, but R. is not forthcoming. For someone who has heard so much, he is certainly full of questions. Suddenly he asks, "Well, what do you think about this business with the Apostles? Do you think W. will join? But" — he shrugs — "M. recommended him, after all. I suppose it might be a good thing."
Did R. know what he was saying? He certainly did; the fox was craftily watching to see my reaction. I must have looked upset. Feel even M. has duped me. Here M. purports to think so highly of my talent, yet he recommends W. & not me!

Pinsent tried to conceal his anger from Moore, but Moore felt the chill. At the same time, Moore saw Pinsent's work was suffering. A few days later, Pinsent wrote:

9.V.13
M. takes me aside today. From the start I know it's about his concerns that I'm neglecting my studies as a result of W.
M. is more donnish than usual & I am resisting — resisting as I have done with every well-intentioned parson or prefect who ever sat me down. I want to ask, "Why even *speak* to me? If mine is such a weighty talent, why didn't you recommend *me*?"
M. is so careful in his enquiry. Remarks that I've been preoccupied. Implies that I've given up too much of myself for W.'s sake. Nothing new here. I've merely thrown Mother over for a new patient.

Not long after this, Pinsent felt pressure from yet another quarter.

13.V.13
Reply from Mother to my last letter. Concerned about my hints at dropping mathematics for classics, possible problems with stipends. More ex-

penses & no money, yet here W. has invited me to Vienna this summer. Feel guilty at the thought of eating lavishly there, while Mother hardly eats at all.

W. tells me I'm too harsh on her. Am I? Am tempted to show him her letters but feel he'd probably find them charming, as w/ his beloved cowboys. Mother is happy. She says we shall not need the grocer, having put in a new garden to replace the overgrown ruin that she planted last summer, w/ its mushy tomatoes. Another litter of cats to overrun the place & the roof still leaking. Says she paid 3 pounds to have it fixed, but the man got drunk & put his foot through the thatch & did not return. Now torrents pour down, but Mother says we have the most glorious swifts in the attic. She predicts that the tufts on the dandelions auger a halcyon summer; & such clouds, & such faces on them! And when, she asks, shall I bring home this Mr. Wittgenstein?

W. says he would very much like to go. He will pay all expenses, of course. And then we shall leave, & naturally I shall feel not a whit guilty about Mother eating mushy tomatoes among the swifts & clouds & cats, w/ the rain dribbling down in pots . . .

And so the trip was arranged: in the third weekend of May, they would visit Pinsent's mother, who lived in the country outside Birmingham. In the meantime, other forces were in motion. Two days before they were to leave, Wittgenstein finally went before the Apostles and gave his speech on "The Nature of Logic." Abstract, exalted, fierce, Wittgenstein kept the Brethren enthralled for ten minutes before he summarily sat down. His election the next day was virtually unanimous.

As it turned out, Russell was quite correct in his warnings about Wittgenstein and the Society. Moore was visibly displeased when Wittgenstein came to him that day to explain his hesitation about joining, his fears that it was not right for him and that he would eventually disappoint the brothers — roughly what Russell had been saying all along. But there was also what Wittgenstein did not say about a certain undercurrent he felt in these ostensibly Olympian discussions. For Wittgenstein, these men were too much at ease, expending too much energy exploring vaguely frivolous topics. He couldn't stand the solemn pauses, the delicious reaching and *je ne sais quoi* punctuated with tweaking innuendoes. That was what he smelled: complacency. Were he to let them, they would have adored him, and this also was his fear, that he might succumb to this decorous ease. To remain honest, he felt he must be even harder, more fierce and impervious: he was the potential criminal who must make himself a judge.

Still, the atmosphere was dangerously attractive, strumming the strings of a side of him that he had to fight, if not expunge. There was the poet Békássy, a British-educated Hungarian aristocrat more English than the English, dandified and severe, with slick dark hair and malodorous opinions he let out like fragrance from a perfume flask. In Békássy was a fulsome whiff of home, the sirocco of Hungarian politics and the Prater, of the booted equestrian who sojourned into the meadows at sunset, having brought his strap and left his horse elsewhere. As for the others, Wittgenstein liked Keynes quite well — Keynes struck him as a clear thinker. But Strachey! To hear him address one of his pets in an urgent whisper as *Pussums, dear* — this gave the candidate the hives. But as he was repelled, so was he faintly drawn.

Of course, Wittgenstein did not say this to Moore, who found his evident agitation difficult to comprehend, if not a bit suspect. Yes, Moore was vexed with him, vexed at these vague complaints expressed as scruples, not to mention the implicit insult that what was good enough for Moore was somehow not good enough for Wittgenstein. Moore wondered what he ought to do. Like Pilate, he had largely tried to remove himself from the proceedings. He had purposely stayed away from the previous night's meeting — a strategic move to sidestep Russell's probable criticism that he was meddling. But now, having tried to do the decent thing, Moore felt duped. Russell would have the last laugh: Moore could well imagine Russell's delight — if not his hand in this — but that was another matter. Moore's immediate concern was that if Wittgenstein waited too long to accept this honor, he would be burning his bridges. The Brethren would certainly be insulted. They'd never take Wittgenstein back if he thought better of his decision.

Wittgenstein's talk with Moore went poorly, and he did not expect his visit to Russell to go much better. But more than just the Apostles was weighing on Wittgenstein then: there was also Russell's theory of types.

In his work developing a proper logical symbolism, Wittgenstein had recently become convinced that Russell's theory was not so much wrong as unnecessary. Wittgenstein had not consciously ferreted this out. Rather, the realization seemed to have found him, like a collision.

Wittgenstein still felt sick about it. He knew it was his duty to tell Russell, but he was dreading it. Still, he felt it could wait. Certainly, he had no intention of broaching the subject that day as he went to tell Russell about his election. This proved an unnecessary courtesy, Moore having sent Russell a curt note about the election that morning. Russell could well imagine Moore's triumph, not to mention that of the gossips like Strachey, who would paint him a grasping opportunist bent on hoarding — or even stealing — the fruits of another's genius. Prompted by Lytton, even Ottoline had entered the fray, asking Russell, much to his mortification, why he had to embarrass himself, and her, with his meddling.

The moment Wittgenstein set foot inside Russell's rooms, he sensed his mentor's smoldering resentment, and it rankled him. At the same time, Wittgenstein felt that his predicament was far from Russell's fault. Rather, it stemmed from the ratiocinations of a higher logic, of which his logic and life were somehow the unhappy result. And again with his election to the Society — with that sudden, ineluctable sense of elevation and the threat of pleasure — Wittgenstein felt a compensatory desire to veer away from that pole and end his life. But even this desire was not enough. To carry it out, Wittgenstein felt, in a blind way, that he must do something deserving of death, and that afternoon at Russell's he found it just as surely as if he'd planned his every move.

By then, the Apostles had been shunted aside, and they were suddenly talking (if indeed they had ever stopped talking) about logic, of its sublime blankness. The *old* logic, said Wittgenstein (meaning, Russell's logic) did not grasp this fundamental truth. The old logic assumed a hierarchy of propositions, building up from axioms, when in fact all the propositions of logic stand on the same level and say the same thing — namely, *nothing*. This, Wittgenstein told Russell, was his great mistake. For the old logic, logic was fundamentally a cog machine: it supplied certain primitive propositions, it supplied the rules of deduction governing their use, and it then said that what results is a *logical* proposition — one that had been pushed through the sausage grinder and thus *made* logical.

In his urgency then, Wittgenstein was hardly building an airtight argument. He was not piercing or succinct. On the contrary, he was thoroughly scattered and staccato. But this only made the force of his invective more fearsome and bewildering. And then, just as if he had planned it, Wittgenstein was attacking the theory of types, Russell's response to the Cretan who called all Cretans liars. Wittgenstein was the confounding Cretan. The essence of Russell's theory, Wittgenstein was saying, was that a proposition could not make a statement about itself. But this, he declared, was only a chimera imposed by Russell's mathematics, for which it was necessary that numbers be classes of classes. In mathematics, this might be expedient, Wittgenstein said, but in logic it held no sway and was in fact useless. Our work in the field of logic might help us better *display* logic, he said, but it could not *supply* or *create* logic: how could we presume to supply what is already there? In logic *we* do not express whatever we wish with the aid of signs; rather, the nature of the absolutely necessary signs speaks for itself. In his theory, then, Russell was only imposing a form on what was already logical and perfect. Clearly, Wittgenstein said, the laws of logic could not in turn be subject to the laws of logic — it was here, he insisted, that Russell's theory broke down. It tried to talk about the *types* it had imposed when one could only talk about the particular symbols. After all, Wittgenstein said, to declare the meanings of signs when establishing rules for them — well, this was certainly wrong. In a correct symbolism there would be no need to invent a system of types to avoid contradictions; the correct sense would be evident in the signs themselves — evident *in advance,* so to speak.

Wittgenstein, by then, was not in control of his voice or his hands; his eyes were gritty slits. There was no question in Russell's mind that Wittgenstein was right: to Russell, Wittgenstein was infallible — sibylline. Without defense or will, Russell sat listlessly in a chair near the lamp. Funny how his hands looked to him under the light, like gloves, so useless and old. Slowly, the blood was draining from his upturned fingers; his breath came in starts. Not that night, or even the next week, would Russell even begin to assess the extent of the damage, much less the further damage that would result, forcing a slow but inexorable change in his life. The wound, Russell assured himself, was not mortal. Russell told himself that his work was like a ship sectioned into watertight compartments, with other doors — sound theories — that could contain the flood when a bulkhead had ruptured. His ship was not sinking, he assured himself. This setback was only temporary. Ottoline had been speaking of an Italian holiday that summer. Yes, they would journey south to Italy, that's where. Ah, he could see them in Venice, so sensual and golden, then on to Naples, the warm Mediterranean. Standing on some sun-drenched terrace with Ottoline, tanned and relaxed, he would be a man transformed. Utterly dashing and charming in his linen suit, he would wend his way through one long party, feeling the admiration of all the ladies as he said, *E una notte serena. Signorina, permetta che mi presenti. Signor Russell . . . Il piacere, il piacere . . .*

But while the hemorrhaging Russell retreated into dreams, Wittgenstein could not stay, not after this. In his own eyes, he was no better than Judas, and Russell was too distracted to stop him from leaving. But then as the door closed, it occurred to Russell that Wittgenstein might really kill himself, and he thought, *Good,* then gave a shudder, as if he had bitten his tongue. Pinsent was asleep when Russell knocked an hour later.

... Russell appears at 1 A.M. in a state. He says W. is "upset" & he is looking for him. Am tempted to ask why W. is upset but I do not, & R. does not volunteer. I ask R. if he has checked W.'s room and he says yes. "You just knocked?" I ask, thinking W. might be inside, hanged. R. knows my fear & adds uncomfortably, "I checked inside. After knocking, of course."

Hands trembling as I dress. All very delicate & queasy; I have the gory feeling of going through some deceased relative's personal effects. We don't want to sound the alarm — don't want to embarrass W. if it is nothing. We are only "looking," & from time to time R., faced with my silence, makes ridiculous excuses: "If only he could rest ... If only he took better care of himself."

For two hours we look, then give it up, promising to notify each other if he turns up. R. says officiously, "I really must speak to him tomorrow." Evidently, R. wants me to agree that this will make everything much better. But all I can bring myself to say is good night. R. is a sad, ruined figure at 3 A.M.; in him there is love, I think, but I cannot warm to him. Still, cannot entirely blame him. If so strong a man as R. is not immune to W., how can I be? At this point, it's doubtful that W. can even endure himself, & I think of him hanging from a pipe, like one with a price on his head.

Flo

WITTGENSTEIN DID TURN UP the next day — no better, no worse, so far as Pinsent could tell. Keeping his promise to Russell, Pinsent said nothing about that night, and Wittgenstein said nothing either.

Even the following morning as they boarded the westbound train for Birmingham, Wittgenstein said nothing about Russell or the Apostles. Pinsent wrote:

I do not count it a good sign that he does not confide in me & sense I am not to ask. Instead, we talk about Mother & what we shall do at home, while I worry if she will have anything prepared. Looking out the window of the train, W. remarks, as if he has just now noticed, "We are on a holiday."

In all, it was a pleasant journey, warm May weather. Yet there was still the same discomfort with money, which remained a barrier between them. Wittgenstein paid for the tickets — second class, quite unostentatious — sliding quiet notes across the cage, then pocketing his change with lowered eyes and a furtive hike of the trousers, as though he were turning from a urinal. Lunch was another hurdle. In the swaying dining car, huddled behind his wobbling water goblet, Pinsent froze as Wittgenstein invited him to order. In that millrace of the spirit, seeking ever purer air, Wittgenstein was increasingly ascetic in his tastes. He preferred the simple and bland — a near vegetarian — but this did not prevent him from suggesting that Pinsent should try the mixed grill or perhaps the York ham and Winchester pudding. Peering up, his red hair fanning across his face, Pinsent asked ascerbically, Why? So you can watch?

Pinsent kept him honest and of this earth — or tried. And actually, Wittgenstein was in somewhat better spirits as they ate their lunch, both staring out at the rolling hills of the midlands. It gave Wittgenstein pleasure to indulge his friend, heir to the life he could not permit himself. Pinsent had his mixed grill with a bowl of mock turtle soup. Knowing how Pinsent loved sweets, Wittgenstein, on the sly, told the steward to bring his friend a raspberry trifle. Pinsent was man alive. He would not refuse these earthly gifts; it was the draconian Wittgenstein who ate humble pie, as quick to deny these innocent pleasures as he was to reject the Apostles, where the food was surely too ambrosial. Wittgenstein would remain friendly with the piercing Keynes, but he could not stomach these other young men, so vain of their brilliance, certain of their place and free with their opinions, and much else.

No, now that Wittgenstein had been offered an Apostleship, he was quite sure that Pinsent would not want one — assuming, of course, that one was even offered. (Pinsent, it seemed to Wittgenstein, was not the trumped-up, obviously impressive sort of man who got noticed for such things; nor was he titled, handsome or rich.)

No, in his ill-guided but well-meaning way, Wittgenstein had other plans for Pinsent. Pinsent, it seemed to him, did not want philosophy — Wittgenstein certainly did not want his friend mucking those stalls. He did not question his own motives; he had no sense of being selfish, or patronizing or presumptuous. If nothing else, he could at least bequeath Pinsent a life free of pain, failure and want. And soon enough Wittgenstein would remove from Pinsent's path the impediment his own life represented. *He* would not be a Blocker, nor would he be greedy: if he could not eat, procreate or prosper on this earth, then he would shortly cede his place to one who could. And so Wittgenstein was going to meet David's mother, to see that all was properly provided for.

•

As they neared Birmingham, meanwhile, Pinsent was worried how Flo would come off to his friend. Pinsent's irreverence about his mother pained Wittgenstein, but then Pinsent was hardly fooled by the court portrait that Wittgenstein painted of his own family. Even more exasperating for Pinsent was how Wittgenstein would paint Flo as some poor, wronged creature — and him the cynical, unjust son. Pinsent said he knew the truth. He told Wittgenstein that he could damned well call her Flo or Bats if he chose — it was he, after all, who had pressed a lock of her hair inside the glass of her photograph. And really, Pinsent told Wittgenstein, if life at home was so awfully cozy, where were the photos of *his* mother and father?

Pinsent was silent and nervous as their motorcab climbed Dalk's Hill, where Flo lived in a cottage of rust-colored stone. It was open farm country, not far from a village set among bowed fields and pastures bound by hedgerows. In the distance there was a slice of river, milk white in the sun, and below that a long swell of slope, mild and green, with cows and a squat stand of trees.

Flo was nowhere to be seen. The gate was gone, and the stones of the walk were slick with brownish-green moss. Last year's rotting apples lay beneath the same snarled limbs, now newly blossoming, and as they approached the door, scrawny cats bounded like rabbits through the weeds. Mind your step, said Pinsent with embarrassment as they picked over broken crockery and a rusty garden trowel where someone had tried to pot something. Pinsent sighed as the door fell open. She never locks it, he said.

Inside, under moss-dark beams, was a murky clutter, a mindscape of half-finished puzzles, hands of solitaire, novels splayed on their spines. Still, it was a feminine disarray, not entirely unattractive. Like giant fungi, blackened oranges spiked with cloves hung from the beams, adding a vinous, spicy scent to the general subterranean odor. And then they heard Flo's conjugating cry:

Dave, Davy, David!

Floating under a mist of reddish-gray hair and dressed in an old gown of silk, lace and tulle, tiny Florence Pinsent barreled down the stairs, then hugged and kissed her son before she abruptly turned to shake Wittgenstein's hand. Oh! she exclaimed when Wittgenstein made an abbreviated bow. David said you had the most lovely manners. And *Sweet William!* You brought me *Sweet William!* Before Wittgenstein could even present them to her, she had thrust her blunt nose into the mottled mass of flowers. Oh! Oh! Waving her hands, Flo hardly knew whether to get her eyeglasses or a vase, she was so prickly excited.

There was no stopping her then. Did you see that rain? Florence Pinsent suddenly wanted to know, gaping up at Wittgenstein as if she had just now seen the Annunciation. Now that was the rain, it was. It passed right over! I prayed it would miss you! I said so and meant it, and it did and didn't, dear me!

Flo's mouth widened as if she had just remembered that her son was indeed here. David, my love, let me look at you! He's so shy, she said, turning secretively to Wittgenstein, her accomplice in this orgy of affection. And *Sweet William* you brought me! Not *baby's breath*, she cautioned suddenly, though no one had suggested it was. Looking around then, she suddenly remarked, Isn't that a queer name, *baby's breath*? Do you suppose anyone knew what *baby's* breath looked like when they named it? I'd call it *sneeze plant* — oh, it makes me sneeze just to look at it! But you know, she said, wagging her finger, perhaps the person that named it baby's breath saw a baby's breath in the winter — when it was steaming, I mean. Clasping her downturned bosom, Florence Pinsent grandly sneezed.

David, darling, resumed Flo, making a pouty face as hungry cats wove underfoot. The fire must have just gone out!

Just gone out, Mother? asked the son, looking at the cold coals.

Then, rolling her eyes, she said mischievously, I don't know what happened, dear. Now he's angry at me, you see, she said, taking refuge behind Wittgenstein. But Davy, she continued in a whiny, girlish voice. Just an hour ago I stirred it. Why don't you relight it and I'll make tea with your lovely Mr. Wittgenstein.

She was a consummate actress, adept at creating little cul de sacs and enveloping silences between people. Taking *her* guest by the arm, she led him toward the unkempt kitchen, saying, I'm so excited that David has finally brought a friend home, Mr. Wittgenstein. David's so very excited about your work. He says it's far more important than his. *I think therefore I am!* Oh, no, David didn't say that — dear me, did you think so? My, no. Descartes René said so. I once tried to read him but I never got very far. I was never *am* enough to think I was, so I wasn't — so here I am! Or *was* —

Mrs. Pinsent flounced to the window to tap at a cat by the pane, then pointed out a cloud that she said looked like the king, gross and fat in his Ascot top hat. Had he ever seen the king, ever? No, no, she scolded, not *Georgie* — she meant the fat, dead one. Edward was his name. She had, once. Seen him, that is.

Queen Flo then decreed they would have tea and Wittgenstein was sent scrounging beneath the cabinets for the kettle, which they set on the gas ring after yet another search for matches. I have the most wonderful biscuits, she said. Mistress of this tea party, Flo giggled with her mouth full and a wondering crinkling of the eyes. They're hazelnut somethings, I think — or filbert. I didn't make them, you know, she said just as proudly as if she had. *Shoo!* she said, driving a cat from the table. And again she went to the window, amazed to see the dolloped clouds massing over the western hills. And you must promise, she resumed, looking a little cross, you must remind me to show you David's numerous awards. Have you any? David has. Oh, but he'll be terribly upset if I boast of him. He's deaf in one ear, you know. Oh, yes. A man pulled his ear when he was a boy. Then argumentatively, I *saw* him! His uncle it was . . .

So began the pattern in which Flo would breathlessly take her guest aside to tell a seemingly pointless story which had the quality of whistling out of tune. Nevertheless, there was a fractured melody to these stories; the mother, however queer and charming, was more cunning and manipulative than she let on. Dimly, through the cloaking sweetness, Flo feared her guest. As the next day began to unfold, Wittgenstein even began to suspect that she was angry at him for usurping her boy. Wittgenstein could hardly blame her — if anything, he shared her fears, feeling that with time he would only bring Pinsent to grief as he had Russell.

Wittgenstein's guilt over Russell was weighing on him heavily now. Shortly before leaving for Birmingham, Wittgenstein had seen his mentor. Embroidering on the subject of his theory of types, talking with all the deliberate cheerfulness of a man in shock, Russell had really been asking Wittgenstein to assure him that his theory was salvageable, that, with time, all would be put to right. Wittgenstein couldn't do it. All he could offer Russell was silence — and not out of spite or anger. There was simply nothing to say: Russell's theory was wrong.

But if Wittgenstein did not grasp Flo's point initially, he did the second day when she asked, Do you know Mr. Moore? Well, he's very fond of David, I gather, but he wrote me saying he was concerned about David's, um, *direction*. Well, of course, I didn't know what to make of it, Mr. Wittgenstein. But then I got another letter from his governor, saying David had been neglectful of his studies. They have such high expectations of him. You see, he has a scholarship, and a very grand one, too.

So odd how Flo went on, so artlessly, as if she were impartial and unaffected by this. Wittgenstein felt as if he were party to a conversation inside her head, or his. She was an artful paradox, was Flo. She knew, for all her apparent artlessness, how to turn the screw. Do you agree with Mr. Moore? she asked after a long, fitful silence. In Flo's own interior logic, no reply was necessary or solicited from the visitor. Speaking into him as if into the telephone, Flo added with a hush of dread, I'm sure you have David's best interest at heart. I know he must help you — he said your work is more important. David's always helped — it's his nature to help. And expect none in return, mind you. Do you?

Mind?

My, no, *help*. Help Davy. Then before he could even answer came the reprise. David has certainly helped me. Oh, indeed, he has! That's David's way, you know.

Flo would say, It was the rainiest rain, the foggiest fog, that David was good because he was good — because he was her Davy David Descartes René, her *am*, so to speak, since all else was, or was no longer. Flo was herself a tautology. I *am* David's mother, she would declare, as if her silent guest might otherwise miss the connection.

It was the silliest thing, how ideas came to Wittgenstein, slowly rising like bubbles to the surface. For months now, Wittgenstein had been on the verge of perhaps his most fundamental insight, but not until Flo had it quite struck him in that direct, offkey way of a revelation, with that accompanying shortness of breath and the air suddenly a pale hue. What struck Wittgenstein with such force then was the notion that although a tautology *says* nothing, it *shows* its form and hence the undergirding structure of logic. On the tensile water, the wobbling rings were settling themselves; on the strumming water, above the freestanding depths, hung an apparent transparency of form without content, of form waiting like life to be filled, true or false, good or ill.

Wasn't life a tautology, singing of itself to itself? Wasn't suicide a contradiction, canceling itself with itself? With Flo, there was a certain parallel. Beneath the patter, she was really asking the visitor to desist and return her son, saying these words not so much for what they said as for what they might show or conjure, since words were magic. Over the hills swept the clouds, bruised and dark. Hovering like a bird in the wind, suspended in that silence before the remark, Flo gaped as the next cloud swept down. Dark the ground, dark the sun. Whoa, cried Flo, clutching her mortified son. That cloud looks like a Chinaman.

And so it was resolved. Out walking the next day, Wittgenstein suddenly thrust a bank draft for ten thousand pounds into Pinsent's hand, saying, And no talk, please, of debt or gratitude. Nothing you owe me. Not even friendship. *Please*, and not another word.

What is this? asked Pinsent. He looked frantic. I don't want this! *No!*

I insist — Wittgenstein put his hand on Pinsent's shoulder. You did not ask me for this, I know. It is not charity. You need this. I do not.

Why? Pinsent's eyes were welling over. Why don't you need it? Pinsent wanted to answer his own question, but again he held back. Answer me!

Never having properly understood money, its power to stun, Wittgenstein was shocked by this reaction. It was as if someone had told him that his potent signature was not backed by gold. Awkwardly, Wittgenstein said, I have more money. Too much money. This is not to boast — it is just a fact. Please, David. *Take it.*

For the wealthy man, this was something of a revelation. Until then, Wittgenstein never would have dreamed it was as hard to rid oneself of money as to have it. Pinsent wrote:

23.V.13

. . . So I took it — provisionally. First I worry where to get it, & now what to do with it & how to keep it.

W. seems relieved. If he has bought peace, I think, then oughtn't I sell it?

For now, we forget it — try. With money I think I can finally forget money, concentrate instead on beauty & spirit, as he does. Only I shall do so in new trousers, w/, I think, a Panama hat & some beautiful braces. I should like such a hat but then wonder if I dare; if it would be too vain.

Later, I am feeling gay. Wittgenstein is whistling. In the pasture, W. calls to some cows in German. Cows love German, he explains, even our English cattle. These are spotted, smooth-horned Guernseys, clopping down. We are enveloped. They are all over us, jealous ladies, butting & nudging for scratches behind their ears to relieve them of the incessant flies.

Later, we eat below a pale field of new grass. Then, toward dusk, something wondrous. Thunder approaching. By the river, the sedge is sweeping up & down like sheets of green silk. It is very high, the grass, & suddenly W. is terribly excited. On the water mayflies are hatching. Like sparks from a burning log, they pour out from the depths — clouds of them, white-white & warbling soundlessly over the water. Sitting on the bank, W. is as under a tent; an insect snow is falling all over him & he is gazing up, overcome. Over the water, the nymphs are a flat white nebula, & then the rain comes beating down, the water sizzling. Exposed out here, we might be struck by lightning, but he, ordinarily so practical, does not care. He doesn't heed me when I call, & then I see what it is. The flies are falling into the water. By the thousands, they are faltering like a white seltzer. The water is inundated & all are dead.

Looking at me, W. says, "Isn't it beautiful? For all to rise & fall for the same beautiful necessity? Wouldn't it be beautiful for us to rise up in light & fall in unison, serving only nature?"

I am appalled. I say, "I think it is jolly good for flies, but not for men. To have all the generations fall like that, in unison? How can you possibly call that idea beautiful?"

Now he is looking at me, not angry, but wistful; it seems I do not understand, tho' I think I do. He says, "You cannot ever be sad for that, not for necessity." "*Whose* necessity?" I ask. "This is only something in your mind! A poet might think it a beautiful thought, but he would not serve it. Was it really so poetic for Shelley to sail out in the storm & drown himself? That was for Shelley; that was not for Poetry."

I can't stand it. Want to tear up the cheque. He knows — he must — that I fear he will kill himself. It taxes & angers me, these hints — he is worse than Mother, how he manipulates me. Who does he serve — who do I? These flies obey another rule. That he has genius I acknowledge, but genius does not have to succumb to itself. I refuse to believe it.

Wedding and Wending

THREE WEEKS LATER, not long after the end of term, Moore was sitting with Dorothy at the head table at his wedding reception as all present, including Russell, Pinsent and Strachey, rose to toast the new couple.

The room was full of mirth and the heat of seventy-five people drinking, waltzing, hobnobbing. In that surfeit of happiness, tongues unfurled. Lytton Strachey, picking up after Moore's older brother Harry, said a few more words on behalf of the newlyweds. Lytton's toast was perfect — eloquent, touching, amusing. Until then, Russell had not planned to speak, but in the elation of the moment, he, too, stepped forth with raised glass and cleared his throat.

What on earth am I doing? he thought as the murmuring died down and all eyes fell on him. *What will I say?* he wondered, hoping that this sudden impulse was more than just the rumbling of the grape. He and Moore were still on strained terms, but Russell felt that after today they might turn a new page. A few warm words, that was all he wanted to say. After all, he could hardly hope to top a wit like Strachey — or could he?

He didn't start badly. There was even a certain piquance as he, an avowed unbeliever, said what a blessing it was to behold an honest man with a good woman on their wedding day. Yes, he continued, warming to his tongue's toothsome twang. *These two,* he said, unleashing his arm, would stand as an example to them all of the outer extent of human hopes. But then with this bibulous reaching, he felt the compensating pull of humor — something to balance and subdue the emotion, like cutting wine with seltzer. Yes, for a generation, he rebounded, Moore had symbolized the best. Nevertheless, he added dryly, he did not do badly. Mrs. Moore would make a man — he stumbled — a *better man* of him.

Here, here!

Moore, meanwhile, felt his bride urgently squeeze his hand, a telegraphic squeeze emitting potent signals of irritation verging on outrage. Even Russell was kicking himself. *Damn!* The way he tripped at the end, this as his eyes hungrily scanned the room for reaction. Oh, God. There was puckish Lytton, busily whispering to Keynes, Leonard Woolf and the attenuated Virginia.

For his part, Moore would gladly have forgotten this gaffe had not Dorothy, her dark hair crowned with a diadem of white cyclamen trailing white ribbons, then hissed into his ear, *What on earth did Bertie mean? He's so perverse.*

Two hours tied and she was already a wife, thought Moore, who as usual was surprised by how much she saw — and how much he missed.

But in that swarm of perceptions, this thought, too, was washed away as Moore covered her pale hand with his own, still unable to get over the gold ring on his finger. When Moore looked again, Bertie was talking to Pinsent; and then that image also vanished as his palsied Uncle Peter, a broken widower, came a third time to earnestly clutch their hands, fighting tears as he gasped for breath or words, wishing only to be near so much happiness. And here was Theodore Llewelyn Davies, an Apostle whom Moore had not seen in five — God, ten years at least! And *Crump!* Crump Davies, his brother! Crumpie, look at you!

This is what heaven must be like, thought Moore, a tide where all of what was formerly, returns. God, but it was spooky to have so much come all at once, like those unaccountable presents covering the table, and all these people who eddied toward them like ghosts, grasping their hands in that grateful silence where words fail and fall away. In the face of such rampant joy, it was hard for Moore to imagine the promise of more joy to follow, and harder still to accept the fact that this joy would someday end. Their joy would be segmented, interspersed with the unhappiness or woes of which they had partaken with that brimming cup of vows. As through a telescope turned wrong end, Moore felt he could see it all, a chain of events linked hand to hand even as they were dancing. Circling dizzily, raising their hands to strain at something grand, straining and reaching before falling back to earth again — what more could he wish than that their love might be a chain of good and a gambol of gladness, begetting good, good people, good, plentiful life, and children, too, to carry on the dance. Let Good begin the dance. All that day Moore had prayed for the grace just to be, for the grace not to think, judge or criticize anyone — not even poor Bertie and his unfortunate toast.

Moore got his wish, pretty much. Later, when he saw Bertie with Pinsent, it hardly crossed Moore's mind what Bertie might be pouring in the young man's ear. Nor would he think of how pleased Russell must be now that events had proved him right: sure enough, Wittgenstein had left the Apostles.

Wittgenstein was the last person Moore wanted to think about. Moore especially wanted to forget the scene Wittgenstein had made two weeks ago, a few days before he went to Vienna for the summer. This was the day when North Whitehead (now off talking to that handsome woman not his wife) had challenged one of his pupils to a rowing race. The three of them, he, Russell and Pinsent, had been there. Russell was rooting for his old partner. The moment the gun went off, Russell was calling hoarsely through his cupped hands, *Pull, North! Pull!*

Whitehead hove strong for the first two hundred yards — not bad for a man over fifty. But then he broke and his young opponent surged ahead, lunging to the finish in long, powerful strokes. North was badly beaten; it was painful to see him sagging over the oars, sucking wind. It was then that Wittgenstein erupted. He said they might as well have watched a bullfight; it was just as brutal and senseless. Russell should have known better than to argue — he said the same later — but instead he came back, You just don't understand the virtue of competition.

Virtue! Wittgenstein snarled. Dogs tearing out each other's entrails — that's what this is! Suddenly his eyes got small; his finger was like a cocked pistol at Russell's nose. *Great works!* he railed. Only *these* have value. This is so vile we don't deserve to live! It smells of the slaughterhouse, your *races!*

Russell was too thunderstruck to respond. Leave him, he ordered Pinsent when Pinsent started after him. Now, *really,* Russell repeated. Do you hear me?

Leave off, said Pinsent with a glare, and with that, he went after him.

Later, they all had different views of the incident. Moore thought it was the Society, that and the pressure of the three of them being together. Russell, on the other hand, thought it was a hysterical reaction to their latest battle over another one of his theories. Both explanations were correct, so far as they went. Only Pinsent knew what else lay behind it: Wittgenstein's father was dying. Wittgenstein's sister Gretl had written him a few days before, but he told no one but Pinsent. Even now, at Moore's wedding, Pinsent was still the only one who knew.

One thing was certain: Pinsent was looking quite prosperous on Moore's wedding day. Moore wasn't the only one to have remarked at this new blue worsted wool suit and the silk cravat fastened with a gold pin. Burnished brogues still squeaky from the bootmaker, buffed to a hue by the man in the loo. And crowning it all, a dark fedora tapped to a rakish tilt with the brim snapped down just so. Flo had also gotten some new togs and would soon get a settlement as well. The roof was fixed and the grocer had been paid — why, there was even a girl to cook and tidy. Flo was goose purple with excitement. They were rich! German money, you know, whole pots of it! Why, Davy was even taking her on a seaside holiday! Oh, it made her head spin to think of it, she did so love the sea. England was surrounded with it, you know.

Much as Pinsent missed Wittgenstein, he was glad his friend was not there with him now. No, Pinsent was flustered enough as he searched the floor for a dancing partner. Oh, go on, he told himself, giving himself a mental push. If he could wear a vain hat, he thought, he could bloody well ask a girl to dance!

For an hour Pinsent had had his eye on her, one of the bridesmaids, a girl about his height, with dark hair and green eyes. She looked shy, the way she kept adjusting her corsage. The soles of his new shoes creaked as he stole across the floor and asked a dance. She didn't refuse! And pretty, too! But he was a clumsy oaf, feeling the heat from her perspiring back as he forced conversation, noticing the heavy smell of her corsage. Katherine, her name was, Dorothy's cousin. Twice they danced before she thanked him, saying, with conspicuous politeness, that she wanted to speak to her uncle. Stiff as he thanked her. About face, his neck flaming. Same old story. The usual rot. And sure enough, he saw her dancing later with someone taller, better looking, more confident. Dratted new hat! Stupid vanity! For his penance, Pinsent left it sitting brazenly on the rack, too dwindled and shamed to wear it home.

Russell was in a similar state. Pained about his toast and now feeling the sag of drink, he was just noticing how the flowers on the tables were beginning to brown at the edges. He could see Moore up on the dais, rubicund and doting, soaring with his bride over life's largesse, gamely sucking the paps from that draining bottle. Ottoline would bloody well be sorry for her neglect, he assured himself. Indignant now, he thought he might even have himself an affair — perhaps this very afternoon! Who, then (since all were susceptible to his charm)? That woman over there, the one with the pretty mouth and promising-looking bosom? Or the more matronly one there with the bored look? A widow wouldn't dally; she would know that life was short. He knew it, too, but for his penance he decided that for now, at least, he would remain the wronged, virtuous one. And couldn't he smile to himself, thinking of old Moore fumbling through his wedding night. But then Russell's mirth bit back, reminding him that the groom, unlike himself, would bring home much more tonight than a hangover.

Then the bar was closed. The musicians were packing up, and a motorcar was waiting outside to whisk the weary couple to their hotel, when Moore's younger brother, Bertie, cut off their escape. Ringing his glass with a butter knife, Bertie Moore announced that the groom would first serenade the bride.

Sing! cried the delighted crowd. Mortified, Moore wanted to crown his brother, but then came the clapping chant:

The-groom-shall-sing! Groom-shall-sing-and-bride-shall-play!

Very well, said Moore with a wince. I'll sing, I'll sing. He looked at Dorothy. *Foggy, Foggy Dew?*

Perfect! cried Bertie Moore. The groom will now sing *Froggy, Froggy Dew!*

There was laughter, clapping and a gay tinkling of glasses as the couple were led to a piano in need of tuning. Arranging her long dress around the bench, Dorothy sounded a few chords while Moore, flushed and nervous, called for a glass of water, then turned to warm up with a sound like gargling. Tie cockeyed, cummerbund sagging, slightly drunk, the groom then turned his girth toward the audience and nodded for his wife to begin.

In her nervousness, Dorothy played the opening chords too quickly, and he started too late, struggling like a rolling ship until at last they merged. Who else Moore's age could have sung so achingly such a naive air? Several women clasped their breasts as he strained to reach the high, sweet, sharp notes, his eyes closed as he mournfully moaned:

> *Song of my youth, song of my heart.*
> *She was a slip of a girl I kissed larking in the heather,*
> *But she skipped away singing,*
> *In the foggy, foggy dew,*
> *In the foggy, foggy dew . . .*

Eating Our Way Toward Cockaigne

MOORE'S SUMMER was both an idyll and a shock — to suddenly find himself a husband and son-in-law shanghaied by meals, chores, budgets. Russell's summer, by comparison, was one of doubt and drift. He fell heavily after that.

For Russell, the feeling was like the outbreak of illness, mounting when he did not expect it, then bursting into fever when it seemed he was at last putting his life and wounded theories back together. The theory of types wasn't the only casualty of Wittgenstein's criticism. The latest casualty had been Russell's newest, and perhaps boldest, construct, the theory of judgment.

This, so far as Russell could see, had been the impetus behind Wittgenstein's outburst at the rowing race. Guilt was the cause of Wittgenstein's fury. To him, that image of Whitehead sagging over the oars was an all too gruesome reminder of how he had just savaged his own mentor's work.

In his better moments, Russell blamed himself for this. It was he, after all, who felt compelled to show Wittgenstein his judgment theory in those last hurried days before term ended and Wittgenstein left for Vienna. In his anxiety, Russell had invited the attack just as surely as if he had dangled fresh meat before a tiger.

Russell was still reeling from that confrontation. And he had had such great hopes for this new theory, which he envisioned as a culmination of logic, physics and psychology. In the most basic sense, Russell meant for the theory to be a model of the act of judgment, of what occurs when we judge something to be true. But, as he well knew, this was tricky, because there remained the problem of accounting for how a person might judge as true what is *not* the case.

But there was much more than this behind the theory. In it Russell was still pursuing his great objection to the idealists' notion that we are never in touch with anything in the world outside our own minds. The task was to determine what we can truly know outside of ourselves, and it required a theory that might, so to speak, open the mind to China trade with the external world. Yet here again the philosopher felt the goad of science, the siren call of the Big Synthesis. Rising to Wittgenstein's own example, Russell felt once more the desire to do something brave and unifying, to sound a chord that would even merge with the new fugues of physics. For lack of a better name, Russell now called his scientific philosophy *logical atomism*. And, much as Wittgenstein disliked *isms*, it was a course that they both were pursuing in their own respective ways, each breaking logical statements down to molecular and even atomic forms that it seemed must somehow correspond with the atomic facts of our sense perceptions — or at least the facts of the world.

No, thought Russell, physicists weren't the only ones doing exciting things nowadays. But, oh, it made his head spin to think how he might unravel this tangled skein. How was he to reconcile the concerns of physics with those of epistemology? Whereas physics exhibits sensations as functions of physical objects, epistemology demands that physical objects be exhibited as functions of sensations. And look at the sorts of things he would have to harmoniously bring together: perceptions, which are purely mental events; abstract properties, such as "greenness" and "softness"; and, externally, quite physical objects such as grass and earth. And even as he had begun plotting out this grand work of unification, he could imagine Wittgenstein cautioning him that names are *not* the names of *things,* that we don't know what names are, except that they are ours to use, pears from a prickly tree.

It was uphill work, but still the work had been progressing. So why, Russell would think in those confused days that followed Wittgenstein's attack, why this acute need to show it to him? Russell knew what he had done the moment he thrust the critical pages in Wittgenstein's hands and bade him sit down and read. Watching him, Russell saw all the danger signs: the foot tapping and chin rubbing, then the sudden irritability as Wittgenstein jumped up. Facing him then, Wittgenstein was trapped; Russell knew, just as surely if he had planned the whole thing, what Wittgenstein would say — that his theory was irreparably, impossibly wrong. Wittgenstein could not even say very clearly *why* it was wrong. He was groping and inarticulate as he explained — more or less — that the theory still could not account for how the mind might judge as true something that was nonsensical, such as, "This table penholders the book." But this again was consistent with Wittgenstein's vision of logic as something as perfect and aboriginal as truth, a thing held aloof from the mind with its carping judgments. Equally damning, Wittgenstein found the theory presumptuous. What need, he asked, had the world, or logic, of a subject mind who judges? This was nothing but a fiction belonging to certain primitive notions of psychology. As far as logic was concerned, mind was the proverbial tree that fell unheard in the forest: in the realm of logic, mind had no hegemony — none whatsoever.

From his side, Wittgenstein was hardly unaware of the irony of Russell's asking him to judge his theory of judgment within a poisonous atmosphere of compounding judgment. Here once more, Wittgenstein felt the mocking animus of logic mimicking their very conflicts. Again, it was this lie of fairness and objectivity — the deluded and, at bottom, mendacious notion that either of them could impartially judge the other's work without regard for his own vision, values or self-interest. But for Wittgenstein the worst lie was Russell's apparent blindness to their predicament. Russell wasn't asking an innocent collegial question, and in judging him, Wittgenstein knew that he was rendering more than just an objective assessment of the truth as he saw it. Even the "truth" was a lie.

Russell's fledgling theory was crude compared to the web of judgments that were then in progress. Judgments of judgments. Judgments in fear of judgments. Judgments fending off further judgments, one's own or another's. Wittgenstein even saw his own grand lie — this pretense that he did not know what he was doing as he killed Russell's theory, like some William Tell who closed his eyes in order to shoot straight.

In the confused days that followed, there were times when Russell could hardly remember what Wittgenstein had said; in his despair, he could but dimly recall why he had even propounded the theory. Secluded in his rooms, Russell felt like a boy conjugating as he thought:

Actually, the reason behind the theory was . . .
Well, if the theory were true, it would enable us to . . .
It was a grand idea, except . . .
With work, my theory could become . . .
But the most remarkable virtue of the theory, if it could be realized, would be to . . .

They managed to patch things up before Wittgenstein left for Vienna. At the station, they both struggled to be cordial, the better to disguise this lie or what perhaps was the finer distinction: the impossibility for either to be honest without injury to the other. Friendly and hale, sad but mostly relieved, they expressed hope for the next year and future endeavors. Lingering there, shaking hands in that second before Wittgenstein boarded, they never dreamed that it would be seven years and a war before they'd meet again.

But matters between them were far from settled, especially on Russell's end. For Russell, there would be the burden of how Wittgenstein's harsh verdict of his judgment theory would temporarily occlude Russell's own sense of judgment. Russell never saw this train coming; it blindsided him. Why, he felt just fine. He wasn't Icarus falling. As Einstein had opined, all was relative, since all was moving or falling at various speeds. Indeed, for all the moving and falling of one's time, it was difficult and perhaps pointless to estimate one's speed or trajectory. Rather, people were like particles in suspension, some floating up, ascendant, while others sank inexorably to the bottom. But, really, it wasn't so bad, this topsy-turvy-dom. Eating one's way into this Land of Cockaigne, m'lord, the bread is verily like cake, fleshly fresh and white. Behold, nuncle, how we burrow through this blighted loaf, through even the air holes and moldy portions, tunneling like weevils to that other, fabled side where one needs bring only his appetite — where, 'tis said, juicy roasted fowls and dainties fly right into one's open mouth!

No, Russell saw no need to despair; he wasn't even *near* the bottom. And anyhow, there were milestones and diversions along the way — Ottoline for one.

Several months before, in deference to Philip's concerns about a scandal, Ottoline had let for their trysts (and hers with Lamb) a little flat in Maida Vale, a middle-class neighborhood located a few miles northwest of Bloomsbury. Their landlady, or jailer, was an older, ill-tempered widow. Mrs. Dood was her name.

Russell hated the arrangement and he loathed Mrs. Dood for being a scrounger and busybody and, as he believed, a reformed prostitute. For him, even the down-at-the-heels Nabob was preferable to this.

Darling, Russell would grouse. I would prefer filth and black beetles to this.

Fine! Ottoline would reply. You find something reasonably clean and discreet for three guineas per month. Be my guest! I've tried.

This would shut him up, but it still didn't ease his discontent. Mrs. Dood insisted that they arrive and depart separately, and invariably it was Russell who would be there first. Ottoline was habitually late, sometimes by as much as an hour. Oh, he hated it. No sooner would he enter the reeking hallway than Alf, Mrs. Dood's rat terrier, would start yapping. Struggling to open the door with his key, he would see the omniscient Mrs. Dood peeking through her eyehole while scratching, scrapping Alf stuck his snoot under the door and loudly sneezed, hoping to catch the intruder's scent.

Inside, the flat was stuffy and shut-up smelling, with the drafty acoustics of a place where nobody lived. The furniture was mismatched, sec-ondhand stuff, the walls bare and the cupboards empty except for a jar of peppermints and the sassafras tea a doctor had prescribed for Otto-line's digestion. A coiled douching apparatus was secreted in the bath, along with a jar of lubricant. Swallowed in a faded green armchair, peer-ing through his arched fingers, Russell would wait and wait, his mood going from expectancy to anger, then to black despair.

Ottoline would arrive with profuse apologies and explanations — al-ibis no sooner made than she expected forgiveness, and woe to him if he showed any lingering resentment. Then she'd climb on her high horse, quick to remind him of what tremendous lengths it took to see him, and never mind the risk and expense. Anxious and apologetic, he was the guilty one then, all the while conscious of the time ticking away. By the time they got down to lovemaking — or bickering about lovemaking — there was no time, and their efforts foundered. Worse, Ottoline's mi-graines were acting up again, making it hard for her to bear his hobby-horsing.

He always brought wine, the libation no sooner uncorked than he was plying her small, upturned breasts through folds of bottle-green silk, fum-bling with the buttons that Ottoline's maid, Brindy, had fastened that morning, wrapping her lady up for him like a pricey parcel. A small heap of discarded underthings fell to the floor: the silk slip and purple stock-ings, the lacy deckle-edged drawers and pointy black shoes shaped like Venetian gondolas. He so wanted to remember everything that he would greedily try to squirrel it all in his memory, so busy *looking* and *remem-bering* that it seemed he missed it even as it was occurring. Like a sweet held in the side of the mouth, he would try to hold these details in mind, sucking on them until at last they dissolved down to nothing. *But here she was in the flesh,* he would tell himself. Here was his chance and he must make the most of it. Oh! he'd gasp. Her lanky shanks! Oh, her rump! *He* was ready in an instant — the Burrower, she called him, always trying to jam himself in, ready or not. This was bad enough, but then in late June, not long before Ottoline took her migraines to a Swiss sanitar-ium, she averted her face from his kiss.

What! he demanded. I hate your squeamishness. What is it?

She was embarrassed to say, but with prodding she came clean, saying that it wasn't just squeamishness. It was his breath.

He was thunderstruck. My *breath?* Why did you never tell me?

Ottoline smoothed his neck. I didn't want to hurt your feelings. Be-sides, she hedged, it wasn't always so bad.

He chewed up one of her mints, then beckoned her to him.

Smell your breath? Ottoline recoiled in horror. I'd rather kiss you!

Then kiss me, damn it!

She kissed him, then drew away, smirking.

No better? Damn! Must be the pipe, don't you think? Well, I shall see the dentist while you're away — I promise.

For all her kindnesses, Ottoline was never kinder than when she was leaving. Then she would revert to her Florence Nightingale self, valiantly striving to put him back together. Still, she could not undo the mark of her leaving — an extravagant kiss, then the rap of her sharp heels down that narrow hallway reeking of boiled mutton. Through the window, Russell would watch her wide plumed hat undulating as she sailed down Sooty Lane past ragged, scowling children and the shrill row house women who called after her: *Will yer look at 'er! Miss Ta-ta! 'Ey, yer Majesty!*

And later, fuming, Russell would be driven down the same public road, with the harpies throwing out their arms, cackling. *'Ere we are, Princey. Throw us a kiss, love! Awwww . . .*

Standing on the platform later, Russell would close his eyes as the shrieking 6:05 enveloped him in pulverizing darkness, dragging and mashing him before he awoke with a shudder, wreathed in steam, and quietly boarded. Second-class carriage — still pinched these days, what with the continuing drain of Alys. Traveling home, he would already be writing his next letter to Ottoline, another relentless analysis of what was wrong between them. And each trip, under the radiant darkness on a hill far out in the country, near Wenden, he would see a ruined stone cottage. Beside the cottage, dark as a shadow, was a fir tree. Standing like an upraised palm, it seemed to beckon or warn him, and with twisted mouth, he would avert his face, feeling, without a clue why, that he would suddenly start weeping.

Then Ottoline left for the spa in Lausanne, where, in addition to the waters, she was given glasses of whole cow's milk cut with brewer's yeast and radium. "I now know why they call it radium," she wrote. With a draught of this heavenly cocktail, she said, she felt like an icon of the Virgin surrounded by rays of hammered gold, her hidden passion. Open to receive were her aching arms — open as if, like the Blessèd *Vierge*, she had dropped the babe. But, oh, so melting she felt as she watched him fall helplessly to earth, poor dear. (She would pray for him.) "Dearest Bertie," she wrote, "if only you could see the world from up here." (*I wasn't invited!*) "If only you could fling away the world with its dross and foolish cares." (*I'm busy and have no money!*) "If only for once, my love, you could see inside my mind." (*Idle bitch! Give me a lamp!*)

Oh, they were torture for him, these psalms that wandered even more than Ottoline's usual letters. In them, she was always reproaching herself for being a basically ignorant woman, while yet insisting, as if something had been denied her, that she had a poet's feel for the voluptuousness of earth. Like a window, she had opened herself to the spirit, she said. Like a radiant window, she prayed that he, too, would open himself to it and quit his atheistic thinking. Really, her letter would continue, it was the most gorgeous summer, such a wonderful age was upon us. And Philip was such a dear, so understanding and undemanding, such a deeply spiritual man, actually. With Philip her mind was free, never weighed like dead fish on a scale. Through the swashing, radiant grass, they would walk down the mountainsides looking for purple gentians, the most intense of flowers, with deep, dark purple cups that reminded her of Christ's passion. And looking down, she saw her mind was melting like the snowcaps. Like freshets, her happy tears were pouring down the valleys as a herdsman blew his alpenhorn. The cows were coming home.

Then toward the second week, she met a Dr. Vittoz, who changed her life utterly and absolutely. For Dr. Vittoz, she kept a diary in which she was to practice eliminating unnecessary letters from words and unnecessary words from sentences, and finally whole paragraphs filled with unnecessary fears and habits of mind that for years had plagued her. By her third week, Ottoline was shedding whole books of fear. And such joyful tears she shed — as through a cloud spent of all thunder, they sieved clear through her. Really, she advised, he ought to try eliminating, ought to try jettisoning all the weight of intellect that only bogged him down and tortured his soul. Really, she said, he ought to try. It was so very lovely to forget — just to gaze out where the snow rested on the mountains and the fat cattle stood knee deep in the grassy meadows. She felt as she did when she was pregnant, full to the paps, like an enormous bulb germinating. It was an adventure to change, and she was changing ever so rapidly — even Dr. Vittoz said so. There were these young girls who danced for them at night in their dirndls, with their hair newly shorn and eyes so impossibly bright. They made her feel old, but then Ottoline eliminated that as well, writing *old,* then *ol,* then, *o . . .*

By the third week she was sure of it: a momentous change was upon the world. There were so many of them up there, Swiss and German, English and French, Italians, Russians, even a Lithuanian. At night they spoke of outbreaks of influenza and said alarming things about money and politics that she did not understand, nor want to. And then one night they made a pact that if ever the world collapsed under a disaster or war, they would come to Lausanne with Dr. Vittoz, where they would work with their eliminating books, washing away dreadnoughts and greed, money and nationalities, so that all the world could partake of this eternal peace and blessèdness. She met so very many people. Among the guests there was a priest and an industrialist, a physicist and his wife. There was even a Hindu, who had given her the Bhagavad-Gita to read. But the Hindu book was so violent in places, like the Old Testament or mythology — why was it, she wrote, that the ancients were so tainted with thoughts of bloodshed and violence, with gods always smiting and breaking into different forms, appearing as burning bushes, swans and such? That was not her religion.

She said she also met an Italian painter — a *Futurist*, he called himself, Vorno was his name. Fearfully beautiful, he was, powerful and dark, with a wolflike face and bad teeth. Every day, recklessly, he would race his bicycle down the mountainside, heedless of sudden turns, animals and drays, people. Vorno said the Futurists gloried in danger, speed and struggle; they loved brutal locomotives, aeroplanes and powerful automobiles spitting flames. Progress, Vorno said, was the sacred economy of life, forever destroying for the sake of onwardness. Yes, Vorno said, he and his comrades were anarchists and murderers, not toothless lap dogs, like these English painters painting nudes and bottles for the licentious rich. Worse were the French — except for Braque, he despised them, too. Sack the museums! Torch the past! Vorno said the human body must be painted in motion — must be shown streaked with savage force lines, like the hideous, blood-streaked face of an Indian warrior.

The other guests thought Vorno would break his neck as he hurtled down the mountain roads, *whisk whisk* in the turns, his head inclined over the bars like a battering ram. Someone said it was a terminal illness that made him so reckless, but Ottoline thought it was his mind. Vorno took the waters, but he sneered at their eliminating. Throw down these idle worries! Rise up and murder the old world! Embrace the evernewness of high-production machines and factories! War was the world's hygiene! War, Vorno predicted, was itself a ferociously beautiful machine, one that would propel mankind into revolutions more beautiful than *The Victory at Samothrace*!

Vorno chilled them, he did. They were all much relieved when he left after a row. It was a scandal, Ottoline said. Missing billfolds, and one guest with both eyes blackened and a fractured skull. Unpaid bills and Vorno's room a shambles, the walls painted with terrible war engines and dynamos and the legend VICTOIRE. The police were into it now. There were even whispers about the wife of the man with blackened eyes — apparently, she was but one of the women he had had, spitting them out, one man said, as a wolf does bloody hen feathers.

With Vorno gone, the guests returned, like atoning monks, to their eliminating, a process that Dr. Vittoz likened to untying the knots they spent their whole lives tangling. Still, looking down from her mountain-top, beholding the world with its fragile lights, Ottoline was tormented by the way her nocturnal mind would busily reknit and knot what she had spent days unraveling. Dr. Vittoz assured her that this was natural. This mischief would pass, he promised. Nevertheless, Ottoline spent much of the night praying, fearful of this beauty that was upon them.

Oh, it made Russell ill, this spirit muck and eliminating. But what Russell most feared was that Ottoline would eliminate *him*.

Alone and adrift, Russell was then writing Our Knowledge of the External World, a series of lectures he was to deliver at Harvard the following summer. His theory of judgment was central to this unifying effort, but his theory, like his confidence, was broken, and his work took another dive.

Wittgenstein's letters didn't help matters. Just prior to Ottoline's departure, Wittgenstein had finally sent word about his father, saying that he would not survive the summer. Wittgenstein continued:

In the afternoon I sit beside his bed, sometimes talking or playing a recorded symphony, but mostly in silence. It is hard to come to this point, when two humans have so little help for each other. I never expected to outlive my father, but now I see that even this will come to pass. It is terrifying, the kinds of mental torment there can be . . .

Russell had replied with a sympathetic letter, but still he hadn't been able to resist asking Wittgenstein if he might better explain his objections to his theory of judgment. Wittgenstein found this imposition enough; Russell did not help matters by adding that Wittgenstein's criticisms had "paralysed" him.

Wittgenstein complied with Russell's request, but his answer was not much help: terse to the point of being telegraphic, he largely repeated his objections, capping them off with what seemed an even more draconian judgment:

I am very sorry to hear that my objections to your theory of judgment paralyse you. I think it can be resolved only by a correct theory of propositions . . .

This was no help. It was an insult. Immediately, Russell sent Wittgenstein another letter — this one distinctly irritable in tone — requesting additional details, or at least some context. Wittgenstein replied:

Please! It is INTOLERABLE for me to repeat an explanation that I gave the first time only with the greatest possible repugnance. What kind of world we live in, or how we judge it, is not for logic to decide.

Evidently, Wittgenstein regretted his harshness. The next day he sent Russell a second letter:

I am sorry I was so abrupt in my last letter. I also want to add that your theory of descriptions is *quite certainly* correct, even though the individual primitive signs in it are not at all the ones you thought. Do not suppose that I take any pleasure in saying this. It is frightful to have destroyed so much and produced so little.

Just now I am thinking of my reaction to you, the day Whitehead lost the race. My reaction was shameful; but the *reason,* it seems to me, was quite valid and important. Our quarrel was not caused by your sensitiveness or by my haste and inconsiderateness. It came from something much deeper — from the fact that, as you can readily see, our ideas are TOTALLY different.

You may say that *we ourselves* are not so very different, but *our ideals* could not be more so. And that is why we shan't *ever* be able to talk about anything involving our value judgments without either becoming hypocritical or falling out. *I think this is incontestable.*

This cannot be cleared up in a conversation, let alone a letter. And this last quarrel was just one of many instances. Now, as I am writing this, I am completely calm. I can readily see that your value judgments are just as valid as mine, and that I have no right to catechise you. At the same time, I cannot impede my work by struggling to find a common mould for our concepts. Months ago I realised this, and I found it frightful, because it so tainted our relations; we seemed to be sitting side by side in a marsh. The fact is we both have weaknesses, but especially *I* have, and in spite of what you always say, my life is full of ugliness and pettiness. But if a relationship is not to be degrading for both sides, it must not be prey to the weaknesses on either side. Now you'll probably say that things have been worked out, and will continue to be worked out. But you see I'm sick of the whole sordid compromise — on your end and mine. So far my life has been one nasty mess — but need that go on *forever?*

I beg you to think this over and to send me an answer *only* when you can do so without bitterness. Feel assured in any case of my love and loyalty. I only hope you will understand this letter as it is meant to be understood.

Russell was still thinking of how to respond to this letter when another arrived:

Dear Russell,

My father died yesterday in the afternoon. He had the most beautiful death that I can imagine, without the slightest pain and falling asleep like a child! I did not feel sad for a single moment during all the last hours as I sat by him, but was most joyful, and I think that his death was worth a whole life.

I will be here two or three weeks more. Then I shall leave for Norway. I will not be returning to Cambridge next term, nor in the forseeable future. I doubt you will approve of this course, but please do not say things we will both regret by trying to convince me otherwise. I can say only that it *is* a course, and that I will follow it insofar as God *permits* me to see it.

Despite our differences, your letters are a great boon to me, and I hope you will continue to write once I settle someplace. Until then, I remain

Yours ever,
L.W.

———

Not long before this time, Russell had finally seen a dentist about his halitosis. Bibbed and reclining in the wooden chair, he closed his eyes as rotund Mr. Geach focused the brilliant dial fixed to his forehead, then probed Russell's gums with a fat finger.

There we are . . . Em — hold there, please. *Hold* —

Peering down, with the air whistling through his hairy nostrils, Geach registered a look of surprise, then disappeared into the other room and returned with a medical book.

Russell took a sip of the bile-colored antiseptic on the stand beside him, spat into the steel bowl and quipped, Is it that bad? He looked up anxiously but only got a finger in the mouth. *Geeeth!* he lisped. *Whahtth ithh issht?*

The dentist exhaled loudly. You'll want a second opinion. You must understand that I'm not at all expert in this.

Russell sat up in the chair. Expert in what?

I see several lesions on your gum. Geach steeled himself, then said it. It's possible you have a cancer.

Russell lapsed back in disgust.

Remember, cautioned Geach, *I'm not sure . . .*

But Russell wasn't even listening. He thought, If it's cancer, I'll throw myself under a train.

One specialist said possibly cancer and sent him to a second specialist, who said quite possibly. Both said it was still too early to tell. The second did remove the lesions, though, then gave his gums a thorough scraping that he thought would end his halitosis. As for the rest, they'd have to see how his gums healed. Eight weeks would surely tell the story.

As a boy, Russell had lost his Uncle Mortimer to mouth and throat cancer. Russell could still see his uncle with a handkerchief, dabbing the ooze that issued like tobacco juice from the red ulcerations on his seared lower lip. Russell promised himself a quick dive under a train before it came to that. Gone in a roaring.

In the meantime, he told no one about the news, not even Ottoline, grimly deciding to hug it close to him, for shame, for pleasure. He could not die, not really. For all his fantasies of death, he still didn't believe he could part from this life, or it from him. Death, rather, was an idea he could explore in much the way his tongue anxiously probed this sore on his gum, rueful and smarting with its presence, like a sweet on a carious tooth. And maybe it *was* better he quit the field now, Russell thought. He knew what Wittgenstein was saying between the lines. Likely his best work was behind him. Well, if so, he thought, he must make room for the younger generation. Wittgenstein could take his place; Russell would still have his reputation. As for his darker thoughts, these, too, he stanched with fantasies of grief-stricken Ottoline, the line of mourners and the lengthy obituaries.

The happy narcissism of death. For days Russell was in a sort of delirium, half anxious, half rapturous with the presence of this death, which lay against his life like a shadow against a hill. He could indulge himself now. He wrote brave, romantic couplets and read the life of Mozart. For the first time in years, he even allowed himself to routinely do the things that he supposed ordinary people do, dining out, going to concerts and taking long rides on his bicycle.

One day he even decided he would get pleasantly tight. Bringing three bottles of wine with him, he went down to the Cam and took out a punt. Ah, the tang of dry, tart wine in the hot, hot sun! The sluggish water was cool. He let his wrist trail in it as he drifted along under the willows fluttering with their tentative green. With each sip, sweat sprang to his skin, flashing cool then hot with the wind's refrain.

Unused to drink in any quantity, he first thought himself crafty, but within an hour he was freely grinning as he rammed one punt, then accidentally splashed a lady with his pole while valiantly fending off a second collision. Oh, he was *sorry*! he cried to the spattered woman and the irate gentleman with her. Percolating his p's as he blathered back, P-p-pardon me! . . . Is the laaady all — *fine*?

Get off the water, you drunken idiot!

As he raised his arms to plead forgiveness, it struck him as funny. He laughed in the man's face and stumbled back, nearly capsizing as he sat with a splat in the dirty bilge water. The day declined. Bottoming the third bottle, he heard the twang of a guitar, then saw a boating party, young swains in cream whites and their young ladies. He stood and, rocking, waved farewell to that, too. Wan and nostalgic, he then lay back across the seat, noticing his feet spreadeagled before him, pointing as they would point for an eternity, useless and skewed. Looking up then, he saw a girl peering down at him from the arched stone bridge, smiling as the sun fanned through her hair. For a moment, he imagined her flame-red hair spreading in strands across his face, and then he saw himself pulling her open mouth to his. But then this image curdled; and, inserting his finger under his lip, he probed that rawness, stunned by the thought of a wild, weedlike growth that would clog his head and choke off his thoughts, even his immortal thoughts! Staring down his half-insensible length, scratching the shriveled nub between his legs, he felt like Gulliver tied by the threads of Lilliputians, dazzled, as blackbirds twittered overhead in a whir of wings . . .

Back at his rooms he fell heavily to sleep, then awoke in stuffy darkness, hung over, thirsty and confused. It took him an hour to wash, eat, shave and settle himself. Shaky, penitent, he then opened Ottoline's latest letter. More bad news. She was prolonging her stay in Lausanne. Another week eliminating.

Enough! Sitting down, Russell dashed off a letter chiding her for frivolousness and selfishness and demanding that she come home. For three scathing pages he continued before a milder, more speculative tone crept in — a foreign voice, older and wiser than his own. By the fourth page, Russell realized he wasn't even writing to Ottoline, he was writing to Wittgenstein. But he wasn't really writing, he was speaking, and the person he was addressing wasn't quite Wittgenstein, nor was he quite Russell. Rather, he was an older, haunted man speaking to a brilliant younger man — speaking in the manner of a Socratic dialogue.

Russell hardly dared breathe for fear it would end. But it didn't end; it only became more urgent. For twenty pages the older man answered the younger man's questions and objections, all the while growing more confused.

With burning eyes, Russell followed the curls of his scratching pen until three A.M., whereupon he fell heavily to sleep. But again at seven, as if jabbed by a current, he awoke and returned to his desk, watching as the phantom hand picked up the pen and resumed writing, transcribing this inner voice.

His bed maker, Mrs. Phelps, was a motherly sort who fussed over him and the other bachelor dons. He usually chatted with her when she arrived, but that morning he dashed back to his desk, still furiously scribbling as she set to work, beating air into his pillows and sweeping.

Why, Mr. Russell! she gasped the next morning when the door opened. 'Ave you been at work all this time?

Paper littered the floor. Hunted, his eyes. Yes! he cried. And, by God, it's good, good, *good*! Look at this! Eighty . . . eighty-five . . . *ninety-five* pages since yesterday!

Well, sir, she allowed, surveying the disarray. That's all very nice, but you ought to sleep, you should. Truthfully, you do look a bit pale and shaky, sir. 'Ave you eaten?

Have I eaten? he asked, uprooting his hair. Who can think of food at a time like this!

Just the same, sir, I'm going to send Mr. Prichert's boy to fetch you something.

Yes, do that, he said distractedly, scrawling another line. And pipe tobacco, please. He pushed some change into her hand. And tea and milk, Mrs. Phelps — and crackers. And *thank you*! God, look at this, will you? I've never had such a run, never!

By the third day, it had grown into a full-blown novel called *The Perplexities of John Forstice*. Forstice, the protagonist, had grown younger and handsomer than the old man who began the dialogues. Nearing forty, prematurely gray and unmarried, Forstice was now a famous physicist, an atheist and freethinker known for his cynicism and cool brilliance.

But then Forstice takes as his student Thomas Graf, a pure, clear-thinking German who debunks Forstice's theory of electrogravitation, then runs off to Norway, leaving his teacher on the Jobian dungheap, plagued by doubts about physics, human progress, himself. Yet here Russell wondered: Was the story perhaps too familiar and self-indulgent, too centered on Forstice? All right, thought Russell, let the outer world mirror Forstice's feverish state. Forstice must have conflict — a war, then, something biblical! And let's, while we're at it, make Forstice more vulnerable and human, not such a fire-breathing atheist. We'll make him, say, a Quaker and man of peace, a sort of Emersonian believer in human progress and the transcendental wholeness of nature. *More!* ordered the Author. *The book must have even more conflict, something splendidly mechanical and Wellsian.* That's it! thought Russell, who was, as it were, the Author's secretary. Nature betrays Forstice! Nature plants a bomb. And not just a bomb but a gravitational bomb developed from the one theory that Graf hasn't savaged — a bomb that can destroy ships and harbors! *Oh, go on,* said the insatiable Author, throwing caution to the wind. *Let the bomb destroy whole cities!*

Russell could hardly stoop to pick up all the baubles popping from his teeming brain. Serve up one war. And one plague. And let's put Forstice in a refuge, a mountain sanitarium or something. Right! He meets a nun, a tall, slender nun named Sister Catherine, who eats peppermints and suffers migraines. And let her also be suffering a spiritual crisis, what with the plague and God being such a beast, letting the world ride to ruin. On the verge of a breakdown, she's taking radium and carrying on with some therapeutic regime called — what? Elimination? No, no, blot that, old boy, we must protect the innocent. All right, then — Subtraction!

But it must be larger, the Author insisted. More characters, then! One Futurist. And a window-breaking feminist and a deranged misogynist like Strindberg. And a Madame Blavatsky and a Kiplingesque imperialist with a little brown Indian boy who calls him *sahib. More!* cried the indefatigable Author. Very well, then. A Prussian militarist and a deposed monarch, an anarchist, a plutocrat and a socialist named Shifsky.

All right, old boy, Russell cackled to himself. The gluepot is simmering! Riots outside the sanitarium gates. London in flames. Swarming like ants across blackened plains, armies leave a tide of plagues, starvation and burning heaps of dead. And all the while in their mountain nest the characters are talking, talking, *talking. But wait!* cried the Author. *What happened to Graf? That's it!* said the Author. *Graf has the antigravity secret that can stop the gravity bombs.*

It was his Ecclesiastes, his *Decameron* and *Masque of the Red Death.* Would Russell ever forget the feeling when, twenty-three days later, he penned that last, poignant paragraph? All his authorial wishes had been fulfilled. There was even a happy ending to ensure snappy sales. Graf had appeared with his antigravity formula, thereby ending the war. Forstice, meanwhile, had undertaken a whole new generation of theories that promised to change the course of physics. As for Sister Catherine, she had gotten off her priedieu and was now Catherine Belusys again. She had stopped her vain subtracting and had begun adding — yes, she had torn off her musty habit and become *Mrs. John Forstice*. Capping off those last pages of Forstice's internal soliloquy, Russell wrote:

Blindly and helplessly, going none know whence, going none know whither, men voyage across this lonely desert. Vainly, they reach for this or that, they snatch the cup of water from each other's parched lips and spill the precious drops on the burning sands, but the infinite pain remains. Day after day, night after night, men look out upon the vastness of the world: the sea beats upon the shore, the sun rises and sets, the starlight reaches us only after years of lonely voyaging through space. But human existence, in spite of all its pain and degradation, is redeemed by any portion, short or long, great or small, of knowledge or beauty or love; and the greatest of these is love. Its sudden rays pierce the astonished darkness of the outer night, and the mirror of sense reveals the undreamed visions of the soul.

It was too perfect. Sitting in his drawers, with a ravished look of locusts and honey, Russell closed his eyes as grateful tears streamed down his face. He felt like a cathedral filled with music, balanced, voluminous, ringing. Surely, this was the best he'd ever written, perhaps even his swan song. Promising himself not to look at it for at least a month, he tucked the manuscript in a drawer, then went out to walk into the early coolness.

Good morning! he said somewhat impertinently to an old lady, who shot him a dirty look in return. He was not deterred. Buying a paper from the stumpy paperman, normally a three-second transaction, he paused to gab, then smiled at two children, who darted away, staring at their feet. Things ordinarily invisible to him — tradesmen, shopkeepers, idlers — all were transformed by his heroic act of imagination. *Hello! Fine day!* Splendid in his new spiritual feathers, the strutting author hailed them all, high or low, bent or straight, smiling with such intense beneficence that their first impulse was to flee.

Ottoline returned in late August, utterly transformed, to hear her tell it. But over the next weeks, her new life unraveled just as surely as Russell's own postcompletion euphoria did.

His philosophical work resumed and foundered, resumed again. Over the next months, he finished *Our Knowledge of the External World,* but he finished it because he was a professional — that is, because it was expected and not because he thought it was adequate. Harder still, he could not even say how the work might be remedied, except somehow to summon that lapsed sense of conviction. Wittgenstein had such conviction, that was what hurt. Russell could feel it in Wittgenstein's letters from Norway, where it seemed something incalculable was happening.

For the time, Russell pinned his hopes on *Forstice.* Ottoline was dying to read it, and he did nothing to dampen her expectations when he told her — and rather conservatively, he felt — that *Forstice,* if not outstanding, was at least quite solidly good. But still, Russell held to his original decision to let the manuscript *breathe* for a month before he or anyone else dipped into it. He was so excited. The truth was, he could hardly remember what he had written.

Ottoline was even more excited when he said that her Lausanne letters had been the inspiration. Sly dog . . . Could he lure her home with a book? Apparently not. As it was, Russell did not see the radiantly eliminated Ottoline until the second week of September — *two* unconscionable weeks after her return, when she finally got around to inviting him down to Studland.

This time, as part of her own new spirit, Ottoline was entirely frank. Straightaway, she said they would not be alone. But to her surprise he did not cavil or moan. This, he was at pains to show her, was part of *his* new spirit, part of the aftermath of *Forstice,* which he said had given him a more stoical, resigned attitude to life. Expecting little, Russell was gratified to see that he rather enjoyed himself during those three days. At bottom, he knew that his feelings for Ottoline had dimmed, but this, he felt, was to be accepted rather than regretted. He was not unhappy or happy; rather, he told himself, he was *provisionally* happy — content for now to see what life would bring, since life must bring something.

Stoic that he was, he didn't tell Ottoline about his possible cancer, though he did say he had seen the dentist. And she had to admit that his breath *was* better, even if sex was not. For her, the most insurmountable hurdle was still the cold buried mass of his intellect — this, like his views on religion, she would never eliminate. For the life of her, she couldn't see the spiritual change he said he'd undergone. Oh, she could see he was changing, all right — and rapidly. Only he was not changing in quite the ways he thought.

Not long after his return from Studland, Russell was relieved, but not very, to be told that he did not have cancer. He was far more anxious a few days later when *Forstice* returned from the typist and he sat down, with trembling hands, to read what he had wrought. Dwarfs had been set loose in the temple of Art — nothing was as he remembered it. Impatient within ten pages, he was pained after thirty, then wincing as he haplessly skipped from chapter to chapter. At last, deeply chastened, he slipped the manuscript into a drawer and went for a walk, this time not saying a word to anyone and indeed wishing to crawl off somewhere and die.

Several people, including Ottoline, said they liked *Forstice,* but he knew, at bottom, that they were just being kind. Still, Russell would outlive *Forstice* and Wittgenstein; by growing steeply, hugely famous, he would survive them all. This was part of the transformation in him that Ottoline saw that summer. She saw it most clearly the day before he left Studland, while peering down through the viewing lens of her Kodak Graflex camera. Ottoline liked snapping her famous friends and guests — fodder for her photo album and the memoirs to come. She thought it immensely revealing, how a person faced the camera. Whereas some ignored or tolerated the lens, Russell clearly welcomed its intrusion. Canting his head, he would strike a triumphant grimace, his pipe poised like a pin to burst the world's worthless bubbles. And yet the way he would draw his chin into his neck! Like a tortoise sucking into its shell, she thought, as he stared back with those cold, reptilian eyes. Yes, even then Ottoline could see that protective carapace forming. Russell was just becoming generally known, and there, peering down into the milky lens, Ottoline could see how the camera's snout made him puff out his character. She could see him striving to show his best, most brazen side, and not the tentative one floating in that haze of light, shrinking from time's judgments.

Ottoline relished the power the camera gave her over him. There! *Like that!* she would order, and there he would stand, at full attention, trying to summon forth his posterity. Framing him in the jiggling lens, Ottoline would wait for perhaps a second longer than necessary, just to see him frozen there, waiting for the shutter's jaws to snap.

Red Sky, Red Water

DEPARTING FROM BERGEN on the *Sweimfoss,* Wittgenstein had sent Russell a short card.

27.8.13.

Dear Russell,
   The coast of Norway is too congenial, so I am going up Sognefjord to someplace where I can *think*. They say that in this constant light birds fly till they fall from the air. May it make ideas germinate! Believe it or not, I am reasonably happy. Like the reindeer, I gorge myself on the summer for there will be longer nights. Despite my moments of *Sorge* (in Goethe's sense of the word), I do not lose courage and go on thinking. Don't you stop either, and do please write soon.
                                                          Yours ever,
                                                          L.W.

   The *Sweimfoss* was now about a hundred miles up the fjord, anchored for the night in a basin among a nest of mountains. Since they'd left Bergen, three days had passed — or four; in that endless daylight, it was easy to lose track of the time. Moored midway between dawn and dusk, the sky was filled with a deep, golden red darkness, a pooling, whorling red like the heartwood of cedar. Peering up into that static Northern summer light, Wittgenstein had the sense of time suspended, floating in place, then resuming like those hypnotized birds above who, sinking, would suddenly remember to flap their wings.
   The *Sweimfoss* was an old, woodburning hauler eighty feet long and low slung in the middle, with a blunt bow that rose like the toe of a wooden shoe. Red cinders flew out her stacks, and oily rust and beads of pitch ran down her white wooden sides. In her hold was the sour, gamy scent of cheese, sour milk, dried halibut, half-cured reindeer hides and other cargo she carried. From the tall steeringhouse aft, the captain would blow his steam whistle as they made their endless stops at lumber camps, villages and outlying farms, where some dawdling boy would lead down a plow horse pulling a sledge to fetch groceries and mail-order tools from this floating post office and commissary.

Wittgenstein wanted a slow, cheap boat where they'd put him to work, and the captain and the mate, who spoke some German, were happy to oblige. Chipping paint. Wiping and oiling the steam engine. Grilling ham and potatoes, salted herrings and easy eggs. It felt so good to be active — healthy, unthinking, physical. Coming around a bend in the fjord, he might see ten miles of glassy water, water sometimes five hundred fathoms deep under a faint gloss of mist. Wittgenstein wished now to be as still and deep as these glacier-carved canyons. Slowly, a peaceful vision sense was floating down over him, an empty-headed gazing, like crossing one's eyes in order to see. Under the four-square light, he would hear the distant thunder of summer avalanches. Looking up, he would see misty flumes pealing down the fjord's sheer rock walls, the water tearing to rags, then to mist that infused his nostrils with the smell of rain. As through clearest crystal, the light streamed through him, with nothing now to impede it. Like a slow rain, the sky was falling, light to air, air to light; like the sound of a single struck key, it left an afterimage that slowly burned on his closed eyelids. *Red sky. Red Wittgenstein.*

It was midnight, and everyone was below asleep. With him on deck the only living thing was a pale brown cow with little knobbed horns who lay kneeling on her forelegs in a bed of straw. She was a sweet, docile bossy with a broad face, long ears and a heavy, four-fingered udder. Earlier, pressing his head against her soft, gurgling flank, Wittgenstein had milked her, thinking about God as the hot milk squirted in the tin bucket, *ploot ploot ploot*. Then as now he had felt the aspect of God. It was the imposition of that single struck key, that sense of being in agreement with the world and at last consigned to it. *Red sky. Red cow. Red Wittgenstein.*

He had been in such a strange mood in these weeks since his father had died: excited, then more subdued, with an unaccountable sense of well-being and happiness. His sister Gretl had not been so sanguine about him — she felt he was much too calm. In fact, she wondered if his father's death had even hit him, or if subconsciously he even believed it. Not believe it? he had asked. In contrast to his feelings at Christmas, Wittgenstein was not angry at his sister for saying this; if anything, he was faintly intrigued. How could he not believe his father was gone? he asked. For weeks, he had watched him waste into a long, dangling ash, eaten up with cancer. As it happened, he was the only one present when the old man finally died.

All that night the dying man had held on, until his family was wrung out with blear weariness. At last there was only Wittgenstein, sitting on a chair beside his father's bed. It was he who went downstairs to tell them it was over, and it was he who then led his mother to the sickroom to see, as it were, what had formed or transformed in that bed, the residue of a life. Approaching the open door, he could see how his mother dreaded what she would find. Why? he wanted to ask. She had already seen the worst. In the space of three months, she had watched her robust husband age thirty years. Why this dread? What was to fear? A few minutes later, when his siblings returned and they all stood mutely by the bed, he found himself wondering what had come over him during those last few minutes. Physically he was standing in the same room as his family, but otherwise he was not part of their world at all. He was forgiven and free, as was his father. Loss there was, but to his surprise there was no longer heat, nor spite, nor anger. What was sorrow? Where did sorrow go after the last spent fumes of a soul? Looking down at his father's wrecked, still warm body, he saw only that a dying man's suffering was over. Was he to be *sorry* for this? The morning sun was on the sill. Shrunk beneath the covers was an animal starved and cannibalized and finally expelled from his own corrupting body. *Sorrow?* Was that the word for this?

No, he thought, the dead don't need the alms of our sorrow. If he was sorry for anyone now, it was for his mother. Frau Wittgenstein gazed helplessly at her children, and then, seeming to think she must say or do something, she suddenly squealed, *I can't* — and covered her mouth with her balled-up handkerchief, ashamed at her outburst. This upset Mining, who clutched her mother and started weeping. The others — Gretl, Paul and Kurt — were distinctly uncomfortable with this scene, which only made them more uneasy about their own contradictory feelings, caught somewhere between *good-bye* and *good riddance*.

As through a glass, Wittgenstein could see their grief in all its guises and shades, its manifold traps. Miserable, guilty, ambivalent, Gretl looked at him as if to say, *And what are you so pleased about?* How was he to explain happiness coincidental with death and not sound callous, unbalanced or vengeful? How to account for this desire to venture out into the free air to watch the light pour like sand through his fingers? An hour before, a debt had been forgiven. The golem had been newly chartered into a whole man. But he couldn't rightfully say this — it would seem crazy, fishy. And not *seem*, either. From Gretl's expression, he could see his behavior *did* seem crazy, but inwardly he was still beaming and did not care.

The preceding two months had not been easy.

From the day Wittgenstein had arrived home, there had been a subtle competition over the sick man, a competition moreover that was largely the sick man's doing. Mining had been the one to care for him, but as his condition grew more severe and compromising, Karl Wittgenstein personally hired two nurses, heavy Slavic women with smooth, dark skin and tightly rolled black hair. Ostensibly, he did this so as not to overburden his wife and children, yet it also gave him a heightened sense of control over not only this uncontrollable disease but his family as well. He would not be hostage to his family's good graces. *He* would remain a sovereign state, with the nurses acting as a buffer between them.

This almost immediately created bad feelings, especially as the nurses appropriated the sick man as their patient, dictating, under the broader fiats of his doctors, meals, sleep schedules, visits. It was uncanny how the nurses would joke, wheedle and even boss him about once the door was closed. Karl Wittgenstein seemed to thrive on it. In the midst of his sickness and his growing helplessness, the two fleshy nurses pampered him in a way he never would have tolerated from Mining or even his wife, who one morning tearfully referred to them as *those prostitutes*. In dictating and enforcing visiting hours, the two nurses also fell into friction with the servants, especially with Herr Stolz, Karl Wittgenstein's personal butler of thirty-four years. The nurses even angered that most unlikely nurse of all, Gretl. Every afternoon, Gretl would bring fresh flowers from her greenhouse. Arriving around four, she would emerge from her car with all the grim vivacity of one on her way to a pressing business appointment. Freud might have lessened Gretl's anger and anxiety, but he needed to do nothing about her psyche, which floated over life like a fulldrafted ship, always managing to displace more pain than it carried. Nevertheless, this impending death was a constant drain on her, and she was absolutely furious when the older nurse told her one day that she would have to leave. Can you imagine? she told Wittgenstein. Asking his own daughter to leave! And in that tone! I looked at Father, but of course he just lay there, letting that idiotic *what's-her-name* speak for him. And I thought, You're even managing your own death, aren't you? Even now you must wrest control, mustn't you?

But it was easier for Karl Wittgenstein to let strangers do these things, and like many invalids, he took a secret, crafty pleasure in being willful and unpredictable, closing off his family even as they were preparing to lose him. The old man did not easily surrender to fatality. Painful as it was for him to move, he still insisted, in those first weeks Wittgenstein was home, on sitting at the head of the supper table. *Careful . . . careful*, he would hiss as two young footmen carried him down the stairs, placing him in his carved chair, then wedging him in with an elaborate assemblage of pillows. Propped up there, valiantly eating his own bland and pitiful portion, he looked like a pasha, albeit a rapidly thinning one, bundled in his smoking jacket and muffler. With his gray hair oiled and combed and his muttonchops carefully trimmed and scented, the old man looked more fastidious than ever, thanks to these two *hirelings,* as Mining called his nurses. And still, greedily, the sick man licked the delicious dew off those last leaves that life held out to him. After dinner, following a sponge bath and massage, the nurses would help him onto the oval settee where, as was his custom, he would play his cello, hugging it to him like a woman as he coaxed forth those last nocturnal groans.

More than ever now, Karl Wittgenstein's home was a factory in which his children took their shifts. Kurt would sometimes play several rubbers of bridge with the old man, who took great pleasure in beating him. Paul's job was to play the piano downstairs, letting the music rise like a draught up the grand stairway into his father's open chambers. At first his father might clap weakly. Later, he would send a footman down to convey his compliments — or, just as likely, to present a piece of criticism scrawled on a sheet. As time progressed, though, Paul was asked to play shorter and shorter pieces. Playing along, Paul would see a handkerchief waft past his eyes. And looking upstairs he would see the nurse who had dropped it as a sign to stop: the old man was asleep.

As his favorite, Mining took up much of her father's available day. Wittgenstein's job was to relieve her. In the corner of his father's room was a gramophone with a trumpeting brass bell, with stacks of records heavy as plates on the table beside it. In the afternoon, after opening the curtains to let the sun beam across the Oriental carpets, Wittgenstein would often crank up the gramophone and play several records for his father. Caruso singing Puccini, Beethoven performed by the Berlin Philharmonic — his father listened and never said a word, careful not to betray the emotion that surely surged within him when he heard great music. Peeping out with those bulgy, watery eyes, the old man rather showed tremendous, cultivated attention, stoical and aloof. Still, Wittgenstein noticed how, when he thought his son wasn't watching, the sick man would tightly shut his eyes, almost shuddering at moments of exceptional beauty. Yet if Wittgenstein ventured to praise a passage later, his father would cut him short, saying, Yes, it was excellent. Very nice. Very nice, indeed.

But Wittgenstein and his brothers felt another unspoken reproach. This came every few days when the old man's solicitors reported to him on the plans he had set in motion to sell all his interests in the Wittgenstein Gruppe. For Kurt, who was titularly in charge of one factory, this was in effect a vote of no confidence — why, his future wasn't even a matter of serious question. Certainly Kurt didn't question it, his own confidence having eroded to the point where he grudgingly agreed with his father's estimation of him.

Had Wittgenstein and Paul shown any desire to assume control of their father's enterprises, it might have been a different story. That developments had passed that point — not to mention the fact that neither wanted a business career — did not make them feel any easier about what Karl Wittgenstein no doubt saw as a repudiation of his life and values. Talking together in the study one afternoon, Wittgenstein and Paul recalled one summer nine years before when their father had attempted to introduce them to the business life. This was the summer following their brother Hans's suicide, when the recalcitrant Rudi was showing many of the same disturbing signs. Kurt, if unpromising, was at least stable: he was working under the stern eye of Herr Graben, one of his father's top assistants. With Kurt in tow and Rudi a losing cause, a worried Karl Wittgenstein instead focused his attention on his two youngest sons, Ludwig and Paul.

Wittgenstein and Paul were then fifteen and sixteen, respectively — old enough, their father said, to learn about the affairs of the world, meaning, of course, the business world. With this in mind, Herr Wittgenstein took them on a tour of his factories in lower Bohemia.

From the start, Wittgenstein felt it was hateful, two princes who had never done a day's work being trotted through plants to watch other men toil. And fearsome toil it was, too, ladling liquid fire and beating red-hot ingots under a burning pall of poisonous yellow smoke.

Karl Wittgenstein would question and reward only his very best workers, and he was carefully advised beforehand as to who deserved this signal honor. Imagine how a latheman feels to explain his lathing to me, the Direktor himself, Karl Wittgenstein told his sons. And for him to see that I thoroughly understand his problems and cares, as if I wore the same greasy black apron. Or for the soot-faced forge operator to shake the factory owner's hand — why, for him this is as if God visited hell.

Wittgenstein best remembered the first plant on their tour, a machine shop in the vast Teplitz works, which made special steel castings for the Imperial-Royal military. At his father's entrance, with the nervous plant manager hurrying before him, the grinding, banging and shrieking of the iron-girdered shop abruptly ceased. Wittgenstein could still remember the feel of the floor, slick with a heavy black coating of grease, carbonized steel and curled lathe filings. Shrouds of yellowy sunlight filtered through the grimy skylights, trickling over the chain hoists and massive geared winches onto the hairy shoulders of the men, all heavily muscled as draft horses as they stood hobbled by their lathes, anvils, punches and presses. Herr Wittgenstein was dignified and charming — the two boys saw the awed, admiring looks of the workers as he walked down the line, more than a man, someone actually *clean,* bespeaking rectitude and prosperity in a suit that his butler, who accompanied him on all his travels, had zealously pressed and brushed that morning. Of the hundred and fifty men in that shop, Karl Wittgenstein personally complimented just four, the shop's top producers. The chosen men were moved beyond words — moved almost to tears, several of them — as the Direktor stopped in the stream of his busy life and told the whole shop, in his gruff and barreling voice, *how much,* and precisely *why,* he valued *this man,* whom he called by name as he seized his grimy hand. This done, the Direktor gave a hortatory speech, emphasizing the importance of their work to the empire. And when the speech ended, they were at first unsure, afraid to applaud. But then with a stutter it started, clapping, then cheers and then the whistle that brought on the grinding, banging and shrieking that continued for two ten-hour shifts, six days a week.

They went through one more plant that morning, and another that afternoon. But at one factory Karl Wittgenstein told his sons to wait outside the foreman's office, saying ruefully, I have to speak to several individuals. From the long bench where they sat, his sons could hear his voice, hunking, guttural. The tempo was all too familiar, and as they sat ashen on that bench, three men and then a fourth hurried through the door with ruined faces. Stripped of their aprons under the gaze of a guard, they were summarily given their pay and their belongings. It was not by accident that the sons witnessed this. Wittgenstein could well remember his father's charged expression, his active eyes, when he returned to bundle the two novitiates inside. And before it seemed they were even through that door, they could see their father's aspect change like the sun. Looking back genially, he said, They all have their story. Always the same story, with variations of course. The sick wife and the children, the sore back, the bottle that calls to them. Believe me, I have heard them all. Look, he said under his breath, with a glance at the workers who were working harder than ever now, with the killing done. Look at these fine men. Do you suppose for a second they are angry at me for this? *Angry?* For sacking the slacker, the drunk who might get them maimed or killed? I did these men a service. Sad and unpleasant business to be sure, but one cannot delegate everything. Sometimes to clear the air, I must see to this personally. Men respect this in a leader. It is not enough to hand out awards. They must see your face. They must see it in both guises.

Karl Wittgenstein's fate was certain. Less certain was his youngest son's. In those last weeks, Wittgenstein increasingly felt the force of his father's critical gaze. As he sat reading to him, he would feel that questioning look like a burning handprint on the side of his face. They both knew the question: *What will you do with your life?*

Karl Wittgenstein made various feints at asking this question. After dozing off during their concert one afternoon, the old man awoke to find his son at his bedside, making those peculiar logical notations in his notebook. Blinking with irritation, the father asked:

Tell me, what does all that business mean?

What? asked Wittgenstein, offering him the scrawled page. These symbols?

His father nodded. Any of it.

Do you really want to know?

Yes. Please explain it to me.

So against his better judgment Wittgenstein explained. His discussion of logical symbology was basic and down to earth, but his father grew increasingly agitated. Yet whenever Wittgenstein tried to end the lesson, the old man insisted that he continue, apparently in the hope that his son would hear his own foolishness. But finally, looking up, Wittgenstein saw that his father was near tears — impotent invalid's tears.

I'm sorry, gasped his father with a heave of his chest. I did not mean to say this — honestly, I didn't — but I do not see what relevance this has to *anything,* or — With a sudden wince of pain then, he hissed, Leave me now — go! He pressed his hand over his face, his voice frantic, and there came a sharp smell. Please! I can't continue this now! Don't you hear me? I said, *Call the nurse! Call* her, will you —

The sick man did not have to call the nurse again. A moment later he was covered with comforting flesh, and Wittgenstein was hurrying down the long hallway, mortified at the coddling way the nurse spoke to his proud father, whom he could hear crying.

Gretl fared no better. For her there was also this criticism, as powerful as it was unspoken. Even now, and ever so subtly, they were still quarreling. Yet Gretl knew that by keeping her composure she would win — by outliving him she would win, for all the good that winning would do.

Her father could see she was winning. She always dressed especially smartly when she came to visit him, the better to remind the sick man of their now vastly differing status. A black dress with bottle-green panels. A veiled hat with a brace of pheasant quills fastened by a diamond signet. With each subsequent visit, Gretl seemed to outdo herself, the better to show herself as one of the secular world of the living, while he, succumbing to his own dark medicine, was fast slipping into that black tarn of his own belatedness, soon to be a face sunk beneath the earth, unheeded and forgotten.

Yet neither won. With a look, the father could undo months of her work with Freud. Several times Wittgenstein found his sister quietly crying downstairs — crying, she said, because she was so appalled at the persistence and virulence of her anger, the way it sunk only deeper without ever emerging into anything else. Wittgenstein also had that anger, but unlike his sister he kept it hidden, even to himself. However buried or transmogrified, though, it sometimes would emerge, as one day when he impulsively told her:

I just want to ask him once, What would you have me do with my life?

But why? she asked. He'll never tell you. Can't you see that? He'd only be relinquishing his advantage.

Yes, but at least I would have asked.

Gretl sat there staring at him. But if he refuses to answer, what's the point of asking?

I don't know. His hands were inert. I suppose so I could tell myself that I had asked.

Gretl had good reason for advising him to let it go. She had put a big question to her father once. She and Wittgenstein both remembered her question. They also bitterly remembered his answer.

Gretl's question concerned Hans. After his death, four trunks containing his belongings were shipped home from Cuba. Like the rest of the family, Gretl knew Hans had kept a voluminous journal. She also knew that those trunks probably contained the many letters her father had written Hans, especially in the last year before his banishment, when their relationship had degenerated into little more than an abusive exchange of notes thrust under closed bedroom doors late at night.

Karl Wittgenstein wasn't about to have his family burrowing through Hans's trunks. He wasn't even about to discuss them, or Hans, who for him was a closed book. Without a word to anyone, Karl Wittgenstein took possession of those trunks. Gretl thought he might even have had them burned.

Gretl found it maddening to have anything withheld from her. But it was more than mere sorrow or curiosity that drove her to ask her father about the trunks. It was revenge. Even at twenty-four, Gretl was exceptionally bold. She told Wittgenstein that she was going to ask her father. She even invited him to hide in the next room and listen. Wittgenstein begged her not to do it, but he was fascinated — fascinated and ashamed that she, a woman, should carry this grievance to their father. He hated himself for being so meek and obedient. A queasy, silent thirteen, he felt like a bent nail that somebody had pried from a door as he positioned himself — quite against his principles — in the next room.

As he had expected, Gretl's initial request was quietly and firmly rebuffed. But Gretl wouldn't be brushed off like a fly. Insolently, she repeated her request, whereupon Karl Wittgenstein took his first swipe at her, saying, Such concern, my daughter. When your poor brother was alive, you could hardly bear the sight of him. But now you want to pick his bones, don't you.

Gretl knew his strategy: he would infuriate her, then dismiss her as a hysterical woman. Calmly she replied, He was my brother. I've a right to see his belongings.

At this Karl Wittgenstein switched tack, adopting a more fatherly tone. Believe me, he reasoned, you don't want to see these things. Your brother was confused.

I realize that, she said. Still, I would like to better understand what happened to him.

And I'm telling you, he said, his voice rising a notch, you won't understand. Believe me, this business will do you no good.

I can be the judge of that, she insisted.

No! he countered, smacking his hand on the end table. *I'll* be the judge of that, and I'll not stand here palavering with you any longer! You haven't the least concern for your brother. You're merely doing this to provoke me! Just as you've done all your life!

Thus began his tirade, his voice booming through the wall to the room where his son stood cowering. For a minute father and daughter traded accusations, and then there came a crash as Karl Wittgenstein knocked down a china lamp, raging, *Get out! Get out!*

Thinking he heard his father coming then, the boy panicked and ran into the closet. Oh, that oozing greasiness in his skin! That shameful, hissing sissiness. Hiding like a moth among these musty old clothes! Like hammer blows came his father's threats. And obstinately, insanely, came Gretl's squealing accusations. Who do you think Hans was — your *property*? Because you *fathered* him? Is that it? And the boy feeling he would pass out then, pinching his thigh in compensation because it was so blackly, murderously good.

But if he was going to ask, Wittgenstein knew he would have to ask soon. Like a fire the cancer was running through the old man. One day the cello was too much, and then it was too excruciating to be moved to a chair, let alone down the stairs to supper. His weight dropped, his skin loosened, his cheeks caved in and his eyes darkened, taking on that glassy, half-expectant look of death. Then came morphine injections, and then the day Wittgenstein heard his father scream, the cancer having so eroded his bones that he had to be moved an inch at a time so they wouldn't crumble.

And then, finally, Wittgenstein did ask, but by then it was too late. He knew it was unfair — perhaps even cowardly — to weigh his father down with such questions, but his anxiety was too strong. He had to know.

Please, he asked suddenly one morning, in no apparent context. Just tell me. If it were up to you, what would you have me do with my life?

Gazing up at him, the old man wheezed, What can you possibly mean, asking me this?

I mean with my life. I want to know finally. If it were up to you, what would you have me do with it?

His father looked one hundred. He looked vaguely like a monkey, a ravaged snow monkey. The old man stared up, uncomprehending.

Can you just answer me that? prompted the son in that cheery, overly loud voice with which people address children and convalescents. Obviously, you have some idea. I just wanted to know. The son waited, then said almost beseechingly, *I need to know.*

The father still had all his faculties, but this was not sinking in, or not as the son intended. His breath faintly popped and whistled through his clogged nostrils, filling the room with a fetor that clung to one's clothes. Feeling frantic, Wittgenstein wished then that he hadn't asked, realizing his utter stupidity as he croaked:

That was all. What would you have me *do*? That's all I'm asking.

Tears sprang up in his father's eyes and ran down his cheeks. Not kindly tears. Tears of rage. With a pop of phlegm, he erupted into a rasping gargle, a drowning, underwater voice:

I . . . don't . . . *know!* — Why do you even ask? — And after ignoring me for years! What do you expect, you jackass — my *blessing?*

It was all out then. With a jolt of pain, the old man irrationally demanded, What are you doing here? *What?*

I'm not doing anything, the son protested. I merely — and he stopped, suppressing a hiccupping breath. Trying again, he said, I only came to ask, to *ask*! But then he stopped again, staring at his father before he added with another hiccup, About what I ought to do . . .

Do? His father's lower lip was jutting out with simian rage. He spat acid, demanding in that gargling voice, But *why ask me?* You're a *philooosopher,* aren't you?

Wittgenstein just stood there stupidly. Then one of the nurses burst in, and he whirled around on her.

Get out!

But Herr Wittgenstein —

I said *get out!*

Something tore loose in him then. Turning back to the bed, he peered down at his father. Is this the best answer you can give? he said. An *insult?* A sincere question, and *this* is your response?

His father was trembling. No words were left, only squeaks. And then came rage-hot tears as the old man gasped, *I . . . don't . . . know!* Is that what you want to hear? Huu-it isn't e-nough to die — I must, I must tell my children what they want to . . . *huu-hear.* So I can be hug-nored, God! — His voice broke off, and Wittgenstein could almost hear the crack of bone as he began again. *Huu-I . . . don't . . . care.* Do-you-hear-that, *philosopher?* Then came another crack of bone, a squirt of tears. *Don't care . . .* and *don't know!*

Why? asked the son, bending down. It was a whiff of a word. Before him then his father's face crumbled like a fire into ashes. Gone was the imploring boy. Wittgenstein stared clear down into his father's squirty eyes as he asked again:

Why?

And the old man, sucking air, said, *Huu-I . . . told . . . you . . .*

Wittgenstein did not know himself then, as he hung over his father's smelly bed or bier. In that ravaged face, he then saw quite clearly his stolen nose, that phantom appendage that had been dangled before his eyes all these years. Nodding, the son said softly, You just now spoke the truth, didn't you? Not only don't you know but you never did, did you? Thank you. In spite of yourself, you have answered my question.

And without another word, he left.

Karl Wittgenstein died four days later.

There were no confessions or tearful good-byes, no parting tales or hortatory advice, no last requests. For Wittgenstein, there was nothing more to say. Looking down at his dying father, he was reminded of a scuttled ship glugging down into the oily, smothering darkness, swallowing up its own confounded history. His father's leviathan of a life was sucking down its own perished past and even taking theirs with it, leaving only bubbles, empty, evanescent and unreadable.

It began as a sloppy, ambiguous death, with no good prospects but an end to suffering. What was the dying man to say? He had had his private partings with Mining and his wife. Wittgenstein, too, had kissed his father good-bye. And later, quite unexpectedly, in his bath, the son found himself crying like a little boy as the warm water gurgled out the tap, sobbing for his cold words to his father, which would stand like the stars.

There was nothing to do then but wait. It was wearying and boring, it dragged on and on. In the aftermath of their quarrel, Wittgenstein had given up fighting his anger and was filled with a bitterness sour as hell fumes. His limbs ached with his own poison. Throughout the night, his father hung on obstinately, from spite or habit, refusing to be dislodged. And finally Wittgenstein reached that point just short of sleep in which he was not thinking, judging or wishing. For all he saw now, his dying father might have been a fly on the wall. His father's face was the very face of Nature, which is always abrading into being, forever unfolding like a slender gasp of flame. Yet within that unfolding, his father's ashen face slowly began to change. Gradually Wittgenstein began to discern a slow transformation in his father's expression. It was the grip of pleasure, a fatal, vivid pleasure that the dying man hugged to himself like the ample curve of his cello. He was not a father anymore. He was released from this life and this family, severed from his frailties and failures, pried loose from the vise of this life and free now to be nothing. *There,* Wittgenstein told him in his mind. *It is enough. It is all right now. It is time. Go. You are forgiven. Please, for God's sake, go now while it's all right . . .*

But the old man only hung on, he hung on and on. Just when the family would think he was gone, he would half open his eyes, asking for a little water as if he had forgotten to take enough for where he was going. Why this delaying? His father did not need water or air, or earth or family. He was ready to take leave of them and they of him, yet he hung on, and grimly they hung on, obstinate in their obligation, not wanting to miss his end. But he wouldn't quit. Relentlessly, he wore them down, and by five in the morning he had them beaten, as ache and restlessness set in and heads began to droop.

The dying man had his way in the end. Poldy said she must have some air, and Mining followed her out. Then Kurt looked at Paul, suggestively tapping his cigarette case. Then they were gone and, with a sigh, Gretl left as well, sneaking out as from a play that had begun to bore her. What possessed him to remain? Wittgenstein would wonder later. Why did he not tell them of this sense he had that they were going to miss the end?

For perhaps a minute Wittgenstein had been staring at his father when the eyes half opened and gave a squirt. And then as his own eyes welled over, Wittgenstein knew why he had lingered there in wonder, sorrow and homage. Neither he nor his father moved. For a long moment they looked at each other, both asking and granting forgiveness — the simple grace to leave. And then without any sign from his father, Wittgenstein instinctively knew it was time: the old man wanted him to leave the room so he could die. Not a word was spoken, not a word was necessary. Without a look back, Wittgenstein stepped outside and shut the door. He waited only a minute, and he was not wrong. Peering up at the ceiling, he knew precisely when his father died. Up, as through his own head, swept his father's soul. Up in one hot gust it went, like a flame sucked up a flue.

Wittgenstein sometimes thought he must be deluded, to believe that his vile old self had died with his father. He thought he must be doubly deluded to imagine that this condition could be permanent. Yet even now, over a month later, he felt no different. His old fear of open space? Over his head hundreds of miles and below perhaps as many fathoms. What need had he of boat or shelter? Sound body. Watertight soul. Sufficient mind. *Red light. Red cow. Red Wittgenstein.*

And staring down at the red water of Sognefjord, his mind said, *Look down into it, into the uncertain depths of the world.* He saw the blood-red surface of the water and upon the water were golden flecks of fire. *But look down deeper,* he told himself, and to his fear he saw that he could. But to look deeper still, he saw he must jettison fear also. And he told himself then that if he truly had no fear he would take off his clothes, and he did. And he told himself he could dive in and the undersky would not be too wide, nor the red water too deep or cold or salty. And there would be no one to see him naked, and what did he care anyway, if he was pure and intent only on this, and this only? And thinking of his father's passing, he saw his new life dangling like a shadow in the water, sliding beneath the fire and depths, saying, *Come merge with me. You cannot walk on the water, man, but you can dive, and dive deep.* And then he was standing shivering and naked on the side of the *Sweimfoss,* smirking because for all the solemnity of this moment, it was so infernally silly and —

Whoosh —

Down he dove with open eyes, down into the cold depths that were red with fire, then black with throbbing pressure. And as his ears popped, he struggled still deeper into the pressure and silence of that aorta, the pulsing heart of the world, hot with the blood of new life and sorrows aching to be dislodged into being. And then the same voice said, *Enough,* and he floated up, his lungs burning and his legs faintly fluttering, watching his own flattened bubbles wobble up toward the surface, where he saw a dull pearl of moon or sun.

With a gasp, he broke the surface. Splashing in the air and red light, he was back again, and *it was cold!* And what a holy ass he was as he shinnied up the rope, grasped the raspy wooden sides and bellied over the gunwale. Splattering water and jibbering then, he saw the cow's broad, inquisitive face. Watching over her nest of hay, she seemed to say, *You are daft, Wittgenstein,* but in his mind he laughingly replied, *But you misunderstand. I am just very, very happy.*

When Love Was Still Green

A YEAR LATER, in late June of 1914, Wittgenstein was waiting on the pier in Høyanger, a town on Sognefjord where he had spent the winter, when Moore arrived on the *Sweimfoss.*

Dressed in a checked flannel shirt, heavy hiking boots and a brown Mountie's hat, Moore looked, after a year of marriage, softer and heavier, as full and plumb as a ripe apple. The brim of his hat left a red crease above his sunburned brow when he pushed it back to get a better view of Wittgenstein, who, after a year of semi-solitude, was himself a changed, if not semi-estranged creature, vaguely feral in the eyes. Gone were the shined shoes and tie, the aesthetical reserve. Tanned and smiling, wearing rough moleskin pants, an ill-fitting woolen workshirt and lumber boots, he looked a bit wild, his wiry hair as shaggy as a roan bull who'd been butting his head against a fence post.

Ho! cried Moore, cupping his hands over his mouth as the thudding boat eased into the slip. Don't you look fit!

Much as he tried to appear hearty and cheerful, Moore was sorely relieved to be getting off this rust bucket after four rough days. From the moment he stepped on the dock, Moore was pouring out his woes, beginning with the day he spent seasick in his berth, clutching the swill pail the mate had tucked in beside him. Scratching, Moore was saying:

And we had the most murderous mosquitoes. Droves of them. And rain. Thick black sheets of it — *for two days!* I didn't know you could get seasick on a fjord; I never dreamt it was possible. As an afterthought, Moore shook Wittgenstein's hand.

But you brought with you so much, said Wittgenstein later, when he saw Moore's mound of luggage assembled on the dock. Never will we get this all up the mountain.

Well, huffed Moore, rocking on his heels. I've read that you have no idea up north, what with the vicissitudes of weather.

I assure you, you will have enough, said Wittgenstein a bit ominously. Some of it we must leave. It is too late to set out today. Tomorrow, yes. Tonight, I have made for us reservations at the Hotel Flaam.

Oh, *good*, said Moore, who frankly was hoping they might spend three or four days more in this pretty town. And then, as they were going to their hotel, Moore dropped a broad hint.

So wearying, travel. I had forgotten.

Wittgenstein shook his head noncommittally.

In a flurry, Moore continued, Yes, it takes a while to settle in. A new country and all. And about mail? Do you suppose a letter to Dorothy would get back to her in *one week's time?*

Impossible. Two weeks, perhaps.

Two weeks! Oh, but she'll be very worried. Then Moore had another alarming thought: And our mail?

A shrug. They will hold it here for us.

You mean we shall get *nothing?*

Attempting to strike a more hopeful note, Wittgenstein said, If we ride in, we will get it, yes.

Oh. Moore looked at him hopefully. It's not too terribly far, then?

Fifteen kilometers. Wittgenstein's eyes rolled up into his head. In the mountains it is hard to tell.

Oh, well, on horseback, scoffed Moore, without the faintest idea what that meant. So it's not too far.

Over mountains it is far. Wittgenstein nodded. Without stops, nine, ten hours at least.

Oh, said Moore nonchalantly. But inwardly he said, *Good heavens!*

·

This wasn't the holiday Moore had planned, not at all. Not that he hadn't tried to wriggle out of it; the wretched truth was, he was trapped.

Originally, Moore and Pinsent were to have made the journey together, but then Moore saw he would have to leave earlier than they'd planned, while Pinsent reluctantly decided to leave later as a concession to his mother, who had come down with a serious case of bronchitis. As it turned out, Moore and Pinsent would pass in Bergen, where they planned to meet one night for a changing of the guard, as Moore put it.

But this was a fortnight away, and Moore first had some business to transact. As a favor to Russell — now at Harvard delivering his new lecture series, Our Knowledge of the External World — Moore had agreed to take down Wittgenstein's dictated ideas, the culmination of his labors for the past year.

But can't he transcribe his *own* ideas? Moore had asked when Russell first approached him about it. I rather envisioned it as a holiday.

Smiling, Russell tried to formulate an answer, then gave up.

No, said Russell with a dry smile. Wittgenstein can't transcribe his own ideas. That, you see, would be *writing*.

But you said he keeps a notebook. Moore was beginning to color. He can't copy it out?

Russell's smile slithered. Well, clearly he can't. Call it anxiety, if you like — you know what a perfectionist he is. He is not ready to publish, not even near, but fortunately he finds speech acceptable — easier, I suppose, to repudiate. I've tried letters, but it's tortuous. No matter what he says, it changes — the ground is constantly shifting under your feet. But really, emphasized Russell, he's quite enthusiastic about the idea of dictating. And obviously you are, shall we say, the perfect medium. You're a trained mind, as opposed to a mere stenographer, and you're — well, basically neutral on the subject. Certainly less suspect than I am, anyway.

Then Moore started squirming. Oh, I don't know, he said, thoughtfully touching the tip of his nose. I'd sooner snatch bait from a trap. After another moment's loss, Moore recovered enough to say, But I'm afraid I still don't understand. Why can't you go yourself?

Well, I would very much *like* to, said Russell, hovering himself for a moment. But you see it will be at least January before I can, what with this American excursion. And by then Wittgenstein may not agree. And besides, he said, brightening — and here was the clincher — Pinsent will be there with you, won't he?

Moore still could not believe he had been stupid enough to agree to it — especially without Pinsent there as a buffer. Already, Moore felt weary, appearing to believe — to Wittgenstein's supreme irritation — that he had undergone a terrific ordeal. Finally, after a drab supper that first night, Moore asked Wittgenstein if they might stay a while longer at the Flaam. Three or four days more, perhaps? Curled around his pipe, with a humbled look, he confessed, I would enjoy a little, em, *transitional* civilization. I've got blisters from these new boots. And as for a *horse*, well, frankly, my piles have been acting up. Moore stuffed his pipe drearily. I suppose you must think I'm a bit of a duffer.

Straining to be conciliatory, Wittgenstein said, A few more days we can wait if you like.

Moore brightened. You wouldn't mind? Actually, I thought you could do your dictating here.

We *could*, said Wittgenstein dubiously.

Several days? Moore pressed, hopeful. You think your dictating may take that long?

Wittgenstein grew tense. I do not know. I have no idea. I am unhappy with the whole scheme.

Moore's spruce chair gave a crack. But Russell said you were quite keen on it.

Anxious to part with my thoughts? Wittgenstein was stunned. Not *anxious*, no.

And not even very willing, it seemed to Moore: tenacious was the word for it. Over two tense days, with Moore acting as midwife, Wittgenstein grudgingly brought forth a year's worth of thinking.

Wittgenstein said, for one, that so-called logical properties *show* the logical properties of language and therefore the universe, but they *say* nothing. He said that in philosophy there are no deductions; that philosophy is purely descriptive. Distrust of grammar, he said, is the first prerequisite for philosophizing. But the swipes he took at Russell led Moore to ask slyly if the second prerequisite wasn't distrust of Russell.

On the contrary, said Wittgenstein acerbically. Distrust of oneself is second. Russell is third. Then comes you, Moore.

Such moments of levity were few. Wittgenstein's prickliness wore on Moore. No sooner would Moore read something back, it seemed, than Wittgenstein would correct him. If Moore interrupted to ask a question, he'd be met with impatience; and if Moore raised an objection, or required too much clarification, Wittgenstein would jump up, shouting:

This is a stupid idea! Idiotic! I hate it, I hate it!

Don't rage at me! Shaking the stem of his pipe. This wasn't my idea.

Rot! Everything I say is *rot*!

Listen, Moore would say sternly. Shall we proceed with this or not?

Whatever do you mean? A look of shock as Wittgenstein motioned him down with his hand. Now, as I *said* . . .

By the time they finished three days later, they were both sour and exhausted. Moore felt as if somebody had been punching him in the ribs. But still, he was pleased with the results, even if he felt, as he wrote Dorothy, that he had played midwife to a rhinoceros.

Wittgenstein was not so pleased, however. The dictator was sick. The next day as they loaded the horses, he was gloomy and silent, feeling that he had offered his treasures to a thief.

With this chore over, Wittgenstein was more anxious than ever to return to the hut he had just built. Manual labor and solitude had been his cure that spring, and it was what he needed now. What he did not need was a guest.

Oddly enough, the blessing Wittgenstein had felt after his father's death had remained with him longer than he'd expected. But it had crumpled under the supreme test — his obligatory visit home to Vienna at Christmas. Like Pinsent, Wittgenstein found himself having to contend with his widowed mother's loneliness and endless worries about him, her worsening health and complaints. True to form, there had been yet another young lady for him to meet — another failure. And then from all quarters came the inevitable questions about why he insisted on leading this hermit's existence away from his family, in the middle of nowhere.

There was also the matter of money — not the lack of money but the harrowing abundance of it heaping up, and with it hectoring solicitors, trusts and endless papers to sign. There was no avoiding it now. It was not his father's money, or even his family's money. No, it was *his* money, mounting, compounding, stock and dividend money with steel jaws to trap him if he wasn't careful.

From all this he had fled, leaving Vienna in mid-January. Once back in Norway, he was better. It was nice to burrow in under the relentless winter — short gasps of daylight followed by endless nights, pulsing with the gaseous whorls of the borealis. Across virgin snows, in applecracking cold, he learned to snowshoe and ski. Several times, he was even seen in church.

His was not a hermit's existence. He was staying in the home of the town postmaster, along with his wife and four children. The postmaster was amazed at the quantity of important-looking mail the boarder received, and it quickly became known that the Austrian was a man of means who struck a bargain without haggling as he went about buying tools and supplies for the spring.

The postmaster's wife, thickset but supple, with gorgeous graying blond hair, saw all this and more in her boarder. She spoke some German and was in the process of teaching him Norwegian. Sitting across from him in a chair, tutoring him, she was like a mother bird stuffing new phrases down his hungry gullet, saying Det er virkeligsnilt av Dem . . . *Det-er-virkelig-snilt-av-Dem* . . . Leaning closer then, she would clarify the grammar, show him the proper position of the tongue, clucking and squirming with delight as he struggled to improve his pronunciation.

Norwegian he acquired with remarkable ease; it was his tutor's more subtle tongue that was slow to discern. But then one day, hearing her full skirts swish behind him, he looked down to see her plump hand sluice through the fold between his shirt buttons. When he grasped her hand, she mistook it for passion, emitting a low midwinter moan. How fearful he found her, bristling with an aurora of sticky, staticky sex. His Norwegian was not bad; he made himself understood. Shamed and furious, seeing to her disbelief that he had nothing for her, the postmaster's wife gave him a real Norwegian lesson then — it was a tongue lashing he would be months getting over. What was wrong with him? she asked. He did not go to the socials that made these winters bearable. He did not talk to the young ladies. Why do you withhold yourself? she asked. For whom? For what?

Sunk in his room later, unable to answer any of her questions, he felt only his own shameful incapacity and contradiction. Much as he wanted to leave, he saw he must stay, since to leave in midwinter would only have invited suspicions. For two tense months he remained there. Looming and unavoidable, smoldering still, the wife made him suffer for having spurned her. At times, he thought he could almost smell her, musty as a sickroom quilt in need of airing.

Spring had saved him. It was a mighty, thunderous spring, which came first with a dripping, then with a roaring and a crashing of ice as roofs and boughs shook loose their burdens. Then in April, with a squeaking and groaning like a nail being wrenched from a board, the ice-bound lakes broke open, the white-hot ice booming and splitting like the surface of a vast, aboriginal egg.

Later that month, driving a heavily loaded sledge drawn by a bay plow horse named Oskar, Wittgenstein set off for the land he had bought the previous fall. Waterfalls unfroze and crashed down the mountainsides.

Under that concerted sun, hardy wildflowers popped up through the melting snow, and the lakes broke clear, flashing up with a hard, blue radiance. With a smack of leather and tinkle of harness chains, Oskar swung a head the size of a woodstove, his flanks and shoulders quivering to dislodge the first black flies. Wittgenstein cracked the reins and up the hill they climbed, the wet, dark earth ripping and squirting out under the sledge's runners with the smell of ripe cheese.

With a neighbor named Nordstrøm and his two sons, Wittgenstein had the foundation dug by the time the first load of lumber arrived on the fjord a few miles below. For two brutal months he drove himself. It took those weeks of hard physical labor just to break his will's dark hold, his pride still welted with the wife's words. But the work redeemed him, his fears melting again in the mountain plenum. In fact, he was quite good until Moore arrived — in his mind, it was Moore's visit that spoiled things. Having surrendered his ideas to Moore, Wittgenstein felt denuded, without an ounce of fat to get him through this next long winter.

Wittgenstein knew, at heart, that this wasn't Moore's fault. But still he resented Moore's intruding presence, and he was sick of Moore's complaints. As they rode out to the hut, Moore's piles throbbed so badly that he hardly knew whether to walk or ride, and so the ten-hour trip stretched into twelve. By the time they arrived, Moore was done in. Spotting the "necessary house," Moore eased himself down from the saddle and took off with that delicate, bowlegged dance step — the green apple two-step, some call it.

Why? Moore asked himself as he crouched over that fulsome lime pit, grunting and slapping. Why was he *here* and not with his young wife? Why not at the Hurley-Burley, where he and Dorothy had passed an idyllic August at the seaside the previous summer?

It was not long after their wedding that Dorothy had insisted on taking him there for a needed rest. This came after Moore had begun to founder on *Prolegomena to Any Future Certainty,* a paper he had been months struggling with. Ironically, it was Wittgenstein who had suggested the topic that day in Moore's office when he refused to say there was not a rhinoceros in the room. Moore's paper sought to respond to such skepticism, but how? The further Moore progressed, the more stale and unconvincing he found his arguments. For a month Dorothy watched his mounting frustration, until at supper one night Moore threw up his hands and declared:

I know it *thus*! *Behold my two hands*! Ergo I *know* there are at least *two* things in the world!

I see, said Dorothy quietly. I'll show you a third. You're exhausted, and I'm exhausted by you. I insist we take a holiday.

Moore didn't protest very hard. Indeed, he was thoroughly relieved three days later when they registered at the Hurley-Burley, a tall, white-shingled hotel near Harwich, on a cliff overlooking the North Sea.

There was a crowd of regulars who convened there every summer, older and middle-aged couples, with many children. Dorothy was among the youngest wives, and when she revealed to Mrs. Noyes that they were only recently married, they were then known as the "young couple" — mascots to remind the older people of when their love was green.

There's rather more burley than hurley here, mused old Mr. Colbeck while sitting beside Moore at grogtime, which began promptly at four on the promontory overlooking the sun-greased sea. By the second day, Moore had heard that dictum repeated a dozen times by the various Burleybacks, or Puffins — the return guests for whom the sameness of those placid Augusts was clearly the best that life could hold.

It was an easy, unmeditated life, a thoroughly common life among ordinary people. Yet Moore had to admit that the life here promised much more good, and certainly a good deal less harm, than many more rigorously applied systems. After supper in the dining room, there were the usual round of skits, impromptu musicales and parlor games. Moore played charades and, with Dorothy at the piano, sang the definitive, three-hankie rendition of *Foggy, Foggy Dew.* Wearing a mop wig and a seaweed beard, he even posed as Poseidon at the Henleys' fortieth wedding anniversary party.

Moore guessed it was partly due to being married and partly due to age that he suddenly found these humble rites so sacred and consoling. Sitting with the men, he could avidly discuss pigeon breeding, garden pests or dog training. There were an endless variety of things to talk about, and once it was learned that Moore was a philosopher, he became the resident authority on virtually every topic. At night, there was always a large gathering out on the promontory. Mr. Glencannon, who only a year ago had lost his lovely wife, Agnes, would play *Mother O' Mine* and *Comin' thro' the Rye* on his mournful bagpipes (sounding like a frightful geese gaggle, as old Mrs. Dovecote never failed to remark). Wearing heavy Shetland sweaters and bundled under blankets in the varnished slat chairs, they would sit for three and four hours at a stretch, talking, drinking toddies, playing euchre. The awnings rippled and the waves pounded the black rocks, sending up a mist that kept people wiping their glasses. Puffing his pipe and holding hands with Dorothy, Moore would stare out to sea, hardly saying a word, while the others disagreed over which constellation was which, or gamely debated whether dogs have souls or God a sex — questions, ultimately, that were respectfully remanded to the able Professor Moore for his considered views.

Mornings, Moore would be up even before the old men to read the paper and savor the sun as it burned off the fog. At the breakfast bell he would be off, heading down the line of steaming chafing dishes, heaping his plate with rashers of bacon and shirred eggs, toast and stewed prunes. God, but he could pack it away there. He could feel the fragrant heat fanning up from the fiery gardens. He could smell the rank sea air that flapped the stiff white linen as he worked away at that holy mountain of food, conscious of the rising pressures of his body stoked with two normal-size breakfasts and four cups of hot coffee.

Seven days a week this was Moore's Sunday morning service. And the body — was it not a luxury liner built for pleasure as well as thinking? *Dorotheeee?* he would wheedle as he crept into the room. *Dorotheeeeee.* Oh, he'd catch her in bed. And didn't he love the whiteness of her breasts below her sunburned neck! Working down the whiteness of her thighs to the red flesh of her ample calves, Bill Moore was in a rut. Sniffing and snorting. Jackstamping in the joy seat of that squeaking iron bed. Long clam-sucking thrusts and a clenching kiss. Then came the whistling, the little rinse in the wash basin before changing into his scratchy black bathing costume. Grinning at her in the mirror.

Yes, a black pleasure ship he was, built for stateliness, not for speed. Offering his arm to Dorothy, Moore would cross the shaky planks that led down the cliffs to the beach. With his pipe clenched in his teeth and his skimmer slanted against the glare, he would step off onto the fine white sand so agreeably hot underfoot. A few older couples sitting fully dressed in beach chairs holding parasols; and then the younger women in flouncy wading gowns and their husbands in banded black. Children running with their pails. Mrs. Marsdon's sturdy black Labrador, Hero, bounding into the foam. Greetings came like alms.

Ah, the young people. Mrs. Moore, do come sit here beside me.

Good Mr. Moore! And how are you, sir, this lovely morning?

Oh, very well, thank you!

Taking leave then of the Burleybacks and bumsitters, parting from his wife, Moore would calmly slog out into the cold, black water. And after him the children would shout, Mr. Moore, your hat! You're wearing your hat, sir!

Lazily waving his hand. The hat's old. It floats. The waves will wash it ashore.

Doing a slow crawl beyond the waves, Moore would spurt and roll over. A sperm whale, he was. From the shore, his black belly resembled a distant island. Timid swimmers found his presence reassuring; he made the sea look so restful and inviting, the golden straw of his skimmer glowing like a halo over the glassy roll.

Moore felt distant and serene as he fluttered along, peering over his belly at the hotel on the little bluff and the folk lying on the sand. From here it seemed he could draw these disparate elements of his life into perspective; it was a way of taking a long look back at his life and wife, staring half in disbelief at that fragile green thing waiting for him on the shore. So odd, he would think, this need to see from afar what could best be seen up close. It was a matter of one's emotional focal length: one was either near- or farsighted, or perhaps not clear at any distance. With his arms waggling at his sides, Moore would daily test the limits of his acuity, drifting out until he felt a kind of pain, like a boy seeing how long he could remain submerged. Sweeping out, he would wait until at last he saw her waving at him, angry that he always ventured out so far, without a care. Then he would bellow back and slog in, feeling secretly grateful that she had called him back. Floating out, he could reforge that bond, venturing forth that he might return, lobbing over the swells to strain the ragged edge of sight.

And now, a year later, as Moore emerged from Wittgenstein's outhouse into the preternatural desolation of that Norwegian mountaintop, he asked himself once again why he felt this need to swim out from his wife and new life? What on earth had driven him here? he wondered, inwardly cursing himself for being such a fool.

For the first time ever in his life, Moore felt homesick — wifesick. This loneliness was a curious feeling. All his life he had prized male company, and he was strangely grieved now to see that he could never return to that life. In his youth, he had always thought he would travel — oh, not widely or adventurously, but freely, whether alone or in the company of other men, cloaked in his thoughts like a weatherproof. This notion was so bound up in his youth that it pained him to find that he was now a confirmed homebody. The question was how he would endure this isolation and wifesickness, not to mention another week of Wittgenstein.

As for Wittgenstein, he was increasingly oppressed by Moore's normality.

Moore was the apotheosis of all that he was not. Moore did not withhold himself from world or woman. Inept as he was in the outdoors, Moore held firmly the bosom of life, snatching pleasure where he found it. Yet despite these frictions, they had their pleasant times. There was still much work to do in the hut, and with Moore's ham-handed help, Wittgenstein finished the bunks and built a shelter over the woodpile. They went for long walks and called over gorges to their cacaphonous echoes. In the sparkling fjord, they sailed a small sailboat Wittgenstein had bought, Moore sprawled in the stern, his boyish face turned up to the sun.

But most of all, Moore loved to skinny-dip in gushing mountain streams. At the first sight of a stream or falls, he would be hopping on one foot, yanking off his trousers. Oh, come *on,* Wittgenstein! he would taunt, slogging into a gorge filled with mist and sunlight. Here Moore was in his element. Here he was again a ripping pleasure boat, whooping as the icy water pounded his flabby white back and dimpled buttocks.

Wittgenstein couldn't stand it. Gone was the grinning novitiate who had dived naked from the *Sweimfoss.* Ashamed and intimidated by Moore's nakedness, Wittgenstein would retreat down the trail and wait until Moore reappeared, half dressed, with his hair awry.

In the evenings before the stove, they read and talked. Frequently they argued about philosophy, but this was the least of their conflicts. Slowly, another competition was unfolding. Within a few days, their relationship began to take on a queer domestic quality, Wittgenstein acting the Spartan provider and Moore the dependent complainer, inept with tools, horses, cooking. Moore resented Wittgenstein's youth and vigor, his contempt for comfort. How could Wittgenstein silently endure this misery? he wondered. Awful food! Lonely nights! No warm Dorothy to crawl up against! Lying in his bunk at night, Moore would wait until his bladder was fit to burst. And then he would charge into the half darkness, there to flail and curse at the mosquitoes that flew like birdshot into his neck while he whizzed and squirted.

Still, Moore had something over Wittgenstein. Twice he had gone with Wittgenstein to his neighbor Nordstrøm's to buy eggs and cheese and even fresh meat when it was available. Nordstrøm had a daughter named Sigrid of perhaps eighteen years, willowy and blond but doorknob plain. Wittgenstein had seen her watching him, but he persistently ignored her. Not Moore.

I saw her eyeing you, he joked as they rode back. You may take a wife yet if you don't watch out.

At this Wittgenstein recoiled, snapping, Don't be silly!

Moore rolled his eyes, happy to get a rise out of him. Oh, you never know.

Please — Wincing. Don't speak foolishness.

After the many small humiliations he had suffered, Moore liked getting Wittgenstein flustered. He dubbed Sigrid the Milkmaid, and after that, when they saw her in the meadows minding her cows, Moore would chime:

Well, well . . . your Milkmaid has come to see you, Wittgenstein.

Moore meant it as a joke, but Wittgenstein only heard the postmaster's wife, until one day he snapped: I forbid you to mention her again!

There was another incident that was to leave a lasting impression on Moore. On no account would Wittgenstein dress in front of him, but one morning, coming through the door, Moore caught him with his trousers down, adjusting a thick black belt that girded his groin and stomach. Glaring, Wittgenstein said in a brittle voice:

I ruptured myself winter last. I must now wear this belt.

Oh, said Moore, turning away. So sorry to hear that.

For Moore, the image lingered, changed to a chastity belt — a hard, self-imposed privation. And then one night, almost in spite of himself, Moore asked:

Don't you find it awfully lonely up here?

Wittgenstein eyed him uneasily. Again, it was the postmaster's wife, posing a question for which he had no answer. He replied:

I am sorry you miss your wife. I am sure I cannot imagine such a thing. No. Wittgenstein shook his head. I cannot.

Oh, it's *terrible!* volunteered Moore, grateful to hear a note of commiseration. Before I was married, I couldn't have imagined missing anybody so much. It's indescribable.

But seeing Wittgenstein's face, Moore realized that he had struck a barrier: there was no point pursuing it; it was a thing beyond Wittgenstein's visible spectrum. Donning a mosquito headnet and coat, Moore then ventured out into the red darkness, into the mild wind where the mosquitoes were singing. For years, Moore saw, intimacy had been his fear; intimacy with a woman had been his girding belt. But now, standing atop that mountain, Moore saw that his darkest fear was loss of intimacy. Intimacy had given him new spectacles. Through love of a woman, he could see clear across the earth. But now Moore felt the stinging fear that his love might be sick or in need, perhaps dead.

Stop it! he ordered himself. Fear of loss was understandable, if morbid, but it occurred to him then that fear of happiness was far the stranger. Fear of happiness, in part, was what had possessed him to float out to sea, and it was just as surely what had driven him north. What it was, he saw, was an almost superstitious disbelief in his new life, a fatal feeling that good could not keep begetting good: sooner or later, one's luck would run out. But this too was curious. After all, why should he, one who so venerated the Good, dread it? Because it might be undeserved? Because it might not last?

And then Moore thought, *What if Dorothy is pregnant?* Think of it: beyond these forests, across a sea, an effect of which he was the cause might be taking root in the womb of a woman curled on her side, asleep. In all the proofs of his ponderous *Prolegomena,* he wondered, why had he never considered this? Amid all that grunting and rooting, in all that sweaty pumping with his face buried in her neck, why had he failed to see all the priapic Good he might be sparking?

Creeping inside later, Moore found Wittgenstein fast asleep. So odd to watch another person sleeping, to see a man bereft of his waking power and stature — just a vulnerable animal craving rest, with his fingers stuffed in his mouth. Up here this man could sleep. Up here a man could lie dead for weeks, with no one the wiser. For a moment as he stood there, Moore had the feeling of them both living in a vacuum, two dimming candles, the last two souls on earth. Staring down at Wittgenstein, Moore wondered what, with none to remember this man, kept his heart beating and caused his lungs to expand? Looking down then, Moore felt the uncanniness with which one life form eyes another, not knowing what it is or how it makes its way in the world, wherein it has carved its little niche. What would ever become of him? Moore wondered. How did Wittgenstein bear this Arctic loneliness? With a chill, Moore realized then that he did not know this man. He did not know him at all.

Two days later, when Wittgenstein returned from cutting wood, the atmosphere broke. Moore had been reading Chesterton while he aired the bedding, and it got drenched in a downpour. Then, trying to dry it, he had trimmed the stove wrong and filled the hut with smoke. Wittgenstein lost his temper.

How can you be such a bloody idiot! Complain, complain, then this!

Damn you! yelped Moore. *Be quiet! Please* be quiet!

Moore jumped up from the table, throwing down his fists. He felt his head was in a tourniquet. He gulped to say something more, choked; and then to his surprise, he burst into tears, stumbling as he lunged out the door.

Moore was staring down at the fjord when the humbled Wittgenstein approached a few minutes later. Touching Moore's shoulder, Wittgenstein said, I am sorry. I know I have been a beast. It is my fault. I am not used to people anymore.

Moore pinched his eyes, then said, It's not a matter of fault. I want to leave tomorrow, and not because of this. I miss my wife. All day long I've been thinking of her.

Green Recruits

IT WAS FORTUNATE that Pinsent arrived in Bergen a day early — otherwise he would have missed Moore in the cottager's lather to get back home. Instead, Pinsent and Moore spent a long evening together, over which Moore spun the whole sorry saga of his days trapped in the wilds with Wittgenstein.

When Pinsent set off on the *Sweimfoss* two days later, Moore's apprehensions were still with him, but over the next days they steadily diminished as Pinsent found the trip to be more what Wittgenstein promised and less the bilious, buggy ordeal that Moore had described. But then Pinsent was younger and more resilient than Moore, and he wasn't leaving a wife — he was fleeing a mother.

Wittgenstein knew all about Pinsent's difficulties. Several weeks before, Flo had even sent him a plea, writing in a scrolling hand that veered sharply up the page:

My Dear Mr. Wittgenstein,
   Despite what David says, I am glad he will be visiting you. If I were younger & if David didn't so mind I would visit you both. I know *you* wouldn't mind, would you?
   I am very most grateful for the money you have bestowed on us you are a Prince even if you do have pots of it; — but Sir, I still worry David will not return to university, & it would be a purple shame for such a bright boy to make his way knocking on doors selling Sheffield cutlery. Don't you agree?
   It would be very good, Sir, if you would kindly tell him this. But PLEASE do not say *I* wrote you, as he wd. be furious. Even as a boy he was always running away from me, such a red-haired gnat, I said; — & you know how *they* are.
   Secondly, Mr. Wittgenstein, you ought to be aware that David is frightfully allergic to bees; — & do be *most* careful walking as I've read a rock or snowball in that part of the world can cause a most unfortunate avalanche! The fourth I forget.

I do not expect such a busy young man as yourself wd. write to me with the long winter only months away. But if so, do; — but if you can't, don't. I will certainly understand in either case.

Gratefully yours,
Florence Pinsent

Pinsent arrived in Høyanger in the second week of July. In his journal, he wrote:

10.VII.14

. . . W. meets me at the dock. Surprised at my moustache; also at my physique, as I admit to lifting dumbbells to prepare myself for the rigours of mountain life. We keep smiling at each other. He is tanned & vigorous looking from physical labour & building his hut.

His English has deteriorated a bit, as Moore said, but he is not nearly as "wild," as Moore joked. No acclimatising for me in hotel as he did for M. We go directly on horseback 15 km., arriving near 10 p.m. W. highly pleased; he says I have fared much better than M. So far, so good . . .

W.'s hut overlooks the fjord, just as he described it. Mosquitoes bad, but not so bad as M. said. We smear ourselves with this evil local tallow &, donning headnets, venture out into the midnight dawn colours, wch. hang like smoke in the cool air. *Slap! Slap!* Through even thick wool they pierce, these little bloodsuckers. Here one pays for the sublime.

Later, sitting inside by the smoking fire, W. has a good laugh at my kit, esp. the Scout manual Mother sent, wch. actually looks somewhat helpful. Knowing that I have just seen M. in Bergen, W. asks if M. is angry. M. *was* badly hurt — hurt more badly than he even let on, I think — but I say little. W. knows I am holding back & adds ominously, "You will tell me if I am being unreasonable." I promise to tell him, then take out a cigarette & light it. W. very much annoyed. Grimacing. "Why do you start this? Such a filthy habit — and so unnecessary." Smiling, I say, "You told me to warn you if you become unreasonable." "Yes, yes. You are right." Watching me light & exhale, he sees I will warn him again too.

11.VII.14

Today we are still on our best behaviour . . . Supper of eggs & milk, canned peas & fish. Make bannock bread over the fire as Mother's surprisingly useful Scout manual sets forth. Wittgenstein's eyes darken when I say I long for something sweet. "Not from you also. All I heard from Moore was food. We are not here to eat." "And why not?" I ask. "We aren't in a monastery."

W. is silent. For him we are, I think.

13.VII.14

When I ask to take W.'s photograph with my new camera, he grows uncomfortable. "No, I am not ready to be photographed. I am still too unapparent, like a larva. Once I become a full human being & man of spirit — then you can photograph me." He smiles. "As it stands, you may develop your film & find no image whatsoever."

A week later, they were fairly settled, though still there were periodic rumblings.

21.VII.14

. . . By now, we are getting fairly used to each other, but W. still has quirks wch. I do not understand. For instance, I ask why he has located the latrine such a distance from the hut. "It is more aesthetic," he replies. "Perhaps so," I say, "but you don't venture out at night into the cold & mosquitoes to relieve yourself!" "Why don't you use an empty tin?" he suggests. "That would not bother you?" "Why should it?" he asks. "I don't know," I say. "I suppose because it's so unaesthetic!"

Tolerance, Pinsent! But why must he brush his teeth for five minutes at a time? Also, his prudishness. *Will not* dress in front of me. Averts his eyes when I dress. Also his preoccupation with cleanliness. Surgical procedures with dishes. After supper, we haul up buckets of water & this doesn't count all the wood necessary to heat it. "But surely," I plead, "one bucket will do." So he sullenly hauls a third & fourth & burns a whole pile of wood to boil our plates, laying them in the grass to dry in the 10 p.m. dawn.

Despite these small frictions, they got along exceptionally well. Handy, hardy, and self-sufficient, Pinsent liked the small daily pleasures of mountain life, the routine of keeping the rough wooden floor swept, the pots scoured, the knives and axes whetted, the woodpile stocked and the tins lined in the larder he built. In reaction to his mother's chronic sloppiness, Pinsent was meticulously orderly, a quality Wittgenstein much valued, especially in such close quarters. Freed from many of these chores, Wittgenstein was again working steadily. Yet this, in turn, evoked Pinsent's own ambivalent feelings of competition — an evanescent sense of drift. To their mutual discomfort, Pinsent even made several desultory comments about being Wittgenstein's "servant" and "wife." Then one afternoon Pinsent saw something hanging on the clothesline.

23.VII.14

. . . W. is on the hillside, reading in the sun, when I see it, black & flaccid, like a corset, with layered webs of rubber. I am still looking when I hear

Wittgenstein call over harshly, "It's a rupture belt." Gratuitously, he adds, "In the spring I ruptured myself — since you are so *curious*."

His voice is daring me — I know he wants to hear nothing more of it, but I say, "Is it wise, all the lifting and heavy work you do? Won't this make it worse?" "I'll be concerned with that!" he retorts. He snatches up the belt & goes inside.

The sight of it curdles me, rather. It's like something found in childhood all shut up in a drawer & best so. Must be torture to wear it, all hot & pinching. Perhaps that is the appeal — his hair shirt . . .

But the rupture belt was girding, as it were, another delicate matter: the question of what they each would do. Fall was approaching and with it the beginning of term. Wittgenstein planned to remain the winter, and it was clear to Pinsent that Wittgenstein hoped he would remain there with him. From his side, Wittgenstein felt selfish for this wish, worrying about the effect it would have not only on Pinsent but on Flo as well. Loath as he was to admit it, Wittgenstein saw there was much truth to Flo's fear that David would shortchange himself for his sake.

Pinsent, meanwhile, had an inkling of something else. Wittgenstein had described the experience of his father's death. The postmaster's wife and then Moore had disrupted that easeful, fecund state, but Wittgenstein now said that he was beginning to recapture it. Implied was his secret wish that Pinsent might share this experience, that together they might undergo this spiritual revaluation. Like a pony feeling the accustomed knees of a rider nudging his flanks, Pinsent sensed Wittgenstein's direction. And as he had done all his life, he stoutly resisted.

25.VII.14

W. has intimated this religious "experience" he had, though he is quick to add that it was not religious in the conventional Christian sense; it had, in fact, no Christian trappings whatsoever.

W. does have an ambiguous relationship with religion from wch. he is, I suspect, a fugitive. I recall how he signed a recent letter: "God bless you — if there is such a thing." It's not the idea of God, he explains — he believes in God (at least as an *a priori*) — it is this "bless" part he discounts — the thought of God going about blessing people strikes him as absurd. ("God has nothing better to do than bless us, or not bless us?") And yet, W. says, if God vouchsafes one ease after a time of torment, is this not a blessing? Yes, this much he understands.

I am more earthbound. W. bridles when I suggest this state may have been mere relief over the end of a painful & difficult death; contradictory feelings about his father, etc. "Then you don't understand!" he retorts. "Psychological crudities cannot account for religious experience."

Later I say, "I do not think you could exist within the confines of conventional religion. You could not surrender to another authority. I think you have your own inward religion." "No," he insists. "That is only arrogance & self-delusion. You must look *out* from the locus of your life; you must look *out* on the world, not caring who or what you are. That is why I am here. Up here I am nothing, really nothing." He looks up. "Ask the wind what you are or if it cares. Ask the animals. They take little notice of me, nor should they."

30.VII.14

My understanding of people is retrospective. If I am quick & perhaps clever in some ways, people may truly tell me anything to my face, esp. in the heat of the moment. They tell me the most atrocious lies, wch. I meekly apprehend with almost gaping mouth. Now I'm thinking of this discussion of W.'s religious sense. Not being religious in the churchly sense, it makes me uncomfortable — I feel W. is directing me in the hope that I shall cultivate a similar sense. Into my hands he puts James's *Varieties of Religious Experience*, commending James for his profound understanding of conversion and the mystic mind.

While regretting my incapacity, I do not feel that I am the least bit susceptible to these mystic states; at least not as I am at present. I suppose one justly fears conversion — the idea that one will feel compelled to shed one's former life like a dirty shirt. But for me it is mostly this fear that W. shall steal my soul & make me a different man, in his image.

As a result of my fears, I feel I must almost arbitrarily make my life in those nooks where W. is not, like the hardy lichen one sees here clinging to the mountain rocks. Well, at least it is kind to the feet. Reindeer also depend on it, I'm told.

2.VIII.14

I am getting more adept at handling our little sailboat. Today, as is often the case, I handle the boat while W. writes. The wind is blowing colder; the water scatters with the wind. When we come about, I call out so W. doesn't get knocked by the boom, since he is utterly unaware of me or the day; or the boat; or of anything. Often he does not hear me. Or remembers, as if just asked, about something he failed to respond to an hour, or a day, ago.

The boat is so smooth in its cutting. The sun comes out & I feel a promise; it goes in, & I feel a chill. Ever since childhood I have felt such — warm sun on my cheek, eyes half shut, feeling the wind & that half-dazed, pleasant sense of foreverness. The sun is out, & it is summer; in it goes & I feel winter gloaming. The farmer's dogs are getting thicker coats, as are our three shaggy horses. My red hair is much too wispy — wrong for this clime. Could I exist the winter here with him? It would be like overstoking the stove. He would drive me out with the heat.

As it turned out, though, Pinsent did not have to decide whether to leave or stay. The decision came when Wittgenstein's neighbor Nordstrøm rode out with a ten-day-old paper, which said there was to be a war. That night, Pinsent wrote:

11.VIII.14
... Wittgenstein, who until several hours ago was ready to vow himself for sainthood, is roused to find it is over a Bosnian who killed some Austrian archduke, who even W. admits was an ass. I ask W., "You mean Austria is willing to risk a general European war to discipline Serbia — and all because of two students?" Suddenly W. is a firebreathing patriot. From the heights a despicable politics emerges. He says these are not students but "revolution-aries," and these unregenerate frontier peoples must be taught a "lesson." "Then you will fight?" I ask in disbelief. "Of course," he says. "And shoot somebody — with a gun?" I ask again in amazement. Stalwartly, he nods, & I walk away in disgust.

They rode into Høyanger the next day. In a three-day-old paper, the most recent they could find, they read that fighting had already broken out. Austria-Hungary had declared war on Serbia, causing Russia to begin mobilizing. Germany had then declared war on Russia and her ally France, and then Britain had declared war on Germany after her forces had pushed through neutral Belgium on their way to Paris. Reports now said that the German armies in Belgium were taking and inflicting heavy losses amid talk of atrocities against the populace. Austria-Hungary, meanwhile, was mounting a punitive operation against Serbia while sending other forces to halt the dangerous Russian advance from the East. Wittgenstein wired his family that he would be home within ten days. Pinsent was waiting with the horses when Wittgenstein emerged from posting his wire. They rode back to the hut in silence. Over the next week, Pinsent's entries became almost telegraphic, the days running down like an old clock.

Attempting to strike a hopeful note, I say, "They predict it will be over quickly." W. frowns: "It will not be over quickly. Not with the Russians."

I say, "You just don't want to miss it." W. says nothing. He has begun to pack.

*

Later W. comes to me. "I have money in the bank at Bergen. I want to give it to you. Your mother can use it." Unnerved by his practicality, I retort, "Wouldn't that be aiding the enemy?" "Stop it!" he says. "This changes nothing between us. Nor between any of my English friends." Nodding, I say, "Do you actually believe that? Do you really?"

*

I am sitting outside, feeling ill. It is afternoon & we have not spoken a word since breakfast. Suddenly he appears & demands, "*Will* you take the money?" Obstinately, I say, "But you have given us money. I can't take any more from you." "For your mother, then!" he insists. "Don't be an ass!" But he sees I won't take it & turns away in frustration.

*

An hour later W. comes to me again, very alarmed with something that clearly has just occurred to him. "You will not enlist, will you?" "And why not?" I ask. He says, "Because of your mother. She has no one else." "Don't drag Mother into it," I say. "Mine isn't the only mother with a son."
   This time I stalk off & hear him call, "You are doing this only to defy me! You said you could not carry a rifle in good conscience."
   "Then I will carry a stretcher."

*

We are eating when, with a look of sudden relief, he says, "But they will not take you! Your deaf ear. This will keep you out." "Only in one ear," I say. "They'll never find out." Then I remember & say, much relieved myself, "And what about your rupture? They won't have you, either!"
   But W. has already considered this. "I will have surgery. My family has also tremendous influence. The army will take me, I assure you. My mother has also two sons and two daughters. And no material cares. But your mother, David — who has she but you?"

*

Nordstrøm rides out. W. tells him we are leaving & says he can take everything, except the horses, wch. he is donating to a church in Høyanger for charity auction. I am packed. Our belongings sit by the door.

*

Later, I say, "What if we became doctors? We could go away & do anything. What are wars or governments up here? You would deny hippopotamuses or my existence, yet you acknowledge governments & races of people avenging themselves. Where is your mystical now? A year from now you may find yourself bayonetting me in the gut."

At this his voice cracks. "Stop! You will be fighting Germans, *Germans*! And I will be fighting Russians. Never will we even *see* one another."

*

Nordstrøm comes with his sons to say good-bye & take away everything. Carrying off our pots & utensils, he leaves us cooked food to eat until our departure in the morning. I am not hungry. The stove is cold, but I don't bother to light it. The oil lamp sputters.

In six hours not a word between us. Outside in the half dark, W. is transfixed. He is sitting on the stool with a hat & the mosquito net drawn like a shroud over his face — looking like a condemned man, I think. I walk down and sit on the hill. There I feel that the world, so full of promise a week ago, has turned on us. Like a bird of prey, the earth has sunk its beak into its own dark breast.

*

It's all up today. On the eaves, I see the wasps sealing up their nests. I have an angry impulse to set their nest & ours afire — let us be off like those dead Norse warriors, pushed out to sea in burning ships. Listen to me — already a bitter, destructive impulse has seized me by the throat.

*

We carve our names above the door: D.P. & L.W. 18.VIII.14. W. is red-eyed & on the verge; he cannot look at me. He says that whatever happens we shall meet here after the war; he says life is always ready to be shaken off & taken up again once you find it. I am not such a mystic or optimist. We will leave the door open for travellers. We will leave the door open so the spirits may depart, but without much hope they will return.

*

In Bergen, before we part, W. asks me to go with him to a church service. Why must he prolong it? For days we have been saying good-bye. But for him I go to this church — what church, I don't know or care. What does he expect? Even if the service were in English, it would be no less foreign to me, dead to song, dead to words. And Wittgenstein thinks I am a *naïf*; if so, I am not the only one. Sitting beside me, his eyes tightly shut, W. seems as if he is praying for a miracle. He is asking the Almighty to speak to him — to take over our lives & gather us unto his cold teat. Yes, I think, the Almighty has a plan for us, but not the one he wishes.

*

I go first. Quick & sweet is how I want it. We promise to write as long as there are mails; we promise to meet here after the war — fairy tales to me as we embrace & I board.

Then the train is starting, swaying and rattling, & I am stumbling into the loo; & then, suddenly, I am crying in spurts into my hand, a wrenching, spilt feeling, knowing somehow we shall never meet again. Whether from your end or mine, it will not happen again, Luddy, not in this world or the next — not ever.

BOOK II

The World As I Found It

When Homer said that he wished war might disappear
from the lives of gods and men, he forgot that without
opposition all things would cease to exist.

— Heraclitus

When the child must be weaned, the mother blackens
her breast, it would indeed be a shame that the breast
should look delicious when the child must not have it.

— Sören Kierkegaard, *Fear and Trembling*

Our Knowledge of the External World

RUSSELL WAS IN AMERICA, winding up his lecture series, when news of the archduke's assassination came from Sarajevo.

Russell had been a rousing success in America, where he was surprised to find himself famous, far more highly regarded than he was as yet in England. His whereabouts and quips were frequently mentioned in the papers, and crowds of four and five hundred packed the halls where he spoke about our knowledge of the external world. At Harvard, home of the New Realism, where his *Principia Mathematica* was already a sort of Bible, he taught several classes and found the faculty and students to be friendly and highly receptive to his ideas, though rather backward by English standards. As for America, he found it barbaric. He wrote Ottoline long letters railing about the disgusting food and the smells in his hotel room, where windows were never opened, about the spittoons and Boston's ossified matrons who, along with their stuporous husbands, gorged themselves at tedious banquets given in his honor. Still, he had to admit he liked the adulation — especially from the ladies who clamored around him after each lecture, nervously asking gratuitous questions and hanging on his every word as he edged toward the door.

They seem to find me irresistibly brilliant and witty, he wrote Ottoline. I find the attention most flattering, and hope I shall not be seduced by it . . .

But in spite of his high-minded hopes, Russell was seduced soon enough by a young woman who came mooning up to him after his third lecture and introduced herself as Doris Dudley.

She hovered there a moment before she added impulsively, You may remember me as *D.D.* — this as she deftly stepped in front of an older woman who had been waiting a good ten minutes for a word with him. We met last year at Oxford — Professor Norris introduced us, *Professor Norris of Princeton?* Russell opened his mouth expectantly, but nothing jogged. With a wriggle, D.D. scrunched still closer, pushing her smiling face up to his, as if they were being thrown together on a bus (the woman behind her cleared her throat indignantly), then said with a telling smirk, I'm the *writer* you met. At which point he raised his eyes, still without the foggiest idea who she was, and said, Ahh — wondering what he should do.

But in fact he didn't have to do anything. With that word from him, D.D. was merrily telling him how much she admired his work and loved England, and how she had come all the way from Chicago just to attend his lectures, all the while blithely blocking the other woman while he signed her copy of that new transatlantic sensation, *Problems in Philosophy*. D.D. gushed: I've never read anything that can make — profundities so, well . . . accessible and, I mean, *interesting* . . .

Oh, she had his attention, all right. She was about twenty-five, rather plain, with thin, catlike lips, a blunt nose, wispy bobbed brown hair and a good, if not excellent, figure, a fact he could not help but notice as D.D. finally stepped aside for the sputtering woman, allowing Russell to better discern the solid rump and frank, uncorseted breasts floating beneath the clingy folds of her white knit dress. There was a certain sweet, beguiling quality about her, careless as a cow and seemingly mindless of the potent and musky heat she exuded. On second glance, in fact, he was intrigued because she seemed so unsophisticated — so peculiarly *American*: her wan earthiness reminded him of some lone pioneer woman, a sort of American Ruth, plain as rain, the opposite of Ottoline.

But, Professor Russell, said D.D., sashaying up again. Professor, about your statements on intuition in philosophy . . .

Ostensibly, she was asking him a philosophical question, but implicit in her voice and every gesture was her willingness — indeed, her eagerness — to go to bed with him. He was so thrilled that he abruptly ended the conversation, pleading a prior engagement, then fled to his hotel room and wrote Ottoline two letters, one for that night and one for the next, already remorseful for what was about to happen.

At his lecture the following evening, with a red-hot horseshoe in his stomach, he saw D.D. sitting in the first row, diligently taking notes. Afterward she stood tactfully off to one side, beaming like a valedictorian as the gaggle rushed up to greet him. This time he was ready for her, having had his blue suit pressed and put on a bold red tie. He had even crunched up a precautionary mint before he winnowed up his papers and skipped down off the stage. Without a word from him, D.D. cheerfully waited until the last of the crowd had left, then followed him outside, ghostly and remotely histrionic as she told him about the stories she wrote and of her dreams of becoming a great writer. For over an hour they talked. Then, as they passed beneath a tree, he pulled her toward him, kissing her roughly, while within, the subdued and impeccable mathematician watched his growling, heavy-breathing alter ego, aghast. Russell felt himself to be the aggressor, but then he was shocked to feel D.D.'s nails dig into the small of his back, as she said in a gargling voice, Come with me, darling. I'm just two blocks away. There'll be no problem.

How odd, he thought, hurrying with her across the deserted square and up the back stairs of an old rooming house with listing floors. She's already calling me darling. D.D. was efficient. Within minutes, it seemed, her blouse was hiked up and she was squeezing her breasts into his mouth, whining and smiling as her slick hair whipped softly from side to side.

Afterward he was even remotely touched as D.D. poured out her grief and loneliness, the relentless pressures of her art and her need for a mentor. Lonely himself, he thought the girl would provide a pleasant interlude. So the next day, while D.D. looked on, stricken, he read *Little Lamb*, a highly charged and disjointed story of how Penelope falls for Charlie, a beer truck driver who runs over her white poodle in a rainstorm.

All that remained of poor Tuffet was a runover rag of red fur, one bag full. Penelope wailed under the beating, bleating rain while the brawny beer truck driver delicately nudged the canine corpse into an empty beer box with a stick.

"Here she is, Miss," stammered the brawny behemoth. "P-p-poor little doggie . . . I-I don't know what to sss-say."

Russell didn't quite know what to say either. Resounding silence as he pretended to savor the final paragraph — the last jarring alliteration — where the repentant Charlie lashes himself to a "tall and terrible tree" in a lightning storm, calling out to God to strike him down as Penelope struggles to free him. Remembering his own misdeeds in his now buried novel, and seeing D.D.'s hungry and desolate look, Russell heard himself say that he thought her story, while not entirely successful, showed definite promise.

Wringing her hands, D.D. brightened and said, Do you? Do you *really*? I want the truth, the total, terrible truth.

Truly, he said, feeling trapped. I would not lie about another person's talent. The story shows genuine . . . potential.

But *darling,* said D.D., wringing her hands. First you said it has promise, now you say *potential.* Sucking the chewed end of her pencil, D.D. thought a moment, then said hopelessly, It's the ending, isn't it? I'm just too subtle. That's my *whole* problem. The white poodle, for instance — did you get the symbol of the paschal lamb? And the fact that there were *three* trees — that doomed feeling of Calvary. I thought of having Charlie nail his hand to the tree with an iron spike. Would you have liked that better?

Frowning, Russell said in a hush, I think not. The ending's best left as it is, I think, though the language might stand a little, ah . . . toning down. *Not much,* he added gently. But a bit. A bit.

D.D.'s bangs gently slapped her face. You don't like it! Oh, God, I knew it, I knew it!

But I *do* like it, he protested.

Thank God, she said, rushing into his arms. I could never love a man who didn't love my work, *never.*

Russell saw another story that was somewhat better than the first, but in his heart he knew where the girl's best talents lay. Nevertheless, she was something new for him — someone modern, rather. Unlike Ottoline, D.D. was always open to his advances, even hungry for him, bouncing and panting, with her eyes rolled back into her head. Even after two weeks, her lust for him hadn't diminished; she said he was a better lover than men half his age, a compliment he didn't entirely believe but was nonetheless pleased to entertain. Indeed, his opinion of D.D. and her writing, though certainly qualified, grew in more or less direct proportion to her desire for him.

As for his letters to Ottoline, they continued, albeit with increasingly fictionalized accounts of his activities. But then after two weeks, burdened by conscience, he came clean — half clean, anyhow. He told his mistress that he had just met a young American woman named Doris Dudley. And lest Ottoline think this was just a dalliance or that he was seeing just anyone, Russell said that the young woman was a writer and was actually somewhat talented. Being totally aboveboard, if not provocative, Russell even said he had slept with Miss Dudley and was really quite fond of her. Yet here he was quick to assure his unappreciative and, he hoped, now jealous mistress that the girl would never displace Ottoline in his affections, much less occupy that innermost spiritual sanctum that he reserved strictly for her.

He was no less candid with D.D. When she asked if he was seeing any women in England, he said, Just one at present. But she's married and we are merely very warm friends. I'd call it a spiritual friendship, actually.

They had just finished making love. Looking at him jealously, D.D. said, But that's what I must have with you! We must be *one flesh*! You must know me, you must!

But I do know you, said Russell evasively.

No, you don't! No man has *ever* known me. But before we finish, we must know each other *completely* — I mean the way Keats said, with our souls fusing — D.D. clapped her hands together dramatically — *solution sweet!*

Russell groaned. I've always hated that line. Much too mushy.

But, damn it, said D.D., reaching between her legs and then smearing the goo on his chest. Sex *is* oozy and mushy!

Russell recoiled as if he'd been doused with scalding coffee. The towel — hand me that towel! You're behaving like a savage.

D.D. pounced down beside him. And you're acting like a damned prude. My being bloody and oozy last week didn't stop you from poking it in. And quit staring at me like that. You look like some nasty old lizard.

Never in his life had a woman spoken to him in this way. I did not *poke* it in, he protested. Certainly I did not *smear* you with it.

He thought that was the end of it, but a moment later, as he was sponging himself off over the little basin by the dresser, he glanced up at the mirror and saw her behind him. Hissing, D.D. had her tongue between her teeth and her thumbs plugged in her ears, her fingers wriggling like gills.

Doris! he demanded. What —

But then, before he could say another word, she had him locked round the neck, panting as she fired her agile tongue into his mouth. And then, just as suddenly, she stopped, gravely serious as she asked:

Do you believe God is watching us?

You mean, Do I think God is a voyeur?

Don't you dare profane him! D.D. was more than just vehement — she looked as if she would strike him. Covering her breasts, she continued:

He *is* watching, you know. If you were more alive, you would see that — you'd feel far more than you do. You think I'm just a whore, don't you! You think I was just put here for your amusement!

D.D., he said, moving toward her. I certainly didn't mean to offend you.

But she pushed him away. I won't have your blasphemy and condescension. I know what you're after, and the free lunch is closed.

•

They lurched back and forth through good days and bad, with Russell hungrily following her sex, half conscious, like a bird bobbing along a trail of crumbs. He had hardly known her a month when his lectures ended, and she invited him to come with her for a week's visit to her parents' home near Chicago. D.D. made it all seem very casual. In view of the short time they had known each other, Russell saw no danger that the Dudleys would feel their daughter was "bringing him home." Besides, he had a paper to deliver at the University of Chicago, and he was curious about the Middle West.

A few days later, after a stopover in Chicago, they arrived by train in Wazooka, Illinois, D.D.'s hometown, where her father was waiting in his fire-engine-red Pierce-Arrow. Portly Dr. Dudley, a well-to-do dentist, councilman and booster, was a mustached man of massive good health who immediately took charge of his daughter and her foreign guest.

Don't you dare, he said with comic gruffness, poking his cocked finger like a pistol into Russell's ribs when he attempted to tip the colored porter bringing up their luggage. You just keep your hands out of your pockets while you're here, Mr. Russell. Here go, Jimmy.

Dr. Dudley then insisted on giving his guest the "cook's tour" of Wazooka. Honking and waving to everyone they passed, he pointed out the new school, the meat-packing plant and the town characters, sitting on crates and busted-out chairs by the ice house and garage. Friendly sorts, rather, only Russell noticed that they all seemed to have the most extraordinarily deformed ears — either too big or too small, and all oddly crumpled. With their lips fat with snuff or cheeks bugged out with chaws of tobacco, they waved and called out things he couldn't understand over the flat plains wind and the noise of the engine.

Big fish in that little backwater, the Dudleys lived in a lofty, white-turreted house that presided over a quiet street of hedge-bound bungalows. A stone wall bristling with a fence of iron arrows surrounded their property, and every morning Dr. Dudley raised a flag into the boundless Midwestern sky with that absurd and flabby American optimism which, to Russell's English soul, was like staring into the void. Mrs. Dudley was a handsome woman, far more reserved than her husband, but active nonetheless in their church and various civic organizations. She was always on the telephone, one of two that seemed to never stop ringing. Gadabout Dr. Dudley, meanwhile, seemed to always be off to another meeting. Scarcely had they finished supper that first night than Dr. Dudley, Grand Mugwump of the Aragolak Oddfellows, came down attired in an oversnug tuxedo and wearing on his head a whole hollowed-out beaver, complete with teeth, tail and clawed feet.

Try this on for size, he said, his laughter like air wheezing from a tire as the hat slid down over Russell's aristocratic ears. Dr. Dudley was showing his guest the Oddfellows' mystic handshake when D.D. groaned, *Daddy* . . .

Now, daughter, countered Dr. Dudley tolerantly, feigning ebullient surprise. I'm just trying to show your English friend how we *are* here in Wazooka.

Russell went along with these rites with the hapless bonhomie of an explorer among aborigines, eating corn on the cob and bloody steaks that "still mooed," rocking on the porch, drinking beer and pitching horseshoes. And without any particular effort on Russell's part, the indefatigable Dr. Dudley took right to him, bringing him downstairs the second night to show him his weapons collection — rifles, swords, Indian war clubs and a scalp of fine red hair that Russell politely declined to handle.

Oh, dearest darling, said D.D., waylaying him afterward, Daddy really likes you. He's never shown that junk to anybody I've brought home before.

Conscious of his age, Russell was rather surprised by this warm reception, but he needn't have been: the prominent Wazooka Dudleys thought he was rich and, best of all, titled, having been told by their daughter that he was next in line for an earldom. The third day, Dr. Dudley dressed Russell in cape and goggles and took him for a long and dusty drive. Presumed heir of all creation, supremely confident, even reckless in his driving, Dr. Dudley showed the greenhorn "God's country" — so many flat and snoring miles of corn, swine, rail depots and cattle. Yet this rich land that Russell found so bleak and unpromising spoke eloquently to Dr. Dudley, who in the sonorous tones of an auctioneer gabbed about endless "deals" involving options, liens, deaths, deeds and probate sales. Lurching to a stop in a cloud of dust, he made a grand sweep of his arm, as if to tell the suitor that if he played his cards right all this and more might be his one day.

Giving him a conspiratorial little goose on the shoulder the fourth day, Dr. Dudley confided, I'll tell you the truth, Mr. Russell. She's stubborn, our D.D. Gets something in her head and won't turn it loose. Guess it's partly me. Wanted a son, got me a tomboy. Well, I raised her to be independent, but, heck, I'll be frank. Her mother and I were kinda worried about her for a while. She was just a little confused, I guess, but I'm glad — darned glad she's straightened out and found herself a nice fella like you. Just wanted you to know that. You're all right in my book.

Russell didn't know how to react to the "glad" part and was sorely tempted to ask Dr. Dudley just what he meant by the "confused" part. But before he could get a word in, the jocular doctor, uneasy after this moment of male intimacy, deftly changed the subject.

That afternoon, though, Mrs. Dudley piqued Russell's curiosity again. As they walked in the garden, she confided her daughter's great admiration for him, telling him how happy she was that Doris had finally brought home someone respectable.

I want to get to know her again, ventured Mrs. Dudley cryptically. For a while I'm afraid we didn't know our daughter.

Really? said Russell diplomatically. When was this?

Stopping to pick a weed their elderly gardener had missed, Mrs. Dudley considered a moment, then said, Oh, after she left the convent, I guess. Or before. But then, seeing this was news to him, Mrs. Dudley got all fluttery, saying, Goodness! I forgot all about the roast.

Grasping, Russell hastily said, You used the word "convent," Mrs. Dudley. I thought you and Dr. Dudley were Presbyterians?

Oh, said Mrs. Dudley, flinching. Well, of course, this was after Doris converted. Much against our wishes, I might add.

To which he, ever the gentleman, replied, Oh, and smiled politely as the mother cheerfully added, But it's all over, quite as if it was, then hurried off to check her loin of pork.

I *refuse* to discuss it! insisted D.D. when he questioned her later. Then, spitefully, she said, I told you that you don't know me! But you know what I really hate? You never even asked!

But hearing this, the suitor didn't want to ask. That night, Friday, Dr. Dudley departed for his Shriners meeting in a tassled maroon fez on which ABDUL was written in rhinestones. Upstairs, D.D. and Mrs. Dudley, who, on second glance, seemed to Russell rather cold toward her only child, had a brief screaming match. Hurried feet and slamming doors. Then, with a transfigured look, D.D. ran down the stairs, saying in a vicious tone, Don't worry about her. She urgently led him by the hand to the closetlike back stairs, where she bolted the door and lit a candle.

I'll bet you never had a nun before, did you? she said. That's Sister John Christopher to you — *bride of Christ*. Do you know how hard I prayed not to be tempted? Do you think for a second it *worked*? They shaved my head and screamed at me. I thought I was nuts. D.D.'s eyes glowed as she pressed closer to him. I've had visions, you know — at night there, under the covers, I was on fire. They were all lesbians. They used to tie me up in wet sheets.

In her open palm, he saw a rolled condom. Her knees wobbled as she hiked up her dress and guided his trembling hands, saying, Do you love me? *Do* you? A nun doesn't come cheaply, you know. For this, you can say ten thousand Hail Marys! Two hundred thousand Our Fathers . . .

In the flickering darkness, her powerful vagina gobbled him in like a Chinese handcuff as a floorboard creaked. And like a loose egg he was cooked — two minutes, done.

Oddly, they got along better after that, both imagining they had come to an understanding, though each had a different notion of just where things stood.

Russell could afford to be kind now that his stint in the alien corn was over. Two days later, he was off for Boston to tie up some loose ends, then bound for England. In the meantime, he didn't want to upset these nice people by telling them that their bohemian daughter and he had not the slightest intention of getting hitched. D.D. understood him, he thought — that was what mattered. And again, the next day, when the Dudleys were outside, D.D. made love to him with impressive speed and ingenuity, reducing him to a gibbering, moaning ninny as she bounced atop him, preening her breasts and lean young stomach before his hot, watery eyes. Russell, in rut, said impulsively, You must come to England sometime!

Bertie, dearest darling! cried D.D. I'd follow you anywhere!

War Trophy

STEAMING across the Atlantic on the *Northumberland* a week later, Russell found himself wondering if D.D. might have taken his overheated words to heart. After all, it was one thing for her to visit him in England (and several weeks together might be rather agreeable, he thought with a grin), but surely, even D.D., in all her wild imagination, could not possibly think that he meant for her to come and stay — certainly not to live or *marry*.

No, he thought, she couldn't possibly be that naive — they were not even remotely suited to each other. He promised himself that he would write her a long letter when he arrived in England, a warm, appreciative letter that would boost her spirits while gently cutting her loose, leaving her a few fond memories and a good deal the wiser. Still, in his anxious moments, he was tempted to send a telegram flatly telling her not to come. But each time he ruled it out as being too cruel — cruel and probably unnecessary, since by now she surely realized that it was only a passing fancy.

With this, then, he put D.D. out of mind, instead absorbing himself in the news of Austria's escalating dispute with Serbia, a dispute that increasingly threatened to involve the other European powers. Russell found the news depressing, but even more depressing was the delight his fellow English passengers took in it. It sickened and amazed him how fierce and irrational, how clannish and thick, they could be, these bland, tweedy salesmen and cottagers and their pale wives — how people who would be morally repelled at the thought of blood sports could, in the next breath, declare their high-minded willingness to pack their sons off to slaughter Germans. Once or twice a day some bilious old fool would come huffing back from the wireless room with the latest news, setting the whole ship astir. Afternoons in the ship's lounge, between darts and quaffs of black and tan, the old poppycocks would prognosticate, matching the French army against the German and England's dreadnoughts against all comers. As for the ship's fifteen German passengers, they were treated with the disdainful correctitude accorded to people about to be deported. The Germans kept to themselves, dining together at two tables at the far end of the dining room and rarely speaking above urgent whispers.

The passage was generally chilly and overcast, with gray girders of light that sheared off into the ocean's gray-black deeps. Russell generally held his distance from the other passengers, working every morning on an article for the philosophical journal *Mind,* then walking the decks in the afternoons, when the ship's lackluster amateur band could be heard practicing *The Turkey Trot* and *Rose in the Bud.* He was gloomy about his prospects in England, unsure what he wanted from Ottoline and even more hesitant about his work. America, in that sense, had been a vacation where he could coast on brilliance and reputation without doing the brutal work that had made him famous — work that, after the blows Wittgenstein had given him, he wondered if he would ever do again. He now had more offers for lectures and books than he could possibly handle, but nothing that seemed to him especially vital or important. Back in Cambridge, he would find waiting for him the notes on logic that Wittgenstein had dictated to Moore in Norway — a Pandora's box that he was almost afraid to open. And for all Russell knew, Wittgenstein was charging off to enlist. Knowing Wittgenstein's recklessness, Russell felt almost sure he would never survive a war, and so Russell found himself faced with the equally depressing prospect of holding a box without a key.

Often in those days just before the war, Russell felt like a fraud. Because for all his expressions of principle and humanity, he saw there was also a nihilistic side of him that was as eager for war as anybody, eager that, for better or worse, life might change. The news, meanwhile, grew worse. Returning to his cabin after breakfast one morning, Russell saw his first iceberg, a glowing, white-hot hull whose heights it seemed he could never scale as he watched it slip by, smoking white against the fog and alive with the cries of birds he could not see.

Three days later, on July 21 — two days before Austria delivered her ultimatum to Serbia — Russell arrived in London. Ottoline sounded cool when he rang her up but finally agreed to meet him that afternoon at Mrs. Dood's flat. After D.D. and almost three months apart, neither of them knew what to do once Ottoline finally arrived, late as usual. Wanting to make himself desire her more than he did, Russell kissed her passionately, but she felt limp and bony. Her mouth fell open, loose and pulpy, and as he drew away, he noticed new wrinkles around her lips.

You're angry with me, he said.

I'm not, she insisted, squirming from his grasp. But I have been thinking that it would be best —

Don't say it — It would not be best.

She clenched her hands in exasperation. You don't even know what I'm about to say! I don't want to completely *end* our relationship, if that's your fear. But I do think it ought to be platonic.

He felt suddenly hot and claustrophobic. You do not. Come, sit down here. You're just angry with me.

Turning away, she said, Please, just leave me a moment.

Ottoline lit a cigarette and began walking restlessly around the room, straightening things that didn't need straightening and eluding his expectant eyes until at last she said:

I do, I think we should cease any further sexual involvement. You need a wife, and I need my peace. Believe me, I was thinking of this before you left — long before you mentioned this girl. Come now, darling, face facts. I can hardly compete with a woman twenty years my junior. Why on earth would I even *want* to? Surely you find her physically more desirable. How could you not?

He sat down, his head splitting as he squeaked, I do *not* find her more desirable.

Oh, please, scoffed Ottoline.

Sensing his comparative inexperience in this new situation, she felt a gathering sense of power and ruthlessness, as she did when she had him pinned in the reflex lens of her camera. Oh, but she wanted to tear off the mask and tell him about Lamb, to say that she knew far better than he the pleasures of a young body.

Come now, she jabbed. Why not admit it? You don't really want me as a lover now. Oh, maybe you *think* you do.

And I tell you, he said on the verge of tears, that's *not* true.

He was trapped, no more able to admit to her than he could to himself that he didn't want her. To say that was like sentencing himself to a future of privation and loneliness. Embracing her, he crumpled down beside her on the sofa, groping for the small breasts that didn't rebound and fill his hands when squeezed, amazed at the lumps and swags on her thighs that weren't on D.D.'s. Ottoline was all atwitch. Elbows poking, feet squirming, she clapped her thighs on his digging hands, her hair filling his mouth like dry feathers as her face slid away. He was like a blind man; he had to remove her clothes just to find her, but all he found was a brittle, middle-aged body like his own. Grazing over her, searching for a spot to start, he probed her like an ache, but she wouldn't be roused. In the end he had his way, but she, suffering all the while, proved her point about the hopelessness of it. Dogged as a tortoise mounting a rock, he gave one last spasm, then lapsed back into the gelid sea of his mind, not even moving as Ottoline rose in silence, her joints cracking as she crept off to wash herself.

Still, she didn't let him get away with it. After a long silence, as they were dressing, she asked, And you actually think she's a good writer?

He was tying his tie, but with this he lost his place, eyeing her miserably as he dropped the loops. Oh, she has talent — some, though not much. She has none of your regalness — she's thoroughly American. We frequently quarreled. I know *we* never fought like that.

Ottoline raised her eyes and he reddened, embarrassed to have referred to them in the past tense. Just to be sure, Ottoline said, So you don't love her?

Grateful she asked, he replied emphatically, Absolutely not.

Skeptical but now faintly conciliatory, Ottoline said, Well, you certainly *thought* you did. Would you care to see your letters?

He knew he would have to swallow this, the ritual abasement. He gave her some digs, but then he played his trump, saying, Darling, I do want to break with her, I swear it. The problem is, I'm afraid she may be coming to England to visit me.

You *invited* her here?

Only once. Very casually. I certainly never expected her to jump at the idea the way she did. We were with her family. I couldn't very well cause a scene.

Ottoline was agog. Couldn't cause a scene? Think of the *scene* when the poor girl finds she's crossed the Atlantic for nothing!

I didn't purposely mislead her, if that's what you think. I rather doubt she'll come, in any case, he added weakly. I sent her a letter yesterday — a very kind letter, in fact — explaining my feelings and saying it would be best to break it off. Russell affected a heartless look. And if she misses my letter and comes — well, I'll simply tell her how things stand with us.

Ottoline parted her hands of this. You'll not drag me into this! Don't you dare! I'll not risk scandal because of your stupidity.

But then curiosity got the better of Ottoline, who snidely demanded, Now, tell me. Just what does this little *writer* of yours look like, anyway?

But D.D. was forgotten over the next days as it grew increasingly likely that England would be drawn into a general European war. Feeling in Parliament about England's entry into war was volatile and divided, and Ottoline persuaded Philip to give a speech urging neutrality, even going so far as to suggest that he might speak to Russell, who, she said, had done considerable thinking on the subject. Philip, not one to let personal matters interfere with the national weal, readily agreed. He even told her to invite Russell to dinner to discuss the matter.

With the war, then, began the gradual unfreezing of relations between Russell, Ottoline and Philip. In fact, there arose between them an odd alliance, as if even Philip sensed that Russell was no longer a true rival for Ottoline's affections.

Yet how sublimely odd it was for Russell, after all these years of being persona non grata at Bedford Square, to hear his name announced in his mistress's home, then to sit across from the guilty wife and his former nemesis, armed only with an arch look, a glass of sherry and a napkin on his knee. In this competition to see who could be the most natural and charming, Russell regaled them for nearly an hour with tales lampooning America. Not to be outdone, his amused host, meanwhile, interjected some able quips and anecdotes of his own, all the while comparing, as Russell did, the amplitude of Ottoline's self-conscious laughter.

After dinner, they got down to business, with Russell holding forth about the four different kinds of wars: wars of colonization, principle, self-defense and prestige. Of the four, Russell felt that the first two, colonization and principle, were often justified. As for the third, self-defense, it was only rarely justified, and then only against an opponent of inferior civilization. But wars of the fourth type — wars of prestige like this one — these, he said, could never be justified, being based on national vanity and offering only the rewards of hubris.

Having made these distinctions, Russell told Philip, who was no more a pacifist than he himself was, that he would have to take great care in crafting his speech. To preserve his credibility, he would have to make it clear that he was not opposed to *all* wars but only to trumped-up wars of prestige like this one.

Watching her politic husband take counsel from her lover, Ottoline was appalled at her own folly, feeling that in her amorous conquests, she had likewise been waging a war of prestige — or rather staving off a feared loss of prestige through failing desirability. Why had she ever embarked on this dangerous course? she wondered. Russell, she saw, was neither as handsome as Philip nor even remotely as kind. So why hadn't Philip been enough for her? And why, when she had a husband who adored her and when — she had to admit it — she was losing her appeal, why did she still feel this urge to squander herself, holding herself up as a kind of Helen, a trophy for the men?

Philip's speech in the House of Commons aroused much hostility but it also helped rally pockets of beleaguered support — enthusiasm that instantly evaporated the next day, August 4, when war was declared and many violently opposed to war turned violently in favor of it.

Ottoline was still in bed when Philip, up all night in various Parliamentary sessions, telephoned, no sooner telling her the news than he burst into tears. She immediately called Russell, who had remained in London, asking him to meet her in Russell Square, across from the British Museum.

Russell had been waiting for fifteen minutes when he saw her coming down the path, egretlike in a watery silk dress that snapped about her spindly, purple-stockinged ankles. A brooding black hat shadowed her eyes, which were swollen from crying. To him, her powdered cheeks suggested the fuzzy wings of a moth; her lips seemed ill aligned, flat, the teeth more equine. He didn't even seem especially aware that he was looking, but Ottoline knew very well what it was. She saw, as he did, that she was now crossing a kind of invisible equator, and that her looks were losing their youthful consistency, causing her to look rather attractive one day, haggard the next. Today was the unappealing, temperamental Ottoline, the Ottoline who expected more, got less and so grew fussy while he grew steadily more remote.

Ottoline gave him her usual pecking public kiss, but turned away when he attempted to hold her a moment, saying, I know, darling, but if it's all the same to you, I'd like to walk.

This galled him — the nerve of her, fending him off unprovoked, especially when he felt almost no desire for her. Picking along the path, dubiously dabbing the red gravel with her toe, Ottoline was in a funk, half oblivious to him as she said:

Isn't it unearthly? I feel as if we're still awaiting the results of some horrible election. Philip was so dashed when he called. He says they're mad, every one of them. Here they are, up all night debating and drafting resolutions, as if they could actually *do* anything in the face of this war lunacy. And the amazing thing is no one cares. No one will even listen now. All they want is blood.

Stopping then, Ottoline rummaged through her bag for a mint. Cracking it like a nut between her teeth, she furiously crunched it up, drawing out her lips as she continued:

I'm taking Julian away for a few days. I don't care where — the seaside or someplace. Anywhere where she won't see these ghoulish mobs celebrating. I can't stand it — the idea of being bottled up in England for God knows how long with these . . . these horror fanatics!

She looked at him, so self-contained and distant, smug. What I *mean*, she added, with an exasperated sigh, is that it's bound to bring down the — I don't know — *values*. And then there's no beauty left but just *ugliness*, and us standing up like targets for the mob . . .

Then, seeing that he didn't know *what* she was saying, she said irritably, My *point* . . . Yet as she struggled, her confidence fell another notch, and she said more grimly, What I *mean* . . . You see, my very point *is* . . .

But then seeing him studying her like a bug, and seeing, to her mortification, that she had lost her point, she collapsed with a groan on the next bench, weeping into her gloved hands.

He sat down and patted her hand, but it was no good. All she felt was his eely kindness, so patronizing and automatic. And his mind *was* elsewhere; he couldn't very well hide it. The day, a Tuesday, felt more like a Sunday, it was so quiet. As yet there were no mobs, no ringing bells or parades. The delirious catharsis of relief and national unity that had greeted the declarations of war in Vienna, St. Petersburg, Berlin and Paris would come over the next days. Nevertheless, the war was rolling. For days now on the Continent, the war's momentum had been steadily gathering, each nation following mobilization schedules that had been drawn up years in advance. Across Europe, endless trains filled with men, field pieces, provisions and pack animals were rolling toward their deployment destinations. With impeccable timing, German divisions were rushing through neutral Belgium on their way to flatten France, while Austria, with all her incompetent bluster, was in the midst of a logistical nightmare, her packed trains hopelessly snarled and delayed in an attempt to make good her threats to punish the Serbs, while rushing to check the feared Russian advance from the east. Exhorted by her ally France to strike quickly, Russia, meanwhile, was struggling to rouse her huge and disorganized forces. While the infantry tried to pull itself together, mounted Cossacks and cavalry reconnaissance units were starting to the front. To avoid the nightmare of the 1904 mobilization, there was also a temporary prohibition on the sale of vodka. Soon enough, though, the vodka would be flowing, and the czar's forces would be trampling fields huge for harvest, dressed in sweltering woolen uniforms designed for parades and expecting, as most nations did, a short, healthy bloodletting that would be over before the leaves fell.

Consoling Ottoline that day, Russell felt more rage than sorrow at what to him seemed a universal outpouring of savagery, imbecility and race hatred. Few generals were as prepared for their war as Russell was for his. His abortive, end-of-the-world *Forstice* had just been a prelude to this; if anything, Russell would come to find it oddly prophetic. Sitting beside Ottoline, he felt more resolute and incisive than he had in more than a year. Like a *deus ex machina,* the war had come to lift him out of the doldrums left in the wake of Wittgenstein's criticisms. And in a perverse way, it was a philosopher's dream. Civilization was about to murder itself, and when it did, Russell felt he would throw off the last moorings and create a better system, one not only more rational but also more just and humane.

For all his certainty about his own course, Russell had no such epiphany about Ottoline that first day of the war. Their love just petered away, hastened by world events — and by D.D., who threw her arms around Russell's neck one night when he opened the door.

Four months had passed. Russell was working against the war and living in London, having moved the week before from Mrs. Dood's to a little flat in the South End.

Oh, dearest darling, said D.D., holding him out to look at him. Thank God you're all right! I've been looking for you for weeks! Why didn't you tell me you were moving? You're not in trouble, are you?

Of course not, he said, drawing back. Nothing's the matter.

D.D. was frantic. Well, then, why didn't you leave word where I could find you? Her eyes watered over. I've been so furious — so betrayed! I went to Cambridge — I even went to your landlady, that Dood woman. She said you'd disappeared.

She told you that? He smacked his hands together with mock fury. The liar! The witch hates me. I specifically told her to give you my address.

On the verge of a hysterical outburst, D.D. faced him hungrily, trying against all logic to believe him. Her eyes were dilated, and her face was contorted in a way he had never seen.

She wasn't just *mean*, D.D. hissed. She was downright *evil* about it. She screamed at me, then threatened to call a constable. But I fixed her! Boy oh boy, did I fix that bitch but *good* by the time I left! Fixed that yappy dog of hers, too.

Well, well, he offered anxiously, trying to calm her down. The important thing is, you've found me. Sit down. When did you arrive, then? Saturday? But you did receive my letters — I sent three. *No?* But of course you know about the overseas mails being disrupted, the submarines and so forth.

D.D. wasn't buying this. Fixing him with the same unfocused glare that must have curdled Mrs. Dood, she screamed:

LIAR! You rotten, mealy-mouthed liar! I didn't get *any*thing. *Nothing?*

Vainly he kept up his patter, trapped, trapped. An energetic cabman was porting up her bags. D.D., meanwhile, was pacing, sniffing for a rival and staring at the floral walls of this hovel that clearly had been let with no thought of *them*.

Cursed luck. Russell didn't even have a spare quid to pay the cabman. Eyeing him with shame, D.D. pushed some notes into the man's hand, then slammed the door, bawling, This place is a goddamned *dump*!

He was all caution and solicitude at first, washing out a cracked cup and lighting the sputtering gas ring to make tea. At first she turned up her nose, but then with a scowl she gulped the tea down. He saw that her hands were trembling, the nails deeply chewed. He thought there was something odd about her looks, too, then realized it was her hair: a still more severe slice of bangs, self-inflicted, nunnery style. And then suddenly D.D. brightened, flashing a minxing look above the upturned cup that made his bowels churn. Hoping to avert an even more excruciating scene, he was about to make his speech, but she spoke first.

Darling, she said, quite as if nothing had happened. We really can't stay here, you know. Mom and Dad will be arriving next month. Not that we have to get married right away, of course, but we can't very well have them find us here.

For some seconds he stared at her, unable to decide whether this was guile or simple lunacy. Then, as gently as he could he said, Doris — D.D., I'm afraid there's been a frightful misunderstanding. It's true I invited you to *visit*, but I never even remotely suggested that we should get *married*. Why, as yet I'm not even legally divorced.

The cup whizzed past his ear. Histrionics and tears. Fearing suicide or a lawsuit, he agreed to let her stay the night, then made the fatal mistake of coupling with her, not just once but several times. His second mistake, caused by remorse for the first, was to agree to read her latest short story, *Requiem for Father Flye*.

Gripping her knees, D.D. watched with relish as he read her story, another of the Penelope Cycle, as she now called it. This tale found the young ingenue in a convent, where she is despoiled by a philandering Jesuit, that hypocrite theologian and scholar of the Virgin Birth, Father Flye. But Penelope gets her revenge. After locking the unsuspecting priest in his confessional, she kneels and, in a disguised voice, recounts their sins before naming their penance — *"Death! Death! Death!"* — hacking open her wrists, then slashing through the screen while Father Flye howls and beats on the door. Russell didn't even pretend to finish it. Rising up, he said accusingly:

How dare you threaten me! Are *you* such a hypocrite? Who seduced whom here?

D.D. reared back as if she'd been slapped. Then she started crying, deep sucking breaths followed by loud moans of rage that nearly drove him from the room. Even when she stopped, she was nearly speechless, gasping to bring up the words:

Maybe I'm just trying to get your lousy *attention*. God knows, I don't expect your sympathy — you don't feel sympathy for anybody, Father Flye! Oh, that's you, all right. First you steal others blind, then ease your conscience by writing another book or something. At heart you're nothing but a goddamned *weasel*!

For nearly an hour, he blankly endured this abuse, hoping that she would tire of it and leave for good. But she refused to give up. With the least kindness from him, she seemed to think everything was on again, while with the least scowl or ill-chosen word, she acted as if she would kill herself.

Two days later, at the end of his wits, he finally called Ottoline, imploring her to talk to the girl. D.D. was only too happy to take her case to Ottoline, who was pained to see that the young American was far more attractive than Russell had let on. Moony as a girl describing her first love, D.D. told Ottoline everything, calmly explaining, with the eerie plausibility of fantasy, how only she, D.D., could "save" poor Bertie. Then came the kicker:

You know, D.D. confessed, I was so jealous when Bertie told me about your spiritual friendship. That was all I ever wanted with a man. She gave a windy grin. I'll bet you'll think I'm awfully impertinent for asking this. I mean, it's absolutely none of my business. But — well, didn't you ever think of having a more, uh, *physical* relationship with Bertie?

Well, no, said Ottoline, trying to pick herself off the floor. No, I suppose I always wanted to keep our little friendship on that high *spiritual* plane.

Oh! D.D. looked positively transported. You're so very lucky!

Oh, I know, my dear, I know . . .

In the end, it was out of sympathy for D.D. that Ottoline made the supreme effort it took to pry her loose from him — if only temporarily.

As for Russell, he was completely unrepentant — defiantly so — when Ottoline exposed his deceits. A year before, he would have begged her forgiveness, but now he just walked away, furious to be bothered with this nonsense when he was busy with weightier matters. Ottoline found his strength and distance appalling. Within a matter of weeks, the war had completely transformed him. And all the while, their relationship was undergoing a similar transformation, existing on less, then on hardly anything at all.

D.D. remained in London, where Russell heard from reliable sources that she had been jailed for prostitution and hospitalized after a suicide attempt. Violent, disheveled, bizarre, she would periodically turn up to plague him at rallies or meetings, once embarrassing him so deeply that he threatened legal action. D.D. was not an entirely isolated case: Russell encountered many confused young women like her at the height of the war. Starved for grand feelings and a cause, working long hours, as he did, at injury to their health, they followed him like enervated ghosts. And, just as lost as any of them, Russell had them — uncontrollably and indiscriminately, one after another.

Then, two years later, in the fall of 1916, Russell awoke in the middle of the night to what sounded like the squalling of a cat in heat. It was D.D., sobbing outside his door.

He was already a man besieged. German zeppelins were bombing London, and the police had him under surveillance for his activities against the war. Almost the moment he heard her, he jumped out of bed, breathing into his hand as he listened to the drunken scrabble of her nails on the door. For ten minutes she sobbed and pleaded before agreeing to leave him alone forever if he would just open the door and listen for five minutes. He set his watch on the table, unfastened the latch and gave her those five minutes. Had his flat been the last refuge on earth, he wouldn't have given her a minute more.

Time's up! he snapped, cutting her off. Thank God your time is up! And with that he shoved her out the door.

The Oracle of Fort Myers

AT THIS TIME Russell was in the process of building his Utopia, a world where man's acquisitive, warlike impulses would be replaced by creative ones and where men and women would rule and love as equals. Yet Russell himself remained an Old World product, completely unsuited for citizenship in his new order. Columbus only discovered the New World — never did he foresee living in his own creation.

Russell was then out of step with almost everyone. Even his staunchest supporters didn't know where to pigeonhole him politically. He wasn't a Fabian or a socialist, wasn't religious, antivivisectionist or vegetarian — why, he wasn't even a true pacifist, a breed he generally found to be Sunday school types whose grand schemes reminded him of fleas proposing to build a pyramid.

His attitude toward the war had evolved slowly. Dead set against the war at first, he then decided that, with war an established fact, the government had no choice but to fight for an early victory, though not a brutal one. Until then — or rather, until England was out of danger — he said he would refrain from directly criticizing the government. Instead, he would hold his fire until hostilities ceased, at which point he wanted a full-scale investigation of the events that had led to war, followed by a public forum on how civilization might be reordered to avoid future wars.

For the first two years, he largely kept his word about speaking out against the government's war policy, but this didn't stop him from speaking out about the politics and impulses of war — and the need for a just peace once the war was over. Taking leave from Trinity, he joined several political parties, organizing, speaking and writing a stream of articles and pamphlets with titles such as "War, the Offspring of Fear," "Why Nations Love War" and "Is a Permanent Peace Possible?"

But his position changed dramatically in 1916, when the government imposed mandatory conscription. Russell saw it not only as an unlawful infringement of liberty but as a clear indication that the war, after two years of butchery and stalemate, was a moral, human and economic impossibility. He joined the radical No-Conscription Fellowship and began an active campaign against the government's war policy. The British authorities didn't know what to do with him. As a writer and speaker, he was too effective to ignore, yet he was too prominent to simply be jailed. As for bringing legal injunctions against him, this carried considerable risk, since it would offer him precisely what he wanted: martyrdom and a public forum from which he could mock the government and espouse his views.

The government was far from stupid in this regard. Indeed, they went to such lengths to ignore him that they jailed six men for distributing an anticonscription leaflet that he had written. Russell wouldn't have this. To shame the authorities into action, he sent *The Times* a letter declaring himself the author of the pamphlet and chiding the government for punishing others for his deeds. This time the authorities had no choice but take him to court, and he made them regret it, ridiculing the government's policies and making the periwigged lord mayor who led the proceeding look like a fool before a delighted throng of reporters. Convicted, he was fined one hundred pounds, which he promptly refused to pay, saying that they would have to jail him. The lord mayor wasn't falling into that trap. Instead, he decreed, under Defense Regulations, that the defendant's books and furniture would be seized and auctioned. This was distressing but it was only a slap compared to what happened next: because Russell had been convicted of a crime — at that a relatively minor political crime — the council of Trinity, led by the militant McTaggart, dismissed him, in spite of a petition in support of him signed by twenty-two dons, ranging from the warlike Whitehead to the anticonscriptionist Moore. Moore even published a scathing letter in *Cambridge Magazine*, thanking the rectors for their patriotism, courtesy and liberality of mind, then suggesting that they end chapel services, too, since *Love Thine Enemies* was plainly subversive.

This sacking was a deep wound for Russell, a bitter betrayal of all he held sacred. Smelling blood, the government, meanwhile, grew bolder in its campaign to isolate and discredit him. After he was offered a lectureship at Harvard, where he thought he might have even greater impact against the war, the authorities revoked his passport, saying that he was liable to make seditious statements. Then, after he made a successful speaking tour of the mines and steel mills in South Wales, they further curbed his freedom, invoking a rule that barred suspected spies from industrial areas. This was a serious blunder: no one, not even Russell's worst enemies, seriously believed he was disloyal, and overnight he was transformed into an object of sympathy, with editorials appearing in his favor, along with a corresponding swing in public support. And he fought back. In those areas he could not enter, he wrote blistering epistles to the faithful, while in those areas he could enter, he was even more ferocious in his condemnation of the war, the government and the generals, who, he said, would gladly butcher sixty thousand men in a morning for a few blood-soaked yards.

No one could have been more warlike in his opposition to war. In his own rising hatred and frustration, in the increasing pitch of his rhetoric, Russell even began to exhibit a certain sadistic streak. Wherever he went now, there would be a police inspector shadowing him, taking notes. Masterfully mugging for the mob, Russell would unfailingly introduce the poor man, then subject him to the most humiliating ridicule, verbally whipping him as a proxy for his enemies as the delighted crowd stamped and jeered.

Inspector, he would say, I have for our most benevolent government a modest proposal. In the interest of greater efficiency, let us end the war today and divide our young men into three groups, killing the first group outright, maiming and blinding the second and driving the third mad with noise and fear. Or better yet, let them kill us all and be done with it! What do you think, Inspector? Tut, tut, old boy, do speak up! Will you clap us all in irons? What do you *think*, man?

By God, he knew now how to get their blood up — how to jerk them to their feet and cow the heckler. Nothing was more intoxicating than the feeling of standing atop that whirlwind. Why, there were nights when, with but a word from him, the crowds would have wrecked the hall and followed him into the streets for a night's rampage. This, he thought, was the exaltation Christ must have known during his last days on earth. At long, long last, he was speaking out, and speaking freely. At long last, the opposition movement was growing into a chorus heard throughout England. But most of all he heard his own strident voice, and in his black periods he alternated between feeling utterly deluded or like a vulturous war profiteer — a Krupp or a Vickers — advancing his own interests over the heaped dead of a war that he could see was only widening. His followers told him he was in danger but this he found oddly consoling, like his periodic thoughts of suicide. And how easy it would have been, in his excitement and weariness, to martyr himself for this noble cause. Martyrdom was easy; it was change — changing one's fundamental being — this was what was hard. In this respect, Russell saw himself, in the later days of the war, less as a revolutionary than as a sort of regenerative creature, a lobster that gladly tears off an appendage in a predator's jaws, knowing that it can drag itself off to grow another claw or feeler, however stunted.

Garsington Manor, Ottoline's new five-hundred-acre estate outside Oxford, was Russell's refuge at this time, even if Ottoline herself was not.

Philip had bought the estate early in 1913 on the advice of their doctor, who felt country air was essential for both Ottoline's and Julian's delicate health. However, it was not until more than two years later, when the house had been redecorated according to Ottoline's extravagant taste, that the Morrells finally took up residence.

Sequestered there with her jesters and freeloaders, the rapier intellects and vaunted opinions, Ottoline had little reason to pine for London. London was soon flocking to Garsington to escape blackouts, queues, food shortages and other lesser wartime barbarities. Before long, there was a stream of genteel visitors who sometimes stayed for weeks at a stretch, and some, like Lytton Strachey, who never seemed to leave, ridiculing Ottoline behind her back while partaking of her eerie, seemingly bottomless generosity.

Gone now were a good many of her young men, lost from month to month in places like Vimy Ridge and Ypres, the Dardanelles and Somme. Every day they would read the long death rolls in the newspaper, sometimes two and three full pages listing those who had gone down. Everybody had lost someone, and it had its effect on Ottoline, who became more extreme and a little more desperate, crossing that zone from demimondaine to grand dame, a now decorated and much scarred social warrior. Within a matter of months, she had quite transformed herself. Scarved as Isadora, gloriously oversparkling, then flinty, Ottoline would hold court, duly accepting the homage of the young men's pecking kisses. The shy gawk who, as a girl, had prayed while her brother, the duke, gave his beastly black masques — the girl still visible at times only a year ago — had been banished. Suddenly, Ottoline had a reputation to protect, and what had been charmingly naive and eccentric about her had hardened into a conscious style. Bitchy, flamboyant, preposterous, she was now a practiced oddity, bristling with vague ideas, impressions, gossip. She smoked Russian cigarettes and sometimes dressed as a Gypsy or a shepherdess, carrying a crook tied with ribbons and leading a pack of pugs. And like all of them, she was deeply afraid, hoarding culture and beauty in the way others did soap or matches.

Set behind hedges and rectangular gardens, the house was built of gray Cotswold stone in the Tudor style, quite light and Italian in feeling, with a triptych of tall gables and arched-and-leaded windows. Below the house was a reflecting pool with pink marble piers and brass gorgon spouts, which required some now unobtainable pumping apparatus to purge it of the green scum that choked it and bred mosquitoes. Ottoline installed marble statues of eyeless Greek gods around its edges and set peacocks loose to roam the brick garden paths. And there, under the great ilex tree, her guests would gather — mostly young men in Panama hats who sat under lacquered parasols with their knees hiked to their chins, talking a mongrel tongue of Italian, French and English and penning verses oft inspired by the chisled loins of the eyeless divinities by the pool.

Garsington was their sanctuary once conscription started. Giving no thought to the enormous expense and complications involved, Ottoline convinced Philip to use his pull to open the manor as a farm where conscientious objectors could do alternate farmwork. Her young men were not nearly as grateful as they should have been, what to have been spared the ordeal of laboring under the hostile eye of some gimpy sergeant just back from the front. The more idealistic ones read Tolstoy and worked, more or less. As for the other Boy Blues, they napped, groused and dawdled, slapping flies and goosing one another in the new-mown hay. At dusk, they could be seen with their rakes and hoes, trudging home for their glass of sherry behind the manor farmworkers who did the real work, keeping their mouths shut for small bribes when the army came hunting for slackers.

Russell often went to Garsington to recuperate. Now that he was sexually out of the picture, he got on quite admirably with Philip, and passing well with Ottoline. Russell rarely stayed in the main house. Instead, Ottoline put him in a little guest house of clabber-colored stucco where Lamb's self-portrait now hung above the mantel, a shrine to another of her lost loves (Lamb, a stretcher-bearer, was bogging bodies through the Somme). Russell paid no attention to the portrait. Like a desert hermit in his cell, he remained most of the day in the little house, writing tracts aimed at a total revision of society, beginning with love and marriage.

Ottoline said the overhaul ought to begin with himself. Sometimes, to goad him, she would eye him wonderingly, as if he were a hopeless case, saying, Poor, poor Bertie. Dear me, where will we find him a good wife? Retaliating for this, Russell would himself muse aloud: Now, where on Garsington shall we find an *able* young man for Ottoline?

Obscurely, each thought — or fondly hoped — the other was sliding into musty celibacy. In their ability to bite and bicker, they were like an unhappy middle-aged couple. One afternoon, as they were sitting in the garden, he looked at her and said, Pity, your hair is going gray. Pierced, she replied, Pity, yours has quite gone.

Ottoline didn't succeed in finding Russell a wife, but she did give him a temporary ally in D. H. Lawrence, introducing the two men at Garsington early in the spring of 1916.

Leading Russell toward the slender young man standing in the garden, Ottoline said, Now, do be patient. Lawrence is a poet, not a logician. He can be opinionated but he really is a dear, lovely man, so gentle and honest, *most* passionate. Now, *her,* she continued, nodding toward Lawrence's big-boned wife, Frieda, who was playing croquet with several men on the flat green below. She's your poster Hun. A *baroness* in case you can't tell. Lawrence is absurdly vain about her lineage — loves to use her crested stationery. Understandable for a collier's son, I suppose.

Frieda's voice sounded, at a distance, like the barking of a large, hoarse dog. She soon pegged out, she did. Laughing, brandishing her mallet, she stepped on one red ball and busted the one abutting it, crying out triumphantly to the vanquished, angular men. Ottoline, like a guide, continued:

Four years ago, she abandoned her husband and three children to run away with Lawrence — I told you that story, didn't I? You don't know the power he has over people. She took right up with him, abandoned everything. Oh, but then she thought better of it — the children, I mean. She was a miserable creature then, a madwoman, completely inconsolable. Several times she tried to see the children, but her husband was shattered — wouldn't let her near them. She's the stuff of Greek tragedy, a Clytemnestra, that one. I don't know how Lawrence bears it. At times, he goes quite mad with her unhappiness. And for all his sex talk, they've had no children. Ottoline sniffed. She has only him to mother now — murder's more like it. They fight like cats and dogs. Not here, thank God, Philip wouldn't tolerate it. David Garnett told me he once saw Lawrence haul her back by the hair and strike her full in the face. Dreadful screaming. David thought he would kill her. Frieda's mouth was bleeding but David said she laughed — *sneered* at him. And then — Ottoline shrugged and brightened — an hour later all was lovey-dovey again! Isn't that the maddest thing you've ever heard?

And you think I ought to meet him? asked Russell dubiously.

Oh, absolutely, said Ottoline, walking on. Lawrence has quite changed my life. But he has had a bad time of it lately, what with *The Rainbow* being banned and no money. You know, no one will publish him now — they don't dare. And because of her, the police have him down as a possible German sympathizer. He hates England now, he's fearfully bitter. He wants to escape and found a colony in America.

Now the alchemist in Ottoline emerged as she said, I do think there's a similarity in your societal aspirations. For England and the world, I mean. And Lawrence does so very much admire your work and your courage to speak out. He told me so.

This pricked Russell's vanity. Nor was he a stranger to Lawrence's work and reputation. Already, he had read, and much admired, Lawrence's poetry. He had likewise been impressed with the opening of *Sons and Lovers* when Ottoline had put the book in his hands that morning. And Russell did want an ally of the visionary kind, as opposed to the rather laborious ideologues he found around him these days.

With his hands stuffed in his pockets, Lawrence, meanwhile, was picking down the rain-soaked path, intently checking the spring's progress, the little stubs of green underfoot and the rude red buds protruding from the branches. For a suspected German sympathizer, Lawrence was not exercising much caution. Even his only suit was a provocation: a Rhenish cut, the color and texture of oatmeal, with too many pockets. Ottoline said he was still getting over a respiratory infection, and he looked it. He was a small, stooped, sick-looking man, not much over thirty, with reddish hair and mustache, weary red eyes, a large jaw and bony hands and wrists. His lips were coarse and sensual, like his thick Midland accent, and his eyes quickened when he saw Ottoline with Russell in tow. The matchmaker had left nothing to chance: Ottoline had also given Lawrence a thorough briefing on Russell.

Ottoline did not stay long after her introduction. Having lit the fuse, she quickly excused herself, saying that she had to speak to the gardener. There was awkwardness and a sense of electricity then as the two men walked along, probing each other with small talk about the spring and the beauty of Garsington.

Lawrence was the first to chafe at this mannered minuet. With a hungry, conspiring look, he suddenly said, Well, now. To the business at hand.

Business? demurred Russell.

That's right, said Lawrence with a nod. I see your face, Bertie Russell. It tells the story. You look tired, man, bone tired, like a fox run across three counties. I'm another fox — aye, a little red fox, panting, with my slack ribs showing. And do you know what the little fox says? He says you must beware the pack, man, the *pack*! Alone they are nothing, but as a *pack* — good God, they'll hound you forever!

Russell was as struck by Lawrence's sudden vehemence as by the image he had chosen: lately, Russell also saw himself as a man pursued. Still, it was somewhat galling to be lectured by a stranger, at that a man some thirteen years his junior. But Russell was even more disturbed to find himself oddly afraid of this frail, clearly frightened man. Lawrence seemed to see clear through him, smiling as if to say, *You can fool them, Bertie Russell, but you can't fool me with your mental dodges and ring-the-rosies.* Russell, making a mental mark, thought, *This man is dangerous.* But as they walked on, he found himself drawn to this menacing quality, instinctively feeling that if he made peace with the danger around him, the danger might spare him its worst.

And soon he felt close to the danger in Lawrence. He could feel the bitterness as Lawrence described the humiliation of submitting to an army physical the week before, of being forced to stand stripped in a line of men while a scabby little doctor with a fag end dangling fingered his groin. Lawrence felt he'd been raped.

What right has the state to poke my loins and peer up my arse as if I were a stud bull? he said. And then to tell me I'm not fit! For lovemaking I'm fit, but not for their filthy war. Lawrence spat with disgust. Dead men, all of them. May their brains burst and their black hearts rot.

Russell found this chilling. And hard as Lawrence was on soldiers, he was no less damning of C.O.s when they later came upon a field where some of Ottoline's charges were working. Two digging a drainage ditch were standing on their shovels while another tried without much effort to pry up a stone. A fourth was off picking flowers. With a savage look, Lawrence turned to Russell:

Why do you bother to save men such as these? Better men are already lying fallow in Flanders. These are unclean. God, how I loathe them, these lilied, fagging public school boys, these lying, foolish cynics. Have you ever listened to their prattle? Blind to truth and the sacredness of life, they are, and they will laugh at *me*! These aren't men or even boys — these are bloody *fetuses*. Let the cannon consume them, I say. They're all done for — aye, and England, too.

Russell had never heard anyone curse with such cold-blooded malice. With a queasy look, he said to Lawrence, Don't you think you're being a trifle harsh? I care for sodomy no more than you, but they are still human beings. They deserve to live as much as anyone.

Living men deserve to live! Lawrence shot back. These are dead.

Giving him a measured look, Russell said, Well, if these are indeed dead, then we don't need a war to kill them.

Lawrence's face blackened, his tone accusing as he said, Don't waste your philosopher's cleverness on me! Let these drones be killed off and be done with it. The war, you know, is entirely biological — Malthusian. Do you seriously believe that all this evolution business, all these ages of lizards and man-apes and bloodthirsty life, were meant to lead to Christ's dying on Calvary and our salvation? I don't, I don't for a second! I believe it has led to this — to decay and death and more death. And thank God, I say. Maggots eat only dead tissue — it's a dying world's way of purging itself of dead matter. *You*, Bertie Russell, you ought to occupy yourself building the new immanent world rather than saving this dying one. And you must speak the truth — I mean the actual truth of blood knowledge — and hang the corruption of this mentalizing nerve consciousness.

Here, Russell lost his patience. *Blood knowledge? Nerve consciousness?* What on earth do you mean?

Lawrence's carotids flared up like two little asps. I mean the truth of the *blood*! Blood consciousness — *instinct* as opposed to febrile *nerve* consciousness and useless intellectualizing. Why do you stare at me? You make me feel fumbling, with your looks. No, I am not being logical, I am being truthful. And if I am not logical, then you as a philosopher must tell me where I do not make myself clear —

But at this Lawrence's voice cracked, and he started coughing in deep, gurgling hacks, so that he had to lean against a tree.

I'm all right, he said, smiling almost pleasurably when Russell started to pat him on the back. Shyly, Russell stuffed his hand back in his pocket and slowly backed against the tree opposite. Lawrence was looking at him, just looking with the profound innocence of one human being coming into focus with another. Lawrence's eyes were like circles in a pool of water, circles marking the spot where a chaste stone had fallen into uncertain depths. Russell feared losing himself in that pool; he wanted to look away, yet he couldn't break from this gaze, which now shone with an almost unfathomable goodness. And then, just when Russell thought he could stand it no more, Lawrence twisted up his nose and laughed. A big brazen boy's laugh. A hurdle had been passed. Beneath it, thought Russell, the man has a sense of humor. Yes, at least he could laugh.

Points of light stood on the new leaves unfolding. On the hillsides, flossy new grass was rippling in the sun. Suddenly Russell felt quite pleased with his young friend. He brushed off the sodden cuffs of his trousers and retied his wet shoelaces, then stood smiling, indicating that he was ready. Lawrence was still eyeing him playfully, on the verge of another laugh. Picking up a limber stick and flipping it around in his hand, Lawrence said:

But *you* are not dead, Bertie Russell, nor am I. And we shouldn't be quarreling when we've only just met — Ottoline would be furious! Come, let us walk some more. Look now, the primroses are out — let us be gay a while and each wear one as a sign in our buttonholes. There, now, he said, threading the stem through the hole. Look down into the flower's throat — *look* as you would smell. Have you seen anything so fine?

You know, said Lawrence, swinging his coat over his arm. You must tell me your philosophy, and I will tell you mine. I know I am foolish, truly I am. But still I love this coming life of ours, and I swear I speak the truth. Truly, I do.

Ottoline's match had caught fire. Later, when she asked Russell what he thought of Lawrence, he said:

He's most wonderfully pure, absolutely passionate and intuitive. I felt as if he saw right through me.

Lawrence was no less impressed. Coming round to him later, like a nectaring bee, Ottoline was delighted to hear his assessment:

He is brilliant, as you said, and he will be useful in our new world. He will be our Zoroaster. Only I feel he needs seasoning. He is too hidebound by *mind*. Yet I feel certain we shall swear *Blutsbrüderschaft*. And I told him we must collaborate on a philosophy to rebuild the world. I

shall speak about immortality and he shall teach ethics. The poet's eyes
twinkled. And after we have changed the world, we shall go to America
and start a jolly colony in Florida, with you as our queen.

With me as *queen*, asked Ottoline fatuously. But what about Frieda?

Frieda? Lawrence thought for a moment. Why, Frieda shall be our
Oracle at Fort Myers. Yes, he said, nodding, I think Fort Myers will be
the eye of our new world.

The New World

TWICE MORE Lawrence and Russell met at Garsington. Letters were exchanged, and then the two men began to seriously discuss this program
in which Russell would lecture on ethics and social reconstruction and
Lawrence on immortality and the new world.

Almost inevitably, though, there were snags. Lawrence, Russell quickly
realized, was not one to be bothered with trifling details or practicalities.
Rather, he wanted to change the world by decree. He seemed to feel he
had only to snap his fingers, had only to write the words, and the reality
would magically appear. Everything was *Let there be!* and *We must!*
Grandly he would say, Let there be an end to this economic thing. We
must burst the bonds of this accursed money that enslaves us. Let industry and communications be nationalized, then every man and every
woman, well or ill, will have his wages and that will be that.

Democracy, on the other hand, was *wrong*. The collier's son had no
faith whatsoever in the wisdom of the working man. Liberty, equality
and fraternity he called the Three-Fanged Serpent. Rather, Lawrence said
there must be an elected aristocracy led by a Caesar. Or better yet, a
Supreme Man and a Supreme Woman, with man dictating the economic
side and woman the domestic. And there must be spiritual marriage, not
corrupt state marriage. The key was Woman. Woman must be the crucible through which Man must strive for his essential blood being, struggling up through her like a drowning man fighting for air.

Russell was alternately repelled and fascinated by these ideas, but he
nevertheless saw them as an antidote to his own rationalism, which he
found increasingly unreliable in the more mystical realms where he now
liked to dwell. Not since Wittgenstein had Russell encountered one who

sent such shivers down his spine. Yet while Russell thought Wittgenstein correct in most cases, he often found Lawrence wrong — wrong and faintly terrifying in his sweeping indictments of humanity.

There was something savage and paradoxical about Lawrence, this frightened man who inspired fear; like Wittgenstein, his knack for exposing anxieties and weaknesses in others was preternatural. Lawrence told Russell that he was blind as a newt, that spiritually he didn't know himself in the least. Lawrence told him that he must be entirely cast forth from the fold of society, that, with a single woman, he must come into newness, bursting forth like a babe into the world.

Russell hungered for this transformation. Already he longed to cease being such a public creature, cut adrift without wife or children. Russell badly wanted the new Canaan that Lawrence promised, but he balked. Standing at the brink of that frontier, he shrunk into his lobster self, paralyzed by the sheer nullity of too much.

And Lawrence, for all his passion, could be stifling. It was always the same litany. London was falling. England was dead. Englishmen *were* dead. And then, just when Lawrence had pushed Russell to the edge with his hatred and nullity, he would reveal the warmth of sanity, in the way he could sing and be gay, or in the humble devotion with which he could knead bread or fall to his knees to scrub a floor.

What Russell found intolerable was Lawrence's muddled thinking. For God's sake, Lawrence, he would plead. In almost a single breath, you tell me that the world is dying and being born, that your colony will be both republic and kingdom, and that London has fallen yet must be pulled down. For once and for all, which way will you have it?

But rant as he might, Russell could not pin him down. Lawrence meant what he meant, he contradicted what he meant, he stuck by what he meant and revised what he meant.

And then, hearing the cock crow, Lawrence said *it was time*. It was time to write down their program. Or rather, he said that at this stage it most depended on Russell — heir to Plato and Heraclitus — to lay the foundation of their coming Utopia, which he would call *Rananim*. Russell did as directed: he drew up their preamble. Moving relentlessly from one institution to another, Russell tried to show that the very institutions that seem to make society work — the state, property, the church and marriage — lead instead to world suicide. Russell was bold, even sensationalistic, in his attack, saying that the disease was disintegration, and the cause, power lust. The symptoms differed but the disease was always the same. He said that states existed only to enforce internal peace and wage external wars, that marriage was to enforce fidelity, morality to protect property and God to justify murder in his name. But Lawrence said it was no good.

No, no, he scolded. Your approach is much too negative.

Negative? Russell was incredulous. You accuse *me* of being negative?

I do, Lawrence insisted. You mustn't waste precious time saying what is wrong. You must instead say what *is* and *must be*. Say what we've agreed on — that acquisitive, murderous impulses must be replaced with the creative life essence and that instead of acting from self, man must act from an essential sense of truth. You must get in the *positive* idea that every living community is a *living* state. That the *fundamental* passion in man is for wholeness of movement, unanimity of purpose and oneness of construction. That this is the *whole principle of construction*.

Russell was in despair. *Truth!* There you go, bandying that word again. And what have you said? All is one! Life is a unity! *Abracadabra!* Russell sat staring at him, trying to soften his tone. Please, put yourself in my position. How am I to make anything out of this? And how, for that matter, am I to make it *intelligible* to the broader public?

Lawrence was indomitable. But you don't understand! The point is *not* to make it popular! Oh, God, do not make it popular. We cannot waste our breath on the mob. We need to get to the root, to chop the snake off at the head! To kill the great falsity of subjectivism.

God help us! scoffed Russell. Now, it's not just truth but *subjectivism*! And everything you've said — it's all profoundly, impossibly *subjective*! You mistake your imagination for truth.

Aye, said Lawrence, waving his finger. And you, *mon frère*, fail to imagine!

Around and around they went, not able to frame even the opening bars of this overture. And then one night, not long after a zeppelin's bombs struck an orphanage, a mob armed with clubs and stones burst in the hall where Russell was lecturing and rushed the stage.

Get out! Russell ordered. *Out! All of you!*

Russell was determined to stand his ground, but fortunately three associates managed to drag him off before the mob enveloped him. As it was, Russell barely escaped, with bruises and a throat deeply gashed by someone's nails. To his shame, he was among the luckiest. Sixteen others were hurt, four seriously, including one man who nearly lost an eye.

After meeting with the NCF leaders, Russell decided to go into seclusion and stop speaking for a few weeks. He and Lawrence were walking through the London Zoo when Russell explained his decision. Lawrence, ill for the last month, had grown a scraggly beard that reminded Russell of a swarm of red ants.

Nonsense, man, Lawrence insisted, appalled by this pusillanimous decision. You can't stop speaking now. Good God, don't you see? The time is ripe, the crowd's ugliness is a good sign! They're ready to revolt. Why, with only a few words from you, they would do so right now!

Russell was incensed. And do what? Hail you as their Caesar? Look! he said, pulling down his collar. Do you see their claws on my neck? *Revolt?* All they're ripe for is murder.

Lawrence nodded. But they would pull down the bloody bunch over us now. Then the war would end and we all could truly begin to *live*. To *live*, Bertie. And a word, a *word* from you is all it would take. Aren't you sick? Aren't you sick to death of it? Death would be better. It's time, I say. You must cast aside all fear and do it — do it for freedom's sake.

Russell stopped short and faced him. You're right. We'll go straightaway to Hyde Park, and *you* can tell the people. You know the mood better than I. You know the word. You, of all people, have the *common* touch that I lack. Well, go on, man! That magical word from you will make it so.

Lawrence's hot eyes bulged. With a look of rage, he admitted, I can't speak to crowds — you know this.

Russell waved him off. Then don't speak this nonsense to me.

Wait! ordered Lawrence, rushing to catch up. God damn you, wait!

I'll not wait, remonstrated Russell. I have nothing more to say to you today.

Russell hoped this would end the matter, but Lawrence kept following, coughing and trying to catch his breath. They passed a clown and a man selling nuts, some children with their nanny. Lawrence was bearing down on him; Russell even wondered if he might physically attack him. But just as Russell was about to confront him, Lawrence streaked by and spat, with a screaming lunge, into the cage of a large male baboon. The ape, bent over with his back turned, whipped around with a hiss.

Hah! cried Lawrence. He spat again, and the ape bounded back, the hair on his spine bristling as Lawrence stared into his hooded eyes, intoning:

Dear, *vile* monkey . . . Pretty, *pretty* monkey . . .

A screech and a shower of dust and pizzled straw as Lawrence lunged with his umbrella. Whirling around, Lawrence flicked the umbrella up like a pointer, the better to show his fellow Utopian the coiling beast, the venomous red eyes.

Look at him, Bertie. So much like you, that hideous *aggressor*, that savage *kaiser* lurking beneath. *Hah!* Lawrence rang his umbrella along the bars, then thrust it at the fanged jaws. This also is you, Bertie, lusting to jab and strike like a man with a bayonet, saying, *This is for ultimate peace.* Why don't you own to your nature? What is the use of you, haranguing the populace with vain talk of nations kissing one another? Give me no more of your lies, moaning about goodness and humanity. You are the enemy of mankind — spiteful and murderous, filled with bestial, repressed desires. Hah, monkey! Wouldn't you love to sink your teeth into my pretty neck? *Hah! Hah!*

But then the blood flooded Lawrence's face, and he began to hack and wheeze. Russell made no effort to help him. Hunched and gasping, Lawrence eyed him with unspeakable loathing, then lurched off, slipping like a shade through the unquiet trees.

That night, during still another blackout, Russell decided that Lawrence was right about him, and as he sat there in his tiny flat, listening to bombs crumple in the distance, he wished that one might fall on him. It was his worst depression since that day on a beach near Ramsgate the spring previous, when, as he stood looking out to sea, with the surf lightly rushing in and not a cloud in the sky, he had heard — or rather felt — thunder, then realized it wasn't thunder at all but shock waves emanating from the massed siege guns in Artois, nearly a hundred miles away. But Russell survived that night and he survived Lawrence, who a week later sent him a letter apologizing for his outburst, saying that in quarreling with him, he had been quarreling with something deep in himself. They never did swear *Blutsbrüderschaft.* Instead, their friendship struggled along briefly before ending in a bitterness that lasted all the rest of their lives. Before the final break, however, Lawrence wrote Russell a letter saying that he hoped Russell would have the courage to stop being a savant and an ego and would concentrate instead on being just a creature. Lawrence also said once more that Russell would never reach the unknown until he had sustained a deep and abiding union with a woman. Anything less, he said, was mere sensation seeking — masturbation.

Russell resumed speaking. Later, to Lawrence's disgust, he even delivered the program of lectures he had outlined. The fashionable and humane thinking public, with Ottoline and Strachey at the vanguard, greeted his ideas with tremendous excitement. But these people, as Russell well knew, were the elect minority. For the rest of England his ideas hardly existed, or did only as very watered-down slogans. And nothing really changed. Not humanity, nor himself, nor even the women who gravitated to him, who seemed alike only in their native unhappiness and eventual dissatisfaction with him.

Later that summer, though, his bad spell broke when he met Lady Constance Malleston, a twenty-year-old actress who went by her stage name, Colette. Russell liked her naturalness and diction. Slender, elegant and well educated, she had waved auburn hair and, that rare thing in England, perfect teeth. Russell had seen her at several meetings before asking an acquaintance to introduce them. Colette told him that she had joined the NCF the year before, shortly after her brother was killed in France.

Of course, my husband's a C.O., too, she added carelessly. Russell must have shown his disappointment, because she quickly added, Harold's also in theater, an understudy to Miles Keegan. He's in Scotland now. We're both quite independent.

At dinner later, she insisted on paying for her part of the meal, and he, owing to his pinched circumstances, reluctantly agreed. Afterward, they drifted outside. It was a warm, clear, moonless evening, and London was nervously expecting another zeppelin raid, the third in three nights. Nine people had died the night before in fires and explosions. The tabloids were filled with headlines like FLAMING FIANCÉE and HERO HOUND and stories like that of doughty little Arthur, the messenger boy who pulled old Mrs. Birme from her burning house. Dropping as much as four thousand pounds of high explosives and incendiary bombs, and flying at heights that often required their crews to suck pure oxygen from rubber nozzles, the airships were portrayed by the press as infernal Jules Verne machines driven by goggled Teutonic insects clad in black leather. For more than a year, the Germans had been making raids farther and farther inland in preparation for raids on London. It had only been recently, and with deep reluctance, that the kaiser had given his permission to bomb the city, and only with the proviso that they spare historic landmarks and, above all, cousin Georgie's palace. For a month the Germans had been making successful raids, and now the German navy was in on it, competing with the army zeppelins to see who could tally the most destruction. In London, the mood was ugly and defiant. A primitive defense system had been devised, but the zeppelins were steadily improving their bombing and defensive capabilities and hence their value as a terror weapon. No longer was it a matter of feinting experimental raids by one and two ships. There were nights now when the coastal lookouts spotted flotillas of four or five of the giant airships moving like long, dark clouds across the Channel. As ominous and slow and out of range as the weather, the zeppelins would begin a slow descent at King's Lynn, every hamlet in their path blacking out as the droning airships swept like a gathering storm toward London.

Russell, meanwhile, was pursuing Colette, but thanks to Lawrence he was being more subtle than usual — tepid, in fact. Yes, Lawrence had rather spoiled his stride with these accusations about being a sexual predator and sensation seeker. Russell was being so mild and tentative that Colette had grown wary herself, sensing that the moralist was having second thoughts, no doubt because she was married.

No telling how long this impasse would have lasted were it not for the bleat of a police whistle, blown by an old warden wobbling down the street on a bicycle that bore the sign KINDLY TAKE COVER. As the streetlights dimmed and went dead, Colette said:

You should come with me. I'm only a few blocks away.

He was only too happy to agree. Emboldened then, he took the liberty of pressing his hand against the small of her perspiring back as he squired her through darkness suddenly filled with voices, blowing whistles, barking dogs and slamming doors and windows. Yet while others rushed by to get to shelter, Colette seemed to feel no urgency whatsoever. She positively dawdled, stopping to play with a maundering cat, then gazing at the stars, remarking, Oh, you can really see them now, can't you? Quite as if you were out at sea.

Watching her, Russell wondered if his anxiety was in anticipation of impending sex or falling bombs. Here, he said, smoothing her shoulder. We ought to be going, don't you think?

Oh, she said. She sounded surprised. Of course. I'm just one block over.

Passing through a narrow, vine-choked archway, they entered the courtyard of her building, where people were now veering toward the shelter.

Shouldn't we go into the shelter? he asked, feeling for her arm. There's time, she said, feeling back. I'm only on the third floor.

Her palm was damp as she took his hand and led him up the narrow stairs, clogged with sweaty bodies hugging bundles, blurting infants, pets.

Cyril . . . Cyril, is that you? Russell felt a jittery hand tap his head and shoulder, then quickly retract when he said it wasn't. Once at Colette's door, he burned six matches while she jiggled the lock.

I've only three more, he said impatiently. Can't I try?

But Colette didn't seem to hear, just kept rattling the lock, all the while chattering about her last role as daughter Winnifred in the drawing room farce *Father's Fond Fairest.*

It just closed at the Whitehall, she said. Ever hear of it? Well, I'm not surprised — it was dreadful rubbish, but popular. As usual, I played an ingenue — I'm always playing precious, conniving little ingenues, giggling to the audience and saying, *But Pa-pa! Oh, Plleee-ease, Pa-pa.* You don't know what a frightful bore it is, wearing patent shoes and some enormous bow in your hair. I'm *dying* to age a little.

Well, said Russell glumly, striking another match. I hope you won't feel you must wear a bow in your hair for me.

Don't be silly, she protested, stroking his arm. You're not at all old. My own father is sixty-something.

The latch broke, and they alighted into stuffy darkness. Can you see? she asked. I hate blacking out the windows, so we can't very well switch on a light. Here. Just a sec —

Before he could object, she handed him a glass of sherry, then gulped hers down, all the while watching him with a faint smile. Bringing his glass to his lips, he found the edge sticky from some previous drinker — perhaps Harold, he thought, as he swallowed it, distastefully warm and sweet. Again he said, I think we ought to go. But Colette kissed him lightly, then slipped a cool hand up the back of his coat as he pulled her toward him. Two sallies before he said again, Colette, I'd love nothing better than to stay but we really must go now.

But she only pressed back, saying, Oh, please, not now. They always pack you in absolutely hours before anything happens. And I hate it, being shut up with so many people, really I do. And the chances are one in two million — they said so in the papers. Besides, they never come over this end.

She gave him no time to object but instead went into the bathroom. Looking around, hearing the familiar running of water, his stomach fluttery now, he wondered if the shoes of absent Husband Harold, the understudy, were in the closet, then dourly figured that this made him the understudy's understudy — Daddy Dearest. And then Colette reappeared, her white skin faintly stippled in the wafer-thin light. She snipped open his shirt buttons with her fingers, then gently laid him down, saying, You know, you really are a dear, lovely man . . .

Her sheets were agreeably cool but did not smell quite clean, and he wondered again if it was Harold or some other young admirer he smelled as her mouth opened into his. Colette was wet and eager, but she was spoiled for him. In his mind, he heard Lawrence wrathfully saying that he was only masturbating himself with her, not yet fit for the new world. Yet who was? Two weeks before, according to Ottoline, Lawrence had been about to leave for Florida with a handful of followers when he suddenly decided, for no apparent reason, to postpone the exodus for a month. He'll never do it now, Ottoline had predicted. Lawrence fears he'll be as powerless in America as he is here.

And hovering over Colette, peering into the little lights of her eyes, Russell wondered if he himself would ever do it — pierce that hard shell and become, as Lawrence said, a *creature*. But he couldn't cede himself to the Eden of this life, couldn't break free from what he was. In himself now, he saw only a man of sublime but basically fraudulent promise, who, like an onion, would peel away through time, layer after layer, until at last he was reduced to a hard, translucent kernel of nothing, attached to nothing. And sexually he was failing. Damp. Limp. Colette, so hatefully patient, was whispering, *There's no hurry. Lie down. We'll just hold each other.*

But he didn't wish to hold or be held. Feeling trapped, he just lay there, sweating and inert, when in the distance they heard the first thumps of the anti-aircraft guns. Then the attacking English airplanes monotonously droning, circling, circling, desperately trying to attain the altitude necessary to attack the airships. Forcefully then he said:

Colette, I insist! We really *must* go downstairs now.

But she only clung to him more tightly. I can't bear it down there in that cellar, she said. I hate it, worrying that I'll be buried alive. But you can go — honestly, I won't blame you.

His male pride wouldn't permit him to leave. For pride, then, he remained. Remained, he thought, for just the same reason the war continued. He was thinking of Lawrence's parable of the war, of the poor dumb brutes who dug coal, the boys from the little towns, the donkeymen and dock workers, the bricklayers and glass blowers, and all their masters, too, the bankers, brokers and merchant men. Arm in arm, in endless legions, they marched out into the salient, there to die in the mud, tide upon tide. First one man went, and because he went, his mate went as well. Because one man went, all men went; and because one man died, they all died, as in a chain, ringing the world from end to end. So Russell stayed. Stayed as the whistles blew, then went silent. Stayed even as the first bombs exploded with a rumbling that persisted in the night air with a whorling sound, like the sea rushing in a shell.

Russell couldn't stand it. He didn't want to die with this woman or with any woman. After all his complaints of loneliness, after all those nights he'd spent wishing to be curled up with someone, he saw he wanted to die alone — even with her, he'd die alone. Fate had tricked him. He did not love, and because he did not, he would die covered with plaster dust with this stranger from a foreign species, coiled within the bowels of a mother he hardly knew.

And now the city was going up. Above the ivy planter on the far windowsill, reflected in the clouds, they could see the glow of fires burning in the west end of the city. And then a draft sucked the curtains out the other window, whisking them up like two waving sleeves. Colette sat up, saying, Do you hear it? I hear it, don't you?

It was the throb of engines flogging the air. Don't go to the window! he ordered, but heedless she ran across the room and peered out, then looked back excitedly. He's just passing by, quite out of line with us! We're safe — he can't hit us from there. Come look.

Russell wrapped the sheet around him like a toga, then crept over and crouched by the sill beside her. Like foghorns came the droning engines. They saw the airship's pointed black nose, the long expanse as it swept by, gigantic and dark. For several minutes they watched as it tacked eastward toward the river, pursued by the nattering planes. Then, as the airplanes abandoned their pursuit, another battery began firing, bursts flashing like lightning against the zeppelin's metallic black skin. He was gone, Russell thought. The last zeppelin had slipped through. All-clear whistles were blowing. Voices were in the air. Below, following the beam of a warden's flashlight, people were emerging from the shelter. Flocking across the courtyard, they were all talking at once, amazed, and perhaps slightly let down, to see that everything was as before.

Russell was peering low over the sill; Colette was stroking his neck. The airship was a mile away now, curving toward the harbor, where a few vain shells were still bursting. And then, suddenly, the airship began to glow, swelling and pulsing with fulminous light before it burst into a boiling sheet of flame that lit the sky. Fiery pieces of fabric whipped up and fell away, followed by two, then three drops of liquid fire — burning crewmen, he realized, as they fell through the darkness. A cry went up. In the streets, and then all across the city, there was a steady, roaring, fist-beating chant, ancient and superstitious, as the exploding airship slid down and down, going dark like a star behind the squat rooftops.

Colette had it right. Taking him decisively by the hand, she said sharply, Come to bed. There's nothing to be gained in watching this.

Now? he asked, with a sickened look.

Especially now, she insisted.

I don't know if I can, he replied, and he meant it. But his groin saw through his scruples, and later he peeled another layer of the onion as he rolled off the sheath of lambskin. Yes, he had managed. He had managed just fine.

Uncertainty

ONE DAY early that fall, as it was nearing evening, Moore was pushing his baby, Nicholas, down the lane in a white wicker pram and worrying about zeppelins.

No airship had ever come within twenty-five miles of Cambridge, which was both out of effective range and strategically unimportant. On the other hand, as Moore well knew from the newspapers, zeppelins were notoriously erratic, prey not only to strong winds, which blew them off course, but to clouds and fog, which confused their crews, leading them to mistake Goole for Hull or forcing them to jettison their bombs over obscure villages or farms. Nothing, it seemed, was impossible for the airships. One crippled zeppelin had blown clear to Norway, crashing in a tiny seaside village, which the papers said was practically enveloped by the giant craft.

Lately, Dorothy Moore would find her husband poring through the papers and magazines, reading lurid accounts of the Raiders. The arrival of Nicholas in June only raised Moore's anxieties. It reached such a pitch that one night Dorothy found Moore on his knees in the cellar hiding candles, medicine and tinned milk in a nook used for garden tools.

What on earth are you doing? she asked, holding her candle aloft as she peered down the darkened stairs. You know perfectly well we're in no danger here.

Almost no danger, he snapped. If bombs can land in Bedford, they can land in Cambridge. In theory, we *are* in range of them.

And in range of lightning and meteors and assorted acts of God, she said in disgust. Good heavens, Bill, what sort of assurances must you have?

Up from the darkness, he bellowed, I'm not asking for *assurances*. I'm merely being *prudent*. PRUDENT!

Oh, bosh, she sniffed. You're just being daft!

·

At first, the war had not especially bothered Moore. Indeed, he found people's reactions to it intensely curious. Why was it, he wondered, that people who were not themselves fighting, or even associated with anyone in the fighting, felt so *badly* about it?

Perhaps I am deficient, he confessed to Keynes. I do truly believe that war is horrible, and I would, if I could, put an end to it. But I do not find myself feeling *miserable* about the war, as Russell so clearly does. Oh, I would, I suppose, if I were on the front, seeing men killed. No, if anything, I find the war quite fascinating, don't you? Most people do — otherwise, why should wars last so long? People love reading about the war. They love it better than football matches or horse races, and they line up in droves to volunteer, even though they risk getting killed — and killed in rather sizable volumes. Politicians like it, as do factory owners and even workers, who with overtime make better incomes, I'm sure, than you or I do. Papers sell better, and there are books and songs written. I'm not being arch, you understand. I just find it curious. Except for widows and war orphans, and so forth, it seems that nearly everyone gets what he wants.

Many had been anxious to secure Moore's prestigious blessing for or against the war, but for the first two years he straddled the fence, leaning distinctly more to the side of opposition but for the most part undecided. In the end, it was not the slaughter in Flanders or even the sinking of the *Lusitania* that finally led Moore to actively oppose the war; it was the imposition of conscription. Like Russell, Moore saw conscription as a fatal infringement of liberty, a law so wicked that for the first time since his boy preacher days he openly proselytized, passing out anticonscription leaflets and even advising nonreligious C.O.s like Lytton Strachey on effective moral arguments they might use in their defense.

Once Dorothy became pregnant, though, the war shrank in comparison to the things Moore worried about. He got her a second maid and was always on her arm, watchful for slippery stairs, sudden drops or sharp projections. In the first months of her pregnancy, when she spent her mornings throwing up, he felt terribly guilty — and queerly cheated — that she should have so much pain while he himself had none. Lying beside her, stroking her stomach, he found himself wishing that he could transfer some of the pain to himself. Considering his own girth pressed between his hands, he would insistently ask, But what precisely does it feel like? — I mean to have something *not oneself* dwelling inside oneself?

Dorothy did her best to explain, but Moore still couldn't imagine it, the feeling of something growing *inside* him, stretching and sleeping, drawing nourishment from his blood. Later, when Dorothy had ballooned out and the baby was furiously kicking, he would watch amazed as it raised eggs under her skin with its traveling foot. And then, cupping his mouth to her stomach, Moore would gently talk to this rambunctious indigestion, this effect of which he was partly the cause, sounding him like his own echo.

Nicholas was born after a hard labor that had lasted all evening and most of the night. Afterward, Dorothy was bedridden for several weeks with a bad case of hemorrhoids — just one more of the ill effects of pregnancy that Moore found so shocking. The baby, too, gave him several scares, first with a persistent cough, then with several weeks of crying and vomiting in the middle of the night, when it seemed they could do nothing to quiet or comfort him. Moore feared diphtheria and croup. He was always jumping to the worst conclusion, mistaking the golden morning light on the child's skin for jaundice, persistent crying for colic and a simple rash for measles. At other times the sleeping child would seem too still and Moore would anxiously place his palm on his chest, relieved to feel him still breathing. To him, the infant always seemed too cool or too hot, exhibiting pains that he couldn't express and emotions that were often unreadable, hiddenness for the child seemingly being as natural as his instinct to suck. Sometimes Moore would just stare at him, seeing in those eyes not his beautiful son but a willful state of nature, a system of flux and even chaos that was always striving for moments of equilibrium, when the child was dry, fed and contented.

Even more complex was the interplay between the child's peace and the father's. Stopping along the lane now, Moore lifted the gauze and peered into the pram with its sour milky smell. Lightly then, he passed his hand over the child's damp forehead before deciding to remove the thin shawl that covered him. And then, morbidly — unavoidably — Moore felt the pulpy, nearly hairless spot on the crown of the child's head where the bones of his skull had not yet sutured. *Achilles heel,* he thought, then reminded of an arctic bird he had heard about whose heart could be stopped by the merest pressure of a finger on its breast.

Worries of this kind would arise from time to time, but despite them, Moore was generally happy, feeling fortunate to be able to immerse himself in such matters when other fathers were struggling just to survive. Now forty-three, Moore had spent several depressed months that winter, when there had been talk of calling men up to the age of forty-five. But when forty became the cutoff age, his relief quickly turned to guilt. And then one day on King's Parade his guilt turned to shame when a militant-looking old woman wearing an arm band suddenly presented him with a white feather, saying with acidic sweetness, A feather for the faint-hearted, dear boy.

In his humiliation, his first instinct was to throttle the old beast, but his second was to think that it was half deserved — that he really was nothing but a coward and a slacker. Moore was still smarting over that humiliation. Conscious of his still boyish face, he was increasingly concerned that his neighbors, many of whom had husbands or loved ones not much younger than he on the front, thought him a slacker. There was no getting away from it. In the streets — everywhere now — there were soldiers. In the stations, there were always wounded soldiers, maimed stumps of lives hobbling or tied on gurneys. In Hall, where Moore still ate two nights every week, officers and old students busily recounted their adventures and talked of all those who would not return. Every few weeks, it seemed, he would hear about the death of some student, neighbor, distant relative or friend of a friend. Loss was one thing, but what bothered him most was how numbing and abstract it all became. With death it seemed he should feel something, something morally immense. But all too often he felt little or nothing, nor could he pretend about it. When a person went away, thought Moore, he was effectively silenced — dead. And when he reappeared? Then he was returned, resuscitated from the dead. You brushed him off and reestablished your mutual life, and so it continued until the next parting.

One notable exception to this feeling, however, was Wittgenstein. To Moore, it seemed odd that painful memories of a person should sustain and refurbish the memory more than pleasant recollections. Even then, more than two years later, Moore was still smarting from that journey he had made to Norway. And Russell, in his own way, had now further soured the whole episode.

Russell had still been away lecturing in America when Moore returned from Norway with the notes that Wittgenstein had dictated to him. Moore thought nothing of it. He left the notes with Russell's housekeeper, along with a message that, if Russell saw the need, he would do his best to explain any sticky points.

Russell thanked Moore for the notebook, but he never questioned him about it. Moore, for his part, thought nothing of it until one morning, months later, Russell dropped by his office with a letter from Wittgenstein, saying, I thought you might find this of interest.

Moore was immediately suspicious. Like a solicitor introducing evidence, Russell explained how the letter, written almost two months before on the Russian front, had been forwarded to Keynes, who, with his high-level treasury connections, was able to get mail from belligerents.

You're sure the letter is not too personal? asked Moore, smelling trouble.

Oh, no, no, Russell insisted. Read it, by all means.

Reluctantly, then, Moore opened the letter. It began on a personal note, then turned testy as Wittgenstein explained various logical points in his notes that Russell had evidently missed, adding, I find it inconceivable that Moore was not able to explain my ideas to you.

Stunned, Moore looked at Russell. What does he mean, why was I not able to explain. *You never asked.*

Russell sucked in his chin. To say I never *asked* begs the point, don't you think? I mean, I thought you would have taken more of an interest in discussing the notes than you did. You must have known that they were cryptic and rather insufficient. I presumed that if you really had understood what you transcribed — well, that you would have been more forthcoming in offering your help.

Moore was popeyed. I *said* that if you needed my help I would offer what help I could. How could I be any more forthcoming? As for the rest, how was I to know what *you* would find sufficient? I haven't been privy to your dealings with Wittgenstein!

Pacing and laboring then, his arms flopping, Moore erupted: Oh, you do take the cake! Why tell Wittgenstein that *you* don't understand? Why, you can bloody well blame Moore! My God, if ever I needed advice on self-serving casuistry I'd come straight to you, Russell! Oh, I would indeed!

Russell was not upset in the least. On the contrary, he had come prepared for this tirade. Now he was the cunning jurist cross-examining Moore:

Did I *say* that you could not have explained? This conclusion is Wittgenstein's, not mine necessarily. I merely thought that you deserved to see what Wittgenstein said. Here Russell couldn't resist a taunt. Of course, if you are willing to sit down and explain some things to me —

Like hammers, Moore's hands fell to the desk. Go to hell! Get Wittgenstein to explain! In fact, as far as I'm concerned, there's no reason why we should even *speak*! Now, for God's sake — out! Please!

But Russell wasn't about to be driven from Moore's office. Out he strolled, perfectly composed, with a faint smile on his face. He was halfway down the hall when Moore, in his burgeoning rage, wanted to call him back — not, God knows, to patch things up, but merely to ask *why,* after so much time, and for no apparent provocation, he should come to start trouble, and moreover to do so over a man who might well be dead. It was astounding. Here was Russell, thought Moore, a man now a major force in England, with more work than five men could have handled. But it still wasn't enough! For Russell, thought Moore, the world must be at *peace*! But, by God, in his own life, there must be tumult and discord, quarreling even with the probable dead and those like him who begrudged him nothing. No, Moore didn't understand. He didn't understand at all.

That, as far as Moore was concerned, was the end of any personal dealings between them. Despite his support for Russell in his expulsion proceedings, Moore swore to himself that he would henceforth deal with Russell on a strictly professional basis, and then only as a last resort. As for Wittgenstein, Moore did his best to forget him. It was easier this way: like Russell, Moore didn't expect him to survive the war. Moore had last heard from him in December 1914, in a card Wittgenstein had sent shortly after he had enlisted. It was a brief, friendly, implicitly apologetic note, saying that his feelings for his English friends had not changed because of the war and that he still very much valued Moore's friendship. Moore meant to reply but, as usual, he procrastinated. He had no idea where Wittgenstein's letter was now.

In any case, Nicholas was squealing. Leaning once more into the pram, rummaging through the covers for the teething ring, Moore wondered why he should suddenly be thinking about Wittgenstein. He hadn't thought of him in several weeks at least — perhaps even a month.

Dipping swallows were clearing the mosquitoes from the sky as Moore pushed the squeaky pram back up the lane. Slowly, the bronzed air was losing its timbre. Night was falling, a clear, cool, moonless night — perfect for airships.

Faster squeaked the wheels. The dusk sky dimmed another hue, and then suddenly the swallows were gone and the air was filled with the first flitting bats, looping and skidding down, then flipping up. *Whap, whap* — gone.

Darker and darker it grew. *Hurry up, Moore,* he told himself, but then, sure enough, Nicky started fussing. Pants wet. Hungry.

There's my Nicky, soothed Moore, bending over again. There's my good, good boy . . .

Moore's back was aching by the time he finally got the child settled down. As he came into the homestretch, he saw Dorothy sitting on the stoop of their cottage. She waited until he came through the trellised gate, then she went up and kissed him, saying, Well, I see you've had quite a walk. You're sweating. And you, she mocked, smacking her lips against Nicholas's cheek as she lifted him from the pram. *Phew!* We're all smelly. See how you behave when you're with your father!

Moore agreed to do the changing. Unpinning the dirty diaper, he was amazed as ever at the sheer volume and oily black pungency of its contents. With the pin in his mouth and his sleeves rolled up, he went through the procedure with almost surgical precision, holding the child by his crossed feet like a trussed turkey as he wiped and washed, then flung on talc.

There, Nicholas, he sang. *We're dddddddddone! We're thrrrrrrrough! We're cleeeean!* He picked the boy up and made a drooling idiot face. *B-gob! Brezzzzeechhh.* The floor shook as Moore danced him out of the room and handed him to Dorothy, who put him on her breast while Moore expired into his chair and reached for his pipe.

Later that night, once the baby was asleep, Moore stepped into the garden to give the sky one last look. Odd, but he again found himself thinking of Wittgenstein, wondering if he was alive and what would become of his ideas if he wasn't. Chilling, thought Moore, how efficiently the world conceals its news, its dead. And then once more he found himself thinking of the goggled zeppelin men, peering down through the polar darkness, nodding and saying *Ja, bombe hier!* Then Dorothy called back:

Bill, for the last time! Come to bed!

Presently, he called, creeping inside. Just let me put a few words in the journal.

Not a tome, she said. You'll not be the one waking up at two.

All right — five minutes.

Still more fear about the zeppelins — be just my luck. Most of all worry about Nicholas. Children the most vulnerable, it seems, though perhaps his father is just a coward at heart.

Another walk with Nicky tonight. Responds more to my voice. Smiles. Clutches my hand. A certain rhythm to his babbling, I think; like a hungry bird, the struggling way he takes the sounds from my lips. Three good b.m.'s for him, one for his pater.

Moore hesitated, then added:

Thinking about Wittgenstein again. Find I'm still angry at him — hurt, tho' I know it's not his fault. Must, in any case, decide what to do. If dead, I suppose I should offer — purely for Wittgenstein's sake — to help Russell with the notes. If alive, I suppose I should write to him, but I hesitate — what would I say? The shame of it, having nothing after all to say.

Later that night, not long after the baby's two o'clock feeding, Moore awoke to talking. It was Dorothy, tossing and mumbling in her sleep:

No, we mustn't go there — not Nicholas. *Hold* the pillow under his head — *catch* it! *Bill!*

Heart pounding, Moore sat up and started to shake her, but then it was over. Mumbling something more, Dorothy pulled his arm around her like a blanket and fell back to sleep. But then Moore had a dream himself. It was all very mixed up, with plummeting bombs and a zeppelin that fell slowly to earth like a planet knocked out of orbit. And then Moore was running with a man who turned out to be the zeppelin commander. The enemy officer was upbraiding him, saying there had been a mistake, an idiotic mistake! Useless charts! The German tore them to pieces. Telescope no good either, nor the sextant. He pitched them into a ditch.

Then the captain tore off his fur-lined cap, and Moore saw that one of his ears had been shot away, the face ravaged. Moore peered for the longest time into the man's face before he realized that it was Wittgenstein. Then soldiers were pursuing, and they were by the sea. That helpless feeling as Wittgenstein stared at him: the uselessness of leave-taking. Wittgenstein's face was draped in darkness, like a lunar eclipse. Moore was trying to smile. And then Wittgenstein turned and dove into the night sea. Churning like a dolphin, he swam to Holland, leaving a broth of shimmering bubbles that stretched clear across the Channel.

Dorothy was trying to roll Moore over when he awoke.

I'm all right, mumbled Moore, sitting up. He bounded out of bed.

Get back in here, Dorothy insisted. What's the matter?

Nothing's the matter. His voice was parched and gruff. I just had a dream. Just a dream. Be right back.

Moore first checked Nicholas, trembling as he slipped a hand under the little gown, feeling the reassuring heart and warmth, the little stutter of breath. Then Moore shuffled down the hall to his study and wrote in his diary.

Dream of Wittgenstein. Zeppelins again. At the edge of the sea, Wittgenstein looks at me as if to ask if it's all right, and I can't help smiling, as if it were, though I know that it isn't; then he is swimming in the sea, and I am still on the shore, but unsure, still unsure.

Must write down what I feel about Wittgenstein.

Nothing Would Have Happened Had Not . . .

SITTING BEHIND a sandbagged trench on the Russian front one morning in the early spring of 1916, Sergeant Wittgenstein of the Austrian Fourth Army was popping lice between his nails and writing in his notebook.

NOTHING WOULD HAVE HAPPENED . . .
   Had not the archduke gone home after the bomb exploded,
   Had not the Russians mobilized,
   Had not the English stayed out,
   Had not a shell splinter been in another state of affairs,
another geometry;
   Had not I asked Pinsent what kind of bird it was in the tree
that day we met,
   Or had the bird alighted somewhere else or not been born,
   Or had a bullet found me first.
   We should have remained in Norway, under Holy Orders.

   Sooner or later,
   What depends on my life? Sad or happy,
   There is only this life, this immediate scheme, which is neither
good nor evil,
   Sad nor happy. Then comes *Not*, the mystery of *Not*:
   Two nots making an affirmation, a possibility,
   Surrounded by another impinging
   Not, annihilating that possibility.

   The world is all that is the case.
   This world divides into facts,
   But because false facts make sense
   With the same logic as the true, we can no more see
   To the bottom of our acts than
   We can with our own eyes
   See our own dark faces. And here is how it stands:
   We see our fate as a fact. We display it.
   But our souls are timebound and blind.

   Now: The simplest fact is: the simplest fact in our
acquaintance.

And the simplest facts are: the facts we cannot explain
or get over:
Had not my brothers been suicides, what would I be?

As a child, I saw the Wittgensteins as a great orchestra.
Now we are a dwindling orchestra. Hans and Rudolf long dead
by their own hands.
Paul, a pianist, loses his right arm to a bullet
while here I have two. (I could philosophize as well with one.)
Kurt, a lieutenant deserted by his men, shoots himself
in the head when Russians storm his trench.
Pinsent, like a brother, dies invisibly with a shell splinter,
while others live for no reason,
Choking on this life as on arsenic.

There is something exceedingly simple here that eludes me!
The human heart
is simple. Life, viewed from a great height,
is simple. The happy life is
the good life, and the happy man, the man carrying out
the purpose of life has nothing to fear, not death, not
even the devil.

Hence I am fearful.

*   *   *

This peaceful morning the sun has risen,
But there is no *logical* reason to believe it will do so tomorrow.
Opening my eyes, I share a world with others. Closing them, I am
on its limits, a lone inhabitant.
Turning my face toward the darkness,
I see that everything I think could be otherwise.
Even God grants exceptions.

As Wittgenstein bent over his notebook, steam rose from the collar of
his filthy gray tunic, slowly trailing over his ears and over the fuzz of his
close-cropped head. From the Russian trenches one hundred and fifty
yards away came trickles of smoke from charcoal braziers, where soldiers
were warming their hands and brewing bitter black tea. Beyond, over a
field of shell holes and barbed wire entanglements, lay a pulverized village, a shallow bluff and a thin line of shattered birches with black
branches, their silver trunks gleaming like glass as the burnt sun rose
behind them.

Below, in the ankle-deep slough of the trench after that night's rain, Wittgenstein's men were bailing and wringing out clothes. Somewhere a mule was bawling. Breakfast was coming. Down flooded communication trenches from field kitchens a half mile away, men would be carrying slopping tins slung on bending poles, troughs of ersatz tea and oatmeal tasting of the greasy soup they had eaten the night before.

For three days the rain had fallen. Rain burst through sandbags and the wattle of sticks revetting the trench walls, rusting rifles, bleaching feet white and soaking their crumbly gray war bread to the consistency of suet. Pumps and bucket brigades were useless against the rainwater: it rushed back unabated, carrying with it hunks of carrion and their own excrement, roaring down with such pressure that it forced up half-buried corpses, bursting from their rotting woolens.

All that night, muddy water had dribbled over Wittgenstein as he lay curled in a warren of hard clay under a corrugated iron sheet. Itching and anxious, he lay there in a sort of stupor, conscious of every noise and fluctuation in the weather as the provident rats skittered along the walls, the rats that in his dreams gnawed his notebook to a fine powder. For a week now, there had been rumors of a gathering Russian offensive. And each night, the Russian deserters that always preceded an offensive crossed over with raised hands, bawling *Kameraden, Kameraden*. Three had made it over the night before. Others, shot down by their officers or nervous Austrian sentries, were left where they lay. The wind was always bringing stenches.

No attack had come, though, just drenching salvoes of March rain. Then around two the night before, about the time Ernst, Wittgenstein's corporal, came to tell him the sentry was being changed, the rain began to blow over. Buckling on his pistol belt, Wittgenstein got up then to check their perimeter. Ahead, the cans and bottles tied to the barbed wire to warn of intruders crashed and tinkled in the gusting darkness; his raincoat ballooned and whipped. He fined a man for smoking, then continued down the flooded trench, which was kinked in a series of rights and lefts, called traverses, so attackers couldn't fire down the length of it or capture more than a section at a time. But this system, so crucial for defense, made it hard to police the men. And the men needed policing.

They were a rotten, demoralized army. Worse, they were a divided army, comprising roughly twelve different, mostly antagonistic, nationalities. Half his men didn't speak more than a few essential words of German: to talk to his Croat, he would have to tell the Czech, who would tell the Slovak, who would tell the Hungarian, who would tell the

Croat — who got it wrong anyway. Except for Ernst, none of his men was reliable, and there was one named Grundhardt who was despicable. Grundhardt was about twenty-five, with dark hair and skin, long, decaying teeth and the sharp, raked features of a young wolf. He was a shameless braggart, with a flair for exaggeration and mystery. Even when they knew he was lying, his naive comrades, jug-eared recruits and illiterates — some men nearly twice his age — were mesmerized by his profane and confident air of experience. Grundhardt told them he was the bastard of a Gypsy whore and a smuggler. Shamelessly, he would masturbate in his dugout, describing his sexual exploits in such detail that those listening would develop vigorous erections. He claimed to have been a powerful pimp and told them of beautiful women in his native Prague who had drowned themselves for love of him. He told them of a sloe-eyed Amazon, a lover of dogs, with tits that could fill a coal bucket — tits, he swore, that could swallow a man's head whole. So help him, he said, raising his right arm, it was the gospel. He had perfumed letters to prove it — juicy pictures, too, showing him with a tart on each arm, dressed in a vulgar suit and hat and standing on the runningboard of a big motorcar.

Grundhardt could turn pure nothing into something. Give him a pea and three shells and he would fleece a platoon of a month's wages. Why, with thin air he could captivate, holding them rapt, sick with laughter, as he applied a lit match to the seat of his pants and expelled shrill gas — grinning as a long tongue of flame shot out, singeing several nearby noses.

There were men in that miserable army who had never seen a city or eaten an orange, fearful, superstitious men who believed Grundhardt when he told them he knew Gypsy curses that could bring impotence, excruciating death, madness and terrors they could scarcely imagine. That he was a thief went without saying, but no one had caught him, or if they had, had never reported him. No one dared; it went against the code. Besides, so long as Grundhardt didn't steal from them, it gave them deep satisfaction to see the little pimp confound authority in an army obsessed with it. What's more, many feared him. He was vindictive. A boy, now dead, who had argued with Grundhardt over a matter too trivial to remember found his cat hanging from a beam in a dugout, disemboweled. Another who crossed him found his boots filled with fresh stool. Justice was swift in the trenches. Several times, late at night, they had taken vengeance, swarming over him with gags and ropes, silently beating him almost beyond recognition as he defiantly flailed and cursed them. But one way or another, no matter what, Grundhardt always got even. There was no getting rid of him; some said murder wouldn't have been enough. Take Antal, the big Hungarian who had thrashed him for cheating at cards. Grundhardt's face was pouring blood when Antal had finished with him. You'll die for this, snarled Grundhardt. And before the Hungarian's eyes, he cut off a lock of his hair, mixed it with blood and spittle and set it afire with harsh, incantatory words. Watching him like a curious dog, the Hungarian shook his head, then punched him twice more in the face. Three hours later, though, when a shell landed too close, Antal was groveling at Grundhardt's feet, begging him to undo the hex. Ever since, Antal had been his dog, protecting him from his enemies and doing his dirty work for small bribes.

It had reached the point that the little pimp was threatening Wittgenstein's authority. He was turning the men against him. But unless Wittgenstein caught Grundhardt stealing or spying or being grossly insubordinate, there was little he could do. Talking did no good, nor did threats or punishments. Wittgenstein made him pull double watches, dig ditches and muck latrines. He ordered him on dangerous patrols. Nothing worked. It didn't even make an impression.

There had been an incident in Galicia that previous summer, during the Russian retreat, when Wittgenstein's men had been part of a column marching through a village where there had been a pogrom. The Russians had fled only hours before, and it was anybody's guess whether it was the Russians or the local peasants who were behind the massacre. Smashed furniture and crockery filled the street, and in the air was the stench of smoldering wool and feathers dumped out of mattresses in search of the gold that it was said the Jews were flying out of Galicia under the wings of storks. Feathers eddied and swirled through the air and stuck to the bloody faces of the dead, who numbered about thirty. Even on the battlefield, Wittgenstein had never seen such savagery. Some of the men had been castrated, others had crosses hacked on their breasts, their earlocks torn from their temples like vestigial horns. There were women as well, raped, then cast off like dead chickens, their skirts dumped over their heads. Not even children were spared. Five were laid out together, smothered like puppies with gasoline-soaked rags; someone had even taken the trouble to fold their hands into little steeples. The only survivor was a trembling old man whose cheeks had been flayed off when they scalped his beard. Now he was an open jaw, his exposed tongue moving like a slug over blackened toothstumps.

The column moved quickly through the street, some men silently crossing themselves. Then Wittgenstein looked back and saw Grundhardt grinning, grinning for no other reason than to taunt him.

Swallowing his deep revulsion, Wittgenstein let the look pass: the army had no statutes against brutishness. Grundhardt didn't let it pass, though; he just pushed Wittgenstein further. The next day they were in another village, another muddy street with more barefoot Jews. As Wittgenstein passed an alley, he saw a small shriveled boy with earlocks scream in pain and drop a coin that Grundhardt had just tossed him. Down the street the child ran, wailing and waving his hand. At first Wittgenstein didn't know what had happened, but then he saw Grundhardt snickering with four simpletons as he dropped the match and tweezers he had used to heat the coin to a dull glow.

You're all on report, said Wittgenstein, running over. And you, he said, giving Grundhardt a shove. You come with me.

Playing for the others, Grundhardt said, What's the matter? We was just having some fun with the little Yid. There any law against us having some fun?

Wittgenstein made him pay for his pranks, but each time it was the same, with Wittgenstein exacting punishment and Grundhardt extracting revenge. Wittgenstein found a putrid rat in his bed, a handful of pages torn from his notebook, his canteen filled with urine. Nobody ever saw a thing.

And sure enough, as Wittgenstein had been making his rounds in the rain the night before, it had happened again. Coming around the traverse, he surprised someone, who vaulted the wall and ran through the rainy darkness, his boots sucking and splashing through the deep mud. Wittgenstein could see from the man's gaiters and *kepi* that he was one of their own. *Halt!* Wittgenstein fired his pistol twice into the air, but the man kept running, leaping over the knee-high roof of a dugout, then disappearing down a snaking communication trench.

Having told the sentries to pass the word, Wittgenstein was about to run back and check Grundhardt's bunk when the quartermaster and three others armed with ax handles and steel billies ran up, telling him they'd lost wallets, a watch, food. Did you see the bastard? asked the quartermaster. I saw him jump the wall, said Wittgenstein. I didn't see his face but I think I know who it is. The quartermaster pushed forward. Just show him to us. Wait, said Wittgenstein, blocking his path. You let me handle it. I don't need you getting my men stirred up. I'll tell you what I find.

The four soldiers became angry and argumentative, and by the time

Wittgenstein settled them down and got back down the trench, he found Grundhardt safely ensconced in his cutaway.

Get up, said Wittgenstein, yanking back the muddy tarp that draped the shelter. He was positive now that Grundhardt was the thief and expected to find him covered with mud. Yet when he tore back the covers, Grundhardt's boots were off and he was no muddier than anybody else.

Stand out, thief, said Wittgenstein with a shudder. He ran his hand under the filthy bedding. You've bought it this time.

But Grundhardt was too smart for his bluff. Who you calling a thief? he said.

Shut up, said Wittgenstein. Like passengers on a sleeping car, several men had pulled back the tarps covering their scrapes and were watching him now.

Look, said Grundhardt, with an insinuating smile. Sarge is getting into bed with me.

Wittgenstein grabbed him by the collar, but Grundhardt just smiled a sick smile, begging him to punch him. He's been asleep! spoke up Moder, another of Grundhardt's toadies, a rag-and-bone man by trade. How would you know, Moder? Wittgenstein snapped, pushing Grundhardt back into his bunk. Where have you been, Moder? Out with Grundhardt? I been sleeping, came the surly reply. Haven't heard nobody. It's true, chimed in Rauff. Stow it, said Wittgenstein, his voice backing down a notch.

He saw he was getting nowhere. This was just what Grundhardt wanted, and Wittgenstein knew he would only further erode his authority by palavering with them. Then Ernst came down. Ernst was about twenty, a tough barkeep's son with a broad back and a crazy crow of a laugh. He loathed Grundhardt and had begged Wittgenstein several times to let him take him around back for a little talk.

Hello there, you ugly little rat, said Ernst to Grundhardt. He looked expectantly at Wittgenstein. What's he done now?

Forget it, said Wittgenstein, throwing down the tarp. All of you, back to sleep.

Wittgenstein started down the trench with their nasty laughter in his ears. Ernst ran after him.

So what happened? asked Ernst. Did you catch him at it?

No. Wittgenstein whirled around, then kept walking.

Oh, come on, said Ernst. Just say you did.

Wittgenstein stopped again. I didn't see him plainly, and I'm not about to lie about it. And you won't, either, Ernst.

But that's just what he's counting on, said Ernst in frustration. He knows you'll play fair.

Wittgenstein drew away. I don't care.

Here, Wittgenstein, said Ernst, putting his hand on his shoulder. Don't be sore. Let's just stand here and talk. I can't sleep anyhow.

I don't want to talk now, said Wittgenstein, softening. I'm not angry with you, I just want to be left a while. Go on. I'm fine. Get some sleep.

Wittgenstein felt ill when he returned to tell the quartermaster that he hadn't found his thief. He saw he was losing, Grundhardt was becoming an obsession with him. His venom was eating right through him, corroding his morals and even his very soul. His legs, which had been giving him trouble, ached from cold and dampness, and he felt a hot gurgling in his stomach as he crept through the forward sap to the Hole, as they called it. Fifty paces from the main trench, just inside the wire, the latrine was a dangerous place at night. Pulling out his Luger and flipping off the safety, Wittgenstein dropped his heavy woolen trousers and sat on the wet and reeking boards, rocking painfully while hot soup dribbed down. The wind kept gusting as the dregs of rain passed over, the last cold drops shaking down from the red clouds where the moon broke through, illuminating the draining field. A fine place to have one's throat cut, he thought. He wouldn't have been the first to have ended thus, hobbled and straining. And unavoidably, the image came to mind: a strong hand grasping his mouth, then the guttered blade gliding up under his tongue and between his teeth as his mouth welled over with blood. With a consummating shiver, he closed his eyes, his insides clenching as the junk crashed in the buffeting darkness.

He couldn't shake it, this soul sickness. Grundhardt lived, and David Pinsent was dead. Wittgenstein had gotten the news only a few days ago, in a letter from Flo that Keynes had forwarded.

January 8, 1916

My Dear Mr Wittgenstein,

I don't know if this will reach you — I hope so, tho' you'll wish it hadn't. David's dead. A shell splinter struck him in the head while he was carrying a wounded boy in a stretcher; Ypres, or some such place. I rec'd a letter from his commanding officer, who said he was one of his finest men, very brave about fetching the wounded, etc.; — the sort of thing they send all the mothers, I expect. It happened months ago now, so you must forgive me, I've been much too ill to write. Tonight I'm staying with a distant cousin and her husband — horrid people; can't stand them. You know how I am. David always said so.

I'm always travelling these days, I never know from one night to the next where I'll be. I often dream of David, which at least is something. There are places where I dream of him more than others, so I keep moving. I hope to God I'll follow him soon. I don't mean to be morbid but it's true. Why dwell on it?

David said he rec'd a letter from you some time ago. He always hoped you would meet again after the war; as I did. Every night I pray for all you lads, even the Germans who killed David. I have letters and some things they sent back. I have his diary as well but cannot open it. David wanted you to have these things, sir, so I have instructed my solicitor to give them to Mr Keynes to keep for you once I pass on.

Mr Wittgenstein, please don't think this is a veiled plea for money; I don't want anything now except my David. If it were possible, I should love to see you. I hope you are safe and remember you in my prayers.

Please don't feel obliged to write but kindly do so if you like. Mr Keynes said he will find me.

Affectionately,
Florence Pinsent

Keynes enclosed his own letter:

Dear Wittgenstein:

I'm deeply saddened to bring you bad news about Pinsent and enclose his mother's letter with distinct uneasiness. Her doctor urged me to read it before posting it, and I hope you'll understand that I did so with the *utmost* reluctance. As you may suspect, she is not "moving" at all; the news was naturally a great blow to her, and her family found it necessary to place her in Blackbriar's sanitarium outside Birmingham after she threatened suicide and would not care for herself. Rest assured she is being well cared for. Relatives, I'm told, are assuming all expenses.

The particulars she relates about David's death are more or less accurate. He died at Ypres the 18th of November of the cause she mentions and received several commendations. His name has been added to the growing roll of honor at Trinity.

I am well and hope you are, also. Bertie is planning to give lectures on how to reorder the world, which certainly could make it no worse. Moore is happily awaiting fatherhood, though I hear he is depressed about Cambridge, which is dreary these days with you and all its brightest lights gone. I know they both would want to join me in offering their condolences and best wishes to you at this very sad time.

Warmest regards,
Maynard

Pinsent's death was not the only blow Wittgenstein had had of late. First there had been the news of his brother Paul, who had lost his right arm while defending the Carso plateau against repeated, and futile, Italian attacks. Then there was his brother Kurt, a lieutenant, who had died five months before, during a Russian counterattack near Rovno. At first Wittgenstein was told only the date and place where Kurt died. Some days later, though, he was told off the record what had happened: the unexpected Russian attack had been a rout and Kurt's men deserted him, at which point Kurt shot himself in the head.

Wittgenstein's ambivalence about Kurt did not soften his reaction. In a family in which suicide and madness ran side by side, this death seemed less a loss than a judgment, as if Kurt were a mere harbinger, to use Pinsent's word, of his own fate. Wittgenstein left for Vienna a few weeks later, but he never told his family the true circumstances of Kurt's death. What was the point? With two sons as suicides already, the truth would have killed his mother — the news nearly killed her as it was. Besides, he thought, who was to say a Russian had not shot him? And what if Kurt had not shot himself? The Russians probably would have killed him anyway.

All that winter the pain had been gnawing its way to the surface, but now with Pinsent gone, it was almost uncontrollable. Wittgenstein was sure he was going to die. It wasn't just soldier's fatalism; he was quite certain, even resigned to it. Yet he was just as determined not to be a suicide, which was doubly hard when death could be had so easily, for just a moment's inattention. To die honorably, he had to want to live, and yet he was dead. Spring, with its coming offensives, only brought death that much closer. And then, just when Wittgenstein had thought he had sunk to the very bottom, he learned about Pinsent.

The irony was that he was at the height of his intellectual powers and he knew it, which should have been liberating but was instead a sorrow, when he saw how little had been achieved for all his efforts. His work stretched from the foundations of logic to the nature of the world, but in his own life that knowledge did him no good at all. He felt like the cormorant, that oily black waterbird the Chinese use for fishing. With an iron ring around its neck, the cormorant can't swallow the fish it catches. But far from discouraging the greedy bird, the iron ring only makes it dive that much deeper, straining against its choker to snatch the biggest fish it can find.

This image of the predatory cormorant seemed to apply to everything in Wittgenstein's life, even his Christianity. Now a disciple of Tolstoy, he carried the New Testament in one pocket of his tunic and Tolstoy's *Gos-*

pels in the other. He wanted to live a life of simple charity and Christian faith, a faith prior to any church. Yet while he found himself faced with all the burdens of Christian faith, he garnered none of the peace that is supposed to come with it. Ethics consumed him: it was what was most important in life, and the key to his philosophy, but it was also fundamentally silent. Ethics could not be taught or expressed; it could only be shown through an exemplary life. And the whole point of his life and work was moral — otherwise what was the point of living? He knew, without being able to logically justify it, that the good life was the happy life. So, as an ethical matter, he had resolved to be happy in order to be good, but he succeeded only in being miserable and therefore false — straining to grasp the essence of life when, like the cormorant, he couldn't swallow it anyway.

And the ring wouldn't release him. Here he was, a good soldier, a decorated soldier, with a reputation for being cool headed under fire and for looking after his men. But even bravery was false when he hardly cared if he lived. At times Wittgenstein envied the cowards, wondering if they weren't the sane ones who truly cherished life. Yet those who cherished life, who were now so desperate they would do anything, even shoot themselves in the foot, to save their own skins — these men for whom he felt so responsible were the ones who, in a pinch, would probably not feel the least bit responsible for him. Lately, Wittgenstein feared he might even suffer Kurt's fate of being deserted in battle, leaving him with a loaded pistol and a choice to make.

Breakfast arrived. Wittgenstein put his notebook away, and was going down to supervise when Ernst came to him and said, We've got a bad problem. Antal's bleeding through his ears.

A crowd of men were standing around Antal's cutaway when Ernst and Wittgenstein got there. Here, move out of the way, said Ernst, pushing through. The big Hungarian's eyes were glazed over. A faint trickle of blood oozed out his ears and his pants were wet about the crotch. He didn't even have the strength to brush the flies from his face. What's the matter? asked Wittgenstein, leaning over him. Antal started weeping. I can't hardly move. I don't feel nothing.

His face was hot with sweat, and his body seemed oddly contorted. Turning to the other men, Wittgenstein asked, Who discovered this? Moder did, someone chimed up. He heard him getting sick last night. Then someone asked suspiciously, What's wrong with him? And someone else replied, Typhoid, stupid. He's got typhoid.

He doesn't have typhoid, said Wittgenstein irritably. Now clear out. All of you.

But even as they were pulling back, more men, some from farther down the line, were crowding up to see, craning over one another's shoulders as Antal lay there in a heap, sobbing. Wittgenstein was about to order them off again, when another man said, If it's not typhoid, then what's he got?

Wittgenstein was losing his temper. I'm not discussing it! Do you hear me? Now, for the last time, clear out!

Rumors were flying by the time Wittgenstein's superior, Lieutenant Stize, arrived, dogged as always by his orderly, Krull. The son of a wealthy chocolate maker now rumored to be a black marketeer, Stize was about thirty, balding and slender, with a narrow collie's face, a thin mustache and protuberant lips, which frequently became bibulous with tots of wine and brandy. Few senior officers, much less front-line officers, were better supplied or turned out than Stize, in his tailored, fur-collared greatcoat, kid gloves and binoculars. Rubber boots were virtually impossible to obtain, but Stize had a pair; and with lice everywhere, Stize had none, thanks to Krull, who would spend hours picking his clothes free of nits before fumigating them with ether. Short, bald and bowlegged, Krull was about fifty and had been with the lieutenant's family from the time Stize had been a boy. Other officers had tried to bribe Krull for his secret source of starched shirts, fresh eggs and fruit, brandy and caviar. Krull told them to keep their money, having already made a bundle on the black market selling the surfeit of chocolate and other dainties from Stize's cache, which not even that truffle swine Grundhardt had been able to sniff out.

Krull was a cool one. At the whistle of the first shell, while his master was cravenly diving for cover, Krull would be meandering along, watching the sky with all the crafty grace of a man who somehow knows he'll come through without a scratch. Stize had no such certainty and spent every possible moment in the safety of the officers' dugout, a deeply mined room thirty-five feet underground that was decorated like a Viennese café, with a gramophone, wooden floors, booths and fake curtained windows painted with Alpine scenes by an officer who had studied under Kokoschka. Stize would have made a brilliant supply officer and, with Krull's help, kept their mess well provisioned with jam and real coffee and even fresh meat. When Prince Primkin admired his patent precision Solingen steel cigar clipper, Stize quickly had one engraved with the prince's initials and, with the most high-flown and abasing rhetoric, presented it to him at his birthday party. Truly, Stize's sole purpose in the war, so far as Wittgenstein could see, was to strengthen his shaky social connections. Stize was especially anxious to ingratiate himself with the prince, a lanky unhorsed cavalryman and wag in his mid-thirties, with a red drinker's face and a sad little belly. The prince loved to cavort with the young officers, but Stize, as a Jew, was not part of that set. Indeed, their main interest in Stize seemed to be his extraordinary ability to procure the unprocurable. That and his willingness, in these days of rampant inflation, to lend sums of money at no interest — that is, when it advanced his social interests.

Stize dearly wanted a staff position, but because he had no connections his petitions went nowhere. If only he could have been a general's aide! Stize was something of a military history buff and could regale staff officers touring the front with tales of Napoleon's troubles in Russia or passionate discourses on the effectiveness of the square against cavalry, complete with faulty allusions to Homeric battles. Of course, these digressions had absolutely nothing to do with trench warfare, but that was precisely why they held such deep appeal for his superiors, with their inbred love of the arcane, byzantine and impractical. The fact was that Stize was one of those remarkable talkers who is knowledgeable about, and good at, virtually everything except what he is responsible for. Stize was positively inspired when advising others on how they might better do their jobs. He was likewise brilliant at inventing unwieldy procedures and unmanageable schedules, and was forever off on some trumped-up business, seeming to truly believe that the success of their sector of the front depended on his tact and diplomacy. He was always full of new ideas. In the washroom of some rear area, he would run into Duke X, a confused eminence with a three-hyphen title, who would hardly have buckled himself back together before the indefatigable lieutenant would be sharing his brainstorm about booting horses to guard against hoof disease and muffle their sound. For the next two days in the officers' mess, Stize would talk up his meeting and his idea, blithely unaware that by then Duke X had forgotten their conversation and his name, remembering only the name of Napoleon's horse or some other tidbit that Stize had left with him. So horses went bootless and Stize's petitions went bootless as well. Around subordinates, Stize was vague, evasive and imprecise, concealing his uneasiness with pompousness and sloughing off problems.

Now, looking at the sick man, working at the pliant kid of his gloves, Stize pettishly said, Well, do you know what's wrong with him?

Leaning forward, Wittgenstein whispered the rumor. Taking a discreet step back, Stize asked, And is it true?

Wittgenstein shook his head. I don't know, sir. But it is turning into a nasty rumor. That's why these men are standing around.

Stize glared at him like an inept waiter who had served him from the wrong side. Well, tell them to *get out*. He was unusually decisive. Krull, he said, turning to his man. Have a stretcher sent back. Then he turned to Ernst. Corporal, why are all these men idling about? Clear the area.

Ernst tried to move the men, but they just shuffled back a few paces, then continued milling. Stize, meanwhile, pretended not to notice this insubordination. In Stize's mind, the men had obeyed: they *had* moved, even if they hadn't moved much. In fact, in view of things, he seemed to think the little maneuver was highly satisfactory. Yes, Stize acted as if he had moved mountains as he stood there, cloaked in arrogant authority while discipline crumbled around him. Turning to Wittgenstein, Stize raised his eyes, as if to ask, Are we through? But Wittgenstein wasn't through.

Sir, he asked. May I have a word with you? Leading him around the traverse, Wittgenstein told him about the previous night's incident and his prime suspect, Grundhardt.

He's a big problem, sir, said Wittgenstein. I wouldn't be surprised if he isn't partly responsible for this typhoid scare.

Stize had heard this before. Here you go, he said, blaming this Grundhardt for everything. I agree the man's a bad apple, but unfortunately we need every apple we can get right now, bad or otherwise. You have no evidence.

I've tried to get evidence, sir. Nobody will report him.

Stize eyed him wearily. Well, then you're stuck with a bad apple, aren't you?

True, sir, said Wittgenstein, trying to contain his anger. But might the bad apple spoil the whole barrel?

The whole barrel? Delighted now to do some truly serious posturing, Stize shook his head with a condescending smile. Sergeant, in this square mile where we stand, there are *countless* bad apples. And that's not even counting the Russian bad apples. In any case, Sergeant, with so many bad apples around us, and with so many soured apples, besides — the lieutenant took a dramatic breath — well, how are you sure that your bad apple is the rotten one? Then, smiling in anticipation of his wit, Stize said dismissively, Make applesauce, Sergeant, make applesauce. Now, I must go. I've a staff meeting in fifteen minutes.

Sir, said Wittgenstein, trying to make one last point. Since you'll be at that meeting, I'd like to remind you of the increased activity our patrols are noticing in the Russian lines. Also, of the fact that they seem to be digging forward reserve trenches. They'll be making rapid progress now with the flooding over.

Stize waved him off. We're watching the situation closely, Sergeant. Intelligence says the Russians have nowhere *near* the shells they need to mount an effective offensive. Their reserves are down, as is morale, and aerial reconnaissance shows negligible movement in their rear areas. No immediate cause for alarm, I assure you. Stize swatted his gloves against his hand and looked around. Ah, here's the stretcher. Good. Very good. I'll notify the medical officer of the rumors — suppose they may want to boil the water or something. You'll be apprised of the diagnosis once it's available.

The men were still milling around as Stize returned Wittgenstein's salute, then left with Krull to make one more pitch for booting horses. And watching them with a grin was Grundhardt, tossing his privates in his pockets like so much spare change.

A few minutes later, once the Hungarian had been carried off and the men had been dispersed on work details, Wittgenstein spoke to Grundhardt. They were alone in an empty dugout dimly lit by a smoking kerosene lamp. The cold earth smelled of mildew and gave off fumes from their urine, an ammonia smell that burned his eyes.

Wittgenstein brought the lamp closer to Grundhardt and said, I don't suppose you know who started this typhoid rumor?

Zealously, Grundhardt replied, It's no rumor. Everybody knows it. There's an epidemic. The Russians gave it to us, the Jews gave it to the Russians, and God gave it to the Jews. I've seen typhus — I know. Like little flies I've seen the children brought from their houses. In the gutters and in swarms by the roads, I've seen —

Shut up! Wittgenstein felt he had to beat him back. Had Grundhardt said that grass was green, Wittgenstein would have denied it. It's not typhus, he said. And if I hear you spreading any more of this nonsense, I'm going to have you charged with sabotage. Do you know you can be shot for sabotage?

Grundhardt stared at him fiercely. Rationally, Wittgenstein could see through his sham — there was something puffed up and ludicrous about him — but even so he felt the hair bristle on the back of his neck. Hunkered like a wolf, with low gray eyes, Grundhardt smelled his fear and exploited it. Floundering now, Wittgenstein said, This is your last warning, Grundhardt.

But Grundhardt just eyed him contemptuously and said, Why should I waste my breath? You'll see — Antal won't be the last.

Later, Ernst laid his hand on Wittgenstein's shoulder and said with a squeeze, Did you get the little rat straightened out?

It was an innocent squeeze, just the corporal's way of establishing contact. How many times had Wittgenstein been walking in the darkness only to feel Ernst clap him on the arm? The gesture meant much more to Wittgenstein than it did to Ernst — that's why it made Wittgenstein so nervous. Besides, Ernst was his friend, and the feelings Wittgenstein sometimes had for him were, to Wittgenstein's way of thinking, not suitable for friends, much less for the army.

In that sense Wittgenstein's friendship with Pinsent had been easy: Pinsent wasn't his type. But the confident, rough-looking Ernst was. For the most part, Wittgenstein had done well at burying his desires, but then a bulging calf, a bare back or a pair of white buttocks in the stinging antiseptic steam of a delousing shower, would spoil everything. Why? Wittgenstein wondered. It was just hair, muscle, skin. Why did he find these details so overwhelming?

In Tolstoy's *Gospels,* the temptations were so homey and simple by comparison. A peasant working in a field would look up and see a devil with little goat's horns peeping down from a stunted tree, urging him to take a drink or a pinch of snuff. But the peasant's sin was small potatoes and his devil a mere pipsqueak compared to the devil of lust. And undergirding it all was despair — these periodic urges for sex were always an index of his despair.

Wittgenstein had told Ernst all about Pinsent. Ernst was a simple man of little education, but he had a good heart and felt sad when Wittgenstein told him about the death of his English friend. Ernst knew what Wittgenstein was going through, and in this respect he was a true veteran: to him, it made no difference that Pinsent had been an enemy. At bottom, Ernst knew that they all died the same way, all twisted in the same attitudes and staring stupefied at the same sky as their eyes welled up with darkness. No, it was only the martinets of the rear areas and the fierce old men at home who felt no sadness for the waste on both sides. Wittgenstein had told Ernst the story of how Pinsent was packed off to Bondock after his father had died, and how on his first day there the red-haired runt lay down in the muddy soccer field, staring at the sky as the bullies spat and kicked him. Refusing to play, not even if they killed him.

Wittgenstein still couldn't get over it. Shaking his head, he told Ernst, I keep wishing Pinsent had done the same in Belgium. Over and over I think of it. What if he had just laid down and refused to fight? What if we all did?

As Wittgenstein said this, he saw Ernst staring hard at him, and then he thought that in a way he loved him. Wittgenstein was now in such a state that for a moment he even fancied Ernst was something like Pinsent. Ernst and Pinsent did share a certain purity and innocence, but that was about it. Actually, they were not alike. They were not alike at all.

Refugees

VIENNA had been covered with snow when Wittgenstein arrived there on hardship leave the previous winter, shortly after Kurt's death.

The long train that had brought him home was rife with noise and drunken soldiers, the passenger cars followed by hospital cars of wounded, and behind these eleven contagious horse cars filled with filthy, half-starved refugees, most of them Jews. It was an interminable journey, with breakdowns and endless stops for water and coal, followed by more frequent stops smelling of death and disinfectant as refugees were turned into the woods to empty slops and hastily bury their dead.

Several times during the longer stops, Wittgenstein walked back to the refugee cars, half from curiosity and half from an impoverished feeling that he might render assistance. The latter impulse stemmed largely from Tolstoy's example, but with the mendicant Christian also came the golem Jew with his empty bucket, having neither alms nor food nor medical training — in short, nothing these tanners and peddlers would have accepted from him. What possessed him to walk a quarter mile back into that little world caught between the war's steel teeth? Not in the least did he understand these people, or the reaction they elicited. How many times in Galicia he had seen them hung from trees and telegraph poles with signs in Russian pinned to their coats, denouncing them as spies, hoarders, vermin. How they rocked and swung, like dark bells, with their legs and hands bound together and a look of stoical renunciation in their constricted faces. In death as in life, these Jews seemed to Wittgenstein to be profoundly uncomfortable in the world, forever outside the fold; their very passivity seemed to encourage murder in the way a rabbit will spur even the most tail-swiped cur to tear him to pieces. This was their lot, these Jews seemed to say. For good times there must be bad times, days when their red beards would hang like fleeces from the trees. Standing amid that hive, Wittgenstein would find himself closing his eyes, listening to these *shtetl* sounds, which nagged him like a melody he could not place.

But there was another reason for Wittgenstein's ambivalence and discomfort, and that was Gretl, who was now learning Yiddish and Hebrew as part of her work coordinating relief efforts between the government and Vienna's many Jewish charitable organizations. As one of the leaders of the Zentralstelle für jüdische Kriegsflüchtlinge, she was finding the charitable alliance increasingly difficult to hold together. In the first weeks of the war, the Russians had quickly overrun Galicia, displacing thousands of Galician Jews, whom the Austrian army shipped west to various refugee camps and to Vienna, where the Jewish population quickly doubled. Working in cooperation with the government, Vienna's Jews managed to keep the refugees from starving that first winter. But the continued influx that spring quickly began to strain the city's own stretched resources, fueling tensions not only between the refugees and Vienna's Jews but with the broader populace as well. The previous summer, when Austria's forces, buttressed with German divisions, had retaken Galicia, further tension arose as it became increasingly apparent that the refugees had little desire to return home. Since many were petty traders, they fell into black market dealings. Many more, unemployed, would be seen standing on street corners, jamming libraries or the coffee houses in the Leopoldstadt. The relief efforts continued, with soup kitchens, subsidies, schools and care for expectant mothers, but not without deep misgivings on the part of Vienna's indigenous Jews. After all, they said, Vienna could hardly feed itself; to continue feeding all these extra people would only encourage them to stay.

A broader problem was the strain the refugees would pose after the war, when they inevitably would find themselves in competition with other minorities returning from the battlefield. Then there were the negative impressions these people fostered — the embarrassment Vienna's industrious, cosmopolitan Jews felt at seeing these primitives huddled on street corners or gawking at passers-by. Perhaps more to the point in these days of frustration and stalemate was the convenient target they made for anti-Semites. Jews were already being blamed for the war, with people sniping at the Jewish black marketeers, the Jewish bankers and the Jewish war contractors who were said to be raping the army with shoddy, overpriced goods. Even among Vienna's Jewish merchants, these village yokels had a reputation for being unreliable in business. Still, for a Jew to let down a Jew was one thing. But for him to trim a goy of his money was exceedingly bad business, especially in hard times.

Gretl saw these as legitimate concerns, but, like other leaders, she was quick to point out that they were still relatively long-range problems. Vienna could not turn out or abandon her refugees, and Gretl urged realism. Until the war was over and the country got back on its feet, these people could hardly be sent home en masse to face starvation and the very conditions that had driven them out in the first place. The community would have to dig deep and be patient.

Despite Gretl's effectiveness in pressing the case for Vienna's refugees, she was having much less success in saving that other threatened population, the men of her family. With one brother crippled and the other now dead, Gretl was engaged in a campaign to get Ludwig out of the army, or at least out of combat. Wittgenstein, however, had made it clear that he was staying put. The question was who would prevail.

Looking out the window as the train crept into Vienna, Wittgenstein could see the massive city huddled under clumps of low winter clouds. A smoky bluish gray in his memory, Vienna now seemed singed at the edges like an old photograph, everything begrimed from the cheap coal they were forced to burn, when coal was available at all. In the station, with its resounding marble ceilings, the lights flickered ominously and the marble stairs echoed with wooden-soled shoes, leather, like most other commodities, being increasingly unobtainable. By the men's room, a pudgy man with a soiled suit darted out from a vestibule. Sir, he hissed. Do you have any cocoa, spirits or other foodstuffs you might like to sell or trade? The man opened a valise crammed with cans and packages. Look. I have some lovely bacon and tinned milk. Choice tobacco? Silk for your girl? Wittgenstein veered away in disgust but was almost immediately accosted by another man pouring out a sad tale, then by a mother pointing to her five railish children. Outside the station, the walks were covered by grimy snow, with only a few tired old men and peasant women to stir it around with brooms and shovels. Here there was no relief, either. No sooner had he fought his way through another gauntlet of black marketeers than he faced a mass of beggars, many hobbling veterans in uniforms with pinned-up legs or sleeves, calling, Sergeant!

Some help for a comrade, sir, a father and a veteran of Lwów . . .

There were no cabs, and the trams ran only infrequently, so he walked home through the dirty slush, amazed, through the dull November sunshine, to see whole trees and houses that had not been gutted. Still, there was an oppressiveness about the city, the shabby dearth and airlessness of a place down on its luck and now too pooped to even keep up appearances. Gretl and Mining's letters were filled with tales of incompetence and corruption, of the endless indignities required just to secure the bare essentials of life. The swans and ducks in the Prater were long since caught and cooked, and those few citizens who still could feed a dog or a cat kept their pets inside. On Sundays, even the relatively well off could be seen lugging around sacks filled with barterables, spending their days setting up tawdry deals for a tough chicken or a bag of mushy onions. The censored news was as inflated as the money. In their desperation, even the most cynical were hungry for miracles, seriously entertaining rumors of trains of food, a secret "bread peace," or an apocryphal scientist who had discovered how to extract starch from nettles.

The rococo angels at the gate of the Palais Wittgenstein were dirty as pigeons. The big house was a ship cut adrift, with no gardener, chauffeur, or footman, no one to scour the stone or reputty the rattling window. The shrubs, once squared so exactingly, had gone wild, and to the side of the house, the faded gazebo lay smashed like a basket under a bough that had fallen during a summer storm. The only sign of life was the black bunting over the door.

The ordinarily reserved Stolz, now the only man in the house, was beside himself when he saw who it was. Flustered, the old servant shook Wittgenstein's hand, then began weeping, dabbing his eyes with a folded handkerchief. Stolz was especially distraught to see his soaking boots. Did you walk all this way, sir? Oh, I wish you had telephoned, I gladly would have fetched you. I'm learning to drive, you know. I haven't been out alone yet, but I'm sure I could navigate the thing in a pinch.

Within a minute Stolz had brought him a snifter of brandy and dispatched Marta, the kitchen girl, to find Mining while he helped Wittgenstein off with his boots. Once he had unbuttoned his gaiters and peeled off his socks, old Stolz looked up mournfully, shamed to see these frozen feet that looked like blocks of lard.

Marta took his wet things. Stolz hurried for bandages. Everyone, it seemed, wanted to do something for him, but nobody knew what to do with him, least of all Mining. Groggy from incessant napping, her way of weathering depression, she lurched down the red-carpeted stairs and threw her flabby arms around his neck. He could see she had lost weight. The skin of her face was sagging, and her hair was flattened to one side. He couldn't stand her overheated misery, her instinct to hibernate like a bear to avoid the want and hunger of this interminable winter. Sobbing and clutching, Mining looked into his eyes, begging some response from him.

I know, he said wearily. I *know* . . .

But she only kept sobbing. Staring into his sister's hot, red face, Wittgenstein felt helpless and panicky. Mining wanted some kind of catharsis, but he was emotionally truncated, numb as a stump. How could he open up to her — to anyone — when he knew he would be shortly returning to the front? If he let himself go, he was afraid he might never stop.

Please, he said, gently prising himself from her grip. Leave me a minute.

Frowning, she said, of all things, Ludi, you're too calm.

I'm not too calm, he protested. I'm just exhausted. I've hardly slept in three days.

Hardly had he succeeded in soothing her than he had his next hurdle — his mother. This, he knew, would be another shock. Ever since Karl Wittgenstein's death, Frau Wittgenstein had been declining, but this last year, with Paul's amputation and her other sons away, the decline was even more rapid, the gray hair going stone white and the face sagging. It was hardest on Mining, the perennial nurse, because the old woman was so unpredictable, weathering a string of bad days, followed by a few better ones before the next bad turn. Stumbling and depressed, cranky and forgetful, then weepy, Frau Wittgenstein was increasingly prey to incapacitating migraines and indigestion, to phantom back pains and now worsening cataracts that encased the world in a cloudy sheath, indistinct and incomprehensible but no less pressing. Because of her failing eyesight, she had insisted on giving up her cavernous room in favor of a closet-size maid's room, where she now sat with her old woman's clutter, her heavy carved furniture deployed around her half like a family, half like a barricade. All day long she would sit wringing her handkerchief while Mining and several maids tried to divert her from the war news, which even censoring could not improve.

Mining thought their mother would find it less upsetting if she saw Wittgenstein out of uniform, so he changed into a sweater and trousers, then followed his sister into the little room. He smelled the old woman before he saw her, a mixture of camphor, cologne and the stealthy, slow sweat of aging, feminine grief. Mining had warned him that she might look groggy because of the sedatives the doctor had prescribed, but even that wasn't preparation enough. She had worsened considerably in six months, and even then he couldn't get over it, to see this most composed and pristine of women now unkempt and phlegmatic, hardly moving when he entered, as if her mind needed time to adjust. The swollen feet on the settee and the gaping look. Wringing the now omnipresent handkerchief as he leaned down to her, saying:

Mother, I'm back. I'm here. I came as soon as I could.

Oh, my boy . . . my poor, poor boy . . .

In her former life, she had been comfortable only with a short, curt hug, but now she clutched him, emitting a feline moan so low as to be almost beyond the conscious frequency. And then before he could disengage himself, her heavy arm caught him round the back, slapping him such that he felt he was being burped.

I'm so sorry, Mamma, he said. And then to his surprise, a bubble like a hiccup broke in his throat and he was weeping, feeling somehow responsible for his brother's death, as if he bore the same disease. But this sudden surge of emotion from him rattled the old woman; it was not her son. Eyeing him in shock, she asked almost scornfully, Where is your uniform? — as if this accounted for his unsoldierlike weeping.

I've been wearing it for days, the son explained. I took it off.

The old woman paid no attention to this. Then you must be hungry, she said plausibly, as if by posing the standard questions she would find the pegs of what had fit formerly.

No, he replied. I'm not hungry.

But she, ignoring him, turned to Mining and asked, suddenly overwrought, I take it they're preparing something special for Ludi? Then, assured that they were, she reached for the next peg, asking groggily, Have you called Gretl to tell her Ludi's home? And Paul — where is Paul?

For the better part of an hour until Gretl arrived, they went on like this, with Wittgenstein and Mining answering their mother's questions and ingeniously raising others so as to avoid the real subject at hand, which brooded about them like the muddy photographs that surrounded the old woman. Encased in their round frames, these portraits reminded him of a clutch of dusty old clocks. Here were Hans and Rudolf, then her husband, and now a tinted portrait of Kurt looking incongruously dashing in his uniform. Four clocks, all broken or stopped, and all of them telling different times, different stories. Wittgenstein just hoped the army stuck to *its* story.

·

As usual, Gretl, in her own oblique way, got closer to the heart of the matter. Toward dinnertime, she arrived in a long black motorcar driven by a young bearded Jew in a leather cap. For Gretl, wartime manners were now the order of the day: newly egalitarian, she let herself out of the car and then bent in the window, instructing the driver. He was a handsome young man, as dark as a Gypsy, and as bold. Instinctively, Wittgenstein hated the impudent way the young Jew addressed his sister, and even more the way she tolerated it, sarcastic but faintly titillated, what with Rolf — now Major Stonborough — off in Poland somewhere.

Lost in the gigantic leather bolsters of the back seat, meanwhile, was a boy of about eight in an oversize coat, wearing earlocks and a yarmulke. Wittgenstein knew well that feral look in his eyes; in Galicia, he had seen hundreds like him, crawling over the army garbage dumps, begging, filching coal, stripping corpses. The boy was ready to bolt, one hand on the door handle, the other on the arm of his little sister, who was clutching a quilted sewing box that Gretl must have given her.

Gretl immediately sensed her brother's aloofness as the long car shot off, winding erratically around the circular drive and narrowly missing the gateposts. He wasn't going to say a word, but Gretl had to have it out in the open, insistently asking, So how do you like my new chauffeur, Abba? He's from Warsaw, really extraordinarily bright — a Yeshiva boy before he studied at the university. He speaks four or five languages and does all my translating for me. A Zionist, of course. He lied to me when he said he knew how to drive, but he's improving.

Knowing this would irritate him, Gretl made a wry face, then brightened, saying, But you look good — well, pretty good, hmmm? I'll never get over you without your hair.

Gretl gave him an impulsive hug, then continued talking, probing through the nervous patter. She, too, had lost weight and was, for her, dressed drably in a black woolen coat, dark green skirt and flat shoes. A beret was pulled over the tops of her ears, and in the tufts of dark hair that hung out, Wittgenstein saw, for the first time, flecks of gray. Gretl explained:

I only dress like this when I'm visiting my refugees — I could hardly come in a ball gown. Don't worry, though. When I shake the rich for money, I dress very prewar, but no jewels. Oh, no, it's dangerous wearing them — so many thieves now. And it breeds bad feelings, so many have had to sell them, you know.

Automatic talk this was, the chatter of exhaustion. Her eyes were dark and circled, and as she walked beside him now, kneading his arm, he could feel an edge of anxiety.

So how are you? she asked. You're all right?

I'm all right.

Good, said Gretl, not sounding at all sure. They were heading toward the house, when she suddenly stopped with a stunned look, then asked: Tell me — do you know how to react to Kurt? I certainly don't. I mean, he was so queer you don't know what to feel. I hate to say it, but for me, he didn't matter — he barely *existed.* But you know, I've had the most incredible feeling that — that it's not his death at all but — I don't know. She looked around, her eyes widening to remember, then said, So you'll be here a week? *Two* weeks?

Six days.

But you'll rest, she said solicitously. And Paul shall be here, and Mining. Poor Mining — Mother has been so difficult, especially since the news. I know she's displeased with me, but I can't hide my feelings — you know how I hate this funerary business. I'm so pressed, I've been terribly busy lately, but for you of course I will make time. But only *six days* you have? That's all the time they could give you? Six days, for a death in the family?

Well, he said, it's not set down on schedules, so much for this, so much for that. It depends on staff levels, one's commanding officer.

But this was the wrong tone. Gretl immediately bridled at his stupid military superciliousness, not to mention his complacency. The idea that *he,* as a Wittgenstein, should subject himself to the whims of the state!

But surely you can get a few more days, she insisted. Then, pushily, Oh, come now. Sure you can.

But I can't, I really can't. He was getting annoyed. You don't understand.

Oh, I know. A civilian.

It's just a different world. Not everything is negotiable.

No, she agreed. For you nothing is negotiable, is it.

She was not one to cry, but then she burst into tears — furious with herself, as if she had spilled something down her dress front. And again for him there was that truncated feeling, a sense of profound emotional clumsiness, as if he were a giant trying to sip from a teacup. Smoothing his sister's round shoulders, he looked at his father's sprawling house and then realized that their world and past, their gentle speech and culture, values and manners — these were anachronisms that were now as worthless, in the world's hostile eyes, as the sagging imperial currency. Ancient world, he thought, your scruples are misunderstandings, and your sacred cows give not milk but thin tears. Wittgenstein saw then what Gretl had been saying between the lines. What she mourned was not Kurt but the slow passing of a family and a culture. These *shtetl* Jews were the first refugees, but by no means the last. If anything, Wittgenstein was amazed, in the aftershocks, to find their fussy little music box world even standing.

Still, he had his own illusions, the memories that soldiers carry around like grubby little photos in billfolds, believing that those at home are as warm and secure for their sacrifices as they themselves are insecure and vulnerable. For Wittgenstein, one such myth was his father's dinner table, which, in his memory, provisioned itself from its own former sumptuousness, serving up dreams, course upon course.

And so, at dinner that first night home, he was in for another small shock. The embroidered damask cloth, the brightly shined silver and the fearfully rare candles in the candelabra couldn't dispel it. The thick brown gravy, the powerful marinade and spices couldn't mask it, and the red wine, long buried in the cellar, couldn't purge it from the palate afterward. Horse meat, and none too savory horse meat at that. Turnips with horseradish. Cooked carrots. Wittgenstein, who could contentedly eat most anything now, looked with shame at his sisters and laid his fork on the side of the plate. The sight of his mother doggedly trying to chew stringy horse meat was almost more than he could bear.

Kurt posed another problem of memory.

What was there to remember? The way Kurt could sit for hours smoking and drinking cup after cup of coffee while reading three newspapers? His rare and unmemorable statements about politics and opera? The Pekingese dog he loved or the young French chef on whose cooking he grew fat before the war?

Indolent and unpatriotic as Kurt was, it was miraculous that he enlisted in the first place. Equally surprising was the fact that at first Kurt seemed to like it, his commission being the first thing in life ever to seriously engage his interest.

Being sent to the front forcibly got Kurt's attention. The last time Wittgenstein had seen him, eight months before, Kurt's natural vacancy had had a different cast to it — Wittgenstein knew the look. Kurt had acquired the habit of morbidly wringing his hands and in conversation would fall into long, vacant pauses in which he sat nervously flipping his foot. The army had also given him a taste for brandy, which he sipped throughout the day, sieving just enough through his gills to remain agreeably submerged.

Even then Kurt didn't say much, but Wittgenstein did recall one afternoon when the foot had suddenly stopped flipping. Wittgenstein was reading. Facing around, Kurt said:

You know, this war is getting rather out of hand. Kurt sat shaking his head. Several months ago, we had a boy shoot his captain. Oh, it was gross hypocrisy for us to stand the boy up and have him shot. Actually, nobody blamed him a bit — the man he killed should have been court-martialed for dereliction.

Kurt clapped his hands together, then wrung them between his knees. I mean, he resumed after a long pause. I have no illusions about myself. I'll be the first to admit that I shouldn't be leading men — no, no, it's true. He drew a sharp breath. But at least I can truthfully say that I *care* about them. That alone makes me more fit than most.

Kurt trailed off again, then lit up with a jerk. Oh, but here's the corker. I found myself feeling vaguely *proud* because I didn't think my men would shoot me in the back. That's it. Proud. Isn't that the end — that morale should sink to that?

Thinking of this as he lay in bed his first night home, Wittgenstein realized that this was probably the most intimate conversation he'd ever had with his brother. What he could not get over was the idea that even the torpid Kurt could be driven to suicide. How? Was it the shame of being deserted? Fear of capture? Or was it, rather, something in Kurt's nature — in his very blood?

But there was no way to know this. There was no way to know anything. Wittgenstein thought of his father's expression for Kurt. A mute shrug. A hapless pass of the hand.

A lost brother was one thing, but to behold one's last remaining brother was another. Thrown together at home, Wittgenstein and Paul felt like a nearly extinct species — a pair of dodos who sense that their best chance for survival is to remain apart.

It was particularly difficult for Wittgenstein to be whole while his brother was not. Between them Paul's missing arm loomed like a third person. It was not a question of ignoring the loss, or of appearing natural about it. Paul wasn't about to let the missing arm go unnoticed; for him, the empty sleeve was an obsession. This injury would not stop him, he said. Why, to hear him, it was as if the arm had been a nuisance — an impediment to his true calling as an artist.

You watch, Paul challenged. In two years I'll be performing in concert halls, and not as a freak, either. In fact, I am in the process of commissioning piano pieces for the left hand. I have approached Strauss and also plan to contact Ravel.

Wittgenstein must have looked askance, because Paul then insisted on demonstrating his new one-handed piano technique.

You see, explained Paul with a frown as the lone hand began to yawn and stretch itself. I realized that I could play by reconstructing in my mind the playing of the right hand — I mean the movement of every muscle and fiber — while playing twice as fast with the left. Close your eyes and I'll show you. I swear you'll hear the right hand playing.

At that, the clenched hand pounced down twice, resoundingly, then raced fluently up and down the keyboard, the loose sleeve flapping. Wittgenstein couldn't keep his eyes closed: Paul's lightning-fast scales, his frenetic arpeggios and thundering chords were making him seasick. In his zeal, Paul never noticed that his brother had opened his eyes. This was more than brute determination; it was a feat of levitation, a virtuoso display of the raging single-mindedness over loss and past. One hand could play like two. Three sons could pull like five, and two even as well as three. After several minutes, Paul was sweating, and Wittgenstein was praying that he would stop. Paul's jaw bulged, his chin jutted out and the veins stood out on his forehead as the hand stammered down and down, bludgeoning the keys, then leaping back up the scale like a salmon plunging upstream. Wittgenstein heard the second hand. In that torrent of notes, Wittgenstein heard hands dead and living. Heard his father, too — the whole sorry orchestra.

On his third day home Wittgenstein's mother called him into her room and said with a glimpse of her former forcefulness, I must know something, and I want you to tell me the truth.

His heart stopped. He thought she was going to say she knew about Kurt's suicide. But instead the old woman asked, I must know what they do about burying the dead after a battle. Surely, they can't bury each man separately.

Wittgenstein sat down beside her and gently explained:

Often they bury the dead in what the Russians call a *brothers' grave*. All the dead — Russian and Austrian — are buried side by side in a large trench. It's not as heartless as it sounds — it's really rather fitting. Not long ago, during a truce, a group of Russians led by an Orthodox priest came down from their trenches and prayed with us while we buried several hundred from both sides. There's no hatred between our armies. The Russians are generally more religious than our men, and they certainly treat prisoners more humanely than the Germans. But as I was saying, we were all standing together, praying and singing. Well, afterward, there was a Russian, an older man, who saw my Bible and said, Here, you must take this. It was a German edition of Tolstoy's *Gospels*. He was a lieutenant, a refined man with a wife and daughter — a schoolteacher, I think. He spoke quite passable German. He told me he had found the book on a dead German and urged me to read it. I suppose we talked for a good twenty minutes before officers from both sides ordered everybody back. Well, we shook hands and that was it. An hour later we were shooting again. Ever since, I've carried that book with me. I'll show it to you later if you like.

Wittgenstein thought this story would comfort his mother, but it didn't. Instead, she covered her mouth with her hankie and started to cry.

I feel so angry, she said. Three boys I've lost — *three!* But you know what I can't get over? None of my boys has ever died at home. They've all gone away and died, and other people have always found them. And no matter what the army says, I'll never know for sure if the man they found is even my Kurt.

Between Wittgenstein and Gretl, meanwhile, there remained the issue of whether he would seek a discharge.

Everyone in the family, including Paul, agreed it was an honorable course, and one in the family's best interest. Certainly, Wittgenstein had done his part in the war — more than his part, they felt, considering that the army had rejected him on his first physical.

It was his rupture that flunked him, but Wittgenstein didn't let that stop him: he had surgery and then had a second physical, this one successful. But even after he had been trained and sent on his first assignment, it took several months and many petitions before he was finally sent to the front. In fact, the army seemed so peculiarly reluctant to send him that he accused Gretl, despite her emphatic denials, of political meddling.

This time, though, Gretl made no secret of her efforts to get him discharged. Still, she hated this perennial role of intriguer, exhorter and advocate; she was tired of always having to intercede with him on the family's behalf. She knew the pressure he was under. She didn't want to spoil these few days he had at home, and she went out of her way, as he did, to avoid unpleasantry.

But he, in the meantime, had another idea — a patriotic idea, which for Austria, if not for her enemies, even verged on the philanthropic. Wittgenstein had already anonymously donated money to artists like Rilke and Trakl, but now he wanted to make another anonymous and far more sizable donation for the development of a new trench mortar.

With this mission in mind, Wittgenstein donned a freshly cleaned and brushed uniform one morning and went to see Herr Brundolf, guardian of the family trust, about disbursing the necessary funds. Herr Brundolf was delighted to see in one piece this young man he had known since a boy, and he was quick to extend his condolences for the family's recent loss. Then, seeing Wittgenstein's impatient single-mindedness — so much like his father's — he said, Well, then, what do you wish to discuss today?

And so, while Herr Brundolf listened, the young sergeant, showing qualities that would have made him formidable in any boardroom, explained in the most serious and lucid detail the urgent tactical need for a trench mortar built to specifications he had developed in accordance with his own careful field observations. The former engineer had come amply prepared, with extensive scale drawings of both the mortar and the 75-millimeter shells it would fire — twenty to twenty-five high-explosive shrapnel shells per minute, to be exact, all delivered with devastating accuracy at ranges of up to three thousand meters. Nothing had been left to chance. It would, he said, save lives and help win battles, and it would be easier to erect, fire, maintain and transport.

Well, then, said the sergeant, concluding this five-minute précis. I figure the army will need at least one million kronen, give or take a hundred thousand. With his gray woolen cap sitting on his squared knees, the sergeant faced the old solicitor, waiting, no doubt, for the man to prepare the necessary papers and send him on his way.

Herr Brundolf had risen to his position of eminence not only through his business acumen but through his ability to carefully hear out the mystifying, sometimes harebrained, but often lucrative ideas that brilliant men will have periodically. At the same time, the solicitor subscribed to the popular and, as it seemed, probable wisdom that the war could not continue much longer — that Austria, having nothing more to gain, ought to press for peace now, before her economy was ruined or she was crushed and forced to accept even more ruinous peace conditions.

Wittgenstein almost immediately sensed these defeatist sentiments in Herr Brundolf. He hated this distastefully *fiscal* attitude toward what, for him, was a war of flesh and blood and spirit. But what really incensed him was to hear Herr Brundolf explain, in the cautious, muted tones of money, that the bulk of his fortune was, in effect, untouchable.

You see, Herr Brundolf explained, the money is invested in various American bonds. Very good securities, you'll be happy to know. And invested in accordance with lengthy instructions your father — your most *prescient* father, I might add — set forth in the addendums to his will. Oh, yes, years ago, your father said there would be a war — of that he was certain. And consider: here, while many of our finest families are on the brink of ruin, your family's fortune has vastly increased.

The sergeant could not believe it. Standing up, he said, Yes, I see we've done marvelously — and all at the fatherland's expense!

When he returned home from his unsuccessful interview, Wittgenstein was even more incensed by his family's reaction to his proposal. Their attitude was a scandal! Cynical! Unpatriotic! Gretl wouldn't hear of it.

Oh, please, she said. You were so grandiose about the money when father died. You refused to discuss it! But now, after years of ignorance about your own finances, you practically accuse us of being war profiteers.

Not profiteers, he said with leveling eyes. *Opportunists.*

She was trying not to get angry, keeping her voice faintly musical, farcical. Oh, stop, she said, making a face. You don't know what you're talking about. The money was invested *before* the war. It's not as if we *capitalized* on the war, buying steel and pork bellies.

No, he agreed, we just capitalized on our good fortune.

And why not? she asked, growing more indignant. Thank God somebody in this country will be solvent once the war is over. And if someone has to be wealthy — Gretl paused for emphasis — well, it might as well be us! And why not? Certainly, we've used our money to better ends than most people. I *know* we can do better than squander it on mortars.

And spend it on what? he retorted. Refugees?

Listen to you! I've spent nowhere near the sum you're asking for.

He lost his patience. That's not the point, that's not the point at all! You just lost a brother, yet you say, in effect, that our money is squandered saving the lives of soldiers but well spent on refugees. Forgetting, I might add, that soldiers — and indeed your very husband — are the ones defending you *and* your precious refugees! And defending you for what? So you can consort with this impudent little Jew who you say is so clever?

He regretted this as soon as he said it. Gretl flew right back at him.

This is outrageous! What do you mean, *consort*?

I mean the way you fawn over him. Your whole demeanor.

I don't fawn over him! Don't be an ass. What on earth are you suggesting?

I'm not suggesting *that,* he hedged, though he knew for a fact that he was. It just annoys me, that you tolerate such impudence from him. But, as you say — he is so wonderfully *clever!*

She looked at him in astonishment. He's not so terribly impudent. And, yes, he *is* clever — so what?

Wittgenstein leapt on this. Oh, of course! All Jews are clever! All Jews have poignant stories. As for those of us on the front — well, we can all go to hell as far as you're concerned. We're not so *picturesque.*

Oh, of course! she said, her voice beginning to squeak. And as for your family — we can all go to hell, too. But it's so very selfless to get yourself killed, isn't it? In the army, you can live out your little Tolstoyan fantasy of the common man, shooting those God-fearing pogrom-loving peasants whom you so adore. So Christian! Such a lover of the common man to pillory me for having an unspeakable little Jew for a driver! Worried you might be a bit of a Jew yourself, is it?

No, not worried, he said, moving toward her in a bottled rage. What I'm speaking about is *seeing clearly.*

Good! Gretl did her best to return his stare, trembling slightly as she said, Then listen to me. No more quarreling or evasions. Yes, you know — you know what I'm talking about.

He knew, and he was moving away. No longer was he the angry patriot. He was the defeatist now, sick to his heart as Gretl pressed in, saying, Just answer me, then. Why can't you leave the army? You've fought honorably. We've paid our share — more than our share. Why can't you leave?

Because I can't.

But you *can*! You can be discharged, I've checked. So why? Mother won't ask, but I can tell you, it will kill her if anything happens to you. So why? Explain it to me.

Gretl was using on him the same arguments he had used on Pinsent, but to no avail. He was trapped. Ripping back and forth across the rug, he said, I don't care what the army says. The army has nothing to do with it. *I* can't. Morally I can't. And not because I'm a diehard. I'm obligated to my men.

Now she was scathing. Oh, don't be an ass! And it's not just patriotism or loyalty, so stop it! Your first obligation is to your family.

Then you don't understand, he protested. You don't understand at all. But beneath his vehemence, he saw that he didn't understand it either — not at all.

·

At home there had been one more thing that sharpened this mounting sense of moral confusion and ambiguity. It was a letter from Pinsent.

This was the second letter he'd received from Pinsent, and again it was sent through Keynes. Military mail, two thin sheets permissible, mangled by the censor's hasty black pen. Not much, but still he knew he was damned lucky to get it. The problem, though, was what to do with it. With each reading the letter changed. Confounding analysis or reduction, cunningly cheating expectations, it finally crumbled to ashes, sucked dry with repeated readings. No way to reconstruct the living from words or traces. No way to tell if Pinsent was not angry or distant, not changed or lost to him in some fundamental way. The letter said:

Dear Luddy,

My platoon has just been pulled back to the reserves after ▓▓ on the line, so I figured I'd better write you ▓▓▓▓▓▓▓▓▓▓▓▓▓▓▓▓▓▓▓▓▓▓▓

▓▓▓▓▓▓▓▓▓▓▓▓▓▓

Diarrhea & duckboards, is all this is; we need life vests, so many of the lads drown when hit or ▓▓▓▓▓▓▓▓▓▓▓▓▓▓▓▓▓▓▓▓ Just as well I'm deaf in my left ear; if I weren't I'd have lost my ▓▓▓▓▓▓

▓▓▓▓ In ▓▓▓▓▓ not long after ▓▓▓ a big shell exploded not ten metres away — killed the whole crew & left me half buried ▓▓▓▓▓▓▓▓▓▓▓▓▓▓▓▓▓▓rs. dug me out with several old corpses that resembled negroes. Another twenty minutes before I fully came around — just in time for the counterattack & then another barrage ▓▓▓▓▓▓▓▓▓▓▓ it's nasty th ▓▓▓▓▓ gan ▓▓▓▓ ▓▓▓▓ o ▓▓▓▓ They call this place the Boneyard.

I'm feeling real low just now. The newer blokes rub me for luck — I'm positively legendary, but I'm feeling used up, Luddy. Dave Arlen, my best pal, gone, Dighty, Bill Bollins, Colin, Alf — all the old bunch and the ▓▓▓▓▓9th ▓▓▓ ▓▓▓▓▓ crock ▓▓▓▓▓▓▓▓ asl ▓▓▓▓ ▓▓ umped. ▓▓ ▓▓▓▓▓ ongs that now bring tears to my eyes.

I'm well liked, believe it or not; the new ones follow me like little ducks, & I teach them how to discern incomings from outgoings, high explosive from shrapnel. "Listen up duckies," I say, "so little ducks don't be dead ducks." "—— off," they say & hit it. "Davie Ducks" or "Dave Love" they call me, what with the endless barrage of letters from Mother.

I wonder what you'd think of me now, whether you'd approve. *Farther*

My God From Thee ought to be our song here. I curse constantly, I smoke, ✕🐄
& I live, as we all do, for my daily tot of His Majesty's rum. Dave Love even
got rid of his tiresome virginity, last of his baby teeth; I had probable 42nds
with a Belgian tart who I think was saying a rosary as I climbed off & the
next lad stuffed his money in the box. Outside, the choristers christened me ✕⠇
with ale.

Funny, but it reminds me of the photograph I took of you before we left
Norway. As you predicted, it didn't develop — the whole roll was ruined —
but then maybe we were both too unapparent then, our features not quite
fixed. But Lord, there'd be pictures now. I just wonder how we'd like them.

Running out of space, but before I close, I'd like to comment on your point
about my "pessimism." Please don't be hurt if I say I think your attitude
carries with it a certain unconscious hypocrisy. It reminds me of that day at
Mother's, when the mayflies hatched out of the water; & how, as that snow
fell over you, you said how very beautiful it was, to see them falling to necessity, serving fate, etc. Oh, you *saw* something that day, Luddy, I've no
question about that; only I think you read it wrong when you called it "beautiful." In your last letter, you say we dare not question reality; that all life is
on the same level, the elephant or wasp, while we can only bend to it. I agree,
so far as it goes. But what you *really* mean, I feel, is that it is good for *you*
to serve it. If *I* surrender to fate or feel that my luck is running thin, then I
have given up; I'm somehow contrary to the purpose of life — contrary to
your idea of me, anyhow.

I feel somehow I'm speaking into an empty tube, with you at the end of
the earth. It's hard when one feels like a coin, sensing that one can fall either
way & suspicious that both may be losers. I wish I could say this better, so
you wouldn't think I was merely being critical or trying for any kind of effect,
esp. when talking, as we both know, only mucks it up.

Like you, Luddy, I do hope we both get lucky. I very much would like to
see Norway & most of all you again. I'd like to live — honest to God I
would — & yes I'd like to do something worthwhile with my life. But this
begs the real question, if life will have me.

Your loving friend,
David

Easter

THE DOCTORS at the field hospital were stumped: though they were quickly able to rule out typhoid as the root of the big Croat's paralysis, they otherwise didn't know what to make of his symptoms. On the other hand, the doctors knew, from long experience, that they did not want to risk alarming the troops with fears of some unknown malady. With typical candor, they instead sent word that it was an endocrinic flare-up, treatable and absolutely noncontagious — nothing at all to be concerned about.

Unfortunately, by the time the good news filtered back to the field, two more men in Wittgenstein's platoon, as well as four men in another, had been stricken with similar symptoms, rekindling fears of an epidemic. Ensconced in the command dugout, busily reviewing new deployment plans, the stalwart Lieutenant Stize was quick to pooh-pooh this epidemic rubbish, shrewdly noting that all the afflicted were "territorials" who, as anyone knew, were prone to hysterical disorders. Yet when Wittgenstein suggested that an appearance by the lieutenant might calm the men, Stize flatly refused:

That's your job, Sergeant. I'm not here to wet nurse this bunch. As you can see, I'm busy.

In fact, Stize was only repeating wisdom gleaned from the officers' mess, that indestructible café-bunker where he and his cohorts were now spending more time than ever. In the meantime, it hardly escaped the attention of malcontents like Grundhardt that the officers were staying far away from what they knew to be a contagious disease spread by bad water (the officers were said to have "special water"), rats, corpses or, in yet another variation, a mosquito found only in the pestilential Pripet marshes. By the next day, when twenty-two more were stricken, panic set in as rumors circulated that half of the sick men had already died from the disease, which was now called typhus, diphtheria, scarlet fever, sleeping sickness and even plague.

At the same time, the Russians were stepping up their own campaign of nerves. Airplanes buzzed over the Austrian trenches, scattering leaflets printed in five languages urging Czechs and other nationals to desert the Hapsburg tyrants, citing devastating fuel, food and ammunition shortages that would soon bring crushing defeat. In good times, such propaganda was scorned or ignored, but under the circumstances it fueled even wilder rumors that the Russians, having poisoned their water and food, were now about to unleash a new and more deadly form of chemical gas.

Wittgenstein felt the rumor campaign mounting against him as well. Coming around a traverse that morning, he had found a group of men standing in simple-minded merriment before a crude chalk drawing of a bug-eyed creature named *Shitgenstein* swallowing the shaft of an enormous cock labeled *Ernst*.

It was as if someone had struck him over the head. Without even thinking, Wittgenstein swiped up a handful of mud and blotted out the drawing. But then as he looked around at his men, he realized that this would only be taken as an embarrassed admission of guilt. Yet wasn't he guilty? It made no difference that he was innocent of this particular charge. The picture expressed a pictorial *possibility*. It was the potent latency of wish, a dreaded connectedness.

Damn it, he told himself, feeling himself dying before them. *Think!* Drive them back.

But seeing the men staring at him, judges now, he realized that here, in the kangaroo court of the trenches, guilt was its own truth. Lies bind reality as much as truth does. Men believed they were sick, therefore they were sick; with their own eyes they saw a picture that pleased them, hence it was true. The picture, open in form, offered itself equally to truth and falsity. The picture was true because he feared it.

How could he have been such a fool? he wondered dizzily. Clearly, they had known his proclivities all along. Steeling himself, he ordered the men off. He was all atremble then, thoroughly smearing it out with mud, when Ernst found him. Evidently Ernst had discovered another drawing, because he looked ready to throttle someone — possibly him, Wittgenstein thought.

Packing his fists, Ernst said, God damn it, Wittgenstein, I've had it! I'm going to teach that little son of a bitch a lesson.

No! Wittgenstein caught him by the arm. Damn it, Ernst, you thrash him and you'll only be dignifying this muck. It may not even be Grundhardt.

Ernst slammed his fist into the sandbags. So what do we do, huh? Let him make bloody fools of us? Christ, he said, raging off. You're as bad as Stize in my book.

More leaflets fell. And then, to give added weight to their warnings, the Russians pounded them for over four hours with their heaviest artillery in a barrage so well orchestrated that the senior staff wondered if the batteries were really Russian. Something was amiss. Ever since their long retreat the previous summer, the Russians were reported to be suffering from a chronic shortage of shells: they hadn't dared use harassing tactics like these. But instead of responding with a galloping wall of fire, the Austrian return barrage was so tentative and thin that the troops became even more disheartened, feeling the enemy leaflets spoke the truth.

Blind as a charging rhinoceros, the Austrian army was incapable of quickly switching tactics to confront battlefield exigencies. The Austrian senior staff had still less patience for, or interest in, frivolous civilian niceties, such as timing. And so, even as the dead and wounded were being carted off after the bombardment — at a time when the epidemic was for the moment forgotten and the troops were most concerned with shoring up their broken defenses — they were instead confronted with medical officers, who arrived with jars of big blue placebos that they promised would stop this "flu."

Stize and most of the other officers were not about to tarnish their prestige (or unnecessarily expose themselves) by being present when these jawbreakers were distributed. That task instead fell on platoon leaders like Wittgenstein. The men were understandably skeptical as he and Ernst started passing out the pills. Still, their native ignorance and herd fear might have led them to trust the efficacy of this sugar medicine had not Grundhardt spat his pill in the mud and squalled, These are worthless!

Standing down the trench, Wittgenstein pointed at him and said, Pick it up! And then, as if obeying his order, Ernst snatched up the muddy pill and rammed it down Grundhardt's throat.

Spit it out! Ernst sneered, cocking back his fist. Go on, you slimy little fucker. I dare you!

Wittgenstein was too late to stop him. But even then Grundhardt managed to turn the situation to his advantage, gagging and coughing so fiercely that the men felt Wittgenstein and Ernst were lashing back — trying to poison all of them.

That was it for Wittgenstein. He immediately went to Stize and insisted that Grundhardt be jailed for inciting unrest. Stize, then being shaved by Krull, wouldn't hear it.

How can you bother me with this nonsense? he asked, blowing a wisp of lather from his upper lip. Here we have an epidemic on our hands, the Russians are poised to attack, and you bother me with *this*? I don't care what he spit out. I don't even blame him. Now go! I have work to do.

Wittgenstein did not know what he was going to do when he emerged
from Stize's dugout. Everyone knew he had gone to Stize about Grundhardt, and when he came back empty-handed, his authority would be a
joke, if it wasn't a joke already. Grundhardt had won. He had even succeeded in driving a wedge between him and Ernst. And now here was
Grundhardt. Wittgenstein had ordered him to wait by the latrine, fearing
that Ernst might kill him. He felt a terrific sense of anxiety when he saw
the little pimp down the trench, smiling that malignant smile. Grundhardt was openly flouting him now, talking to two men when Wittgenstein had ordered him to stand at attention and not to speak to anyone.
Wittgenstein hardly knew what he was doing. He must have said something to the two men because they parted from his vision like sheaves of
wheat, and suddenly he found himself alone with Grundhardt. Wittgenstein was walking behind him, enraged now, with an ungodly clapping
in his ears. And then Grundhardt turned to him with that nasty smile.
Scratching his crotch insinuatingly, he then casually raised his middle
finger to scratch his long nose — just, it seemed, so Wittgenstein could
see the chalk under his nails. Wittgenstein wasn't made of iron. He
snapped then — snapped so suddenly that he fairly overwhelmed himself
as he pounced on Grundhardt, his thumbs locked on his windpipe as he
said in a voice that issued deep from the pit of his stomach, *So you think
you can outsmart me? Think so!*

Struggling up with blood-engorged tongue, gurgling with rage, Grundhardt clawed at his hands as Wittgenstein hauled him up by the neck,
then slammed his head down so violently that the black mud spattered
up into his eyes. No telling what stopped Wittgenstein from killing
Grundhardt. Certainly it was not a matter of conscious choice or some
inner sense of decency. Wittgenstein simply felt a stab of revulsion and
yanked him up by the collar. Coughing and gasping, Grundhardt spat
and jerked away, wiping his purple face with a mud-drenched sleeve.
Trembling, Wittgenstein felt utterly crazed, like an animal facing a natural predator, a hamstringing wolf who had now cut him from the fold.
Kill him, said a stricken voice. *Kill him while you still can.* But over this
came the quailing instinct of civilization, the astounding notion that even
now this matter could somehow be negotiated, tidied, explained. But
here Grundhardt was eons ahead of him; Grundhardt knew they had
long passed that primal meridian. With his gray wolf eyes burning
through the bitter black mud, Grundhardt scraped a long nail under his
throat, a pig slit, slow and deep. Then, trembling like a berserker, he bit
his thumb so hard that it cracked as he growled, *I'll kill you for this, you*

cocksucker — you kike. I swear to God I will. And then in a little wind he was gone, slipping like a greased turd down the trench.

It wasn't like Ernst to apologize. But he must have been sorry for his outburst, or perhaps just lonely, because he came to Wittgenstein a few minutes later and said, Want to hear our latest intelligence? Ernst laughed that crazy crow of his, then said, The Russians will attack by tonight or tomorrow because their deserters say they were issued clean underwear yesterday. They swear it's a sure sign. It's the only time they get fresh skivvies. Just before a big battle.

Wittgenstein stared at him in disbelief, then burst into laughter. The situation was so black and hopeless that they needed a good joke. There'd been another artillery duel, and they'd just lost a man whose life had splashed away while they struggled to lash off his shattered legs with lengths of telephone cord.

Still laughing, Ernst said, Honest to God. That's what intelligence says. I heard it from some corporal down the way.

Trying to keep the comic momentum going, Wittgenstein said, Well, that reverses what Napoleon said. But then, looking at Ernst, Wittgenstein realized with embarrassment that Ernst, of course, would not know *what* Napoleon had said. Quickly he added, About an army fighting on its belly, I mean.

Still not sure what he meant, Ernst nodded sagely, saying, Well, we shoot from our bellies, all right.

Wittgenstein looked at him with chagrin and said delicately, Actually, what Napoleon was talking about, I think, was the soldier's need for *food.* Napoleon would have thought it unmanly for soldiers to shoot lying on their bellies as we do, let alone from trenches. Wittgenstein pulled himself back, realizing that he was waxing pedantic. Quickly, he added, But then Napoleon didn't have to contend with machine guns or barbed wire.

Ernst grinned crazily. Or Russians in clean underwear.

Wittgenstein clapped his hands together in delight, famished for Ernst's naturalness and good sense. But Ernst still didn't clap him on the shoulder.

The clean underwear proved a better barometer than expected, because later that afternoon the Russian bombardment began in earnest, with hundreds of artillery pieces — field howitzers, long-range heavy artillery and gigantic, high-arcing mortars — all firing at once, emptying the contents of whole freight cars with each salvo. Within an hour, the sheer volume of shells fired put to rest any lingering doubts that the Russians were short of shells. Everything the Russians had done wrong for the past two years they now did right, as carefully registered shells blew huge holes in the Austrian wire, destroyed buried telephone lines and silenced many of their biggest guns.

As night fell, the rocketing shells lit up the sky for a hundred miles. The Austrian lines were in chaos. Greasy, high-explosive smoke choked them and singed their nostrils. Whole men disintegrated in a bloody sleet, while those left alive lay dazed and helpless, bleeding profusely through their ears and noses. Violently, the atmosphere was contracting, expelling men from the womb of life, which didn't want them anyway; they couldn't even scream or catch their breath before the next explosion punched the air from their lungs. Men filled their pants with diarrhea and drove their fingers into their ears to drown the pile-driving concussions. Wittgenstein found buried men, hysterical men, fetal men and men reduced to jumbles of smoking rags and limbs. He saw bodies with their clothes blown off tumbling high into the air and crazed rats racing in circles. Even more unbelievable were the wounds. Men gnashed their own arms to dim the pain, begging to be killed. There were men so torn and riddled with shrapnel that nobody could believe they were alive, while others fell stone dead without a blemish, struck down as if by God.

Probably the men would have broken and run had they seen any reasonable chance of escape, but there was no chance. By midnight, order was breaking down badly, and the officers were checking their weapons for fear of mutiny. No stretcher bearers were available, no food had arrived or would arrive, their water was almost gone and their defenses were a shambles. Yet here when critical military communications were lost or destroyed, the rumors ran unchecked, streaking through the air like an electric current. It was as if they were all suffering the same dream. Anything was believed. Whole companies of Czechs were murdering their officers and marching over to the Russians. The Russians had a new gas that drove men berserk. Why, it was even rumored that Grundhardt was a spy — a captain in the Russian army.

The one thing certain about Grundhardt was that he had vanished. No one had seen him since the bombardment had begun, yet now everyone was talking about his daring escape, unable to imagine that he was more likely lying dead somewhere. Not Grundhardt, they said. He was too slick. Besides, they said, nobody that evil ever got killed. They came up with countless ingenious dodges that Grundhardt could have used to escape. That Gypsy son of a bitch! they said. How he had fooled them!

They seemed to feel it an honor to have been conned and stolen blind by him and suddenly saw every stupid, willful thing he had ever done as another master stroke, all part of his vast plan.

Wittgenstein let them talk — at least these wild fantasies about Grundhardt diverted them and eased their terror. Stize, meanwhile, felt vindicated in his wisdom when Wittgenstein told him about Grundhardt's disappearance.

I told you you'd soon be rid of him, Stize was saying. But then a shell came whistling over and he dove for it, his eyes wobbling in their soot-blackened sockets as he skidded down the trench on his knees and elbows. All that night Stize had been careening around, too spooked and green — and too tipsy with shots of brandy — to distinguish near shells from passing screamers. It was almost touching, the mothering way Stize hugged his crotch as the next shell shrieked down and exploded in the reserve trenches two hundred yards behind them.

Seeing he was the only one who had dived for it, Stize scrambled up as if he had merely lost his footing, then quickly added, Anyway, he's probably been blown to bits. Well, good riddance, I say. Adopting a more casual air, the lieutenant handed Wittgenstein a few lumps of gold foil, saying, Here, then. Have some chocolates.

Wittgenstein didn't know what had gotten into him. In his own inept way, Stize was suddenly trying to act the part of an officer, braving shells to periodically check on him and the other men. At this late hour, Stize was even displaying a spirit of unexpected benevolence, handing out a small fortune in chocolates that the bandy-legged Krull carried for him in a field pack. Finding a group of muddy, miserable men in a bomb scrape, Stize would steel himself into a casual grimace as the beam of his flashlight found their hostile eyes. How are we doing? he would ask. Then before anyone could answer — or not answer — he would say, Good! Well, I'll tell you, they're getting worse than they're giving, I have that on good authority. Here, he said, reaching into his goody bag. Have some chocolates! That's the stuff! You men carry on!

In his heart, he must have known this bluff talk didn't fool anyone, but it helped calm him, his chatter growing more absurd the more frightened he became. And he was more jumpy than ever now, having heard that that essential personage Prince Primkin had been ordered to evacuate at his earliest opportunity with his four young aides. Stize was trying to be a good sport about it. Shaking his head resolutely, he told Wittgenstein:

The prince very much wanted to stay but I told him he must go. Really no choice. And do you know what the prince said to me then? He said,

Carpe diem — that's our regimental motto, you know — and I said, By God, you go ahead, Rudolph. (I call him Rudolph, you know. No hanging on protocol for him.) Yes, there you go, old chap, I said. Never you mind about the old chocolate maker. *He'll* find his way home.

But Stize was not so sanguine when he returned a few minutes later. His gas mask had been stolen, and he had heard from the prince that three officers up the line had been shot by agitators.

Stize continued: He told me I'd better watch my back, and then — here Stize proudly pulled a small pearl-handled revolver from his pocket — he gave me this. Stize flicked on his flashlight so Wittgenstein could see it better. See his initials on the barrel? There's an inscription, too, from his father, the grand duke. Well, you can imagine how I felt. He even wanted to give me a card for some debts, but naturally I refused. Staring at the pistol, Stize was like a boy who likes to scare himself with stories of hobgoblins. God, he said. Only hope my hand doesn't shake if it should come to that. Should do the job up close, though, don't you think? Bloody fanatics. Heard some have to be shot three and four times before they go down. Always been excitable. Even giving speeches in school. Terrified me. Well! he said, slipping out his flask with a shiver. Enough of that. Have a drink. Go on — do you good. Never tell a soul. No? Well, then — Glowering as the brandy bit back. Surely, they'll tell us to fall back. I mean, they can't very well expect us to fight to the last man. Not with this bunch we have here. I'm sure they'll be sending up fresh reserves. Have to.

Wittgenstein couldn't get rid of him. Again and again, Stize returned that night, filled with spurious war lore, staff rumors and misinformation. First he had heard that the Russians positively would not attack because it was Sunday, then, on the contrary, that they were the most murderous on Sundays, when they were all sure to be raging drunk and wearing shirts specially blessed by the priests to ward off bullets.

Between the men and Stize, Wittgenstein hardly had a moment all night to speak to Ernst, who was silent and gloomy as dawn approached and the bombardment began to die down. It seemed as if there was something to say — something forgotten or unsaid in their leave-taking — but at bottom, he realized, there was nothing to say, nothing at all. He felt oddly humiliated by this, humiliated in the way he had felt once when his father had slapped him, snapping his words off in midstream. And now that life was breaking off, all he felt was silence, an abiding, humbling silence. Not a consoling silence: it was as cold and impersonal as fate, but at least it was real in the sense of being how things stood: an end to life's delusions.

By that time, most of the men were sleeping or in that general attitude, the living almost indistinguishable from the dead. Ernst, meanwhile, had taken some men to bring up crates of stick bombs and ammunition, and Wittgenstein was watching the Russian lines, when he heard someone yell, *Hold it, you yellow bastard!*

Turning then, he saw, illuminated by the flashes of an automatic pistol, the blood-streaked face of an officer who was firing into the darkness. Cursing, the officer slapped another clip in his pistol, cocked it, then lurched toward a dugout and flung the door open, bellowing down, Get the hell up here, you miserable cowards. The Russians are about to attack! Do you hear me, he yelled, brandishing a stick bomb. *Out!* Out right now or I'll kill you all myself!

Shots rang out. Screaming, the officer pulled the fuse ring and flung it down, bringing pandemonium. But it didn't explode.

You, Sergeant! he yelled, running over to Wittgenstein. Give me a stick bomb — *now!*

Saluting, Wittgenstein lied. I don't have one, sir.

The officer, a major, stuck a bent cigarette in his lips and struck a ghastly profile, with blood oozing down his shako cap. Then give me a light! You at least have a *match*, don't you? Looking away, the major mumbled, Goddamn idiots . . .

Sir, said Wittgenstein, who now could smell alcohol on the major's breath as he rummaged through his pockets for a match. I respectfully suggest that you seek medical attention. There's —

But the raging major stared into his eyes, bits of spittle on his lips as he flipped the cigarette up and down. Don't you think I know that, you goddamned bumpkin? I'll be damned if I'll take guff from some simple-assed son of a sausage maker like you. The major was working himself into another fit. God *damn* you! he roared, suddenly jamming the hot pistol barrel into Wittgenstein's neck. You've got five minutes to get these sorry bastards up on the line because when I come back I'll be bombing dugouts and shooting traitors, especially *Czech* traitors. One just shot Major Springer. I've been after the little bastard all night. They have a special whistle they use to signal the Russians. Ever hear it? Sounds like a partridge. You know what a *partridge* sounds like, don't you, straw foot? Still holding the pistol at Wittgenstein's throat, the major thoughtfully mumbled something to himself, then presented the bent cigarette in his slobbery dog's teeth, snarling, Now, light me up, *asshole*.

The match flared. Wittgenstein was considering grabbing the madman's pistol when the major whirled around and fired. There! There he goes! Over *there*, God damn it! Are you blind, too?

The major charged off into the darkness, cursing and firing. Then, several minutes later, Stize ran toward Wittgenstein with a muddy handprint on his face.

Did you see him? Just now! This major, some lunatic, slapped me as I was coming out of the officers' dugout. Prince Primkin was right behind me with his orderly. He was just about to leave, and the man struck him, too. Knocked him down! Just raving with the blood pouring from his face. Stize patted his pockets for a cigarette, then continued. And that's not the worst. They want us to fight to the *last* man. And the Russians are certain to attack. Did you hear? They were issued fresh underwear yesterday — underwear and *vodka,* so they're all sure to be running amuck. Prince says it's a sure sign. Apparently the wretches think they can't go to heaven in dirty underwear. And watch your back. There's this whistle the Czechs are using to warn the Russians. Goes like a cuckoo or something —

Cutting him off, Wittgenstein said impatiently, Sir, it's nearing daybreak. I think we ought to deploy the men.

Stize shook his head rapidly. Right! About to say the very same thing. Good. You do that. Reinforcements are coming. Prince says they're sure to call us back. Got to. Bloody suicide to stay here.

Wittgenstein pulled away from him wearily when Stize pulled the little pistol from his pocket and asked meekly, By the way, will your pistol cartridges fit this thing? Blasted thing's unloaded. Meant to catch the prince before he left. *No?* Stize wavered a moment, staring at the pistol, then said, Well, look here, then, I'll find some bullets and be *right* back. Good! Very good!

A cold morning breeze was blowing as Stize disappeared again. Over the Russian trenches, the first faint streaks of dawn were beginning to appear. Wittgenstein was trying to collect his thoughts when an empty tin struck him on the elbow — a warning, followed by a little edge of laughter as he turned and heard the snap of a fuse ring. He knew who it was, and turned, fatalistic, as Grundhardt flipped a stick bomb at his feet. No time to throw it away or run. Wittgenstein could hear Grundhardt cackling as he scuttled off. But the joke was on both of them, because this one didn't explode either, though for Wittgenstein it might as well have.

The mad major was perhaps not as mad as he seemed. The Russians did attack shortly after dawn, and it was only because the Austrian first lines were deployed that they even delayed that onslaught.

Some reinforcements arrived just before the attack, but they weren't in much better shape than Wittgenstein's own men, who were almost docile after a night's pounding. While the machine gunners locked and cleared their guns with a peremptory coughing, Wittgenstein and Ernst situated the men, handed out stick bombs and bandoliers of ammunition, then ordered them to load and fix bayonets. They were barely ready when the first Russian wave rushed out in a probing maneuver, covered by a thin smoke screen and a walking barrage laced with rifle fire. Stumbling over shell holes in long brown coats and tall fleece caps, most of the Russians were summarily cut down by return fire and the chugging, water-cooled machine guns that swung back and forth, dropping them in clotted heaps, some crumpling, some sitting abruptly, some blown back onto the ugly spike bayonets of those rushing behind them.

The first wave was decimated, as was the second. But those who got through managed to clear paths through the remaining wire for the third and fourth waves, who by then were whooping and cheering, impeded only by the bodies of their comrades.

The noise was deafening and it was difficult to follow targets or get more than glimpses of what was happening through the bursting shells and drifting smoke. Ernst, six or seven men down the wall from Wittgenstein, was firing and urging the men on; in the confusion, Wittgenstein never had a chance to settle accounts or say good-bye in that veiled, awkward way of men before battle. To Wittgenstein's amazement, Stize was there, too. Wittgenstein never expected him to return, yet there he was, glowering and hung over, frantically pacing back and forth to keep from trembling, almost enraged now that he realized he was trapped with nowhere to run for instructions, with no other business before him but to be sacrificed with his more expendable men, without even the prince there to see him valiantly waving that unloaded pistol in the air.

Stize probably surprised himself that day. He was helping feed bullets into the machine gun after the second gunner was killed, when he himself was shot through the throat. Wittgenstein was too busy cranking the hot bolt of his rifle, firing at glimpses of coats and arms, to be able to do anything about the chocolate maker as he lay there, bleeding to death with Krull bent over him. Nor was there anything to be done about Ernst a few moments later, when Wittgenstein paused to reload and saw him lying at the bottom of the trench, with his legs flung over his shoulders and the side of his head blown off. The Russians were nearly on them by then. Some of his men had fled, while others were wounded or feigning wounds or death or else frantically throwing down their weapons and holding up crucifixes, having heard that the Russians wouldn't shoot a man holding a crucifix. Wrong again.

There was no time to turn the men around; there was no time to do anything. As the first Russian attackers neared the trench, Wittgenstein and others nearby flung two and three stick bombs each over the breastworks, but only a handful exploded. And then the first Russians broke over them, a gang of six or seven, young and green. The Austrians who were still fighting were mostly the brawlers, the mean-eyed ones who loved it. A bearish man beside Wittgenstein dropped his rifle in favor of a pickhandle bristling with nails and a sharpened railroad spike, exultantly cursing as he broke the back of one boy in midair, then took another down at the knees, splattering his brains like a toadstool. Wittgenstein had never been caught in a dreaded hand-to-hand fight, assuring himself that it would be better to sacrifice himself, Isaac-like, than stoop so low. But he saw hobnailed boots and a bloody face in the sky — then ducked as a Russian bayonet sank like a javelin into the sandbags opposite. Whipping around, he shot the man pointblank in the face, then winged a second, before a third swung from behind and leapt on him with his rifle. The pistol went off and dropped, but as Wittgenstein fell, either he managed to put his boot into the man's groin or else the man just stumbled — no telling which, it happened so fast — and Wittgenstein wrenched the rifle from his grasp and pounced on him. The Russian was barely a boy, a yearling soldier with a square face and queer Mongol eyes. The boy knew he was dead, so fearstruck that when he screamed only air-starved steam rushed out. It was Grundhardt again. Grundhardt was all Wittgenstein saw. Like a wounded rabbit, the boy was squealing in hot, panting little breaths, his muddy hands frantically tearing at Wittgenstein's tunic, when the steel rifle butt stove down, a glancing blow that tore the skin from the side of his forehead. The broken boy shuddered and bucked. Fear raised the rifle up. Something was set in motion that couldn't be stopped. Dizzily, Wittgenstein aimed, then rammed the butt home with one final, lusting grunt, crushing bone to jelly as a tardy, sickened impulse told him the first blow would have done it.

Then Wittgenstein was scrambling over gelatinous bodies, clawing up as out of a bloody bucket. Everyone who still had legs was running then. Ahead he saw Krull, Stize's orderly, hopping nimbly over the shell holes, like black Peter with his sack of chocolates. And behind him hundreds more were running as through a fire storm, going up in geysers or falling gored on their faces as the rallying pursuers shot them down. Wittgenstein's pack was slapping his back and his blood was splashing. His chest could hardly contain his lungs. The miracle was that he was actually running to save his life that day, running with no thought of his book or of anyone but himself, bawling, *Nicht schiessen, nicht schiessen!*

The Russian offensive was a rout for the Austrians, who in the next week were driven back forty miles, losing some two hundred big guns and more than three hundred thousand men, killed, captured or missing. What had been an army was now a frantic, fleeing mob bent only on saving itself, stripping the dead, abandoning the wounded — even taking their last drop of water — and murdering anyone who got in its way. Hundreds drowned in the crush to cross a flimsy pontoon bridge across the rain-swollen Styr. Russian planes bombed and strafed the bottle-necked columns, and bands of Cossacks mounted on the hairy Kirghiz ponies cut down stragglers. And complicating everything were hordes of refugees, who were driven from the roads into the forests, where they hid, competing for the spoils with scavenging packs of deserters from both armies. Yellow Units, they were called, murderers and thieves who hunted in packs, like wild dogs, the all against the all.

Unable to find his own unit, Wittgenstein fought with remnants of various other units during two days of rear guard skirmishes with the Russians while the main army escaped. And everywhere he went, he looked for Grundhardt. He knew this was madness, and yet, if anything, the sheer improbability of ever finding Grundhardt made their meeting seem all the more inevitable. If he saw a soldier with Grundhardt's general build or coloring, Wittgenstein's heart would fly into his mouth. But when he called out Grundhardt's name, some weary stranger dragging a rifle and bedroll would turn around, puzzled by his wild stare.

Finally, an officer sent several squads back to a virgin stand of birches for a full night's sleep, Wittgenstein's first in weeks. Exhausted and desperate to forget, most of the men were out the second they lay down. But Wittgenstein only grew more agitated as he lay there listening to their tormented mumblings, watching them twitch and whimper in their sleep like dreaming dogs. This was not sleep, nor was the sleep life, nor was life the end. Beasts walk the earth — he saw that now. Hirsute and engorged with themselves, they rose like erections, spilling and stealing and cutting the generations down like corn.

Now the picture of his life cast its shadow across the world. Bitterly, he thought of how fiercely he had fought to save himself. And for what? Flatulent heart. Fraudulent life. The shadow ran through his empty heart as through a sieve, spilling lies in the vain hope of distilling even a few grains of truth. He had no faith, and yet he felt faith's desires — a castrato's urge, singing to only a dim memory of music, pretending that one is, after all, human, born of woman and earth. No, it was quite clear: he had no soul, but still he felt the pain of one, the phantom pain that amputees feel from missing hands that still play empty rondos and fugues. But by far the most excruciating pain was how, once severed from the soul, the unmoored mind persisted, gliding along like a monstrous shark, swimming for no other reason than to force raw life through its gills, swimming like sperm to ovum, seeking life, seeking death.

He desperately wanted to weep but every pore was plugged; he thought he would explode there under the stars, surrounded by the sleep-talkers and skittish horses who stood dreaming on their feet. And then Grundhardt was there; he was sitting right beside him. His face was black and vacant and the sharp little triangles at the top of his skull, like the ears of a cat, only confirmed Wittgenstein's suspicions. Dragging between his legs was a thick cock or tail with a meaty club head that, when Wittgenstein looked closer, resembled an ace of spades. Loathsome, the insistent way Grundhardt stropped and fondled it; Wittgenstein felt his sphincter lubricate and tighten in apprehension. He didn't argue when Grundhardt said that many others were writing the same book as he; Wittgenstein had long suspected as much. God is wasteful. How else to explain why so many men of genius — so many Darwins —are simultaneously put on the world to die in their prime so that one might propagate some peculiar species of idea? Were ideas so precious? Effortlessly, sketching equations in the air with a smoking fingernail, Grundhardt was making all kinds of logical connections that so far had eluded Wittgenstein. Wittgenstein was amazed at how he had underestimated him, that master metaphysician. Grundhardt had, for instance, devised an equation — a sort of ballistic triangulation — by which he could plot the path of bullets and so slip unscathed through the steel fusillades in the way that air slides between raindrops. But when Grundhardt sketched out Wittgenstein's own ideas, the signs swirled into nonsense and the logic went awry, causing Wittgenstein's once majestic propositions to wilt over him like spaghetti strings until he groaned with mortification. With eyes as low as the Dead Sea, Grundhardt said contemptuously:

How often I've watched you scribbling in your idiotic little book. But you were right about one thing: everything you think *is* otherwise. As for the rest, *logician* — you might as well as put a big fat *naught* before all you think . . .

Wittgenstein could only vaguely follow the rough outlines of Grundhardt's masterly and intricate condemnation, which, like Luther's complaint, ran on forever, far exceeding his own meager powers of reasoning.

Every Jew, Grundhardt was saying, was a contradiction, which, like all contradictions, pointed in two directions and so came to naught. Every fairy, on the other hand, was a tautology, which was to say an empty copulation, arrow pointing to arrow — a vain cancellation.

For Wittgenstein, there was of course no rational way to refute or deny this wizardry, but then of course he was quite out of his depth — Grundhardt must have read his mind. In his shame, Wittgenstein's only wish then was to be crushed. But here again Grundhardt quite saw through him, sneering, Don't *presume* to choose your own punishment — I'll be the one to decide that, not you . . .

This was pure capriciousness: commanders were always deciding to do what their subordinates had suggested, then presuming they had thought of it first. So, seizing Wittgenstein by the buttocks, Grundhardt flipped him over and straddled him, hissing like a King monkey as he rammed himself down into the roots of Wittgenstein's molars, splitting him like a chicken with his throbbing malice, driving him down into the rich black mire even as Wittgenstein was ruefully acknowledging, finally, the sublime pleasure of his dominion.

Grundhardt was saying, Your little book is not the least bit original — kikes are always unoriginal. Would you believe what fresh underwear could cost you? But of course not, etcetera. Just now Count Primkin, etcetera. And Pinsent, too, etcetera, etcetera. And Kurt and Ernst, and even Stize, etcetera, etcetera, etcetera . . .

And holding him down, chattering in his ear like a ciphering cricket, Grundhardt kept monotonously repeating the word, which applied to everything, a string of deaths and failures of which he, Wittgenstein, was the natural conclusion — absurd, thought Wittgenstein, when he had denied the causal nexus.

It was almost dawn when Grundhardt finally released his victim. Looking up at him as his ruptured bowels cohered, Wittgenstein saw that he had been suffering from a blind spot and that Grundhardt had spontaneously filled that void in the way that lightning fills lakes with scalding new life. For what seemed like ages, Wittgenstein stared into the black square where Grundhardt's head should have been, stared at it even as Grundhardt, casting his malign shadow over the world, drifted away, a figure only slightly darker than the general darkness.

Again the late spring rains came. And with the rains, the Russian drive, like virtually every major offensive of the war, ground to a halt, the forces blocked by the very devastation that had enabled them to break through in the first place as mules sank to their shanks and wagons keeled over and feet sucked out of boots.

As the Russian offensive lost steam, fresh Austrian divisions were brought up, stiffened by crack German divisions. Skirmishers on both sides threw up little mud furrows and began burrowing until, within a week, both sides found themselves living once more in trenches. Forty miles ahead or forty miles farther back — it didn't make much difference to the man swinging a pickhandle. White flags appeared. The last wounded were hied away, and the dead were stacked like ricked wood on wagons and carted off while Russian and Austrian soldiers did some hurried trading. Obscurely, inexorably, bubbling to itself like an ulcerous oyster, the cannibal earth was slowly coating their leavings with a lustrous varnish of rot and rust, mulch and metamorphosis. Cherry and apple trees foamed with blossoms, and gusts of returning birds blew over the hills.

Sent to the rear to rest and be reassigned, Wittgenstein was fed and deloused, then given a clean cot in a depot where he slept for thirty hours, rising near noon the second day. Walking around the village later, he felt human for the first time in weeks, his turmoil having subsided to weary grief and puzzlement as he noticed, as if for the first time, the outcroppings of this teeming spring, which seemed so sudden and unaccountable.

Wittgenstein reported to his unit the next day, but the grilling he expected about the collapse of their lines never came for the simple reason that the army wanted to bury the incident. The only question Wittgenstein encountered was that of a wheezy sergeant suffering from hay fever, who pinched his fat, gurgling nose with a soaked handkerchief and impatiently asked for the names of the dead. Wittgenstein gave him the names — as many as he knew, anyway. But when he asked to see the list of those accounted for, Grundhardt's name was not on it. Wittgenstein never heard of him again. In fact, the only person from that time he ever heard about was Prince Primkin, killed with his horse by a freak bolt of lightning on the parade grounds at Lemberg.

Wittgenstein sent letters to the families of the dead, the longest and most truthful going to Ernst's family, the shortest and most stretched to Stize's. Ernst's mother thanked him for befriending her boy and invited him, please, to visit sometime. Stize's father, on the other hand, wrote him three turgid pages on his crested stationery, strongly suggesting that his son was deserving of a medal and urging him to attest to the fact.

By then the Germans had taken over their lines, and Wittgenstein had another platoon, this time under a German lieutenant, a drop forge op-

· 355 ·

erator raised from the ranks who had the stomach of a hyena for the murder of that summer. Helpless to change what he saw, Wittgenstein could only change his attitude. So, as most front-line soldiers do eventually, he acknowledged the relative helplessness and insignificance of his lot — that he was indeed no different from the elephant or the wasp, as important, as insignificant.

Then one day he was leafing through a badly written safety manual when he saw a photograph of an automobile accident, with skid paths drawn in and white circles marking certain significant objects: a broken road sign, a pair of smashed glasses, a lady's glove. The objects in the picture, he saw, connected with objects in the narrative, just as words connect with the things in the world they pictured. The picture reached right out into reality, and reality was unutterably contained in what was pictured, hence connecting, in a true picture, the scheme represented with its representation.

The picture grew into a theory of language and logical form, and this theory, in turn, was combined with other theories until it grew into a book. However, by inscribing a limit on what *could* be spoken about, Wittgenstein had also managed to isolate what could *not* be spoken about in any meaningful way: God, the mystical, ethics. But since, for him, these things were the most important things one could ever think about, there were actually two books. There was the written book, and then there was the larger, more ambitious work, which suggested the immensity of all the written book had left out. This was the book of silence, of silence and the awed resignation before silence.

Wittgenstein was commissioned a lieutenant and sent to fight in the mountains of Italy. A few months later, when the war was nearly over and the Austrian army was again falling apart, he was walking down a road with two other men and the completed manuscript in his pack, when he was captured by a platoon of Italian soldiers and put in a prison camp.

Ironically, Russell was himself in jail then, serving a six-month sentence for having made statements "likely to prejudice His Majesty's relations with America." This action stemmed from an article in which Russell had suggested that if American troops proved no good at fighting Germans, they still might be used to intimidate British strikers. It was not exactly the sort of transgression he expected to be jailed for, but he said, rather laconically, that he supposed it would do as well as any since the authorities obviously wanted to punish him. He made a ripping martyr. Jauntily, he told the press that prison would afford him some much-needed time for reading and relaxation — he thought he might even dash off a book. But this was just a pose. The truth was, Russell found prison life a misery, confiding to friends that he felt like a dusty book on a shelf. It was springtime and he was in love, longing for the slender thighs of Colette, who was then starring at the Piccadilly in *Winnifred Takes the Cake*. But cruelest of all for him was Colette's naive honesty, which was so like his own. Wouldn't Ottoline have smiled to hear Colette tell him about her latest lover, this young Bolshy who had come to England to spread the word about the Russian Revolution! Still, Colette said it was nothing — all very casual. She swore she'd make it up to him.

Oh, please, Bertums, she wheedled. Don't you know how *hot* for you I am?

So deliciously naughty, his puss-pussums! So saucy and sly, nipping at his fingers through the speaking grate during her weekly pilgrimage to the Tomb. Well, she just *had* to tell him about it. And where was the harm? she asked, adding, I'm sure you'd do the same if the situation were reversed.

I would *not*! he protested. And to tell me this *here*! Where I'm *power-less*!

But *darling,* she pleaded, sounding so dainty and coquettish. This has nothing to do with *us*.

But it has *everything* to do with us! he insisted. Have you no *faith*? Can't you spend a night *a-lone*?

Wittgenstein, then, was the very last thing on Russell's mind when he received a card from an Italian prison camp. It was the regulation twenty-five words or less, the English rusty:

I am prigionere in Italy but have written a book that, I believe, solves all our problems. Please write! It will shorten my prison.

It was 1919. The war was over. The world was starting up again, but there they were, Russell in a cell reading Descartes and steaming over Colette, and Wittgenstein behind barbed wire, staring at a wall of blue alpine air, furious that such chaos should be loose in the world when he had written a book that he felt had solved all the fundamental questions of life and philosophy!

In a way Wittgenstein found it anticlimactic, and somewhat bitter, seeing these photographs in the newspapers of jubilant enemies posing together after the armistice. Despite his relief, he felt he would be years thawing from this. And there was something dispiriting in it — to see men suddenly reconciled, embracing in the satiety that seems to come only after a period of vast bloodshed.

Yet even the war, as Wittgenstein remembered it, had had its brief moments of peace, including one he would never forget. This was the Easter peace of 1916, not long after that battle in which Ernst had been killed. Sweet buns and liquor had been promised that day, and some said there might be colored eggs — maybe even ham. It was early morning. Breakfast and inspection were over, and he was getting ready for the open-air mass, thinking that it would do him good to take part in a peaceful act with others.

From the Russian lines, meanwhile, drifted smells of baking bread and roasting joints of meat, along with the tentative toots and lumberings of some band. He could see a towering dais and atop it an altar surrounded by religious standards — red and yellow silks on long poles that swirled and eddied in the wind. Tired of the weeks of heavy fighting, the Russians were feeling restless and playful. Some were hollering over good-naturedly and waving, while others, exalting in their new freedom, basked in the sun in plain view. Then the mischief started. Someone snatched an officer's hat from his head and sailed it over the trench to delighted hoots. Soon, two then three hats were sailing back and forth, and then the hat throwing stopped and a surging, riotous cheer went up as over the Russian trenches rose a giant bedsheet banner proclaiming in German: CHRIST HAS RISEN!

Wittgenstein was still staring at the banner, wondering what they were up to, when several Russians broke from their trench and went cavorting down their lines, waving their arms and shouting. An officer jumped up and ordered them back, then made a fool of himself by chasing them, drawing taunts and whoops as others ran out and joined the melee. And then the gates opened: knots of men swarmed out of the trenches, whooping and dancing, waving branches and flinging their hats into the air. Wittgenstein saw a man being tossed on a blanket, smiling as he turned lazy somersaults in the sky. There was a man juggling, another dragging a shaggy white mascot goat, and what appeared to be a circus troupe — Gypsies and fakirs, monkeys and a bawling bear. Soon everyone was into it. With a flourish and a beating of drums, the band struck up and started marching down the hill. Then, in windy white robes and miters, bearded Orthodox priests climbed over the berm of the front-line trenches. Lifting their golden staffs in blessing, they slogged down the hill, followed by an unruly mob of worshipers carrying icons, tall crosses and standards emblazoned with thorned crowns and hearts of flame.

Down the hill swept the Russian army. Down in droves they came, carrying crossed Easter buns, seed cakes, vodka, balalaikas and accordions as others ran ahead with wire cutters, chopping lanes through their own entanglements. Then midway they stopped: the band struck and all fell silent, leaving only the sound of the wind and the giant clouds plowing over like archangels in the sun. For one interminable minute, the two armies stood face to face, studying each other like a far oasis. As he eyed the round, sunburned faces of his enemies, Wittgenstein thought that army looked like a ripe brown wheat field sweeping up and down. In his hands, Wittgenstein was holding the gifts he would give that day, his copy of Tolstoy's *Gospels*, picture postcards, a bar of soap — anything at hand. In return, he would be given seed cakes and painted eggs, a small broken doll and a coin, swigs of vodka — tokens redeemable for some measure of his broken faith.

Two vast armies facing each other, two extreme poles of existence. And the next thing he knew, the dam was broken: the Austrians let out a cheer and he was charging down that hill, where he suddenly found himself engulfed, the two armies meeting like the swollen headwaters of two rivers. Russians were grappling on his arms and energetically patting him on the head. Thousands had risen from the earth. Wittgenstein felt as if he were present at the Day of Judgment, differences and alliances alike suspended as Jews frolicked with Cossacks and honest men with thieves and murderers. Talking was useless on such a day; with no recourse to speech, they could only touch, gesture, point. Adrift in that walking amnesia, they couldn't keep their hands off each other or ward off each other's piquant human strangeness. Wittgenstein could see men mutely nodding and moving their arms with tears in their eyes, the spell broken only when they tried to speak. It was nearly dark before order was restored and dawn before the wire was repaired and the carousing stopped. Until then, they sang, clapped, waltzed, bawled, exchanged addresses, beat drums, howled like dogs and hung together in knots, atrociously drunk and wearing one another's hats while pictures were taken. One Russian told Wittgenstein that stoves could have flown on such a day, but in the forests and on the roads, refugees were eating cooked weeds and dying like little flies, and a few hours later, the revelers were falling as well. Like the corn and the seasons they fell, but still this work, necessary or not, could not be called *beautiful* or *complete*. Christ had not risen high or for long, nor had he risen for everyone that Easter Sunday.

BOOK III

The World Revisited

BEACON HILL, 1931

With their eyes all creatures gaze into
the Open. Only our eyes, as though turned in,
on every side of it are set about
like traps to circumvent its free outgoing.
What is *without* we know from the face
of animals alone, for even the youngest child
we turn around and force to see the past
as form and not the openness that
lies so deep within animals. Free from death,
we alone *see* death; the free animal
has its destruction always behind it
and before it God, so when it moves, it moves
into eternity like a running spring . . .

— Rainer Maria Rilke, *The Duino Elegies*

Reunion: Summer 1931

THERE HE IS, said Dorothy Moore, hurrying down the station platform. That's him over there, isn't it? With the cane? You never told me he walks with a cane. Is he lame from the war?

Lame? asked Moore, who frankly had never noticed. I don't know. No, not lame. I have no idea why he carries that thing.

It's so annoying, remarked Dorothy with a sideways look. You never tell me the interesting things about people.

That's because I so *dread* the interesting things about people, said Moore, returning her look. As I am dreading this weekend.

The man with the cane was Wittgenstein, and Moore and Dorothy were meeting him at Cambridge Station to take the train to Petersfield, on the South Downs, where Russell and his wife, Dora, lived with their two children at Beacon Hill, the progressive children's school they had started four years before. It would be a reunion of sorts, but it wasn't a social visit. The next day, at Russell's, Wittgenstein was to stand for his doctorate, with Moore and Russell as his examiners.

It had been a good two years at least since Moore had seen Russell, and probably ten years since Russell had seen Wittgenstein; and it had been at least seventeen years since the three of them had been together. The prospect of examining Wittgenstein at this *Viva* was reason enough for Moore to be uneasy, but he had others, one being the perhaps volatile chemistry among the three of them, and another being Russell, who for him was still persona non grata. Ever since their row during the war, when Russell had accused Moore of not understanding Wittgenstein's work, Moore and Russell had studiously avoided each other. Moore guessed he had not seen Russell more than a handful of times during those years, and then typically in some unavoidable public context. A few bland pleasantries and he and Russell would quickly move on. They had little to say to each other.

Still bitter about his expulsion from Cambridge during the war, Russell had also been keeping his distance from Trinity. It was with deep reluctance, then, and in a purely official capacity, that Moore wrote to Russell asking if he would examine Wittgenstein for his doctorate. To Moore's surprise, Russell agreed, though he said that, because of commitments at his school, they would have to conduct the *Viva* at Beacon Hill. Russell did add that Moore and Wittgenstein — and Dorothy, too — were most welcome to stay there. While not keen on the prospect of spending two or three days with Russell, much less a horde of children, Moore had to admit this was an exceedingly decent offer. Russell was under no obligation to examine Wittgenstein, nor at this point was Russell on especially good terms — or really on any terms — with Wittgenstein. This, Moore figured, was largely a result of frictions brought on by the book Wittgenstein had published after the war, though certainly there were other factors, not the least of them being time and distance.

Wittgenstein was another story. The war, it was said, had unmoored him. Other than his stint in the Italian prison camp, no one knew exactly what had happened to him, but for years word had it that he was slightly "off." Moore discounted most of these rumors, but he had heard from fairly reliable second- and thirdhand sources that Wittgenstein had become quite religious. Russell was doubtless the source of these stories, and Moore, knowing Russell's tendency toward exaggeration and his antipathy to religion, took them with a grain of salt. Still, Russell had been the first and, for many years, the only one from Cambridge to have seen Wittgenstein after the war, when they met in The Hague in 1919 to discuss Wittgenstein's manuscript. From what Moore gathered, it had been a tense and difficult meeting. Apparently, Russell thought Wittgenstein was suffering from nervous exhaustion, and Wittgenstein was typically impatient with Russell's questions about his manuscript — questions whose answers, to *him* at least, seemed obvious. According to Russell, Wittgenstein said he had undergone some sort of mysterious conversion. But then so, in a sense, had Russell, with his now outspoken sexual views and aggressive socialism. Certainly Wittgenstein must have disapproved of Russell's politics and anti-Christian views, but then so did a good many other people. A few months after meeting with Wittgenstein in The Hague, Russell traveled to Russia to meet Lenin and see firsthand the fruits of the Russian Revolution. Wittgenstein, on the other hand, was apparently continuing to undergo some kind of internal revolution. It was all very murky, but Moore did know that, sometime prior to this meeting with Russell, Wittgenstein had given up his quite sizable fortune, apparently in the Tolstoyan belief that money was evil, or something to that effect. Moore knew this because he remembered hearing that Wittgenstein was so poor that he could not pay his train ticket to The Hague. Russell had to pay his passage, taking, at Wittgenstein's insistence, some expensive furniture that Wittgenstein had left in England before the war.

The manuscript of Wittgenstein's book had been passed around Cambridge. Moore had read and admired the book; in an appreciative letter to Wittgenstein around this time, Moore had even suggested a title for it. Moore had a poor recollection of dates and chronology, but it seemed to him that some time after his meeting with Russell, Wittgenstein renounced philosophy. The story got murky here as well, but apparently the decision was partly precipitated by Wittgenstein's disgust with his book, which had been published after much difficulty and then only after Russell had promised the publisher that he would write an introduction to it. As promised, Russell wrote his introduction. Moore thought it was a rather good introduction, but evidently Wittgenstein felt it was completely wrong and misleading — so misleading that he finally tried to stop publication of the book. Fortunately, Wittgenstein was too late, however, and the book was published anyway, first in German in 1921 and then the following year in an English translation that appeared under the Latin title that Moore had suggested: *Tractatus Logico-Philosophicus*.

Moore knew only the bare facts of what had happened next. Having given up his fortune and renounced philosophy, Wittgenstein virtually disappeared, going off to teach school in a little Austrian village called Trattenbach. A gifted young protégé of Moore's named Frank Ramsey, who in fact had helped translate Wittgenstein's book, made the journey to Trattenbach in 1923 in the hope that Wittgenstein might resolve some questions he had about his work. As far as Moore knew, Ramsey was the only one from Cambridge who ever saw Wittgenstein during that so-called lost period, and it was not an altogether cheering sight. Austria was in bad shape after the war, and so, apparently, was Wittgenstein. Ramsey told Moore the village was a poor and dreary place. Worse, said Ramsey, Wittgenstein was embroiled in tensions with the villagers. For the life of him, Ramsey couldn't see why Wittgenstein chose to stay there — "intellectual suicide" was what Ramsey called it. Mysteriously, Wittgenstein one day remarked to Ramsey that he had undergone a painful but necessary operation on his character. It had been a kind of surgery, Wittgenstein said, a surgery of the most radical nature — certain limbs had been lopped off. But Wittgenstein maintained that he was better off for it, though certainly diminished and weakened. Wittgenstein told Ramsey that he harbored no illusions about himself or his talent. Six or eight years was about as long as anyone could expect to do this kind of logical work before being ruined by it, at least in the case of a marginal and basically derivative talent like his own. Not, Wittgenstein hastened to add, that this was any great loss to philosophy. In fact, he said, it was no loss whatsoever. Having said all he had to say philosophically, he had turned to the world of children, feeling that it was better to persist as a benign spirit among children than as a ghost among men.

With Wittgenstein apparently having consigned himself to silence, it was a great surprise when he returned to Cambridge in 1929, clearly as sharp as ever, with a mass of new written work. Wittgenstein told Moore he wanted to get his doctorate so that he might make a living teaching while he developed a new philosophy. At least, Wittgenstein said, this was what he planned to do if Cambridge would have him. Moore told him that it was not a question of Cambridge wanting Wittgenstein. The question, said Moore, was whether Wittgenstein really wanted Cambridge.

As for Russell, he had his own problems, one immediate problem being his need of money.

Married ten years now, Russell and his wife, the socialist and feminist writer Dora Black, had two children, a boy of ten named John and a girl of eight named Kate. Russell and Dora also had thirty-five pupils, nine teachers and a house staff, not to mention two cars and the upkeep of the school's buildings and grounds. Certainly, Russell had not begun the school as a profit-making venture. On the contrary, he had begun the school for personal, social and experimental reasons, and in the full expectation of *losing* money, but not on a scale like this. At times, Russell's life seemed to him like a sorry ledgerbook, with one debit row for employees, forever pinched and begging advances, and one for children, forever eating, getting sick, breaking bones and smashing things.

Even then, during the early years of the depression, America was where the money was, so every summer, just to meet the staggering costs of the school, Russell was compelled to leave his children and spend weeks on tour, talking himself hoarse in New York, Boston, Chicago and points west. Not that touring was completely bereft of rewards. Besides affording one a chance to exercise one's fame and opinions, there were always eager, attractive women and, with them, exciting nights of dalliance and only slight pangs of regret in the morning. Russell had written that it was inevitable and probably healthy that husband and wife should have their occasional infidelities, at least so long as these episodes did not intrude on family life. Russell believed this a matter of reason, yet he also knew that for one of his Victorian-bred generation it was difficult to completely shake the deeply ingrained feelings of shame that society had implanted. In all likelihood, Russell thought, he would never entirely shake them. But he hoped that at least his children and the generations to follow might be free of these fears, thereby fostering a world less pent up and violent, or rather more happy, tolerant and humane.

In the meantime, though, in these seedy American hotels where he stayed, there was this unpleasant residue and the longing not so much for his wife, who could wait, but for his two children, who could not. The children were now the focus of his life, and he found it harder and harder to be separated from them. And increasingly he resented it, the loneliness and the frantic pace of his touring schedule, then the inevitable guilt and disorientation upon his return, when he saw how much his two children had changed even in that seemingly short interval.

Ironically, it was because of their children that Russell and Dora had begun the school that now kept him away twelve weeks every summer. For more than a year after John was born, Russell and Dora had researched schools and educational philosophies, reading, among others, Freud, Froebel, Montessori, Piaget and Margaret McMillan. They also looked with despair at the English school system, where coeducation was virtually nonexistent, where children routinely received religious instruction and where boys were typically given some form of military training. In its tendency to perpetuate class hierarchies, intolerance and aggression, the system was already bad enough. To someone like Dora, long active in the campaigns for birth control, sexual education and legalized abortion, the system seemed even more disastrous in its propensity for fostering repressive sexual attitudes. In their marriage, Russell and Dora had eschewed the possessive notion of husband and wife, but then marriage, at least as they viewed it, was not really the problem. It was the fundamental dishonesty of society's patriarchal heritage that finally shackled and killed love, insisting on fidelity at the price of either frustration or dishonesty. They wanted both to be free, and they wanted nothing less for their children. After all, if boys and girls were not educated together, not taught from earliest childhood to work and play and cooperate in a miniature society of children, how could they ever grow into free men and women, living and loving as equals in a free society of adults?

Russell and Dora were in general accord on these principles. The problem was finding a school that could properly promote them. More liberal schools were of course closer to their liking, but after examining the situation more carefully they had concluded that there was not a school anywhere, not progressive, Quaker, Montessori — not even Summerhill — that could give their children the humane, nondogmatic, practical education that, in their view, was crucial to peace and social progress.

This was the genesis of their school, and once they decided to go forward with it they had no trouble finding students. Rather, the problem all too often was finding *normal* children, as opposed to problem children; or, as was more often the case, problem children with problem parents — incompetent, irresponsible, often divorced parents who often had trouble paying their bills and, still worse, trouble taking back their problem children once their other problems had become insurmountable. Such parents did not want to be presented with more problems: there would be loud denials and accusations, the problem parents swearing that, in fact, their children had not been problems until they had come to Beacon Hill. And didn't the brochure plainly say that Beacon Hill, though designed for the normal child, was also specially suited for the "exceptional child" — to wit, the "gifted" (problematic) child? Why, several of the more cunning problem parents had threatened the white-haired headmaster, saying that because the school had been negligent on one count and clearly fraudulent on another, he could either wipe their debt clean or else face long and certainly messy legal action.

Such were the miseries of running a school. But there were also considerable pleasures. Most of the children were good, normal, loving children who ranged in age from four to eleven. The Beacon Hill staff was also excellent, its teachers willing to work long hours with demanding, outspoken children who were encouraged to question *everything*. Filled with admiration for the Russells and believing themselves to be on the groundswell of a new movement, Beacon Hill's teachers tended to be talented, intellectually venturesome and progressive. Happily for the headmaster, they also tended to be young, idealistic and female.

Even so, it took more than trips to America to float the school. By night, the headmaster was the ever more popular journalist and author, tossing off myriad articles and books to stave off his creditors. Yet this, too, had its satisfactions. Russell liked seeing his name and ideas in print, and he was proud to be able to hold his own in the practical, pecuniary world that made the higher world possible. Russell wrote like he lived — quickly and easily, often brilliantly, in long, lean, lucid sentences. No subject was too daunting and none too trivial. If the Hearst papers or *Vanity Fair* wanted an article on the morality of kissing or the social implications of bobbed hair, they would quickly have it. Russell rarely revised and he never looked back, taking workmanlike pleasure in his better efforts and quickly putting out of mind his poorer ones. Having finished a book entitled *Marriage and Morals* two years before, he was now at work on its sequel, *The Conquest of Happiness,* along with an article — or rather a foregone thesis — that *Parents' Magazine* had assigned him entitled "Are Parents Bad for Children?"

As for the rest, Russell had little direct connection with philosophy or academia now, and he was taken aback by Moore's letter asking if he would be willing to examine Wittgenstein. Russell had worked hard to get Wittgenstein's *Tractatus* published, and he had been sorely irked when Wittgenstein sent him a letter rejecting his introduction, saying with an evasiveness otherwise foreign to him that Russell's ideas about the book did not survive in translation and "left only superficiality and misunderstanding."

Russell, though disappointed, was certainly not surprised when Wittgenstein suddenly announced that he was going off to teach school in lower Austria. Despite the tensions between them, Russell and Wittgenstein still corresponded at that time. In one letter, Wittgenstein spoke of his decision as "my good deed" and said he intended to haul the peasants "out of the muck." Russell still could vividly remember Wittgenstein's first enthusiastic letters from Trattenbach, which he described as a "sound old roof" and "a peaceful nest of a place." Wittgenstein said the children were especially charming, thoroughly simple and unaffected. They loved to hear him whistle and would sit open-mouthed with their chins resting in their hands while he read them tales from the brothers Grimm. Less charming were their backward parents. From the start, they were suspicious of the new teacher, but Wittgenstein nonetheless felt they were appreciative — good, hearty peasant folk, in the main.

Russell wasn't surprised as this rosy picture gradually changed for the worse. In 1920 and 1921, with Dora Black as his companion, Russell was living in China as a guest of the Chinese Lecture Association. Defiantly unmarried and openly sharing their quarters, Russell and Dora made headlines, carrying scandal to British consulates from Tokyo to

Peking, who anxiously wired London for instructions as to whether the libertine couple should be officially received. The Chinese were far more broad-minded than the English, not caring a bit about Russell's personal life. Revolutionary students and moderates alike welcomed the great thinker with a reverence and enthusiasm that he found almost embarrassing, importuning him, as a sort of latter-day Lao-tzu, to kindly, if he would, please, sir, enlighten them in the halcyon ways of social revolution and lead their backward country into the twentieth century. With Dora, Russell toured Peking and the surrounding provinces, speaking to students, officials and sundry delegations on topics ranging from mathematics to education, and from syndicalism to the Boxer indemnity. Russell liked the Chinese, and he was greatly encouraged by what he saw in China — especially compared to what he had seen in revolutionary Russia, where he had expected to find the embodiment of his political dreams and had instead seen poverty, gross inequality and mass persecution on a staggering scale.

As for Wittgenstein, his eyes seemed to have been opened as well, his letters from Trattenbach turning sour, then bitter. In a matter of months, his snug little nest had become "a disgusting swamp of humanity." In the aftermath of the war and the wild inflation, the money-grubbing Trattenbachers had sunk to the "very bottom," Wittgenstein said. Past the bottom: the reformer now claimed they were the most wicked and debased people on earth. Indeed, their only saving grace was the children, but with such drunkards and ignoramuses for parents, he feared the children would also perish.

Russell was then in a good period of life — too good to be spoiled by these doom-ridden reports from the barrens. Oppressed by Wittgenstein's unhappiness and irked by his naiveté, he wrote back, "If you think the Trattenbachers are wicked, then you ought to go to Russia as I did last year. Then you will have a better appreciation of the relative scale of wickedness and inhumanity. The people of Trattenbach are no better or worse than people anywhere else in the world."

How glad Russell was not to be around Wittgenstein in those years! His fame was steadily growing, and he was terrifically busy with various writings. Russell was even involved in politics again, having unsuccessfully stood for Parliament as a socialist candidate in the 1922 and 1923 elections. Wittgenstein and his narrow concerns seemed quite foreign to him, and their relationship dribbled down to almost nothing — a card or two, usually around Christmas, but blessedly remote. Then around 1926 or so, Russell got a rather mysterious card from Wittgenstein saying that he had left Trattenbach some time ago. He gave no reason. He said that for his sister Gretl he was designing and building a spare modern house, pruned of the usual clutter and, he hoped, the usual pretenses. Beyond that, though, Wittgenstein said, he didn't have the slightest idea what he would do with his life.

That was the last Russell heard from Wittgenstein until he received Moore's letter. Wittgenstein after a doctorate! What a howler! And wasn't it vindicating for Russell to have Trinity come crawling to him — and better yet making Moore the messenger boy! Still, despite all the old doubts and anxieties that the *Viva* would inevitably dredge up, Russell felt almost morally bound to examine Wittgenstein. Moore was another matter. Russell had little idea what Moore was doing, though he figured, snidely, that Moore probably wasn't doing much. True, Moore had published *Philosophical Studies,* a collection of his articles, in 1922; and he had been elevated to full professor in 1925. It was also true, as Russell thought with some distaste, that Moore was now editor of the prestigious philosophical journal *Mind.* Still, as Russell sometimes felt compelled to tell himself, Moore's output was minuscule compared to his own. But here Russell's feelings were basically preemptive: as he well knew, Moore and his other old colleagues didn't think that he was doing much either, opinionizing from the popular pulpit and squandering himself on children.

Russell was painfully aware of the irony that he should be writing *The Conquest of Happiness* at a time when he was feeling exceedingly thwarted and unhappy. That, he thought, was one of the disorienting things about writing, to be describing or analyzing emotions that one was not then experiencing. Russell certainly thought he had been happy far more than he had been unhappy, yet he had experienced little of what might be called joy. In his ruminations about the book, and in his general unhappiness, Russell had been trying to remember not just the times of happiness in his life, which had been many, but times of joy. Real, not figurative, joy. Not passion or triumph, or even boundless love, but pure splashing, beaming, unqualified joy. And Russell could think of but one instance: fatherhood. Indeed, fatherhood seemed the one bright spot in his life now that his second marriage was foundering.

Miss Marmer, one of the teachers at Beacon Hill, was not a joy or even an especially bright spot in his life, but she did offer harbor of a kind. Miss Marmer was very understanding about these things. Best of all, Miss Marmer was also discreet and undemanding, with no apparent expectation of anything more lasting. Of late, Russell had been seeing more of Miss Marmer, what with Dora shutting him out of their room. Not that Russell wanted *in*, especially; it was more a matter of principle, or rather a battle of wills, with Russell wanting *in* expressly because Dora had shut him *out*. To be still more precise, Russell wanted *out* the man who then was living inside his wife's room, the man who was consoling her and, as he sometimes thought, plotting with her against him. Higgins was an American, and he was no stranger to Beacon Hill, having lived there all the previous September while the headmaster had been away in America. Higgins had seen after things in Russell's absence. As a matter of fact, Higgins had fathered the child that Dora was soon to deliver.

Sometimes, while walking with his son John on the nearby chalk bluffs, in the sharp sea wind, Russell would say, Strong men seek the mountains; wise men of virtue seek the sea. And John, a bright and inquisitive boy, with a snarl of dark hair, would ask, Which do you seek, Daddy? And Russell, beaming down at his beautiful bark of a boy would reply, I seek both of course, saying this with all the self-sufficiency of fatherhood, as if he were the same man at all times. But at night, cut off from Dora and feeling neither strong nor wise nor fatherly, Russell would find himself seeking something else. Miss Marmer had become a regular harbor then, as a matter of fact.

The Innocent

SUCH WAS THE SITUATION that morning as Moore and Dorothy were hurrying down the platform to meet Wittgenstein. Or rather, this was the situation until the Moores saw a large, rough-looking man barge excitedly over to Wittgenstein. The man's face was heated, his back was broad, and he was gesticulating emphatically. Dressed in canvas shorts and sandals and an open white shirt with rolled sleeves, he was smiling and spreading his big arms, nudging Wittgenstein with a gaping tale he seemed to be gathering out of his chest, his voice resounding over the station din like the cadenced woofs of a bow saw.

For a moment then, Moore thought — or wanly hoped — that this human spectacle was someone Wittgenstein had run into at the station. But, no: Wittgenstein seemed to know this man, whose story he was following with deep, if uneasy, attention, all the while tapping his slender cane.

But who's that, Bill? whispered Dorothy, sidling up to him. You never said he was bringing a friend.

Well, if he is, muttered Moore indignantly, it's certainly news to me.

With that, there was the flurried press of greetings and introductions. Wittgenstein was saying hello to Dorothy, whom he had met only once briefly, before the war, and Moore was paying the porter, who was staring at the vagabond pack and roll at the big man's feet. Pointing to a corrugated cylinder with leather straps that hung from the pack, the porter said to him, That there — that's a Heinie gas mask case, id'nit? From the war.

Beaming with a broad punch of a face, the big man said, Sure. That is so, brother.

The porter went white at the sound of the man's heavy German accent and said quickly, Didn't mean nothing by it, mate — by Heinie, I mean.

The other man shrugged affably. In it I keep only food now.

The porter looked puzzled. The German wasn't much past thirty — young to have been in the war. He said, You was in it, were you?

The German nodded. Arras. Verdun. Then the Somme, and wounded bad. Then here in the prison camp two years.

Sorry 'bout that, mate, said the porter, with a troubled look. A bad time, that was. A better time for you in England this trip, eh? He turned to Moore respectfully. Begging your pardon, sir, mum. For my interrupting, I mean. I was just very surprised, is all.

The German threw up an easy hand. God keep you.

Said the gaping porter, easing off, You, too, mate.

With a look of discomfort, Wittgenstein resumed his introductions. This is my close friend Max Einer. Max and I met in Austria after the war. He arrived unexpectedly last night, and I wonder if you would mind if he came with us. I thought Russell would have room. Max is not fussy about where he sleeps, and he will make himself useful. There are always jobs to be done at a school.

Sure, agreed Max. Anywhere I sleep, he said, pointing to the pack.

Well, said Moore in a laboring voice. It's certainly fine *with me* if Mr. Einer comes, but of course I can't speak for Mr. Russell.

Oh, said Max offhandedly. This Russell and I, we will be fine, Moore. Always, Ludwig tells me about you, Moore, and also this Russell. Always I told him I will meet you. So this is *gut*. And this nice lady, he said, gesturing to Dorothy. This is your wife, Moore?

Moore, unnerved by his astonishing forwardness, said protectively, This is Mrs. Moore, yes.

Dorothy Moore, she added, offering an uncertain hand.

Oh, *Dorthe*! said Max knowingly, with a loutish grin. Boyishly then, as if he had known her for years, Max gave her plump arm a squeeze, then looked around happily now that all was settled. And after that Max called her *Dorthe*, just as he called Moore Moore.

And Max did make himself useful. With Max there was no need for a porter. And with the likes of Max barging down the crowded aisle with two armloads of luggage, they had absolutely no trouble finding good seats.

And he was charming, if not bewildering, in his way. It was not from uncouthness that Max so quickly assumed familiarity with everyone, it was rather a matter of intense belief. By Max's book, no man had hegemony over another. Max detested convention, pretense and falseness of any kind. He ate with whatever spoon was nearest and spoke his mind, no matter who was present or what it cost him. In court once, after a brawl in which Max had beaten three men unconscious, the magistrate sentenced him to three days more in jail for refusing to address him as Your Honor. The magistrate lectured and threatened, but Max was recalcitrant: he took those three days in jail, then six days more for his continued stubbornness. Max would have been jailed a thousand times had not the local priest interceded. This was in Trattenbach, toward the end. Having long acted as Wittgenstein's apologist and defender, Max never flagged in what he saw as his duty to his best friend on earth. Once released, Max found those three and gave them another pounding for other ugly tales they had spread. But he didn't stop there. Down by the tavern, bloody and enraged, he battered down a door and beat two other men senseless, then with loud oaths dragged them into the street, daring anyone to utter another word against him or his friend. In his way, Max considered himself a man of the Gospels, a friar of sorts.

There was an extraordinarily healthy, unkillable presence about Max. On one thigh was a red scald from the flame throwers his shock battalion had used in the war. A bullet had gone clean through the meat of his other thigh, and shrapnel had torn a bite from his left calf. There were mustard gas burns on his back and his left ear was as nicked and crumpled as a tomcat's where shrapnel had shredded it.

Now, other passengers were looking over their magazines at the garrulous German. Children stood on their seats to stare at him. The warm air sweeping in through the window carried his smell, causing those nearby to stir nervously in their berths like horses who had caught scent of a bear. It was a faintly vinegary and beery smell, mixed with the scent of the cheap talc used by the barber that Wittgenstein had taken him to that morning to get him cleaned up for the trip. How do you want it? the barber had asked. Short, said the indifferent Max, who carried no comb but his hand. The barber had not been able to keep him still, and as a result, Max's thick brown hair had been clipped short and erratically. With his long broken nose and little creased, predatory eyes, finely etched and crinkled about the edges with fist cuts, he looked like one of Dürer's stony peasants. For Moore and Dorothy facing him, he was a little too close. His seat creaked with him; he was like a bucket threatening to slop over, uncontainable. They saw dirt caked under his toenails. His legs were hairy and heavily muscled, and his ankles were scratched with thistles. Alarming, too, was that aggressive bulge in his crotch, his thighs spread wide to the world — of this, Max seemed as open and unaware as an animal of its own steeping sex. Huddled beside him, subtle and watchful, Wittgenstein seemed almost birdlike.

At first, Dorothy Moore couldn't quite picture them together. And yet there was an unspoken intimacy between them, as if their separate oddities had knitted together over the years like a human island, populated with its own peculiar flora and fauna. Wittgenstein was distinctly uneasy; each time Max opened his mouth he seemed afraid of an upset. They were about an hour outside of London, the train having fallen into a comfortable shipboard rocking as they passed plump, loaflike hills, narrow sweeps of forest and fields scattered with dirty gray balls that, on second glance, one realized were sheep. They were talking about Russell's school. Dorothy Moore was slowly brushing the underside of her chin with her finger. Comfortably curled into herself in her chaise, handsome and suitably older, she was like a plump cat. I understand you taught school yourself, Mr. Wittgenstein, she said. How old were the children you taught?

She saw Wittgenstein's eyes focused on her, piercing, like pencils. Slowly he was rubbing his pressed hands together, saying, They ranged in age from eight to thirteen. Peasant children, very poor. The village was barely a big ditch. This, you see, was where Max and I met.

Ah, said Moore, nodding. It seemed now that he could connect them.

Dorothy remarked, Isn't that interesting, though. That you and Mr. Russell — philosophers — would spend years teaching children.

I did not turn to it from philosophical interest, said Wittgenstein abruptly. On the contrary, my aim was to turn completely *away* from philosophy. Not wishing to seem overly harsh, Wittgenstein ventured a smile, adding, But I understand what you mean. It amuses me too that Russell should himself be teaching now, following in *my* humble footsteps. Ten years ago, he thought I was quite mad to waste myself on children.

Scoffed Moore, Now people think the same of him.

Be nice, intoned Dorothy, lowering her eyes.

I am being nice, protested Moore. But between you and me, I don't know how he stands it at his age — having all those children underfoot. And from what I understand, Bertie has some wild little Indians. Glancing at Dorothy, he said, I told you Hawney stopped there last year. Moore smiled in anticipation, then said to Wittgenstein, Hawney's a don at King's, a historian of some merit. At any rate, Hawney hadn't been there an hour when he saw one boy push another down a flight of stairs. Bertie told him that was nothing — why, the month before a girl had put a needle in her little brother's soup, then sat there giggling while the little fellow choked.

Oh, quit! protested Dorothy, making a face. You know Hawney hates children.

Oh, does he now? Well, one day Hawney and Bertie are sitting outside when they hear the most dreadful caterwauling. So they run round the house, and there they see a little girl tied to a tree, just screaming her heart out while the other children are busily piling rubbish and sticks around her. Bertie nearly fell over. Oh, she's Joan of Arc, said a little boy. Hawney said Bertie was fit to be tied himself. As they were freeing the girl, Bertie turned to him and said, What am I to do — suspend the teaching of history? Can you imagine if we taught the Spanish Inquisition?

Wittgenstein and this Max were staring at Moore with looks of stern disapproval. Max said, This is not good. The children must have order, always. In Ludwig's school, always there was good order.

Oh? Moore looked at him, bemused. It was extraordinary, to hear this profuse, unrestrained man speak of order.

Eyeing Max with displeasure, Wittgenstein said, I was firm. The children knew what I would tolerate and what I would not. But there is certainly a good deal more to teaching than keeping order.

Indeed so, said Moore with a mischievous nod. Peering over the rims of his glasses, Moore then remarked, Well, I do hope the children are clothed when we arrive.

Oh, go on, said Dorothy, giving him a little nudge with her shoulder.

But it's true! Moore insisted. Hawney said Bertie lets the children run about like little aborigines when it's hot. *I'm dead in earnest,* said Moore, peeping delightedly around the company. Apparently, the local parson and his wife live nearby. Hawney says the children will saunter over to the parsonage to be fed milk and cookies. Oh, just as pretty as you please, they come, and, mind you, not one stitch! The parson and his wife are very good about it, I understand. I suppose they view themselves as missionaries. But it does aggravate Bertie terribly, the religious ideas the children bring back. Hawney says the children are rather fonder of Demeter and fairies than Jesus anyhow.

Now Max was shaking his head in vigorous disapproval, and Wittgenstein was picking a piece of lint from his trousers with a distinct air of distaste. Unable to resist, Moore went on:

I heard another tale, you know. Sucking in his cheeks in anticipation as they looked up, Moore said, Well, when Bertie first opened the school, the parson naturally stopped by to offer his greetings. So he knocked on the door, and when it opened, he saw a little girl. And, lo and behold — Moore slapped his forehead — the child was stark naked. Good God! exclaimed the parson. To which the little girl replied, *There is no God*, and slammed the door in his face.

Wittgenstein laughed with surprise at this, but not Max. Folding his arms in disgust, Max didn't say another word for ten minutes — a long time for him.

Moore, meanwhile, was getting curious. Normally he was not one to pry, but finally, a bit anxiously, he asked Max to divulge what, in England, is considered a somewhat private matter. Moore asked the young German what kind of work he did. An innocent question. A natural question. Max thought nothing of it, and without a hint of humor or irony he replied:

God's work.

But there was a question that Moore and Dorothy did not ask. It was about the cane.

Sensing their curiosity, Max said, Ludwig's stick? You wonder why for is the stick?

Cane, corrected Wittgenstein. I acquired it while I was teaching. Then, with a look at Max, he added, To use as a pointer, not a rod.

Injected Dorothy with a note of relief, Oh, then your legs are all right? I thought it might have been something from the war.

No, no. Wittgenstein brushed this off. I bought it in Vienna one Christmas — 1922, I believe. Quite on impulse.

Sure, cut in Max. To stick at me, with his stick. When Ludwig is angry he pointed at me this stick.

Cane, corrected Wittgenstein again. And not to point. To punctuate. To punctuate a point.

This is so, *huh?* asked Max, defiantly dropping his jaw with a crazy gleam in his eyes. To puncture — to puncture me he pointed, see? Like the motorcar's wheel to puncture, so?

Not wheel — *tire.*

Wheel, tire — the same. Ludwig don't think I will know this word "punctures," Dorthe. And so I learn good your words, Ludwig. Puncture Max with your stick, so?

Cane.

Cane, stick, wheel. The same. The same.

Later, Max took down his pack and started rummaging through it. Moore and Dorothy could not help looking at what was clearly the kit of a seasoned traveler. It was a military pack, stitched and restitched and attached to a homemade wooden frame webbed with strong jute cord and canvas fixed with brass sailing grommets. On the top flap of the pack was a hand-drawn cross, runed and black, like a crusader's cross or the German Iron Cross. Inside, all was as meticulously and economically laid out as an apothecary's cove: fishhooks and other things in watertight bottles, coiled rope and canvas, candles and matches, a sheath knife and hatchet, spare clothes. Max withdrew a book wrapped in oilcloth and proceeded to unwrap it with all the ritualistic care of a man who owns only a few essential things. Even before he untied the string they knew it was a Bible. It, too, had been through a war, and looked it. Battered and mildew spotted, it had a greasy handmade cover made of tallow-hardened sailcloth marked with another black and clotted cross. It was a labor itself, that book. As Max opened it, they could see pages blackened with heavy underlining and spiraling notes in German — indictments written in a heated hand. Seeing that part of the book had been torn away, Dorothy Moore said:

It looks as if you lost part of your Bible.

Not lost, said Max with a snort. I pulled it out. The Old Testament it was. Five years behind I see this is all lies made by the desert Jew. To show God with such filth, yes, and so *cruel?* To make of God such a *murderer?* I say this is *evil.* Men make murder, not God. God does not trick or lie — he does not tell Abraham to kill his son, then break his word. What God would tell Ezekiel to bake his bread over human filth and the filth of beasts? In these books are two Gods, the Jew God and the Christian. Both cannot be.

Wittgenstein sighed with irritation at what was clearly an old argument, saying, Oh, drop it, Max. You're talking nonsense. Who are you to decide what God would do or be, or which God is the true one? The story of Ezekiel *is* disgusting, but it speaks of an experience we cannot comprehend. God is different things to different men.

Sure, Ludwig! said Max, reddening. And what do you say now? You say we cannot know. But truly now, you say I am wrong. How is this? Sure, you are just like me, Ludwig — as bad in your thinking. So take your old murderer Jew God — your bloody Yahweh. God save us from this Yahweh. Thank you, I will eat my bread with bee's honey, not this fool's honey. Not even a dog would eat what Ezekiel did.

John the Baptist was fond of locusts, mused Moore, attempting to inject a note of pleasantry.

Max only shrugged at this. Insects are not unclean. Several times, in hunger, I have eaten such. Worms also. Good for birds, good for Max.

The effect of this pronouncement hung on for a while, but then it faded as Max began talking about his travels. This was a different Max, a sunnier Max, a man with a free wind about him. To hear Max talk, it seemed the world was unbounded and undivided, without mountains or oceans or borders but only the grace to be. In the face of eternity, time was as water to him, with one place quite as good as another. Max was amused by Dorothy's questions about chronology, the pointless accounting of where, when, why and how. That one place was the effect of the last, or that life should devolve from successive occurrences or reasons — this to Max was as foreign as concepts of privacy or property. Stories, faces, kindnesses Max remembered, and he gave of himself freely: anyone who needed his help would have it, and for nothing. Of a place there persisted for Max only the snap of a good apple, impressions of certain curious plants and animals, or memories of the local provender ripening by the roadside. Max's sense of direction was extraordinary. Forgetting roads, mostly oblivious to the sights, he knew with the unerring compass of a migrating bird the declination of the sun and the local constellations visible at that latitude, in the advancing season. He had been many places. He had been to Greece, to the ruins, which for him were holy, even if pagans had built them. He had gone to the holyland, too, and to Palestine. As an ordinary seaman, firing boilers and chipping rust, he had shipped to America, Argentina, Chile. He was fairly good at picking up languages and dialects. For a while in Chile he had even lived among Indians.

Dorothy said, I gather you went to Palestine before you tore out your Old Testament?

Um, before, yes. Gretl, Ludwig's sister, said I should go there, to see. All right. I go. There I work. On their farms — *die Kibbutzim.* These are different people, different Jews. On a different standard they live. Not money but the land. This much I can respect. To build again a ... a *Charakter.* For a peoples this is much work.

Now Moore's ears were up. Character? he asked.

Max nodded. Sure, Moore. A people's *Charakter.* To rise — to make of themselves a different life. To grow to men. This is *Charakter, nicht wahr?*

This was queer. With his hands folded on his stomach, his eyes half closed and his mouth half open, Moore was now considering what Max had said. For the longest time, Moore sat there, breathing in starts, formulating his reply. Wittgenstein, meanwhile, was growing increasingly uncomfortable with the turn the discussion had taken. Finally, Moore said:

I'm sorry, Max, but I'm afraid I do not understand where *character* enters into this. It seems to me that the Jewish peoples and Zionists have gone to Palestine not to rebuild their characters but to rebuild, or rediscover, a life. Or to escape the old life. But not, I would say, for want of *character.*

As Moore was saying this, Max popped open the gas mask container. In plunged the fist. Out came a handful of grain, which he dribbled into his open mouth. Moore could see the muscles working in Max's temple and bulging lower jaw. Then Max's eyes slowly floated up, and he said:

In America, they have the Negro peoples. As slaves they come there — a steel — a *stolen* peoples. Still today, I think, they are the slaves, still stolen. In America, very bad do I see this fear in their faces. On the street, the Negro will not look at you. In New York I am told by a sailor that they want to go back to Africa, these Negroes. This wonders me. The little Jew, he wants to be the big Zion Jew. The Negro to be again African. Many peoples want their Zion land. Africa I think is their Negro Zion — in Africa I think will be better for them. In New York, I am thinking these things to me, *ja.* So one day I think to ask these Negroes if they will go back to Africa, to their hot Negro Zion. But, Moore ... they *will-not-talk-to-me!* It is this fear in them. Like that — Max struck his hands together — they run away.

Moore was walleyed. Staring at Max in incomprehension, Wittgenstein half groaned, You never told me this. I know I never heard this.

Max was still chewing, unconcerned. Ummm, sure, this happened. Oh, but one Negro — this man, he will talk to me. He knows this Zion, sure. Oh, he is a fast-talking, black-black, this man. I can hardly understand his Negro talking. He says they are buying a big ship, an ark. He wants to taken me to his church. All right. Good. I go there with him. Here are black Negro men, Negro ladies wearing the white dress, to the floor. Terrible, terrible it was! Such shouting! On the floor they are falling. Max flopped his arms spastically. Like this, *elektrifizieren*, they are doing, huh? Never do I hear such noise, such singing! I hope to God never again will I hear such singing. You know me, Ludwig. Not much I fear, but from there I run. Max grinned. I know it when the devil touches me!

Wittgenstein and the Moores sat there at a loss, not knowing what to say. Max, meanwhile, went on chewing, his little eyes now trained out the window, fastened on something else. Max's stories frequently had this effect.

Succession Song

Toward noon, they entered Liverpool Street Station, where they caught a taxi through the city to make their connection at Waterloo Station. They were hungry by then, so after settling their seats and luggage, they all had lunch in the dining car. They were already outside London by the time they had finished. The train was rapidly picking up speed, the cars coursing and swaying as Moore followed Dorothy through the narrow aisles back to their seats. It was treacherous, crossing between the jamming, shuddering cars. Dorothy half closed her eyes, the gritty wind pummeling her ears as she clasped Moore by the arm and stepped across the caged couplings. If only he were more nimble! Frightened he would loose his footing and be sucked under the wheels, she shouted, *Quickly, Bill, quickly! All right!* he shouted back. *Just go on yourself!* looking as if he would sneeze, with his tie flapping up into his red face.

By the time they reached their seats, they were passing London's outlying suburbs. The little streets were giving way to increasingly green stretches where the sun became more steady and the westward distances more blue. The car was warm, and as Dorothy pasted down the wing of Moore's collar, she saw a fine sweat on his brow. I'm quite all right, he huffed, repairing his silvery white hair with one careful finger. Now, *really*, he repeated under his breath. Just leave me. Very well, she replied. But she eyed him a moment longer, not altogether sure.

As this was going on, Wittgenstein had noticed a rust-colored bird sitting on a stone wall. What was that? he remarked. Must be some kind of thrush — it's too large for a wren.

I'm sure we can find it, volunteered Dorothy, pulling her field guide from the wicker creel in which she carried her birding things. Flipping the pages and biting her lip. One eye on the book and one on Moore, who by then had ebbed into a pall of aloof and weary abstraction.

It was then that Max snatched her binoculars from the creel and trained them on the far hills. Grinning foolishly, he said, I will show you birds tomorrow, Dorthe! I will show you the things. Tomorrow we will go together out.

At this, Wittgenstein snapped, Don't invite yourself, Max! Mrs. Moore might want to be by herself.

Max looked at him with hurt surprise. It seemed not to have occurred to him that Dorothy might not want him along.

Dorothy could see his feelings were hurt and she spoke up. Oh, no, we might go tomorrow. In the afternoon, perhaps.

But then she was stuck. The idea of going birding with Max was somehow incomprehensible, but she couldn't very well withdraw her offer. In her nervousness, she began telling a silly little story about an old man she had known, a Mr. Collie, who kept finches. Yet no sooner had Dorothy begun the story than she realized it would bother Moore. Stuck again. She had no choice but to finish it: the story was dangling from her lips like a long string of spaghetti.

Of course, male birds are the ones that generally do the singing, she said, resuming her story. Well, Mr. Collie had one particular pair of which the male was an exceptional triller. Oh, a regular little Cock Robin he was. All day long he would be preening and singing. The female was just a drab little thing, and quiet. Hardly made a peep. She just kept to herself on her perch, fluffing and nipping at herself. Anyhow, Mr. Collie awoke early one morning and heard the male singing away. He didn't know what was the matter. It was still pitch black outside, and of course the cage was hooded for the night. Caged birds almost never start singing that early.

Well, he lay there for the longest time, hoping the little bird would quiet down, but he just kept trilling away. So finally Mr. Collie crept downstairs to see what was the matter. And when he found what it was, he couldn't believe it. The male was lying at the bottom of the cage, stone dead. He'd died during the night, you see. It was that little female who was doing all the singing. And not just singing, mind you, but singing *his* song — exactly. Mr. Collie said it was as if she had spent her life as the male's understudy, listening so she could take up after him. Isn't that the most peculiar story? Oh, it sent a shiver down me when I heard it, I don't know why.

But looking at Moore then, Dorothy knew why, just as he did. It was the unspoken part of the story — the loss part lingering in the background, hooked like an old coat behind a darkened door.

No wonder Dorothy Moore shrank at this story of succession. At times, she felt like the female canary herself, the way she had to take up for Moore, paying the bills and maintaining the house with the help of their two boys. But of course there was more to it than that. Increasingly, they felt the nineteen-year difference in their ages. At thirty-nine, Dorothy was a handsome woman, plump and abundantly healthy — if a tad dowdy — in her plain flowered frock, rolled-over ankle socks and scuffed oxfords. Moore could hardly keep up with her. He found her energy and enthusiasm astounding. Dorothy was always ready to hike for miles, or get on her bicycle, or do rubbings or dig for fossils. He, on the other hand, was slowly retiring from life's more strenuous activities, having reached the age at which he craved inward peace and privacy. Most telling of all, he was at the age when men acquire a fondness for stale puns and seemingly pointless jokes — jokes that, to Moore's delight, made Dorothy and the boys wince and hold their noses. The jokes were silly, but the reason he told them was not. Moore loved this tomfoolery; it was his deepest intimacy. Well, he'd say to the boys after telling some stinker, I guess your father's just an old fool. But the old fool was not getting simple. He was just testing the waters, seeing how it felt to think of oneself as old. At fifty-eight, Moore was finding it all easier to imagine. With his white hair and his face now pale and wrinkled around the eyes, Moore had quite lost his boyish looks. He was also thinner, having lost his epic gut to seltzer water, digestive pills and late moderation prompted by proddings from Dorothy and his doctor about his high blood pressure.

No, Moore did not expect to last, but then men seldom do. Oh, no, he fully expected to go first — not soon, necessarily, but first. This was sporting of him. Why, it seemed somehow chivalrous, spreading one's life like a cloak before the woman that she might pass over it unscathed. After all, there was only so much mutual time and air between a man and woman; this life is not free for the breathing. In a sense, dying seemed to Moore a selfless act, as if by dying he would bequeath that much more life to Dorothy. And yet in another sense Moore felt cowardly and guilty, realizing that he vastly preferred the idea of going first to hanging on like old Collie, wifewrecked, with only shrill birds for company.

They had been traveling for a while when Max got up to stretch his legs. Wittgenstein took the opportunity to speak to Dorothy:

Please do not feel you must go with Max tomorrow. I'll talk to him. He may even forget it. Max's eyes are always bigger than his stomach.

Oh, I quite understand, she said, passing it off. He is a bubbling pot. But it is charming in him.

That's *true*, said Wittgenstein, nodding. He seemed grateful that she had noticed Max's good points. He *is* charming — I forget that. And absolutely generous and pure. Wittgenstein thought about this for a moment, then added, And please do not misunderstand me. I am not suggesting you should *not* go with him tomorrow. In fact, I am sure you would find it tremendously rewarding. Max has a most amazing eye. I don't know how he manages to find or see the things he does.

Wittgenstein appeared slightly agitated. He kept starting and stopping, as if all his thoughts of Max were afterthoughts. Closing his eyes, he resumed:

If only he weren't so stubborn. He has no sense. He doesn't even have fear — not even fear to preserve himself. My sister Gretl is a cultured woman. To see her, you cannot imagine her tolerating for one second a man like him. Yet she is very fond of him — like a headstrong son. Of course, they quarrel. He thoroughly exasperates her at times. Oh, he'll *work*. He'll work his heart out for anyone — for nothing — for a bowl of soup. But will Max take a job? Absolutely not. It's quite out of the question. The mere idea of taking money — and I mean honestly earned money — morally offends him. Name one account in the Bible of Christ's taking money, he'll say.

Wittgenstein dismissed this with a wave of his hand, then continued, We thought last year he was going into the monastery, but no. When he travels, he gets into trouble; when he stays put, he gets into trouble. My sister thought it would be good for him to see me. It was she who bought him his ticket.

Oh, really? said Dorothy, a come-on so he would tell them more about his friend.

But Wittgenstein abruptly changed the subject when he saw Max ambling back down the aisle, hauling himself along the seat tops like a gymnast.

And not long after that, Wittgenstein himself got up, leaving the Moores alone with Max. Clearly, Max suspected that Wittgenstein had been talking about him, because he smiled and said with a glance at Wittgenstein's departing back:

Ludwig thinks I talk crazy. I know this is true sometimes. Just now I think: Max, you are a Zionist looking for your Zion. This is how it is for me, you see. Always am I changing. And I am a bad man. Now you smile, Dorthe, but is true, is the true! I am a looking man. Ludwig also. Ludwig is worse in his looking. His sister sends me here, you see. Because she thinks he works too hard.

Oh, said Dorothy. So she sent you here?

Max nodded. Sure, to see after him. This is a good woman, this Gretl. She gets me out of the jail when I fight these two men. Max made a guttural noise in his throat. Communists. I don't hurt them so bad. In Vienna, you know, everybody knows Ludwig's sister, Frau Stonborough. Oh, people, they are surprised that I will know this great lady. Well? She sends me to Palestine, to see this place. She thinks this will do me good to be with Jews, to see myself these peoples. All right. I look. For me this is good, I think. If too long we stay, as I think, we become a church. No, I will not be a church. I hate all these lying churches.

They crossed the wealds, rolling, softly wooded land capped with high lopsided hills whose broad backs broke off into flaky scarps of seamed chalk — the same chalk that whitened the notched roads the hills enclosed and the squiggly stone walls that ran in every direction. Wittgenstein and his companions dully watched it pass, the roads enclosed by hills, the trees hemmed by clouds, the land receding to sea, and all this dissolving into the private, mutual life that intimacy enfolded. Slowly, a certain awkwardness set in. They found themselves running out of words. Perhaps the barrier was the Moores: the barrier of marriage, a private language enclosed as if within parentheses from public view. Or perhaps it was more the two foreigners enclosed by English, a tongue that made Max, transmogrified, sound foreign even to Wittgenstein, as if he were hearing a translation of a translation.

It was something of a relief, then, when around two-thirty the train pulled into Petersfield, where they were to meet Russell. For Moore, who had arranged the trip, it was also a minor embarrassment because they were over an hour early. Earlier, while squinting through his bifocals at the timetable, Moore had apparently strayed into the wrong column.

It was just as well, really. Wittgenstein wanted a word with Max, and Dorothy wanted a few minutes with Moore — time to collect themselves and compare notes. Moore and Dorothy were quite agreeable when Wittgenstein asked if he and Max might take a short walk. It was too pleasant a day to sit inside the station. The platform was almost empty, so the Moores said they would wait there, with the luggage.

And so Moore and Dorothy found themselves sitting silently together in the summer air. The sun warmed the pavement, and the billowy clouds carried the sense of the sea, though it was ten miles distant. Moore patted his pockets, reassuring himself of their return tickets. Dorothy refolded the tops of her white ankle socks. Finally, she asked:

Did it bother you, that story I told about Collie?

Moore looked around at her. You never told me that before, did you?

I thought it would upset you. Dorothy waited a beat, then said, We still haven't sat down, the two of us, and drafted a new will.

Moore stared ahead uncomfortably. There are things I'd rather do. No, he admitted after a moment, it was not a terribly happy story. Grasping the bench, Moore stretched out his trousered legs and surveyed them, like a carpenter eyeing a pair of crooked beams. Then he asked, Would you mind if we talked about something else? It's not an especially good time for it.

If you wish, she said. But there is never a good time for it.

He sighed and rested back. They'd let that string dangle for now.

Knowing Moore's sensitivity to what he considered gossip, or at least malicious gossip, Dorothy felt she had to move slowly in broaching her next topic, the subject of Max and Wittgenstein. Dorothy was no gossip, she was just more open and direct than Moore in her opinions of people. Still, there were unspoken rules between them, rules governing gossip and countless other matters. Hence, while Dorothy might discuss with Moore the matter of Max and Wittgenstein (at least so far as was seemly), it was understood that she mustn't do so too soon, or with too much relish. So, after waiting a decent interval, she said quite by the bye:

Wittgenstein hardly seems to have aged. He must be — what? — over forty now, I guess. The years seem not to have been too hard on him, for all that. He looks closer to thirty, I'd say.

Moore knew as well as she did what she was getting at, but he hung back until she said:

Well?

Well, what?

You know perfectly well what I mean. I mean Max. What do you make of Max?

I guess I don't know what to make of him, said Moore carefully.

Well, what do you make of that business about the Jews and the Negroes?

Moore sighed. I don't know, it was one of those things you wish you hadn't heard. I remember Wittgenstein looking at me then, begging, I think, my indulgence — I was certainly very embarrassed for him.

Moore trailed off, rubbing his hands, then continued, But with Max, you're tempted, I don't know, to make some recourse to *reason* — as if the problem were a simple matter of understanding. Or of overcoming some powerful misapprehension. But it's not a matter of *proof* or *instruction*, I don't think . . . Moore trailed off, then said by way of amplification, And it's all the worse when its roots are religious. You heard what I started to discuss with Max. And I don't mean to suggest that he is by any means stupid or unsubtle —

On the contrary, I think he's extremely acute.

Well, he *is*. But as I say, I didn't think talking would be any use. Nor, apparently, did Wittgenstein. I can't tell you how often this seems to happen to me. Someone will say something. And — and it's so miserably wrong, and so — Moore reached with his arms — *odious*, well, my mind just blackens, and I see there's absolutely *nothing* to be said. People talk of epiphanies, but *that* — when absolutely nothing can be said — that, for me, is a kind of small death. And it is a shame, because for all that, Max *is* likable and, I think, rather extraordinary — if extraordinarily misguided.

Moore looked up at her, and she knew that he wanted to drop this discussion, too. And so they fell back to the day at hand, to the neutral, ordinary things — the grass bent like wires in the sun and the fidgeting sparrows washing themselves in the dust by the roadbed. For five minutes then they sat in silence. Then Dorothy said:

Tell me this much. Can you quite . . . *see* the two of them together?

Moore shrugged. As *ideologues,* I suppose. There is that kind of, I don't know, *zealousness* about them. Moore glanced at her suspiciously, then asked, That is what you meant by "together," isn't it?

Well, I didn't mean it *that* way. Which way did you think I meant?

I *didn't* think, he said with a scowl.

Oh, you did, too, think. If it wasn't on your mind, you wouldn't have asked.

Moore puffed out his cheeks. What do you mean! It most emphatically is *not* on my mind, and I don't wish to discuss it!

She saw this would lead them nowhere. Oh, all right, she said after a minute, touching his arm. I don't want to quarrel. Loath as you are to admit it, we *might* just enjoy ourselves, you know. I'd *like* us to enjoy ourselves this weekend. So don't be putting yourself in a mood. Lightly then, peering into his clouded face, she said, Come on now, Bill. Give us a smile.

This was a game between them when he was feeling grumpy. Oh, quit now, he said with a wince. Like an unwilling bear, he pulled his head away, trying not to smile.

Dorothy coaxed. Oh, come on now. Give us that charming smile. Smile for us like you're going to smile for your good friend Bertie Russell. Don't be coy.

Moore knew she wouldn't relent. Looking around then to see that no one was looking, he gritted his yellow teeth into a grimacing smile and emitted a low growl.

There we go, she said merrily. There's my good bear. Now, don't you feel better?

No!

Even to the South Pole

OUTSIDE THE STATION, meanwhile, Max was making a beeline for the pub, with Wittgenstein in pursuit.

Max! warned Wittgenstein as his friend pulled open the pub door. Max, I'm not going in there with you. I'll not have a repeat of last night, either.

Oh, come on, said Max, who, like Wittgenstein, had fallen back into German. I'll only have a couple. We'll be back in plenty of time. You're not coming? Well —

Max!

The heavy door swung shut, and Wittgenstein was left standing there like a fool, stiff shouldered and red faced, tensely tapping the cane. Max was so expert at manipulating him! And as usual Wittgenstein saw he had no choice. Either he could stand outside, impotent and angry, or he could go in and vent his anger, in which case he would still be playing right into him.

When Wittgenstein did go inside, he found Max berthed by the taps in the low afternoon darkness, draining one pint while the barmaid drew another, watching him like a robbery in progress. This was another side of Max. In Trattenbach, Max had always been deeply abstemious, never touching a drop of alcohol. But now it seemed there was a deeper rupture between Max's beliefs and what he did, as if all that mattered, in the end, was the sheer will to believe. Wittgenstein went up and stared him in the face.

Have you forgotten your promise from last night? Or were you too drunk? Because if you want to be an ass and carry on, you can stay here. I'll not have you embarrassing me.

Oh, come on, groaned Max, giving him an affable paw on the arm. Get down off your high horse, will you? I told you I'm only having a couple. Who are you? My wife?

Max knew this last remark would sting Wittgenstein, and it did. With that, Max changed his demeanor. Here was sober Max — God-fearing Friar Max.

Come on, Ludwig, he said after a minute. Just give me twenty minutes. I'll be fine. Was I not fine today?

No, said Wittgenstein with a glare. You were not fine. Why must everything be an article of faith with you? Don't give me that wronged look. You know exactly what I mean. I mean your jag about Jewish *Charakter*. Or that story about the American Negroes. What were the Moores to say to *that*? What was *I* to say?

Hunkered down on his elbows, Max glowered at him. It was true, it was a true story.

You needn't convince me of that. Wittgenstein watched the glass tilt up, then asked, Would it be such a betrayal if you put your beliefs aside for a day — a week? You'll say we will not agree on this. Very well. Then we will not agree. But why can't you accept it in others? Russell's an atheist and a socialist. If you can't accept that, stay here. Russell advocates infidelity. If you want to fight with him about infidelity, stay here. It's very simple.

But now Max was nodding. His feelings were hurt. So I won't shame you — sure, I understand. Max is fine pal when you're with the yokels. But around your big-shot friends —

Oh, shut up, groaned Wittgenstein, looking away. Either you're making something more than it is or you're making it less. Shame is not the point.

Then what is the point? asked Max, signaling the barmaid for another. Admit it. You're ashamed.

Wittgenstein snorted with disgust, but again, as the night before, he found himself looking into those hard little eyes, seeing that same mixture of goodness, intolerance and brute intransigence. They were back ensconced in their native language, enclosed within this other culture. Yet from what Wittgenstein could see, his friend made no better sense in German than he did in English. Max said he had come to England wanting to talk, but they had done no honest talking — none at least of any duration or consequence, and none of it very calm, either. But Wittgenstein was now thinking that Max, whether he knew it or not, wanted it this way. Ever since he had arrived, Max had seemed to want to stay in public situations, the better to avoid Wittgenstein's relentless gaze. Wittgenstein had been quite unprepared for his arrival. Alone in his room at Whewell's Court at Trinity the night before, Wittgenstein had heard a loud knock. But no sooner had he opened the door than Max leapt out and seized him in a bear hug, shouting, *Surprise! Surprise! Surprise!* as he bounced him up and down.

Max had then dropped his pack on the floor and announced he was starved. Wittgenstein suggested Woolworth's, the lunch counter, where the food was cheap and good. But Max wanted no Woolworth's — it was beer he wanted. And so he pulled Wittgenstein into the Green Mask, a working-class pub down the lane, where he wolfed down two fish dinners, carrying on simultaneous conversations with Wittgenstein and men at two other tables as he mashed, shoveled and chewed, washing it all down with two glasses of milk and three pints of ale. When they finally left three hours later, they were on different planes — the wet and the dry. Standing upstream of him, Wittgenstein waited in exasperation while Max drunkenly straddled the alleyway, talking in a rush amid his own healthy spurting and splashing. Then came the affable arm, locked like a horse collar around Wittgenstein's neck. Time for the Big Confession jag.

Max always finds his pals, he'd said in beery German. Always! No mat — no mat-ter what! If you were in South America — even the South Pole — Max would find you . . .

Drink may have dulled Max's mind, but it only exacerbated his already deep sensitivity to imagined slights. He grew argumentative. Did Wittgenstein doubt the lengths he would go to for a friend? Sucking and stammering, dryly clacking his tongue, Max backed Wittgenstein against a brick wall with a heavy forearm, saying, Do you think I take friendship lightly? Do you think friendship for me is just *talk*? Just the farting and rumbling of beer?

Wittgenstein was fed up by then. He told his friend to calm down. But not being a drinker, Wittgenstein didn't know how to talk to a drunk.

To Max, Wittgenstein only sounded punctilious and disgusted, and the big man gibed back at him, mimicking Wittgenstein's precise German phrasing:

Oh, I know what you say. You say, But Max, you are not acting *reasonable*. And he sneered the word, saying, *reeee*sonable, so that the spittle flew.

Wittgenstein couldn't move. Max's raging jack-o'-lantern face was pressed into his as he blathered, You are right, Lurr-wig. Gretl is right. Sure, I am animal — is a fact! I am not too *reee-sonable*! Reasonable man would stop. But Max is not reasonable and does not stop. Oh, but *you*. You can be so ver' superior now, huh? Sure, in Trat — bach you tell me, *Don't hurt those men, Max*. Let them speak lies and filth. And the boy, that Franz. Sure, let them take him — let him roll with the pigs with his father. It is all right, your poor hands are tied. But Max, see, he does not like, and his hands are not tied! His head is too hard!

Wittgenstein could still remember how Max had watched him with those black little eyes. It seemed as though a film of ice had formed over the dank pond of their past, and Max now wanted to smash through it — wanted to smash it just as he had smashed the faces of those men in Trattenbach. Until then, Wittgenstein had never known that Max held such resentment against him. He had seen Max's anger unleashed, but never against him, and certainly never like this. Doubtless, Trattenbach was part of it. But influence was also mixed up in here. This, Wittgenstein could see, was Pinsent's legacy: the disciple's compulsion to settle accounts and declare his immunity to further influence.

Max! Wittgenstein shouted, shaking him by the shoulder. He felt as if he were calling across a gorge. It seemed as though Max could hardly hear him, but then something else took over. Suddenly, Max's anger broke. Wittgenstein didn't know what had happened; it was as if Max had had the wind knocked out of him. His arms flagged, and his will seemed broken, as if he had suddenly seen something in his rage. But what Wittgenstein most remembered were Max's little eyes, so glazed and frozen, like the stunned stare of an animal killed unawares. And then there was the way Max had lumbered home, here like a driven beast, there like a child begging forgiveness.

Wittgenstein wasn't having this again. When the barmaid brought Max another, he put his foot down:

That's enough. No more, do you hear me?

One more.

You already had that one. Why must you fight me?

Max stood there open-mouthed, goggling at him. Fight *you*? That's a laugh! Oh, you like to think I'm a hard man, Wittgenstein, but you're harder — much harder. Frau Beck — I remember she once said to me, He thinks he's Jesus Christ, doesn't he? He thinks he is Jesus Christ among us peasants.

Wittgenstein whirled around in a fury. That's enough from you!

Max caught him by the arm. All right. I'll stop if you will.

I want to go, said Wittgenstein, seeing other drinkers staring at them. I think you ought to stay here. I can meet you here Tuesday.

But Max was wise to his threats. Oh, come off it, he said, waving him off. I told you, I'll be all right. Look! Max stood back from the bar with his arms extended. Am I not all right? Do you see me weaving? Forget Russell — I won't bother him. I'll keep my trap shut. I promise.

I mean it!

And I told you, I promise.

Max was standing at bum's muster. Of course Max would go to Russell's. Max's arms were outstretched like an aerialist, and he was smiling. For a moment then, he was the old, irrepressible Max, Wittgenstein's former guide and translator, the intermediary between Wittgenstein and the people he wanted to haul up from the muck. Or so it was until the Trattenbachers dragged the schoolteacher and his impressionable disciple down with them.

Back in Trattenbach

IT HAD BEEN the other way around in Trattenbach, that sodden toadstool sitting between two sloven mountains. There, it was Wittgenstein who had been in bad shape, and it was Max, a beefy boy of twenty-one, a year out of the English prison camp and just back, disillusioned, from revolutionary Russia, who had pulled him out of his trough. Without Max, Wittgenstein never would have stayed as long as he had in Trattenbach, hanging on for almost five years. Then again, without Max, Wittgenstein might have had the sense to leave before the villagers had turned completely against him.

Wittgenstein wasn't the first would-be reformer the villagers had driven away. Before him, there had been Father Haft, Wittgenstein's friend and ally and Catholic Trattenbach's sole clergyman. Tall, big-boned and gaunt, with an acne-pocked horse face, Father Haft was a gruff and inflexible ascetic who fasted on Fridays and feast days and gave away most of his pitiful living allowance. The priest was the type who was unable to keep a crumb for himself while others were in want, and he wore himself down to no purpose. Few could have emulated or equaled Father Haft in self-denial, least of all his poor parishioners, who thought a priest ought to have more dignity than to tramp around in worn black gabardines and broken-down boots, without even an um-brella to stave off the rain or a pot to piss in. Father Haft couldn't have cared less — he had nothing but contempt for his parishioners. Like Witt-genstein, the priest was an educated man from a good family, but having come from people of some means, he had no interest in hobnobbing, as had his deceased predecessor, with the mill owner and the more prosper-ous villagers and outlying farmers. To Father Haft, these were piddling fish in a piddling pond, and they now found themselves battling the zeal-ous young priest for control of the crumbling church, which they seemed to feel was a God-granted concession for their own benefit.

From the day Father Haft arrived, they had hated him, this fierce bearer of bad news. From his black gallows of a pulpit in the gritty church he contemptuously called Our Lady of Perpetual Disrepair, Father Haft was forever berating his grubbing parishioners for the peevish smallness that left them growling and scrapping at each other like hungry dogs, then circling like a pack at the approach of outsiders or the threat of progress.

These were the days, soon after his awakening but before the fervor, when Max would still enter a church. Every Sunday, in fact, just after the Epistle, Wittgenstein and Max used to slip into the empty choir loft, where they would sit for the next half hour, cackling with delight at Father Haft's jeremiads against his parishioners. On deaf ears the priest's sermons rained; in resounding silence they suffered him, this threadbare rich man's son from Linz. (For them everyone outside Trattenbach was thought to be rich.)

Why, Father Haft wanted to know, why were these people so blind to the good in others and so unconscious of the good in themselves? A camel sooner could have passed through the eye of a needle than a Trat-tenbacher could have been gathered into Father Haft's nutlike ascetic's heart. Only Wittgenstein, Max and a handful of others seemed to meet with Father Haft's grudging approval, and even they regularly fell from grace. Every week, Wittgenstein and the priest met for discussion and mutual criticism, groping together for higher states of the good that, in the villagers' jealous eyes, made them too good, thereby preventing them from doing much good at all. Father Haft claimed that man must be a moral witness, but he didn't know where to stop in his moral denunciations. One of his most memorable and histrionic sermons concerned a drunkard who had frozen to death in plain view of the village's main street. Showing himself weak with hunger and exhaustion, his voice low and tremulous, then growing staccato, Father Haft described the Lord's pain as He died in the snow with that drunkard. Kneading his fingers into a clove of rhetorical essence, drawing out his attenuated words as if he were pulling a needle through Christ's still quivering Sacred Heart, Father Haft claimed that Christ had suffered a second Calvary with his poor son Alois, the toeless, babbling drunkard. Yes, said Father Haft, looming down from his pulpit, there was left and right, and right and wrong; there was life and death, heaven and hell, Good Samaritans — and Trattenbachers! The priest rose up to smite them, his vestments flapping, they would say, like the devil's wings. And so it was at every sermon. Father Haft would lean down from his pulpit as from a fiery hell chariot, heaping them with abuse, begging for an outpouring of Charity and Spirit and receiving in return only a torrent of hatred. At times even the self-styled evangelist Wittgenstein thought his friend and cellmate had finally pushed them too far.

It took some doing, but after numerous complaints to the bishop about the Jesuit's heresies and abuse, the villagers succeeded in booting the priest out of town. And later, much later, after Wittgenstein's trial, they would proudly say that after they drove out the priest, they gave his crazy friend the schoolmaster the sack as well.

And to think that Wittgenstein had once called Trattenbach "a peaceful little nest of a place"!

Many times afterward, he would try to recall just how the villagers had seemed to him at first. Certainly, they were not as wicked as he thought in the end. Nor, for that matter, was he as blameless as he had thought all along.

Quite objectively, though, Trattenbach was a poor and ugly town — even the Trattenbachers said so. Not far from Trattenbach was a place known as the Gates of Hell, an iron mine that for generations had killed and crippled the region's men, at least while there was any profit in it. But now, as the joke went, the Trattenbachers were safe from damnation: the Gates of Hell were closed. Slammed behind them, was more like it. Those left behind mostly eked out a living as subsistence farmers or unskilled laborers. The more "lucky" worked at the little textile mill or at another local sweatshop, sewing cheap girdles. Among the women, a few even turned to prostitution — mostly of the seasonal or itinerant variety, often to feed the children while their husbands nursed the bottle.

So hell was closed and heaven drifted along, never farther, never closer. The mountains brought nothing either; they only hogged the light and held the clotted clouds that drained the rain and hemmed in the fog, which hung for days like a blight over Trattenbach's ashen hovels. Helmeted and turreted, with spearlike roofs, the houses were as dented and squashed together as the stunted fortress folk who dwelt within them, scheming, brooding, breeding, snarling at one another. It seemed that every wall in Trattenbach needed a coat of paint — paint or dynamite. Wittgenstein could remember slopping through the filthy slush during the winter, his eyes burning with the cheap soft coal they used. Slowly, like a web, the soot sifted over the town, caking everything, to the point he would feel he was scraping between abrasive sheets, his face sparking with the malice he felt seeping out from those scabby walls.

Without the sense to leave and only his own inflexible pride to keep him there, even he could see he had outlasted his potential to do the place any good. But of course poverty was what had brought him to Trattenbach in the first place. Ugliness fell to the poor. After all, he had not renounced his wealth to minister to prosperous people in scenic surroundings. And it was the poor who needed him, he thought. But here, like Father Haft, Wittgenstein failed to see that while he had chosen poverty, the villagers had no such choice, and knew it.

Later, when Wittgenstein had come to realize the extent of his arrogance, he saw that he had been bewitched by an image. This was the idea that poverty and misfortune were something that could be communally *shared* by assuming poverty's outer manifestations. But poverty wasn't brotherhood or comradeship; it wasn't bread that might be broken and distributed like alms so that its hardships might thereby be diminished. Father Haft's and Wittgenstein's chosen poverty was nothing like the trapped hopelessness the villagers knew. But for the elect, for those philanthropists for whom poverty was a vocation, God had removed the meat but reserved the broth, the essence, of poverty; for Father Haft and Wittgenstein, unlike the ignorant villagers, there was poverty of the spirit in full knowledge of one's condition. Knowledge also was a sickness, and Wittgenstein and the priest well knew this predicament, knew it in all its depth and breadth. Spiritual poverty or material poverty — which was the more painful, and painful for whom? At first, Wittgenstein was inclined to believe that for the person of superior intellect, the anguish of spiritual poverty was a far deeper anguish, grossly speaking, than that borne by an ignorant person in the face of hopeless material poverty. But later, when Wittgenstein became more sensitive to the pain of ordinary people, he realized that God, in His wisdom, had apportioned pain according to one's lights, so that these two pains, while qualitatively different, were psychically equal, a bountiful table spread for all.

And the truth was, Wittgenstein needed the poor then to assuage his own impoverished spirit, which at that time, just after the war, was immeasurably poorer than theirs. The aftermath of the war was crueler to Wittgenstein than ever the war had been. At least during the war he had been able to salvage a soupçon of self-respect. But now that the mobilization was over it seemed as if his spirit were mobilizing against him, reducing him, like the rest of Austria, to a state of complete rottenness and decay.

Why had he ever come to Trattenbach? he wondered. Until the very end, Wittgenstein never dreamed that the feeling against him was so bitter and virulent, so deep-seated. Yet why had he come to the village but to debase the currency — to challenge the values of these poor farmers, mill workers and day laborers? And if he couldn't rouse these troglodytes from their hideous ignorance and lethargy — if they were to continue their slavish allegiance to Austria's hemorrhaging money and remain stuck in this stupefying wallow they mistook for a life — then he figured he could at least save their children.

Wittgenstein knew the villagers found him forbidding and peculiar. How could they not? They had only to take one look at him, let alone hear his impeccable high German, to know he was a cultured gentleman from the city. They weren't fooled for one moment by his conspicuous, aggressive poverty. They could spot him a mile off in his cast-off army coat, swinging that cane and carrying a notebook under his arm — that spying notebook in which it was said he jotted down misdeeds that Father Haft would blast them for on Sunday. Still, Wittgenstein felt it was inevitable, and probably healthy, that they fear him. And if, as Max said, they took him for a wealthy eccentric — a *baron*, no less — well, then so much the better. Every St. Paul wants his Ephesians to know that he was formerly a Saul.

How Wittgenstein would have loved to have seen their greedy eyes gorge with the fortune he had given away before coming to Trattenbach! In the disastrous inflation after the war, when Austria's fat blotter bills were devalued two and three times a day, when money was being carted and valued almost by weight, his wealth could have done much for the war orphans and the widows whose savings had been wiped out. For that matter, it could have done much for his former comrades, the maimed or unemployed veterans whom he would see sleeping in parks and doorways. Yes, Wittgenstein could have done many good deeds with his money, but he still heard Tolstoy counseling him that to give money to the poor was like spreading disease. Common people couldn't be trusted with money; it went to their heads like cheap wine. Besides, though Wittgenstein could himself renounce the accumulated power, the hegemony, of this money, he instinctively felt the need to preserve it in his own people. In this respect, he would always harbor the instincts of a man of wealth.

His family, in any case, was rich beyond corrupting. As a result of her highly successful wartime relief work, Gretl was now Herbert Hoover's personal representative in Austria, charged with overseeing the efforts of the American Food Relief Commission. Frau Wittgenstein had died of a heart attack early in the spring of 1920. Freed from her mother's care, Mining was again overworking herself, helping Gretl and running a grammar school for poor children. As for Paul, he was away most of the time, traveling across Europe giving highly acclaimed one-armed piano concerts.

Wittgenstein was not so lucky. On his return from the Italian prison camp, he had found Vienna's half-starved populace chopping down the city's woods and hauling it off in rattling wagons and wheelbarrows. But the worst thing for him was realizing that he was now one of the wealthiest men in Vienna, the bulk of his fortune safely sheltered in America, earning vast sums in interest. It was hell for him to have so much while others had so little — to feel so indelibly the guilt and responsibility of old money, which had accumulated so long in the sun, concentrated in power like the bee's honey. The weight of this stacked money only dragged down his drowning soul. Wittgenstein had hardly been home a week when the guilt of his wealth became unbearable. Amid their happy relief at being reunited with him, Mining and Gretl felt his anxiety rising like ripples on a lake. He talked not at all, then talked in a rush, with alarming, vertiginous complexity. He couldn't think for thinking, couldn't sleep for dreaming, which was thinking, too, since all was thinking and all thinking, dreaming. *Music!* He craved music, but music was also thinking and was always being played a hair too slow or too fast, like conversation, which made him, in his anxiety and impatience, want to speed to a point that was never forthcoming amid all the jabber. *It was the house,* he would think, it was the Palais Wittgenstein, that bloated pastry stuffed with dead dreams. He loathed the house. Steeped in the soil of an earlier culture, it was just like himself, an anachronism. If only he could have died in a moment of brilliance! If only he could have been a star in the sky! But now he felt himself being hurled into the furnaces of a featureless future, another useless war relic to be scrapped and melted down.

The ripples mounted into waves. His nights were interminable. One night, hearing a dog howling, he remembered the scavenging, corpse-eating dogs during the war, how their cries carried for miles in the crystalline night air, amid the rumbling of the war trains laden with men, horses and explosives. His peasant soldiers said the barking dogs meant that someone had just died, a not unreasonable belief, since men were always dying and dogs were always barking. It was true what the peasants said, he thought, the dog did have the most intimate connection with death. Wittgenstein must have drifted off then, because later he awoke and heard the dog bark. Three times, distinctly, the dog barked. And then it stopped like the crowing cock that signaled Peter's betrayal. For twenty minutes, Wittgenstein lay there in a sweat, praying that the dog would bark again to prove it was not a sign but a dog, not a curse but a simple cry. But the dog did not bark again, and Wittgenstein realized that he was furiously biting at the twisted end of his sheet, tearing at it like a dying man in his hateful big bed of money.

That was the end for him. The next morning, Gretl received an urgent call from Herr Brundolf, the family's solicitor, asking her to come to his office immediately. He said it was her brother Ludwig. He was in a state of great agitation, insisting that he be forthwith and forever relieved of his entire fortune.

After much cajoling, Gretl managed to get her brother home from the solicitor's office, but nothing could shake his resolve. Paul and Mining and other members of the family were hurriedly called and consulted. Sanitariums and temporary conservatorships were discussed. Wittgenstein was incensed by their questions. He insisted he was of sound mind and said he would go to court if necessary to be freed from this accursed, mutating money; when that didn't work, he even hinted at suicide. Gretl told Mining that it would have made a great drawing room farce had it not been so tragic.

For two weeks, Gretl managed to stave him off. Then early one spring morning, when the weather was rainy and gusty, Wittgenstein called Gretl to the window. Pointing to a man down the street who was struggling with his whipping umbrella, Wittgenstein said in a voice drained of emotion:

You know, if you did not know there was a heavy wind outside, you might see that man tumbling along with his umbrella and think, How ungainly and clumsy. And so unnecessary, all this man's vain twisting. But, big sister, your window is shut. In the end, you do not know, and cannot theorize, what forces drive the man. And look, he said, pointing. The man is being driven down the road.

Since childhood they had spoken to each other in this way, using similes and parables. Wittgenstein had made his point. Gretl gave in to his wishes and followed them to the letter as quickly as possible. This was just as well. The truth was, he was then in no condition to see after his own affairs.

With that done, there remained the larger problem of what Wittgenstein was to do with his life. Actually, he had given away two estates: having written a book that, to his mind, answered all the essential philosophical questions, Wittgenstein had literally worked himself out of a job as a philosopher; and having given away his fortune, he was bankrupt but no better off. As he saw it, if he could be of no further use to himself, it was only fitting that he make himself useful by doing something of service to others. Indeed, in following this path, he would be continuing a family tradition, pursuing a course of which even his father might have dimly approved. It was Mining, with her connections with the new school reform movement, who suggested teaching. Wittgenstein seized upon the idea and spent the next year in the teachers' training college, the Lehrerbildungsanstalt. The school had virtually nothing to teach him, and he hated it. Every day his face stung with the almost unspeakable humiliation of sitting at a little desk, submitting to the tutelage of various sincere but inferior minds whose thoughts he was expected to absorb and parrot without question or protest.

Wanting to break with the past, he refused at this time to live with Mining in the Palais Wittgenstein. Nor would he accept Gretl's clearly *pro forma* invitation to live with her and Rolf. Instead, he took a little room on the Untere Viaduktgasse, close to the teachers' college but, as he well knew, much too close to the Prater meadows, where toward dusk the young men would gather like feeding deer among the enshrouding trees.

All that summer there was a siege in him as various moral props gave way. He was not a star in the sky but only a shallow vessel, a spittoon. Now there was only sex, wrenching spasms of uncontrollable, indiscriminate sex. Again and again, there he'd be, stripping and sucking the salty dog from some rimmed cock that stood bent like a swollen jugular in his mouth while some stranger's strong legs strummed in the wind. Unwilling to rationalize his guilt, unable to forgive himself and start afresh, utterly glutted with his native rottenness, he had sunk to the very bottom. Sin reeked from his pores. Indeed, at times, the only sign of life he discerned in himself was his surging erections, uncoiling down his trouser leg on trams, in class and in other inappropriate places, quite mentally unattended, like a dog that had snapped its leash. There was no fighting it. Battling like an exhausted swimmer against the tide, his will would inevitably collapse before a torrent of anxiety that drove him into the Prater, there to kneel beneath the sucking stomach of some unemployed butcher or mechanic with nocturnal eyes, the type who'd no sooner finish than he'd be shaking himself off as if before a urinal while Wittgenstein delicately turned away, spitting the eggy spunk like poison into the bushes.

There was another precedent in Wittgenstein's decision to take up teaching the poor. Count Tolstoy himself had taught school for a time, instructing the little peasant children on his country estate, Yasnaya Polyana. But Trattenbach wasn't Yasnaya Polyana. For all their backwardness, the Trattenbachers weren't real peasants with red noses, nor was he a God on his own estate, teaching the fearful children of his humble servants.

This was where Max came in. Max could deal with these people. Max could speak their language and so became Wittgenstein's intermediary in the most ordinary transactions.

They met at Trattenbach's dank little cellar cinema about six months after Wittgenstein had arrived in the village. Wittgenstein had bought a bag of nuts and was sitting on one of the wooden seats, waiting for the show to begin, when this lunk with a broad calf's face pounced down beside him and started talking in midstream as if he were resuming a conversation rather than starting one. Never before had Wittgenstein seen this young man. He thought he was some disturbed person, the way he was carrying on about cowboy pictures and Russia and full of impertinent questions. Ignoring him did no good; it only drove him on. Fumbling and gesticulating, sprawling into Wittgenstein and glaring into his eyes, the stranger would punctuate his jokes with an obnoxious laugh, then immediately goose Wittgenstein on the shoulder with an excited *But listen to this!* as he launched into another wild story. As the stranger continued talking and carrying on, Wittgenstein suddenly felt the bag in his lap rumble, then saw the fellow cram a dribbling fistful of nuts into his mouth. *Gaggmmmm*, the man mumbled approvingly, crunching and shaking his head like a feeding horse. Good and fresh, huh?

Shock kept Wittgenstein from believing that this young hooligan had just helped himself — it was impossible. But then, sure enough, the bag rumbled again, and Wittgenstein plainly saw the freeloader's ham hand haul out a second fistful of nuts and mash them into his mouth, chewing fitfully as the lights went out and the screen flickered. At this, the man jumped up in alarm and called back to the projectionist, *Hold it! I'll be right back!* Then he barged down the aisle to fetch more nuts, not because he had devoured Wittgenstein's bag, but simply because he had a tooth for nuts.

Within a week, they were inseparable. At first, Max reminded Wittgenstein vaguely of his old corporal, Ernst. But he soon realized that Max was far more intelligent and perceptive than Ernst. There was something preternatural in him. He had an uncanny knack with people, an idiot grace that enabled him to get away with almost anything. Even those in Trattenbach who thought Max a wild good-for-nothing couldn't help but like him. Children would bring Max home like a stray dog, and within minutes he would have their parents enthralled as well. Wittgenstein saw Max work his magic on many people during the tramps they took through lower Austria during those summers. Max's way of addressing complete strangers in midstream, as he had done with Wittgenstein in the theater, was quite typical. But by Max's ideal and inflexible logic, this made perfect sense: if all men were his brothers, then it stood to reason that they were all familiar to him. Wittgenstein remembered the way a farmer, a complete stranger, had once squinted into Max's eyes, asking, Don't I know you? And how Max had stood back like a prodigal whose image would shortly float into focus, mesmerizing as he said, Don't you, brother? *Don't* you? . . .

All the world was Max's larder, property, for him, being another arbitrary and artificial barrier obstructing human commerce. Do you see up there? Max would say to Wittgenstein as they hiked along. The old lady who lives in that house makes good black honey bread and apple jam. Whereupon Max, with the powerful instincts of a bear, would walk straight up to the house to be fed by the old woman, who would be delighted by his company, and whom he'd repay by tearing down an old shed for firewood or fixing her roof.

Then there were Max's stories — wild, convoluted stories, one leading to another, like jokes, like parables. And because Max feared no one and would talk to anybody, he heard everything until it all ran together as in a powerful dream. Only later, while retelling some preposterous tale, would he realize that too much didn't fit, whereupon a scandalized look would crease his face and he would say, That man lied to me! unable to comprehend why anyone would do such a useless and despicable thing.

But had Max been more critical, had he been more discerning and cautious — or less gullible — people wouldn't have felt the freedom to tell him the things they did. Max had none of his later harshness and inflexibility then. He was young and had a marvelous freshness and purity of insight, which Wittgenstein found immediately arresting. Max was really a philosopher, of sorts, a behemoth deeply submerged in the midst of life. He was so much a part of his surroundings, so deeply imbedded in life, that it was hard to imagine anything bad ever befalling him. And when something bad did happen, Max laughed it off — *became* it, sunny as the young grass, happy to be reaped for the fullness of sprouting again.

By all appearances, even the war had been this way for Max. It seemed to have passed right through him. Still, there was something distinctly martial in Max's nature, no doubt about that. Standing before Max, one knew why men's eyes were not fastened on either side like those of cattle. One could see why man's predatory eyes were aimed squarely ahead like the wolf's, seeking rather than avoiding — blind. For fifteen months, until he was badly wounded and captured during a German counterstrike near Thiepval, Max had served in a crack batallion of shock troops specializing in surprise night assaults using flame throwers and stick bombs. There would be no moon and no stars visible under the dark clouds, no bombardment and no covering fire — nothing but speed, surprise and their own youthful ferocity. With cork-blackened faces, they would come sprinting down on the first paralyzed sentries, who would hardly have cried out when rocketing jets of flame sucked the air from their lungs. The Black Death, the French called them. For Max, it was how the Angel of Death must have felt passing in a hot wind over the blood-smeared doors of the Pharaoh's Egypt. It was the war which taught Max that men really had spirits: the boy could feel that turbulence as the souls of the dead took up in a greasy torrent of burning petrol. So exhilarating, how death liberates the mind. Fire cannot harm fire, and death is impervious to all harm. Max and his cohorts were a hot black wind chasing arcs of immolating liquid fire. To Max, the advancing sheets of fire felt like nothing, a summer wind. He was seventeen. In the enfilading darkness, he was a black death angel, invisible and invincible. Lost in his blackened face, his snarling open mouth looked disembodied, like a bite torn from an apple. Faced with the wobbling whites of his eyes, men gave in to the last panic of death, hearing their coshed skulls crumple as they sunk into the sulfurous fens of the Land of Lamentation. The Black Death broke the French lines. They did not stop, and they did not care, hurling stick bombs and hurling themselves in vengeance, hurling themselves to no purpose but to inflict death and terror, since ultimately they would be repulsed. Max was one of a new breed of specialized soldier, carefully selected and highly trained; he was that one man in a thousand ideally suited to this savage, cut-and-run fighting. In this reverse Darwinism, the strongest and fiercest tended to be the first killed, while those few who survived were propelled into a new consciousness. Older men — men over the age of about twenty-five, men who cared about life and knew themselves to be mortal — found the extreme stress and horror of this butchery intolerable. They broke down under it; their psyches were too well formed. But for the uncreated man, for the germinal man within the street youth from Nuremberg — for a big, sprawling, easygoing reform school boy, who, when pushed into a fight, would go berserk, heedless of any injury, severely beating bigger, older boys, beating two and three boys at a time even — for such a boy, this rough comradeship and terror seemed intensely natural, an ideal.

Fire cannot harm spirit, and time holds no sway outside of time. For the boy, the horror was never quite real, or rather had quite gone past reality. In those frenzied minutes of killing, like a weasel ripping through a hen house, the boy told himself that it would soon all be past, and as something past would no longer be real and thus would no longer matter — which was to say, it had never happened in the first place. The reality of it was thus quite magical. He was decorated and it never touched him. He was wounded many times, several times seriously, but it touched him no more than did the death of his comrades, sewn in pits in one long black sleep. By the dozens, and in every attitude, even in slumber, he had slaughtered his enemies, English, French, territorials. He killed so much that at last it seemed he had entered a condition of nature, showing neither malice nor mercy, sorrow nor anger. And after a battle, he would immediately forget everything, the men he had murdered, the comrades he had lost. He would tolerate no killing of wounded or prisoners and treated captured enemies with all the courtesy he showed his comrades. Still, it was clear to him that his own life did not matter, and so, in the end, nobody's life really mattered.

All men have stories that they tell themselves in order to account for their misfortunes, and Max was no different. Max had told Wittgenstein the general outlines of his story, which, like most stories, had developed into a kind of personal myth. Before God, the boy soldier told himself, no one mattered. Before God nothing else was real and so was all a dream; and since all was a dream, the man of reverence could only surrender to the dream's perdurable power. First Max's mother had died, and then his father; and then his shiftless uncle took him for a year until he too died, drinking himself to death as Max's father had. From the age of seven the boy was raised by the city, in a pound for children. Max rarely spoke of his childhood, but he told Wittgenstein that with the death of his parents he had early lost his faith in life in the usual sense. And then, having lost all faith in the efficacy of life, he found his faith in God on the Western Front. With God, all made sense. Max realized that he was not made to live: clearly, the world had not massed all its powers of destruction in one place so that he and his comrades might live to a ripe age. One day in the lull before a battle this dawned on him, but instead of feeling betrayed, Max felt only stupid, like a boy who had just learned about sex, wondering why he had not seen it all sooner. With that, many things became immediately apparent. For one thing, the boy understood that this was not just any war. Of course, the boy had never then heard of divine right or anything like that, but he understood, in an almost teleological way, that it was not General Falkenhayn nor even the kaiser but God almighty who was sending down their battle orders. This, he supposed, was for the good. In the end, Max told himself, all would be raised and righted: the dead were not really dead and the living were only living provisionally, like beasts in a barnyard, waiting for the whistle that would carry them from their funk holes into Kingdom Come. Ultimately, all men, on all sides, were engaged in a common assault on a destiny not of their choosing and indeed quite beyond their comprehension. If God sacrificed the majority of mankind to save the few who were worthwhile, then this, by Max's book, was to the good; if a nation did the same to perpetuate itself, then this, too, was to the good. Bees and ants and animals with their young did this thing, surrendering their lives for the good of the species. It was all part of the same process, the individual stoking the great engine of life which ran for no reason but God's pleasure and aggrandizement. Whole forests that no human eye would ever see would rise toward the light only to come crashing down; whole generations would joust their ascent, ramming and splattering up out of the thundering spume like salmon, thirsting for another element. Under the showering destruction of His own hard and unfathomable radiance, they would shield themselves, like fire in the midst of fire. This, for Max, was the mystical. And so it was one day some years later, when Wittgenstein and Max were walking at dusk in the mountains near Trattenbach. They had ascended out of a valley of darkened firs, climbing toward the buoyant light of the ridges, when Max reared back, then pointed in amazement to a misty teepee of light lodged in the cliffs. This was how he imagined God, he said. Like a hunter, Max did not move, his eye narrowing and his mouth half open to swish the sounds swirling through the cold, iron-tasting air. Till darkness shrouded his face, Max stared at this faintly pulsing triangle of yellow light, watching as it guttered into darkness. Straining to see what held his friend in thrall, Wittgenstein wondered if the blindness was his, the occlusion of his sophistication. Try as he might, he did not see the God who had shone His face over the water. All Wittgenstein saw was a crag scalloped with light — a blank and fearsome image vaguely like the vulgar but oddly apocalyptic etchings in Max's cheap Bible.

Evangelist

WITTGENSTEIN called himself an evangelist during this time in Trattenbach. Father Haft was especially rankled by this term, and one day, during one of their weekly mutual criticism sessions, the priest demanded that Wittgenstein explain himself.

The priest charged that Wittgenstein was spiritually incoherent. He said he had heard Wittgenstein speak with awe of the Day of Judgment, but he had also heard the schoolmaster say that he did not believe in an afterlife, or rather that he found the notion of an afterlife unbelievable. So, too, Father Haft had heard Wittgenstein speak with awe of God — of the mind of God, above, and prior to, his own. But to speak of a personal, loving God, let alone to speak of God as part of some divine Trinity — this Wittgenstein said he found unintelligible. As for confession, Wittgenstein said he could appreciate it as a beautiful *idea,* like a kiss or a prayer. But he could not kiss or confess — unless, of course, one took the sacrament of confession to be a process akin to these criticism sessions, which were more inquisition than confession.

But how, asked Father Haft angrily, how can you possibly call yourself an *evangelist*? That the *idea* of God can inspire awe and fear in you but not belief; that you can thirst for the justice of a Day of Judgment but not for an afterlife; that you can pray while having no illusion that anything will come of it and while loathing, as you say, the *materialistic* view of prayer as *asking* — how am I to make any sense of this?

Wittgenstein chafed at Father Haft's scorn, his face reddening. Then, as civilly as he could, he replied, I believe in the Gospels as stunning examples of human goodness — as expressing fundamental human truths. And I try to live by the example of the Gospels. But I don't pretend to be officially *sanctioned* as, say, you are, Father.

Go to hell! cried Father Haft, smacking the table with the heel of his palm. Now you must insult my office, too! This is just your damned pride, Wittgenstein — stinking, delusionary pride! You're much too clever for your own good but still stupid enough to think that if you were smarter you would be better off. *Evangelist!* An evangelist of one — or *two*, counting this one here, he said, pointing to Max.

I am my own church! protested Max.

A *church*! snapped Father Haft, leaning across the table. You're another fool! I don't know why I bother with you, either.

Fortunately for their nerves, Wittgenstein and Father Haft weren't always fighting. While at the teachers' college, Wittgenstein had taken up the clarinet, and as an adjunct to these mutual criticism meetings he began playing waltzes and songs from Viennese operettas with the priest, who accompanied Wittgenstein on a beat-up hockshop violin — his sole luxury.

Later Wittgenstein and the priest formed a chamber group with two other men. Playing guitar and sometimes harmonica was the village shoemaker Halt, a bachelor and a vegetarian who collected matchboxes. On piano was Halt's boon companion Epp, another eccentric, who carved manger scenes and the Stations of the Cross in walnuts and ran the cellar movie house, where they would practice after the Sunday matinee.

Epp joined only under the provision that they would admit neither Jews nor women to the group. Halt strongly seconded, and Father Haft, who didn't much care for Jews either, readily went along. Well, then, Wittgenstein, asked Epp, how do you vote? Feeling the vestigial Jew pawing at his insides, Wittgenstein found himself wanting to object not so much on moral as on aesthetic grounds. It all seemed so distasteful, this Jewish business. And so beside the point.

Why are we even discussing this? Wittgenstein asked. Are there even any Jews in Trattenbach to exclude? We might as well concern ourselves with Eskimos.

Of course there are Jews, insisted Max. Are you blind?

At this Wittgenstein shot back, Who asked you? You're not a member of this group.

And I'm telling you there are Jews! Max insisted. Don't tell me there aren't. I'll show you some.

This was Max's unpleasant side, when his face blurted up like a blood sausage and his eyes got hot and squinty. Recognizing that he himself was a difficult and opinionated man, Wittgenstein was inclined to overlook this side of his friend. Everyone has his shortcomings, and this was as yet a minor part of Max's character. Besides, it was hard to entirely blame a person when one knew what had shaped him. Nuremberg was a Jew-hating burg, and for one whose childhood memories included beating up Jew boys and snowballing families going to synagogue, these views were the precipitate of a far deeper process; they had simply become part of his lore. Only periodically, when Max would produce *Protocols of the Elders of Zion, Master Types of the Nordic Race* or some other greasy pamphlet on the Jewish conspiracy or miscegenation (one of Father Haft's hobbyhorses), would Wittgenstein take his friend to task for his gullibility.

Still, it was easy to overlook these foibles in the overall scheme of Max's evolving character. And Max was so *unformed*: there seemed no way to auger what he would become, nor did Wittgenstein want to unduly pinch his still pliant character. What's more, Wittgenstein was optimistic, tending to think that as Max evolved as a man these concerns would shrink in comparison to weightier matters.

Yet in another sense, Wittgenstein felt a queasiness and ambivalence that was uncharacteristic of him. Many times Wittgenstein considered telling Max — if only so he might put his prejudices in better perspective — that he was of Jewish lineage. Yet he hung back, afraid of what his friend's reaction might be. Wittgenstein inwardly berated himself for this, telling himself that he was not Jewish enough to make such an admission worthwhile, but reproaching himself for being Jewish enough to keep silent about it. And, at bottom, Wittgenstein couldn't entirely disagree with Max's assessment of Jews. Prompted by Max and others, in fact, he was beginning to do some thinking himself about the Jewish character, though perhaps less how it applied to a people than to how it applied to himself as an example — or a symptom — of that people.

This was part of the radical surgery that Wittgenstein mentioned when Ramsey visited him in Trattenbach around this time. He thought that by looking at his racial origins, he might find in himself the flaw that had knocked him off his star. Several times, during this period he found himself looking in the mirror, examining the prominent nose, the faint but telltale weakness in the jaw and the epicene smoothness in his prowlike forehead, a morphology realized out of a heredity that was itself a vast system of ancestral composites that were at once advancing and declining. To Wittgenstein, it seemed that the only antidote was the resolve of character, even if that character was a basically Jewish one. It is hard to stand above one's own height, but he felt that by a monumental act of will — say, in the way that Freud had succeeded in psychoanalyzing himself — one might be able to amputate a dead or ill-formed limb and grow a better one. Sex was an instance of this. If thy eye offend thee, then hie thee to Trattenbach, where one will not be so tempted. But Jewishness, it seemed to him, was more slippery and ambiguous, less susceptible to such radical surgery. Kraus had the idea, exhorting fellow Jews to resist their Jewish tendencies. Wittgenstein saw that it required constant vigilance, not only from himself but from external agents like Max and Father Haft, who effectively kept the Jew in him bottled up and aware.

But race was hardly a constant concern with him and Max. Rather, it was a kind of leitmotif. In fact, with all the paradoxicalness of prejudice, Max was quite civil to Jews and stood as ready to help one in genuine need as he did a Christian. By the same token, if there was intolerance, there was also music, of a sort, during these Sunday sessions of Trattenbach's own Meister Players. Such playing! Wittgenstein hated Epp's banging, melodramatic piano style, which better suited shoot-'em-up cowboy pictures than a dreamy waltz. Epp, on the other hand, thought Wittgenstein, as the leader, was too hot-headed and opinionated. As for poor Halt, the guitarist, he tended to wander and miss his cues, while pent-up Father Haft hacked at his violin and Wittgenstein struggled to keep them together while blowing his lamentable clarinet.

Max was almost always there, and he never failed to fall promptly asleep, sprawled on his back with his arms outstretched, deaf to the world. Except for movies or marching, Max didn't see much use to music. Wittgenstein didn't blame him — sleeping was probably as valid a response as any to that noise. *Max!* Wittgenstein would shout when it was over. *Max, wake up!* Odd, the things one will recall of a time. The image of Max sleeping through those sessions was one of his best memories of Max or of Trattenbach. It seemed the very emblem of human tolerance, how Max would groggily sit up, scratching the back of his head and saying with a yawn, *That was nice!* just as if he'd been listening all along.

Suffer Me the Little Children

AT BEACON HILL, in preparation for the arrival of his guests that afternoon, the headmaster was trying to put his own house in order.

It was a very full house that weekend, and it was brimming with tensions that had driven the headmaster to his study-roost, an old semaphore tower that rose forty feet above the main house. The house sat on the crown of a hill, and in the days before the telegraph, the tower had been part of a string of semaphore stations that stretched from Portsmouth to London carrying news and official communiqués. Signal boys had once stood on the floorboards of Russell's study, working the beacon that blinked the news of Nelson's victory at Trafalgar, along with details of various elections, coronations, wars and accords. And as Russell sat up there at his nicked desk, he liked to think that he, too, was transmitting news of a kind to millions of readers thirsting to be improved and one day freed from various unsavory ideas they had been taught from the cradle by parents and educators who, like parents and educators of every generation, thought themselves thoroughly enlightened and modern in outlook.

Quiet and snug, with a spiral stair and a heavy trap door that could be thrown down to drown the din of dinner or the bedlam of bedtime, the tower was by far the best thing about that otherwise ugly, sprawling white house. Having grown like an atoll over the years with various ill-conceived additions, the house had no coherence as a home. As a school, however, it was almost perfect, with many large, high-ceilinged rooms that served as classrooms, nurseries and offices. Despite the portrait the press had painted of Beacon Hill as the "Come As You Go School" — feral children and fauvish adults in primitive conditions — the school was quite well appointed, with a tennis lawn and garage, a long shed that served as a laboratory and another strewn with paint, sawdust and plaster of Paris where the children were taught art and carpentry.

Russell and his wife were always giving tours to visiting journalists or the parents of prospective pupils. In her part of the tour, Dora was often at pains to make it known that the children showered twice daily, that their matron was a trained nurse and that "free school" did not mean anarchy, especially with regard to the children's welfare and safety. Russell, picking up where she left off, was wont to talk volubly about the frightening expense of providing lavatories for so many, not to mention the intricacies of boosting the school's heating and electrical capacity and modernizing the kitchen. The hill and the area around it were subject to terrific electrical storms, but here Russell was careful to point out that the children's safety was always of paramount concern, no matter what the cost. As a case in point, the headmaster would direct the visitor to a stump where, several years before, lightning had split a great oak like a stalk of broccoli. And then walking up the hill, he would show his visitors the elaborate network of lightning rods and copper cables he had had attached to the house and outbuildings and to the larger trees. Russell was exceedingly proud of those cables; he liked to shake them, as if to reaffirm his own high prudence and fatherly rectitude, anchored like them into the ground. No, with such cables, he seemed to say, one need not fear lightning.

It surprised and sometimes saddened friends and visitors to think that so vast a mind should be so consumed with such mundane matters. At times, it sorely exasperated Russell himself, who would be hounded into his tower lair, which he had furnished with the rugs he had brought from the Orient and the bust of Voltaire that peered down disdainfully from the file cabinet. From his desk, Russell could see for miles in every direction. To the north, beyond grassy hills patched with whorls of gorse and purplish heather, was a deep, dark wood. East and west were more hills, and to the south, barely visible but understood in the summer disturbances, was a gray slice of sea and the mild green landhead of the Isle of Wight. Yes, the presiding tower gave the headmaster a necessary sense of control over the unruly school and its denizens. Sitting on the windowsill were a pair of powerful binoculars, through which he had spotted several children who had wandered off and had caught many more getting into serious mischief. The headmaster also kept a police whistle handy, blowing one blast to warn the wrongdoer and three blasts in an emergency, as when, a week before, he had seen smoke rising from a shed that a boy had set afire with a filched cigarette.

Looking down now, Russell could see the blackened frame of the shed and the kidney-shaped body of grass where the flames had been racing toward the garage before they were beaten down with wet blankets and the garden hose. Near the shed now, bombing the beetles with little clouds from a pump sprayer, was old Tillham, the caretaker, a crusty old local man and mumbler who did obscure and mostly useless jobs of his own devising. And farther on, by the swings and teeter-totters, Russell could see a flock of children, among them his pride, his John, running higgledy-piggledy with their new teacher, a nubile young Belgian named Lily Loubry. And with the sight of this girl came a certain feeling of disbelief and estrangement that Russell had experienced at various times during his life. Typically, Russell associated it with standing up suddenly. A feeling of faintness, the world suddenly twittering and drained of color and with this a sense of incredible disbelief at what was otherwise a given: that he should be himself, a presence named *Russell,* and that this fast-unraveling skein of sensation should actually be his life — that his life should have slipped to this point. That day on his bicycle in 1902 when he had suddenly realized that he no longer loved his first wife — that had been such an instance. This time, though, the situation was vastly more complicated. It was also much less logical, what with his wife pregnant by another man and his two children hanging in the balance.

Russell and Dora had both wanted brave, fearless children, children hungry for life. And they had gotten them, the children of their dreams. Above all, Russell's fear was that of an orphan, the fear that, with the dissolution of his marriage, his children's easy faith in life might be irreparably broken. Russell knew it didn't take much. At the age of three, the boy, John, had had no fear of heights: he would have run off the chalk bluffs by the sea had Russell not held his hand. Then one day Russell took the boy to the edge and, while trying not to unduly scare him or break his spirit, calmly explained that if he fell from that height, he would break like a plate on the rocks below. The boy knew how a plate broke. Afterward he had a healthy respect for the height and the rocks below. But Russell saw nevertheless how the boy skirted that danger, always pushing and probing it, wondering at that miraculous transformation, from a whole plate to a broken one.

And as he stared down now, Russell couldn't get over it either, that height from his love. In the yard below, the speeding children looked to him like figures in a Brueghel painting. Crowded, rowdy, unmanageable, the scene seemed completely fabulous in perspective. It was that strangeness which strains intelligibility without ever becoming intelligible, hanging there in the way that a sail will crease the outermost rim of the sea, neither approaching nor receding, never resolving the eye's mounting anxiety. Russell was watching the children play — or rather, he was watching the young teacher who was watching the children play. Snap-the-whip, they were playing. The force was too much — they couldn't possibly hold on, nor could he stop it. He might as well have been the man in the moon, for all he could do. Round and round by the crotchety apple tree, the squealing line hurdled down, the children's upturned faces like blank plates when, *snap!* — a hand broke and down they went, tumbling down the dumbles as their teacher gaily clapped, her bobbed hair turned up like a smile as the headmaster thornily peered down, considering.

In truth, Russell's relationship with Dora, shaky as it was, had worsened in that month since the new teacher had come to the school. This was partly Dora's doing. After all, she had agreed to hire the Belgian girl, if only as a kind of guilt offering. Then again, Russell had been doing his best to make his wife feel guilty.

Whatever else, the Belgian girl was startlingly beautiful. Harder for Russell to bear, she seemed maddeningly unconscious of her beauty, filled instead with a sympathetic warmth and enthusiasm that seemed partly a result of her youth and partly a result of spending so much time around children as a maid and nanny. She was dressed carelessly enough that morning she came to be interviewed, bare-legged, in sandals and a simple print dress that buoyed into a high scoop of bosom. Her lips were full and creased in the middle, and her nose had a long Gallic septum made for the ring, refined but not too. Only he noticed that her ears were abnormally large and pointed — inquisitive, he thought, pricked like a doe's ears, alarmed at what he portended. Russell especially liked how, when she thought he was not looking, she would tug at a strand of her straight bobbed hair — how she would suck it, then quickly tuck it behind one large ear, her eyes tilting up, a vague hazel blue.

Certainly she was nervous around him during their interview, but Russell judged that a good sign — a subconscious quickening to him, the wise, gay-spirited headmaster. And really the poor girl was hired before she sat down. He had it all mapped out as he talked to her about the school and England and Brussels. He was exceedingly nice to her, but even then he was queerly aware of feeling resentful toward her, resentful *in advance,* almost knowing even then that she was sure to spurn him eventually. It seemed unfair. Here he was the interviewer and she the interviewee, and yet he felt as if the roles had been reversed, as if he should try to please *her,* a mere girl still wet behind the ears, with none of his worldly attainments. Still, he found it amusing, in a cat-and-mouse way. She seemed to have little idea just who he was, or what sort of school Beacon Hill was, presenting herself quite innocently as a girl who simply adored children and wanted a job teaching. As if that were the whole of it! No, he thought, she was much too casual about her beauty; it was inconceivable a girl could have gone twenty years with such looks without realizing it was a trump to be played. She was being coy, he thought, but he would catch her — and he eyed those earlobes that begged to be nipped and sucked before he worked down her long throat to those plumb breasts that promised to be so magnificent, though he wondered what kind of nipples she had. Fat and pink and protuberant? Or, still delightfully, tiny hard buds on big bells of bosom? Like a girl, she squirmed a bit in her hard chair, and for good reason, he thought — her panties must be sticking to her ample bottom on such a warm day. The sun was streaming in, athwart her. Her upper lip glistened with perspiration. Hesitating at an answer, she ran her tongue around her mouth. She said she had walked there from Petersfield that day — she very much liked to walk in the open air. Faintly, he could smell her, earthy and careless and overheated like wet hay in the sun, her thin white socks drooping over her slender ankles. And oh, those sturdy calves, which touched when her clenched knees touched, a sure sign to him that she was the type to get exceedingly wet very quickly.

She was unused to the chase, he thought, or else she would have been more cautious. She was like one of those trusting Galápagos creatures, knowing no natural predators. Having spent a lot of time around children, she was quite open and free, but where children took her openness at face value, he of course read it much differently. The girl was not stupid in this respect, she was just young. Nor was she completely naive. She had spent the past two years working in England and spoke excellent English. Yet midway through that prolonged interview, Russell vainly insisted upon speaking to her in French, which she said, quite guilelessly, that he spoke well and, when he protested that he did not, nervously added, without the faintest notion of being funny, that she meant he spoke French well for an Englishman. *Hoof, hoof, hoof.* His big, hoarse laugh brought a blush from her, whereupon he hastily apologized and praised her for her candor — charmed.

He liked her even better when he took her into the classroom and saw how good she was with the children, especially with his own children. Dora interviewed her next. Afterward, Dora said she preferred an older, plain-looking woman who was unquestionably better qualified. Yet here Russell reminded her that, as they had both found, the best teacher was not necessarily the one with the best credentials but rather the natural leader who could guide the children while learning right along with them. Dora did concede this point, though more from weariness than conviction. Seeing that he had his heart set on the girl, she simply gave in to him, though not without a parting dig:

So have her, then. I'm sure you know what you like.

As do you, he said snidely, eyeing her big belly. That's *evident*.

Dora's eyes blazed. Never one to miss a blow below the belt, are you!

Yours was the first blow, he said with that bland, smiling self-control that he knew would further infuriate her.

She made a move toward him, at once menacing and looking as if she would fall. She had accused him once of trying to make her so mad that she would miscarry, and he had told her then, with all the treacly malice he could muster, that he dearly wished she would. Dora called him a murderer, and, at that moment, she meant it. Such a knife edge their emotions were on now. Russell in particular had an aristocratic disdain of domestic squabbling and unpleasantry, but lately even he was primed for upset. Dora still loved him. Under the present awkward circumstances, her problem was how to express it. Part of her said that she must fight for him in the traditional feminine way, but this was so foreign to her nature. She was not a woman who lived on her feminine wiles; quite the opposite. Yet even her blunt earthiness — a quality he once had found so refreshing after Ottoline and Colette — worked against her now. Dora saw almost no way to express her conflicting loyalties in a way that he would have found honest or intelligible — her swollen belly gave the lie to anything she might say. Feeling him slipping from her grasp, Dora instead felt increasingly compelled to lash out — to scatter the birds since she could not entice them.

A stout, direct, strong-willed woman of thirty-seven, Dora had stringy, dark gray-streaked hair, which she carelessly sheared herself and braided on either side of her head like Danish twists. She was, at bottom, a kind, motherly woman, with a mythic, hieratic quality that the orphan in Russell was much drawn to, if with a faint edge of fear. Dora, in any case, had none of his cool, murderous reserve. If she could be quick-tempered, she was probably better off for it, being in most cases just as quick to forgive and forget. But now he had pushed her too far. She was a pregnant lioness, and she would not, on any account, be pushed around by him. She scared him — she knew that much — and in her fury that day, she drew close to him and uttered: Hear this, you arrogant son of a bitch. I'm not the only whore in this house, not by a long shot.

Dora burst out of the room then, but five minutes later she returned to find him slumped in a chair, clearly as devastated as she was by the viciousness of this exchange. Never in ten years of marriage had they fought like this, and that day they vowed, as they had vowed before, never to let it happen again. Dora hated the way she was acting. It made her feel so crazed and driven, so horribly biological, falling against her will into the stereotypical role of spurned wife turned shrew. But she couldn't help herself. I don't want to fight with you, she insisted. I'm not trying to call the kettle black — it's my fault, too — but you egg me on. You seem to want to bring out the very worst in me, Bertie. Really you do.

He apologized then. He had tried terribly hard to avoid bitterness and hypocrisy. He did not expect Dora to be faithful when he wasn't, but illegitimate children were another matter, another matter entirely. This, he had written, went against the biological basis for marriage and could be a source of intolerable strain. And with modern contraceptive techniques, he added, there was no need for this to happen.

But it had happened. Like him, Dora was too open and principled — too defiant — to lie, and he believed her when she told him it had been an accident. Nonetheless, it did seem possible to him that Dora had subconsciously let down her guard, so badly had she wanted another child. But then so had he. That's what hurt most. Another man had given his wife what he couldn't, and after several years of trying. Worse, he had all but asked for it. On the lecture circuit in Chicago the summer before, during one of those inevitable late-night depressions in his hotel room, he had written her saying that if he couldn't do the job, then maybe someone else ought to do it.

On a purely rational plane — as a simple means to produce a desired end — this might have been the practical thing to suggest. Within the scope of their beliefs, it might have even been politically courageous — proof against outdated moral systems and the commonplaces of bourgeois marriage. But there is nothing political about the emotions, and Russell realized all too soon that there was no rationalizing another man's child in his wife's womb. It broke his heart. In his books Russell had championed the need for freedom and openness in marriage and warned of the alternative — jealousy, poisonous jealousy, and all that it engenders: man jealous of man, family of family, nation of nation, the whole prurient, pent-up legacy of paternalism, colonial oppression, hatred and war. It was the jealous cuckold, the shamed and raging man or nation made a fool, who was the murderer of civilization. Jealousy was the misery of miseries, a vestige of man's savagery, like the appendix or foreskin, forever useless or festering. And what was the origin of male jealousy in marriage, he had written, but the fear of false parentage?

Robbed of his power of parentage, the would-be father was finally a nothing, a bounding cur that doesn't know his offspring from what dribbled down the leg of another.

Yet what was he now, thought Russell, if not jealous — stupidly, spitefully, maliciously jealous? For years, he had been a teacher of men, urging civilization to reach for its highest. But here, in himself, he felt his hopes for civilization die. The child was an intruder: it was not his, and in his heart he knew that nothing would ever make it so. It shouldn't have mattered, he thought. For a genuinely caring species that truly loved life and didn't cling to vanity, it would not have mattered. Even with certain *animals* it did not matter. And yet for him and his kind it did matter. It did, indeed.

As for Dora, Russell tended to attitudinize: great men require many loves, and ten years with any woman was about his limit. His love for her, while genuine, had never been especially passionate. Certainly he had never loved her with the intensity with which he had loved Ottoline or, later, Colette. He still regularly corresponded with Ottoline and Colette. At fifty-eight, Ottoline was now too old for him. Not *quite* as old as he, but well past her prime — certainly too old, by his book, for affairs. Colette was still ripe for him, though, still beautiful and available. Funny, he found himself thinking more and more of Colette lately, rooting through old letters and photographs, wondering how it might have been with her. They had come close to marrying in 1920. The problem was children. Realizing he was getting no younger, he had wanted to start a family immediately, but Colette had wanted to wait a year or two. Surely, he could wait a year or two, she said. He wasn't that old yet.

Dora, on the other hand, was eager to start a family. Dora was also ready to accompany him to China, whereas Colette had been again unsure, begging him for more time to think about it, if only a week. Thinking about Colette now, with his second marriage a shambles, Russell wondered why he had been in such an all-fired hurry. He couldn't wait. The next thing he knew, he and Dora were on a steamer bound for China. Dora was a good, sturdy woman to travel with, fearless, resourceful and free. Russell was her hero. They were not mere lovers, she thought, they were socialist comrades, and she imagined them striding side by side into a revolutionary future, banners waving as they stoutly sang *Ich hatt' einen Kameraden*. The Chinese certainly liked the indefatigable Miss Black, who, if anything, was more defiant in her views than Russell was. The frozen looks, the snubs they got from the Europeans for sharing the same quarters and "subverting" the Chinese — these didn't bother an inveterate bourgeois basher like Dora one bit. They can all bloody well stuff it, she liked to say, and that pretty much summed up the couple's attitude. Skidding over the cheap glaze of social convention that gilds human society, they careened across the Orient with all the careless aplomb of geese landing on a frozen pond. And by the time they returned to England a year later, the die was cast: Dora was six months pregnant. She very much wanted the child but saw no reason to marry. However, the eventual lord was adamant that his child not enter life as a bastard, and six weeks before the boy was born, Russell had his way.

Despite their present tensions, Russell still loved Dora, in a peculiar, somewhat possessive way. Nor did he entirely rule out the possibility that some rough *modus vivendi* might eventually be worked out, if only for the children's sake. Russell told himself that he should adopt a wait-and-see attitude. And he must, in any event, try to be decent. It was an odd, rubbed life that he led, and he was long used to a heavy load of confusion and ambiguity. His home, after all, was a school, and his personal life and even his family sometimes seemed like an unwieldy public experiment. Russell was aware that by dissolving his marriage he would be making a public admission of failure, which was to say he would be turning his marriage into a public event, within the stream of public discourse. To be sure, this was a lonely, bile-producing and quite humbling prospect, but he nonetheless found it a comfort that he could make this admission of failure under the guise of his own public persona. This public persona was often a burden and a nuisance but it also offered escape, affording him a sort of second skin — a slick chameleon suit that he could wriggle out of when it became psychically necessary. The public and the critics assailed a mere empty suit, a distant, distinctly public self, not his real self. In this context, personal pain as such had become a somewhat abstract concept to Russell. *He* was not himself in pain; *he* was actively searching and discovering in the hope that from his private pain and discontents he might extrapolate some broader prescriptions for the public weal. Above all, he told himself that he must be honest and consistent and not hypocritical. After all, if he and his wife — the fundamental social unit — couldn't broker a civil solution to their problems, could he expect any better of the world?

Dora felt these same pressures and ambiguities — the family as part of a school, the school as family and social experiment. This tribal creature, the Family School, was easily as much her creation as his, but she, unlike him, was less burdened and blinkered by a public sense of herself. Like him, she wanted to be decent and reasonably discreet, but even with the tremendous pains they took to conceal their tensions from John and Kate and the rest of the school, they were abundantly evident and only begat further tensions, further politics. It got so bad that there were days when Russell and Dora would have to call a truce so they could emotionally regroup. This was what happened following their quarrel about hiring the young Belgian.

Wait, Dora had said, taking his hand that afternoon. Just sit down here with me, dear. Just let's rest here for a few minutes.

That "dear" rattled him. They had not slept together, or even touched each other in weeks, and he was tense as Dora eased him back on the creaking bed. In its way, it was an act odder and more improbable than sex, and more eerily intimate, how they lay there together, talking and staring at the ceiling. For half an hour they lay there, trying to summon enough feeling that they might walk peacefully downstairs to dinner without upsetting the thirty-five children and thirteen adults who would all be watching them, the putative "parents" of this unwieldy extended family.

A month ago this had happened. Two days later, Lily had come to the school, and Russell, in his unhappiness, found himself bitten, then stunned, then absolutely captivated by her.

Dora, meanwhile, was looking forward to his annual summer departure for America, praying that he would be gone before the baby arrived. As a matter of patrician principle, he had offered (though clearly without much appetite) to remain with Dora until the baby came. Quite sincerely, she thanked him but said that this would not be necessary. Higgins would be there with her.

Higgins, an American journalist and socialist in his mid-thirties, had been with Dora on and off during her pregnancy, but at nearly two weeks this was his longest visit, with no end in sight. Russell had tried to be decent, but he could not get past his jealous rage at this usurper twenty years his junior who was stealing his family. Russell was fond of belittling Higgins around Dora, with digs about his sponging, his parlor socialism and lackluster career as a stringer for the sleazy Hearst papers. Even more effective were Russell's gibes about how Higgins was now licking the boots of Henry Luce for a berth on his new magazine, *Fortune*.

Russell hardly missed a beat when Dora pointed out that he himself had written for Hearst until he had made the mistake of declining the magnate's imperial invitation to be his guest at San Simeon. It didn't matter that Higgins was a respected journalist and activist, or that he had offered Dora money, which she had declined. Russell didn't care about his distortions. Lately all he cared about was that Higgins vacate for those three days that Wittgenstein and Moore would be there. In fact, once he left in two weeks for America, Russell said, Higgins could stay to his heart's content. Three or four days! That was all he was asking! Dora refused.

I want him with *me*! she insisted, the more to emphasize the fact that he, Russell, had deserted her. Tell your guests anything you want. He won't compromise you.

It was the morning his guests were to arrive, and Dora, who had been having a hard pregnancy, was ill in bed with a splitting headache. So Russell did what he thought was the sensible thing: he went straight to Higgins about the matter.

Russell caught Higgins in the upstairs hall, on his way to Dora's room with a glass of water. Russell was casual and businesslike. He even managed a feeble smile as he explained, I'm only asking for three days. I'll be happy to pay for your hotel. And, by all means, if you feel the need, you can certainly come by. I really think it would be best for all — and Dora especially. I do think it would be rather less strained, don't you?

Tall and balding, pettishly fingering what Russell called his Public Enemy mustache, Higgins said at last:

It's Dora's decision. If she says so, fine — I'll leave.

But as you well know, Dora *won't* agree, said Russell, with an edge to his voice. That's why I'm asking you. He hung back momentarily, then added, I am trying to be decent about this, you know. I think I've been uncommonly decent about everything. You might try putting yourself in my place for once.

I'm very sorry, said Higgins coldly. Dora is my concern, and Dora needs some aspirin. Now, if you'll excuse me . . .

With his comparative youth and size, Higgins was more than Russell's match. But as the American walked by him, Russell, in a flash of rage, fantasized throwing him over the stair rail — fantasized but then watched in astonishment as his young rival strode into his wife's room and quietly shut the door.

Are Parents Bad for Children?

ONE MORE PROBLEM cropped up that afternoon before Wittgenstein and the Moores arrived.

Dora was still in bed with a headache. The children were outside playing, and Russell was secluded in his tower study, struggling to complete his *Parents' Magazine* article, "Are Parents Bad for Children?"

In the downstairs study, meanwhile, one of the teachers was reading when she felt a cold drop of water strike her on the leg. Looking up, she saw beads of water dribbling along the ceiling. Then there came a crash as the chandelier in the next room collapsed under a hundredweight of water. The teacher ran into the hallway, where she saw water lapping down the stairs like a lazy falls. Running up, she found the next floor completely flooded and water slopping out of the lavatory, where two sinks were stoppered and the faucets wrenched on full blast.

In his study upstairs, Russell was just becoming aware of the commotion when he heard Dora below, banging on the bolted door. Hurrying down and opening the door, he met Dora's distraught face as one of the teachers came splattering down the hall with a pile of soaked books. Dora was holding her throbbing temples with her thumb and index finger, and now he, too, felt sick.

What happened? he asked. Did a pipe burst?

Dora dropped her hand. He plugged the sink and left the water running.

Russell slouched against the door jamb. Who had him? They were supposed to be *watching* him.

Miss Gilmer had him. She said she *was* watching him. Dora closed her eyes, then said with a weary pass of the hand, It's a wreck downstairs as well. A ceiling collapsed — the room where Wittgenstein was to sleep. Of course, he denies it . . . Dora trailed off, then said almost imploringly, Bertie, I can't stand any more of this. We've got to get him out of here.

I'm trying, he said. But what can I do? The detective —

Forget the detective, she broke in. We can't wait for your detective to find his mother. It might take another month, and God knows what he'll do in the meantime. I'm frightened he'll set the house on fire or injure one of the children. He's beyond us. We've got to get some institution to take him — and I don't mean next week, either. I've a very bad feeling.

Russell was rubbing his face with his hand. I know, he said, looking up. You're right, but, my God, the expense! If the detective doesn't find his mother soon, he'll ruin us.

The boy in question was Rabe Peck, a fat, freckle-faced American boy of nine who had started at the school about six weeks ago — right about the time the new teacher did.

Even Russell had wondered if his distraction with the new teacher wasn't partly to blame for his poor judgment in admitting the boy to Beacon Hill. Dora wasn't the only one to suspect that his brain had been in his trousers that day. Miss Marmer, Russell's most senior teacher and current mistress, was also furious at him for the decision — doubly so that he had made it without consulting her.

One thing was certain: hard as it was to find a good child, it was often that much harder to find a bad child's parents or wheezy maiden aunt once one was desperate to give him back.

Rabe Peck wasn't the first such child they'd been stuck with. The teachers even had a name for these children — "hot potatoes." Rabe Peck was some potato: to be exact, he was a six-stone hot potato with a club foot who liked to snuggle up to adults while making warm puppy noises — and then swipe their cigarettes. It was Rabe who had burned down the shed. In his short stay at the school, Rabe had so distinguished himself that the teachers had nicknamed him Rape. The children called the fat boy Puffo or Stiffer for the way he dragged his foot. Later, when his bed-wetting was discovered, they found an even crueler name: Wee-wee. Several of the boys had a way of saying the name so faintly under their breath, and at such a freak pitch, that it was almost inaudible to adult ears. It was pure torture for Rabe. A teacher would be calmly conducting a class when Rabe, for no apparent reason, would fly into a rage, screeching and bucking and throwing anything in reach. The boy couldn't stand teasing.

Rabe had shown little sign of his problems the day his mother brought him to Beacon Hill, arriving one morning in a hired car piled with baggage. Accompanying Mrs. Peck and her son was an older Negro woman wearing a worn blue suit and white gloves, with tightly rolled hair and skin so black it had a bluish gun-barrel cast to it. The woman hung back so as not to upstage her extravagant mistress, who fairly leapt from the car, exclaiming about the view, Look out there, Rabie. Id'nit lovely!

Standing discreetly behind them, a little smudged, the Negro woman, Mrs. Price, looked out over the countryside but didn't say a word. She politely declined Dora's offer to show her the school while Russell spoke with Mrs. Peck, just as she politely declined her offer of a glass of iced tea. Her accent was deep and her phrasing was emphatically precise and grammatical. Mrs. Price thought she would sit up on the porch, if that was all right. Do you want to sit with me while Mr. Russell speaks to your mother? Mrs. Price asked the boy. Standing like a lump by the car, the boy sullenly shook his head, his fat arms dangling like dead fish. Very well, then, said Mrs. Price, who then went up on the porch and sat down. Mrs. Price was obviously used to waiting. Stoical and sovereign, she carefully teased off her gloves and folded them on her lap, ignoring the openmouthed stares of the other children, who then were drifting out. Most of them had never seen a colored person before.

Mrs. C. Randowne Peck of Columbia, South Carolina, was a plump whirlwind in white perched on two-tone patent pumps. Gay, petty, imperious, with a deep southern drawl, she was a remarkably unconscious woman who clearly was accustomed to doing exactly as she pleased. Hardly had she sat down in Russell's office than she pulled off her shoes and without a thought began rubbing her swollen red toes, all the while talking. She said she was very sorry, she'd forgotten the boy's report cards, then launched into a complicated explanation that Russell politely declined to hear, saying, That's quite all right. Oh, thank you, she said, emphasizing that she would wire the States and have complete transcripts of the boy's record promptly sent to the school. But then she remembered something else she'd brought and withdrew from her purse a letter from Miss March — Miss March of *Miss March's School in Savannah*? she asked, her voice rising in inflection. Oh, it's famous throughout the South. Rather progressive, too.

Russell took the letter that Miss March had written on her own engraved stationery, solemnly extolling Rabe's sterling qualities. Mrs. Peck, in turn, took Russell's questionnaire and with a gold-nibbed pen thoughtfully ran down the standard medical list, checking *No* to problems such as *Fainting Spells, Tantrums* and *Bed-wetting*. The Beacon Hill questionnaire also contained a box concerning marital status in which Mrs. Peck mischievously crossed out *Divorced* and wrote in "Remarried," saying coquettishly, That sounds so very much nicer, don't you think, Mr. Russell? Russell laughed, then admitted that he was "remarried" himself. It never occurred to him to ask pert Mrs. Peck how many times she had remarried.

As a rule, Russell disliked Southerners, but in a peculiar way Mrs. Peck grew on him as the interview progressed. Though on the surface she seemed flighty and somewhat scatterbrained, he could see that this was something of a ruse. Beneath the patter, the woman was clearly quite shrewd, in charge of a successful importing business that she said required frequent travel, which unfortunately took her too often away from her sensitive son. Not, she hastened to add, that he would ever have any trouble reaching her through her London office. I'm always available, she said, withdrawing from a silver case a handsome engraved card that showed a quite substantial address in Belgravia. Mrs. Peck added, Miss March, God rest her soul, never had any trouble reaching me.

As for Rabe, he seemed quite bright and inquisitive, shy and eager to please — perhaps too eager, thought the schoolmaster, adding in his notes that he "might suffer from a lack of confidence." The boy said he liked arithmetic and science. He also liked reading a whole lot, especially Dickens and books about animals. He really liked animals, he said. He wanted to be a veterinarian.

As for his queer high-pitched laugh and the way he squirmed in his seat during the interview — well, Russell did notice this, but he didn't find it especially alarming. The boy did seem a little shy around the other children, but this wasn't so unusual either, especially for a heavy boy with a game foot. Still, the foot wasn't all that severe, and Mrs. Peck did not fail to add that Rabie had two extra pairs of special built-up shoes, as well as a third pair specially made for athletics. She was ecstatic when Russell said, rather officially, that they would want to put the boy on a diet, providing, of course, that they decided to take him. Why, I agree with you one hundred percent! said Mrs. Peck. Then, unable to contain herself, she said how much she admired *Marriage and Morals* and his thought-provoking articles. Say what you will, Mr. Russell, she added impulsively, forward-looking Southerners are listening to you.

Wonderful! said Russell. Perhaps in that case they'll enact an anti-lynching law. That would certainly be very forward looking.

Forward looking, agreed Mrs. Peck carefully, but not very likely, I'm afraid.

They talked for a while about the South and the Scottsboro lynching case. Then Dora met with Mrs. Peck and the boy, but she was feeling unwell again and, after a few minutes, had to excuse herself. Russell, meanwhile, was too preoccupied with fantasies of Lily to spend much time weighing the decision. And really, Russell didn't have deep feelings either way about the boy. Actually, he thought he was being rather coldly

practical about the matter. Summer was coming, and they would be short
of students and short of money. The truth was, he was too strapped to
be turning down a paying prospect.

Rabe cried when his mother kissed him good-bye. Mrs. Price also
kissed the boy — pointed a warning finger at him, too. Later, Russell
would find himself thinking about Mrs. Price, remembering how much
more refined she seemed than her mistress, as if it had fallen on her to
care for tarnished custom in the way she did the family silver. Then again,
the family silver was probably in hock, because two weeks later Mrs.
Peck's London bank returned her check for insufficient funds.

For a couple of weeks, the boy did a fairly good job of fooling everyone — everyone, that is, except Miss Marmer.

His bed-wetting was the first sign. Rabe had been there three days
before it was discovered, but once discovered, it quickly worsened with
the stress of discovery and the taunts from the other children. And soon
there were other signs: the anger and manipulativeness, the fibs, fantasies
and implausible stories.

Almost from the first, Miss Marmer felt there was something not right
about him.

I'll say it again, she said out of the blue one night when she and Russell
were making love, I think you've made a terrible mistake with that boy.

And I think you're being typically hasty, said the headmaster, undulating over her.

Au contraire, she insisted. You're the hasty one — as usual. Slow
down!

She could be acerbic and a know-it-all, Miss Marmer. Whatever her
deficiencies in dealing with adults, though, she did know children. But
Rabe wasn't the issue here; what Miss Marmer was really miffed about,
Russell saw, was his growing preoccupation with the girl. Not that Miss
Marmer ever would have overtly expressed jealousy, let alone emotional
need. She was far too proud and independent for that. From the start,
Miss Marmer had said that she knew there could be nothing enduring
between them, and that that was exactly how she wanted it. Hadn't she
told him that she shuddered at the thought of spending a weekend alone
with him — with any man? She would feel as if she were suffocating.

But if Miss Marmer was not the marrying kind, neither was she, at
thirty-eight, a celibate spinster. She loved sex, and by her account had
had many affairs. She said she preferred being a mistress, which seemed
so much more sexy and knowing, so much less claustrophobic than being

some man's "cow." It seemed to Russell that being a mistress — a tempt-ress — better fit Miss Marmer's exaggerated romantic image of herself. No one knew what she *really* felt, she seemed to say, implying that within her small bosom there welled a vast gulf of solitude and great unknown passions that she would carry to her grave without ever divulging to anyone, especially a man. She adored the gush of opera. She was Mad-ame Butterfly, she was Carmen and Isolde. She likewise adored the so terribly apt poems of that literary lioness Edna St. Vincent Millay. And, perversely, like many intensely private people, Miss Marmer was prone, in spite of herself, to say some queasily revealing things. Entering her claustrophobic, candlelit room late one night, Russell found her reclining in a long negligee with bowed sleeves, reading Poe's "Ligeia." Oh, why did Poe, such *genius,* have to die so wretchedly, in a gutter? she asked rhetorically. Then, with a queer, self-satisfied smirk, she closed the book, confidently saying, *I* could have saved him.

For close to a year now, it had been almost perfect. Dora looked the other way and the solitary, faintly sibylline Miss Marmer asked only that he be punctual and *adagio,* then *andante,* then *presto!* Also, that he bite her rear end. Yes, Higgins aside, it had been rather all right until that girl had come along.

The boy, meanwhile, was exhibiting more disturbing signs. For instance, there was the way he would bite his arm when he was excited, gnawing it and shaking it like a flipper and laughing with wild glee. Then there was the way he liked to talk about death, especially gruesome death — fires, automobile wrecks, dismemberments and the like.

On the other hand, Rabe genuinely craved affection, and he was no fool in knowing where to seek it: once they put him on his diet, he at-tached himself like a barnacle to the cook, Mrs. Bride.

Mrs. Bride told Russell that she liked the boy, but there was an incident with him one day that she said had certainly made her wonder if the poor lad was not, well, troubled a bit. It happened in the kitchen. Watch-ing Mrs. Bride sharpen her knives, Rabe asked if he might test the blade on his thumb the way she did.

I should have known better than to give it to him, Mrs. Bride told Russell. Oh, he was just aquiverin' with excitement, you know, like — like a dog about to get his supper.

Finally, reluctantly, well-meaning Mrs. Bride gave in, but for all her warnings, he immediately — and she thought purposely — drew the blade across his thumb. It cut me, it cut me! he squealed.

OWWWwwwww . . . It was not a serious cut, but Mrs. Bride remembered how his eyes gorged at the bright beads of blood, then how he stared at her, almost drunkenly, as if the cut symbolized some special bond between them. Nor could she forget how he had thrust the thumb in his mouth, mournfully sucking it like a sour candy, before he jerked his head around to gnaw at his other arm, which had begun flopping uncontrollably. Well, sir, said Mrs. Bride, concluding her tale to the headmaster. I told him to stop — oh, I scolded him, I did. Well, I ran to fetch the gauze. It was awful. When I got back, his poor arm was covered with red teeth marks. I didn't know what to think, sir. I thought it must be the pain.

Mrs. Bride told Russell this only after several other incidents had surfaced. One day a teacher had found Rabe in the garden, sticking pins into slugs and singeing them with matches before melting them with salt into bubbling pools of mucous. To the now seasoned headmaster, this cruel behavior, though certainly disturbing, was hardly unprecedented. Russell prided himself on his ability to talk — and listen — to children. He took the boy into his office and asked him why he had tortured the slugs and what he was angry about. After all, Russell said, trying to catch the boy's downcast eyes, one didn't torment innocent creatures because one was happy. There were tears. The boy said he was sorry. He said he was mad at his mother for leaving him, said he was mad about his diet and all the teasing. This much was true. The boy also gave his solemn word that he would come speak to the headmaster if he felt such impulses again. Russell was no sentimentalist about children or the powers of a good old-fashioned talk, but he guardedly thought the session might have done some good. Yes, he thought, with work the boy might turn out all right.

But that good feeling quickly evaporated as the bed-wetting continued, along with the tantrums, fighting and destructive behavior. Then a week later, there was real cause for alarm: one of the smaller boys ran in hysterically one afternoon, saying that Rabe had held him captive for an hour in the bushes as his "nigger slave," jabbing at him with a sharpened weed fork, forcing him to eat weeds and dirt and threatening to kill him if he told anybody.

Of course Rabe strenuously denied the story, just as he later denied the fire in the shed — that is, until two girls came forth and said they had seen him in there with a cigarette, giggling and showing off as he puffed away. Among the staff there had been considerable debate about what to do with the boy. Professional pride was involved. Beacon Hill was not a school to give up easily on a child, but Rabe soon persuaded them otherwise. The problem now was Mrs. Peck. She seemed to have disappeared. Russell had hired a detective to track her down, but the detective wasn't having much luck either. Three days before, he had sent Russell the following telegram:

TO: Mr. B. Russell STOP
FROM: A. N. Pip
RE: MRs. Peck STOP
1. Peck's imports belly-upSTOP
2. Boy's Farther a fugitive — in Bolivia, biGamy and morals chargesSTOP
3. Boy's legal guardian, Mrs. Peck's mother, a senile lOOney in church HomeSTOP
4. Miss March ran school for DEAF STOP Lives at the Home w/old lady Peck STOP
5. RE: Relatives taking the boy STOP Not on yr. life STOP
6. Request yr. further instructs & prompt remit of $250 bal before proceed further STOP
Beft Regards
DAVIS INVESTIGATIONS

A Modest Proposal

IN THE AFTERMATH of Rabe's latest scourge, the Beacon Hill disaster detail was hard at work. The upstairs resounded with the slap of mops and the bang of pails. Russell had one group bailing, another watching Rabe and still another making inquiries into institutions that might take him — and fast. Russell had a hundred things to do, but now he saw it was nearing 3:30. Wittgenstein and the Moores were due at the station in thirty minutes.

Russell was grateful for an excuse to get out of the house. Finding Miss Marmer, he said with his usual daytime formality, Miss Marmer, I have to pick up my guests, and Dora is feeling ill. Would you mind terribly taking over?

But Miss Marmer wasn't having this. Don't you think you ought to stay here? she asked. Why don't you send someone who's not so busy to fetch them? Then, as matter-of-factly as she could, she added, Lily. Lily might go.

The school's egalitarian principles notwithstanding, Miss Marmer was a great believer in the virtues of seniority and dues paying, especially where the Belgian girl was concerned. Lily was pliant and young, and with good cause she feared the brittle Miss Marmer, who was a stickler about what she broadly called "professionalism." Russell had warned Miss Marmer several times not to be ordering the girl about; for that matter, Russell had told Miss Marmer several times not to be telling him what to do. Still, he saw that his aide-de-camp was right: it wasn't at all a good time for him to be leaving. Mindful of his male sensitivities in this respect, Miss Marmer was careful then to soften her tone, saying in the soothing voice of an efficient secretary, You're busy now. I understand. I can tell her for you.

No, he said pointedly. *I'll* tell her. You stay here.

And on second thought, Russell rather liked the idea of sending Lily. He felt her attractive presence would express something of himself, of the power and dynamism of a man mostly surrounded by women. But of course, on a more practical level, it was an excuse to talk to Lily. Russell needed an excuse now.

Miss Marmer was not the first teacher whom Russell had slept with, not by a long shot. Among his staff, Russell was notorious for making quick and startlingly frank advances to the new teachers. Successful advances, too: it was a point of considerable pride to him that, with the exception of two or three women (who had left the school soon after), all had readily — and, he thought, happily — accepted his attentions.

Miss Marmer knew this, of course, and she knew, as Dora did, that it would be only a matter of time before he approached the girl. Here Miss Marmer was caught between what she regarded as her sovereign duties as the most senior teacher — duties that called for professionalism and objectivity — and those instincts that had once made her such a formidable competitor in ladies' lawn tennis. At the same time, Miss Marmer was objective about herself. She readily acknowledged that she was plain. She said this the very first time Russell had approached her a year ago. It happened one day when they were alone in his office, arguing about what to do with a certain child. There had always been a certain tension between them. So that day Russell told her that he believed the tension was sexual, and then, like a doctor writing out a prescription, he said that, to reduce this tension, they ought to sleep together. He wasn't self-conscious in the least about it. How could he spread the light of sexual freedom if he did not first expunge these tensions from his own life and those around him?

By Beacon Hill standards, Miss Marmer was a bit strait-laced, and he thought (and even faintly hoped) that she would be shocked. But instead Miss Marmer managed to shock him. Standing up and smoothing her hands over her blouse and skirt, she turned, so he could get a better look, and said matter-of-factly, like a job applicant, Well, I am pretty good in the sack, whether or not you know it. Oh, I know my face is nothing special, but at least I was blessed with a pretty good figure — don't you agree?

Her figure was decent enough, especially her legs, but he came to realize that she had rather a thing about it. I know I haven't much up top but . . . what do you think of my rump? she would ask before lovemaking, hefting it in her hands for his scrutiny. Critical, detached, apprehensive, she was like a woman trying on clothes, holding her body up to herself like an old dress and, with him the mirror, preemptively pointing out her flaws before he had a chance. During sex, it excited her to have him grab at her and praise her body, and she craved this reassurance all the more when the new teacher arrived. Again and again, she would say to him about the girl, Isn't she pretty? Don't you think she's pretty? searching his face for any sign that he thought the girl was more than pretty or, conversely, that she, Miss Marmer, was the plainer in his eyes for the girl's beauty.

Miss Marmer always took it upon herself to orient new teachers, meaning, implicitly, to tell them what was what and who was boss. She liked to think that she was warm and approachable, though with adults — and especially with rival women — she was neither, being more the Girl Guide leader, trying to uphold a code with which she was at once unfamiliar and profoundly uncomfortable. My door is always open, she liked to tell the newcomer, sounding, for that, a bit forlorn since no one had ever taken her invitation.

Miss Marmer gave Lily the obligatory tour. And she did her duty, telling the girl, as though describing the house ghost, not to be shocked if the headmaster made a pass at her. Miss Marmer made it clear, from her tone, that this was an eccentricity to be humored and fended off — certainly not to be accepted. What Miss Marmer did not know was that the other teachers had already given Lily the lowdown on the headmaster and the arrangement he had with his most senior teacher, whom they waved off as a self-important twit, though they did admit she was good with the children. Derisive, gossipy, all holed up together in a room, they had given Miss Marmer a good hiding, calling her Mother Superior and Miss Glorious Excelsior.

Russell, meanwhile, was on tenterhooks, wondering when to make his plea before the girl. He couldn't read her. She seemed so innocent, and such a prize, that he felt he had to exercise extreme caution. He tortured himself for two weeks before he finally called her into his office one morning.

Sensing what was coming, Lily was skittish. Russell paid no attention. He interpreted this as mere shyness, perhaps even the flush of anticipation. As always at such times, he came straight to the point. He said that he liked and admired her, and that, though he knew he was not as young or desirable as he once had been, he was a vigorous lover who had much to offer a girl her age in the way of worldly wisdom and friendship. It was a very nice, even touching, little speech, and she listened carefully. God, but she was a beauty! Her knees were pressed together and her toes were slightly turned in like some ungainly girl's, her breasts huddled protectively between her arms and that randy hay smell wafting off her. His old heart was pounding and his hands were clammy, but he pressed on, telling her how as he grew older he found that the only way he could delve into the psyche of a woman — to really *know* her in the deepest soul sense — was to sleep with her.

She could not have doubted his sincerity in telling her this. He was not old, he seemed to be saying. The mind was eternally young. There was no shame but in dishonesty, he said, nor was there virtue in celibacy. On the contrary, he said as if he had mounted a public podium, prolonged celibacy was harmful for anyone working around children — witness the Victorians and the sadistic, prurient impulses rampant in the public schools, not to mention the fearful legacy of the various celibate church orders. Russell explained these things with the same rapt and passionate plausibility with which he would have explained asteroids or Kant or the need for world disarmament — as a beautiful and time-proven fact of human existence that he had, as it were, identified like a curious shell he had found on an eternal beach. He was honest. In response to her puzzled, somewhat suspect gaze, he acknowledged that this view presented some problems. Certainly, it did not account for how he might ever get to know a woman whom he did not find physically desirable. Nor did it explain why — Socrates and the Greeks notwithstanding — he did not apply the same standard to men.

Russell freely admitted these problems. It was terrifically hard, he seemed to be saying. The times were so new. She had to understand that he was still pioneering this new life, trying to hammer down provisional solutions to these age-old problems until better solutions came along. And then he also told her, lest she think him a humbug, that he and Dora had an understanding. He quickly added that he certainly did not — and could not — expect fidelity from a girl her age. Yes, he said, he would be quite content to share her with younger men, thinking to himself that here again he was being exceedingly generous and realistic.

So saying, Russell beamed her his characteristic wry smile, that irreverent, confident and, it seemed, forever *youthful* smile that had for so long carried him forth, like a carved figurehead plunging into the exhilarating foam of life. He really thought he had carried it off. Very well, then, he said ebulliently, I've had *my* say . . .

He sat back to hear her answer. And she was *so* shy. Dear, dear child, he thought, the better to let his fundamental goodness shine through, that she might speak up. And why did they even need words? She could respond with a simple embrace, a kiss!

Lily, meanwhile, was staring at her feet and winding a strand of hair around her finger. Playfully, he peeked down at her, hoping to catch her eye, her trust. But then she looked up, and he felt the blood slowly drain from his face as she stuttered and struggled to explain that, while she *liked* and very much *admired* him, she did not . . . *could not* . . .

He had told himself she was naive — perhaps a virgin still, intimidated by his candor. Then he'd remembered she was a Catholic, and Catholic educated. Of course! It was the revenge of the celibates, of the frustrated sisters and life-hating Gallic clerics, blocked men suffering from carbuncles and piles!

But predictably enough, his feeble rationalizations bit back at him. He turned dour. He was old and unsightly — a bloody fool to think a girl that beautiful would have him. His self-pity turned to rage, then to jealousy. In his desperation to find a rival, he even found himself casting a baleful eye on poor Mr. Brewer, the music tutor, a pale, spindly youth with dandruff and acne.

For a week these recriminations burned. And then, in spite of all reason, Russell found himself hoping she would have a change of heart. Mooning like a seventeen-year-old, he fantasized confessions, happy coincidences and misunderstandings, a sudden epiphany as they flew into each other's arms. Stuck on his *Parents'* article, he shot an afternoon writing a sweaty story entitled *Her*, which he promptly burned, cursing himself for being such a blasted fool.

This was roughly the point where he found himself that day after Rabe had flooded the house, when he went to ask her if she would go to the station with the old caretaker, Mr. Tillham, to meet his guests. She was upstairs mopping when he found her. It is no trouble, she said, and then she followed him downstairs as he described Wittgenstein to her. In an old album, he even managed to find a twenty-year-old picture of Moore. Lily was more at ease than she'd been in a week.

Oh, I am sure I will know them, she said attentively as they walked outside.

I would much appreciate it, he said, struggling to seem natural. I really must stay here. I hope you understand.

They were standing out on the porch, close enough that he could inhale that musky scent. She was looking out across the hills. Sneakily, guiltily, he stole glimpses of her long and lickable neck, squeezing the image behind his eyelids, a little death for wishing. Then they heard a roar as addle-headed Tillham brought the long black car around, skidding to a stop with the engine racing. Fumes tumbled across the yard. Clenching the wheel and peering out through the windshield with his mouth agape, Tillham looked like some ancient Druid who had just been granted a motoring permit.

In exasperation, Russell called down, Pull-off-the-*choke*. He suggestively jerked his hand back and forth. The *choke,* do you hear?

Lily smiled at him — smiled warmly, he thought, before she ran down to the roaring car. Russell forgot the old man. He forgot Rabe. All he saw were Lily's sturdy thighs as she swung the door shut. The tongue hadn't saliva enough for what Russell had in mind. He didn't just want to have or hold or even enter her. He wanted to *wear* her like a glorious coat, one sleek with luxurient youth and promise, with many, many colors.

Tryst Complicit

PROFESSOR MOORE? . . . Professor? . . .

Moore jumped when he heard her calling his name. His first thought, for some reason, was that it was bad news: something had happened to one of his boys.

But he soon brightened when Lily walked up and explained herself. And he positively beamed when he learned that this striking young woman had recognized him aided by only an old photograph.

A photograph? asked Moore, fishing. Bertie with a photograph of me? Why, how old a photograph, I wonder?

Dorothy scoffed, There'll be no living with him now, my dear. Of course he hasn't aged in thirty years. Not at all.

Friendly and good-natured, the Moores were making a concerted effort to put the girl at ease. This was their way, of course, but they were working at it all the harder to compensate for the strangeness of Wittgenstein, who hung back with a vague air of distaste. Was it Miss Loubry he was bothered by, or was it Max, now so playful and talkative, if not tipsy? Wittgenstein was curt and aloof when they introduced him to Russell's emissary. Not Max. Before they could even introduce him, he barged forward, saying, And I am Max.

Until then Lily had been bright and outgoing, but when he confronted her, her voice faltered. She nervously repeated herself in a breathless singsong, saying, Yes, I am Lily. I teach at the school. How very nice to meet you . . .

Now her youth told. Unsure of what else to do, she turned and pointed to the car, black and dusty in the white sun, with Tillham standing beside it, scowling. Sizing up the four of them and their baggage, Lily said with some concern, I hope we will all fit.

Oh, this is done, said Max, snatching up bags. Now he was securely in his element. Come, he told her with an engaging smile. I will make this do.

It was a squeeze, but they managed it, Max heaving luggage up on the roof rack while Wittgenstein meticulously tied it down. Max then selflessly suggested that Wittgenstein and the Moores should take the more ample backseat. This was generous of him — why, he was even rather insistent about it, holding the door as Dorothy climbed in, followed by Moore and Wittgenstein. Max then wrenched open the front door and motioned the girl in, briskly saying, Here. First you . . .

Lily hesitated, flustered, then scooted across the hot leather seat, whisking her thin blue cotton skirt over her knees as Max, fresh from the Green Mask, squeezed his sweaty bulk in beside her and clamped the door shut. From the cavernous backseat, Moore asked uneasily over the roaring engine, Are you quite sure you have sufficient room there, Max?

Max looked back with a grin. Sure. It is good, Moore.

It was hot and close, and Moore, who sometimes suffered spells of car sickness, loosened his tie and slowly cranked down the window. Muttering and fidgeting and reeking of insecticide, Tillham jerked out the clutch — rocking their heads back as the engine popped and stalled in a cloud of blue smoke.

Yer must ter leave me more room ter drive, Muss! growled Tillham to the girl.

Lily had no choice but to squeeze closer to Max, and with a shudder they were off finally. Outside Petersfield, beyond the valley, the road grew hilly, slaloming through gentle swells of downland. On their left, they again saw the hump of Black Down, and Moore repeated half audibly, "Green Sussex fading into blue, with one gray glimpse of sea."

What was that? asked Wittgenstein with an air of disapproval.

It's from a poem, said Moore. Tennyson, I think. Yes, Tennyson.

I hate Tennyson.

Yes, well, mused Moore, raising his eyes. He was a favorite of my youth. Taste of a bygone era, I'm afraid.

As Moore said this, he was looking at Max and the girl. Nor was he the only one. With his eye on Max, Wittgenstein added, Browning I've never liked, either. Or Hardy.

Indeed? asked Moore. And tilting his nose to the window, he gulped air, wondering if it was him or if the car was indeed faintly weaving, this as he suppressed a desire to tell Wittgenstein, *Well, you know I hate Schiller, and often Goethe bores me as well.*

Dorothy, feeling the pall, chimed in, Oh, look! There's a hoopoe. Then, seeing that no one had the least idea what a hoopoe was, she added, A golden-crested bird. It makes this *hoop-hoop* call.

Whoop-whoop. It was Max's voice. Call of the wild.

Sensing that he was mocking her, Dorothy said pricklishly, Yes, it's a relative of the kingfisher. Then, somewhat provocatively, she asked, Have you ever seen a kingfisher, Max?

Sure, guffawed Max, yawing around as if to say, A stupid answer to a stupid question.

And tell me, dear, asked the indefatigable Dorothy, trying to draw poor, trapped Miss Loubry into this struggling conversation. (*Yes,* hissed Dorothy in response to Moore's simultaneous entreaty, he *is* weaving.) Em, tell me, Dorothy continued, is Mrs. Russell one for walking? I'm something of a birdwatcher, you see. I thought I might ask her to trot about with me tomorrow.

Lily turned around with surprise. Mrs. Russell hasn't been feeling too well, ma'am. She is, um, very large.

Large? asked Dorothy, wondering for a moment if the girl, with her uncertain English, meant that Mrs. Russell was fat. Seeing her perplexity, Lily hesitated, then said, I mean, the baby.

Oh! Dorothy glanced at Moore, who seemed a bit pale. We haven't heard anything about a baby, have we? No, she said to Lily, I guess we haven't. Well, that's marvelous. How soon is Mrs. Russell due?

The girl seemed uncomfortable with this question. Two weeks, three.

My — Dorothy raised her eyes — that *is* soon, isn't it? I hope we're not coming at a bad time.

Oh, no, Mrs. Moore. Lily seemed alarmed, afraid she might have said the wrong thing. Mr. Russell is most extremely anxious about your visit.

Mordantly rolling the whites of his eyes for Dorothy's benefit, Moore muttered, We're sure he is.

But with that, Lily grew silent again; the whole car did. Dorothy felt a sisterly concern for the poor girl, who surely had to be uncomfortable, thrust up against, and surely sticking to, the overheated Max. Even Moore appeared a trifle concerned. Trying to ease the girl's awkwardness, Dorothy attempted to divert her with further questions, neutral questions. The sea — was it still cold this late in the season? And the Iron Age hill fort mentioned in her guidebook — was it worth seeing?

The young teacher seemed grateful to talk, if increasingly nervous and distracted. Max was curiously quiet, though, his head cocked slightly, as if he heard distant music. Maybe it was the way the girl squirmed once that made them wonder. Or maybe it was the way she suddenly got silent, her neck flashing with red gooseflesh. From the curmudgeonly Tillham, there was no sign whatsoever. It was all he could do just to keep the long black hood aimed down the road.

Max, meanwhile, was in a little reverie. He was fixedly admiring Lily's breasts, noting how they jostled, so high and fat and firm. (These trick brassieres couldn't fool him, he could see they were nice.) She knew he was watching, and she rubbed her hands together to stop from trembling as she chattered on about the weather, which had been unusually hot, and the children, who had been unusually naughty on account of it — oh, especially one boy, she said, one very bad boy . . .

But then she lost her train of thought, and was suddenly and discordantly silent as Max spread his legs and, with his right hand, slowly loosened the tumescent seam of his crotch with a coaxing, cuddling gesture. Without the least hesitation, he then slyly slipped his right hand under his folded left arm and inquisitively squeezed her breast, cupping and assessing its weight. A good, firm tit, all right. And no complaints. So, he ran his rough fingers down the perspiring underside of her bare thigh and fondled the hollow beneath her knee, then gradually kneaded her sturdy calf, which throbbed in his hand as she stared at the ribbon of road glowing like a long, crumbly chalk stripe over the swelling hills.

From dips rose abrupt hills, then rocky outcrops and sky, where stray sea birds trailed their wings in the gloaming light, which clung to the earth as vapor does to trees. The seat was high; Max and Lily were quiet as cats. From the back, Dorothy and Moore could see only their two immovable heads. Yet there was electricity — complicity — in the air, as Max slid his fingers under the girl's buttocks, Jack Horner style, then coaxed a slow, imperceptible urging from her as she stared ahead.

But Lily broke this reverie when the square tower of Beacon Hill came into view. And she sat bolt upright when she saw the headmaster standing atop the long drive.

As in Circles

RUSSELL'S ANTENNAE were up the moment he saw Lily squashed in beside Max. And when he saw that shamed look on her face, his suspicions were even more inflamed, as if the girl had somehow lied or tricked him, faithless as Dora.

Max was first out of the car, but he wasn't nearly as eager to help Lily out as he had been to get her in. Russell was now the focus of his attention, the girl forgotten as he strode up and introduced himself, with that exuberant punch of a face.

The public man in Russell, the veteran of countless receiving lines, was expert at bestowing an icy greeting on the aggressive lunatic and fond gaper. It didn't deter Max. It was Max's nature to form quick, sensitive impressions of people, and he must have detected something in the look Russell gave the girl. Or else Max simply decided that, since it was inevitable that he and his freethinking host would be at odds, he might as well make the worst of it. Whatever it was, Max was subtly antagonistic to Russell from the first. Poor Lily, meanwhile, didn't seem to know what had happened. Head down, stepping nimbly across the yard, she looked as if she'd been thrown from a horse.

So much was happening at once. Luckily for Russell, his children, John and Kate, were there. Vying for his attention with several other children who had run out, they were creating just the kind of happy domestic scene — or smokescreen — that he needed, with his nerves in an uproar and Dora so conspicuously absent. Oh, for God's sake! he thought, seeing Miss Marmer. She had heard the car and was now out on the porch, nosing around — just in time to see the headmaster's jealous stare as the shamed, stiff-shouldered Lily veered across the lawn and went inside. Russell then saw Miss Marmer herself glaring — at *him*. The truth be known, it was more than just Russell's stare, or Max, that Lily was trying to escape.

Fortunately, Russell had regained his composure by the time Moore and Wittgenstein approached. Moore spoke first:

Bertie, he said in his best I'll-try-if-you-will voice, how are you?

Quite well, answered Russell ebulliently. And how are you?

Quite well, too, said Moore, spreading his hands across his stomach. A bit worn from the trip, but otherwise fine, thank you. Isn't it lovely here.

Well, that was pleasant — quite enough for starts. Wittgenstein came next, not fond, but bracingly literal as he shook his old mentor's hand and said, I have thought of you often.

And I have thought of you, said Russell truthfully. Then still genial but with a slight catch in his voice, Russell said, So, coming back into the fold, are you?

Am I? asked Wittgenstein, somewhat at a loss. Then pointedly: I didn't know I was ever *in* the fold.

No, admitted Russell with a coolish smile. No, I guess you never were in the fold, were you.

That was all Russell needed to convince himself that nothing had changed between them. Even with the first words out of Wittgenstein's mouth, Russell saw that same thorny obstinance, that innate unwillingness in Wittgenstein ever to concede a point or let a simple thing be. And so it went during those next few minutes: stops and starts and polite probings, each of them summarily deciding that it was hopeless, feeling that everything and nothing had changed and wondering why they were even pursuing it.

Wittgenstein, meanwhile, still had Max to account for. But even as Wittgenstein was preparing to explain his companion, Max, now feeling combatively comical, pointed to the children and said to Russell with a vacant look:

But, Russell — I see the children wear today the clothes. It is for Ludwig that you dress them?

The remark caught everyone off guard. Wittgenstein flashed Max a killing glare. Then the flushed Moore, manfully taking his medicine, spoke up:

He's referring to something I told him I had heard — how in warm weather you sometimes let the children go about unclothed.

In other circumstances this might have been a disaster, but fortunately Dorothy, who had hung back while the three got reacquainted, came up at that moment to offer her greetings, saying with a broad smile, Bertie Russell.

Dorothy Moore, returned the master glad-hander. So good to see you. Then artfully, he said, Max here — I take it I may call you *Max?* he asked patronizingly. Well, Max was curious why the children are wearing clothes. And in answer to your question, Max, it is true we used to let them run naked on warm days, or when they were exercising. Shame, you see, is taught like anything else. Unfortunately, as the school grew, we took on older children who had been taught the old way — that the human body was a matter for shame and sniggering. And then there were the newspapers, which of course exaggerate everything. So we tend now to avoid it, and I must say it's rather a pity. Those early days before all the ruckus — those were our Eden here, in a way.

Despite the wistful note at the word "Eden," Russell was doing a bit of probing with this Biblical reference. He was especially sensitive to Wittgenstein's newfound religiosity, remembering Wittgenstein's air of disapproval at his freethinking ways after the war. Russell also saw the wooden cross around Max's neck, causing him to wonder what manner of man this ox was, though he had an idea. In the meantime, Russell's patronizing explanation had had its effect on Max, whose stubborn ears were back. Max took hard reckoning at this one who thought himself so slick. To him, there was nothing more hateful than to hear a sworn atheist bandy the Bible.

As it turned out, Russell sized up Max rather shrewdly. He could see that Max was not nearly as simple as he let on, just as he could detect, amid the expansive gestures and masking playfulness, the German's clouded hostility.

Wittgenstein saw all this and more. Pointedly, he said, *Max* — let's take off the bags.

Trying to smooth things over, meanwhile, Moore said to Russell, Well, Miss Loubry tells us that congratulations are in order.

Congratulations? asked Russell.

I mean the fact that you're to be a father again.

Oh — Russell nodded hastily. Yes . . . She is that — pregnant, I mean.

Due soon, I'm afraid. I thought I had told you. Actually, Dora's upstairs with a bad headache, unfortunately. Should be down for dinner, though. I see I am very remiss. She did ask me to offer her greetings.

I'm sure you both must be very happy, ventured Dorothy.

Oh, indeed, said Russell evasively. Indeed. But Russell didn't look so happy, and in his anxiety to deflect the conversation, he said without thinking, But here . . . Let me introduce my own two children . . .

Russell inwardly cringed as he said it but didn't dare dig the hole deeper by qualifying it. Shepherding forth a round-faced, brown-haired boy with sheer blue eyes, Russell said, This is my son, John . . . *my fearless explorer.* And this, he said, patting the pudding-bowl bob of a slender girl who presented herself at vulnerable, pretty-please attention, this is my daughter, Kate.

This was done efficiently, if somewhat hastily; the guests scarcely had time to do the requisite handshaking and talking before Russell rather ostentatiously introduced some of the other children who had run outside, as if to make it plain that at Beacon Hill there were no favorites.

Max seemed to have a knack for children. Showing off, he held two happily squealing boys upside-down by their feet. The children were drawn to him as to an inviting tree, and not just children, either. Lily, Dorothy noticed, had come out again and was now sitting on the porch, her expression somewhere between wounded and wistful. And then, rather suddenly, Russell began his standard tour narrative, pointing up to his tower, then to his prize lightning rods, all the while stealing looks at Lily, who was pretending not to be looking at Max.

They saw outside themselves as in circles, as in pictures, each opening into another, a little at a time. By the car with Max, meanwhile, Wittgenstein was feeling very much *out* of the picture. Russell, the school, the children, the long time away — it conjured a lot in him, mainly loss. Untying the ropes on the roof rack, Wittgenstein had watched as Russell introduced his children to the Moores, noticing not Russell's daughter but the boy, the son. And it was not just the boy but the bond that Wittgenstein felt; it was Russell's deep and abiding pride as he squired his splendid son forth to say a few words to Moore, whom he explained like a piece of history. Russell, he knew, would not give *him* such an introduction. He was all too keenly aware of a certain clubbishness in the way Russell introduced his son to Moore, as if Russell were conscious of Moore not merely as a fellow father but, as it were, a *real* father — a father with sons.

Looking at them then, Wittgenstein was filled with envy and grief for the unfairness of it — that for some people life could swiftly change for the better, while for others like himself, it seemed to never change, the general direction of life, with all its manifold defects and deflections, seemingly foreordained in its downward trajectory.

But Max was also weighing on Wittgenstein's mind then. Wittgenstein was furious at him for having embarrassed Moore, and now, in his jealousy at seeing Russell with his son, he was all the more ready to vent his anger on Max. Speaking under his breath in German, Wittgenstein warned him again about Russell. And then, almost against his better judgment, he added:

And quit your games with that girl.

What games? Max demanded.

You know perfectly well what games. Do you think I'm blind?

But Max wouldn't budge. With a shrug, he said, I don't know what you're talking about, Wittgenstein. That girl means nothing to me.

Looks That Alight Like Flies

BUT DIDN'T YOU THINK it was peculiar? Dorothy was whispering to Moore during the ten minutes they had alone in their spartan room before rejoining the others downstairs. And what about the way Bertie interrupted me and said, *But let me introduce my own children.* Quite as if they were *his* children and not hers! Who does he think he is? Abraham?

Dorothy was on to something. Maundering Moore was changing his socks as she continued:

And what about that woman standing on the porch? You saw her. The queer, athletic-looking one with the dark hair? Don't give me that lost look — you saw her staring at him. Staring at that poor Lily, too. As Bertie was —

Well? Face red, Moore was leaning over the bed, pulling on his left shoe as he said, I don't see what you expect me to say. That it's *odd?* Well, of course it's odd — I expected as much, so why bother about it? Can't we, *please,* go down and have a glass of sherry? Can't we merely *sit* for a while, without the analysis?

We can, said Dorothy dubiously. Only I feel more comfortable knowing. It's not mere *nosiness,* you know.

Moore put on his other shoe, then stood up as Dorothy, flicking a toothbrush, said decisively, Very well, then. But do admit this much: there *was* something going on between Max and Miss Loubry in the front seat.

Moore closed his eyes. I don't know that. Nor do you. Not for certain. Moore added evasively, I heard no protest from her.

Oh, come *on*, said Dorothy, dropping her head. The poor girl was probably petrified.

Now Moore was getting agitated, thinking she was calling his courage into question.

Then why, if you *knew* — why didn't you tell me? I'd have spoken up. And anyway, where was Wittgenstein, if it was all so obvious? Moore stared straight at her, then said, It's hard to act when you're not sure. And I'm not so blind, either, I'll have you know. I see rather more than you think.

Dorothy nodded emphatically. I know you do. You also *think* more than you think. Or *say*.

So? said Moore, drawing himself up. I suppose I find it necessary. As they say in cooking, reserve some of the liquid.

Well, you might reserve a little less liquid.

So I might, he said in that brusque way he had when he wanted to sever a conversation. Dorothy did not want to press it and followed him outside, where they found the hallway empty, the doors shut.

But who else stays up here, I wonder? whispered Dorothy as they started down the unlit back stairs. Careful, she said, and she clutched his arm, ever aware of his worsening vision in the dark. *Oop* — she held him back — Wait, there's water there. Do you see it? To your left, my sweet, to your *left*. Mind the water . . .

Moore sorely wanted a drink, but first Russell took them for a short tour of the grounds. Here Russell was much the squire. Wanting especially to dash any image of the school as being primitive or ill-equipped, he took special pride in showing them the laboratory and then, mostly for Wittgenstein's benefit, the workshop with its child-size benches.

Russell could scarcely manage a screwdriver, but he sounded quite savvy as he led Wittgenstein to the back of the shop, saying, And here is our wood lathe.

Taking his cue, Wittgenstein turned the screw and felt the edges of the wood chisels. He nodded his emphatic approval. I had no idea, he said. Most impressive. And the children use these machines?

Well, replied Russell, only the older ones use the lathe. But they use them quite ably, just as they do the chemicals in the laboratory. Oh, some cuts and splinters, but nothing serious — it's the child who has never seen these things who seriously hurts himself. Yes, we think handwork and practical instruction are most important. There's much more to education than academics, don't you agree?

Here again Wittgenstein was in vigorous agreement, saying, I gave some of my boys such instruction. More in the standards of craftsmanship than technique. We did not have such fine tools available, unfortunately.

And not your girls? asked Russell, unable to resist. They received no instruction?

They did not take such an interest, said Wittgenstein with a look of discomfort. Many of the boys were from farms and had some experience with tools. The seeds were sown already.

I see, said Russell, but he did not press it. Feeling he had redeemed his school from the status of a nudist colony, he was a good bit more relaxed. But as they crossed through the dusky beeches that enclosed the tennis lawn, Russell saw his guests eyeing the burned grass and the gutted shed, whereupon he — ever the punster — remarked, Well, every school has its bad apple. At Beacon Hill, we have a Peck.

Russell was explaining his pun and the situation surrounding it as they went back inside.

I'll tell you more about it later if you've an interest, he said as he led them down a long hallway, past a wall the children had painted with a seascape of starfish, sea horses and a Viking ship. But first let me conclude my little tour by showing you the children's dining room.

Then we won't be eating with them? asked Moore, trying to disguise his relief.

Oh, no. We do eat with them often, but not tonight, no. Rather to the annoyance of his guests, Russell continued in that same nervous, somewhat pedantic tone, We always introduce guests to the children. After all, this is the children's house. We do try to spare them from that class sense of two quite separate worlds, one for adults and one for children, with different rights for each. We feel these introductions relieve the children of that forbidding sense of *foreignness* that visiting adults carry with them. I know I always hated it, that seen-and-not-heard syndrome of our parents.

So saying, Russell ushered them into the brightly painted dining room, where the children could be heard amid a clabber of utensils and scraping stools. In its smell, the warm room was redolent of Hall, with an aroma of overcooked meat and vegetables and, mixed with it, the slightly sour custard smell of children, happily sunburned and dirty from a long day playing in the hot sun. Lily was there. Besmocked and helping with the serving, she flushed like a grouse when she saw Max loom in the doorway, inquisitive, predatory. Stealthily, she slipped back into the kitchen, evading not only Max and the headmaster but also Miss Marmer, who was supervising the meal. For thirty minutes, Miss Marmer had been awaiting the headmaster, and it was on her cue that the children jumped up and repeated in a hilarious, faltering singsong:

Wel-COME — come-to — Bea-Con HILL — to-Bea-con Hill — to Hill . . .

It was charming how the children giddily clapped and laughed. But *look,* Dorothy whispered to Moore, look for God's sake at that queer boy gnawing on his arm as if it were a great red drumstick!

I would guess, ventured Moore, that that's Bertie's pyromaniac.

Lovely. Then — just so there'd be no confusion later — Dorothy said with a veiled look toward Miss Marmer, *That's* the woman we saw on the porch — the athletic-looking one I mentioned.

But there was no need for Dorothy to point her out. Smiling nervously, Miss Marmer tiptoed over, leaning a little too close to the bewildered guests as she introduced herself with spectral friendliness as *Winnifred Marmer.* Lily, not wanting to be accused of lollygagging, had reemerged from the kitchen with a pitcher of milk — fresh *pasteurized* milk, Russell added — that she seemed to take forever pouring as she fluttered there, staring at Max. Miss Marmer, meanwhile, made a point, either for Russell's benefit or out of simple curiosity, of going up to Max and peering at his great chest while asking in amazement:

And you, sir? Are you an athlete?

Nein, said Max, giving her a murderous flick off with his eyes.

Russell didn't tarry then. But as they were leaving, Dorothy and Moore saw once more the looks zipping from Russell to Lily to Max to Miss Marmer. And then on Miss Marmer's cue the children jumped up a second time, shrilly singing:

GOOD-night-GOO-night-night — night . . .

Oh, *that* was him, was it?

It was out of an embarrassed sense of politeness that Dorothy feigned surprise when Russell identified the arm-gnawing boy as his shed burner.

They were drinking sherry, and Russell was telling of his woes with the boy, or rather about the woes of schoolmastering, which led to another short disquisition about the school and its educational methods. These, he said, were essentially eclectic, experimental and evolving, with new approaches being tried as others were discarded as impractical or ineffective. Of paramount political importance to him and Dora, Russell said, was that their school be as "uncoercive" as possible. Sitting back in his chair, Russell was saying:

The key, I think, is to reduce external discipline to a minimum. By setting the child largely free, he can, for the most part, learn on his own, and at his own speed. Not that it's easy. Trusting the impulses of children is often very difficult and trying, but we're convinced that this is the only really good way that children learn. You can't just *teach* democracy. We feel we must try, as a school, to *be* one. In fact, our school council is comprised of children and adults, each with only one vote.

And they don't take advantage of that? asked Moore.

Oh, sometimes they do, of course. The child who has been overdisciplined always does at first. For a week he may go wild, but usually he quickly gets over it, especially once he's been around the other children. Last year, the school council voted out all rules. We didn't oppose it. Russell smiled. For a day we had anarchy, but since everyone did what he pleased, the children saw they also had no regular meals, or bedtime stories, or anyone to mend their clothes. Two days later, tired, grubby and sick of jam and bread, they most gratefully voted back all rules. I must say it was an exceedingly valuable lesson. How many adults know what anarchy is really like?

As Russell had expected, though, Wittgenstein and Max looked dubious. Gulping his second sherry, Max said cheerfully, So they are free to burn down your little house.

Shed, you mean, corrected Russell.

Shed, house, sure. Max broke into a grin. They learn about fire!

Well, intoned Russell, with a look of irritation, this, I must say, is the exception. Rabe Peck is his mother's creation, not ours. Normally, when we have a child given to abnormal sexual fantasies — morbid preoccupations with sex or violence and the like — we encourage him to talk about it to his heart's content. The normal child usually quickly gets over it, but our shed burner, I'm afraid, is beyond that. We don't claim to be able to help children with problems of his magnitude. But again the problem is usually the parents. My friend A. S. Neill — the one who runs that allegedly daft Summerhill school the papers are always attacking — well, he has a boy of six who craps his pants six times daily. Neill's was the only school in England that would take him. Evidently the boy's mother, a quite wealthy, educated woman, ventured to teach the child by making him eat it.

Strangling the sherry decanter, Max said with a laugh, Give this burner to your friend Neill!

I'd like to! hoofed Russell agreeably. Everyone laughed — everyone but Wittgenstein.

Now Ludwig, continued Max, spilling a bit of sherry on the sideboard, Ludwig, he was a strong teacher in our town. Oh, he made the children learn good, but, *whack!* you know, when they do the bad things or will not hear. But they learned this way, the children.

We just discussed this on the train, Wittgenstein broke in petulantly. Max makes it sound as if all I did was keep order. In fact, I was part of the reform movement in Austria after the war. On the whole, it was very enlightened — very progressive, our system, especially compared to the drilling of the old state system. I disciplined, yes, but I took great pains always to be consistent. Consistency is what children need most. More than sheer brute discipline.

And a certain amount of compulsion, agreed Russell with a knowing look and a nod to Max. Not to mention *sheer instruction.* This, I think, is where Dora and I differ with Neill and other liberal educators. As we've learned here — and rather painfully, I'm afraid — certain steps do have to be taken to impart a requisite amount of learning. Much as we want to create an atmosphere of freedom, we know that children can't completely be turned loose and be expected to get it all themselves. To our chagrin, we've also found that steps also have to be taken to keep the bigger ones from terrorizing the smaller ones, which inevitably means you're stuck with putting them in classes, as if you were breeding chickens. With a hapless smile, Russell added, Like it or not, the school really does become a kind of microcosm of the state, with all the same virtues and deficiencies. One wishes we didn't need the police and the army, but I'm afraid that, to some extent, this is the case. The mystery, it seems to me, is how to instill order and discipline without stifling the creativity that stems from these same chaotic, generative impulses. Seeing he was nigh on making a speech, Russell looked at Wittgenstein, then switched course. But as I recall, it was not the children but again the *parents* who were your problem. Russell laughed to himself. I'll never forget that one letter you sent me — the one you sent me in China? You know the one I'm referring to?

I remember, said Wittgenstein with a rueful expression. When I wrote that the Trattenbachers were rotten?

"Wicked" is the word I remember.

I said wicked? Wittgenstein asked. Well, if I did, I was wrong — they were much too small to be called *wicked*.

Oh, they was not so bad, scoffed Max, growing more sociable with the warmth of the sherry. Why bad? These people have no money after the war — you English see to that. And they fear of this one, he said with a nod to Wittgenstein. Sure. They fear him because they think he is rich and talks like rich. Then something occurred to him, and he said excitedly, Ludwig! Do you tell them how you fixed the big train engine?

What's this? asked Russell.

Wittgenstein frowned, then said, A locomotive had broken down. It was the only train linking the village with a mill on which the village heavily depended. Several engineers came to look at it and said it couldn't be fixed — not in the village. They said it would have to be shipped back in pieces to Wiener Neustadt. For the village this would have been ruinous. Wittgenstein sat there like an engine idling, then hurried the story to conclusion, saying, So, I asked to examine the train. And after an hour, he said with a shrug, I fixed it.

Max threw his hands up delightedly. Oh! Oh! He found a way, this one! He found a way! God, the tongues start to do this, said Max, clacking his fingers together. That was when Ludwig's trouble starts with this people. That was the start, sure.

Moore, intrigued now, asked, But how did you fix the engine, Wittgenstein?

With the hammers, interjected Max.

Sledgehammers, corrected Wittgenstein, acting as if this were nothing. I saw the engine was frozen. So I positioned Max and ten other men around the train with sledgehammers. And then I had them strike certain spots at different intervals to set up a sympathetic frequency — a rhythm to free the structure.

Moore almost upset his sherry. Can't you see him, Bertie? he said with a sideways look at Russell. Conducting them all like a great glockenspiel?

Sure! Max sat nodding. They think Ludwig is crazy. Max touched his forehead zanily, then went on, Half the people, they are there to laugh at him, such a rich crazy man. This one who thinks he is so smart, you know, with this boom-boom, tink-tink. And, then . . . Max's eyes got big. The train engine, *it moves!* And they *looked* at him, these peoples, and they get all quiet. Sure, they think he is — Max touched his head again, this time superstitiously. And then, *ffssst!* Like that, off Ludwig is. Gone!

My God, said Russell, raising his eyes. They must have thought you performed a miracle, Wittgenstein.

This was too much. Wittgenstein was disgusted. Nonsense! It was no miracle. Please . . .

Wittgenstein had just managed to change the subject when they were interrupted by a knock. It was Russell's son, John, who ran to his father and said in a breathless whisper, Daddy, Mrs. Bride says you're to come to dinner now. She says everything will be mush if you don't. Are you coming?

We're coming, said Russell, standing up. Tell her we'll be sitting down in five or ten minutes. Have you called your mother?

Mr. Higgins says she's coming now.

Good.

As the boy ran back, Russell turned to his guests and explained, Mr. Higgins is an American friend of Dora's. He's been spending the past few days with us.

Oh? Standing nearest the host, Dorothy perked up with polite interest, naturally expecting that Russell would say something more about this other guest who would be at dinner. But, oddly, Russell said nothing, and Dorothy, wanting to break the awkward silence that followed, remarked, Your John seems a lovely boy.

Russell sprang to life at this, saying after a moment's hesitation, You know, I do hate to brag, but he is. And fearless — God! Fearless of heights, water, horses. *My* fear is that he will be destroyed in the next war.

It was queer how this came out, to mix morbidness with such enthusiasm. Russell did not say "next war" as anything but a certainty, but to Moore and Wittgenstein, who felt no such certainty, it sounded only cranky and political, part of his unpleasant, propagandizing side.

A Son

RUSSELL AND HIS GUESTS were just starting down the hall to dinner when John ran back to his father and solemnly asked a word with him.

We'll only be a moment, said Russell to the others. With that, he led the boy, all huffy and disheartened, to a nearby alcove and listened for a minute before sending him off with several carefully chosen words and a squeeze on the shoulder.

It was a thoroughly ordinary transaction between a father and son, but again Wittgenstein felt that sense of loss and envy, that longing that he had felt outside earlier, when he had first seen the two of them together. What a cruel contradiction, not to desire women and yet to desire a son: to Wittgenstein it seemed that one impulse should have canceled the other. Even then, six years after it had happened, Wittgenstein still found it hard to believe that he had once asked a man to let him adopt the man's own blood.

The boy Wittgenstein had asked to adopt was Franz Kluck, a poor farmer's son. Franz was the most gifted pupil Wittgenstein ever had in Trattenbach. Every night after school, in the little room he occupied above the barren grocery, Wittgenstein gave Franz and a few other of his brightest boys additional lessons in Latin and Greek, geometry, biology, German literature. At eleven, Franz could recite Schiller and Goethe, write Latin verse in hexameter, discuss Pythagoras, identify local rocks and plants and follow a topographical map. At home, his father, who was drunk whenever he could scrape up the money, beat him for coming home late and ridiculed him for his airs — for reading books and for speaking correct German and not the local dialect. Franz's three older brothers were as terrified of their father as they were jealous of their brilliant little brother. Their father encouraged them to pound sense into Franz, and the beatings were especially vicious when he was drunk and urging them on. In an effort to force the boy to drop his stupid books and confront real life, the brothers once mashed his face into steaming hot guts. Sitting on him, they poured schnapps down his throat and tickled him till he blacked out. Several expensive books Wittgenstein had lent the boy returned with broken bindings and shit-splattered pages from having been heaved against walls or flung into the pigyard. Once, after Franz had accidentally left the door open, his father made him stand for hours in the freezing cold without a coat. Not long after that, Herr Kluck went on a binge and nearly burned down the house.

Most nights after their study sessions, Wittgenstein would walk the boy part of the way home. The slender mountain road was dark but strewn with interesting rocks, and the sky was usually swarming with stars. It seemed they were always stooping or pointing, or examining something by the light of a match, but inevitably as they approached Franz's house the boy would grow anxious and depressed. Wittgenstein knew how he felt — he had felt much the same as a boy. He knew the silence and tensed shoulders, the sick stomach. More, he knew the resentment that turned back in on a boy, especially a brilliant one, compounding the senseless pain of adult whims and cruelty into a circuitous and self-fulfilling logic: imagining biting back the dog that had bit you, then in guilt biting yourself more bitterly than the dog ever could.

Franz knew his stars because he knew the night. Knowledge of constellations came later, once one saw a logic, a fatal organizing pattern, to one's life. Then came the obsessive building, the spiraling systems, the fantastic and oppressive apparatus to account for what could not possibly be put right, or justified. For Franz, it was the father who, in one breath, could punish him for an open door and in another declare his sovereign father's right to burn down his own house if he liked. For Wittgenstein, it was the father whom he could remember once calling him a pig for eating three of the doughnutlike *Krapfen*. His voracious father, on the other hand, might eat four or five at a sitting without being branded a pig, and for no better reason than because *he* was a *Vater*.

Wittgenstein understood this night-entranced boy; he understood him all too well. As a boy, Wittgenstein, too, had made a study of the stars, especially after Hans killed himself in Cuba. Winter stars, the boy had found, were hypodermic — hot, piercing and fearfully accurate — but the summer stars, especially, he imagined, the southern stars of Cuba, were warm and hypnagogic, like overripe blooms, like bitter drugs and pistols clumsily aimed. Wittgenstein could remember habitually pinching himself under the table in his father's august presence, finding that the smaller pain, which he could control, tended to blunt the larger one, which he could not. When this failed, there was the roof, where he could peer out as through a tube into that vast and mindless sky in which so much music had been lost and wasted, wasted as Hans had himself been wasted, leading the boy to fear that the world, which seemed resoundingly closed, would run out of numbers or melodies or places to bury people, until life itself was exhausted as he himself was exhausted by the father in the study below, coaxing moans from the boy-sized cello cradled between his knees.

The grown man knew his stars well enough to know that Franz was sincere when he turned to him one night before heading down the path to his house and said he wished that he, Herr Wittgenstein, were his father. Letting down the warm formality with which he disguised his love, Wittgenstein said he wished the same.

That was the origin of the idea. Afterward, it seemed to Wittgenstein that the whole scheme had been rash and ill conceived, but that was because it had all gone so impossibly wrong. Yet the truth was, there was nothing sudden about his decision. Wittgenstein had examined every phase of his adoption plan — and every possible stumbling block — in meticulous detail, to the point that, for months, he could think of little else. And certainly, he never would have dreamed of suggesting adoption if Franz had not first broached the idea. Franz was a very pure and serious boy, but Wittgenstein had nevertheless been careful to give him plenty of time to weigh his decision. In the meantime, Wittgenstein brought Franz and the rest of his children by train to Vienna, where they stayed with Mining and Gretl while touring buildings and museums and going to concerts, cafés and the Prater. Later, Franz even succeeded in getting his father's no doubt insensible permission to go once more to Vienna, this time alone, to spend a week with Mining and Gretl as a trial to see how he liked it. And when Franz did like it, Wittgenstein made still more plans for a whole new life. Everything was set forth. He and the boy would live with Mining in Vienna. He would get his doctorate and teach, and during the summers he and his son, Franz — Franz Wittgenstein — would travel, touring England and Russia and Palestine, maybe even America, on and on.

Then came the day that Wittgenstein went with his mediator Max to talk to the boy's father. They found Herr Kluck stooped in the muddy pigyard below the decaying house, grimy, bristled and pitifully small compared to the monster the boy had described. That he was a brute and an ignoramus was beside the point; he was still a father, and that, no matter what Wittgenstein told himself to the contrary, made him immeasurably more than he, an oddball with no wife. Even as he began talking to Herr Kluck, Wittgenstein realized that the whole scheme was ridiculous. Had Max not been there to steady him, he easily would have turned around in disgust and walked away. Afterward, Wittgenstein thought he must have been out of his mind. Did he really think that Herr Kluck, this father of nine, for whom children were basically cattle, would simply give his son up for adoption just because some crazy man from the city wanted to raise the boy as his own and educate him? If nothing else, Herr Kluck had his pride. What did he care that Wittgenstein was willing to send Franz home to visit whenever he wished? Herr Kluck said the boy was no good anyhow. He would just run back home.

Max wasn't fooled. Max knew the story. He knew what was running through Kluck's sodden brain, between those crusted wads of hair stuffed in his ears. He knew Herr Kluck couldn't allow himself to be indebted to this reputedly wealthy man. To give the boy outright, even as a gift, to imply that this rich man could give the boy things that he couldn't, much less to imply that these things had any worth — for Herr Kluck, as Max knew, this was unthinkable. *Selling* the boy, on the other hand, driving a hard bargain as if the boy were a bull or a pig, this would have brought Herr Kluck recognition as a clever operator, ridding himself of a mouth to feed, and for cash money, to boot.

Max pulled Wittgenstein aside when Herr Kluck, with a shrug and grunt, walked away — a typical bargaining ploy. Max was extremely fond of the boy. The orphan in Max had a large emotional stake in this adoption. Max had already throttled Franz's oldest brother, Klaus, behind the tavern, showing him, in the most graphic terms, what he would do if he or anybody else laid another hand on the boy. Franz, then, was a kind of second chance for Max, who badly wanted to make right for Franz what had eluded him in his own life. Standing in Herr Kluck's pigyard, faced with his friend's sudden lack of resolve, Max was on the verge of tears.

What's wrong with you? he asked, staring into Wittgenstein's shamed face. You said you want him — *do* you? The old bastard won't *give* him to you, I'll tell you that right now. But he'll *sell* him to you. Just show him the color of some money. Just a little money — he'll take it. Get him drunk and he'll trade you the boy for a bottle. Hell, I'll do it, if it's so distasteful to you! Hey! Come back here!

But Wittgenstein's pride got in the way. Not even for the boy's sake would he buy him — it was disgusting and out of the question. Wittgenstein walked away. He actually walked away, abandoning Max just as surely as he did Franz.

Of course the story got out, Herr Kluck saw to that. Soon it was even said that Wittgenstein offered him a fortune for the disappointed boy, whom afterward people eyed with wonder, as if he were a walking sack of money. Wittgenstein even received several half-decipherable notes offering children for sale — good Gentile stock children, the notes said, girls and boys, and pretty, *Herr Lehrer*, all ages.

The incident with the broken-down locomotive, then, had only been the start of Wittgenstein's misfortunes in Trattenbach. Miracles aren't necessarily good or fortuitous occurrences, much less happy ones. There are miracles of belief, and there are miracles of disbelief in the face of the dazzlements of belief — miracles of overcoming the lies and evasions of one's life and time. Thus, on the one hand, there is the spectacle of a powerful man being unhorsed by a gust of light, while, on the other, there is the powerless man living with the seemingly incredible belief that one day the light will strike him, turning him, for one dazzling moment, into light itself. For Wittgenstein, in any case, the worst and most unbelievable miracle was that, after this failed adoption, in the absence of belief and in spite of all reason, he remained in Trattenbach, with the hardest revelations yet to come.

Commonplace Miracles

DINNER was not a success.

Maybe it was Dora's reserve, the way she politely rebuffed Dorothy's first shy attempts at friendliness. Or maybe it was the uncertainty about just who this Higgins was, sitting protectively at Dora's arm. Higgins didn't exactly seem to be a mutual friend — not to judge by Russell's snide remarks and Higgins's cold silence.

Also, there were the constant interruptions. The children were taking a bus trip down the coast the next day to tour some Bronze and Iron Age sites and do a bit of bathing — and there were last-minute problems with lunches and the bus and who among the staff would be going, since it was a Saturday. The other problem was what to do with Rabe. Taking him on the trip was hardly an appetizing idea, but then, as Dora argued, it made better sense to bring him to a ruin than to risk his turning the school into one.

Then it was 8:30. Distant thumps and caterwauling. Time to say good night to the children. We always make a point of it, said Russell, ceremoniously helping his heavy wife up from the table while the proletarian Higgins slouched over his plate. When Russell and Dora returned, they seemed silent, strained. Had there been words, perhaps? Once more the telephone was ringing. Once more, Miss Marmer peeked in with profuse apologies, this time to say it was the solicitor, long distance.

Russell looked distraught when he returned. Uncapping the decanter of sherry, he said, The solicitor thinks we ought to hire another detective to find the boy's mother! I told him the expense of one is ruining me as it is. Then leaning toward Higgins, Russell said archly, Two more weeks in America. That's what it will cost me, Higgins. *Hoof, hoof.*

It was probably in retaliation for this crack that Higgins leaned over to Dora then and said, I know one very good detective — several, in fact.

Do you now? asked Russell, bristling with fears that the plotters had been making inquiries about him. (They wouldn't trickle poison down his ear!)

In their unhappiness, Russell and Dora were almost oblivious to how they were coming across to their guests, for whom their life was like an open bureau filled with things the visitors politely tried not to see. Dora hardly seemed to care at that point, sick of the whole pretense of it. She had barely eaten half her dinner when she excused herself, taking her sick headache back to bed. Higgins was no more discreet, excusing himself five minutes later. Russell wanted to brain him. The fellow didn't even have the decency to leave by the other door.

It was easy to feel sorry for Russell then, left to fend alone with his guests and the constantly ringing telephone. Wittgenstein had been noticeably quiet. So, for that matter, had Max, who was looking bored. Suddenly, he rose from the table, without excusing himself.

Oh, said Russell hopefully. The lavatory, should you want it, Max, is down the hall — to your left.

Max nodded in acknowledgment, then went out. Ten, fifteen minutes passed. Finally, unable to contain his curiosity any longer, Russell excused himself, saying, Oh, dear, I forgot to tell Miss Marmer something. I'll be back presently.

Russell knew what he would find, and sure enough, he found it. They were standing by the banister. For a moment, Russell didn't know what to do. Leaning against the wall with her hands behind her back, she was simple and easy — easier, certainly, than she had ever been with him. Did he detect a trace of sauciness, of rising anger in her eyes? He expected the girl to blanch and shrink with shame, but instead she faced him, querulous, but standing her ground. Max stood near her, saying with his hostile little eyes, *Move me, you old goat, just try.*

Russell felt his gorge rise. He would not be a hypocrite, would not enforce a code of morality he found basically false and hateful. So be it, he told himself. The girl was free, if she had no better sense, or taste, in companions. Russell felt almost fatherly, if flimsy, in his concern, which even he knew to be suspect. I was looking for Miss Marmer, he offered as if he needed an excuse. There was galling sweetness in her voice as she said, I am sorry. I have not seen her. And then she waited as for a poison to take effect, knowing that they, as two, were stronger than he.

Russell made a point of finding Miss Marmer then, but not to talk school business. They ducked into his office and shut the door. Miss Marmer could see his need and seemed pleased.

Well, she said drolly, you'll have to be doubly quiet with your *guests* beside us.

There'll be no problem, Russell replied. I saw Moore nodding. They'll be going up to bed soon.

I'll be waiting, Miss Marmer said, and then a duskiness crept into her

voice. She was a moaner, she was, and she was slowly curling into herself
like a cat drunk on catnip. Moving her shoulders slightly, she looked as
if she would loop across the rug and start rolling on her back. Do you
know how I'll be waiting? she asked, and then she gave another slight
squirm to get his juice up, to show him what he would be having upstairs
later. A familiar dish: throat of pearls and lipstick, the clop of her black
mules and the silk kimono that he liked to spread over her perfumed
buttocks like a peacock's fan as she bent over and slowly touched her
toes, flowering for his breathless adoration like the sucking purplish
anemone. Opera would be playing — Puccini, probably — and he knew
he would find her usual lubricity as through her rather small teeth she
panted, *Don't stop — don't, dear — don't.* This was harrowing. In sex
she was another person. In fact, he sometimes felt squelched and squeamish at this woman's rasping *meeooww.* After all, there was what the
libertine doctor prescribed for civilization's ills, and then there was the
other truth, that there should be pleasure, certainly, even abandon, but
only so much as was seemly. Why, a fellow of his years was liable to
rupture himself, straddling the grunting goddess of the Golden Mean.

After this interlude, Russell returned to the dinner table. To his surprise
and relief, Max himself returned a few minutes later. The horse wasn't
out of the stable.

Russell had been right in gauging the Moores: Moore was suppressing
yawns, and Dorothy was getting restless. Even Wittgenstein was tired.
They all were tired, but there was still a certain tension, a scratchiness in
the conversation, which was being passed round the table like dry bread.
Here, just before they all went up to bed, were the opening shots of Wittgenstein's *Viva* the next day. It must have been the story about Wittgenstein resuscitating the train that started it. The talk turned to miracles —
what they were and whether, in this age, there were any. Wittgenstein
and Max were both disgusted when Russell again provocatively suggested that the incident with the train might be rightly termed a miracle.

Call it intuition — mechanics, said Wittgenstein. It was no miracle.

Then Max spoke up, saying, in effect, that miracles were an extinct
phenomenon, the last having been performed by Christ and the Apostles.
The rest — the saints and their acts, the holy relics — were all lies and
blasphemy. Max continued:

Christ started his life as Lord at Cana, to turn the water to the wine.
And at the last dinner, he turns the wine to blood. Looking vehemently
round the table, Max concluded, In this there is *much* to know. But no
one, even Russell, wanted to ask just what.

Taking a sip of sherry, Russell then turned mischievous. Invoking the shade of Voltaire, he said to Max, God, you would admit, set the world in order. God knows all things. How, then, do you explain, Max, why he who knew and made all things would violate his own order by letting his son work miracles in order to make ignorant men believe?

This is mere enlightenment cleverness, interjected Wittgenstein, trying to preempt Max's fury. Voltaire assumes God must always be reasonable. A venerable old clock maker. This accounts for nothing. You might as easily say that Christ performed a sort of miracle by having the fortitude *not* to perform one. Here I refer to when the devil tempted Christ in the desert, daring him to throw himself down from the mountain since it was written that angels would catch him.

Russell's face grew red. His sudden anger was quite unaccountable as he suddenly said, Yes, and Jesus might have performed another miracle that day! I mean when the devil showed him all the world's kingdoms arrayed there below. Christ might have united the world forever in a single stroke. But what instead does he do? *Nothing!* A thousand wars since, and he wastes himself with circus tricks — raising corpses and making idiots speak!

At this, Max lunged up, sneering. So smart you are, Russell! I know not much, it is true. But about God or war I will say you know not *one thing*! Not *one*! And I will say to you all good night.

But this is only a discussion, protested Russell weakly as Max burst through the door.

For all his frustrations with Max that day, Wittgenstein was instinctively protective. Rising to go after him, Wittgenstein shot back at Russell, Well, now maybe you see! Not everyone is *reasonable*, Russell, not even God. Voltaire never understood this, either.

Dorothy and Moore said their good-nights shortly thereafter. As they crept back through the long hallway to their room, Dorothy scarcely knew where to start.

Oh, come now, she whispered. You mean you didn't feel the friction between him and Dora? And what about that Higgins? I mean, didn't it seem a trifle odd to you, him leaving so soon after Dora?

Not really.

Oh, come on, Bill. You astound me.

And you astound me.

Why must you always act as if it's so distasteful? hissed Dorothy, pulling him back by the arm. What passes between us is intimacy, not gossip. I wouldn't *dream* of saying this to anybody else. Where is the shame in admitting to *me*, your *wife*, what you see? Can't we have this much between us?

Moore stood glaring at her. I just don't feel that everything bears recounting or comment, that's all. He started off again.

But *why*? she asked, tugging his arm again. Where's the virtue in that? And anyway, why should anybody care — or know — what we think? I hate it when we attend the same event and come away with utterly different impressions of people and what happened. I sometimes feel as if we've been in completely different *rooms*.

Well, he said mulishly, so, in a sense, we have.

Oh, quit! she hissed. Save that nonsense for your *Viva*. And please, don't fall right asleep on me. And don't groan. All day long, I've felt like a pair of bookends, with all these people wedged between us.

There was light under the door of the next room, where they could hear, as through a wire, the tinny sound of some aria being played on a gramophone.

What is that? asked Dorothy. Verdi? It's a little late, I'd say. You'd think Bertie might have told us who's sleeping in the room next to us.

Pretend you're in a hotel.

I *feel* I'm in a hotel, thank you.

As if to banish the chill ghosts of this otherness, Dorothy then started unpacking, hanging up clothes, filling drawers and arranging brushes and bottles along the dresser. Moore, meanwhile, took his towel and kit and went down the hall to wash. It was after ten, but the drafty house was still noisy, especially on the children's end, where the children could still be heard chattering like crickets in their beds. But outside, too, there were voices and laughter, diffuse and indistinct in the distorting night air. Hearing a door open, Dorothy looked out the window and saw a man — was it Wittgenstein swinging his cane? — walking across the crackling gorse in the wind. A while later, as she was plumping up the pillows, she saw a woman disappear around the side of the house. The man was gone.

There's certainly an awful lot of activity going on outside at this hour, she said to Moore when he returned.

At this they heard the toilet flush. Faint footsteps — a woman's steps, it sounded like.

Dorothy was standing by the bureau, looking tense. Moore scowled. Oh, stop it. Go on and get yourself ready.

I just don't like it, not knowing who it is. Leaning against the bureau, rubbing her arms, Dorothy said, At least she could turn off that opera.

·

Moore was fast under the covers when she returned.

I'm not asleep, he said before she asked.

Not yet, you aren't.

She climbed into the bending bed, and drew up to him with a sigh. For some time she lay there, and then she said, You know, I couldn't stand it, having to share my children with others, as they do. I can't imagine it. Apportioning out love like that. Always having to be careful not to show favorites, the complete lack of privacy. I couldn't conduct my family on those terms, so publicly. I guess I'm too private and selfish. I suppose I am.

Moore rested there with his mouth open, feeling her full warmth on his chest, the outside coming inside, that infusion of intimate peace as he expired further into the bed.

I felt that myself earlier, he said finally. He's such a public man, Bertie — public in ways I'll never be. I can't imagine it, having such an appetite for that arena, to be willing, as he is, to make such grist of one's life. Perhaps it's because he was an orphan. Maybe that's why he's made himself such a ward of the greater weal.

They lay there a while longer, then Dorothy said, Do you know what this place reminds me of, vaguely? That hotel we stayed at in Harwich the summer before the war. What was it called? Something to do with Macbeth. You know the place I mean.

He surprised her by remembering it straightaway. The Hurley-Burley, you mean.

That's it. Oh, my . . . Remember that old Scotsman who played the bagpipes? And you singing after supper while I played the piano?

That was *Foggy, Foggy Dew* I sang.

And that birthday party — no, no, an anniversary, it was. The one in which you played Poseidon, holding that pitchfork with your weed wig? God, they had some types there. Dorothy sniffed. They have some types here.

The window was inclined into the summer air, the air that moved the curtains. Looking troubled in his recollection, his face glazed with moonlight, Moore said, You know . . . I distinctly remember hearing that they pressed the hotel into barracks during the war. And — that's right — somebody told me the hotel burned down. God, I can't remember where I heard that, but I'm fairly sure. Positive, in fact.

Burned down? she asked disappointedly. You never told me that.

Oh, this was years ago I heard it. Or did I read it?

Air belled the curtains. Light sustained the air. Side by side, they were looking up to look *out* at their life, looking up at the time staring down.

The sea was so glassy there, Dorothy said. I don't know that I've ever seen you so relaxed as you were then, floating on your back. The other guests were all so much older than I — by now a good many of them must be under the ground. Do you remember that old lady, the one with that huge black birthmark on her neck who read tea leaves? She was always in a tizzy whenever you went for a float. *I'd watch him if I were you, dear,* she'd tell me. Over and over she'd say it. Scaring the daylights out of me. Saying you were liable to fall asleep and slip under the waves. You don't know what I used to go through, waiting there — I hated you staying out there so long.

Moore shifted around. Suddenly he was wide awake. I remember you complaining, but you never said it bothered you *that* much. Why did you never tell me?

Dorothy lay a long time without answering, anxious, tugging at a strand of hair. Nudging her, he said, Well?

She hesitated, then said, I didn't feel I could. I didn't want to be a worrywart. I knew how you loved the water. And you mustn't forget — you were so much older than I. I might have seemed independent, but I was still a girl in ways, there were still things I couldn't tell you. Dorothy turned to him. Her eyes were moist. Didn't you ever think of me sitting on the beach, waiting for you?

But of course I did, he said, pulling her closer. I was always aware of you up there, tugging at me. Didn't you know that?

He thought she was going to cry then as she said, I was so idealistic then, still the bride. My eyes were *this big.* I remember I used to think that if we were truly tied you would finally read my mind and know to come in. But you never came in when I wanted. So I sat and sat, fretting and watching for you like a dog tied outside a sweetshop, wondering why you had to do it.

But why did you never tell me? he remonstrated. I don't know why I swam out so far . . . Moore took a long breath. I never expected to marry, I felt such a duffer then. Being forty, I mean, with my fellow's meals and fellow's rooms — I thought I had long passed the point of being *eligible.* I simply couldn't believe it, married after all those years. I had no perspective, I felt I needed to pull back to see our life — I had to swim off a distance. Not that I completely *wanted* to, you understand. Oh, even as I was wading out I would be thinking of coming back in. In a way, I felt as if it were a little daily ordeal so we could be reunited — to properly think of myself as *this* man, paired with *this* woman. The idea that even apart we were bound. Oh, I know, it was the *simplest little thing,* but somehow I couldn't quite grasp it. For the life of me I couldn't get the hang of it — having you there.

They hit a rock then: able to think back no further, they lay for some minutes in each other's arms, thinking of the miracle of this time and of that ultimate separation, when they would succumb finally to the undertow of fallow earth. It was that sad old matrimonial song. Two by two, or in twain, the partners went up like Noah's beasts into an unknown ark, with theirs and all theirs after them following them into the ground. It was bitter in its way, the necessity of this life, and yet they hung on to it so doggedly, clinging to each other with that odd longing for something that is already there, but only provisionally, so long as they could sustain themselves on these hypnotically recurring tides, under the receding eaves of this light.

Moore didn't last long in this swimming. He was the first to go, while Dorothy, as usual, was still lying wide awake, with his slumbering weight athwart her flank. The house groaned, it carried sounds like a telephone, with a pinging undersea sound. Sometime later, half asleep, Dorothy heard a child crying, then later still, the sound of a man's cautious footsteps, followed a few minutes later by the delicate but unmistakable creaking of springs. And then — this was unusual — Dorothy awoke, roused from a dream, with Moore inside her. Grappling and struggling against her, he was half asleep as the bed bobbed and rocked, the two of them blundering like sleepwalkers into completion.

At five, had they been awake, they might have heard somebody creaking down the steps. But they heard nothing and did not remember their long dream together, until two hours later when their host crept back up the stairs to wake them for breakfast.

A Synoptic View

MAX was the first up that morning — first after the cook, Mrs. Bride, who arrived at five-thirty, after breakfast for her own family.

Whatever else, Max had not lost his common touch. He soon charmed Mrs. Bride, who spread before him two normal-size portions of kippers and eggs, which he was sopping up with a slab of bread when Russell came down at six-thirty for his morning tea.

Max liked to earn his keep, and the evening before, he had told Russell that he would do some odd jobs that Tillham would have taken forever to do and botched besides. But Mrs. Bride spoke for Max first.

Might I have him early this morning, sir? she asked Russell. He promised to fix the back sink, and I have several things else. T'wd be a help.

Why, of course, said Russell, who at that point was far more concerned with keeping Max busy than with anything he might accomplish.

Russell was in a slightly better mood, but only slightly, having kept something of a vigil for Lily the night before after the Moores had gone to bed. As he had stood there watching from his tower study, the headmaster had done some very involuted reasoning to justify his spying. He saw the light go out in Lily's room — a signal? Well, Max wasn't with her, that much was clear. Following his blowup, Max and Wittgenstein must have gone walking, because Russell later saw them return across the downs, a broad shadow and a slight one.

Staring down from his tower, Russell found himself beset by all sorts of crazy and not-so-crazy fears. The sensational premise of his article "Are Parents Bad for Children?" seemed almost diabolically prescient now. Late at night like this, especially when he was working, it was sometimes painfully clear what would happen with Dora and the children. He could see it all very mathematically, as if their predicament were a sprawling and unwieldy theorem based on an immutable logic that only he was cold and abstruse enough to see. Still, the truth came to him slowly now. He was well past the age of being thunderstruck, or of even wanting calamitous moments of vision. Rather, Russell now saw the truth by degrees, the light trickling down like dust motes in the general disarray. The dust might be brushed away or tidied, but it was always accumulating. He knew, at bottom, that it would not work with Dora, and that it would not work because he did not want it to work. Despite his high-minded feints about leaving the matrimonial door open, he did not want Dora, not really. In a way, he was even grateful that Dora had given him the perfect excuse. He was not willing, at this point, to impose on himself a life of quiet misery by working out some modern, selfless, perhaps even progressive marital arrangement. He remembered how he had told his guests of their desire to create an uncoercive school so they might break the violent and oppressive "form" of society. But the form, he saw, was in his mind; the coercion was that of his own intractable drives and habits. This was his downfall. It was this, he saw, that had led him to fail in the face of his own splendid vision. And of course it was comparatively easy to change one's mind — to emend or retract one's ideas — but the course of one's life still persisted with all the sickening inertia of a derailed train. Here the public mask was useless, and his children, the fruits of his choices, were still oblivious to the subtleties of his evolving program, lost to his neat distinctions and the history he was writing. None of this missed him. Nor did he miss the irony that, once again, he would find himself playing the part of pacifist in spite of his natural lust for combat, especially now when, at bottom, he felt *hors de combat.*

No, he wouldn't have his children treated like small and miserable colonies caught in the tidal pull of two large, belligerent nations. He wouldn't object. He wouldn't bloody Dora, or himself, in a fruitless court battle to wrest the children from her. He could see it all quite fatalistically. Dora would get the children and the school. And then old Higgins would step in and sweep up all the cards — everything.

There was much pain to undo by the time Russell finally tiptoed up to Miss Marmer's room. It was better sex than they'd had in weeks. Whatever else, it gave Russell a huge and priapic pleasure to be having his while his old rival lay snoring away in the next room.

And having had good sex the night before, Russell felt he could be more conciliatory with Max this morning, saying, I'm sorry for having angered you last night. Truly, I didn't mean to.

Max's forearms were resting across the table. Still chewing, he passed this off with an indistinct smile. Last night I was in anger, he said. Not today. Ludwig and me, we talked outside, in the dark. This does for me good. I know I have anger. This is bad, I know. I work hard to stop my anger, but still it comes. Max shrugged. There it is.

Russell said abruptly, I do want to pay you for your work today. Let me at least give you something.

No, please — Max spread his flattened palm across the table. This is good between us. I need no money.

Russell smiled. Have children and you will.

This was more tail pulling, and Max knew it. Russell could see Max's rising anger, and as he turned, he was smiling just as he had two hours earlier when he crept past Moore's door.

After Russell had drunk his tea, he woke the Moores. Then he went into the study, where Dora was spending a few minutes with John and Kate.

It was a relatively new ritual, this fifteen-minute family gathering every morning. Fifteen minutes a day wasn't long for a family to have together, but for the school's other children, it was a major show of favoritism. Russell and Dora were keenly aware of this, but they felt that for the present the potential damage from inattention far outweighed the passing frictions that John and Kate would suffer at the hands of their envious schoolmates.

From almost the day Beacon Hill had opened in 1927, the Russells, as a family, had been hostage to these pressures. In fact, the constraints that the school would place on family life was probably the drawback that Russell and Dora had least considered in their decision to open the school. But if Russell and Dora were ill prepared for this, John and Kate were that much less so. Having spent their first years in quite ordinary and happy family life, they suddenly found themselves having to share their parents like toys or clothes or any other of the school's semicommunal property. As the elder, John had been the first to feel it, realizing that if he was shown *any* favor, or even the hint of it, he would sorely pay for it. And of course it was something to live down anyway, like being the preacher's son. It wasn't much better for Kate, and since there was no fighting it, the two children retreated, vainly trying to be anonymous. It was an impossible position. They felt encased in bubbles, not quite Russells and not quite children in a place that was not quite their home nor even quite their school — at least in the sense that it was a school for the other children. It wasn't fair. The other children could escape. They could spend the holidays in a home that was really a home and not a school as well. Not John and Kate. Like cast-off toys, they had to remain behind during the holidays, sleeping in rooms suddenly full of empty beds and eating at a long dinner table with two people who were suddenly not just "Dora" and "Bertrand" but "Mummy" and "Daddy."

These were not the only pressures. Even if Beacon Hill had robbed them of their parents, John and Kate felt responsible to the school in ways that the other children did not. For one thing, they were both acutely conscious of money, which there was never enough of. And they were even more conscious of time, which, like money, their parents never had either. Still, if the school was a thief and an intruder, it was at least familiar. Before this baby came along, money, time and rival children had been the threat, but now it was something else — something to do with love, or split love. The children didn't analyze it; they simply felt it, a sense of abandonment and insecurity that was not much different from what their parents felt, with life crumbling around them. For all of them, this crisis manifested itself as a lack of love, yet this was largely an illusion. The problem was not the lack of love but rather the confusion of too much pent-up, twisted love contesting at once, so that everything was thwarted and disguised. Their parents were drawing apart, and in the process they were pulling the children apart as well. To the children, it simply felt like another kind of belt tightening, as at the dinner table, where, as a matter of economy, they could spread their bread with either butter or jam but not both. Not both.

Russell was the biggest loser in this game. Dora was pregnant and sick — *she* had their sympathy. All he was doing, though, was leaving for America. Kate, in her hidden way, was taking it especially hard. No longer was she Daddy's girl — now she was Mummy's girl, all wrapped up in the baby, wishing, in a way, that she *were* the baby, bundled under her mother's loose Russian peasant smock. Intellectually, Russell understood this. He knew all too well how children shunt back and forth in their loyalties and affections, but now he was abnormally sensitive. John especially felt the pressure of his need. As his sister went over to his mother, the boy, like one in a sharply heeling sailboat, leaned to the other side. But most of all, John was simply withdrawing, edging away into himself even as his parents pressed closer, increasingly smothering and insecure.

Dora and Russell were blind to their vying. Almost against their wills or better judgment, they both played the game, seeing who the children most gravitated to — who they asked first, hugged harder, seemed the gladder to see.

Dora had beaten him there that morning. She was sitting on the sofa with Kate — Mummy and Kate and Baby. Kate, with her hand on Dora's stomach, was monitoring the baby. Entering the room, chirping with all the overanimation of guilt, Russell said, Kate-Kate-Kate! He gave the girl a kiss, then made a perfunctory peck at Dora. Kate, preoccupied, exclaimed, Mummy, I felt him kick. He's kicking more. I'm sure it's a boy. A girl would never kick so much, do you think?

Russell had no appetite for this. Ceding Kate to Dora this morning, he went over to John. But his approach was all wrong, too needy and sudden. The boy was terribly slow to wake — Russell should have known better than to expect much from him at this early hour. John's face was pale, and his dark hair was matted to one side. Sleepily, the boy was checking his little bag for the trip they were taking down the coast that morning. Russell was speaking to him — at him — about the mysteries surrounding the Long Man, the ancient 231-foot figure outlined in chalk on Windover Hill, where they would be going that afternoon. The boy had already seen the Long Man. He'd seen him several times. But still Russell rattled on, outlining the various theories about the figure, until he broke off, realizing that John was only half listening.

It was always like this before he went on a trip, only now it was worse. For weeks Russell had felt the children shrinking from him. Harder still, Russell felt himself running out of time to atone for his leaving, which John and Kate saw as part of a broader desertion. The children loved the beach, so in his desperation that morning Russell upped the ante, telling John and Kate that he would take them to the beach the next day with the Moores and Mr. Wittgenstein.

In ordinary circumstances, John in particular would have been overjoyed at this. Now he hardly seemed to notice. He just turned to his mother and said, Mummy, will you please . . .

That was all it took. For Russell, it didn't matter what the boy asked; what mattered was that he had asked Dora and not him. That was it — Dora's match, her fourth in as many days.

Max was hard at work under the sink, thrusting and grunting, when Russell returned to the kitchen to get more tea. The floor shook. He saw Max's gaping thighs, then the big red wrench as the frozen steel fittings shrieked and gave way.

Russell fled upstairs, but that was no better. At the top of the stairs, he heard loud accusations. It was Miss Marmer. She was shouting, shouting at Lily. But the unbelievable thing was that Lily was shouting back — shouting tearfully but shouting just the same. Russell was too late to tell what it was about. The door burst open, and Lily shot past him, down the stairs. Then Miss Marmer flew out, looking as if the girl had flung a bedpan in her face. Miss Marmer was even more furious when she saw him standing there. Russell had barely opened his mouth when she cut him off.

This is my affair, not yours! Every time I see you, you're mooning about, *sniffing* after her. Now stand off!

Loaded with fifteen children and five teachers, the old red bus, salt-eaten and bug-eyed, left at nine for their day trip. Miss Marmer was in charge. She was also taking personal charge of Rabe, who looked quite chastened, all but shackled beside her in the front seat, directly behind the driver.

It was a beautiful morning, warm and sunny, with a good clearing breeze blowing in from the sea. Russell and Dora and the other teachers were there to wave good-bye as the merry bus pulled away. The children waved and called back, excited that there would be singing and bathing and a promised stop for ice cream, a rarity at that nutrition-conscious school. But where was Lily? Russell heard one of the teachers ask. Probably off sulking somewhere, or cowering, he thought. Russell was certainly glad he wasn't on that bus.

Standing over in the garden, Dorothy and Moore watched the old bus lumber off. Dorothy was off herself for a day's birding. They were an incongruous pair, Moore in his ill-fitting morning suit, as prescribed for *Vivas,* and Dorothy in her old green skirt, walking shoes and oat straw hat. She was well equipped for the day, with binoculars, canteen and the wicker creel containing her lunch and other gear. She was glad to be getting away. She and Moore had heard the commotion upstairs between the young teacher and Miss Marmer. They had also seen the strain of Russell's forced gaiety at breakfast.

Giving Moore his instructions for the day, Dorothy said, All right, now don't be getting too heated in discussion. And don't let Bertie get under your skin. We've another day here, remember.

She kissed him and started off resolutely, burrs already sticking to her socks. Moore called back, You be careful yourself. Not to twist an ankle or something. Have you your whistle?

I have mine, replied Dorothy with a cagey smile. Have you yours?

Colloquy

IT WAS A FOREGONE CONCLUSION that the two examiners would give the candidate his doctorate, but they weren't letting him off the hook that easily.

Promptly at nine, the *Viva* convened in Russell's office, where the examiners were at first quite jovial, hazing the candidate for not having worn the prescribed morning suit.

Mr. Wittgenstein, said Russell imperiously. We note that you are improperly attired. Do you fancy, sir, that this is an examination for a paper-hanger's permit? Taking his cue, Moore leaned toward the candidate, saying in an anxious stage whisper, I could lend you a tie. It would vastly help your chances.

But these frivolities soon ended and then, inevitably, the bickering started, with the two examiners squabbling about who would ask the first question.

You're the professor, said Russell to Moore with a dry smile.

True, said Moore with a nod. But it was you, Dr. Russell, who guided Mr. Wittgenstein's early work.

Oh, come now, said Russell, turning a shade obstinate. I thought I was merely the poor bloke you asked to look on.

Here Moore detected a faint note of challenge in his tone, as if Russell wanted to prove his long-standing claim that he, Moore, had never understood Wittgenstein's early ideas, much less this new work.

Very well, said Moore, the color rising in his cheeks. I will start. So saying, Moore composed his thoughts for a moment, then began:

Mr. Wittgenstein, I find your early work admirable in its attempt to achieve a synoptic view of all that we know, and, equally important, of all that we cannot know. This you do by inscribing, as it were, an arc defining the relative *limits* of things: knowledge, consciousness, language, the world. In the *Tractatus* in particular you attempt an ascent of the absolute, and yet you do this with profound humility before the limits of what you say that human understanding will never penetrate or surpass. You say that what we cannot meaningfully speak about we must pass over in silence. You say the meaning of the world must lie *outside* of the world. What is curious, though, is that you yourself step outside this limit to speak of things that, as you say, are beyond the scope of logic or intelligible speech — things such as ethics, eternity, God, the mystical. In your book, Mr. Wittgenstein, you move from a state of natural facts within the world to arrangements of those facts as depicted through concatenations of language, which is undergirded by logic, or what you beautifully refer to in almost Homeric style as the Great Mirror. This mirror — logic — in turn, reflects the underlying structure of the world, just as it mirrors the inner workings of language. You say that words picture facts in the world, that they *display* them. You say that logical pictures can depict the world, and yet you also point out that language often disguises what it discloses.

Here Moore paused, then continued:

It is a terse and rigorous book. At times, it seems as if it was painful for you to say even *one word* more than was necessary to express your meaning. Indeed, I might say that, in its compression and elisions, your work reads at times like a great poem. At the same time it is true that the book's very terseness — its attempts to capture essences in declarative, oracular statements — leads to tremendous difficulties in interpretation. It is an ideal world you picture, Mr. Wittgenstein. It is a calm, classical and, above all, hierarchic world. Now, Dr. Russell, in his introduction to the *Tractatus,* notes that your concern is to determine what the conditions would be for a logically perfect language —

That is Russell's assumption, injected Wittgenstein. It is not mine.

Though, I might add, broke in Russell, that Mr. Wittgenstein has always shown a marked antipathy for anyone who would presume to summarize, much less comment on, his work.

Moore was insistent. Will you both kindly let me finish? Please, let us all *try* today to dispense with old squabbles. Or shall I yield to you, Dr. Russell?

No, no, said Russell, feeling he had won his point. Please do continue.

They started and stopped, but they didn't get far. The telephone rang, the solicitor again. And when that was done, they got sidetracked with terminology and other wrangles that shot another hour, until Mrs. Bride brought them tea.

Then from outside came a clatter. Looking out, Russell saw Max raising a large wooden ladder, preparing to fix a section of loose gutter on the back of the house. Moore, meanwhile, was saying to Wittgenstein:

I recall when Ramsey visited you — oh, my, this must have been seven or eight years ago, when you were still in Trattenbach. Anyhow, you told Ramsey that the point of the *Tractatus*, for all its talk of logic and language, was actually *ethical*. Now, I thought this was an intriguing thing to say. After all, you say little in the book — at least directly — about ethics.

To discern, said Wittgenstein. To discern clearly. This, as I see it, is an essentially ethical pursuit. But, you see, it was what I did *not* say in the book that seemed to me the most implicitly ethical.

Moore was nodding, compressing his hands excitedly. Oh, absolutely. That was exactly my point. Your comment made me quite read the book again. And it struck me as being most curious, as if all your labors in logic were such that, by establishing what you *could* speak about intelligibly, you might isolate what you *could not*. Which, as I gather from Ramsey, you felt was more important anyway, this being the ethical and mystical part.

Moore folded his hands, then continued:

I hope I am not getting too personal. I don't mean to get sidetracked into the history of the work and what you felt about it later. But — but I gather that by then, a good four years after completing the book, you were rather disenchanted with the whole enterprise. In the book, you said your propositions were like a ladder that one must ascend in order to climb beyond them. At which point, you said, the logical climber would view the world aright and would finally see that your propositions were nonsensical.

If he was not too dizzy, remarked Russell wryly.

Moore ignored this and continued. But, as I say, when you spoke to Ramsey in Trattenbach — well, I gather you were by then rather *disdainful* — if that is not too strong a word — of your earlier thinking.

Foreign, corrected Wittgenstein distractedly. That would be a better word for how my early thinking struck me. Already by that time, some of the book's aspirations were growing *foreign* to me.

Moore nodded as this sunk in, then charged off again, saying, But I recall, Mr. Wittgenstein, that you told Ramsey that you wanted nothing that needed to be reached by a ladder. You said that you were looking for something far more humble, a village and not a vast metropolis, or something to that effect. Oh, I remember Ramsey saying he had a terrible time yanking answers out of you. Moore glanced up at the ceiling, a reaching look. You know, I just now recall Ramsey mentioning a friend of yours! A large, rough-looking, happy-go-lucky fellow. That would have been *Max*, I guess?

Wittgenstein compressed his lips. Yes, it must have been. He nodded. Yes, they did meet.

Russell, meanwhile, was noticeably distracted. For twenty minutes now he'd been glancing out the window. Looking around, Moore saw Max grappling with the gutter from the top rung of the ladder.

Oh my, said Moore, turning to Wittgenstein. I hope he doesn't fall. Is he all right there, do you think?

He's fine, said Wittgenstein brusquely. Now — Wittgenstein took a breath — as for your question about Ramsey. The point is that it was then difficult for me to think about the book. I felt like a leftover season, with no weather that would have me or even carry me away. Wittgenstein thought for a moment about this, then added, You see, I was losing faith in the usefulness of an attempt to find the *last word* about language. Formerly, I was under the illusion — the common illusion — that there must be a key, or keys, to this puzzle. I was captive to the illusion that, because there is a prior order to the world, there must be an *essence* to language — that my inquiries would yield a unified and utterly simple solution of the purest crystal. Much of this problem, I think, can be traced to this . . . *scientific* craving, this craving for *generality* that seems to permeate our thinking. And the point is, we are philosophers, not scientists. Science is not our affair at all. Like me, Russell, you've taught young children. But consider how children acquire language. Consider, for instance, the way a child finds it almost impossible to believe that a word could have two entirely different meanings. But watching children, you see that, even when a word is used according to its so-called intended meaning, it is often used entirely differently in different contexts. Words are not that precise and scientific. On the contrary, words are very approximate and indeed often need our help, as when we emphatically *point* and say, I mean *that* broom — that broom over *there*.

So we are necessarily delving beneath the surface of the ostensible meaning of a word, brushing off the dust and accretions of the years — the full burden of memory and association — to reveal its grammar. By *grammar*, incidentally, I mean the way a word is *used* in a particular context. And consider all the different ways we use words. Play acting. Telling a story. Guessing a riddle. Describing a pain. There are countless ways in which we use language. These activities — the speaking of a language — I call *forms of life*. But within those forms, there is almost limitless variety and shades of distinction.

Ah! said Moore. Then you do, in your way, still find yourself looking for the essences that you say you rejected. Universals, of a kind.

Wittgenstein wrinkled his nose, then replied, The essences within the ordinary, if you like. Or essences beneath the surfaces of our ordinary language. But again the point is that these essences are always shifting beneath our feet. And you see, even as philosophers, I believe, we are mostly unconscious of these nuances. Using language is like riding a bicycle: we don't think about how we do it, we simply do it. At the same time, language is so natural that much escapes us, and it leads us, as philosophers, into a great many confusions. This, then, was part of the slow change in my thinking. And it was this, I think, that made it so difficult for me to respond to Ramsey's questions . . .

Despite his effort to give the impression of deep and serious attention to the *Viva*, Russell was finding himself distracted by what was happening outside, especially when Lily walked past the window.

The little tease was doing it on purpose! thought Russell. She must have known he was inside, watching her as she looked up at Max. But that was all Russell saw. One peep and the show closed: Lily walked out of sight. And the maddening thing was, Russell could sense her there, the minx. Standing by the side of the house, she was clearly tormenting Max, who was now staring down at her from the ladder. God, will you look at him, Russell thought. Just like one of Pavlov's dogs — the salivary chime.

At the same time, Russell sensed the rising annoyance of his colleagues, who, though facing away from the window, were well aware of his distraction. Trying to rouse himself and forget the girl, Russell then took the offensive, saying to Wittgenstein:

Well, being a philosopher who prefers simplicity, I must say, Mr. Wittgenstein, that your new work creates countless problems in its sheer, and I might say undisciplined, *variety*. Enormous problems, in fact. What can we apprehend when each sentence — each word and expression — must be identified and explained? That's not philosophy, that's a laborious taxonomy.

Wittgenstein immediately felt Russell's pressing the attack. He pressed back, saying, My aim is not to seek ease or neatness. And, again, I think you're dazzled by that search for a mathematical *essence* — for the tics and conventions of formal *elegance*. As I say, language will not be tied up in this neat, formal way. This was part of Ramsey's problem . . . Here Wittgenstein visibly hesitated, then came out with it. Do not misunderstand me, I greatly respected Ramsey. Ramsey was tremendously useful in helping me to clarify my thinking. But if you'll pardon me for saying so, I would describe Ramsey as a *bourgeois* thinker.

Moore slapped his knee, incensed at this slight of his brilliant protégé, dead the year before at the age of twenty-six. Russell was insulted on general principle, knowing, in effect, that Wittgenstein was saying the same of them.

I beg your pardon, remonstrated Moore. But I take deep offense at your remark about Ramsey. In fact, I find your statement extraordinarily patronizing and insulting. Especially when I think of the pains that Ramsey took to *clarify* your work.

Now wait, protested Wittgenstein. Just now I said as much. Digging his grave deeper, the candidate then explained, By *bourgeois* I mean that Ramsey wanted to tidy up the affairs of a particular philosophical and intellectual community. He didn't want to reflect for long on the *essence* of a problem, or its manifold difficulties. What Ramsey really wanted was for these problems to go away — to be declared trivial and laid to one side. But, you see, I do not think the philosopher should belong to *any* community.

Oh, come on! scoffed Moore, losing all patience. And what, pray, will *you* be, Wittgenstein, when you ally yourself with the Cambridge academic community? And what makes you so sure there is such tremendous regulated orthodoxy in our thinking? This is incredible! Moore dropped his arms and looked at Russell. You act as if we're an intellectual church order or something! As if we all subscribe to the same creed!

Oh, no, said Russell with a blazing look. What the candidate *means*, is that we don't subscribe to *his* creed — whatever *that* is.

But Wittgenstein wasn't budging. Nodding fiercely, he put both his examiners on notice then:

There is community. There is community, and there are *many* shared values and assumptions. True, I share many of these essential values, but you both know me well enough to realize that, even if you *should* admit me to the company of philosophical doctors, much less to Trinity . . . Moving his arms in his agitation, Wittgenstein seemed, for a moment, to hover in the air, whirling like a dervish before he continued. Even if you *should* do this, I will never be a part of your community, nor of anybody's community. Not that I won't bear your community my most sincere goodwill. But Cambridge will never own me, nor will philosophy, nor the church, nor the country, nor the various charities. Oh, I might, I suppose, have dedicated my life to the glory of God. And of course I have tried as much — fruitlessly. But to say that *this* was my intent would be chicanery — I mean it would be misunderstood. And so you might say, Russell, that what I am doing is not doing philosophy at all. So, you might say, humanly speaking, that I am *completely outside the fold.* I do not entirely deny it. Clearly, I do not understand the values and aspirations of this age, insofar as it has any that *I* can discern, with its fatuous science and pathetic delusions of progress. But then I freely admit I am narrow. But understand this — if I should do your community *any* good, however unlikely that seems, it will be as an outsider. *That* much is clear.

It was as if the entire room were suddenly covered with broken glass: Moore and Russell sat there mutely, not knowing which way to move to avoid the shards. But even now Russell was torn in his attention: Lily was at the foot of the ladder, talking to Max. And then there came a knock — Mrs. Bride was waiting outside with their lunch.

When Russell next looked outside, Lily was gone and Max was coming down off the ladder. Then Max started around the side of the house.

Oh, my, said Russell, pulling out his watch. I see it's already one-thirty. Why don't we break here for lunch? If you'll excuse me a few minutes, I'd like to place a call. Shall we resume around two, then?

And before they could even give their assent, Russell was out the door. There was uneasiness then when Russell left them. In silence, they began eating. Several minutes passed, then Wittgenstein said to Moore, I hope you at least understand my point about Ramsey.

I will *respect* your opinion, said Moore measuredly, pausing in midstream over his soup. That is not to say I agree with it.

Silence and sandwiches, a desultory chewing. Wittgenstein went to stand by the window. Max was gone, but Wittgenstein had caught a glimpse of him and the girl — enough to see what was in store. He found it oddly distancing to stand there helpless before this feeling that was developing in him, in the midst of this other colloquy. Granted, Wittgenstein was not comfortable with what would certainly happen next, with the sex part. But this was nothing new. For Max, there had been other women — other "falls," and still more painful falls for the women he contemptuously discarded once soiled. Even this, Wittgenstein could accept. What he absolutely could not accept was Max's hypocrisy in stormily disavowing any interest in the girl — the idea that he could so baldly lie about it.

How was it possible, wondered Wittgenstein, that a basically good and sincere man could act without any apparent consistency, saying one thing and blithely doing another? Wittgenstein stared out the window with wonderment and a feeling of dislocation. Did words deserve the primacy we gave them? Were *words* "moral" in the same sense that *actions* were? We say, thought Wittgenstein, that Max had not "meant" to sin, saying this in the way we might say that Max had not meant to lie. But of course this revealed problems hidden in the grammar of the word "meant." There was, for instance, the question of whether Max was using "meant" to designate an intended action — what he had meant to *do* — in the same sense that he might have said that this, after all, was what he had meant to *say*. Worse, we would likely be using "meant" once or twice removed, using it to cover Max's first lie by successively re-explaining what he had *really* meant. Ethics was such a misery, thought Wittgenstein. Words were so slippery, and metaphors were all the more so, being instructive in almost equal measure to their power to distort. And in the end, words only evaded: our words could not justify, and further words and actions only muddied our questionable original intentions like a picture that has been too often erased and revised. No, thought Wittgenstein, good or evil (if those were quite the words) were not to be broken down like salt in a crucible to get at the truth — it was a hollow nugget that clinked into the alchemist's dish. Somewhere in the process, the spirit escaped.

Say it, thought Wittgenstein. Max was in pain. That was the "meaning" this "sin" expressed, and though this sin no doubt had a root somewhere, it had no "reason." It was simply pain, disfiguring scribbles over a once pure page.

If the conscience is not an ethical organ, thought Wittgenstein, might it at least furbish the mind with a decent recollection? Looking out across the hills, he felt an impulse to sleep for weariness. The truth was, Witt-

genstein vividly wished to die at that moment. But then he realized that
even death was just another metaphor for something else.

Heirs

MOORE HAD GOOD REASON to be offended by the epic ingratitude of
Wittgenstein's remark about Ramsey. But patronizing or not, Wittgen-
stein's feelings about Ramsey were more than just a lack of gratitude.
Ramsey was an unpleasant reminder of other things.

When Ramsey had first met Wittgenstein in Trattenbach in 1923, he
was not yet twenty, but in Cambridge he was already widely regarded as
the most promising young man to have come down in a generation —
meaning, since Wittgenstein. Moore took tremendous pride in his brilliant young protégé and fellow Apostle. It was Moore who introduced
Ramsey to the *Tractatus*, and it was Moore who wrote the letter of introduction that Ramsey enclosed with his own letter to Wittgenstein, asking if he might come to Trattenbach to discuss the *Tractatus* with him.

Wittgenstein was at a low ebb when he received Ramsey's letter. His
attempt to adopt Franz Kluck had just failed, and the witch-hunt that
would eventually force him out of the village was just starting in earnest.
Responding to Ramsey's letter, Wittgenstein wrote, "I'm afraid that I
have little to offer in my present state of mind. But you are certainly
welcome to come, *if you really think it will do any good.*"

An older, less enthusiastic man might well have been put off by Wittgenstein's gloomy letter, but Ramsey immediately sent a wire providing
the full details of his arrival. This pleased Wittgenstein. Depressed and
lonely, he was curious about this young man whom Moore had spoken
about so highly, and he knew the arrival of a cultivated foreigner would
set the village buzzing. Wittgenstein thought it was sad, and certainly a
sign of how low he had sunk, that he should feel the need for such os-
tentation, but he couldn't help it. On the heels of his humiliation at the
hand of Herr Kluck, Wittgenstein felt a positive hunger to remind himself
and the Trattenbachers — as if they needed reminding — that he was a
worldly, influential man with distinguished friends.

Ramsey never did see why Wittgenstein chose to waste himself in Trattenbach. Even the children seemed scarcely enough to justify such lone-

liness. In a letter he sent to Moore shortly after his arrival, Ramsey wrote in part:

He looks younger than he can possibly be; but he says he has bad eyes and a cold. Still, his general appearance is athletic. He's clearly fond of the children, who, in turn, seem fond of him despite his strictness and the tremendous demands he places upon them. This is especially true of his cleverest boys, who are like a small tribe, but *his* tribe, with his intensity and even his mannerisms. The villagers stare at us. I don't think Wittgenstein is at all conscious of the effect he has on people.

Ramsey was especially struck by a class zoology project that had begun when Wittgenstein found a dead cat in the road. Wittgenstein plopped the cat in a burlap bag and carried it back to his room, where he skinned it, then boiled the carcass to bones in a big black pot. His excitable landlady was grievously upset when she learned that he was cooking cat in his room. Are you so poor? she wanted to know, and not without some cause. The smell — remarkably like venison — had permeated the grubby little grocery downstairs, where the teacher's eccentricities were already a favorite subject of conversation.

Wittgenstein could not be bothered with the landlady's female squeamishness. The cat was duly cooked, and when Ramsey arrived, he found Wittgenstein and his boys restringing the skeleton by drilling tiny holes in the bones and fastening them together with fine brass wire. In another letter to Moore, Ramsey reported:

I mention the cat because I feel as if Wittgenstein did the same in the *Tractatus,* leaving me endless bones to pick as I try to drape his elegant skeleton with flesh and skin. So far, we seem to average about an hour per page, or about five pages per day, before his clever boys come trooping in wearing boots and knickers and little black hats. They're so *very* solemn and respectful, almost rapt when he talks. They call me Herr Doktor and are like greedy young birds with their questions about university and England. As for our cat, Ilse, she is a headless, tailless biped! But she's coming along! I know there may be many ways to skin a cat; but have you any idea how many bones there are to one?

But for all Ramsey's enthusiasm, it was hard blowing life into cold coals. Wittgenstein said he was sorry for this, and he warned Ramsey, lest he wind up the same way, that there came a time when a man had to drop such thinking if he was not to be completely wrecked by it. Ramsey was no Pinsent. He never became Wittgenstein's protégé, and, unlike Wittgenstein, he never lived long enough to quit philosophy. Still, as Wittgenstein sat there eating with Moore that afternoon, he was not sorry for what he had said about Ramsey, nor could he join with those like Moore who would wonder aloud at all Ramsey might have done had he lived. Wittgenstein had seen too many promising young men die in the war to indulge in what-ifs.

Heartless or not, this was how it was and how it would be. Because as much as Ramsey helped Wittgenstein clear the ground for his new work, Ramsey was inevitably somewhat stunted as a thinker by the higher stories of Wittgenstein's influence. And thanks in part to Ramsey, Wittgenstein could now roam on, unbothered by bourgeois questions of influence or gratitude, drifting over the landscape like a grazing cow called History, which had broken down the fence and wandered off, not even bothering to look back over what carefully tended gardens she had trampled and uprooted.

Ramsey wasn't the only casualty of Wittgenstein's thinking. Another was Friedrich Waismann.

Waismann was a member of the Vienna Circle, a group that arose partly in response to the concerns and aspirations of the *Tractatus*, especially in its desire to separate the realm of significant statement from that of nonsense. The dream *was* attainable, and the group's early members looked to Wittgenstein to lead them toward an age of scientific philosophy based on logic and empiricism and, above all, freedom from the muddles of metaphysics.

The first time Wittgenstein encountered this little group, waiting for him to help them throw off the last heresies and lead them, clear-eyed, into a new day, he felt a deep sense of sadness. *They* were the heretics. They took up his logic but cast aside his mysticism, never understanding how inextricably the two were bound. But in them Wittgenstein saw something else that nauseated him: it was the growing shadow of his own influence, as reflected in strong, sophisticated intellects surrendering not just to his ideas but to the sheer force of his personality — to a hateful *style*. It made him fearful and ashamed, all the more so because there was a side of his personality that craved the attention. Faced with the harsh mirror of their admiration, Wittgenstein did what seemed the only decent thing during that first meeting: he read these antimetaphysicians the passionate metaphysical love poems of the Indian poet Rabindranath Tagore.

Moritz Schlick, one of the leaders of the group, got along well with Wittgenstein — better, at least, than the more abrasive (and less deferential) Rudolf Carnap. Schlick was the first member of the group to establish a relationship with Wittgenstein, albeit an often delicate one. This was during the period after Wittgenstein had returned from Trattenbach, when he was engaged in building Gretl's house, frequently with Max as his second in command. Building this house was more for him than just a favor for his sister. In asking her brother to undertake the house, Gretl also knew the work would provide him with a needed refuge.

Gretl often acted as his intermediary in those days, and it was she who arranged the first meeting with Schlick. Having led the members of the group through two years of intensive analysis of the *Tractatus*, Schlick came as a votary, and the meeting was a success. Wittgenstein especially appreciated Schlick's highly cultivated personality. Schlick also came at the right time, when Wittgenstein was feeling the first surge of new ideas. Sensing this, Schlick subsequently introduced Wittgenstein to his young associate Waismann, largely in the hope that Waismann might get Wittgenstein's chaotic thoughts into a systematic and publishable form.

The Vienna Circle dreamed of making philosophy a handmaiden to science, and Waismann was no less willing to make himself a handmaiden to Wittgenstein's evolving thinking. For the past four years, Waismann had virtually dropped his own work while fruitlessly trying to systematize Wittgenstein's ideas. That it was proving an impossible task was certainly not because of Waismann's skills as an organizer and creative midwife. Rather, the problem was the speed with which Wittgenstein's ideas were changing — that and Wittgenstein's inherent dissatisfaction with his own productions. Wittgenstein was like a molting bird, all swatched and patched and unclear, wondering at his own wild growth, with no idea, or concern, about what kind of bird he would become. Poor Waismann, meanwhile, was trying to turn him into a definite kind of bird with a definite shape. Twice now Waismann had ordered Wittgenstein's new ideas into the scope of a book, but each time Wittgenstein had rejected it, saying that the ideas in it were far too flawed, that his thinking had changed and was changing still.

It would have been an act of kindness, even humility, for Wittgenstein to have told Waismann to abandon this doomed undertaking, but he would not do this. Wittgenstein was nothing if not pragmatic in this regard. He thought Waismann was brilliant and capable, certainly, but otherwise unoriginal. But then this was not altogether surprising, since

Waismann was a Jew. As Wittgenstein saw it, it was part of the Jewish nature to understand another man's work better than he himself understood it. Nor was Wittgenstein attributing to Waismann anything that he did not clearly see in himself. In perceiving this deficiency in Waismann, Wittgenstein was no less aware of the essentially derivative nature of his own talent, which stemmed largely from Russell and Frege, among others.

Jewish reproductiveness — this was how Wittgenstein termed this characteristic one day in conversation with Max. It was an ill-considered and irresponsible remark, and Wittgenstein immediately regretted having said it in Max's presence. Certainly, Wittgenstein did not mean for Max to view it as being in any way in sympathy with the various racial theories that were then surfacing with renewed vigor. But it was too late. Max immediately latched on to this as another important insight to be added to his Jew lore, that rag-bag of jokes, pseudohistory and scurrilous "scientific facts" culled from various strident newspapers and pamphlets.

In any case, it seemed to Wittgenstein that if Waismann could not get on with his own work, he could at least help him get on with his. After all, he reasoned, it didn't matter, in the end, who did the work, just so long as someone did it.

This at least was what Wittgenstein told himself. The truth was, Wittgenstein was anything but adverse to what Waismann could do for him. Wittgenstein had once told Waismann, and emphatically, that he was not yet willing to speak about his ideas in public. Nonetheless, he was secretly intrigued several days after this pronouncement when Waismann took the hint and nervously asked, after a floundering and abasing preface, if *he*, Waismann, might give a paper on Wittgenstein's mathematical ideas. Wittgenstein gave a laboring sigh, a look of distaste. But despite these feints, Wittgenstein, much like Pontius Pilate, was finally willing — if not compelled by the world's barbaric curiosity — to accept "Waismann's idea" and send his work forth like the condemned to a fate of almost certain incomprehension. There was nothing else to be done. Why, Wittgenstein even went so far as to provide Waismann with an outline of what he was to say at the mathematical conference held in Königsberg in 1930. Nor had Wittgenstein objected — or failed to subtly jerk the wires — that past year when Waismann had presented several other papers on his views in Vienna.

Unfortunately, things had not gone so well when Waismann attempted to write a paper of his own. In his preface, Waismann said that conversations with Wittgenstein had provided "valuable stimuli" in the development of his ideas. The master was not at all happy when Waismann sent him a complimentary copy along with a humble letter of thanks. Instead of an appreciative letter, Waismann received an icy rebuke pointing out that Waismann's alleged original ideas had not risen like marsh gas from the mere *stimulation* of their discussions. Rather, Wittgenstein said, Waismann's ideas had come directly from his own, and not just from conversations, but from dictations and unpublished typescripts.

Waismann was of course devastated, all the more so because the mistake had been so unconscious. Even now Waismann was struggling to draft a formal acknowledgment of his error. But how was he to explain it? Overinfluence? Inundation? A *mirage*?

In the meantime, though, this Sisyphean undertaking would proceed apace, with Waismann rushing to complete another version of the master's ideas for his almost certain repudiation.

Pain and Its Language

RUSSELL DID CATCH a glimpse of the lovers before they disappeared.

He had run up the stairs to his study roost, to comb the hills with his binoculars. And there, in a sweep of the horizon, he had caught them. Max had a blanket under his arm. He saw her willful back, her windblown hair. Then they were gone. Over the hill.

Why did he feel so sick at this? he wondered. Did he begrudge her her youth and vigor? So leave her be! he told himself, but he only continued to feel more hurt and furious — furious in a way that even he could see was absurd, as if he were a virtuous father concerned for his daughter's welfare.

Never mind that Max had unstopped the leaky drain, repaired the stove, torn down the shed and fixed the gutter. Walking through the empty school, Russell saw only ruin, incompetence, disrepair. Out then in the garden, he heard *whizzz-ick . . . whizzz-ick*. It was old Tillham, the caretaker, poisoning the afternoon with noxious white puffs from his beetle sprayer.

Russell veered away. It was all hitting him again, a bad attack. Russell missed his children — even when they were there with him now, he missed them, missed them *in advance,* as it were. And with this loss, he felt the sour heart and the heaviness, remembering, as if he had ever forgotten, that he had a ladybug with a lover, and that their house was burning, burning, with the children all gone . . .

He was just weary, and mad. He wanted to take John and Kate and chuck the rest — Beacon Hill and Dora, this ungrateful girl, his guests. And then, full to his gullet with anger, he walked into the kitchen and caught sight of Dora, red-faced and unhappy, almost sloshing in her awful fullness. She made him sick. The cook was out. Dora punctually put down her cup, her mouth hard, just daring him to say one word. And then, before either of them knew what had happened, they were at each other's throats, he in his morning suit and she in her sloppy peasant smock.

With Higgins upstairs and the children away, there was nothing to stop them. This was close, vicious fighting — the fighting of experts. Violent gestures and inflections were needed to expel their words into utterance. Russell's throat was so constricted that he had the distinct sensation of choking, but it was punctilious choking, with the faintest film of composure and a heavy coating of malice. Russell struck first, and struck deep, when he chastized her, pregnant or not, for neglecting the children and the school. Look at you, he said. You spend half the day in bed — implying, by his tone, that it was an idle slut's bed.

But Dora wasn't shamed. She lashed back. I've seen you staring at her, she said, and he quailed when he saw that her lower lip was trembling with rage at his arrogance and insensitivity. For a moment he thought — or thought that she thought — that he might strike her. But at this his hand recoiled as from a fire, and his will was shattered. Standing powerless before her, he knew almost exactly what she would say, but at the same time he was morbidly curious to hear it. Dora had him by his self-esteem. Their sexual life was over, but even so he was listening to her like a man at a sentencing, apprehensive to know if his wife still considered him a functioning sexual being.

He was not disappointed. Dora went for the jugular, sneering. Bloody old fool. Everybody's seen you staring at her. And she's gone with him, you know. Off for a *holiday,* I'm sure.

Russell was watching her mouth. He was watching the words form on her lips. It seemed he could actually watch the words well up, whorling and wobbling, then softly exploding like smoke rings over his face. It was the oddest, most disembodied sensation he had at that moment. But the most remarkable thing was that, even at a time when he deserved nothing from his wife, he still craved something, even if that something was only pain.

He had to steady himself after he left Dora, his hands were shaking so. It took him another ten minutes to collect himself in the study before he was ready to face Moore and Wittgenstein, but by then he was shot for any kind of serious discussion.

They turned to Wittgenstein's new work, but Russell found it hard to conceal his hostility to what he saw as a profoundly misguided enterprise. Still bristling about Wittgenstein's bourgeois remark, Russell stopped just short of calling the work irresponsible.

Where does it lead — or end? he asked Wittgenstein. To *plow,* as you say, over the entire field of language — one might just as well try to name every star in the sky.

Russell felt almost betrayed. How could Wittgenstein do this to his talent? he wanted to ask. Suddenly, Wittgenstein made no sense to him whatsoever. Seeing him now, Russell could hardly imagine the shy, tortured young man who used to collapse in his rooms before the war, looking as if he could not endure another hour of this life. But that wounded young man was gone forever. Today, it was a hard man that Russell saw before him. How did he endure it? wondered Russell. How did he make his way through the world, seemingly attached to nothing and accountable to no one, following only his own brute instincts? To Russell then, Wittgenstein seemed like one of those ancient cairns that one sometimes sees in England — a pile of rocks sitting in the middle of nowhere, as if dropped from the sky, saying, *Take me or leave me,* and never insisting, as had the breathtaking peaks of his youth, just to be beheld.

They argued for an hour before they hit upon a subject they could sink their teeth into: Wittgenstein's examination of the language we use to describe pain.

Of all his new work, Russell and Moore found this pain business the most difficult and confusing, and by far the most odd. As Wittgenstein explained, though, it wasn't pain, per se, that had led him into these inquiries. Rather, it was the way our expressions of pain revealed the misleading nature of the word "I" as a representative for the self with its pain. Wittgenstein was saying:

We all have had pains, aches, sadness. We know how these things feel. But how do we express them? How, linguistically, am I to suppose that you, Russell, have the same pain that I have — that we are, so to speak, related in our pain? For when I say that "Russell has a pain," I am referring to a physical body — to Russell's body. But when I say, "*I* have a pain," I am not referring to my own physical body — "I" does not denote a possessor. Here, I would commend Lichtenberg's suggestion that instead of saying, "*I* think," we ought to say, "*It* thinks." After all, you must agree that it is philosophically curious, this spectacle of the self soliloquizing to itself about its woes like Hamlet to Yorick's skull.

Moore let out a guffaw. Russell, though, was looking increasingly uncomfortable as Wittgenstein continued, But let us consider another example. Compare the statement "Russell has a gold tooth" with the statement "Russell has toothache." At first glance, these two statements may not seem to differ, but in fact they are quite substantially different in their grammar. One immediate difference is how each might be verified. For while Russell can readily open his mouth and show me his gold tooth, he can't very well show me his pain. Or take another instance. Suppose Russell tells me that he has an ache in his side —

Hold it! protested Russell. First, you put pains in my teeth and now you put aches in my side. Next you'll be putting words in my mouth. What is your point?

My point, said Wittgenstein, is that you don't seem to see it as a problem.

No, countered Russell. My problem is that I don't see it as *much* of a problem.

Now Wittgenstein was pacing. And I would say that you're merely trying to sweep the problem under the rug with the usual appeals to common sense — the appeals that commonsense philosophers always use.

Oh! exclaimed Russell, rolling his eyes at Moore. So now we're *commonsense* philosophers, are we?

But I thought we were merely bourgeois philosophers, quipped Moore.

Wittgenstein tried to explain, but the subject of pain was then too charged and messy to be discussed in a strict philosophical sense. And for Russell, it was particularly unpleasant, discussing pain in the abstract when he was feeling pain in the particular. This pain was a séance, of sorts. Pain was a medium of human exchange, like body heat or love; it was a sort of litmus that could be used to detect the human presence, tracing how it learned and grew, and the way it remembered. Pain, Wittgenstein strove to explain, was an as yet uncharted territory, a wide and various language with a kind of anthropology. Consider its wide variety, with grief, sorrow, anger and anxiety, and distinct languages for each.

Indeed, pain seemed a kind of vault for the psyche, much as in polar regions one may find whole frozen mastodons, perfectly preserved. The men were speaking. Electrically, if imperceptibly, the pain was flowing. It was well past four, getting late. Dorothy was overdue now, as was the bus. And what of Max and Lily?

Russell could hardly stand it, this squirmy, queasy talk of slow, dull aches and stabbing pains. He looked at Moore for succor, but Moore seemed to be following the discussion with his usual cheerful interest. Wittgenstein was examining a whole alphabet of ailments. Having begun with a discussion of the problems with the inexactitude of the word "where" — as in "Where is the pain?" — Wittgenstein was back discussing problems with the use of the word "same" — as in "We share the same pain."

But as Wittgenstein continued his colloquy on pain language, other events were taking place outside. Russell saw Dora walking down the road with Higgins — no doubt looking for the bus, which was now forty minutes late. Then, a few moments later, Lily flew in the back door, her face streaked with grief.

I wonder what is taking that bus? Russell said. But going to the window then, he saw no bus. All he saw was Max, emotionless, as he pulled down the ladder and carried it around the side of the house.

Standing beside Russell, wondering if Dorothy was back, Moore said, It rather looks like rain, doesn't it?

And then, as if at Moore's suggestion, the storm appeared: Russell saw dark clouds piling up on the horizon and the leaves showing their dusty white undersides. And then he saw Dora and Higgins standing farther down the road, watching the coiling storm. Such reports the eye carried back. One's wife, one's love, one's children on a bus — their lives were as clothes stretched on a line. It seemed unjust, so unbelievable to stand there in awe and fear, powerless before this fiction called life.

And then, as he heard the thunder approaching in the distance, Russell felt real pain, afraid the children might be caught out in a lightning storm or in an accident. Wittgenstein, meanwhile, was summing up. He regretted the unclarity of his remarks about pain language. He recognized that his discussion had been hard to follow, but he had not yet had a chance to explore this question of pain with the thoroughness it deserved. Words were like buckets, he was saying. Each word carries only so much, but the odd thing was how a word might carry more than its measure of meaning, so that it spilled over in flood.

Then Moore, who had been patiently listening for over an hour with scarcely a word, stopped him and said, But I have one question, Wittgenstein. Why all this talk of pain? You may think this a foolish idea, but couldn't one as well approach these questions from the standpoint of *pleasure*? For instance, I just thought of the curious fact that, while we can say, "He has a pain," we do not have a comparable expression such as, "He has a pleasure."

This *was* odd, and Wittgenstein blinked, looking away for several seconds before he turned back to Moore and said, That is curious. I don't know. I will have to think about it.

But the buckets, as it were, were spilling over. Because for all this talk of pain and knowledge of pain, Wittgenstein ended the discussion when he saw Russell's stricken look as the wind started blowing. And the miracle was that, for all the poking and analysis, the language worked. It was in perfect, sentient repair then as Wittgenstein touched Russell's arm and said in a firm voice, Now, you are not to worry. I'm sure the children are fine. Let's go outside and wait for the bus.

Dust was blowing off the road. The temperature was plunging. The tangled trees were lifting and crashing, and the grass was beating down, light, then dark, in furrows. And in spite of their anxiety, it was cool and exciting there in the windy darkness. Staring into the outer elements, feeling, in the most animal sense, the world battening down and scurrying for cover, they each gathered into themselves like pockets, hoarding their own limited warmth. First they saw Dorothy, waving as she crossed the cloud-shadowed hills. Then Max came over, his nostrils flaring as he looked up into the gloaming sky. Doors and shutters were banging, and then the remaining staff and teachers came out. Skirting the crowd, avoiding Max, even Lily emerged, solitary, bruised, rubbing her arms. And how odd it was for Russell, standing like a spurned groom in his morning suit, as Dora walked up to him. Arms folded, squinting, she gave his hand a replenishing squeeze that nearly brought tears to his eyes in the strong wind.

Now everyone was waiting, standing poised against the storm. A white flash. Jagged summer lightning leapt up the sky, crazing and cracking in hot green stitches. They all jumped at the boom, and Russell said loudly, as much for himself as for the others, I'm sure they're just late.

Thunder was pounding and the wind was whipping, plangent with the first hot fusillades of rain. Standing beside Dora, Russell felt himself trembling. First the flash, then the crack — first the dread, then the mounting panic, cleaving and clawing the sky. In the rising panic, one could feel the approaching pain as one could smell the rips of electric rain. Russell was wringing Dora's hand. In the panic they were parents. Against the rain, they were all gazing up in wonderment, all suddenly as backward and small as their forebears who had dwelt in huts. A distant tree went up in a bone-white blast. Puddles were forming. The ground was drenched and sizzling. It was looking bad, but then, just as swiftly, it changed, changed so resoundingly that Russell could hardly believe it as Dorothy, peering through her binoculars, said, *Here they are!* and then they all saw the old red bus come barreling up the drive and splash to a stop. And then the door opened and the sunburned children jumped down and everybody hurried inside laughing and talking all at once as the rumbling sky flashed white with an awful crack, then broke black again with the wonderful heavy warm rain.

Confession

THE CHILDREN had a dog named Daisy, a long-eared, white and liver-spotted mutt that lived at the school with three other dogs and four cats. Old and fat from under-the-table feedings, Daisy was a favorite who waddled in at meals and lay the rest of the day like a beached seal in the sun. She could lie for hours on her back with a look of utter, insensible pleasure — smiling, the children said, as they rubbed her big spotted belly. Digging her nose in the grass, Daisy would grandly sneeze and the children would say, God bless you! as if their old grandmother had learned a trick. (The dog knew nothing but her name.)

So it was sad when, after the rain, the children found Daisy lying dead and stiff in the grass.

Max was playing with the children when they discovered the dead dog. Barefoot, bellowing, Max was chasing them around the house, racing after them impossibly fast with his arms stretched wide. The children screamed in joyful fright as he snatched them up and carried them off, a raving robber-god raising them like offerings to the sky.

Max! they cried. *Me, Max! Me next!*

With raised arms, the children vied and cried for their turn to be swept aloft by him. But then a girl found the dog, and the children quickly gathered, repulsed but curious, then crying for Max, since the teacher watching them had momentarily stepped inside. Max knew a poisoned dog when he saw one, and he knew justice. Examining the dog's muzzle, he said, She is by poison killed. The old man's poison for the flowers, she was fed, I think.

The children immediately knew, or thought they knew, the culprit. Rabe did it, they cried, and they pointed at him, screaming, Slug! Fat wee-wee-face! Come see what you did to Daisy!

Knock-kneed, cowed, Rabe was standing by the spigot, his mouth gaping as Max turned with one stabbing finger, shouting, *You!* Boy! Come *here!*

Max didn't wait. He hurtled toward the boy at full speed, running with his arms pumping and his eyes bugging out. Instinctively, Rabe grasped his crotch. At the last second he tried to run, but collapsed in a puddle as Max seized him by the neck and hauled him aloft by the seat of his pants. It was just like the game they had been playing, only this time it seemed that Max would dash the boy's brains out on a tree. In the war, Max had had a particularly deep response to the shrieks of the wounded horses. On balance, a fat, twisted boy like Rabe was probably worth much less to him than a good horse or a dog. The children had never seen violence — not like this. The older children squinted and screwed up their faces, and the smaller ones started to squeal. In his rage, Max didn't know what he was doing. He had Rabe by a hank of hair, snarling as he repeatedly mashed the boy's scream into the dead dog's slobbery muzzle, the better to see his crime.

Russell was outraged when Max dragged the hysterical boy in to him and demanded that he be punished. How dare you discipline this child! he roared, pulling the boy from his grasp. He is my charge, not yours, and I will handle him as I see fit. Now, out! Out, do you hear! Out and not another word!

When Wittgenstein heard what had happened, he ran upstairs and found Max throwing things in his rucksack. There was no reasoning with him. Max insisted that Russell had ordered him to leave, and that suited him fine, he said. He would not stand another minute in this place with godless people who let such wickedness go unpunished.

But what makes you think Russell won't punish him? asked Wittgenstein in German. Russell's quite upset about what the boy did. But can you blame him for being angry with you? You don't discipline other people's children.

Right! said Max pointedly, lunging for the door. You, if anyone, should know that.

Wittgenstein moved to block the door. What are you doing? Must you insult me, too?

But Max wouldn't listen. Pushing him aside, he trooped down the stairs, out the door and down the road, not caring that he was miles from anywhere, with more rain in store. Wittgenstein practically had to run to keep up with him. Why are you doing this? he was asking. Come back to the house, will you? Just for the night. Then if you like we can both leave in the morning and go somewhere. I have some money.

But Max still wouldn't listen, so Wittgenstein stopped talking. They walked a while in silence, then Wittgenstein tried once more:

Max, why are you doing this? The other night, when you were drunk, you said you would follow me to the ends of the earth. Now you're running away.

Max stopped. I'm leaving, not running. Russell can go to hell with his whorehouse!

Max started walking again, fitful, fugitive looking, but then he stopped short, saying: Ludwig! Stop here. I will confess to you now.

Wittgenstein didn't want this. Who am I that you should confess to me? he asked evasively. Confess to God.

Darkness was falling. They were standing in the open road, with the land rising away in long rolls. Every now and then a drop of cold rain would fall.

Max said, Do you remember in Trattenbach? Do you remember when we would criticize each other with Father Haft?

Criticize, yes. We did not confess.

Max wasn't listening. He said, To confess is manly and cleansing. It is also a sign of trust and respect. This much I owe you. I will confess to you, and then I will mend my ways. Listen — do you think I am sorry for that boy? No, I am not sorry, not at all. I'd as soon have killed him, had he been mine. It's that girl I'm talking about, that little bitch you warned me to keep away from.

Wittgenstein could barely look at him, he was so disgusted.

Well? Max insisted. Are you hearing me or not? I'm not talking to the wind.

I hear you, replied Wittgenstein grudgingly, and then he bent into himself like a crag, saying, Go on, then. Confess if you must.

I lay, said Max with a sigh, I lay with her. Today. I tried to ignore her — oh, I know you don't believe that, Ludwig, but it's true! I *did* try, but she kept hovering around me — you know how they do.

Wittgenstein scowled. Don't blame her. Last night I warned you. *Twice* I warned you.

But she was the first spark —

Oh, stop it! Better never to confess than to *half* confess. That's vile!

Max accepted this. All right, he said. You are right. I should have had better control — Max let out a snort — since *she* obviously couldn't, a woman. Sin is over quickly.

Yes, and so are confessions.

Listen to me, said Max. I say this before you and God. I know I asked to come here with you, but I wish I had never come to this place. Don't sneer — it's hard not to think filth in such a whorehouse. Among atheists. And I don't care what you say — Russell is not a good man.

Wittgenstein was repulsed by Max's self-righteous air. He wanted to say again that Max was not being consistent, that he *made no sense*. But he saw there was no decent or understandable way to say this, not in the dark, in the middle of nowhere. Max, in any case, was in no mood for a sermon, and Wittgenstein was in no mood to fight with him or beg him back, seeing that it wouldn't have worked anyway. But the hardest thing, Wittgenstein realized, was that he was not sorry to see him go, though he felt guilty about leaving him in such a sorry state. Wittgenstein told himself that he would see Max later, at a better time. He told himself that they would meet in a better time and place. But there was nothing left to be said, not then. Max grasped Wittgenstein hard by the shoulders, then started walking with big pumping strokes into the darkness, that black beauty he would lay with that night before waking with the first birds into the amnesia of dawn.

Regret

RABE was a good icebreaker: thanks to him, there was suddenly plenty to talk about at dinner that night. The mood was almost convivial, even remotely festive, the Russells and their guests being thrown together like semiestranged neighbors meeting at a house fire. Uncoiling from the strain, Russell uncorked three bottles of wine and offered a toast to Wittgenstein, *Philosophiae Doctor*. Here, here! said Moore, who made a second toast, which Wittgenstein shyly acknowledged with a sip of his nearly untouched glass.

Conspicuously, there was no mention of Max, and Wittgenstein shortly excused himself and went up to his room, thinking, as he had been thinking all night, of Max's confession. Wittgenstein remembered the wartime confessions — long, winding lines of men standing under the open sky, waiting to kneel before a black-frocked priest seated on a camp stool with a scarlet stole draped around his neck. Here were no screens or buffers, no cloaking anonymity. Here was just a man with bowed head kneeling before seated justice, just another sinner whispering his crimes into the impassive ear of God. To Wittgenstein, there was something manly and incongruous and innocent in the sight of fighting men on their knees, frankly unburdening themselves before a big battle. Many times he watched this scene, wishing that he were good and simple and brave enough to get in that line, if only to feel, for once, the ease of speaking his soul into another human face. But he couldn't do it, not even at the price of salvation could he do it. Dying would have been easier than confessing before so many eyes. The Russian lines were closer to him than the face of that priest.

Outside, a steady breeze was lifting the branches, the rain having purged the sky of its heat. Resting his feet on the bed rail, letting the air sweep under his legs, Wittgenstein could hear the children idly peeping in the darkness, resisting sleep. Humans, he thought, are the only animals that fear the dark. But where the child sees the darkness as being without, the adult sees it as more a cumulative seepage. With each year, he feels his mind accumulating not just fears but pains and regrets, groaning like an old thatch roof under ages of snow.

Wittgenstein was thinking of something he had regretted for a long time, something that had happened once in Trattenbach. In a flash of temper one day, he had struck a girl — struck her without thinking, and then much too hard. She was, by his book, a stupid, indolent girl. Age ten and prematurely developed, she was from bad stock and lazy, given to the most idiotic lies and snitching from the other children's lunches. He couldn't remember what she did that caused him to strike her, but he remembered being particularly annoyed because he had been so patient and reasonable with her, assuming she would naturally follow his reasonable example. It infuriated him for her to spurn even his kind forbearance — children are so self-centered and ungrateful. He had given the girl every chance to redeem herself. Knowing that she would certainly lie if he confronted her before the other children, he spoke to her privately, after school. Just tell me the truth, he said, and not at all unkindly. But she lied.

Liar! he barked, and with the heel of his hand, he gave her a chop across the face — a blow so hard that he heard her neck snap as she fell back into a desk, badly banging her elbow. Seeing him go white, the girl knew instinctively that he had overstepped his bounds. Like a baby who has taken a bad tumble, she hesitated, half from surprise, half to judge his reaction, then started howling and holding her limp arm, squealing, You broke my arm! You broke it, you broke it!

Shut up! he said, so frightened that he nearly clapped his hand over her mouth. It was a matter of survival. To apologize or show concern would have been tantamount to admitting his guilt, so he steeled himself, telling her, as if to make it so, that she was not hurt, that she must get up, stop crying and *never* lie to him again.

The girl wasn't lying when she promised to tell her parents. The next day while the children were eating lunch, the district school inspector arrived and asked for a word with him. Wittgenstein knew immediately why the man had come, and he was nervous. At the same time, he knew that with his unblemished record there was no real need to lie about the incident. The girl's arm, though bruised, was not broken. A slight reprimand, perhaps a formal apology to the girl and her parents, and the matter would be over. But he couldn't do it. To apologize to these people, to admit that he wasn't always in full control and completely effective as a teacher — it was intolerable to his already bruised pride. Besides, no incident was too trivial anymore. Here, he thought, was just the ammunition the villagers wanted. With this, they'd pull him down like a wounded stag and destroy him. Wittgenstein told the inspector that the girl was lying.

The girl was a better liar than he was. Wittgenstein could see from the inspector's eyes that he knew he was lying, but because it was his word against the girl's, and because it was his first such incident, the inspector let it pass with a warning. But that was not the end of it. Inevitably, the story got out, and Wittgenstein, the cooker of cats and buyer of boys, got an undeserved reputation for brutalizing his pupils. This hurt him. In remorse, he tried to turn away from corporal punishments, but that proved even worse: having established discipline with the rod, so to speak, he couldn't adopt milder methods in midstream. Almost immediately, the children sensed his reluctance to discipline them and started testing him at every turn. Even Franz Kluck began acting up.

It was around this time that the fainting started. One unusually hot day, a rather anemic boy named Glöckel fainted. Wittgenstein quickly revived the boy, gave him water and some cookies, then sent him home with a letter to his father recommending that he not be put to work that evening. But hardly had Glöckel gone than the other children began to complain of the heat, insisting that they, too, should be sent home. Drink water if you are hot, said Wittgenstein, pointing to the water jug. Ordinarily, that would have been the end of it, but then a boy named Frank, one of his worst clowns, wilted onto the floor, obviously faking. Get up! ordered Wittgenstein. There was a great uproar as he yanked him up, moaning and rolling his head, then sat him in his desk. But where two weeks before, he would have boxed the boy's ears, Wittgenstein gave him a stern warning — a joke.

There was one more fainter that day, and three more the next. By the fourth day, Wittgenstein was desperate. Hardly had he hauled the first fainter off the floor than the second slumped in his desk. And even as he sent them to the corner, a fourth fainter fell out — Franz Kluck, grinning like Judas as Wittgenstein thrust him back in his seat.

This was too much. I'm fed up with all of you! he roared, smacking his rod on the side of his elevated desk. For the next ten minutes you can all wallow with the *pigs,* for all I care. But when I return, I promise you that any other fakers will be severely punished!

Yet here, he saw, he had boxed himself in again, promising what he was afraid to deliver. He was trapped, and they knew it. Even as he left, there were delighted squeals and taunting pig grunts. But when he returned, they all raced to their seats, biting their lips to suppress giggles. Wittgenstein resumed the lesson. For almost an hour they were quiet, but then he detected the same telltale restlessness and whispering. It was Frank and his cohorts again, averting their faces to hide their smirks.

I'm warning you, he said ominously, and then there came a hush — broken by a loud groan as Frank slumped to the floor.

Wittgenstein saw that his authority was at stake. He had no choice but make good his threat. This time there was no heat. He was thoroughly businesslike about it. Hauling Frank up by the arm, he thrust him back in his chair, then drew himself up and resolutely slapped him. It was a thoroughly regulation slap, not at all hard, but Frank played it up. Like a cowboy in the pictures, he splashed out of his seat and sprawled ignominiously on his face. Quit your playing, Frank, or I'll give you another! Over the next few months, Wittgenstein would hear these words again and again, because when he turned Frank over, the boy was bleeding profusely through the nose.

That ended Wittgenstein's career as a schoolteacher. This time there were charges of brutality, which Wittgenstein resolutely denied. Serious as they were, the charges were administrative, not criminal. He could have left Trattenbach then, but in an effort to clear his name, Wittgenstein fought the charges. In his desperation, he even agreed to submit to a psychiatric examination, meeting four times with a psychiatrist who finally pronounced him withdrawn and depressed but otherwise normal — not, in any case, brutal and sadistic. Ultimately, Wittgenstein was cleared of the charges, but in the meantime, Max didn't help his cause by beating up those three men, including Frank's father. In court later, Max refused to repeat to the judge the things the men had said. Herr Frank and his sneering cohorts should have known better than to taunt Max as he was being led off to jail. The judge and Wittgenstein both warned Max to forget the matter. It did no good. When he was released, Max went on a second rampage, then lit out, never to be seen in the village again.

To the end, Wittgenstein was genuinely perplexed about how he could have bloodied the boy's nose. It wasn't until several years later, when he was back in Vienna building the house for Gretl, that he received a letter from Franz Kluck explaining how Frank had jabbed a sharpened pencil in his nose as he lay on the floor. Franz's letter was a typical schoolboy confession, hurried, brief, incomplete. Franz said he was sorry for not telling the truth about what had happened that day, adding that he had wanted to but had been ashamed — but ashamed of what, or of whom, he did not say.

Father Haft's successor, Father Schöttl, was still in Trattenbach, still stuck there as pastor of Our Lady of Perpetual Disrepair. Father Schöttl was one of those self-appointed reporters who periodically feel the need to fill others in on the drab news, whether or not they want to hear it. Every Christmas Wittgenstein received a card from him, and the news was always the same. The village was as bad, if not worse. Hilda Mueller, the girl he had struck, was a tramp — she had left the village, unmarried and pregnant. Herr Kluck had long since drunk himself to death. Now out of school and working for a grocer, Franz Kluck was about to take the civil service exam in the hopes of becoming a postal clerk.

Franz and Wittgenstein still corresponded occasionally. Wittgenstein knew that the young man still harbored dreams of going to university, and had Wittgenstein wanted he certainly could have gotten Gretl to finance his education. But he told himself that the young man was probably better off where he was, leading a simple life without unreasonable expectations. Actually, Wittgenstein thought quite a lot about Trattenbach. After the trial, he had sworn never to go back, but by now he was becoming curious. Often, he would imagine slipping back into the village in disguise, there to walk like a spirit among the people to see firsthand how it had all turned out. But of course this was just another fantasy, much like these late-night thoughts of confession.

Floating Out to See

EARLIER THAT NIGHT, not long after Max had left in a fury, a delega-
tion of distraught children had gone to Russell to make known their
anger at Rabe.

Bertrand, we think Rabe should be punished for killing our dog, said
John, the apparent spokesman for the group. We also think Rabe should
be made to bury Daisy.

There were about eight children, and Russell invited them all into his
office to talk about it. Gathering around him on his big leather sofa,
the children were angry and upset, and he was amazed, as always, by
the child's fierce and seemingly innate passion for justice. Russell and
Dora had done much to try to cultivate this instinct. Under the auspices
of the school council, the children had their own court, and they had
their own code of punishments: two nights with no dessert, hoeing the
garden — that was about the extent of it. But Rabe, Russell explained,
was a case quite beyond their court.

Rabe is sick, he said. He needs the help of doctors, not punishment.
Punishment is wicked when it can do no good. For all we know, Rabe
couldn't help himself — and that is assuming that he did indeed poison
Daisy. And, mind you, we do not know for a fact that he did. For all we
know, Daisy may have died of old age.

At this John spoke up. But Rabe told Max that he did it.

Well, now, replied Russell. I expect you'd have confessed yourself, had
Max throttled you the way he did poor Rabe.

That was mean of Max, said six-year-old Mary Berry, bouncing on her
seat.

Yes, it was mean, agreed Russell, falling into that conspicuous, somewhat homiletic voice of his alter ego, the Headmaster. Finding guilt is
not easy. Then there's the problem of what to do once you find it. Why
did Rabe poison Daisy — if indeed he did poison her? Why has Rabe
done so many other bad things? I, for one, think that Rabe did these
things because he is sick and unhappy. A happy boy would not torture a
poor innocent animal.

You mean Rabe is sick so he made Daisy sick? asked a red-haired boy
named Alf.

But Russell could see that this was already getting sticky and hard to explain, the children's idea of sickness being something one catches rather than something that is passed down, instilled or whatever. And of course there were other questions. Inevitably, the children wanted to know where a dog like Daisy went when she died. Russell told them frankly what he thought: the dog simply died and was no more. He did add, though, that in a sense Daisy would live on through her puppies, who would carry, and pass on, a piece of Daisy just as the children carried and would one day pass on to their children pieces of their own mummies and daddies. But at this Russell saw several of the children, including John, screw up their faces, as if *he* were leaving, and he realized that they were all afraid of his leaving, of the long leaving. So leaving was the quotient, but the content, again, was pain — pain and the dread of pain, since all was leaving. And then Russell remembered how as babies in their baths, John and Kate would dip their hands into the water, looking at the liquid, then at their hands, and then at him, aghast, not knowing how to separate either their hands from the water or their own bodies from his. And with this anxiety ran another fear: that he might somehow vanish as in a game of peek-a-boo, eclipsed like the sun, never to be restored.

It was unlikely that Russell could have approached these matters with greater care or sensitivity, but still he was afraid that, no matter what he said, the children would be somehow scarred by the dead dog, the unbalanced boy, the violent man. The main thing, though, was that he was explaining, having learned that often it wasn't so much the explanation as the sheer care of explaining that matters most to children. But his explanations weren't just for the children's sakes; he, too, took comfort in explaining, which was as necessary for him as for them. The children were spread around him like a quilt, a warm, arm-splatched quilt that smelled of sticky skin, of flesh and rain and earth. The children seemed to act as if he were telling them a story, and so in a sense he was. Outside, it was already dark, getting ready to rain again. This was about the time that Wittgenstein was standing out on the road, hearing Max's confession — another less happy, less satisfactory explanation.

Late that same night, in a literally eleventh-hour effort to rid themselves of Rabe Peck, the desperate school finally found a place in Salisbury that agreed to take the boy, sight unseen, for a suitably exorbitant price. This was Vale of Muir Lodge, an institution desperately short of funds and full of empty beds and restraining jackets.

This is nothing but robbery! cried the headmaster, looking pigstuck as he held the telephone. But after spending an hour dickering with the blackguard who ran the place, Russell finally struck an agreement by which Vale of Muir would take the boy for a two-week evaluation period — *and* with the proviso that if they did not themselves keep the boy, or were not judged suitable, they would secure an appropriate institution that would take him until his mother was found.

Miss Marmer readily volunteered to take the boy to Salisbury the next day, being all too glad to get away from Beacon Hill — and the headmaster. And later, after Russell had settled matters with Vale of Muir, Miss Marmer gave him another night's harbor, and not such a bad night, either. The truth was, Miss Marmer felt badly about her outburst that day, when she had railed at him by the stairs during her quarrel with Lily.

So, early the next morning, after Russell had crept from her room, Miss Marmer took Rabe Peck down to the car, where Tillham was waiting to drive them to the station. Earlier, Tillham had dug a grave for Daisy and laid the dog in it, just as Russell had instructed. Unfortunately, though, the old man had not dug a grave-shaped hole but a round hole, as if he were potting a tree. In fact, when Russell looked into the hole, he wondered for a moment if it was a shrub or piece of rooting, what with the way Tillham had bundled the dog in a ball of twine-bound burlap.

Dratted old nitwit! muttered Russell to himself, knowing all too well the child's natural concern for orthodoxy and consistency. He knew the children would be disturbed by the unusual hole, and, sure enough, they were.

But that's a *round* hole, huffed Rose, who had seen her grandmother buried. Graves aren't supposed to be *round.*

A grave can be any shape, Russell replied carefully. Certain primitive peoples used to bury their dead in clay jars. Really, my dear, there is no right or wrong way. It's merely a matter of *custom* — I mean the way different people do things.

But where's Daisy? squealed Peter, one of the smaller boys, clutching Russell's leg as he peered down into the hole.

She's down there, said Russell, taking the boy's arm reassuringly. Daisy's all wrapped up in that burlap there. Quite nicely wrapped, as you can see.

Is she a mummy? asked another boy, with an astonished look. Has Mr. Tillham made her a mummy?

But with this, little Peter, still clutching Russell's leg in confusion and having heard something about a mummy, bawled: But I still don't *see . . . Where's Daisy?*

There were some tears, and several of the children said some kind words about the deceased, who had never bitten anybody or even barked very much, and who in her day had dropped many a litter. Then, after this eulogy, the children tearfully sang *Oh-where-oh-where-has-my-little-dog-gone*, the only dog song they knew, while Russell fiercely rubbed his face, trying not to smile.

Russell wanted the children to see death as a thoroughly natural process, but he needn't have worried. Scarcely had the children filled in the dirt and covered it over with grass and wildflowers and a turtlish stone with DAISY painted on it than they were asking when they could get another dog. And then they were off, Daisy, for the time being at least, forgotten.

That was all. When Mr. Tillham returned, Russell took John and Kate, along with Wittgenstein and the Moores, to an isolated beach below the cliffs. It was a huge, luminous day, and the white chalk path that cut down the cliffs to the beach was steep and difficult for them, encumbered, as they were, with baskets, blankets and chairs.

John, said Russell preemptively, John, mind you — But, waving his arms in the speeding wind, the boy ran whooping down the path like a young goat, heedless of his father's shouts.

Picking down the crumbling path, they saw the boy on the beach, lunging at the chopping swells that cracked like eggs against the black rocks, then ran foaming down their mussel-crusted sides. John was quivering with excitement as he ran up to his father, begging, May we swim now, Daddy? May we?

You may, said Russell sternly. But only if you mind me. Didn't you hear me calling you back up there? Russell lit his pipe and sent him off with his sister. The boy had no fear of the water. Waiting for the first good wave, he took a step back, then charged into it, squealing as it bowled him over.

John! cried Russell.

Suspended under that white bombardment of light and mist, the boy was deaf to him. So let him go, Russell told himself, but he hung on, so powerless as the next wave rocketed down, consuming the squealing boy with the sound of a distant explosion.

Sitting up higher on the beach, in quite a different element, Wittgenstein was watching Russell and the boy, feeling the same pangs but keeping them well hidden. Truly, Wittgenstein felt a little queer being alone at a beach among these family people, without even Max there as a buffer. And for the Moores and Russell, it *was* rather queer to see Wittgenstein in such a setting — to see him partake of something purely pleasurable and without purpose. Remembering Wittgenstein's prudishness in Norway, Moore was correct in his prediction that he would not bathe, but to his amazement and Russell's, Wittgenstein did go barefoot, rolling his trousers above the knees. Free from the *Viva* and now Max as well, Wittgenstein did seem more relaxed, in his way. Digging his feet into the crusty sand and working it through his toes, he talked to Dorothy for some time. And later, he took John and Kate exploring, happy to lose himself in the sun's drumming heat. He didn't at all mind their calling him Ludwig. Like an abnormally bright child, he answered their questions, but in his answer he always sought to subtly recast the question, returning it like a piece of sourdough in the hope that they might use it to make something more.

As for Moore, it wasn't long before the waves coaxed him into the water. Not since the reading parties of their undergraduate days had Moore and Russell seen each other in bathing dress. It was a bit of a shock as the clothes came off, to be subjected to the harsh mirror of one's contemporaries. The two men tried to seem natural about it, but there it was — old man's skin, all tucked and puckered and flabby white, hanging off them like filets of haddock. Oh, God, they thought, it had really happened. They were old. Then came the poking, the joking. Not much different, humm? jested Moore in his ancient black woolen one-piece. Not much, said Russell, immodestly sliding his thumbs down the latex belly band of his very moderne black trunks.

The two men walked down to the skiffles where the children were playing in the sand. Moore didn't want to intrude. Russell was telling the children about the Spanish Armada as Moore waded out into the deeper water. Behind him, Moore was aware of Dorothy, perched like a nesting bird on the beach in her beige bathing suit. All that morning he had been aware of her, floating up in him like a water beacon. He swam out a short way and rolled over; spat and closed his eyes. His lungs swelled and contracted. The water rocked. Forever it rocked and rocked, and he became even more forcibly aware of Dorothy's presence, beaming down on him like strong sunshine. It had been so long since he had floated, but what he had lost of his former buoyancy he had gained in perspective. Without Dorothy, Moore knew, he would not be floating so confidently. Oh, he might be wading, might be standing much diminished in the shoals, staring at his white legs, bent and foreshortened in the water. But, no, he would not be floating.

Intimacy is like a stream within a stream: there is the tantalizing life without, a numinous loom with its light and air and vast trees; and there is the rich, dark, mutual life whose language and nuances are quite invisible to those standing on the periphery. This had been the case the day before. Moore had seen that something was bothering Dorothy when she returned from her birdwatching. He had still felt her unease at dinner, but it was only later, when they were in bed, that Dorothy revealed what it was about. With her binoculars, Dorothy had seen Max and Lily that afternoon. She said she had started to call to them, but then she saw the blanket under Max's arm and thought better of it.

I don't know why I looked at all, she said. Oh, I stopped looking immediately once I saw what they were up to. I'm sure you think I'm a horrid peeping Tom, but it's true.

Moore assured her that there was no cause for shame. Curiosity was natural — very natural. Even as they were discussing this under the covers, they could hear another opera playing in the next room. They still didn't know who it was in there, but Dorothy had her theories. In his reserved way, even Moore was getting curious. He was even more curious when he went down the hall to wash and smelled strong perfume — a cloying, almost swampy fragrance. He couldn't get it out of his head. All that night, the music seemed to continue; in Moore's imagination the perfume all but soaked through the walls, filling him with crowded dreams.

Moore always relieved himself in the early morning, and when he blundered down the hall, half asleep, he smelled the perfume even more strongly. He was sitting on the toilet, waiting for his cramped bladder to unknot, when he heard a door creak open. Moore froze on the seat, his heart pounding. He heard whispers, then slow steps picking down the hall and down the stairs.

The voice and footsteps were unmistakably Russell's, and as Moore sat there the whole sorry situation suddenly became clear to him. He took no pleasure in it. He would have put it right out of his mind had it not been for Dorothy's complaints about his reticence. So he told her about it. Told her for intimacy's sake — to repay her for her own secret.

Ironically, then, Russell's ill fortune had become Moore's good fortune. All that morning Dorothy had been especially frisky and affectionate, grateful for this confidence he had conferred on her. Life is bad. Life is good. How does one ever decide which version is truer or the more pervasive? Moore's face was now a mask on the surface of the ocean. His legs were fluttering, and his hands were undulating at his sides. Only as much is learned as is forgotten. One swam off just far enough to discern the shore — just far enough that one could say that one had seen it floating there, one's wife and life given sensuous shape on the shore. Moore slipped out just far enough to see this, and once he had seen it, he knew, at this stage of his life, that he need venture out no farther. No, Dorothy had no cause for worry this time. Moore didn't stay out long.

BOOK IV

The World After

Repentance is not a free and fair highway to heaven.
— Henry David Thoreau, *Journals*

Anschluss

IN SEPTEMBER OF 1938, six months after the *Anschluss,* Gretl's butler Frick came to her, his face white with panic as he told her about an SS *Sturmscharführer* who was waiting downstairs to speak to her.

Gretl thought it odd that the SS would send only one man: when the SS came, they typically came in force. Gretl knew this not only from friends who had fled or gone into hiding but from her own experience a few weeks before, after her ex-maid had reported her to the Gestapo as a Jew harborer. Ever since, Gretl had been expecting a call in the night, and now she thought they had finally come to arrest her — perhaps they figured a *Sturmscharführer* was more than enough for one old lady.

Having more or less prepared herself for this, Gretl only hoped the Nazis would spare Mining and poor Frick, who had been so brave and loyal about staying when all her other servants had given notice. The loss of her house staff had been a heavy blow, but under the circumstances Gretl could hardly blame them for leaving. All over Vienna servants were leaving good situations, while their former employers were hastily departing for worse ones. Most of Gretl's eleven servants had gone with regret, many of them tearfully, but all had left in fear, taking with them Gretl's resigned blessings and a generous severance. Knowing that their mistress would not dare report them under the circumstances, several of Gretl's newer servants, including the maid who reported her, had even left with a little something extra, stuffing their bags with silver, food, clothes and other booty, no doubt figuring that Frau Stonborough would not need these things where she was going.

Arriving with a six-man SS contingent, the Gestapo inspector who had come that first night was a mild-faced man with thinning hair who might have sold insurance in his former life. Dressed in a dark suit with a swastika armband, he was not in the least imposing or sinister; if anything, he was quite matter-of-fact as he opened his briefcase and produced blood papers for Gretl and Mining.

Gretl still had her health, but Mining was now hugely overweight and ailing, with arthritis, a bad heart and a left arm that had swollen twice the size of her right following the removal, two years before, of her cancerous left breast. Ever since Rolf's death from leukemia four years before, Mining had been living with Gretl, and she was now Gretl's greatest worry: Gretl thought her sister would have a coronary right there when the SS came through the front door with rifles and drawn pistols.

Panting like a stricken animal, Mining just stood there, white-faced and staring, holding her fat dimpled arm. Gretl wasn't doing so well either. She felt the blood slowly draining from her head. It was late, very late, and she remembered hearing how the SS made their arrests late like this, when people were asleep and thus more docile and confused. The ploy worked. Gretl's mind was quite blank with fear, and her legs were weak, but she felt she must remain standing or else relinquish all control. She grasped the table. The Gestapo inspector was reading some idiotic charge against the Reich, and her right leg was falling asleep. Then her left leg began to tremble, and she looked at the SS troopers, thinking of what they say about dogs — how even the most vicious dogs are fine until they sense the fear that gets their blood up.

Gretl felt fear now. It was like death by exposure, starting in the legs, then traveling up the spine until it addles the brain, making one dizzy and desperate for sleep. *Stop it,* she told herself, telling herself that she must think not only for herself but for her poor sister. With her fleshy bulk sustained by this now feeble heart, Mining looked ready to topple over.

Liebste, Mining, es macht nichts, setz Dich hin, said Gretl oversweetly, begging her to sit. But no sooner had Gretl said this in an effort to somehow ease the situation than she looked again at the young, black-gloved SS men blocking the door with their rifles, their peaked caps and black suits luminescent with a meaningless sorcery of braid and insignia. They were like leashed dogs, she thought, they were like lean and hungry Dobermans, hungry to snap and roust *den Juden* from her house. *Mining,* Gretl said more forcefully. Mining, darling . . . please sit down while I speak to these men.

It seemed that her only recourse was to resort to a forlorn and absurd kindness, as if mere breeding would show, or matter, at such a time, much less suggest to these men that they should follow her kind example. Trying to fight paralysis or sleep, Gretl found all kinds of delaying, distancing questions coursing through her mind. This was the part that no one had been able to prepare her for. In all the times she had heard people describe this now familiar experience, no one had been able to properly convey the shock that would hit her, much less the silly things she was liable to say. In her shock that night, she did not know, or did not want to admit, that for the first time in her life, she was powerless — an old nobody. She was freezing to death and didn't quite believe it; in her powerlessness, she was being sucked down, yet she still fought it like death, focusing on her sister's fear so as to ward off her own, saying as to a child, *Mining, listen to me. You must sit down . . .*

But Mining only managed a confused, stricken look, and in that moment Gretl saw her big sister reduced to the mute dependency of a child. Cradling her heavy left arm like an infant over the nonexistent breast, Mining looked at her, then more indignantly at the inspector, and squeaked hysterically, I'm very sorry — *I'm sorry but I will have to sit!* And then there was Gretl's jarring panic as her sister blundered back, collapsing into a slender chair that made a sickening crack as Mining's heavy, varicose legs gave way.

The perspicacious inspector clearly viewed himself as a scalpel, not a meat cleaver; he was visibly discomfited by this unpleasant scene. Please, Frau Stonborough, he insisted. Please, both you ladies must sit and rest yourselves.

But with Mining's tumble, Gretl's fear turned to rage. In her contempt for this imbecile, Gretl thanked him with an edge of sarcasm, obstinately saying that she preferred to stand, *danke.* The inspector felt her contempt — he was all too conscious of that gulf of class she represented — but instead of taking offense, he took even greater pains to show that he was not some party thug, that he was indeed a man of discernment and civility. It was really quite pathetic. The inspector's manner was one of ceremonious disappointment as he explained to Gretl, in the most muted tones possible, that the Reich was prepared to treat her and her sister *as Gentiles,* but that as bona fide friends of the Reich they could not break the law by harboring those of Jewish blood. The inspector said this on a hopeful note, assuming, naturally, that the two women would find it a profound relief. But Gretl was not relieved. Suddenly she was furious, telling him in the prickly voice she used on recalcitrant tradesmen that she was a Jew and did not wish the Reich to consider her anything *but* a Jew.

At this, the inspector glanced with vexation at his men — the woman was obviously mad — and repeated, as if it were an incontrovertible scientific fact, that she was nonetheless a Gentile; her blood papers were quite clear on that point. At Gretl's remark, meanwhile, Mining had pulled herself up from her seat. Her eyes were swimming. Gretl could see exactly what she was saying. *Are you mad?* Mining was asking. *Do you think that, as a Wittgenstein, you can say* anything? Mining hadn't forgotten the facts. She hadn't forgotten the people lined up outside the consulates, frantically seeking permission to emigrate. Nor had she forgotten those already interned in SS camps, or murdered. Many had committed suicide in the first violent days of the *Anschluss,* when shops were wrecked and Jews were attacked by roving mobs. On the Kärntnerstrasse and Graben, down streets of smashed and boarded-up storefronts with *Jude* scrawled in white paint, Jews had been forced to get on their hands and knees to scour the paving stones. No one had been spared. Even rabbis and decorated war veterans had been publicly humiliated. With their own beards, Hassidic Jews were forced to symbolically scour the stones while the mobs howled and the fun-loving SS men prodded them with their riding crops or rode them piggyback by their earlocks.

In her way, Mining was far better prepared for this than Gretl was. Age and sickness had taught Mining something: if nothing else, she had learned what it is to be powerless. All her life Gretl had laughed or scorned away the bad, the crude, the idiotic. Never had she been powerless. Never in her life had she been in a situation where something couldn't be worked out; the family politician couldn't yet comprehend these politics. Characteristically, Gretl had labored under the delusion that because the Nazis were disgusting and fraudulent, they could be scorned away by their betters as having no moral power — as if moral power meant anything against guns and tanks. Yes, Gretl saw that she was quite deluded in this late hour. They were no longer Wittgensteins: they were nobodies — Jew harborers, or at best pawns the Nazis might keep around while it was expedient to show the world that it wasn't so bad, that Vienna still remembered with gratitude her best citizens.

Gretl didn't know what had gotten into her just then; the words had just leapt out. She wasn't heroic, she was scared to death. Besides, there was nothing she could do now. That knowledge was what broke her, as the soldiers brought down the people who had been hiding upstairs. Gretl was standing with Mining, trying not to cry. And then she was crying anyway as her friends — an old doctor, a schoolteacher whose husband and son had been seized, a lone girl of fifteen and a family of four — were led outside. Out they filed, past a gang of kerchiefed youths wearing swastikas and carrying nasty little eagle-headed daggers on their belts.

And there they were loaded into a tall black van and taken away, never to be heard of again.

After this, Gretl knew she could not remain in Vienna. Every Jew who could had left by then, and any left were struggling to get foreign entry permits or were in hiding. After months of harassment, Freud had been deported, and then only after heavy diplomatic pressure had been put on the Nazis. Not that this stopped them from confiscating nearly everything Freud owned. What did they care that he was old and dying? To them, he was just another rich Jew to turn upside-down and shake before discarding. Freud was the linchpin. If the Nazis were willing to publicly mistreat a man of Freud's stature, then it was clear they would stop at nothing to make the Ostmark, as Austria was now called, *judenrein*.

Gretl wanted to throw bombs. She knew she could do no further good by staying in Vienna, and yet for weeks after the Gestapo incident she did nothing, absolutely nothing. At first, she stayed out of stubbornness and anger, feeling that they had no right to drive her out of her own city. But then her anger wore her down and she fell into despair. Yet it was despair of the worst kind — the humbling, debilitating despair that she recognized as the despair of the *old*. She was sixty-one. Oh, a young sixty-one — a mere girl of sixty-one, her more charitable friends would say. And hearing these innocent blandishments, Gretl would cock her head wistfully, wanting to believe them and then playing the same game, telling these flatterers, in turn, how good they looked, shaving off a few guilty years. But now the strain told. She looked sixty-one, she thought — looked a good sixty-six or seventy. And for the first time she truly felt old and useless, felt the creep of decrepitude. It was as if somebody had knocked the wind out of her. Bad enough she had to largely fend for herself for the first time, but she now had the additional burden of caring for Mining. She hated it. It just was not her nature to play nursemaid, and Mining knew it. Mining felt guilty for needing her help, and Gretl felt doubly guilty for not giving it more freely. And then Gretl would find herself getting irrationally angry. Angry at life and the Nazis. Angry at herself! Angry that goodhearted Mining, who had nursed her father and mother, should have such a spoiled brat for a sister, and at that an incompetent brat who could scarcely iron a blouse or cook.

Every day her son Stefan would call, asking when she would leave, and every day she would stall, becoming increasingly inert and helpless. She just didn't feel resilient or adaptable enough to be uprooted to a new country. And what will I do without my friends? she would ask, willfully forgetting that her friends were gone, or dead, or else trying desperately to scrape up *Reichsfluchtsteuer* and other Nazi ransom taxes with what remained of their seized or frozen assets. And this was when they could even find a country that would take them, in those times of worldwide depression and unemployment.

Above all, Gretl had reached that intractable age where she could not endure the idea of leaving her home. She loved this modern house that her brother had built for her. It reminded her of one of those lacquered Chinese boxes, dark and luminous, with well-fitted doors and clasps that locked, and everything of exactly the right proportion. Perhaps she best liked the house for being so unlike life, especially as it was at present. The house was like a dream unfolding, revealing a tall door, then a slender hall and a labyrinthine stair that spiraled down with the skewed but haunting logic of prime numbers. In the center of the house was a glassed-in elevator that her brother had specially designed. At times these days Gretl would find herself thinking up excuses to ride it up, then down again, watching, amid its whir, that slow, devolving hierarchy of steel and glass, light and darkness. Living in that house with its books and paintings, she sometimes felt like a monk in the Dark Ages. Yes, she would think. This was why she was staying in Vienna. She was holding a few precious things for safekeeping until men learned to read again.

For a few minutes she would feel a little better with this fantasy, but then she would find herself getting angry again — blaming life and the Nazis, the chaos of Austrian politics, on and on. But of all the things she blamed, she felt the strangest was this urge to blame her culture. In her mind, even Gretl could not help scorn the notion. One might as well blame the weather, she thought. As if culture had planted the knife and welcomed Hitler! As if culture should have prevented this like a kind of moral prophylactic! Just like you, Gretl, she would think. Always looking for a boogieman or culprit. But still, if her culture couldn't stop Hitler — or even had invited or created Hitler — then why not feel betrayed by it? And how strong or deep was culture if the river could be diverted into a grotesque Teutonic religion of Bayreuth festivals, of garlanded girls and men in lederhosen, blowing hunting horns?

If not vaguely ludicrous, these questions were certainly pointless in her present predicament — Gretl was all too aware of that. She knew that she was woolgathering and avoiding, but she couldn't help herself. She was so preoccupied and forgetful these days. Up and down the elevator she would go, her mind wandering, then stuck like the humming electric panel that was waiting for her to push 1, 2 or 3. Very well. Down she would go. But then she would remember something upstairs — a book she needed or a light she had left on. And so up again with a whir, watching the floors pass, feeling herself lofting up invisibly like a rising body of heat. *Chunk*, the doors would open. But standing there, she would hesitate. The light she thought she might have left on was, as she very well knew, off. The book was downstairs or unimportant. And the fact was, she was stuck. *Don't be neurotic!* she would tell herself, now on the verge of tears. But looking down, she would see the perforated toe of her shoe — an old lady's black shoe, soft as the plush lining of a coffin — tapping the threshold of that stone floor. And such elegant black stone it was, a polished slate like onyx. But God, how it showed dust. It was so unspeakably dusty and untidy — it was like her whole life! But it wasn't dust or forgotten lights that were tormenting her. Dread was what it was, a dread as debilitating as malaria. Deep breaths as she stood by the door, amid that insistent humming. Toe tapping. Not wanting to step off, yet oppressed by the thought of the shutting doors and then the slow drop, floating down like the dust.

The other anxiety was where they would go. They couldn't decide. America? Mining would suggest. Ugh, said Gretl. France? Even worse. England, with its bleak, chilly weather? Italy! Italy, so gorgeous, so warm and sunny. Gretl spoke beautiful Italian, and they had some distant cousins there. But the disgusting politics! And so dirty! Switzerland, then — Switzerland, where years before Gretl had so shrewdly put the bulk of her fortune, just as her father had done before the first war. But the Swiss were so stodgy, and she was feeling so old, buried beneath this dust. And so it would press down, the heaviness of long, slack days when the two old sisters, afraid to go out and too depressed to even listen to a radio symphony, would look at each other and start weeping — weeping as once their mother had wept, with their handkerchiefs balled in their fists.

Death's Head

Now, after having spent weeks adrift in that house in the wake of the first SS visit, Gretl was told that the SS was there again. But to send only one man? Mining was asleep, so Gretl came alone down the elevator, her heart fluttering as the door opened. Once again there was that hesitation, the toe on the threshold as she saw the SS *Sturmscharführer* in his black bulletproof suit, his legs encased in two punishing cylinders of gleaming black leather.

It made her flesh crawl to see his shoulders covered with this braid and regalia, which reminded her of skittling insects. The *Sturmscharführer's* back was turned, and he was looking with wonder at the geometry of her house, with its ribbon windows and lyre-like radiators. Gretl would never forget the silver death's head insignia on the tall peak of the cap he held under his arm as he turned and said with a respectful nod, Frau Gretl. And then she saw that big shovel of a face and realized that it was Max. Max, who had laid the floor on which he was standing and helped build the geometric stair beyond. It was impossible. To see Max dressed up, to see him contained in a uniform, no less, and so dour and reserved, with none of that wild profusion she remembered — at first this was a shock, but then it all fit with the most awful logic.

Neither she nor her brother had heard from Max, or of him, since that "scene," as Gretl called it, at Russell's school. Ludwig had given her a full account of that visit, and its distressing end. Still, Gretl had expected it all to blow over. She never thought it would be the last of Max. Never one to give up, Gretl had even made inquiries about him, as had her brother, but these never produced anything. So finally, reluctantly, they concluded that Max was dead — killed in a brawl, found along a road somewhere or perhaps dead from drink.

Wittgenstein dreaded Gretl's questions about him. For years, every time Gretl had seen her brother, she would say, And you still haven't heard from Max? just as if it had been last week that Max had left, and not four or five years. No, Wittgenstein would say bitterly, I haven't heard. And if I haven't heard, I won't, so we might as well forget it. Well, Gretl would say, unable to put it aside. I just can't understand it. Something really must have happened to him, don't you think? And then with a pained shrug Wittgenstein would reply, Of course something happened. Something always happens.

And looking at Max now, Gretl saw that something had indeed happened. She was not altogether surprised, either, feeling that she was seeing something she had glimpsed years ago but had pushed back in her mind. Once, she had even raised the possibility that Max might have joined the Nazis, but Wittgenstein rejected it as being beyond Max; he said it was pointless speculation and slander of the dead. But Gretl was well aware of Max's anti-Semitism and his hatred of communists, his lingering bitterness about the war. Like her brother, she had clearly seen his dark side; and like him she had suppressed it because Max was so extraordinary, because in him she saw so much more good. Not that Max's bad points were always easy to ignore. Gretl remembered Max making some asinine remark about Jews, and how she angrily told him that the Wittgensteins were Jews by blood. Max refused to believe her. You Wittgensteins are not Jews, he had insisted. Even if you say you are, you are not. And even if you are of Jewish blood, there is nothing remotely Jewish about you.

Max didn't care when she showed him old family pictures and memorabilia: her great-grandfather's prayer book with its thin silvery pages and a Kiddush cup engraved in Hebrew. Max was woefully ignorant about Judaism, and he was typically disbelieving when presented with physical evidence. *He* was not a materialist. He didn't care what was written or fixed on photographic paper. For him the past was a vast fabrication to be shaken off in the way a tree sloughs its own leaves. Gretl found his denials incredible. She gave him a good tongue lashing, but, like her brother, she viewed his excesses as a comparatively small price when stacked against the greater rewards of knowing him. And of course Max had not always been the troubled man she last remembered. Moreover, he intrigued her. For an intensely curious woman like Gretl, this was in itself an irresistible asset, and it was partly a result of how Gretl had changed in the wake of the First World War. Relief work had been a profound awakening for her. The refugees expressed another realm of existence, one quite apart from that select and, as she now saw, intensely sheltered milieu in which she had grown up. Gretl wasn't the only one whose eyes had been opened by the war, and Max appealed to her in essentially the same way he did to her brother. The best thing about Max was that he was so utterly unlike them. In his sweaty way, he was like a breath of fresh air — such an antidote to their refined world. In his crazy, unrestrained freedom, Max had once seemed to Gretl to be the purest expression of the lower class and the promise of that class. In the beginning, at least, Max had conveyed the liberating and still rather novel conviction that men and women could learn and grow, that life need not run forever on the same fixed rails of tradition and class. For Gretl, Max was a letter from the frontier. He didn't hunger for what she had. Unlike most people, he didn't stand in awe of her. He loved to tease her, and she took strange delight in his impertinent remarks. And Max, in turn, adored her and probably listened to her as much as he did anybody, including her brother.

But now as he stood before her, she found nothing to say. Gretl's social gifts quite failed her in the face of the big, gale-voiced regimental ser-

geant. Gretl wanted to ask him what he thought of himself in his black
suit gleaming with SS lightning runes and death's heads. She wanted to
ask him how many defenseless Jews he had kicked with those big boots,
strutting about like God Almighty. And most of all she wanted to ask
him what had happened to his kindly Christian God — why He had
turned so vengeful and Yahweh-ish, turning a good man into a beast?
But she was too sick and frightened to say a word. And Max himself
seemed at a loss for words. At first, Gretl thought he was testing her
nerves, the way he seemed to stare through her. He was standing stock
still, but his suit was so tight that he creaked like a windlass as he faintly
rocked in that black pistol harness. He must have been forty or more but
he didn't look it, trim and vigorous as ever. His hair was cropped short,
and there was a red dent in his long Dürer nose that she didn't remember
— token of some brawl, no doubt. Lightly, his restless hand was patting
his thigh — patting it, she thought, as if with an absent riding crop. Max
then took a breath — clearly this was extremely hard for him — and said
with a glowering, exerted look:

I am not here in any official capacity, Frau Gretl. I come here out of
duty to you and your good brother to tell you that you are under suspicion and must leave Vienna as soon as possible. I can see to papers or
any other arrangements that must be made for you and Frau Mining and
Stefan to safely leave Austria. I can also give you money if you need it.
But you must not wait. Please. In a week, I may be unable to help you.

Max looked like he wanted to say something further, but something
stopped him and he just stood there, his boots creaking, looking captive
and extremely uncomfortable now that he had unburdened himself. He
could not have been there five minutes. Afterward, Gretl thought that she
must have thanked him — if only automatically — and yet she couldn't
remember saying another word. Handing her a blank card with his telephone number written on it, Max told her to call him, saying that if she
did not, he would call on her again in two days' time.

That was the extent of it. Having reached the ragged limits of entreaties, words or even looks, Max then gazed at her — looked *out*, it
seemed, with those two trapped little eyes. Gretl did not say good-bye to
him as he turned and walked out the door, black as the devil. It occurred
to her that he must have come at personal risk, and yet she did not feel
grateful for anything but the fact that he left quickly, without pausing to
pass pleasantries or good wishes. Yes, that was like Max — he would
not play false by invoking any of life's ordinary offices under intolerable
circumstances. Done like a true soldier.

Max wrote Wittgenstein after his visit. His letter arrived the day before Gretl's did.

9 September 1938

Dear Ludwig,

I am sure you will hate me now when I tell you that for the past two years I have been a member of the SS. To say this to you is like leaving you on the road at Russell's — a clean break. All I will say is I do this for the reasons of honor and belief that you will never understand. I tell you this not to confess — with God's work there is nothing to confess. I say this only to reveal to you who I am and to urge you to convince your sisters and nephew to leave Vienna immediately. Tonight I went to Frau Gretl and offered her my help in getting the three of them safely out of the country. I can make all arrangements, but I warn you like I warned her that she must act soon, as she is under suspicion and may soon be arrested as an enemy of the Reich.

I know better, Wittgenstein, but others will not. Years ago, your good sister told me that the Wittgensteins are of Jewish blood. (Why was it you never told me this?) I told her that you are not Jews in the true sense. This I learned from the wise Jew Weininger who knew that the Jew is not simply a victim of his own blood. The Jew is he who falls to the female sickness of his own will. This is not the way of your vigorous family, but others in the movement do not often see things how I do. I do my job, and they are my sworn comrades to the death. But know this much — God is still above, and Max is still his own church. Never does he forget a good turn or an old friend.

As you would say, I am getting off the track. I will end here. Do NOT come to Vienna. Don't be stupid. You can do your sisters no earthly good and will only get yourself in hot water. Listen this once to me. We will forever be strangers now, but I ask you now to please accept my help as a parting gesture of respect. Let me do for you and your family this final good deed.

God keep you,
Max

Sex and Character

MAX'S LETTER cast Wittgenstein into a depression that only deepened the next day when he received Gretl's letter, telling him all about Max and the first incident with the Gestapo, which she said she had kept from him, not wanting to upset him with things he was powerless to change.

Gretl, in any case, said she had decided to take Max up on his offer of safe passage and told Wittgenstein that she would contact him once they were safely out of Austria. Wittgenstein passed an anxious week before he finally received a wire from Gretl saying that the three of them — Mining, Stefan and herself — were in Switzerland, where they planned to stay a month before leaving for New York, the only city in the world that met Gretl's basic criteria of being great, cosmopolitan and an ocean away from Europe.

Having his family out of Vienna relieved Wittgenstein's immediate fears, but it still did not break the depression that Max's letter had brought on. What especially bothered him was Max's reproachful question of why he had never admitted his Jewish origins. Wittgenstein felt like a moral coward — a liar. It made no difference that he had never actually denied his Jewishness. The fact was, he had never acknowledged or firmly stood up for it with Max, Father Haft or other anti-Semites. Even in England, where prejudices were more subtle, his Jewishness had been a matter of fairly conscious omission — which was to say, he had lied.

Now, once and for all, Wittgenstein wanted to see the truth of his life, no matter what the truth was or what it cost him. It was not for mere goodness' sake that Wittgenstein resolved to do this: it was a matter of moral survival. Not since his days on the eastern front had he been so shaken. Now, in this summer of darkness, with his native country having fallen, Wittgenstein's past was seeping over him with thoughts of Max, the radical, self-anointed Christian wearing SS death's heads, and Otto Weininger, the sex-crossed, self-hating Jew who had written *Sex and Character,* a book that for Max had been an explosive. Yet here, too, Wittgenstein saw that he had nobody to blame but himself: it was he who had introduced Max to Weininger, having once shown Max a copy of *Sex and Character* while they were living in Trattenbach.

Weininger had stimulated Wittgenstein's own thinking for good and bad, and in directions not necessarily suggested by the poisonous major themes of *Sex and Character.* Weininger was only twenty-two when he had written the book, and he committed suicide in the fall of 1901, not long after its critical reception — indifference and opprobrium, mixed with ecstatic acclaim from several prominent anti-Semites and misogynists, including Strindberg, who said the precocious young doctor had finally solved in his virile book the great problem of Woman and Sex.

Despite its obvious faults, and for all its haste and malice, *Sex and Character* was a dark work of genius that was as extraordinary in its

scope as in its ambition to radically reorient thinking about questions of
sex and ethics, freedom and will, crime and salvation, slavery and eman-
cipation and, ultimately, the fate of mankind. For Weininger, the way was
narrow and labyrinthine, growing progressively darker and more airless
to the sarcophagus, wherein lay the truth. Life was man's Original Sin.
Good was guilt, shame was health, and death, which lay beyond the
goring poles of sex, was man's salvation. Eternity was man's rightful
woman. Woman was man's death and cross. Thus, Weininger said, the
female sex could be grossly divided into prostitute or mother, but in
either case woman amounted to the same thing. Completely unconscious
and malevolent, utterly without soul or will and unknown even to herself, woman was an erotic ghost — a syphilitic orifice capable only of
sucking out man's soul, pulling man down from higher pursuits with her
shrill, idle desires for sex, pleasure, children, perpetuation — life. Spiritually, said Weininger, the most debased man was incomparably higher
than the most advanced woman. Yet complicating these distinctions,
Weininger said, was the fact that both men and women were bisexual, such that each man and each woman, to a greater or lesser de-
gree, contained the seeds of the other sex, a fact that accounted for
why there were masculine women and feminine men and all shades in
between.

In his vaunting ambition, Weininger went on to discuss more than just
these ideas in his book, which proceeded from a discussion of male and
female plasmas to the laws of sexual attraction; from questions of homosexuality and pederasty to "characterology," his own "science" of
character; from discussions of genius to considerations of memory, logic
and ethics — and from there to still other questions: the problem of the
"I," motherhood and prostitution, erotics and aesthetics, the essentially
female nature of the Jew, and finally the ultimate problem of woman, the
ruin of mankind. Here, the moralist was quick to add that this tragedy
was man's fault, not woman's. Devoid of soul or conscience, and without
any intellectual or moral faculties to speak of, woman could not be held
accountable for her sirenlike temptations. Man had let her pull him down
with her Judas kiss.

For Weininger, there was no middle ground in this question. What was
called for was a complete spiritual revaluation of society. There must be
an irrevocable sundering of the sexes — a draconian spiritual hygiene.
Certainly, Weininger said caustically, there was no *moral* reason to perpetuate the human species — what man had ever entered into the act of
coitus with the idea of perpetuating the race? The only thing perpetuated
thus, he said, was universal guilt and anguish, the insolvable riddle of

life. Rather, said Weininger, the only decent course was to renounce sex entirely and thus to allow humankind to wither like a dead fruit so that Spirit could at last flourish and ascend out of the world.

Above all else, Weininger's book was a young man's effort — Wittgenstein found it inconceivable that an older man, accustomed to the realities of compromise, could have produced such a work. Wittgenstein could remember reading Weininger's remorseless self-autopsy as a boy and even as a young man, and wanting to die. Weininger was nothing if not searingly honest, nothing if not pure and burning in his insane idealism, which was less a moral state than a self-imposed death sentence: no inquisitor could have prosecuted his case with less pity when faced with what he took to be the rancid and pitiable facts of humanity as embodied in his own foul life.

At fifty, Wittgenstein saw Weininger much differently. He acknowledged Weininger's influence and saw that there was much in his hasty book, besides the more sensational themes, that was highly original and worthwhile — if only as a goad to thinking. Wittgenstein did find Weininger philosophically stimulating in his discussions of logic and ethics, genius and character and other more general questions. On the other hand, Wittgenstein could clearly see Weininger's manifold faults. He could see the obvious errors, glosses and unconscious evasions, could see the artful but forced conclusions, the logical leaps and wild exaggerations of legitimate points. So too could he feel Weininger's thwarted sexual drives and tortured doubleness, could feel, in the overheated, often byzantine prose, the alternating fear and exaltation of Weininger's pathological egotism — his overarching ambition to write a great and revolutionary book that would not so much save the world as cure it into extinction.

At times, Wittgenstein could even laugh at Weininger. Once, Wittgenstein had said to Max that everything Weininger said was absolutely true — if one put a *not* before it. Wittgenstein could still hear himself saying that it was the enormity of Weininger's mistake that was great. But this mistake, Wittgenstein saw, was also his own, and now he too had been bitten by the stretching and circling of Weininger's black prophecy. For Wittgenstein, *Sex and Character* was one of those books read in youth that, for better and worse, hold a lifelong and uneasy claim to one's moral and mental map. Certainly in his youth, the book had been too rich and ripe for his delicate and enervated constitution. *Sex and Character* entered his blood like a malaria, stimulating dreams that he now saw he would spend his life periodically sweating out.

Thinking of Weininger then in that period after the *Anschluss,* Wittgenstein saw the fantastic delusion of his own life. Toward sundown he would walk in the Cambridge Backs, through tall brakes and drifts of green. The frogs would be starting with a roaring. Darkness would be collecting in the drains. Toward the breathing dark, in coves of cool above the water, were little globes of flies that he would brush from his eyes. Each year, there were always the same flies. Each year, there were always the same dreams, always the same slow trail of days to be brushed from the eyes so that one might capture a few good things like lightning bugs before it was too light to see and then too dark ever to go back.

If only he could have been an inch higher than the truth, or just to the right or the left of it. But he couldn't climb outside his own skin or exceed his own height, nor could he see his own sin while knee-deep in it. And here, when his own influence was mounting, Wittgenstein saw that he was not a single man but a composite — a concatenation of the various influences that went under the name or tag of fate known as *Ludwig Wittgenstein.* This was only a further burden, because with what he took, consciously or unconsciously, of another life to make a mental life of his own, he accepted also a portion of that person's fate, evading and accepting it at the same time. In this sense, then, Weininger was certainly a part of him, just as he and Weininger were both, in some way, a part of Max. This, he saw, was the burden and paradox of influence: to wonder what truly is yours while yet accepting responsibility for it.

He thought he had been vigilant, no sleeper in the hay, but he saw that even vigilance was not good enough. Flicking his cane before him, switching through the sharp grass, he told himself now he had been an ass deep in hay, and deeper still in his own evil-smelling fool's honey. What had ever led him to believe that character would tell and protect? What had ever led him to believe that genius would prevail over a flawed character and thereby keep one from being snatched by the sleeve into that fulsome, earthbound machinery that grinds up the generations, then stamps them out again into fresh abominations? What good is philosophy if it does not improve one's thinking about important questions of everyday life? And of what use is genius if it comes to no earthly good? For so long he had waited on his genius and time of vision; for so long he had spurred it, urged it, called it names. And then after its first storms, after the flood had abated and he realized that neither he nor the world was any better than before, how he had sought in Trattenbach to bury his genius alive, seeing all too bitterly that if genius was the catalyst, the agent of vision, it was, at the same time, an impediment to normal human life. What had genius brought Weininger? And why had he, Wittgenstein, believed he could transmute Weininger's deranged thinking to his own, quite different ends? Did he imagine that discrimination and character, high culture, would bind and protect the mind from a Weininger? Did he think that sickness might be distilled into a curing serum, an inoculation against itself? Did he think that the storms of history forearmed the world against further history? There was no protection. Truly there were things not to be seen or heard, books that didn't bear reading, ideas too unspeakable to be entertained and stories that didn't bear repeating. One didn't *entertain* Weininger. *Sex and Character* wasn't some illiterate, ghost-written *Mein Kampf* filled with false pieties. One didn't patronize Otto Weininger, or laugh, for long.

Above all, Wittgenstein could feel Weininger's root sickness and revulsion in the face of his unforgivable Jewishness — his doubleness. Yet, as Max had pointed out in his letter, Jewishness, for Weininger, was less a matter of race than an essentially feminine condition — an infirmity of the mind. Anyone could be a Jew, according to Weininger, Jewishness being not a race, people or creed but a tendency of mind that is most conspicuously evident in Jews. The Jew warned the true Aryan to guard himself against such traits: the rootlessness and irreverence, the lack of fixed beliefs and the resulting fixation on material things rather than spiritual values. Conversion, if it was sincere, might help, but it was no real solution and still less any salvation. True, as with homosexuality, the Jewish character might be partly combatted by frankly facing one's deficiencies, but ultimately, Weininger implied, the only sure cure was death, death, for him, being a moral condition, like Heraclitus's transforming fire, whose life fans up with the death of earth. Thus Weininger maintained that Christ was the greatest man in the history of the world because he had conquered man's greatest enemy: the Jew within. Judaism was Christ's original sin, Weininger said, and Christ was, and would remain, the only Jew in history to conquer the spiritual death of Judaism through his death on the Cross.

Could Wittgenstein have been surprised that all these ideas found an immediate home in Max? Though Wittgenstein was inclined to agree with elements of Weininger's basic diagnosis of the Jewish character, he thought his chapter on Jews was among the craziest in the book. He told Max this; he told him this several times — forcefully. It did no good. If Wittgenstein could not completely put the book in perspective, certainly Max could not. So why, Wittgenstein asked himself, had he ever shown Max this awful book, so steeped in nullity, death and self-hatred? Hadn't he known the effect it would have? Or had he just been curious about Max's reaction, wondering what it might reveal of Max's own attitude toward him, the Jew within?

Over and over, Wittgenstein asked himself this question, but each time the answer came down to this: ambivalence. Jewish lineage he had, but no true allegiance. He was philosophical. About Jews he could say, in an echo of Weininger, that even the greatest of Jewish thinkers was merely talented. Certainly, he could say this about his own talent, which he thought was the useful but essentially unoriginal Jewish talent for clarifying the ideas of other men, Gentile men — men of authentic genius with original minds. Wittgenstein did not mean this in a disparaging way. He was only trying to be realistic. After all, it was precisely because the Jewish mind was being measured by standards that did not fit it that it was consistently over- or underestimated. But, again, he thought, this was an evasion in the face of — ambivalence. So what, then, was at the root of this ambivalence? But his concentration was broken. It seemed he couldn't look that deep. His will faltered and his mind dimmed — with ambivalence, empty ambivalence.

For so long Wittgenstein had been forcing back his past, his youth, that it came back with redoubled force that summer, with memories of his native city and his boyhood.

Vienna was such a small town at bottom. Or at least it was small within one's milieu — so long as it was the right milieu. Certainly, Weininger, a contemporary of Wittgenstein's brother Hans, would have known who the Wittgensteins were. So, too, Weininger must have known about the brilliant Hans, a dandy and aesthete like himself who moved in the same general intellectual circles. Hans, in any case, certainly knew who Otto Weininger was.

It occurred to Wittgenstein that his father might well have known Weininger's father, Leopold. They were men of the same mold. Leopold Weininger was not a wealthy man, nor was he Karl Wittgenstein's social equal, but, like Karl Wittgenstein, Leopold Weininger was a self-made man, a prominent goldsmith and art expert who fashioned miracles of gold and enamel in the tradition of Cellini. The two fathers were also alike in their passion for music, which they followed with a devotion that could only be described as religious. It now seemed to Wittgenstein that in this age of low culture people no longer listened to music with quite that same feverish intoxication: they had lost the necessary powers of concentration. Karl Wittgenstein possessed the necessary concentration.

Music moved the unmoved mover; it shook him to his depths. Gone was the ocean of reserve, the brute deliberation — the dikes would burst. There he would be at two A.M. after a concert, pounding the floor, humming the theme and swinging his arms in wild oblivion, unaware of the boy peering down the grand red-carpeted stairway. Nobody was permitted to enter his father's reverie, nobody was to speak or intrude upon the sacred Art Experience. It would have been like shaking a man in prayer — like throwing cold water on the backside of a man engaged in sex. What did his father, this vampire, derive from music? He must have been starving; what he sought seemed more than art could decently provide. The boy, too, was starving but did not know it. He was shocked, certainly. He must have even felt slightly betrayed to see his father behave in this way — to realize that there was another father whom he did not know and would never be permitted to know. The boy might have felt more had there been much left to feel, but it seemed that his father had used up all the feeling, inhaled all the air, gulped down all the life and gnashed up all the coal and ore to make iron, and with iron, money, so he could gorge himself on solitary art feeling in the middle of the night. This was the Dionysian man. But there was also the Apollonian man, the idolator who could confess to his wife once, after returning from the symphony, that he had felt guilty warming a plush seat while others played for him like demons, saying that for *decency's* sake he should have gotten down on his *knees* to behold such a torrential mountain of music! Even forty years later, Wittgenstein remembered this with humiliation, feeling even then, as he had at age ten, that his father had somehow said something unspeakable, that in some fundamental way he had profaned himself, making of art an altar.

From what Wittgenstein understood, Leopold Weininger was much the same way. Wittgenstein could well imagine the melancholy that must have fallen over Leopold Weininger, that idolator of Wagner, after the exaltation of these musical evenings, when Siegfried had slain the dragon Fafner and won Brünnhilde — when the tumult of the orchestra collapsed and he returned to the listless banality of his comfortable house with his invisible wife, his four meek daughters and his three sullen sons. This was the same pattern with Wittgenstein's own father, who would crash through the house the next morning finding everything out of place, his sturdy factory of a house filled with disorder, mendacity, conspiracy, disobedience. Leopold Weininger was no less a tyrant. Wittgenstein had heard that he would fly into sudden rages, bludgeoning the air with his fists, then lumber off into days of crushing silence, when no one, least of all his wife (whose very absence in these stories perhaps spoke for itself), dared ask him what was wrong.

But there was one fundamental difference between Karl Wittgenstein and Leopold Weininger: Leopold Weininger was a practicing Jew who raised his children as Jews. At the same time, however, Leopold Weininger was a bitter anti-Semite who had nothing but contempt for these Dreyfusards and Zionists, believing that, in the main, Jews had no one but themselves to blame for their misfortunes. Leopold Weininger was, by nature, an angry, accusing, unreflective man, and he did not perceive his views as being traitorous or contradictory. It was a severe blow to him when the rabbi told him that his son Otto had officially resigned from the synagogue. This was Otto's break from the Pharisees, his declaration of holy war and the beginning of his public ministry. Leopold Weininger apparently sent his cruel son a wounded *et tu, Brute* letter, asking him how he could do this — to publicly humiliate his father and sever himself from the fold of his own people. But this was nothing compared to his reaction when Otto's book came out and he read his son's cold-blooded attack on womankind and Judaism. Leopold Weininger was thunderstruck. He couldn't believe his son would say such things. He seemed genuinely perplexed and at the synagogue even professed not to know where his son had gotten it, nor to know why, with such a decent and hard-working mother, he would express such loathing and contempt for the opposite sex. For Leopold Weininger, *Sex and Character* must have been an unpleasant mirror. But then didn't Otto Weininger write that the most virulent anti-Semites are apt to be Jews? That we loathe in others what we most loathe in ourselves?

Wittgenstein could still remember finding *Sex and Character* at his brother's bedside. This was not long before the break, when their father banished Hans from the house. Wittgenstein was twelve, and the Blocker made him feel it. But Hans made him feel much else, now directing his self-hatred and spleen at him in the form of subversive, belittling barbs that implicitly questioned the boy's worth and sexuality, as if the worst — meaning, that he would wind up like Hans himself — were foreordained. Hans's own homosexuality cried out, and yet, as if from some unspoken injunction from their father, who scarcely could not have seen it, it was strenuously ignored like some obnoxious family ghost — ignored to the point that his younger brothers had to swallow their own personalities to make room for Hans's: two or three such ghosts in the Palais Wittgenstein would have been impossible.

Besides his interest in music, Hans delved into biology, physiology and genetics, as well as the divinations of palmistry, phrenology, astrology and tarot. His library was filled with books on these subjects, and whether they were written by learned men or by quacks, Hans seemed to burrow through them with the same indiscriminate zeal. Reading and taking notes, he was a man obsessed with tracing his lineage, as if he belonged to a secret and separate race with its own craniums and hands and its own shrouded history to be divined by timbre of voice and density of chest hair as extrapolated over various Pythagorean formulas of width of palm in relation to length of foot. And with these books were other books, expensively bound folio editions with ponderous scientific titles containing photographs of expressionless naked men. Here were tattooed men, hairy bushmen and hairless Chinamen; here, too, were madmen, murderers, freaks and monstrosities with prehensile toes, gaping craniums and pinched faces, each specimen carrying below it a pseudoscientific caption noting certain race-linked irregularities: generally hirsute, muscular or of the sometimes horse-sized sexual organs.

These forbidding picture albums both excited and repelled the boy, and it was while looking for them in Hans's cache that he found *Sex and Character.* Wittgenstein could vividly recall being drawn to the word SEX in the title and opening the book to what seemed the first page and having his eye drill down to the incriminating word "homosexual," his stomach burning with anxiety as he pored over the text, wishing he had never found the book but unable to put it down. Surely, much in that strange book must have gone completely over his head, but now, nearly forty years later, he remembered less of what it said than the indelible feeling that it evoked: shame and an overpowering sensation of corruption and death in the querulous, high-pitched voice of a guide who seemed to say: *I know how you are because I am the same.*

What most struck the boy was how much Weininger sounded like his brother — or vice versa. It wasn't just the ideas, it was that distant, attitudinizing tone, seemingly so detached and scientific, when the feeling, at bottom, was more akin to hysteria. Hans was a human tuning fork. Playing the piano with his preternaturally slender fingers, he was one quivering nerve ending, rising to an impossible pitch of grace and perfection — then collapsing on the least note of dissonance, which only he could hear. Critical as his father was of him, Hans was far more critical of himself, until at last his father didn't have to criticize him at all. Hans didn't have the stamina to contain his enmity toward his father. His hands would tremble and his face would break out with nervous eczema, weeping with a glutinous poison that would dry and flake off in a yellow crust. At other times, he would be struck down with brutal stomach cramps that would leave him doubled up in bed for days, writhing and sobbing in agony and frustration at pains that were meant as much to punish him as to punish his father. But Karl Wittgenstein wasn't about to be manipulated by this whining hypochondriac. He fought back by not bothering about him at all. It was all in his head, Karl Wittgenstein would say to his wife when she would beg him to see his son. Then, reddening, with even more justice and certainty in his voice, Karl Wittgenstein would say: *No, I absolutely refuse to see him when he is doing this to himself* — saying this quite as if the head, with its vague and immaterial feelings, did not experience pain.

Hans had a high, contralto voice that quailed and quavered around his father and grew even more stretched and anxious around his circle of male friends. Karl Wittgenstein loathed them, these wealthy idlers, these vain popinjays, as he called them, cologned and bespatted, wearing mouse-colored gloves and hats and preposterous, severely cut suits. Furtive, secretive and exclusive, Hans and his friends were always glancing around and gathering in corners, always disappearing and hastily shutting doors, where they could be heard whispering in a rush punctuated with mocking, hysterical titters that left Karl Wittgenstein fuming.

Wittgenstein could remember Hans and his circle discussing the book, and he could remember himself reading it and clearly seeing in his own nature virtually every fault that Weininger enumerated. He remembered going through a terrifying period in which it seemed he could actually *smell* his sex rising over him like gas. He could smell it issuing from Hans when he was around his friends, and he could smell it in his own smoldering glands, cooking in his own urgency. This was the period when he would climb out on the roof, seeking air yet feeling burdened by a vastness that magnified his own paltriness and rottenness. He was Jewish and he was Catholic, and he knew, without being able to admit it to himself, that he liked men, which made him an invert and sinful, part man and part woman while combining the worst features of each. He didn't go to school, didn't mix, in his strangeness, with other boys. He had only his tutors and siblings and Otto Weininger, so that it seemed that across the world people were reaching the same impasse, with no decent way back and no decent way forward but through the black egress of death in which everyone would either be cleansed and made decent or else rendered forever incapable of inflicting further evil. This was the dialogue the boy heard; this was the full range of possibilities. He was out on the roof and Weininger was now out on a limb. Weininger must have felt the pressure, with Hans and others, too, speculating whether he would follow his own moral code and cede either to celibacy or to death, the ultimate celibacy and immaculate conception, thereby making himself the second greatest Jew in the world's history and the second Christ, bearing a new and everlasting covenant of universal death.

Wittgenstein remembered this, and he remembered Hans's morbid excitement when Weininger did finally kill himself, shooting himself in the chest after having checked into the same hotel room in which Weininger's god, Beethoven, had died. Wittgenstein still had Hans's copy of *Sex and Character* with its meticulously underlined passages and his emphatic marginal notes — notes that Wittgenstein could not read now without feelings of queasiness and embarrassment: *So true! As I myself have felt! Duly observed in K.P. Can I be this way? YES! A fundamental insight that must be ACKNOWLEDGED!* In the front cover of this book Hans had glued a now brown clipping of the notice — or rather, proclamation — that Weininger's clear-thinking father had placed in the papers the morning after his son's suicide:

Our poor son, Otto Weininger, *doctor philosophiae*, yesterday morning of his own free will took his own life. His friends will please note that the funeral will take place at 4:30 Tuesday afternoon at Matzleindorf Cemetery.
Vienna, October 5, 1901.   HIS PARENTS

Even as a boy, Wittgenstein had found this notice odd and cold. It still chilled him, with its unflinching restraint. Even more peculiar was the mention of free will, as if for that the Weininger family was absolved from any blame for Otto's carefully composed suicide — this while unwittingly fostering the myth of his death as an act of moral courage in a dissembling city of men who flew between their wives and mistresses like fat bumbling bees. Surely, Weininger would have approved of the notice, Wittgenstein thought — why, he might have even written it himself, so well did it contribute to the legend of the fervent, sex-crossed young man courageously gulping the hemlock that his corrupt and moribund culture had given him to drink.

What Wittgenstein still did not understand was why, as a boy, he had felt so driven to attend Weininger's funeral. Partly homage, partly morbid curiosity, partly a desire to observe Hans — Wittgenstein supposed it was all these things. But it still did not explain the desperate sense of urgency that made him lie to his tutor, Herr Mössbauer, about a doctor's visit, then slip behind the house and change into a dark suit that he had smuggled out the night before.

Wittgenstein was certainly the youngest of the many uninvited onlookers who came to Matzleindorf Cemetery that day to pay homage to the now famous — or at least notorious — young doctor. There must have been a hundred or more of them, but they had none of the cohesiveness of a crowd. Scattered over the cemetery grounds, they came alone and they stood alone, dubiously loitering at a barely respectful distance among the packed stones and the tangled black trees whose leaves were just beginning to turn at the edges. It was an old Jewish cemetery that was cluttered with the generations, a babble of stones. Down a hill that might have been a vineyard rose a forest of stout mausoleums with worn stars on their eaves and ancient plots where families lay interred — whole generations stretching from massive black marble monuments down to sunken and listing tablets, some barely the size of cobbles and washed clean of any earthly identity. It was not the boy's first funeral but it was his first suicide, and it was several minutes before it dawned on him that all of the uninvited onlookers were men. Later, he would learn that, just as there are those who make a practice of attending weddings and trials, there are those who do the same for suicides. They were all there: shabbily dressed students and intellectuals, unhappy bachelors or lowly civil servants wearing sloven cravats, idlers and drunks and even wealthy-looking scions like Hans and his friends, whom he could see to his left, darkly and carefully dressed and clasping bunches of closed white roses with drooping heads.

The boy was standing — or half hiding — beside a large tree, leaning out imperceptibly to get another glimpse of Hans, then leaning back again to watch the funeral on the little hillside below. On the red gravel drive was a train of carriages and several motorcars led by a black, glass-encased hearse drawn by six blinkered black horses. Wittgenstein could remember the horses shaking their silver harnesses and the white pine coffin like a loaf of unbaked bread as the pallbearers slid it out. Up the hill climbed the procession; up the hill after the cortege bearing the slowly rocking coffin, the bunched mourners clambered behind the rabbi in his black robes and white shawl. Wittgenstein especially remembered how, before beginning the service, the old rabbi looked hard at them, the uninvited, as if to say they should either disperse or come down. But no one moved. They all just stood there, too shameless to leave and too furtive or hostile to join in the Jewish service. And by then even more men were drifting down the hillside, emerging through the clotted trees. Everywhere he looked he would see another solitary face, another somber stranger holding his hat over his privates, as if to conceal a grievously spreading stain.

Of that day, Wittgenstein also remembered the rabbi's singing, wrenching utterance, ancient, mournful, guttural — spoiled when a heavy, unshaven man nearby snorted in disgust, then held his nose for all to see. The next thing Wittgenstein remembered was a man to his left pointing to a sturdy, petulant man with hawklike features in the funeral below and telling his companion that this was Herr Weininger, *der Vater*. The boy thought the man must be mistaken. Dressed all in black with an improbable little black yarmulke on his large head, the man looked so fierce and irritable that the boy thought he was a bad-tempered undertaker, not the grieving father. But then he saw the rabbi grasp him filially by the arm, saw his weeping wife and daughters, and his more inert sons, standing desolately beside him. Wails were heard as the gravediggers lowered the coffin with thick leather straps. He saw a chair being hastily brought forward for an old woman who had collapsed. Someone else was being led away. All around Leopold Weininger, people were weeping, yet he never flinched or faltered, never betrayed the slightest sign of ordinary grief. Even when the rabbi handed him the shovel and motioned toward the mound of freshly turned earth, he didn't flag. Leopold Weininger didn't merely sift a few ceremonial grains of dirt over the coffin. Resolutely, he stoked the shovel deep and cast a full burden down, the thin pine booming like a drum as he thrust the shovel at his son and turned away.

As the boy stood watching Leopold Weininger that day, he was also watching Hans. Hans seemed to be dreaming, his long adenoidal neck stretching out of his celluloid collar, stretching, it would seem later, to see his own destruction in the face of this father who displayed about as much remorse as his own father would a little more than a year later when they placed Hans's own ashes in the family crypt. Naturally, Hans's funeral was not as well publicized or attended as Weininger's, but that day the boy would see some of these same curious figures watching in the distance among the jagged stones and trees, all as lost as Hans or Weininger had been in those thorny and inexplicable thickets of character.

As it turned out, in fact, there were two ceremonies for Weininger that evening, the second closely following the first, once the mourners had gone and the diggers had hurriedly filled in the grave. The sun was down and darkness was falling, but Hans was there until the end, waiting. Without quite knowing why, the boy was also waiting, watching as Hans and his friends carried the larval white roses down to the gravesite where several dozen others had gathered like solitary chessmen among the glowing stones, staring at the freshly tamped dirt and going through their obscure devotions.

Hans was still there when, through the trees, Wittgenstein saw a yellow ball of light from an oil lantern carried by a bearded watchman, an old Orthodox Jew wearing a long and tattered greatcoat that nearly reached his heavy boots. Bellowing, hoisting the lantern aloft like a censer as he slogged down the hill, the watchman exorcised them like sullen ghosts, then stood defiantly by the grave as they vanished into the pooling darkness. The boy left then. The ground was broken with treacherous roots. Like glowing keyholes, the blanched white stones loomed out at angles. He was walking fast, hopelessly late, when a man who smelled of tobacco blocked his path, his hand outstretched and his face obscured by hat. The stranger asked a hushed question. For a second, the boy thought he had misheard him, but then he recoiled and started running, tearing through the gabled oaks and over the conjoined bones of the dead with this, the first time ever he had been propositioned.

Confession

FOR DAYS Wittgenstein thought about these matters in his past. And then one night Moore received an urgent telephone call from him, saying that he wanted to come over immediately and make a confession.

Sitting in the parlor, ensconced in his big overstuffed chair with his vest askew, Moore was looking agitated when Dorothy Moore asked who had called.

Moore roused himself and said, That was Wittgenstein. He says he is coming over to *confess*. You heard me correctly. Well, what was I to say to *that*? Moore shifted around uncomfortably, then added, He specifically asked that you be present.

Me? Dorothy leaned against the doorway. What on earth would Wittgenstein want to confess to *me*?

Moore dropped his arms in urgent mystification. He picked up his pipe and started rummaging through his vest pockets for a match, his voice rising, slightly gargly, like a boiling kettle, as he said half in protest, Well, I don't know. It was all so sudden. I suppose I could have told him you were out or something, but he caught me off guard. With a huff, Moore stopped going through his vest pockets and reached into his trousers, saying, Don't ask me what on earth it's about. He'll be here any time. Damn it!

Here, said Dorothy, producing a box of matches. *Here* —

Plumping down on the leather hassock before him, Dorothy Moore girlishly wrapped her fleshy arms around her skirted legs, thinking. It took her a minute, but then she, too, got the itch, scowling, *Owwww,* I don't like this — She jumped up and started straightening. Should I make a pot of tea, do you think?

Moore struggled out of his chair, the sucking chair with ash-strewn arms and clutter all about, the chair that held him more powerfully in its grasp with each passing year. Stiffly standing, he blustered, No, no — don't bother with tea. And quit your fussing.

I'm not fussing, she insisted, whisking out of the room with a glass and some stray magazines. Just wait here for his knock. And I'm making tea.

And I promise you, he called back, your tea will just sit there.

You sit, she said, misunderstanding him. I'll be out in a second.

The *tea*! trumpeted Moore. I said the *tea* will sit! He's coming here to *confess,* not to drink tea!

But Dorothy put the kettle on anyway, and they waited. It was raining, a Thursday night, a good two weeks since they had seen Wittgenstein. In fact, they had been wondering what had happened to him. In the year since Moore had retired and Wittgenstein had assumed his chair as professor of philosophy, it had become customary for Wittgenstein to visit Moore on Tuesday evenings, and not just to confer a kindness on an old colleague. Wittgenstein valued Moore's curiosity and civilization, and he still relied on his forthrightness, never having found anyone who could so gently, almost naively, probe and criticize his germinal thoughts or find the precise way to express a tricky concept. Besides discussing philosophy, Moore and Wittgenstein read and discussed Freud, St. Paul, the writings of the Desert Fathers and Spengler's *Decline of the West.* Knowing how Wittgenstein hated the "gesticulations" of Schoenberg and Stravinsky, and how deeply he distrusted modernism, with all its rashness and obstreperousness (If only modernism, like Luther, could have waited!), Moore even took the devil's role one night and played Wittgenstein some of his son's jazz records. Quizzically perking his head and scowling at the splayed notes, Wittgenstein played Louis Armstrong's "Potato Head Blues" five times in a row before admitting that, while it definitely had *something,* he could not presume to judge it: the experience behind it was simply too foreign.

Much as Moore looked forward to these discussions, he did not depend on them, nor did Wittgenstein. This was not from any lingering distance or ill will; it was simply how it was with them. Between them there was a certain bond, but it was not, after all these years, an especially sentimental bond, being based more on trust and respect than on what might have been called affection. Moore had his own life. He was not forgotten. There were still the fitful writings and occasional lectures; there was also the mail begging favors, and the students and former colleagues asking advice, not to mention his Saturday discussion group and the fortnightly meetings of the Moral Science Club. Moore took this with the matter-of-factness of the accomplished old: this was his life, and he neither underestimated nor overestimated it. Yet at the same time, Moore was slowly distancing himself from these things, not because of his mind or his hearing, which were both excellent, but because of a deeper instinct that was slowly weaning him from life, counseling him not to rely too much on pleasures that might end tomorrow, what with the frail state of his health.

Dorothy Moore frequently participated in her husband's discussions with Wittgenstein. And sometimes, reluctantly, she was forced to end them when she felt Moore was getting too excited for his weak heart. With Wittgenstein a now frequent visitor, she knew pretty much what to expect from him, though she was never entirely sure. Dorothy was still smarting from Wittgenstein's reaction one night about a week after the Nazis had occupied Vienna. The strain on him had been evident, and out of concern she had asked if his sisters were safe.

Of course! he said, bristling as if she had asked a completely idiotic question. The Nazis would not dare bother them. They're much too well respected.

Dorothy had dropped the matter then, but now as she and Moore sat there waiting for Wittgenstein's knock, she wondered if anxiety about his sisters wasn't partly the source of this confession. It has to weigh on him, she said to Moore. You said so yourself when we saw him last.

But this only set Moore off. Well, I'm sure it does, he said, leaning forward in his chair. It *must*. But for God's sake, *don't* say a word! You don't know how he is when he gets in these states. Already, Moore was puffing and anxious. My word, no. You'll never see me delving into personal business with him. I don't unless he asks, and even then I'm most extremely careful not to upset him. Damn it, Wittgenstein! Gripping the armrests and glaring at the door, Moore roared, I want to dispense with this nonsense and go to bloody bed!

Bill, said Dorothy, easing up to peek through the curtain. Calm down. I think that's him coming.

A few moments later, they heard the stamping of shoes followed by Wittgenstein's emphatic knock. Opening the door, Moore saw him standing stricken on the stoop in his wet mac, flicking rain off the tines of his umbrella. He walked straight inside. Moore had almost shut the door when he realized someone else was standing off to the side. Oh, Mr. Skinner, he exclaimed. I quite beg your pardon!

It was Wittgenstein's shadow, a slender innocent named Francis Skinner, who for four years now had been Wittgenstein's almost constant companion. Moore knew the young man only by sight. Francis did not accompany Wittgenstein on his Tuesday visits, and in all the times Moore had seen them together, he had spoken to him but once, and briefly. Francis was deeply, painfully shy. At times the young man's shyness would get so bad that even Wittgenstein would shout in exasperation, *Francis, speak!* Whereupon Francis, with a slightly foolish smile, would hunch up his shoulders, speak a few guilty words, then clam up again.

Piercing-alert and efficient, Francis was twenty-six but looked a beardless seventeen — "Saint Francis," Wittgenstein sometimes called him, this silent secretary and sounding board for his ideas. Francis was the only man in Cambridge who had ever been heard to call Wittgenstein by his Christian name. Two years before, he had accompanied Wittgenstein on a month-long trip to Russia, where it was rumored they planned to emigrate, first to study medicine, then to work as doctors among the poor. Moore had heard these rumors, including some nonsense that Wittgenstein was now a confirmed Marxist. But to this Moore paid no attention. Francis and Russia, the little cult that surrounded Wittgenstein — these were aspects of his successor's life that, to tell the truth, Moore preferred to ignore.

Under the porch light, meanwhile, Francis was still wiping his shoes. To Moore, it looked as if he was about to genuflect — the way he was scraping his feet and shaking out his coat was itself a small act of devotion.

I'll only be a second, said Francis, his face cast down from the light. I don't want to wet your floor. But then Wittgenstein gruffly called back:

Francis! Get in here! Then to Moore he said, I brought Francis because I want him to hear this as well.

Standing in a puddle in the hearth, his hands stuffed in the pockets of his dripping black mac, Wittgenstein faced them with a forbidding glare, as if he were waiting for silence to begin a lecture. Moore didn't know whether to stand or sit. Dorothy, meanwhile, was looking to Moore for direction. Fortunately, Francis sensed their confusion and, with the invisible prompting of a born courtier, pointed to the diminutive hassock, saying in a firm, precise voice, I will sit here, Professor and Mrs. Moore — if, of course, you don't mind.

Oh, please — do make yourself comfortable, said Dorothy, grateful for a chance to break the tension.

Wittgenstein did not make himself comfortable. He just stood there glaring as they took their seats, feeling their way down into the cushions. Straightaway then, he began his story. It was wrenching to watch. Stammering, halting, then urgently pushing on, Wittgenstein told them then that he was a Jew by extraction and that for years in England he had behaved with despicable cowardice by not admitting to his "origins," which even then he made to sound shrouded and vaguely shameful. He told them this and then he told them about Max. He told them how for years he had misled Max about his Jewish origins. Not only had he misled him, but he had led him astray, when with more honesty and persistence, he might well have saved his friend from moral destruction.

At this, Wittgenstein stopped, and they slowly settled back, thinking with relief that the confession was over. But then, impulsively, as if these two "crimes" weren't enough, Wittgenstein told them about the girl he had struck in his class in Trattenbach — told how he had hurt her arm, then lied about it, and for no better reason than to prop up his own revolting pride at being a good teacher when clearly he had been nothing of the sort.

With this, Wittgenstein stopped again — stopped dead — seemingly shocked that he had run out of crimes, with nothing more to say. This silence was hard enough on his little audience. But by far the worst thing, Dorothy later said, was to see him standing there, half panting, as though he were waiting to see if there would be any *difference* — some relief or burden lifted. Yet clearly there was no relief, just sorrow and weariness. Moore knew it was no time to tell Wittgenstein that he vastly exaggerated his guilt, that people had known or assumed for years, from his name alone, that he was of Jewish ancestry. It would do no good to say this now. In his present state of mind, Wittgenstein wanted only guilt and censure, not understanding. Denying any possibility of forgiveness and forbidding any expression of sympathy, Wittgenstein wanted them only as witnesses to that guilt, that hereditary link that at once proves the past and haunts the future like the light traveling from some long-snuffed star.

It was devastating, to sit there like fools, able to do nothing but witness this man's pain. They could hear the rain drumming. Opening and closing his mouth as if there had been a change in the air pressure, Moore felt angry and cheated. Dorothy was staring at her hands, upturned in her lap. As for Francis, he was nearly overcome. Numb and trembling, forcing back tears, he was all gathered into himself in the leather hassock, which could be heard faintly creaking with his forlorn rocking.

Blurting an abrupt thank-you, Wittgenstein started for the door. Moore followed and, as he let him out, said reproachfully, You are not a patient man, Wittgenstein. Whereupon Wittgenstein, this most impatient of men, turned to Moore with a look of genuine surprise and said, as if this were one further blot on his life, I'm sorry. I did not know that. No, I did not.

What? Moore was incredulous. You mean you don't know how impatient you are? But look at you! You're too impatient now even to accept forgiveness.

Forgiveness is not at issue! Wittgenstein insisted, looking away. Truth is not a matter of forgiveness.

Perhaps, said Moore skeptically. Nonetheless, you might have the humility to forgive yourself. Guilt just as surely brought you here as truth or goodness did.

I see, labored Wittgenstein, with a halfhearted nod. I will try, Moore. As best I can I will try. Good night.

Outside, it was still raining. Wittgenstein pumped out his umbrella and pushed into the leaning downpour. And after him, balancing precariously with his outstretched umbrella, Francis followed him to their next stop, the second of three sessions where Wittgenstein would purge himself that night, like a man crossing himself three times.

Eggs About to Hatch

WHEN THE WAR CAME a year later, Wittgenstein and Francis volunteered to drive an ambulance, only to find that Wittgenstein, at fifty-one, was too old and Francis was too sick, so sick that he died a few months later from acute poliomyelitis — another heavy blow for Wittgenstein.

Besides Francis, Wittgenstein had for years surrounded himself with other young men whom the other dons would sometimes snidely refer to as his Twelve Holy Disciples. These young men did not number twelve, or even seven, and yet as much as Wittgenstein loathed the term "disciples" and all it implied, it more accurately described the relationship than did "friends" or "students." Wittgenstein did not consciously try to create this kind of relationship, and yet as much as he tried to discount or ignore the magnitude of his influence, he could hardly help but be aware of it. And in his way, he was a tyrant — not a tyrant like his father, certainly, but a tyrant just the same, sure in his instincts, inflexible in his opinions, harsh in his judgments and exacting in his expectations. Jealously absorbing himself into the lives of his young men, he soon took over everything. He remembered birthdays and delighted in giving them durable, well-made gifts that he bought after lengthy deliberation at Woolworth's, where vulgar questions of "taste" were finally subsumed by a healthy utility. If his young needed money, he would give it, if they were sick, he would care for them, and if they were tied to their mothers, he would soon tie them to him. And if they tied themselves to some girl, or got married, he would quietly acquiesce and retire until they sought him out, affecting to be slightly surprised — though he was greatly relieved — that they would want to bother with an "odd old bachelor" like himself.

But soon these young men were leaving for the war, and then Francis was dead and Cambridge was sad and empty, denuded of yet another generation. Wittgenstein knew his innocent young men, like the prototypal Pinsent, would never be quite the same after seeing war, and this pained him deeply. At the train station, seeing off Tom, a young physicist entering the army, he said, If you should fall into hand-to-hand combat, you must give yourself up to be slaughtered.

Wittgenstein gave this order as if to say, *You must not let yourself fall below this point,* the natural assumption being that this was the stance Wittgenstein himself had taken in the last war. Unable to break from Wittgenstein's gaze, Tom nodded that he would do as his mentor advised. Tom had been instrumental in helping him settle Francis's affairs — especially in handling Francis's mother, who had long resented how Wittgenstein had taken over her son's life. Mrs. Skinner had hoped that Francis would be a doctor or at least a professor of philosophy, not some man's shadow. But Wittgenstein, knowing Francis's intense shyness and nervousness, had urged him not to squander himself in the wasteland of philosophy. Instead, he advised him to take up something decent and peaceful and manual. So the gifted prize boy — the wrangler and winner of scholarships — had taken up auto mechanics, thereby scotching the brilliant career that his mother had planned. It was a tense funeral.

Tom was another of these brilliant, tongue-tied, mother-tied boys. Handsome Tom standing on the platform with the enormous bags his mother had bought him, bags bristling with silly snaps and zippered compartments that he would certainly never use. Guileless Tom, so mild and loving, with the bewitching widow's peak and dark doe's eyes. What would they ever do with him in the army, this lollygagger with the soft heart? Tom couldn't even pass a worm on the sidewalk without stopping to carry it to safety.

Walking home later, depressed, Wittgenstein wondered why he had even given Tom his advice. Surely, Tom would be killed in hand-to-hand fighting — the notion that he would defend himself was almost ludicrous. But then Wittgenstein, now the careful reader of Freud, realized that this dictate was not for Tom but for himself. What he was really telling himself was to accept Tom's fate, so like that of the worm wriggling on the hot sidewalk after a rain.

Not long after Tom's departure for the war, Wittgenstein took an indefinite leave of absence from Cambridge and went to London, where he first worked for more than a year on the wards of Guy's Hospital, then for a doctor in the War Ministry.

While working for the doctor, Wittgenstein used his engineering and mathematical expertise to design a laboratory experiment that could simulate and measure the effects of shock. To this end, Wittgenstein, aided by an electrical engineer, designed and built a machine that registered pulse and respiration by means of two steel styluses that zigged and zagged across a roll of calibrated graph paper, charting the two functions in black and red ink. Using himself as a test subject, Wittgenstein conducted many shock experiments from 1942 through 1944. At first he did this by subjecting himself to various physical and mental exertions, but later he was able to inject greater realism in these experiments when he learned that Tom had succumbed to amoebic dysentery in Burma, and that another young friend had been blown up in Antwerp when a German V-1 missile struck the magazine of his docked cruiser. And then close on the heels of this came a letter from Gretl saying that Mining had died in her sleep in their Central Park West apartment.

Wittgenstein had told himself that Max was dead, or as good as dead. Yet this merely helped him dispel any thought of Max: deep at heart, Wittgenstein couldn't imagine a berserker like Max ever dying. Unknown to Wittgenstein, though, Max was dead, killed in the failed assault on Stalingrad along with most of his elite SS Panzer division. Across Russia, they had come to this. Out of the vast yellow spaces, with the villages blazing before them and the *Einsatzgruppen* extermination units working to their rear, they had stormed across the land only to find their tanks stopped by a network of great earthen dikes dug in subfreezing temperatures by thousands of starving women and old men. And there, finally encircled by the Russians, without even the fuel or supplies necessary to attempt a breakout, they died by the thousands that winter. Under a thunderous megadrome of firelit clouds and snow, they threw up their souls in blasts and left behind them only miles of frozen meat under the rubble and eddying drifts. The Nazis did not last. They did not prevail to kill all the miles and all the souls. They did not last, and there was no Easter reunion, and for their comrades who survived there was only starvation and cannibalism and abandonment by their own command. They did not last, but after them, and in spite of them, there was still the all-weathering earth, turning like a gnawed bone into the chemical bubblings of spring with her subtle hygiene, the final disposing of things — elements to the earth, the wild energy to the air — framing the disturbances of things to come.

For Wittgenstein, it was not the sheer extent of the catastrophe that he felt, or the daily news of it, so much as the sheer antediluvian depth of it. It had been so long in coming. For this, whole ages of hatred had been stored up like explosives. For this, whole ages of culture had been in a long and steady decline. Probably the decline was greater than even he realized, but then Wittgenstein had to remind himself that, as a product of that culture, he, too, had been in decline and so had failed to gauge, in even crudely relative terms, the speed of the world's descent. He found it hard to think meaningfully or incisively about these things without succumbing to moral mawkishness, or without merely using the fabled past to cudgel the present for its shallowness and malignity. Nonetheless, he found himself wondering if people of every age had felt this way, or if instead he was living in a Cain time that didn't proceed according to the heart or the logos and that, like language itself, seemed to far outstrip his or anyone else's ability to understand it, much less stand outside it. Philosophically, he found himself returning to the same questions in the way the painter returns to earlier subjects. As a young man he had wondered if there was a prior order to the world and, if so, where its value might be found. But now he wondered not only where value might be found, but how it was transmitted, a path of inquiry that inevitably led him back to that harsh medium of memory, pain. *Where do you feel a grief?* he would write. *Is the absence of feeling a feeling? . . .*

Like an artist sketching his own immobile hand on the table, Wittgenstein carefully mapped this anatomy layer by layer, drawing with such deep and concerted attention that he might have been startled to see the hand twitch to dislodge a fly — how odd to realize that the hand was, after all, one's own. And finally, he found himself wondering as much what the pain said as where in the world it *went,* the pain of the years and the generations. At Beacon Hill, Moore had been the first to ask him, *Why pain?* And many times since, Wittgenstein had found himself wondering if it was indeed a bit perverse, this effort to classify the variety of pain expression like a naturalist. More, he wondered if this abominably complicated, slippery and amorphous stoop work even really amounted to philosophy — if he was not instead adding to the already rampant confusion. Language was the text, but pain, it seemed, was the subtext. Indeed, he found himself wondering at times if this aspect of his admittedly strange investigation didn't amount to a kind of experiential biography. Like a message inserted into a bottle, the record of this pain could only be flung into the oblivion of one's time in the slender hope that it might eventually drift into a wider sea or better time. And like that message in a bottle, there remained the wish to see one's life and time at a kind of sea level, neither too high nor too low, both within one's time but somehow apart from it, riding high and dry over the sea like a message in a bottle. But the problem, again, was in the communication: it was the sense that this pain must not only be put into words but must somehow be given a kind of emotional "english," be it a moan, touch or grimace. And then of course there was the notion that the pain is already *in* our words, that these pendulous fruits are already overburdened, poised to fall, so dark and heavy, at the least provocation.

Someone is in pain, he would write. *Someone is in pain — I don't know who.* The water buoys up, but the pain presses down until we become mostly unconscious of it, displacing the pain as we do the mounting pressure of the air. Peering into his soul, he would try to give this pain a name or make of this pain a lesson, or to make of the lesson a *reason* that might serve to ward off this pain that comes the way of all darkness, filling the world as the light slowly fails. And what had pain to teach, he thought, but sufferance or denial of pain — still more tricks of a mind clotted and dwarfed by its own productions. Or, in yet another variation, there was the desperate and fruitless attempt to fool the pain by creating another, lesser pain to drown the memory of the first pain, that bucket which is the heavier for being so empty. And so out of the emptiness of the past, the pain hurls down. Out of an awful vastness, the pain of the generations descends upon its heirs to be chocked down and sweated out, then blotted out and finally lost in a recurring flood that may yield mystery and even moments of vision, but never the peace and sufferance of eternity, shuddering like thunder against the closed depths of the sea.

In such an age, Wittgenstein thought, one could only have the will and humility to put one foot in front of the other. Often he would think his impulse had quite dried up, and yet for years, for better or worse, he had not been so productive. But still there were the critics like Russell who said that what he was practicing was not philosophy and in fact was nothing less than the fall of philosophy — the product of a misery almost Miltonic.

Of course, Russell's antipathy to Wittgenstein's work came partly in reaction to his own stormy fortunes. For Russell's work, this was a period of critical "reassessment," which, he joked, was a kind of scholarly purgatory prior to embalming. Now that his major work was assumed to be safely over and out of vogue, it was being critically declassified and even broken down into saurian periods. But then it wasn't his "work" that the critics spoke of now, but rather of his "achievement" — and then usually in the past tense. And, alas, his achievement, while indubitably "major," was, like a mountain viewed from a distance, somewhat smaller and less impregnable than it seemed originally, when no one had yet scaled it or even seen it very clearly.

Russell found it eerie at times, walking around, breathing air, being somehow anterior to his own work. But he never lost his sense of humor, and many a Lilliputian tasted the hot cat of his wit. And at bottom, Russell maintained that it was all silliness anyway, this modern fame and reputation business. After all, he had been slandered and vilified for years — especially in America, where as recently as 1940 he had even been publicly charged with lechery and indecency and tried *in absentia* in connection with a course on logic he planned to teach at New York's City College. But now, having undergone a lengthy period of virtual public leperhood in which he could scarcely earn a living, he was suddenly, absurdly respectable! Beyond respectable, in fact. He had assumed Great Man status. Everything was coming back to him. To be famous and young was nothing — a fart in the wind — but to be famous and *old* vouchsafed him a sinecure of public veneration, his days one long retrospective honorarium, *per diem* and podium unto death. Even his old loves were becoming retrospective. In the last years of her life, until she died in 1938, he had resumed his romantic correspondence with Ottoline, sniffing the perfume of her letters and remembering, much to the chagrin of his young third wife, someone much younger and gayer and now ageless. And then, with his third marriage doomed, Russell was fondly corresponding with Colette, loving her better from afar than he ever could for long up close.

Then came the atom bomb.

If the Americans had not invented it, Wittgenstein said, Russell would have to have done so himself. But what was so terrible about this boogie bomb? asked Wittgenstein. If it was an especially bitter pill for mankind, well, so be it, he said, hoping it might spell an end to the hegemony of our disgusting soapy-water science. And it was so safe to hate, Wittgenstein said, this bad boogie bomb! Who didn't hate War and Hunger and Death? Who, for that matter, didn't love and yearn for Peace and Prosperity? These were *safe* politics, said Wittgenstein. What if the sky was falling? To his mind, this bomb business was little more than a meal ticket for Lord Chicken Little, with his Labour card, his fine sentiments and his ladies-in-waiting. And this was the man, Wittgenstein mused, who at the Moral Science Club shook his fist at *him*, saying that *he* was the source of the confusion!

Russell, in the meantime, was flying around the world, lecturing heads of state and exploding small bombs for peace in world assemblies and lecture halls. Then one day he was on a plane headed for Sweden, where he was to deliver a speech on the need for nuclear disarmament. Russell had dozed off when he felt a violent jolt. He thought they must have landed. His attaché case had flown into a bulkhead and his papers were scattered across the floor. Damn — the papers were soaking wet when he scooped them up. Someone must have spilled a drink. He was patting his suitcoat for his glasses when he felt water welling into his shoes. Then he heard someone in the forward section screaming in a loud gargle. Surf was washing over his legs. He tried to stand but was yanked back by the seat belt as he heard more choked screamings. Clawing and slapping at the snap, he broke the belt and slogged down the listing aisle. Waist deep in cold water clogged with bobbing suitcases and pillows, he was struggling out when some young man — one of the crew, he guessed — pushed him violently toward the hatch. And Russell remembered thinking, *It will not be me!* And like a newborn, he took one big, defiant breath, then dove down and somehow pulled himself through the sucking vortex — expelled into the suddenly somnolent sea.

Then his suit was bubbling over his back, and he was wriggling like a polliwog toward the dull light of the surface. And there he found himself in the open gray sea. He was a mile or more from shore, but never did he flag. Fully clothed, he was seen swimming toward the approaching rescue boat — swimming, the papers said, like no seventy-eight-year-old lord had ever swum before.

LORD RUSSELL SURVIVES FATAL AIR CRASH . . . *Nineteen Die,* read the headline in the London *Times.*

Below the headline was a picture of him sitting up in his hotel bed in a bunchy borrowed robe, primly holding a cup of tea as he posed for photos and fielded questions from the reporters who had crowded into his room. Yes, he said for the hundredth time, he felt lucky. Yes, he explained, he was most happy to be alive — and yes, he was sorry, most terribly sorry for the dead and their families. No, he never caught cold. Felt fine, truly did. Of course he'd speak that night — so long as he got his wet trousers back from the valet. My secret for living? he asked, cannily repeating the reporter's question. Heredity and lack of worry. Then inclining his head toward the next question, he asked, What? What's that? Will I *fly* again? Why, of course, he said, peevishly. Yes, of course I'll fly, and so should you, young man. Keep flying and you might live to be a hundred — that is, if mankind hasn't destroyed itself by then. Next question.

After weathering the war in New York, where Mining had died, Gretl finally returned alone to Vienna late in 1947.

It was, of course, a changed city, a captive city destroyed in areas by bombs and shelling. It was also a divided city, filled, in her sector, with rude Russians who both helped and aggravated an already bad situation, bringing with them even more chronic shortages, along with blackouts, queues, bureaucratic bungling and other annoyances.

Money for her was no problem, but her needs and desires were on a completely different scale, and she lived there from sheer doggedness just to be in her native city. As almost everywhere in Europe, there was an acute housing shortage, and it was a triumph for her after a few months to move from her tiny hotel room into a small apartment in a faded three-story building on Rotenstern Gasse. Gretl was hardly overjoyed at the prospect of living in Vienna's Russian zone. But it was an apartment, and the location wasn't too bad, being just a few blocks from the International District, as the Ring was now called. It was an old building, with dirty, shrapnel-pocked wall reliefs outside and a lobby of cracked marble and tarnished brasswork, where in the afternoon the old ladies gathered. Peacock Alley, Gretl called this gauntlet. Perched in their beat-up bentwood chairs, gravely nodding, they would watch ogle-eyed as she passed — *die Kaiserin* — dressed in her dark prewar furs and smart veiled hats trimmed with sharp feathers.

By Gretl's standards, the apartment was barely servant's quarters, but it was enough. To get back her own house, which the Russians had turned into a police stable, was beyond her strength or desire at that point. Even to seek restitution or simple justice for what was hers would have taken more years and energy than even a far younger person would have had. And why chase the past? She was convinced the house would one day be reclaimed as a monument of sorts; it would not be lost. Without much regret, she let it go.

And much as she made fun of it, Gretl loved her shabby little apartment, with its bad plumbing and the decomposing scrollwork that edged the cracked ceilings. Still, a coat of fresh paint could not dispel the history of the place, which had slowly gathered like the dust on the hinges. Deep in the recesses of one of the closets, wedged behind a board, she had found an old copy of the Passover Haggadah marked in places with hairpins. Later, in her bedroom, a workman found a rumpled, brownish photograph sandwiched behind the window molding. It was a picture of a mother and son. Wearing a starched white blouse, the mother was dark haired and nicely *zaftig*, holding a dark-eyed boy of about three on her lap. But such a superstitious place to stick a photograph — literally under the woodwork, as if in the hope that it would one day be found in memory or accusation. More troubling for Gretl, the workman turned up a second picture of the boy. This one showed the boy a little older, four or five perhaps. Sitting on a bench in short pants and a big cap, he was smiling and snuggling with a snarly lion cub with thick, ungainly paws. Where had the picture been taken? she wondered. The zoo? The circus? Had the boy a father? Gretl didn't know why she would find herself staring at that picture of the seemingly brave boy with the mirthful eyes and that big floppy cap. Even to herself, she couldn't quite explain why it struck her so, bringing forth a chill. No explaining why the photograph seemed to her prophetic — why she felt so sure that the boy and his mother were now under earth, or why at night she would sometimes grieve to think that they were probably not even buried in the same place. Not even buried together.

For Gretl the whole city was a little haunted with this new life going on in their midsts, where formerly the old life had dwelt. At night, the pipes shuddered and moaned, and the reeking hallway was filled with children who slammed doors and ran down the resounding marble stairs. She was a curiosity among her neighbors, who, like everyone in Vienna, had of course never, never supported the Nazis. And who could blame them — a captive people. All were Hitler's victims. The devil was dead, and the Nazis were gone. All were Viennese again. And look, business was improving! The cafés were slowly reopening, and the shops now at least had some goods on their shelves — it did not do to be asking silly, morbid questions of people who had lived through air raids and Russian plundering, followed by months of near starvation after the war. To ask questions was to be somehow sick or mischievous, not forward-looking. To ask questions was mean-spirited — *ungrateful,* like not cleaning one's plate.

So be it. Gretl didn't rock the boat. She minded her own business — the old, she wryly wrote her brother, have no choice but to mind their own business since nobody minds them. It was Gretl's way, this bitter-sweet humor. She said she was old and funny looking, but in fact she had her hair done three times a week and cut a far more elegant figure than she was willing to admit in her tailored clothes. Besides, being an old fuddy-duddy made for a better story in her comical letters to her brother: better to play an old character than to just be another old lady shuffling down the street, pulling her little wheeled grocery cart. Her letters were now peppered with exclamation points and words typed out in capitals: "I DIED . . . I tell you, that woman is such a BITCH!" Reading them, Wittgenstein could hear his sister's still throaty laugh and run-on stories. She said that her apartment reminded her of a lifeboat filled with those few things she had managed, with Max's help, to rescue from her former life. There was the portrait Klimt had done of her, still young and dark haired, wearing a long white gown. There were also a few Chinese vases, the black lacquered writing desk and the old family pictures in their stands — things completely out of scale and now too lavish and grand for this silly, pinched life of hers.

And she was so amazed with her silly old self. Her telegraphic letters would proclaim these small daily triumphs: "ARRIVED CARRYING MY OWN BAGS . . . I RODE THE TRAM . . . A REAL PROLETAR-IAN." Twaddling along in her furs, she said, she felt a bit like dispos-sessed royalty, in truth, a little deshabille. Almost all her friends were dead or gone, but she found several old, dear friends and managed to make some new ones. These were mainly "old Jewish ladies" — obstinate returnees like herself, who used too much rouge and perfume, wore feathered felt hats with veils and rolled their stockings over their knees, having grandly given up garters and girdles. All except Gretl had copious cats ("I'M SICK OF HEARING ABOUT CATS!"), and they met every Sunday at the Café Alte Backstube, where, at a marble-topped table in the corner, they gabbed away the morning before going to a symphony or play, and then on to Zur Linde or Schöner's for a glass of wine and maybe a bite to eat.

It wasn't much, Gretl said, and yet she had learned to love this unlikely, untidy life of hers, which gradually took another unexpected turn. She had a Russian girl named Katerina who cooked and kept house for her. Gretl soon took a deep fondness for her and her five-year-old boy, Alyosha, whose father had been killed in the war. Finally, Katerina and Alyosha came to live with her and became her "little family." So Gretl had no need of cats. She had the boy, and the boy had a doting "auntie" who spoiled him terribly. She took Alyosha to the theater and the opera, to museums and the Wurstel Prater. Letting down her cultural defenses, she even took him to some of those silly American dance movies that her brother was always urging her to see when she needed a lift. Ach, *Top Hat*. Ach, Busby Berkeley. For the boy's sake, she even suffered Disney's *Mickey-Maus* and then *Schneewittchen*, dozing amid all with the gamboling dwarfs and furballs. But in her present state, even Disney would creep up on her. When Snow White ate the poisoned apple and lay dead in the crystal casket, she suddenly found herself clutching the squealing Alyosha, "SOBBING LIKE AN OLD FOOL."

And slowly along the way, Gretl discarded some of her sophistication like so much useless ballast — or discarded, rather, the imperious standards and expectations of sophistication, which she said was half finickiness anyhow. It wasn't just old age. Gretl said she was not one of these "ADORABLE, SOFT-HEADED" old ladies who love all children and always remember birthdays, and yet she felt herself changing. And it was so odd, she said, the things she took pleasure in, pleasures so small that they seemed to peep at her like the little sparrows on her window ledge. Here, suddenly, were all the small, insignificant things she had never noticed, the people on the street, the slow turn of the seasons, the way things grew. Modest as they were, these pleasures were real, and they drew her along, enticing her to nibble at the crumbs strewn along the path of this unlikely life, which seemed to have reserved for her only such things as befitted her diminished appetite. Wasn't it odd, she wrote, the way old women, like young shopgirls, live on sweets — little tastes of things, scarcely enough to fill a bee? And wasn't it the most amazing thing, how this life could accommodate everyone at his own pace? Whatever it was, it seemed enough to her now. Just to watch her silly little plants growing on the windowsill was good. It seemed to her that she had even learned to love on a different scale.

Gretl had had some seven months of this cramped contentedness, when she felt a lump that became a pain that became cancer. And then she was hooked like a struggling fish to decline and death. Oh, she hated it. It seemed so unfair to die with this horrid pain, diseased and dressed with sores and dwindling down to a stick — to die ignominiously like her father, filled with the smell of her own fetor. It was so ugly and humiliating. She was the first to admit that she was a chicken about these things; she was a perfect baby about it. At night she would cry in Katerina's young arms. And then she would get so stupidly furious at Mining, the deserter, furious that she should have died cleanly without this horror and without even being there to care for her. And then there came the day when, with the sharp dread of panic, she decided to stick her head in the oven while she still had the strength. She got as far as turning on the gas and getting down on her knees. But she gagged at the first whiff, as sickened by the gas's rotten marsh smell as by the sharp familial shame it evoked, a stench of smothered anger. For so long this anger had lain dormant, so subtle and virulent. Like an ineradicable stain, it now bloomed in her blood, spreading through her body like this cancer. Never did she think she could have sunk to this point. Never did she imagine that she would suffer this rage and desperation against things that had happened longer ago than it seemed human flesh could endure or even remember. And now to be pinned like a moth to this life with this pain and rage. And, worse, to have the way out closed to her — to be not innocently, insensibly old, nor even wise! To be nothing but bitter, harboring this senseless fury against the impervious ghosts of the ageless dead. To the dying old woman, this was a pain beyond reckoning.

Gretl was through the worst of these metamorphoses by the time she told Wittgenstein about her cancer. And he came immediately, closely followed by her son Stefan and his American wife, Shirley, who flew in from New York.

The family scrupulously kept their promise to let her die at home. For seven weeks that spring, Wittgenstein watched his sister die. He wished he could have died for her: if there were one person in the world he would have spared the shocks of this life, it would have been her. Yet for all Gretl's squeamish fear of doctors and the instruments of the sickroom,

Wittgenstein was amazed at the extent to which she finally inured herself to invalidism and then to the prospect of death. And in a way he had never seen, he realized that even death was a language which, like everything else in this life, must be learned. He had seen so much death, but this death he watched as if it were his own, and he learned from it. This death put his life in such relief that it seemed he could finally see the wonder of this *once*, this once-to-be that life held forth. To behold death in the face of this once, he knew there could be no reincarnation, and he thought it a blessing, to have this once to swell forth, then to be enfolded like a seed into the sheltering darkness of eternity — to be lost in time among such furrows as the sea makes.

He was jealous and saddened by her leaving, but in the end, he forgave her this death, which he had watched so closely. He gave her leave to die. And softly Gretl groped her way into it, like somebody prying open a door and creeping down a dark stair. She was careful. Like him, she had never quite known what she was religiously, but so much did she want to be sure now that she sent first for a rabbi and then called the next day for a priest.

With that there was nothing anybody could do but keep her drugged. Anger was gone. Will was gone. Every cell in her was slack and fatal, yet there was still life or pain or both, which she gripped like her son's hand even after it seemed she was barely conscious. Gretl was generous in death. Unlike her canny father, she did not die in secrecy. Rather, she died with everyone present, not even minding when Alyosha, busily playing with his toys and asking audible questions, tiptoed over to her bed and stood there open-mouthed, watching his old auntie like an egg that was about to hatch.

The Blessing of This Life

WITTGENSTEIN NEVER RETURNED to Vienna after Gretl's death.

Two years before, he had left Cambridge for good, with the distinct feeling that he had only a few good years left to complete his work. His instincts were right, as it turned out. He stayed for a time in London, then he had a fairly good year living and working in a little cottage along the Irish coast, where he tamed two summering terns to feed from his hands and filled three notebooks with remarks. Later, he went to America for several months, staying outside Princeton, New Jersey, with one of his young friends and his new wife. Quite unexpectedly, he liked America, was amazed at the lavish American plumbing and more amazed still by the cars roaring down U.S. 1, all so thunderous and new as they passed the orange-roofed Howard Johnsons. Wittgenstein even picked up some American slang and after that might be heard to say with relish, Hot diggity dog! I'm hep. Or, Let us case the joint.

One day during his American visit, Wittgenstein was walking on the meadowlands of a nearby farm with his friend and his wife. The friend was to be a father, and his young wife was as full as life is full when one looks in the right places and in the right frame of mind. Wittgenstein was happy for them. At sixty, he still had his bad periods — not black periods as in Trattenbach, but blue periods, when he could not work or think productively. But he was generally happy, and certainly happier, on his good days, than he had been at any other time in his life. Other than calling it old age, Wittgenstein didn't know how to account for this enclosing feeling of lightheartedness, which reminded him of Gretl's letters during the last year of her life.

But on this day, while walking in the meadow with the young couple, something else took hold of Wittgenstein: a feeling of perfect ease and grace. They were talking about the heavens, when it occurred to Wittgenstein that the three of them might represent the movement of the sun, earth and moon. Suddenly he was quite excited about his idea. The husband and wife didn't quite know what had gotten into him, but they were intrigued and happy to go along with the game.

You, said Wittgenstein to the wife, you cannot be running. Not in your condition. You, then, will be the sun.

So saying, he sent her off. Slowly circling the wide meadow in her long dress, counterbalanced by her oblong belly, she stared at her feet in concentration, her long strawberry hair sticking to the perspiration on her freckled back. Infused with the game, Wittgenstein was shaking his head excitedly, telling her she must go much slower, yes, and rove out much farther to be the mothering sun, traversing millions of miles in her sweep.

Now you, he said to his young friend with a chopping motion of his hand. You, then, will be the earth. You will circle round your wife, the beautiful sun, and I, the little moon, will circle round you both.

But you will wear yourself out, his friend protested. The moon is the most strenuous part.

I assure you, I'll be fine, Wittgenstein insisted with a smile. Now catch her. Very well, then! Here we go . . .

The moon, it's true, is small and comparatively insignificant, but it circles both earth and sun and causes the tides to well. The husband gamboled around his wife. Ambling stiff-legged in daft circles, flushed and laughing, Wittgenstein had to run twice — three times — as fast, revolving around the husband, around the wife, around the meadow high with summer, with the grasshoppers sharply churring out before him like bits of chaff. Whirling in his round, Wittgenstein wanted to marry the world. Two solar years they covered, the wife looking cautiously forward, meeting the eyes of her revolving husband. And whirling around them in incantation, dizzily spinning in his own outer orbit, Wittgenstein was wishing, as he had wished for Gretl, that he could make life good for just these two, that one good thing might stand, fixed like a star in benediction over this fragile time. No, no! he insisted, so daftly happy when his concerned friend, the earth, protested that they must stop. Running and spinning and waving his arms, he continued until he collapsed on the warm clover, laughing and panting with the sun in his face.

Wittgenstein had been back in England for some months when he felt a pain in his groin. Stoic that he was, he ignored it for several weeks, until one of his young friends, a psychiatrist, prevailed upon him to see a very good older doctor by the name of Bevens. This was in early March of 1950.

Wittgenstein went to see Dr. Bevens, but he allowed the doctor to examine him only after having secured his solemn promise to tell him the complete truth, whatever it was. Such precautions proved unnecessary, for Dr. Bevens was a blunt man. After some tests and a second examination, he told Wittgenstein that he had cancer of the prostate and had, at most, a year to live. At this Wittgenstein only shrugged. He was not surprised. He had long suspected that something like this was happening, and he was strangely relieved to know the truth. It was as if, after having lived for years as a fugitive, he had been caught by the rightful authorities. Yes, Wittgenstein was tremendously grateful to Dr. Bevens for his honesty, and when he left, he gave him his heartfelt thanks, as if the doctor had given him something of inestimable value.

Dr. Bevens warned Wittgenstein that he would have only a few good months before he would need looking after. This was what Wittgenstein feared most: despite his experiences working in the wards during the war, he shared his sister's aversion to hospitals. As a rule, he didn't think much of doctors, either, but he was highly impressed with Dr. Bevens, who, it turned out, was no less impressed with him. Dr. Bevens knew that Wittgenstein had no family left, and he could see his visible distress at the thought of ending his life in a hospital. This troubled the doctor, and the next day, after discussing the matter with his wife and several of Wittgenstein's friends, Dr. Bevens told Wittgenstein that he and his wife wanted him to live with them when the time came.

Wittgenstein gratefully accepted the doctor's offer, and eleven months later, he died in the doctor's house. It was a painful death, but it was still a fairly good death as deaths go. Besides Bevens and his wife, most of Wittgenstein's friends were there, and until almost the very last, Wittgentein was conscious, with a copy of *Black Beauty* on his night table, along with the philosophical remarks he had written out that morning.

In the months before, while he was still able, Wittgenstein had made the rounds, saying good-bye to various people he had known. Moore and Dorothy were first among those he visited, and it was a good visit. Unlike that night when he had come with Francis to make his confession, Wittgenstein was matter-of-fact and strangely cheerful as he told them about this thing that was so certain — he rather gave the impression that he was going on a trip. Although he walked a little slower than usual, he did not look, or act, infirm, nor did he dwell on his illness, which he treated more like a minor inconvenience as he spoke to Moore about his philosophical papers and other business that he wanted to put in order.

In another man, such matter-of-factness might have seemed strange, a mere mechanism of avoidance. Yet Wittgenstein was so genuinely at peace that he put them at ease and left them feeling oddly hopeful, as if at last he had laid some hard things to rest. He told the Moores that he was leaving the next week with a friend for his hut in Norway. Red-faced and ailing, Moore was now seventy-seven. Dorothy was a healthy fifty-eight. Moore had long relinquished thoughts of travel, but he told Wittgenstein that it sounded magnificent, his plan to go north late in the summer. Yet even as he said this, Moore thought of the indescribable loneliness he had felt on that Norwegian mountainside thirty-six years earlier, reft from his wife. The memory of Wittgenstein shipwrecked in that hut as a young man reminded Moore of the loneliness that Christ must have felt when the devil took him on the mountaintop and showed him the world below in all its glory. But St. Luke, it seemed to Moore, had it wrong. It was not godliness that had made Jesus spurn the devil's temptations. It was not mere goodness nor spite, nor had Christ been holding out for something higher. Rather, thought Moore, Christ spurned the devil because to accept what the devil offered was not in his nature. That was all. It simply was not his nature.

Wittgenstein promised the Moores that he would see them when he returned, but it didn't turn out that way. Moore missed the funeral, but several times he visited Wittgenstein's grave in St. Giles's churchyard, in Cambridge, where in 1958 Moore was himself buried, and where in 1977 Dorothy was buried beside him, just a few feet from Wittgenstein's grave.

In the intervening years, neither Moore nor Dorothy ever contributed, as Russell did, to the various memoirs or gospel accounts about Wittgenstein. But for Moore and Dorothy there were those odd, insignificant things one remembers about the last time one sees someone, things that only later take on significance. Thus they would recall how he took a second piece of cake on that last visit, and how, as if they had just then noticed it, he would sometimes gently slap his forehead when he thought of something. They likewise recalled watching him walk down the street afterward. Walking in quite his usual way, really. And yet in his step there was something, em, so telling or *mortal,* or so *something* (though he was just walking), as memory moved in and began its subtle redaubing of the thing remembered.

Before he died, Wittgenstein did make that last trip to Norway.

A young poet named Tony accompanied him, the two of them arriving in August, when the nights were growing colder and the sky was still smoldering at midnight, still that same pooling, whorling red.

Fourteen years had passed since Wittgenstein had last been there with Francis, but the hut was still in good repair, its tangled sod roof having been patched repeatedly through the years by a succession of hikers or hermits who had passed by or pilgrimaged there.

A full set of pots and skillets were neatly stacked in the pantry, along with matches and scouring powder and a mildew-spotted note in English kindly asking the guest to clean out the ash box of the stove and leave wood and matches for those who came next. There was a peculiar human history about the place. On one wall hung an old guitar, on another, a set of binoculars. In the cubby they found cards and a chessboard, while behind the bunks there was now a long shelf lined with books in various languages, including a German edition of the *Tractatus* and an Agatha Christie that Wittgenstein, now addicted to detective stories, was pleased to see he had not read.

It was almost eerie, the place was in such perfect order. Even the damp, smoky-earthy smell of the place was as Wittgenstein remembered it. Unwittingly, he and Pinsent had even begun a tradition in August 1914, when they had carved their initials on the beam above the door. Now the beam and door and sills, the eaves and rafter poles, were scarred with initials and dates, with limericks and formulas, stories and riddles, jokes.

Here I am, Wittgenstein said excitedly to Tony, pointing to his L.W. above the door beside the D.P. And here I am again — with Max this time . . .

They were all there — his initials with Pinsent's in 1914, then alone in 1921; later with Max in 1925, 1926 and 1938; alone again in 1933 and then with Francis in 1934, 1935 and 1936. Over the course of an hour, while Tony sat tunelessly strumming the five-stringed guitar, Wittgenstein found them all, superstitiously running his finger over the deeply incised letters, then going out to walk, a little overcome.

Wittgenstein had his morbid moments, but it was generally sweet for him in its way, the ragged end of this season. He had forgotten how small and concentrated in their essences the hardy mountain flowers are at that altitude — how they gouge the eye with their spectral brightness. In the distance, hot coils of golden red light slowly effused in the darkness over the glowing snow tips of the mountains, the bending sky pressing down over the earth like a wide bowl. Wittgenstein had the old sensation of having his hair slowly being pulled up by the roots. Under the hot magneto of that sky, it seemed the light did not refract or reflect, but rather *extracted* a color clear from the molten depths of the earth, drawing it up through the flossy tips of the grass heaped in the rocky meadows like a manna snow.

There is a certain palette of approaching death, a vividness one sees in the late work of the great masters, when a last few things work themselves free and the colors come fluid and true without much effort. There was something of this radiant, brooding clarity in Wittgenstein's late work. Wittgenstein was writing a series of remarks about the nature and perception of color — of colors as subtle as odors and as mysterious, in the discontinuous light, as the mind's efforts to discern them. To discern: this finally is the holy work of the mind.

In religion, Wittgenstein had once written, every level of devoutness has a certain form of expression that makes no sense at a lower level of devoutness. Beliefs, by virtue of being beliefs, are not reasonable. Faith, then, is not to be explained, or refuted, by reason, nor will faith of a higher order of devoutness always be properly understood by someone at a lower level. Wittgenstein did not think of himself as especially devout, but he was devout enough to realize that he had fallen short of what might be attained in this life, and he was still unreasonable or vain enough to thirst for something outside it. There is beauty outside the mind, and in spite of all evidence or reason to the contrary, there is a stream of life outside this one. Even in the darkness the mind moves. In the darkness the mind can move a long time, moving in almost the way sound travels at night, when an occasional star deigns to drip down. On that mountain, in the stealthy darkness, Wittgenstein liked the way his mind moved, and he was grateful to leave a few thoughts in good order in the modest hope that others might come after him to polish the humble skillets, sharpen the knives and carve something else above the door.

At the end of a life people assign it a weight or a general trend, a moral trajectory. They ask whether it was sad or happy, failed or successful, asking this just as if there can be some consensus after the self as remembered is safely consigned to the common estate of history, which is ultimately everyone's destiny and thus everyone's business. Like a willing weather, the spirit moves through time, and against its time. Thus the spirit is dry when all outside it is wet, cold when all is hot and confused while all others are certain. The spirit wonders at this difference, while those outside see the spirit coming in the guise of a man and try to form an opinion of what the weather must be like inside, some saying calm, others saying stormy, and still others saying that it is an impertinence to ask and better not to know, though in fact nobody really does.

Just before he died, Wittgenstein said to Mrs. Bevens, Tell everyone that I've had a wonderful life. Of course, it wasn't like him to exaggerate, and his friends found it troubling that he would say this. To them, Wittgenstein's life seemed many things, but not wonderful, and in the end they did not know if he had merely been trying to put them at ease or if in fact he had found his troubled life wonderful. But this, in any case, is what he said.

Acknowledgments

I would be ungrateful if I didn't thank a number of people who helped with various aspects of this book.

First, I want to thank, above all, my wife, Marianne Glass Duffy, without whom I likely wouldn't have found this world or any other.

I also wish to thank Marjorie Perloff, who was there to continue my wayward education when it really began — out of college. And I want to specially thank Tom Lachman, whose editing, blunt advice and enthusiasm were vital to the most formative stages of the book, and to my very development as a writer. My thanks also to Chris Zylbert for her copyediting during the formative period, and for many fine comments that helped sharpen the book.

Many people say no to a writer, so I'd like to thank those who were the first to say yes: my agent, Malaga Baldi; Jonathan Brent, editor of *Formations;* Bradford Morrow and Deborah Baker of *Conjunctions;* and finally, Katrina Kenison and Corlies Smith at Ticknor & Fields.

I'd also like to specially thank Martin Morse Wooster for his excellent additional research and advice, and Timothy Dickinson, who offered many other valuable comments and saved the manuscript from some serious errors. My gratitude also goes to Janet Silver, whose manuscript editing, in conjunction with Katrina Kenison's editing, has done much to improve the book.

My thanks go to others who helped in various ways: Tommy Caplan, Ken Ludwig, Lillian Kowitch, Mòniek Engel, Laurie Parsons, Gwen North Reiss, Frances Padorr Brent, Slaton White, Michael J. Weiss, Steve Fennell, Dr. Robert Anthony, Harry Liebersohn, Dorothee Schneider, Heidi Glang, Gabriele Glang, James Glass, Jack Duffy, Muffy Stout, Robert Sherbow, Marge Binder, Ken Nesper, Sid Gudes, Clarissa Chapman, Bill Maly and the other understanding folks at Labat-Anderson, Inc. Finally, thanks to Steptoe & Johnson and Washington Area Lawyers for the Arts.